SILENT CHILDREN

BY RAMSEY CAMPBELL
FROM TOM DOHERTY ASSOCIATES

Ancient Images
Cold Print
The Count of Eleven
Dark Companions
The Doll Who Ate His Mother
The Face That Must Die
Fine Frights (editor)
The Hungry Moon
Incarnate
Influence
The Last Voice They Hear
The Long Lost
Midnight Sun
The Nameless
Nazareth Hill
Obsession
The One Safe Place
The Parasite
Silent Children
Waking Nightmares

Ramsey Campbell

SILENT CHILDREN

A TOM DOHERTY ASSOCIATES BOOK • NEW YORK

SILENT CHILDREN

Copyright © 2000 by Ramsey Campbell

This book is printed on acid-free paper.

A Forge Book
Published by Tom Doherty Associates, LLC
175 Fifth Avenue
New York, NY 10010

www.tor.com

Forge® is a registered trademark of Tom Doherty
Associates, LLC.

Design by Lisa Pifher

ISBN 0-312-87056-6

First Edition: July 2000

Printed in the United States of America

0 9 8 7 6 5 4 3 2 1

For Poppy Z. Brite,
who helps me remember how strange I am

ACKNOWLEDGMENTS

Jenny helped as always, not least by finding some scenes more disturbing than I'd realised they were. Good, say I. Are our children in here too? They must decide—it's inspiring to have them around, at any rate. As to research, some American details were supplied by my friend Pearl Elsasser. Barry Reese advised me on care in the community, Asa Casey was the medical advisor, and Cyrelle Mace was responsible for the tour of London and its suburbs.

SILENT CHILDREN

ONE

Terence was following the boss through the trees, down the slope that led away from the hotels to the wide bright trembling sea, when he couldn't keep quiet any longer. "I know what I saw."

"That's as may be," said Mr. Woollie as if imitating Terence's loudness might make him lower his voice. "Let's wait till we're out where you want to go and you can tell me all about it."

"In the kitchen at that house." Terence was on the edge of confusion, unsure if Mr. Woollie understood, unable to judge how loud he himself was speaking. "It wasn't a worm with a funny head, was it? It wasn't a worm with earth on the end."

A helter-skelter in the forest on the slope sent a little girl twirling down toward the promenade, a gull seesawed in the blue air above her, and for a moment Terence couldn't distinguish which of them was uttering a plaintive scream. Mr. Woollie leaned sideways toward him, his grey caterpillar eyebrows squeezing his reddened eyes thin and revealing pale cracks in his broad leathery forehead, and gestured with one large calloused hand at children trotting to the playground. "Let's keep it to ourselves for now, shall we? We don't want little ones upset when they've come for a lovely day out by the sea."

Terence might have felt as guilty as Mr. Woollie seemed to hope he would if he hadn't heard two boys in fat white shoes and shorts garish as cartoons, laughing just ahead of him. "A worm with a funny head," chortled the boy with a back like a wall half-stripped of pink wallpaper.

"A funny head," his friend repeated, his voice even shakier with mirth.

"That's the style," Mr. Woollie said. "Let's have a laugh or let's have nothing."

"It wasn't a head. I'm *saying* it wasn't, that's what I'm *saying*. It was a nail, a nail on a finger."

Neither boy looked at Terence—they were busy laughing at a woman's voice from a public lavatory window: "How are your bowels performing today, dear? Are they behaving themselves?"—but at least a dozen people below them on the slope did. "Come along now," Mr. Woollie said, and dug a thumb into the crook of Terence's elbow. "If you make any more of a scene they won't let you on your boat you want to go on."

His tone was telling everybody that Terence wasn't like them, that he was one of the people they tried to stay away from in the street and shouldn't be taken too seriously: he was talking as if he'd no idea what Terence meant even though Terence had done his best to explain to him yesterday. But he was leading Terence down to the sea that always calmed him as not even his medication did, and Terence didn't want to seem ungrateful when the Woollies had taken care of him for so long, Mrs. Woollie mothering him at the Haven while her husband trusted him enough to take him out on building jobs. He watched the broken line of boats swaying on the edge of the water close to the start of the mile of pier, the bunch of them swaying on their stalks of ropes, pods emptied of their seeds on a tree in the wind. He brought his mind more under control as the keeper of the boats, a wrestler dressed in trunks that sprouted black hair wherever they had the chance and with all the muscles of his arms tattooed, turned to examine his customers. Now Terence saw that each boat was rocking like a cradle, and began to hear a lullaby in his head, though not the words. "Two for an hour's worth," Mr. Woollie said.

"Handled a motorboat before?"

"Many a time, and with a lot younger than him in them." When the man blinked less than happily at Terence Mr. Woollie said "It's his treat. He's been looking forward to it. He wouldn't spoil it for the world."

"Keep out from under the pier," the man said, having visibly decided to forget about Terence, and pointed a finger black with hair along the coast. "Stay well clear of all the danger flags."

Terence hadn't realised there was supposed to be any danger. As he planted his right foot between the two low benches that spanned the boat, the floor lurched and he went staggering helplessly forward to trip over the pointed end of the boat and sprawl in the jittery water—except that Mr. Woollie had grabbed his arm and bruised it. "I've got you. Turn round. Sit down now. Sit down."

He sounded exactly as Terence's parents used to—the sullen urgency, their voices willing him not to be an embarrassment—and Terence had to do as he was told. He watched Mr. Woollie sit opposite him and pull the string to start the motor once the tattooed wrestler had thrown the rope at him. The boat steadied itself and eased itself away from the swaying of its companions, and then there was sea all around Terence.

As the seafront shrank away from him he saw the red flags shaking their warnings at him along a stretch of wet sand past the end of the promenade. They were too distant, and swiftly more so, to mean anything to do with him. A train chugged along the pier, and he pretended the boat was racing it—would have emitted appropriate noises if those mightn't have made his boss think worse of him. When the train reached the end of the pier first, he contented himself with willing it not to start back until the boat was past it, and that was a kind of victory. Off it chugged again, carrying an assortment of dolls for return to the hotels a mile away. The trees were dragging the hotels down into the green fuzz that was squeezing the children's playground smaller, muffling the tiny squeals that could have been of panic. The sounds reminded Terence of something the boss had said. "Mr. Woollie?"

"Talk to me, Terence."

"Did you have children?"

"What's making you ask me a question like that?"

Those were too many words, and Terence had to struggle free of the tangle of them. "Because you told the man you'd had some in a boat."

"A long time ago."

Behind Mr. Woollie, to the left of the pier, a long thin gleaming blade rose from a bird sanctuary to vanish and reappear further along the coast, where the trees had crushed the playground almost to nothing. They pressed it down into the sea and followed it with the hotels, and the paddlers and swimmers near the beach were only cries and shrieks. "How far are we going?" Terence said.

"That's up to you." As if this were part of the same answer, Mr. Woollie stared at him and said "What did you want to tell me?"

"I don't . . . tell you . . . you mean . . ." Terence felt the waves splashing up into his brain to wash away his thoughts. "About . . ."

"What you wanted everyone to hear when we were coming down to your boat."

"You know, Mr. Woollie. Just before we were pouring the concrete at the house in, where was it, you know, Jericho Close."

"Never mind telling me what I know. It's bad enough you're seeing things when you're supposed to be capable of doing a job, when Adele and me have been doing our best to get you back in the community. What are you trying to make out you saw?"

"I did see it, and you did, because you threw some earth on it and banged it down, remember? I thought it was a worm coming up at first, but it couldn't have been, because it wasn't moving. Maybe it had been, but now it was just sticking up."

"A bit of rubble. That's all you saw, a bit that needed smoothing over."

"But you always say we can't do that. We've got to dig out anything like that before you lay the concrete." That silenced Mr. Woollie—his eyes and mouth shrank as though the receding coast had tugged at them—which emboldened Terence. "Anyway, it wasn't only us that saw it," he said. "Hughie did."

"Hughie's worse than you when he starts. If you ask me you set each other off, and that's what anyone will say if you tell them. If you want to talk yourself out of being trusted on any more jobs—"

"That's not true, Mr. Woollie."

Mr. Woollie's eyes grew so small that Terence could barely see them watching him. "What's not true?"

"Hughie told the doctor yesterday, and I did, and she didn't say we'd made it up."

Mr. Woollie's eyes closed, and his face set like concrete. "What did she say?"

"She said she was meaning to have a word with you anyway."

Mr. Woollie let go of the rudder and wiped a hand over his face, which might have been why it began to glisten. "That's what you get for trying to help people," he said. "For thinking they've enough sense to keep quiet when it's good for them."

Beyond him Terence saw the pier retracting itself like a lifeline he'd failed to grasp. He wished he hadn't spoken, not if that was making Mr. Woollie neglect to control the boat. A wave splashed against it, spraying Terence's face, and he tasted the salt that would fill his mouth and nose if there was an accident out here at sea. "I want to go back now," he said.

He wouldn't have minded if his voice had carried to the tiny people on the pier. It seemed not to have reached Mr. Woollie either until his eyes revealed slits of themselves. "We've got nowhere yet," Mr. Woollie said, then cut the motor. "We need to quiet you down."

"I don't like it this far out. It's too deep."

"Just about deep enough, more like."

"Let's go nearer the beach," Terence begged.

Mr. Woollie's eyes widened as if Terence had inspired him. "You're taking charge, are you?"

"I just want—"

"I heard, and you'll get it. The boat's all yours. Change seats and you can steer."

Terence supposed he should take that as an expression of trust, but he was too nervous. "You" was as much as his mouth could manage as he watched Mr. Woollie rise into a crouch.

"I'm finished, Terence. It's your turn."

"I don't want to," Terence pleaded, digging his fingernails into the underside of the seat as Mr. Woollie straightened up and swayed above him.

"You can't always have what you want, Terence. You sound like a little child whining, do you know that? What do you reckon the doctor would say if she could see you cringing like that? What do you reckon your parents would?"

"Don't care," Terence wailed, gripping the seat so hard his nails bent, as if that might stop Mr. Woollie and the boat from swaying, whichever was causing the other. "You aren't meant to stand up in a boat," he protested.

"Not by yourself you aren't, that's right. Get up now, quick. Come this side of me before we lose our balance," Mr. Woollie said, jerking his clenched face leftward.

"You're making it do it," Terence cried, hanging onto the seat with all his strength. "You sit down and it'll stop."

Water sloshed over the left side of the boat, then the other, so that he was terrified that the next time it dipped, the boat would scoop up so much water it would start to sink. Spray stung his eyes, but he saw the coast tilting as if the world were getting ready to throw him off into the sea. He saw a line of people waiting for a train at the end of the pier, closer than the distant swimmers but dismayingly far away, and every one of them had their back to him as they watched a train start toward them. "Stop it. You're doing it. He's doing it," he yelled.

Nobody heard him except Mr. Woollie, who lunged at him. "Come here, you damned—"

Terence threw himself aside, trying to hold on to the slippery wood with one hand. His weight sank that side of the boat into the water. Mr. Woollie floundered across the empty stretch of the seat, and his purple face squeezed his mouth small. His impetus carried him over the seat as the side of the boat opposite Terence heaved up. There was a large flat splash, and Mr. Woollie was in the sea.

Terence saw the waves rub out the splash. He was expecting Mr. Woollie to reappear in the same spot, but when the purple face heaved itself above the water it was several arms' length further out to sea. It spluttered furiously and sank again, and Terence tried to make his stiff brittle body do something besides wait for the head that looked enamelled with greying hair to pop up somewhere else like someone who was trying to amuse a child. It might have been a hundred yards away when it reappeared, grimacing like a mask as unreal as the situation felt to Terence, as unreal as the finger in the earth was supposed to have been.

Didn't people who were drowning get just three chances? The idea released Terence from his trance, allowing him to notice that his side of the boat was lower than the other. He was inching himself toward the middle of the seat, clutching at it in a panic that almost blinded him, when Mr. Woollie's head bobbed up, twice as distant. It glared an accusation at him, so fierce he imagined that was capable of keeping it afloat. Then it vanished as if the glittering blades of the sea had chopped it up, and Terence thought at last to shout for help.

The sea shrank his voice and flattened it, even when he pointed his mouth at the pier. He'd hardly cupped his hands around a shout when he had to grab the seat in terror. He made himself let go in order to direct his shouts, only to panic and clutch the seat again. It must have been minutes later—by which time he was weeping so hard he could barely pronounce the syllable he kept repeating— before somebody on the pier noticed him out there alone on the sea.

TWO

One day, Leslie promised herself, she was going to sell the man in the tweed hat a record: perhaps the day he came to her and Melinda's shop without his hat pushing his large pink ears wider as if to help them strain to extract every nuance from the music in the air. As always, he'd gone straight to the secondhand section before risking the temptation of the full-price racks, and now he'd strolled to the month's bargains, where he was weighing a box of Wagner in one hand while he fingered the top button of the jacket of his tweed suit with the other. He took some time about replacing the fat box on the shelf and pinched the bridge of his expansive ruddy nose before turning toward the counter. "Which other versions of the *Ring* do you carry?"

It was a game, Leslie knew, but playing it came with the job. "All the best ones. I own the one you were just looking at, the Solti."

"Ah yes, the worthy Georg. A solid fellow. Too studio-bound in this instance, however."

"You might like the Bohm, then. That's live at Bayreuth."

"Every cough and rustle of the audience and lumbering of feet onstage faithfully reproduced, no doubt. Not for me."

"How about the Furtwangler? We've had more people fall in love with that than any other recording."

"With the recording? It must be getting on for my age. Maybe I should take that as a sign I've still a chance in the romantic stakes, would you say?" The customer, if that was the word for him, let his briefly speculative gaze drift over Leslie's face, then tugged his hat down as though to contain himself. "Thanks so much for indulging me. I hear it rumoured young Rattle may attempt the cycle. I believe I'll await his reviews," he said, and let himself out of the shop.

She watched him cross Oxford Street once the two-way parade of buses and taxis and venturesome bicycles allowed him. As he disappeared up Wardour Street toward the film distributors and sex shops, she asked Melinda "What was your customer wanting to sell us?"

Melinda copied out the catalogue number of an order to phone through before she straightened up, rustling with all the layers of lace meant to make her body seem as small and pretty as her face. "A pile of discs for types who'd be afraid to come in here."

"I thought I saw *Mellow Out With Mozart.*"

"You did, and there was *Tremendous Tschaikovsky Tunes.*"

"*The Best Bits of Beethoven?*"

"That as well, and *Open Up to Opera.*"

"Never *Don't Back Off Bach.*"

"Afraid so. I was polite, all the same. But did you see the Haydn operas went? And the Gardiner Beethovens to that old chap who'd heard the finale of the Eighth, and he took the Dvořák quartets as well. And we mustn't forget the student you persuaded to brave Elliott Carter."

"We aren't doing too badly for a couple of girls who used to work at His Mistress's Voice," Leslie said, and the phone rang.

Melinda turned down the disc of *The Lark Ascending* and lifted the brass receiver of the antique phone they'd chosen to go with the oak panelling the shop had acquired in its incarnation as a specialist in all the coffee there was. "Classical Discount," she said, and with hardly a pause "Yes, she is. It's your mother, Les."

"Maybe she wants my advice," Leslie joked, and accepted the heavy receiver. "Yes, mother."

"Perhaps if you occasionally took mine, you'd have reason to be grateful."

It wasn't an accusation so much as an expression of her constant disappointment with Leslie, with her having done only just as well at school as her parents expected, falling short of the university they'd considered best for her, graduating from the university she'd enjoyed for three years only to find work in HMV, and as for her life since then . . . "I have, you know, mother," Leslie said gently. "You just don't notice when I do."

"Name me one occasion."

"None of the ones when you tell me to do things you know I won't so I'll feel I've let you down." Leslie kept that to herself, not a new experience, and said "This isn't why you rang, is it?"

"I fear not. When I drove to collect Ian he wasn't there."

"Oh dear. Could you have missed him?"

"You should know there's very little I miss. He was meant to be in detention yet again, but he'd failed to present himself."

Leslie's grimace was so fierce that a man examining the display of standees in the window moved away quite speedily. "What's his crime now, do you know?"

"I made it my business to find out. He and his usual cronies were caught smoking. The solitary crumb of comfort, if it's that, is they were only cigarettes."

"Takes after me at his age, don't say it." When her mother took her at her word Leslie said "He'll be home. He knows where his dinner is. Maybe he just didn't want you seeing him in disgrace again."

"I fear I've almost grown used to that. Perhaps if you were to show a little more concern about his behaviour—"

Leslie interrupted only partly because an idea had suggested itself. "It's Thursday, isn't it? That used to be Roger's day off. Maybe Ian's gone to him."

"Perhaps I can leave you to ascertain that."

"I'll call now," Leslie said. Her enthusiasm deserted her as soon as her mother rang off, but she dialled the number that, however much she resented it, she found readily available in her head. The phone hadn't finished ringing twice when a breathless voice demanded shrilly "Hello?"

"Hello, Charlotte. Is Roger there?"

The phone emitted a clatter that suggested it had been flung away. "Mummy, it's Roger's old wife," the eight-year-old shouted across at least one large room.

The phone took its time about speaking again. "Leslie. How are you? How's your business?"

"Fine."

"I'm very glad to hear it," Hilene said with a genuineness Leslie found harder to cope with than she thought insincerity might have been. "What can I do for you?"

There was no use retorting that she'd already done a great deal more than enough. "Ian isn't with you, is he?"

"Well, no, he wouldn't be. It's not our day for him, is it?" With so little change in her voice it was clear that her daughter had stayed in the room Hilene said "You haven't hidden your friend Ian anywhere, have you?"

The giggles that provoked must have been accompanied by an outburst of Charlotte's vigorous shakes of the head. "No scent of him here, I'm afraid. Is there some trouble?"

"He's at the puffing stage. Silly boy and his silly friends couldn't even wait to light up till they were away from the school."

"Gosh, I thought we'd impressed on him how dangerous they are. Nasty smelly cigarettes. They make you ill, but you can't stop smoking once you start, so don't you ever touch them."

Only the words, not her tone, made it clear that most of this was addressed to her daughter, and all of it felt like a rebuke to Leslie, who retorted "I didn't expect him to be there, but I thought I'd better check."

"I'll tell Roger when he brings the car back from being fixed. Poor old thing, it's starting to show its age."

"That gets to us all," Leslie told the younger woman, younger by only two years that weren't worth resenting, and was about to ring off when Hilene said "If you ever need to talk about Ian, please know I'm here."

"Yes. Thank you, Hilene," Leslie said with an effort that involved squeezing her eyes shut until she replaced the receiver. She opened them when Melinda laid a soft, warm, slightly moist hand over hers. "How bad this time?" Melinda said.

"He's wandered off to be by himself and feel the world's against him. I remember how that used to feel."

"So he won't be with his friends you don't like at least."

"They're locked up at school for a while. Maybe he's somewhere he doesn't want to be with anyone," Leslie said almost without thinking, and then her eyes widened as her mind did. "I know where he is," she said, and saw Melinda know it too.

THREE

Less than an hour later the train drew into Stonebridge Park. It hadn't quite halted when Leslie edged the door open and jumped onto the platform to dash down the ramp to the main road. No doubt her fellow commuters took her for one of themselves, in more of a hurry to get home than they were. Most of them followed her across the road into Wembley and dispersed themselves through the streets of the suburb, and before she'd crossed three streets she was alone with her hurrying footsteps.

An airliner hauled a ragged strip of cloud across the wide blue sky above the broad red roofs. A bat patted a soft ball in some child's back garden, a lawn mower drew long deep purring breaths. Here was the house where she'd kept hearing someone in an upstairs room practicing the solo part of the Trumpet Voluntary once ascribed to Purcell, each rehearsal a little improved, but the window was silent now. Here was the front drive where she'd seen a large dog and a kitten that would have fitted in its stomach lying back to back in last year's midsummer sunlight while they took turns to pant, but the concrete was deserted. The memories were awakening others she was going to have to face. Ahead was the junction with Jericho Close, and now here was its corner where the paving stones had cracked and sunk under the weight of a builder's lorry or some other vehicle, and she could see to the end of the cul-de-sac—to the house that was pretending to be as innocent as its equally whitewashed partner.

It still looked like hers. It was the only house that had been just hers and Ian's. Her curtains still bordered the windows, and as she walked swiftly up the short quiet discreet road, her mirror framed by wooden blossom on the front-room wall greeted her with a flare of sunlight. It might have been a warning, or an indication that she ought to notice what she already had: the For Sale sign had been broken off its pole, and a curtain was swaying to a halt in the smaller of the two front bedrooms—Ian's room.

She unlatched the gate and lifted it the half-inch necessary to prevent it from catching on the rogue fragment of the jigsaw path, and saw the For Sale sign propped against the inside of the low chunky wall, crushing a dandelion that had invaded her flower bed. She marched along the path and reached for the bell push to summon Ian. Then, wanting to discover how the house felt to her, she slipped her keys out of her handbag instead and, with a stealth she couldn't explain to herself, opened the front door.

For a moment her hall looked as it should. The plump green carpet extended itself up the stairs, at the foot of which the phone sat on its table, though the line had been cut off for months. Her collection of wonderfully dreadful record covers, starting with Beethoven and Glenn Gould in the cab of a truck, still decorated the wall over the stairs. But the hall led past the front room and the dining room to the closed kitchen door, glossy as sweat, pale as fear. She reminded herself that Ian was upstairs and made herself pad quickly down the hall to rest one hand on the painted wood, which was chilly and slick. She pushed and felt the metal ball of the catch lose its grip on the socket with an almost imperceptible click, and the door swung inward.

Whiteness almost blinded her: the white of the wall cupboards, the cooker and dishwasher waiting in patient silence, the tall refrigerator humming its monotonous note, the slitted blinds at the windows—the new floor. She thought concrete was floating above it until she saw it was only a fan of sunlight that was turning the dust white. She clenched her fists, and when they began to relax she ventured a step into the room.

There was no use her pretending: she no longer had a sense of treading on a hidden grave. Nevertheless her mouth was dry, and so she crossed to the sink and lifted a glass down from the cupboard and filled it from the tap, having run that longer than she ordinarily would. She raised the glass and took a tentative sip, and then a mouthful. It wasn't just cool, it was calming, and tasted as pure as water ever did.

She finished it as she gazed out at the back garden. Her side of the hedge was as tousled as a five-year-old's hair. At the end of the strip of lawn that was brandishing weeds at her, the umbrella of the garden table drooped like a neglected flower against the alley wall. She turned away to be confronted by the open cupboard full of items there had seemed to be no point in moving until she and Ian had somewhere else of their own to live. She was feeling altogether less compelled to retreat off the new floor than she'd expected when she heard the stair immediately below the landing emit the creak even the thick carpet couldn't hush. She set the glass down on the pine table and paced into the hall.

Now that Ian knew he'd been heard he let his weight drop on each stair, every step a declaration of defiance. He swung himself around the end of the banister and lolled into the hall, confronting her with his thirteen-year-old bulk as though he didn't care whether it impressed her as more than a gawky object, too much of which he didn't quite know what to do with. His black school blazer with its scuffed elbows didn't help his image, nor did his reddish hair that refused to lie down no matter how much he sprayed it, and even his necklace of a tie that was dangling its strangulated knot failed to create the effect it was meant to have. He couldn't know that in him she was seeing a version of her own awkward adolescence, of the compulsion to rebel even against oneself. Perhaps he didn't realise he had Roger's broad square face and her eyes, as apparently sleepy as they were keen. She mustn't let any of this, nor her surge of exasperated affection at the sight of him, divert her from dealing with his behaviour. She was opening her mouth when he spoke in his new mostly deep voice. "Can we come back to live?" he said.

FOUR

"Will you listen to what she's proposing now, Edward." To Leslie her mother said "Sometimes I think I don't understand you at all."

"She has to make her own decisions, Ivy," her father said, but Leslie had the impression of being discussed like a customer at the bank he managed when he added "She's old enough to live with the consequences."

"They aren't consequences just for her. There's a child to be considered."

Outside the picture window the expansive houses of Wealdstone paired off toward Harrow. Whenever Leslie came to it the street was as quiet as a waiter in an expensive restaurant, and now the evening had muted its sounds further while toning down the sunlight, but the quiet fell short of her parents' house, where at times it seemed no conversation was complete without the accompaniment of some tape of their old favourites. Just now John Lennon was demonstrating how several repetitions of "her" were hidden in "too," which failed to lift the concern that weighed down her mother's long face toward the mouth. "Do you hear what I'm saying, Leslie?" she said. "I hope you aren't going to retreat into one of your sulks, or you'll be having him take after you in another of the ways you've discovered you don't like."

Leslie restrained herself to glancing at her son, who was perched on the edge of a soft fawn leather armchair, his legs in purple calf-length shorts wide apart as he leafed through an Internet magazine she could tell he wasn't actually reading. "You're being considered, aren't you, Ian? You want to move back."

"Right," he said without looking up.

That was the maximum enthusiasm he and his friends would let themselves betray about anything just now, but Leslie's mother took it for reluctance. "How can he," she said, leaning toward Leslie and lowering her voice, "if he knows . . ."

"He does."

Leslie's mother turned her face to him, but was apparently requiring him not to hear what she was about to murmur when he spoke. "They found a dead girl under our floor."

"Careful with the old tongue if you don't mind," Leslie's father said, his plump ruddy face still looking for a reason to be optimistic so that he could relax at the end of the day. "Sensitive souls present, remember."

"Thank you, Edward, but I'd like to hear it all."

"The man who fixed our house did it. My dad's aunt's house dad gave us when she died, and when mum and dad sold their old one we had the money to do things to it."

"And enough left over to help your mother open her business. Your father tried to do his best for everyone at least."

Whatever rebuke that was meant to contain, Leslie ignored it for Ian's sake, and he gave a shrug of his kind of agreement with her mother's words to hurry past the interruption. "Hector Woollie was the man we got. His wife runs a home for loonies and he had some of them helping him. He used to murder kids and bury them where there was going to be concrete. Only when he buried the one in our kitchen she wasn't—"

"We're cognisant of the facts, old chap. No need to wallow in them."

"Let him speak up for himself, Edward."

"One of the loonies saw a bit of her when they were putting in the concrete. We were staying here out of the mess, so we never saw. Then the loony started telling people, and his boss tried to drown him and got drowned instead. So the police brought the loony round to our house and said they'd have to dig it up, so we had to come back here again."

"Leslie, I don't know how you can stand the way he talks," her mother said. "I thought we weren't supposed to use derogatory terms for anyone these days."

"It's just his way at the moment, isn't it, Ian? I don't believe making too much of it will help. Anyway, look, we weren't talking about Ian to begin with."

"No, we were discussing something else that makes as little sense to me. Isn't your house still up for sale, or is that another idea you've abandoned?"

"I never saw anyone that was seriously interested in buying. They just wanted to prowl around the house, and I'd rather not think why. And sorry, but—"

"Allow me the floor for another moment. We're not wholly insensitive, whatever you may think. We realise you'd prefer to be living somewhere you could call your own, and your father would be prepared to arrange a loan for you. Tell her, Edward."

"Just until you shift the house you've got. We'd use it as collateral. It's not the kind of loan I can swing for everyone. Too little profit for the bank."

"Thanks, dad. I appreciate it." Behind him the Beatles were finding more syllables than melody in "ride," and she couldn't help raising her voice. "Only I was going to say before, I haven't abandoned anything. We're set on moving back in."

Her mother exhibited her open hands and let Leslie's unreasonableness weigh them down. "Whenever we have a conversation I feel as if we might as well not have had it at all."

"I think that's a slight exaggeration, Ivy, do you?"

Leslie's mother allowed the silence to answer for her, the Beatles having paused for breath between tracks, and then she said "Make an effort for me, Leslie. Try and help me understand."

"I have been."

"One more effort," she said as she might have addressed toddler Leslie on the toilet. "Give me one good reason why you insist on moving back to that place."

This melodrama of an argument and the impossibility of avoiding such confrontations while Leslie and her son were staying here was one, along with the oppressiveness of being treated like not much more than a child, but these were among the last things Leslie could say. "Help meee," the Beatles shrilled, and she was reminded of an old film she'd once seen on television—reminded of a fly with a man's head emitting that cry while a spider reeled it in. She'd found the image both absurd and frightening, and now she had to tell herself those words had no bearing on her future. She and Ian needed to return to the only place he seemed to regard as home, where she could ride out his adolescence and do her best to bring him up without her mother's attempts to help aggravating his behaviour. She managed to reduce all that to an answer she could risk uttering, one that her father might even persuade her mother had some sense in it, given time. "It's a challenge," she said.

FIVE

Leslie had finished unpacking the toiletries she'd returned to the bathroom and was sharing a proprietary smile with herself—a smile that the halves of the mirror on the wall cupboard couldn't quite fit together—when the doorbell rang. "I'll see who it is," she called, and ran down the stairs that were once again hers.

She felt the front-door latch snag, its familiar trick that no amount of oil had overcome. Janet Hargreaves from the adjoining house was on the path, wiping her lined leathery forehead with the back of one hand in a gardening glove. "I just wanted to welcome you back," she announced loudly in her hoarse cigarette-ridden voice.

"I'm glad I am, Janet. Will you have a coffee? Ian's being mother."

"That's a promising development, isn't it? I'd better not, thanks," Janet said, lifting one earthy boot to demonstrate the reason. "Ring the bell whenever you want a chat. I just had my old man on the mobile from some motorway services over the border, and he agrees you made the right decision, whatever anyone else says."

"Anyone being . . . ?"

"Whoever they are. As Vern says, they'd own up to who they were if they were anyone worth knowing."

"I'm lost. Who's been doing what?"

"Don't say you haven't been seeing the *Advertiser*."

"I cancelled it while we weren't here."

"I'd have thought the estate agent might have shown you," Janet said, so obviously unhappy to be the bringer of the news that she almost took hold of her mouth with an earthy thumb and forefinger. "Shall I dig them out for you? They're in the recycling heap."

"You're kind."

"You'll see," Janet said and stumped off, scattering earth into the cracks of the path.

Leslie glanced along the hall. Ian was sprawling on a pine bench in the kitchen, one elbow on the table just about holding him up, his feet drumming on the concrete as the percolator kept him waiting. Beyond the kitchen window Melinda was raising the umbrella over the garden furniture, having provided herself and her car to help Leslie and Ian move. In the distance a church bell celebrated the hushed bright Sunday afternoon that eventually brought Janet back with an armful of issues of the *Wembley and Sudbury Advertiser*. "You aren't in all of these, I don't think," she said as some kind of reassurance. "I'll leave them with you, shall I, and get back to my spinach."

When Leslie saw the headline on the topmost newspaper she folded the bundle and jammed it under her arm to carry it past Ian. He was only tapping the floor with one heel now; it sounded not unlike an impatient finger. "I'll be down the garden," she said, as unnecessarily as his expression told her it was, and stepped into the spotlight of the sun.

HOUSE OF HORROR TO BE SOLD, declared the headline, as the bundle she dumped on the garden table spread itself. Staff reporter Verity Drew summarized the history of Leslie's house and expanded the headline to a paragraph, and that had been enough to start a correspondence. "Outraged Ratepayer" demanded why the house couldn't be compulsorily purchased by the council and torn down. "Concerned of Cricklewood" suggested this might damage the adjoining property but felt the motives of anyone who bought the house deserved to be questioned. "Retired of Wembley" recommended that any profit from the sale should at least be shared with the victim's family, but "Suburbanite" went further, insisting that anyone who touched the money would be tainted and quoting the Bible to prove it. Melinda was reading each item after Leslie, muttering "Ridiculous" and "Pity they've nothing better to do" and "I hope you aren't letting this get to you, Les," when Ian made his way to them, spilling not much of the contents of two mugs of coffee. The moment he'd set the mugs on the table he swung back toward the house. "Ian?" Leslie said.

"What?"

"Don't you want to see what we're reading?"

He took his time about turning the left side of his face to her. "I know."

She'd guessed as much. "Since when?"

"When it says. Stu showed me at school."

"Why didn't you tell me?"

He spoke toward the house, and she almost didn't hear him. "Thought it'd put you off coming back."

"It hasn't," Leslie said so vehemently that Melinda patted her hand, and more gently "Thanks for the coffee. Aren't you having a drink?"

His unequivocal answer was to slouch into the kitchen, where he filled half a glass with grapefruit juice and topped it up with lemonade. As he fed himself a gulp he screwed his eyes tight shut before letting them relax. "I take it that means he's enjoying it," Melinda said.

"I have to tell myself that about quite a few things. Maybe our parents had to about us."

"That's, you'll tell me if I shouldn't say this, but I wouldn't have expected to hear that from you."

"There's nothing like having a child to make you wonder how it was for your parents."

"That's a reason I'm never likely to have," Melinda said, immediately followed by a smile that didn't feel the need to be forgiving, and had little else to say until they put down their mugs with a united thud. "I should be on my way. Unless . . ."

"Don't miss the beat, Mel."

"I was just thinking if you wanted I could phone Sally and say I was staying here tonight, if you'd appreciate the company. Only don't let me make you feel you need it if you don't."

"That's really thoughtful of you, but I've got a young man about the house."

"Then forget I even thought I should offer."

That didn't help as much as it was meant to, but Leslie had realised what should. "As long as it's on your way home, could you give me a lift to Cricklewood? Me or us."

"The more the, I oughtn't to say merrier."

Ian was at the kitchen table, his elbows resting on it like clipped wings. "I'm going to visit the little girl's grave," Leslie said. "Coming with me?"

He stared at the floor and shook his head. "May go to Shaun's."

Her expressing disapproval of his friends would only make him more determined to keep them. She said as much to Melinda as the Volkswagen chugged through Wembley, and then no more during the twenty minutes it took to arrive at the church, a long concrete box practically featureless except for a triangular spire and a few coloured windows of various angular shapes. The Volkswagen puttered away toward Highgate as Leslie followed the flat white path beyond a metal sketch of gates. A railway ran behind the church, and a goods train spent some time ticking off its many wagons along the track, after which the churchyard grew quiet as stone except for a rustle of litter caught in the poplars beside the path. White headstones shone under the lowering sun, black ones glared like negative images of their neighbours. Leslie was close to where she remembered she had to go when a woman in a black tracksuit emerged from the church.

She was about Leslie's age but prematurely greying. Her plump sullen face, lined not unlike a balloon starting to deflate, wobbled as she stalked toward the gate. Leslie moved out of her way, having spotted a wreath leaning against a small thin headstone that did indeed belong to Harmony Duke, 1991–1999. REST NOW BABE, the gilded inscription said. Leslie crossed the chunky turf and had just reached the grave when the woman demanded "What are you after there?"

Leslie turned, thinking she ought to have acknowledged her with more than a passing smile, and met her pinched gaze. "Mrs. Duke . . ."

"Reporter, are you? No more stories. We want leaving alone for a change."

"I'm not a reporter. I—"

"You're not another frigging social worker," Mrs. Duke said, suggesting the opposite, and turned her fiercely dry eyes toward the grave as though to reassure herself her daughter hadn't heard her swearing. "If they'd kept their snouts out of our business Harmony might still be alive."

"I'm sorry," Leslie said before she realised that might sound more like an admission, but Mrs. Duke didn't let it interrupt her. "They made out she was at risk from the bloke I was living with," she said, close enough for Leslie to smell mints on her breath. "He'd gone with a girl he didn't know was under age, and you wouldn't have either if you'd seen her, like it was anyone's business but ours after he'd served his time, so when Harmony went missing they went for him and me as well like I knew he'd done it, and never looked where she was till it was too late."

"That's . . ." Rather than complete her thought, Leslie felt safer saying "I'm not a social worker."

Mrs. Duke's scrutiny felt like a weight on her face. "What's she to you, then?"

"I own the house where, where she was found, Mrs. Duke. I nearly came to the funeral, but I stayed by the gate, so I felt I had to come now."

"Why?"

The question was so hostile Leslie couldn't help being compelled to produce a motive more specific than in fact she was aware of. "I feel—not responsible exactly, but if we hadn't had the house fixed up . . ."

"You should."

Leslie thought it best to turn to the grave. She interleaved her fingers and gazed at the inscription so hard that she heard the words in her head. "I'll leave you alone now," she said once she was certain her voice wouldn't sound as though it were borrowing some of Mrs. Duke's grief.

As Leslie stepped back from the grave the other woman stepped between her and the path. "Selling the house, are you?"

"I've given up on that. We've moved back in."

When Mrs. Duke only stared, Leslie paced around her. She was on the path when she heard Mrs. Duke snarl "Living where he did that . . ." Leslie glanced back to see her crouched over the grave, a stance that looked both protective and threatening. "Stay away," Mrs. Duke said through her teeth. "You and your brat stay away from her and anything to do with her."

SIX

The thuds as regular as heartbeats Leslie heard as she stepped into Jericho Close were indeed coming from her house. They were the bass line of one of any number of albums Ian liked just now—she wouldn't have been able to distinguish which. Not much more in the way of music was apparent once she'd let herself in. She shut the front door none too quietly and called "Ian, I'm home."

He either didn't hear or didn't think an answer was required. At least he'd switched on the oven when he'd come in from school, and the house was greeting her with the spicy aromas of imminent dinner. She sprinted upstairs to shy her bag and her linen jacket onto her mockingly wide bed, then she knocked on his door, knocked harder. "Ian? Ian."

"What?"

Since this was as much of an invitation as she was likely to receive, she inched the door open. A roar of guitars and a snarl of harsh torn voices had been awaiting her cue. Ian was sitting on his bed with his back against the headboard, his shoed feet on the quilt, schoolbooks strewn around him as he glowered over scribbling in an exercise book. On the walls the overlapping posters for loud films and louder music fluttered their edges as she stepped into the room. "Let's have the window shut. No need to share your tastes with the whole neighbourhood," she said, picking her way around the assortment of obstacles on the floor, and had to lean all her weight on the half-open sash before it would deign to slide down. "How long do you think you'll be?"

He scribbled no more than another line and slapped the book shut. "That long."

"No hurry. I can slow dinner down."

"Don't. I'm going to Shaun's after."

"Turn that down a bit. A bit more so we can talk."

Ian jabbed the button of the remote control for his miniature hi-fi stack until he judged even she had to be satisfied. "What?"

"Do you know if Harmony Duke has a brother at your school?"

"Rupe Duke."

"You know him?"

"Seen him round."

So that was how Mrs. Duke knew Leslie had a son. As if this explained his not having mentioned the other boy, Ian said "He's only half her brother. His dad wasn't hers or the one he's got now."

Was there anything else Ian hadn't told her that she ought to know? She was trying to think of a question sufficiently casual not to aggravate his defensiveness when the doorbell rang beneath her feet. She made for the window again, stepping over a sprawl of dog-eared magazines about martial arts and motorcycles and teenage female pop stars wearing very little on the little there was of them. A woman was subsiding into a wheelchair on the path.

By the time Leslie opened the front door the woman was levering herself erect with one hand on the chair to poke the bell push with a crimson-nailed forefinger. Beneath a cap of close-cropped artificially silvered hair, her sharp face pale as china blinked long lashes in what might have been reproach at Leslie's slowness. "Careful," Leslie was unable not to say as the woman fell back into the chair and planted her fists in the lap of her ankle-length brown dress. "Sorry if I kept you waiting. I'm afraid I need to go to the bank."

"I beg your pardon?"

"I've no money you'd call money in the house."

"May I ask whom you're taking me for?"

"Nobody. I mean . . ."

"I'm not collecting for the disabled, nor selling door to door." Having paused for Leslie's silence to betray she'd had such possibilities in mind the woman said "Leslie Ames? Verity Drew."

She raised one hand, either offering it to shake or negligently indicating herself, and Leslie was about to reach for it when the name registered. "You're from the *Advertiser*."

"It's good to be famous. Is it convenient for me to ask you a few questions?"

Leslie wondered how many interviewees had been too abashed to refuse. Discomfiture wasn't her primary reason for saying "I wouldn't mind a word." She retreated as far as the stairs, then saw how high the doorstep was. "Can I—"

"Please don't trouble." The reporter tipped her chair back, at the same time grabbing the sides of the doorframe, and in a moment she was speeding down the hall, barely allowing Leslie time to dodge. "So this is the room," she said as she came to a halt by the cooker.

Leslie turned the oven down a setting. "It's my kitchen all right. Would you like a drink?"

"I don't, thank you."

"Tea or coffee, I was meaning."

"Thank you all the same."

"Not even a glass of water? You look hot."

The reporter's gaze flickered to the taps and then to the pipes that led under the sink into the floor. "I'm comfortable as I am, thank you," she said, though her shoulders shifted. "Perhaps I can start by asking—"

There was a screech of pine on concrete. Leslie hadn't meant to pull the bench out quite so vigorously, and almost flinched as the reporter did. She sat on it and thumped the table with her elbows. "Let me ask you something first. Why was that story of yours news?"

"I take it you mean my piece about this house."

"The house of horror, as you called it, or whoever wrote the headline did."

"I'm responsible for it, I assure you."

"I suppose when the paper's so local you might be." As Verity Drew sat up straighter as though her raised eyebrows had hauled her erect Leslie said "But however local it is, I don't see why selling a house, and that's all this is now, is news."

"Quite a few of our readers did, Mrs. Ames."

"After they'd been stirred up, maybe. Why did you?"

"Why did we decide it was worth reporting? Some people—"

"Let's stay with ones who've got names. What were *you* thinking?"

"I believe the public has a right to know what's being done with the site of by far the most horrific crime that has ever appalled our community, especially when it's slap in their midst."

"As you see, nothing's being done with it. I'm back."

"Which brings us to the subject I wanted to raise. Can I ask you about it now?"

"What do you feel is worth asking?"

"How you feel about returning to, returning here."

"To the scene of the crime, I suppose you stopped yourself saying." When the reporter only gazed expectantly at her over the notebook that an ample pocket of the brown dress had proved to contain, Leslie said "It wasn't my crime, perhaps you'd like to keep in mind. I was just coming back to my favourite house that I'd lived in. And maybe you'd like to consider that your paper made it impossible to sell the house except to people you wouldn't have wanted in it, I can tell you."

"So would you say there were any feelings you had to overcome before you could be comfortable?"

"What do you think? There still are. I feel sad and worse than sad whenever I think of the little girl, and sorry for her family. Don't you?"

"This isn't about my feelings, Mrs. Ames," the reporter said, and immediately contradicted herself by starting so violently she almost dropped the notebook. For a moment Leslie felt as if the kitchen had grown cold as the underside of concrete, as if the sunlight had turned into clinging mist, and then she saw that the presence behind her was Ian. "How long have you been there?" she said with a laugh that surprised her by not being nervous.

"A bit."

Verity Drew pressed her lips together, erasing their tinge of pink. "I wonder if I could have a brief chat with your son," she said, and set about turning the wheelchair toward the hall.

"That's up to him."

"In that case," the reporter said, though Ian had expressed no enthusiasm, "let's adjourn to another room."

"What for?" Ian said, lounging in the doorway.

"I'm sure a big boy like you must have understood my meaning.

I'd like to hear how you feel about living here," the reporter said, and wheeled herself toward him.

"I mean, what's wrong with doing it in here?"

"I should prefer not to. Just let me past and you can tell me all about your feelings."

"There's nothing wrong with it, is there, mum?"

"Not as far as we're concerned, but if Ms. Drew, I assume it's Ms., if Ms. Drew isn't happy—"

"It's Mrs.," the reporter declared as if Leslie had cast doubt on her marriageability. "Will you please let me out of this—"

"Thought you wanted me to say how I felt."

"Yes, as I made clear, when—"

"The same as my mum. The same as she said, that's how I feel."

"If you say so. Now will you just—"

"Aren't you going to write it down?"

"I'll remember. Believe me, I will," the reporter said, her voice barely under control, and flattened her hands on top of the wheels preparatory to driving the chair at him.

"Ian." However much the reporter deserved to suffer the effects of the atmosphere she'd created, Leslie felt that was enough. "Don't tease," she said.

Perhaps she should have omitted the last word, because the reporter fixed her with a look that contained no gratitude. As Ian advanced into the kitchen the reporter accelerated down the hall, not quite along the tracks she'd already dug in the carpet, and didn't slow until she was past the stairs. By the time she'd levered herself up to seize the latch and pull the door open, Leslie was there to assist her in maneuvering the wheelchair over the step. She'd hardly taken the handles when the chair lurched forward. "Let go of me," Verity Drew almost screamed, bumping the chair down onto the path. She twisted round to glare at Leslie and caught sight of the picture above the stairs of Beethoven in a truck. "Can't even take good music seriously," she muttered in something like triumph.

Leslie strode to open the gate and close it with pointed gentleness as soon as the wheelchair was past. She stood in her doorway and watched Verity Drew pack the chair and herself into a Mini, and as the car swerved away with a rubbery squeal she closed the front door. "She's gone," she called into the kitchen, "and we aren't going to care what she writes, are we? It can't touch us. We're here for as long as we want to stay. What happened is over now."

SEVEN

"Mummy, look at the children in the clouds."

"That one's bouncing on a cloud, mummy."

"And those ones are dancing in a ring on one like we dance at ballet school."

"That one wants to sleep on his cloud, doesn't he, only the others won't let him. Why is he laughing about it? Why have they all got the same face?"

"Ask the old man, Felicity. He drew them."

"I don't want to, Rosalind. You ask."

"Stop being rude to the gentleman, both of you. You'll have him thinking you're no better than all these children let loose to roam the streets without their parents. I do apologise. I assure you they've been brought up to respect their elders."

"No offence, madam. Your little charmer was only speaking the truth. When you're as old as I am there's no point in pretending you aren't."

"Why is he speaking like that, mummy? Has he hurt his mouth?"

"Felicity, I'm utterly surprised at you. You know perfectly well not to make personal comments. Just you tell the gentleman you're sorry."

"But I only—"

"Never mind turning on the squeaky tap. I want to hear a sorry from you as well, Rosalind, or there'll be no pony lesson for either of you."

"Mummy, that's not fair. It isn't *fair*."

"Seriously, madam, don't upset them on my account. I don't mind if children laugh at me. Let's have a laugh or let's have nothing, that's what I say. Do you two want to see the funny bunny?"

"Yes."

"Yes, please."

"Please."

"I should think so too, Rosalind. You're supposed to be setting your little sister an example. Now just see whatever the gentleman is so kindly going to draw you and then we must be trotting off to piano practice."

"I don't need to draw him. Here he is. What's up, doc?"

"Oh, mummy, the poor old—the old gentleman has hurt his mouth."

"Don't worry about that, Felicity. I'm not crying, am I? Don't you think the rabbit's funny? Ehhh, what's up, doc."

"Say thank you very much, both of you, and here's some extra pocket money each to put down for the gentleman."

"Thank you, Mr. Rabbit."

"Yes, very much."

"That's it, Felicity. Wave goodbye now. And excuse me"—the young blonde blue-eyed mother leaned toward him, her tailored grey suit releasing a hint of discreetly expensive perfume—"but maybe you ought to pop round to the hospital and have that looked at in case it gets infected."

She and her daughters weren't quite out of earshot down the newly cobbled alley opposite when the smaller of the two blonde girls remarked "His drawings weren't very good, were they, mummy?"

"At least he's trying to earn himself a little cash, Felicity, and he isn't taking any younger person's job."

"He mustn't have any children of his own to look after him," the older girl said.

"He hasn't got anyone to make faces for," her sister agreed, as a group of chattering Japanese tourists put paid to the sight of the two children skipping along hand in hand with their mother. He was gazing after them as if doing so might bring them back when the chalk drawing on the flagstone between his splayed legs began to turn red.

Nobody else saw. The tourists and students above him were ignoring him except to avoid his drawing, as though nobody existed below the level of their stomachs. He wiped his mouth with the back of his hand, then his reddened hand on the side of his boot, and dug in the rucksack lolling beside him for a pocket mirror, which he held in the palm of his hand and raised in front of his face.

He'd have said that was an old man if he'd stepped out of its way in the street: shaggy faded hair, eyes cracked by seeing too much, caved-in cheeks dragged down by weeks of stubble. Only the mouth could do with being more collapsed. He dabbed at a last trickle of blood with the sleeve of his raincoat and ran his tongue over his aching gums, then he lifted his top lip and twitched the lower. No wonder the little girls hadn't been impressed: the glimpse of the remaining teeth in his lower right jaw spoiled the effect. He'd had enough of the rabbit—there were better things he could do with his face. He dropped the mirror in the rucksack and saw a woman watching him from the doorway of a souvenir shop.

Weren't pavement artists supposed to use mirrors? She was looking at him as though wondering how much of a criminal he might be—as though she knew he'd stolen the chalk from a shop across town. As soon as she withdrew to deal with a customer, he grabbed the rucksack and the very few coins that had been dropped for him, and lurched painfully to his feet, treading on the telltale drop of blood that had fallen on the curly yellow hair of the child trying to sleep on the cloud. He pivoted his heel and felt the child vanish like dust—felt himself grinding the stone thin underfoot, thin enough to give way beneath him, revealing the secrets it hid.

He wasn't really feeling that, he had too much control. He lifted his foot and saw that the child's face had become a pale blur smeared with dark red. He'd never seen anything like that elsewhere, and there was no reason why it should affect him. He shoved his meagre pickings into a trouser pocket and thrust his arms through the straps of the rucksack, and put some crowd between him and the erased child.

Now that he was on the move he was better than unobtrusive. Nobody wanted to spare him more than half a glance, especially once he set about rooting in waste bins. He found himself three newspapers and clamped them under his arm while he searched for somewhere he wouldn't be overlooked while he read them. He was out of the bustling streets and on the far side of a ring road that smelled of several lanes of hot traffic when he chanced on a park.

Several people as decrepit as he hoped he looked were asleep on the grass under a blue sky with a white sun carved out of it, others were drinking and even talking on benches. Eventually he located a bench with nobody on it or near, facing a lake that contained ducks and litter, and within earshot of a children's play area. He sat on someone's spray-painted initials and unfolded a newspaper, and sang to himself whenever he heard a child cry or scream. He was turning the pages of the second newspaper when a headline and a photograph turned off the sights and sounds of the park in his head.

CONTROVERSY MOUNTS OVER SALE OF MURDER SITES. Of the five houses in the areas of London where the bodies of children murdered by builder Hector Woollie had been discovered, four were still for sale despite protests from the families of victims. Leslie Ames, owner of the site of Woollie's final crime, had now withdrawn the property from the market and was living there with her thirteen-year-old son. A photograph showed the house with a FOR SALE sign outside. "*Not for sale,*" the caption said.

The words went away, and there was only the photograph that might have been the house itself, reduced to handy pocket size and stripped of everything—colour, surroundings, occupants—irrelevant to the memories it held. He caressed it with his fingertips and resumed singing the lullaby the cries from the play area had urged out of him.

"Now I lay you down to sleep,
Close your eyes good night . . ."

It had almost been perfect that time. The medicine had done its job. He only wished he'd realised sooner what else it was capable of besides keeping his employees' minds normal or at least in check. The little girl hadn't struggled at all once he'd given her the pills he'd said were sweets: there had been no clenched fists, no mouth grimacing for air, no toothmarks on the underside of the pillow, just a trace of saliva that had faded as he'd watched. As he'd wheeled her in the pushchair to the van, the pillow behind her head, an old couple out for a stroll had smiled at the sight of a child peacefully asleep. That was the image he'd brought away with him—that and the memory of the concrete, white and smooth as a sheet drawn over a slumbering face.

Even if she'd wakened before the sheet had covered her, he was sure she hadn't panicked. Though she'd managed to poke a finger out of the earth, there had been no sign of a struggle, no upheaval of soil. It must have felt like a dream to her, he thought, if she had even been aware of groping through more than darkness. He'd spread earth over the finger with the side of his boot and trodden it down, promising himself that next time, if there had to be a next time, he would double the number of pills.

"Angels come your soul to keep,
  Close your eyes good night . . ."

He was having to sing more loudly, because the sounds of the park had started to get to him. A little girl was being dragged away from the lake where her toy boat had lodged on litter in the middle, and screaming louder as her older sister swiped at her head with the back of a hand. He bit into his raw gums so as not to imagine the kind of home the girls came from, the lives they led. The world was full of children who deserved to be given some peace, but there was nothing he could do about that now. If Terence and Hughie hadn't seen the flaw in his workmanship before he'd had time to put it right—if he'd found a way to deal with them before they'd told anyone else . . . He hid the lullaby under his breath while he used his longest fingernail to cut out the photograph, which he slipped into his shirt pocket. He dumped the papers in an over-flowing concrete bin as he made himself only stroll out of the park.

Having just felt helpless in the case of one child, he was anxious to avoid them. He mustn't risk intervening, not yet, not until he didn't know when. Whenever he heard a child in distress, any number of them in the increasingly uncared-for streets, he sang to himself. In less than an hour he was free of the city and tramping along a devious road toward distant woods that were hauling the sun down, and the only squeals he heard weren't of children but of pigs. Very infrequently he met people out for an evening walk, and ranted at them well after they were past him. "How's your feet? Don't want to swap them for mine, do you? Any idea where I can get some new ones? Maybe some doctor would give me a transplant. They can do anything these days, the doctors. It's a good old world, never been a better. . . ." There was nothing like pestering strangers to make them want to forget you, nothing like playing the madman to conceal how sane you were—no trick like drawing attention to yourself to convince people you had nothing to hide. But he was going to have to hide while he finished changing his appearance, and when he came to the edge of the woods he left the road.

At least he was certain nobody was looking for him. He'd swum underwater to the pier while all the attention had been on Terence in the boat; he'd moved toward the shore when nobody was watching, so that by the time the coast guard began searching for him, he'd been able to stand on the ocean bottom and cling to one of the pier's supports, only his head above water, disguised by a clump of seaweed. Once it was dark he'd made his way along the water's edge until there were only screaming birds to see him emerge. On an otherwise deserted stretch of promenade, he'd found a drunken tramp asleep on a bench in a shelter, only his right arm in the raincoat he must have struggled to pull off because of the heat, and had relieved the man of it. He'd spent the night feeling the salt dry on him in a hollow on some wasteland, having pulled bricks out of the earth to make himself something like comfortable. By the time shops started opening nearby on the edge of town, his clothes had been sufficiently dry, and sufficiently concealed by the long raincoat, for him to risk buying a new outfit and a rucksack in a charity shop. An incinerator on a rubbish tip had taken care of his old clothes once he'd changed in a public convenience, and then he'd been well on the way to becoming his new public self.

Tonight would see it finished. Though he seemed to be alone in the woods, he followed the gravelled waymarked path until he was miles from the road and the twilight started filling in the cracks in all the trees around him. He sat on a grassy hillock facing a fallen tree, having planted two large stones to brace his heels against. Even if nobody could be looking for him, he wanted to be certain nobody thought they saw him. He fished out of the rucksack the pliers he'd snatched from a do-it-yourself shop and clamped them to the outermost of his remaining lower teeth. As he bore down on the pliers with both hands he began to sing, soon more indistinctly and higher and higher. When he wasn't able to keep up the gurgling lullaby he did his best to laugh.

EIGHT

When Ian came home from school he could tell that his mother had got ready to say something serious to him. What she said, however, was "Do you want to help me shop?"

He hated that—her making him wait to find out which of the things he'd done she was going to bring up. He hadn't been caught smoking since they'd moved back to the house; he hadn't skipped detention either, and the couple of stupid detentions he'd been given for nothing at all had been short enough that he'd arrived home before her. He'd hung around with Shaun and Stu and Baz nearly every night, but he knew she was hoping he would grow out of them if she didn't go on about them. Maybe the subject she was holding back might even turn out to be interesting, if that wasn't too much to expect. "All right," he mumbled, though it was more of a wish.

On the way to the supermarket, she only asked him boring stuff, what kind of a day he'd had at school and whether he'd thought any more about what he wanted to do with his life. Two women gossiping across the gate of a front garden with a Victorian streetlamp in it fell silent before resuming their chat, and he knew they recognised him and his mother from all the publicity—knew that was why his mother raised her voice just slightly to suggest he ought to work toward staying at school after he was sixteen so as to qualify for a better job. The games adults played with one another bored him even more than most of the stuff they talked about, and why should they expect him to grow out of anything when they never grew out of those? His answers were growing shorter until they hardly emerged at all, though he didn't particularly want to make her feel bad: it was just that since his father had found himself another family to live with, and for quite a while leading up to that, Ian had kept experiencing the sensation that a slab had been laid on top of his mind, a weight as dark and heavy as it was insubstantial. Thoughts could lift it if it didn't squash them into pointlessness, but more often he needed something outside himself to free him of it—right now, swinging a supermarket trolley up the ramp and driving it at the automatic doors to see if they were fast enough to get out of his way. It might have been more interesting if they hadn't, but they did.

He was following his mother out of Frugo twenty minutes later—minutes that had felt slowed down by hushed thin music and the pace of all the trolleys, not to mention how half the customers had seemed not to want to be noticed watching him and his mother—when an orange-uniformed assistant some years older than he was and with a good deal more acne to show for it accosted him. "Where you prowling off with that, mate?"

"Just to unload it at home," Ian's mother said. "We'll bring it straight back."

"The other boy lets us," Ian said.

The assistant ignored him. "Where's your house?"

"Just in Jericho Close."

"Jericho Close."

"That's what she said. What's your problem?"

"I've got none with most of it."

"Don't have one with our house either," Ian said. "It's our house."

Delight not too unlike contempt dawned on the assistant's face. "Thought you were them. The manager won't want you taking that there."

"Think we're going to bring a body back in it?"

"Shut that, saying bollocks like that. You're as bad as—"

"Forget it, Ian. Leave it now. Excuse me," Ian's mother said, and stepped between the assistant and the trolley. "We'll do without. We can manage."

Ian grabbed the two heaviest carrier bags and pretended they needed no effort while the assistant was watching. By the time the

five-minute walk home had lasted ten minutes, the increasingly
flimsy handles were cutting into his fingers. He did his best not to
let his mother see the trouble he was having, but when at last the
kitchen table took the weight she caught his hands and turned
them over to wince at them, then kissed them. "I'm sorry I made
you do that," she said.

He only looked at her, which made her say "I wonder what
you'd think of a notion I've had."

"Don't know."

"If you aren't in favour no pretending, promise?" She waited
for him to shrug before she began loading the refrigerator. "How
do you think you might feel about having somebody else in the
house?"

"Who?"

"Nobody just yet. Only it struck me we've a bedroom going
spare and I wanted to know what you'd say to the idea of a lodger."

"Don't know."

"Just the idea. Nobody's going to be moving in unless we both
approve of them. Do you want time to think about it? You could
tell me tomorrow when you come home from Hilene's, or whenever you decide. I don't want to put pressure on you about it."

"You're not."

"I wouldn't advertise it round here. I thought of putting a notice in my and Melinda's window."

"Go on then."

"You think?" Much more neutrally she said "Will you be telling
your father?"

"Don't you want me to?"

"Up to you," she said, and saw that he wasn't convinced. "Let's
see if it happens and then he can know, do you think?"

"If you want."

"It doesn't always have to be what I want," she said, so wistfully
that he was preparing to mumble "It isn't" when a car door
slammed outside the house.

His mother one shut the freezer, which emitted a frosty breath,
and ducked into the front room to glance through the window.
"Must have heard us," she amused herself by saying. "Here they
are."

Here was another one of the games his parents played, she
meant or ought to mean. He wasn't going to ask who had turned

up with his father. He stayed in the kitchen and fed himself a drink of sharp sour grapefruit juice from the carton while she waited for the bell to ring before opening the door and straightening her mouth to greet his father, who responded by throwing his head back an inch and pushing the upper lip of his broad square face over the lower. All this performed, Ian's mother said "He isn't quite ready. He's been helping me shop."

"They're good at that when they don't have to dig in their own pockets, aren't they?" Ian's father seemed to wish he hadn't said that, because he added hurriedly "We're early, I expect. Whenever you're set, big feller."

Perhaps Ian's mother didn't like being talked past, because she drew almost imperceptibly aside. "Will Charlotte come in for a glass of something?"

"I think she's best left in the car if we don't want hysterics."

"That must be hard on you," Ian's mother said with, he suspected, as much delight as sympathy. "What sort of crisis do eight-year-olds have these days?"

"Anything can turn into a drama. There's no knowing what until the curtain's up." He hesitated before saying "Don't let it bother you, but she got herself into rather a state on the way about coming here."

"I'm sorry to hear it. About what?"

"Well, obviously, about . . ." He waved at the kitchen. "You won't be too much longer, will you, Ian? We'll both end up with a headache if her highness decides to create."

"I'm surprised you told her at her age," Ian's mother said.

"I can promise you we didn't, but unfortunately she overheard Hilene reading some of your press coverage."

"Hilene can be rather audible, can't she? Are you waiting to be invited in?"

"I'd better stay where Charlotte can see me, otherwise her siren's liable to go off."

"That would never do. You might want to consider putting on a spurt, Ian, before anyone gets the impression I won't let your father in the house."

Ian dumped his drained glass in the sink and went upstairs to grab his shoulder bag, into which he threw his toothbrush and deodorant and skin soap and hairbrush and another pair of the jeans he was wearing and a Drilled Skulls T-shirt followed, to placate his mother, by socks and underpants for the morning. All that should be enough for an overnight stay, but he wasn't going to let anybody think he'd rushed because of Charlotte, and so he stalked to his window.

She was in the front passenger seat of the Peugeot, squandering the leg room he needed a lot more than she did. She'd drawn up her knees in a long dress like a tube of floral wallpaper, to wrap her arms around them, and was pressing her small, slightly pudgy face against the window, her breath swelling on the glass as though she were trapped beneath it. She was keeping a proprietary gaze on Ian's father, which made Ian bare his teeth just as she glanced up at him and showed him most of her tongue.

He'd shoved the window open, intending to yell one of the words she wasn't supposed to hear or know, when he realised what he'd done. Pushed that high, the sash always stuck. "Dad," he called, "can you fix this?"

"Can't your mother?"

"It's my window. I can't shut it."

"It won't matter overnight, will it? We're meant still to be panting for rain. It's not as though anyone is likely to—" Perhaps Ian's mother had communicated some rebuke to him, because all at once he dashed upstairs. "Let's get it dealt with and be on our damn."

The last word had greeted Charlotte's protest that was well on the way to a scream. "Don't, Roger. Roger, come back."

He sprinted to the window and ducked out. "Here I am, Charlotte. Just shutting this and I'll be there."

Perhaps she didn't hear him for her cries, because she only raised her voice. Either she'd forgotten how to operate the window or she was too busy clutching her knees and pressing her forehead against the glass, on which her breath kept transforming her face into a wide-mouthed blur. Her distress struck Ian as no more than she deserved, not least for being allowed to call his father by his first name. He watched as his father leaned hard on the sash and brought it down, muffling Charlotte's cries a little. "Are you ready, Ian?" his father was already saying. "Come along at once."

"Roger, where are you? Don't stay in there, please don't, please." Charlotte's pleas had drawn Ian's mother to the car, and she was trying to persuade the little girl to open the window as his father ran out of the house. The clamour stopped instantly, leaving the adults to sidle around each other at the gate while Ian trudged after his father.

"You want him back for dinner tomorrow, do you?" his father said.

"Of course." To Ian his mother said "Be good" as a preamble to an unavoidable kiss greeted by a giggle from Charlotte. She craned around to make a face at him as he sprawled onto the back seat, glimpsing the wink of a net curtain opposite the car. His father swung the car out of Jericho Close and used the mirror to frown at him. "Ian, did you do that on purpose?"

"No."

"Hmm." That was bad enough—the sound adults made when they didn't want you to be sure whether they believed you—but Charlotte made it worse. Dry-eyed as though she had never lost her composure, which Ian suspected to have been the case, she told him "My mummy says she doesn't know how you can bear to live there."

"Now, both of you try to get on together," his father said as she turned her back on Ian, and that was when he knew he hated her. He was glad he'd found a way to frighten her. He only wished, as long as he'd been accused of it, that he had meant to. Another time he would.

NINE

LARGE SUNNY ROOM IN FAMILY HOME;
FIVE MINUTES FROM TRAIN TO WEST END;
BREAKFAST AND EVENING MEAL IF REQUIRED

It had been her idea that Ian should stay overnight with his father and the rest of them, Leslie reminded herself. However unforgiving of his father she might be, she didn't want to pass that on to Ian. Her fury of a year ago occasionally flared up out of its ash, but she'd accepted that she would never be sure of the details of Roger's behaviour—whether while Leslie was being soothed by music in the basement of HMV, he'd begun by sympathising with his colleague on the top floor over the disintegration of her marriage and then had made more than his sympathy felt, or whether the cause and effect had been more the opposite—and there was no longer any point in caring. If she herself had turned out to be less or other than he'd thought he was marrying, that was surely part of the experience of marriage, and he should have talked to her about it instead of to Hilene, as Leslie was sure he had. Still, now all that mattered between them was that Ian didn't lose whatever relationship he needed with his father, and that was even worth her spending tonight by herself in the house.

So far that hadn't proved too daunting. Listening to favourite music without its being even slightly overshadowed by her sense of Ian's automatic dislike of it was a treat in itself. The Bach cello suite had emerged from introspection to celebrate with a dance, and then another. The final throaty chord faded, and as the last suite began she tore the page off the message pad and deposited the screwed-up wad on the plate with the remains of her lasagna.

LARGE SUNNY ROOM IN FRIENDLY HOUSE

Of course she would have to tell anybody who responded the history of the house, but when she imagined doing that, the advertisement hardly seemed worth writing. The only way of being sure to fail was not to try, and she'd learned never to be satisfied not to. She scrapped the page and started on another.

LARGE SUNNY ROOM IN SUBURBAN HOUSE;
FIVE MINUTES' WALK TO DIRECT LINE TO WEST END;
CONTINENTAL BREAKFAST AND EVENING MEAL IF REQUIRED

Room with view of sunset, the sight through the dining room window suggested she should have written. A version of the yellow afterglow had appeared in a bedroom over the wall at the end of the garden, and except for the area lit by the small chandelier dangling its tears above the table, her house was growing dark. She gathered her plate and utensils and tall glass printed with white lipstick that was milk and carried them to the sink.

As the fluorescent tube jittered alight the floor appeared to shift, and a shiver sent a tear down each of her cheeks. She was remembering the photograph of Harmony Duke she'd kept from the *Advertiser*—a school photograph in which the little girl had been even younger than she'd had the chance to be. The small bright-eyed face smiling proudly with a hint of self-consciousness had put Leslie in mind of Ian when he'd started school—Ian bringing home a painting of two big pink lollipops and one sucked small that she and Roger had realised just in time was a picture of the family, Ian helping her to garden by building a Lego scarecrow complete with a sign that said NO SLUGS, Ian reading the SQUIRREL WALK sign in a nature reserve and solemnly commenting "Rabbits might know, but not squirrels." There were still moments when she glimpsed that innocent child in him, however hard he worked at denying it, and she thought it might be the basis of some of how he grew up, particularly if she didn't draw his resentful attention to it. There would be no growing up for Harmony Duke, no protracted clumsy adolescence. Leslie imagined Mrs. Duke calling Harmony's name into the growing dark, her voice turning harsh with rage that perhaps had given way to panic—she imagined calling Ian's name like that, and closed down her thoughts. As soon as she'd washed up her dinner things she walked no faster than she ordinarily would out of the kitchen, and kept her back to the darkness as the glow of the tube fluttered and died and the Bach danced itself to an end.

The compact disc lingered over the echo before halting with a faint whir. The abrupt silence, broken only by a whisper of movement in the kitchen—the contraction of the glass tube—caught her wondering what to do next. There was no use wishing she'd accepted Melinda's invitation to join her and her partner for a night on the town, not when Leslie wouldn't have known until she joined them how the girlfriend might feel about it. Time to watch one of her films Ian couldn't stand while she had the opportunity, and she turned off the compact disc player before slipping *Meet Me in St. Louis* into the video recorder.

She was able to lose herself in the film: the soft bright nostalgia, the colours more vivid than life, the sense of a family as close as surely some families were, the studio allowing Judy Garland to act her age at last, the seasons passing fast as a dream of a year . . . Winter came, and she found her head sinking in time with the large soft monotonous snowflakes, and started awake with a breathless impression that there was a lost child in the house.

Little Margaret O'Brien was smashing a family of snow people to bits because she and her family were about to move away from their home, but Leslie's impression seemed more real than the film, and perhaps as near as the unlit hall. She was holding her breath and straining her senses when the phone shrilled in the hall.

As it repeated itself she clutched at the remote control to pause the image on the screen. In the midst of the pale crumbling figures the little girl trembled—eager to be released from her unnatural stasis—as Leslie snatched the door open. The light from the room framed the lower half of the stairs and the phone on the table ahead of them, and helped her reach for the switch of the hall light, which drove the darkness back into the kitchen, where the concrete floor gleamed like exposed bone. Now she was fully awake, and as she lifted the receiver her sense of any presence other than herself was extinguished. "Leslie Ames," she said. "Hello?"

Several breaths invaded her ear before they admitted to having a voice—a man's, so far as she could judge. It didn't speak, only hummed a simple tune over and over, until she recognised that the low repetitive sound belonged to a lullaby. With it came the rhythmic noise of some kind of improvised percussion instrument held close to the phone, the kind of item someone might make to amuse a child: she thought the caller might be shaking a handful of small hard objects in his fist. She'd asked him several times who he was, and once what he wanted, when he expelled a breath in her ear and was gone.

She cut off the droning of the dead line and bent a fingernail against the digits that would identify the caller's number. When a recorded voice informed her that he had withheld it, she silenced the message and stared almost blindly down the hall. There was no point in pretending not to wish that soon she would have more company in the house.

TEN

"You're right," Melinda said. "He's watching us."

Two red double-decker buses cruised by, close together as elephants on parade. Once they'd passed, the man was still staring fiercely across Oxford Street at the shop. His grey hair sprawled over the collar of an old tweed jacket, his fists bulged the pockets of a baggy pair of slacks the brown of dried mud. The fists jerked against his hips as he darted through a gap in a selection of taxis to the concrete island in the middle of the road, and from there to the crowded pavement. His large loose face, the redness of which was concentrated in the eyes and the nose swollen out of shape, bent heavily toward Leslie's advertisement in the bottom corner of the window full of Ives and Copland and Bernstein and Glass, then his gaze swung to meet hers as he pushed the door inward.

Her stomach tightened, yet she felt relieved. He was here to be confronted at last—he was more than just an impression that she was being watched. She'd suffered intermittently from that since the wordless phone call almost a fortnight ago; she'd begun to feel watched both inside and outside the house; and yesterday she'd been so convinced she had been followed to work that she'd spent too much of the day watching the street and growing tense whenever anyone seemed about to enter the shop. Now he had, and Melinda would hear whatever he had to say for himself, and if anything threatened to get out of hand they had company, a man of about Leslie's age who was peering at a leaflet he'd slipped out of a box from the secondhand rack. He didn't look up as the red-faced old man jabbed a finger at her, bestowing a smell of stale tweed. "Can't you do better than that?" he said in a voice that was mostly effortful breath.

She remembered how his displeased gaze had moved from her notice to her. She straightened her back and planted her hands on the counter. "What would you suggest?"

"Where do you think you are?"

Even if Leslie hadn't had enough of questions, Melinda had. "We're in our shop, and so are you. If there's something definite we can help you with—"

"You're in Britain. Better than that, you're in England. If you're supposed to be dealing in serious music, what's all this American stuff doing in your window?"

Leslie swallowed a laugh that might have come out hysterical. She was reflecting how much of her sense of the world her situation had invaded when he began to wave his hands as though invoking the kind of music he approved of, not the Copland ballet score that was dancing in the air. "It's beyond a joke. It's taking over," he complained. "There's nothing to see in Leicester Square but American films and American restaurants and hot-dog vans for people who talk like Americans and spell like them too, I don't doubt. We need a few laws to keep what's left English," he told the customer who'd abandoned squinting at the tiny print of the compact disc leaflet and was regarding him wide-eyed. "Don't you agree?"

"Excuse me, sir, but I don't think I'm the person to ask."

Leslie snorted and covered her mouth, but the revelation of an American accent only enlivened the interrogator. "You people come for the Englishness, don't you? Aren't you here to get away from everything you left at home?"

"Makes sense to me."

"Of course it makes sense," the tweedy man said as though the American had dared to contradict him. "You won't claim you enrich us, will you? Except with tourist money. I'll give you that."

"Me personally? I'm not sure I'd even—"

"Not you personally, but let's take you if you insist," the man said, turning his back on Leslie and Melinda as they managed to interrupt only each other. "You won't have written any"—he flailed at the dance overhead—"*music*, will you?"

"Just a bunch of books."

"Ah, books. Works of American literature. May I ask what kind of a name you've made for yourself and with what?"

"While there was a market for it I wrote horror."

"Most American of you," the tweedy man said, and confronted the women. "Do you feel you must bow to the market too?"

Leslie waited long enough to be sure of sounding calm. "I can't speak for this gentleman, but I think we've had enough of you."

"How surprising," the man said, redder-faced than ever, and held off letting himself out of the shop until he'd prepared an exit line. "Country and western," he protested, baring his teeth at the music, "even worse than jazz." With that he tramped off towards Tottenham Court Road, and Leslie and Melinda gave each other a look that might have led to mirth if the American hadn't broken the silence. "Sorry if I was the cause of that somehow."

"Whatever makes you say that?" said Melinda.

"It seemed like it might be the thing to do."

Leslie was taking in his appearance: grey eyes that looked eager for the unexpected, wide lips poised to smile, long nose that turned up at the end as if to deny some cliché about itself, broad face nearly as right-angled as the red crew cut on top. "I hope we didn't make you feel that way," she said.

"You make me feel just fine."

The women shared a pause before Melinda lifted one eyebrow. "Is that the kind of thing people say in your books?"

"Some do, sure enough."

"And can we ask what becomes of them?"

"Some of them make out okay."

"I can see how they might," Melinda said with the faintest hint of censure, then relented. "Are you here working on a new book?"

"Researching one."

"You'd rather not say any more about it at this stage," Leslie guessed.

"Talk about it too soon and the chances are you never write it," he said, and looked impressed with her perceptiveness.

"Will you tell us your name at least," Melinda said, "in case we've heard of you?"

"I don't believe you will have. Jack Lamb."

"Do you know, I think that does ring some sort of bell. I could almost swear I've seen it on a cover or two recently."

"They'd have to be imported. I'm only published in the States."

"Then maybe we'll see you in print here soon. Leslie, save me from making more of a fool of myself in front of our delightful customer."

"I just wanted to say, Mr. Lamb, that if our window enticed you in we should apologise for everything you had to put up with."

"Your window did, ma'am, but you haven't a thing to apologise for, either of you."

"If you say so. I mean, good, thanks. Is American music your territory?"

"Some. Stuff people like who aren't as expert as you two have to be."

"So what were you looking at before?" Melinda said.

"I don't honestly remember, except trying gave me a headache."

"But you say our window brought you in."

"The notice about the room to let did. I was going to inquire when you started talking about that guy who came in. Would it still be available?"

"Couldn't be more so," Leslie told him. "You're the first to ask."

"You're kidding," he said, so surprised that she couldn't help taking it as a compliment. "I guess you've only just advertised it."

"For most of a fortnight."

"Maybe I'm plain lucky. Would you say it was quiet enough to write in?"

"It certainly is when my son's at school, and if you need it to be when he's there he'll have to use his headphones."

"It's a room in your house."

"A big bedroom, that's right." His gaze was lingering on her, and she felt absurdly in danger of blushing. "There's plenty of space for a desk if you need it," she said.

"Would it be okay for me to view it soon?"

"Perhaps I should tell you about the house first."

"Why don't you do that when I've seen it and got the feel of it. I like to keep my first impressions innocent. Comes with the job."

"Nothing wrong with a bit of innocence now and then, is there, Leslie? You could take Mr. Lamb now if you want and I'll lock up."

No glance at Melinda was needed to confirm she was hoping Leslie might acquire more than just a lodger. When Leslie thanked her, Melinda had the grace to keep her astuteness out of her smile, but there was no mistaking what she continued to think. "See you tomorrow," Leslie said firmly enough, she hoped, to put paid to any misplaced romantic notions. Right now it was sufficient that, as she emerged into the crowd with her new acquaintance, whom she didn't think she would mind having both as a friend and a tenant, she no longer felt watched.

ELEVEN

They had almost reached Shaun's when he shouted at Ian. "Our Crys wants to see in your house."

"Wants to lie on the floor in the kitchen," Baz improvised at the top of his voice, "and stick her ear on it and listen to the worms."

"Wants to see the kid's head come up out of your sink," yelled Stu.

They were having to bellow because Shaun lived on the North Circular Road. Ian might have objected to how they nearly always ended up at Shaun's, where the traffic noise and the smell of petrol followed you into the house, if Shaun didn't have most of their good ideas. Baz stole a magazine from just inside a different Soho sex shop every weekend and hadn't been grabbed once, Stu had already dropped acid several times and said things like "Where's the fucking focus on this thing?" while he clutched at the sides of his head, but it was Shaun whose right cheek bore the scar from shoving his face through the glass of a bus shelter when he was twelve to show a gang he wasn't scared of anything they could do to him. "Let's show her," Ian hollered.

A lorry several times the size of Shaun's house rattled the insecure glass of the windows as Shaun stabbed the lock with his key on a chain with a skull. Ian was first after him into the token hall, where they had to sidle past a bicycle with one wheel missing and some bits of the furniture Shaun's father kept attempting to build so that he would have another kind of job to try for. Baz heeled the door shut as they followed Shaun into the front room, where shabby chairs faced a television crowned with a video recorder and cable box. The furniture left space only for a plasterboard bar in one corner, where three bottles of spirits hung their heads on the wall. On top of the bar a quartet of crumpled empty cans of Skol guarded the corners of a car repair manual bristling with yellow slips of paper. The boys had hardly thrown themselves into a chair each as Shaun set about switching channels when his big sister Sharon appeared from the kitchen, pushing seven-year-old Crystal ahead of her. "Someone let her sit before she spills her juice," Sharon shrilled, and more directly to her brother "They haven't kept you back at school for once, then, so I needn't rush to work."

"Don't know what you'd have to rush for. They must be hard up, anyone who'd pay to watch you wag your arse on a table."

"Never mind joking someone who's got a paying job, Shaun Nolan." Since she'd ducked to pat her elaborately careless heap of blonde hair in front of the mirror above the electric fire, she appeared to be addressing herself. "You wait till you finish school and you're out of work like dad."

"At least he doesn't have men looking up his arse, and I won't either."

"We'll see, won't we. Turn that down and let her sit before she stains her dress, and you've got to stay in with her till mum gets home." Without waiting to see if any of this was likely to be obeyed, Sharon stalked out ahead of her hot spicy perfume and was gone with a slam.

Baz shoved himself out of his chair, writhing his shoulders as if someone might need to be punched. "Sit here," he told Crystal. "We don't want you messing your pretty white dress."

Stu looked at the ceiling and found nobody there to observe his grin. "Not yet," he added.

"Just park your arse there, Crys, and finish that," Shaun said, flicking through the channels. *Crackpot Jackpot* flashed by, and *Driving Me Crazy* with its harassed clown of a driving instructor, and a talk show in which teenagers were screaming and bleeping at their weepy obese parents while an audience howled and catcalled to prove themselves normal. When Crystal glimpsed *Hocus Focus* and the camera that magicked its owner into the scenes of its old photographs, she perched on the vacated chair before Baz could reclaim it and began to wail. "Put it back on. Mum says you have to let me see my programmes."

Shaun switched the television off and aimed the control at his sister as though it might work for her too. "Shut that. Do it, bitch. Leave your drink if you aren't going to finish it or you won't get your surprise."

The instant he stopped speaking Crystal's tears brought themselves to an end, reminding Ian of the girl he was expected to think of as some kind of sister. "What is it?" Crystal sniffed.

"Wouldn't be a surprise then, would it? It's at Ian's."

She downed half her black currant juice so that its place in her plastic mug could be taken by a hollow gasp. "She said I can't go out."

"Shar did, but she's not here. Now you have to do what I say or you'll never know what your surprise was going to be."

She hadn't asked to visit Ian's house at all, and Ian might have been angry with Shaun for trying to deceive him, except that all four of them often said things the others were supposed either to know weren't entirely true or to find out soon enough. "It's special," he said. "It'll make you special."

He knew that would get to her—it might have done so to him. He felt contempt for them both, a contempt that squashed his thoughts. When Crystal emptied her mug, daubing her mouth with purple juice, he grabbed her plump warm sticky hand for as long as it took to pull her out of the chair. "Wipe it," Shaun said in disgust, and Ian felt as if he were obeying as he rubbed his hand dry on his trousers while Crystal smeared her wrist with her mouth.

The noise of the traffic swallowed the slam of the front door. The boys marched in single file across the road, Crystal in the middle of them with her hands over her ears to shut out the screech of brakes and furious blaring of horns, and into the park, a lot of green with some muddy water cutting through it, and kids walking home across it, and people taking their dogs for a shit. The slab on top of Ian's mind made his surroundings mean less than nothing to him, and sometimes he wondered if his friends felt that way too, not that he was about to ask. They crossed the park so fast that Crystal had very little breath to wail about how much further they were going, but when they reached the gates she stopped to look maltreated. "Hurry up," Shaun said, and when that didn't shift her, "or you won't see your new friend."

"What friend?"

"A special little girl," Ian offered, and felt a flicker of excitement reach beneath the slab as Shaun said "She wants to play with you."

Not much was happening in the streets. Kids with keys were letting themselves in, and cartoons were uttering short bursts of words together with a good deal more noise beyond quite a few of the sets of net curtains, but otherwise the houses were keeping their occupants to themselves. The boys had hurried Crystal almost to Jericho Close when a white Astra, its back seat heaped with bags of food, cruised past them and stopped with a gnash of the hand-brake. The driver's window slid down to extrude the grey curls and then the crimson-lipped determinedly tanned remainder of the head of Mrs. Lancing, who lived in the corner house. "Ian," she said.

It wasn't a greeting so much as a summons. "What?" he just about responded.

"Is that the little one who was making all the fuss outside your house the other day?"

"No."

"I hope you won't be upsetting her the way you did the other little girl."

"Right."

"What do you mean by that, Ian? Just you wait until I've finished speaking," Mrs. Lancing called after him. He grinned at hearing her voice rise only to find it hadn't quite enough breath, but he was even more pleased by how her comments must have improved his friends' opinion of him, though they couldn't question him in case that put Crystal off. Instead they followed him down Jericho Close to his house.

Everyone but him stayed behind Crystal on the narrow path as he twisted the key in the lock. When he turned from pushing the door open, however, she had retreated a step and was tugging at her right-hand bunch of hair with one sticky fist. "Where is she?" she complained.

"She can't come to the door. I said she was special."

"What's wrong with her?" said Crystal, her mouth on the way to drooping, one sandal digging at the path. "Can't she walk?"

"She's just asleep. You've got to wake her."

"Why can't you?"

"She doesn't like boys to," Ian said, and saw his ingenuity impressing his friends. As soon as Crystal ventured forward, almost leaving the sandal with its toe stuck in a jagged crack of the path, he said "Come on and I'll show you her room."

Crystal hesitated with one foot over the threshold. He saw Stu think of pushing her into the house, and looked at him hard enough to prevent it. "Why did the woman in the car say the little girl made a fuss?" Crystal said.

"About coming in a house she didn't know, just like you. She's used to me and my mum now. She likes it here just like you will."

When Crystal stepped forward he felt as though his friends' admiration for his technique had given her a stealthy shove. The moment she was past the door the boys crowded after her, and Shaun shut it while Ian blocked the way upstairs. "Want a drink before you see her?"

"You made me thirsty walking so quick."

Her using an accusation as a demand lost her any sympathy he might have had to suppress. She followed him to the kitchen and sat where he pointed, on the bench at the far side of the table from the hall. The back door was locked, and the key wasn't in it. He watched the floor, where the shadows of her thin bare impatient legs made the concrete or something beneath it appear restless, until Shaun and the others filled the doorway. "What am I supposed to give her?" he asked Shaun.

"Something with water in."

The door of the refrigerator cast a shadow like a trapdoor creeping open in the concrete. "Want some red stuff?" Ian said.

"What is it?" Crystal said, so suspiciously that the boys in the doorway covered their mouths.

"See what it says on it," Ian told her, and laid the bottle on the floor.

He watched her grip the edge of the table to lean down. Her little finger touched the concrete as she took hold of the bottle by its neck and dragged it to her with a scraping of plastic that seemed to grow louder in his ears once it had stopped. She hauled herself into a sitting position and stood the bottle in front of her, but gave the label no more than a grimace for being unfamiliar. "Is it sweet?"

"Try it and see," Ian advised, and carried the raspberry juice to the sink, where he filled a glass almost to the brim with juice before adding a glass of water. There must still be some of the little girl under the floor close to the pipes, he thought, however much of her the police had cleared away. The notion sent a shiver of excitement through him as he stooped to place the glass on the floor.

"Stop putting it down there," Crystal protested, but leaned off the bench to reach for it, her bunches swaying on either side of her intent face. The shape of a little girl's hand swelled up out of the concrete beside the glass, then vanished as her closing hand met its shadow. Ian saw her fingers tremble as they gripped the table while she concentrated on raising the glass. He saw Baz and Stu itching to speed up the game, and Shaun scowling at them. Then Crystal had the glass and lifted it to her mouth, not spilling a drop. She continued to grasp the edge of the table as she tilted the drink into her mouth.

Ian saw an inch of unsweetened juice vanish at a gulp, and held his breath. He watched her suck her lips in and her eyes start to water. Her head jerked up, and she tried to stand the glass on the table fast enough to give her time to reach the sink, but she was only in the process of swinging her legs off the bench when the contents of her mouth proved uncontainable, hitting the floor with a loud flat splash.

There was a silence that emphasised how the stain was seeping into the concrete. Not until Crystal glanced up, looking ready for an argument, did Baz say "You've done it now."

"Better say you're sorry quick," Stu advised her.

"It wasn't sweet." When her complaint brought no response from Ian, not even a blink, she muttered "Sorry."

"Not to him," Shaun said.

She tugged at her hair. "Why not him? Who?"

"The little girl," said Ian. "You've woken her up."

Crystal tugged so hard her head began to cant as though the floor was drawing it sideways and down. "Where is she?"

"Under where you spat. You'd better talk to her before she comes to see who spat on her."

Crystal shoved herself in a single movement to the far end of the bench. Her heel caught an upright of the table, and her sandal flew off, slithering across the concrete toward the stain. "Don't want to," she wailed.

"You've got to. She knows you're here."

"If you don't talk to her she'll follow you home and get in your bed," Stu said.

"You've got to lie on the floor," Baz said, "so you can hear her."

"If you don't she'll come out," said Shaun, "and you won't like how she looks."

Crystal stared at him, her mouth pulling itself out of shape and releasing a trickle of red as though she had bitten her tongue. "This is where mum and dad were talking about and they stopped when I came in," she cried.

"Where the little girl was buried, that's right, under there, and now you're going to see her if she doesn't think you're sorry enough."

"She's got worms for eyes," Baz assured her.

"And her entrails are all hanging out with insects crawling on them," said Stu.

Ian thought the last two were going too far, at least for him, though they were causing Crystal's mouth to wrench itself into progressively more interesting shapes. For him it was sufficient that the new floor and all that it was meant to conceal had grown intensely present, its whiteness vibrating, the stain gleaming like the irrepressible mark of a death. "She made your shoe come off," he said. "She made it go to her. You'd better listen so you hear her. Listen hard and you will."

Crystal's eyes turned unwillingly toward the stain as though it, or something whose location it marked, had fastened on them. The rest of her appeared to be unable to move except for a slight quivering. Ian willed his friends not to give in to the temptation to make her jump, because he was sure that if they waited she would hear what she'd been told to hear. But he wasn't expecting to hear it—a muffled scraping like the sound of a buried finger trying to draw attention to itself.

The concrete appeared to flutter, having grown thin as a sheet that was about to be flung off. Then, as his friends swung round to stare along the hall, Ian realised that the sound wasn't in the kitchen. He'd heard car doors slamming near the house, but there was no reason why they should have anything to do with him. He was facing the front door, which was the only course of action his friends seemed able to think of, and there was no sound in the kitchen except for a tentative whimper from Crystal, when the door swung open and a stranger stepped into his house.

TWELVE

"You mustn't be doing too badly if you can afford to park off Piccadilly," Leslie said.

"I'm still trying to get my head around some things about England."

That might include driving on the unfamiliar side of the road, and so, as Jack Lamb turned the hired Nova along Park Lane, she confined herself to directing him. An ambulance racing to the children's hospital nearly made her send him into the wrong lane at Paddington, but once they'd escaped the hot clogged fuming streets under Westway, there wasn't much for her to do except tell him to carry on. The Grand Union Canal came to find the road and swung away again, taking with it a barge brighter than a florist's display, and the car was following an elongated lorry that wagged its drunken rear at them through Kensal Green when Jack said "Say, did I offend you somehow?"

"Not that I noticed. What makes you ask that?"

"Just that you've been quiet for a good while, but don't let me intrude if you've got things you need to think about."

"Nothing that won't keep. I just thought you might want to concentrate on driving."

"Am I that scary? I've been trying to take care."

"You're fine. I've never felt safer," Leslie said, and found she wasn't exaggerating out of politeness after all—he certainly never made her feel compelled to brake with her feet against the front of

the cabin, as Roger used to whenever he saw the slightest opportunity to overtake. "So how long have you been over here? Is this
your first time?"

"First time out of the US of A for Jack Lamb, and as I said to
your friend at the shop, just me, not my books."

"Let's hope before long it's both. And by the way, I wouldn't
want you to think I was laughing at you back there, just at that
awful man not realising where you came from."

"No mistaking that once I open my mouth though, huh?"

"Not much," Leslie said, and waited while he braked as the
lorry swayed left into Harlesden. "So how long has it been?"

"The cops would be after me in California," he said, and she
had to deduce the offence was having flashed his headlamps to
invite a woman in a Mazda to steer across his path. "Forgive me,
you were asking how long . . ."

"How long you've been in the old country."

"Got you. Just a few months. I'm staying with some friends in
Hampstead that I met at a concert in the Bowl. That's as close as
some of us Hollywood types get to your kind of music."

"I should think that must be pretty close."

"You wouldn't if you'd heard half the audience applaud whenever they thought the symphony was over. At least I knew better
than that. It was apologising to Charles and Liz because I'd heard
they were English that started us getting acquainted."

"So are you in films? That's to say, are your books?"

"I'm not a performer in either sense, I have to tell you. Wes
Craven's office asked my agent about one waste of paper, but that's
the only query I ever had a name for."

"It's researching your new one that's brought you to England,
then."

"It's the people who are making me want to stay."

"Tell me if I'm asking too many questions."

"I don't see how. You'll want to know about me."

That struck her as somewhat presumptuous, yet disconcert-
ingly true. She'd known him less than an hour, and she had no
idea how he might react to the disclosures she had still to make,
and so there was no point in liking him as much as she already did.
At least now they'd crossed the North Circular Road, requiring her
to direct him through the suburban streets. In two minutes they
were in sight of Jericho Close, on the corner of which Mrs. Lancing,

never a favourite neighbour of Leslie's, was in conversation with another woman. The Nova swung into Jericho Close and cruised to the end. "This is it," Leslie said.

So it was, and she didn't feel ready. Was she going to take him through the house before she told him what he had to be told? Apparently so, because now she had climbed out of the Nova and was preceding him along the path. She reached for her keys and heard someone calling her name—rather more than calling. Mrs. Lancing's partner in conversation was approaching with a purposefulness that drove all expression out of her face, which looked tightened by the ponytail that rendered her head too small for the large frilly blouse blossoming from her terse skirt. In a moment Leslie recognised her from having exchanged not much more than guarded greetings with her once at the school: Shaun Nolan's mother.

What had Ian been up to now? Nothing, Leslie suspected, that she wanted Jack Lamb to hear as his introduction to her household. She unlocked the front door and gave it a push. "Go right in," she said, and faced Mrs. Nolan, only to find her staring into the house. Before Leslie could turn she heard a little girl's cry along the hall.

She felt as though her keeping the secret of the house had caused it to manifest itself. As she swung round she had to grab the doorframe for fear of losing her balance. At first she couldn't see the child whose cry she'd heard, because Jack had stepped over the threshold and was blocking her view. "Hey, guys, what's been happening here?" he said.

The response was a rush of small feet. As if his appearance had proved too much for her, a little girl in a white dress and wearing a solitary sandal bolted out of the kitchen. He held up his hands to show they were harmless and dodged aside, and she shoved past Leslie onto the path. When her unsandalled foot caught on an edge of the jagged paving she fled one-legged, each hop jarring a whimper out of her. "Come here, Crys," Mrs. Nolan said in a voice too loud to be addressed solely to her, and flung Leslie's gate open so hard it rebounded from the wall. "Come here, love. What have they been doing to you? What's he been doing?"

It was clear from the look she aimed at Leslie that she wasn't referring to her own son. The mute accusation only aggravated the rage Leslie turned on Ian. "Just what have you been up to?"

He hadn't quite managed to produce the expression of bored

innocence his friends had achieved. "Showing her where it happened. She wanted to come."

"Sweetbreads to that, Ian, gonads. I can see how much she wanted to be here, so you explain—"

Mrs. Nolan was louder. "What did he do to you, Crys?"

"Excuse me, Mrs. Nolan, but I see four boys in there. I don't think there's any reason to assume it was all Ian's doing. If you'd like to come inside we can sort this out, I hope."

Crystal flinched against her mother and clung to her. "Not in there," she pleaded.

Leslie saw Jack not knowing what to do except stay in the hall and look neutral. The prospect of his tenancy was receding fast, and she felt angrier than ever, not least with herself for regretting that so much in the midst of everything else. "We'll go in the front room," she made herself suggest.

"We'll be going nowhere in there, Crys. One little girl may have come to harm, but you won't be another. Get out of it, Shaun, and bring the other two while you're at it. I don't want you near this house again."

Ian's friends obeyed readily enough by their standards, Shaun carrying a sandal like a trophy. They were passing the stairs when Jack stretched out a hand. "Listen, maybe you should stick around till this is sorted out."

"It's all right, Mr. Lamb, let them go. I'll get the truth out of my son."

"I wouldn't like to think what you'd get out of him or anybody who wants to live in that place."

Though Mrs. Nolan meant that for Ian and his mother, it was Jack who responded, levelling his fingers at himself. "Could be I'm one."

"Might do some good to have a man about the house," Mrs. Nolan said to nobody in particular, and to Jack "Have you got any idea what kind of place this is?"

"I believe I've figured that out, yes."

"God forgive you, then, if you have. You're as bad as her, and look how it's affecting her boy. Come away, Crys, and you, Shaun, and the two of you as well. You can be a bit less friendly with him in the future, Shaun. We don't want you ending up like him."

Leslie's anger nearly forced her mouth open, but a row in the street would only leave her feeling worse. She watched Mrs. Nolan

herd her children along Jericho Close, the other boys trailing behind. When she saw Mrs. Lancing hurry down her garden to accost
Shaun's mother, Leslie closed the front door with a gentleness that
felt like a slow-motion slam.

At least she wasn't angry with Jack. "I don't mean to sound
rude," she said to him, "but what do you think you've figured out?"

"Did I read about your house?"

"I don't know what you may have read. I don't know you that
well."

"This is where a little girl . . ."

"Was murdered by a man called Hector Woollie while he was
doing building work, and he buried her under the kitchen."

She'd wanted to get it said, but her brevity sounded callous to
her, as though the secret of the house was becoming simply a part
of her life. She thought she'd alienated him until he gave her a
careful smile. "That's what I thought," he said.

"I should have told you when you asked about the room."

"I can see how you might have decided that wasn't such a good
idea."

"Sorry," she said with a gesture that was on the way to reaching
for the latch. "So . . ."

"I wasn't planning to go anywhere unless you want me to
leave. I'm not like the lady who just left, I hope."

"I'm sure you aren't," Leslie said, withholding her delight—
there was still Ian to be dealt with and taken into account too. "I'd
better introduce my son. Ian, I said we're going in the front room."

"That's okay." As though to reassure her that he was harbouring no reservations about the house or anybody in it, Jack strode
into the kitchen and proffered his hand. "Ian, Jack Lamb."

Ian stared at the hand for only a moment before shaking it.
"Hi."

"You can hear where I'm from, and I've written a bunch of
horror books, so now you know all about me."

"Are you after the room, then?"

"If you'll both have me."

Ian gave a shrug that risked betraying some enthusiasm. "Fair
enough."

"Can I take that as a vote for me?"

A grin succeeded in escaping onto almost half of Ian's mouth.
"Expect so."

"Good deal. I've a feeling we'll have lots to talk about once I've settled in."

Leslie couldn't be sure if he was gently mocking Ian. "I'll show you the room so you can decide," she said, "and then I'll want a few words with you, Ian."

"Say, I hope you won't be embarrassed to have me round the place," Jack said to Ian. When the answer was even less than a shrug he turned to Leslie. "May I?"

Though he'd swung an open hand toward Ian, she had no idea what he was asking. "Why not," she nonetheless said.

"Okay, so listen, Ian. Let's not pretend I didn't see the situation when I came in. What was all that about exactly? What were you trying to do?"

"Just playing with her." Ian saw that wouldn't suffice, and made to shrug, but Jack raised his eyebrows. "Teasing her," Ian admitted. "Scaring her a bit."

"Is that your kind of fun?" Having waited until Ian shrugged, Jack said "Are we going to be honest with each other?"

"Maybe."

"Whose idea was it?"

"All of ours. Shaun said she wanted to come."

"It's your house though, isn't it? If you hadn't brought her nothing could have happened. Or did you need to see someone being scared like you sometimes are?"

"I'm not scared," Ian said fiercely.

"Well, good. No reason why you should be of anything here, is there? And I'm sure your mother isn't either or she wouldn't be living here." Jack looked at her for agreement, then gave her a wry smile instead. "Excuse me. I haven't been in the house more than a few minutes and already I'm taking over the show."

"You've done nothing I'd call wrong so far."

"Then I'll just finish. Ian, would you say I saw you at your worst when I came in? Is that right, mom?"

"He can be pretty decent when he wants to be, can't you, Ian?"

"I know it. How's this for a deal, Ian? Don't let me see anything bad about you again and you never will about me."

"Okay," Ian mumbled, if with a shrug.

"I can tell your mom wants to be proud of you, so let's give her plenty to believe in," Jack said, pretending not to have seen the boy blush. "Maybe I should see the room now, though there'd have to be a huge trick being played for me not to like it."

Leslie conducted him up past the framed record covers and opened the bedroom door. Sunlight was waiting in the room to demonstrate how white the quilt and the wardrobe and the rest of the furniture were. The subtle pattern of the discreetly green wallpaper looked overexposed or just starting to develop. "Told you," Jack said, kicking off his shoes, and lay back on the quilt, unselfconscious as a child in a holiday room. They hadn't discussed terms yet, Leslie thought, but she knew they would reach an agreement, and so she could acknowledge to herself how glad she was. Little as she liked to agree with anything Mrs. Nolan had said, he seemed capable of having such an effect on Ian that she might indeed be able to use this man about the house.

THIRTEEN

"Who's got my teeth?"

"What's Tom lost now?"

"Says his feet have gone."

"His what have?"

"Feet, I said. Has the wine messed up your ears as well as your eyes now? His feet."

"Shut up, can't you, and let me sleep."

"His feet have what?"

"How do I know? Gone like your ears and your eyes and the rest of the lump on top of your neck. Watch out the old women don't put it in the soup with the rats and all the stuff they get out of bins."

"What's gone now? It's full of thieves, this place is. They'd steal the lice off your head if you hadn't been sprayed. Smuggled a few of those in past the security last night all the same, I did. You've got to have some company. If you're quiet enough you can hear the tiny blighters talk."

"Isn't anybody listening? It's my teeth is gone, can't you hear? I'm naked without them."

"The lot of you shut up. Shut up, for Christ's sake."

"He isn't here. He stays upstairs, him. Got more sense than to come down here and smell us lot. He'd fall off his cross with the pong of some of us."

"What's someone saying about teeth?"

"It's old Tom. Couldn't be anybody else. Says they've run off like his pockets were supposed to have last week."

"Don't you go saying it's like my pockets. I just couldn't find them, that's all. Someone woke me in the middle of the night and got me all confused, and I'd still value knowing who. Teeth aren't pockets. They was under this pillow and now there's nothing, look. All of you look."

"We're looking. Might find some of your brain as well if you're lucky. It rolls out of your ear in the night, you know, and then one of the old women has to stuff it back in so you can wake up. I saw her doing it. She's your favourite, the one with the hairy blob under her chin who always gives you extra rats' tails in your soup."

"Don't you try confusing me, Bill Buncle. I'm not confused. I know someone nicked my teeth, and I'm having them back."

"There they go, under Carl's bed. Chatter chatter chatter."

"What's under my bed? God, it's a beetle, a bloody great beetle."

"It's your boot, you daft drunk sod."

By now the wakeful voices had strayed out of the middle of the dormitory beneath the cathedral and ended up beside the wall. "Shut up and let me sleep," he snarled at the owner of the boot, but it was no use. When at last exhaustion had proved stronger than the aching of his raw gums and the throbbing of his blistered feet and the relentlessness of the caged tube of light above him, a dim glow that clung like a coating of dust to the ranks of restless sleepers huddled under blankets, he'd seemed to sleep for hardly a minute before being wakened by a shrill wailing, a cry that had threatened to become so much worse he'd thought it must be Biff. Even when he'd managed to remember that there were no children in the place, the impression had persisted as the dull glow beyond his eyelids held his eyes. The world outside was full of children, and how could he avoid them all? The notion of their helpless suffering made him want to pull the rough blanket of the narrow trestle bed over his face, but he knew the women who ran the refuge wouldn't let anybody linger in bed, and he mustn't draw attention to himself: he had to pass for just another of the sweepings of the streets. He wasn't like them, and that was why he could pretend to be. Pretending to the extent of sharing the communal toilets and showers with them didn't appeal to him, however. He eased his stiff legs off the bed and pulled it away from the wall to retrieve the rucksack it had been protecting, and picked his way through the maze of grumbling dozers to the stony corridor.

The showers faced the toilet cubicles and the urinals with their pouting lower lips across a double line of sinks along the centre of the white-tiled room. The light on the tiles was as sharp as the smell of disinfectant in the air. Apparently none of the cubicles had ever benefited from a bolt on the door, and so he jammed his rucksack against the hinged inside of the door of the cubicle farthest from the corridor before lowering his clothes and trusting his buttocks to the scrawny plastic seat, which tried to sidle from beneath them. As in all the refuges he'd used, the paper on the roll was clinically harsh, the kind he'd dreaded every morning as a child but which Adele wouldn't have in the house or the care home. Adele had been all softness—her plump body, her yielding breasts, her hugs, her large dark eyes constantly on the lookout for a way to help someone. Never mind had been: still was, and now—

Footsteps were approaching the tiled room. He pressed his buttocks together and shut down his thoughts in case they somehow drew attention to him. The light quick footsteps halted at a urinal, where he would have expected the early riser to greet the day with a resounding hawk and a copious spit. Instead he heard an eventual trickle that sounded too thin for a grown man's, at the end of which the footsteps veered toward the middle of the room, and somebody began to whisper in a small high voice.

It sounded like a child, perhaps more than one. Had someone who worked in the refuge let their children use the toilet? Children would surely make more noise than that unless they knew he was in the cubicle—of course, they could see the rucksack under the door—and were discussing him. Except that the more he strained his ears, so hard his face ached almost as fiercely as his gums, the more he thought there was only one voice, one child whispering to itself. Why was it making sure he couldn't distinguish its words? Suppose the child's life was so dreadful that it couldn't be articulated even in a whisper? He didn't think so—he was beginning to suspect a trick. He craned forward and seized his rucksack, and then he did the unexpected: he snatched the rucksack away and threw the door open and lurched out of the cubicle as if he'd been tugged by his tube of limp flesh that even Adele had never seen, not even while they were labouring at making their son in their dark bed. The shackles of his trousers had sent him stumbling away from the

cubicle before he grasped that no child was to be seen in the tiled
room.

Yet it was still whispering, and now he could hear its message.
"Biff," it was repeating, "Biff." Was Biff able to whisper at last to
make up for all the screams he had uttered in life? Was he trying
to convey that he'd found peace? "Biff," Hector called, tugging his
trousers high enough to let him shuffle to the centre of the room.
In a moment he saw the mouth that was whispering to him—the
stiff greenish circular mouth of a plughole into which water was
trickling.

Had whoever was responsible crept out of the room? He
couldn't recall having heard them leave. Perhaps the whisper had
been a trick they'd tried to play on him so that he would betray
himself—but of course that made no sense, and he mustn't start
thinking such things just because he wasn't fully awake. He was
supposed to act confused, not be it. He twisted the tap, bruising his
fingers, until the whisper gurgled into silence. He was so intent on
hushing it wasn't until he looked up that he noticed two of the
vagrants he was trying to resemble staring at him from the corridor,
each with a hand on the other's arm.

They must think him as mad as one of Adele's residents. The
idea clenched on his mind, robbing him of the ability to move—
and then he remembered that he was meant to be an outcast people would prefer not to have near them. He took hold of his waste
tube and wagged it at the men, calling "It's good morning from me
and good morning from him." When they looked suitably disgusted
and convinced of his daftness he retreated into the cubicle and sat
on the unstable seat, his heels pressed against the door through the
rucksack. Once the showers began to hiss and splash he managed
to finish his own activity without emitting any sound that would
remind anyone he was there. At the least stained of the sinks he
confined himself to washing his hands and face while he gripped
the rucksack between his ankles. He dried himself on the plain
rough towel he'd been issued, and dabbed at the sodden cuffs of
the overcoat he'd worn even in bed, and spat a little blood into the
sink before heading for the breakfast hall.

He could think of so little to say to any of the loudmouths and
ranters and babblers who wandered in after him that he was glad
when it was time for prayers and hymns. Behind the counter at
the end of the wide cardboard-coloured room full of trestle tables,

women put aside their ladles and spatulas to hold up their prayerful hands while a blurred smell of porridge and bacon descended upon the gathering like the promise of a reward for their devotion. He wasn't about to pray or sing hymns—no matter how desperately he'd prayed, it had done Biff no good. Instead he murmured "Now I lay you down to sleep . . ." in the midst of the prayers and sang it for a hymn, and didn't care if the priest in a polo-necked shirt who was leading the chorus noticed. At last it was time to shuffle to the counter as if his trousers were still around his ankles. The woman with the spatula gazed at him out of her pale toby jug of a face topped by a froth of white curls that spilled down the back, and eventually declared "New face."

How could she know he'd made himself one? His picture shouldn't have been in the paper for weeks. He felt as though it had fitted itself over his altered features—that she was watching it stiffen them into itself. His mouth had begun to grow unworkable before he understood her. "Came here yesterday," he said.

"Let's have a name, then."

"Bert. Bert Walker."

"You won't be wanting to hang around me."

Her gaze hadn't shifted—he wasn't sure she'd even blinked. The queue behind him was trying to distract him with several impatient voices. "Why not?" he demanded.

"Not unless you've got some teeth to put in there for me."

She was saying he wouldn't be able to deal with her bacon sandwiches. "I'll have to make do with porridge," he said, sidling along the counter to her colleague, who dug her ladle into the tureen of bubbling white sludge and raised her shrunken bright-eyed face, unwrinkling her leathery neck. "You'll need to get them seen to," she advised him.

"What?"

She doubled her volume and halved her speed. "You ought to get yourself fixed up with some teeth."

From a nearby table came a dull clang of metal against china, and a shout with some consonants missing. "What's that about teeth?"

"Not yours, Tom. I'm telling our new friend he needs some."

Hector turned from the counter with his bowl of porridge glistening with milk to find toothless caved-in Tom watching him. There was a seat on the bench opposite Tom, and he took it, hitching up his rucksack on his shoulder. While he waited for the porridge to stop steaming, he found blood on his gums with his tongue and ignored the way Tom was tugging at his own lower lip to expose the lack within. At last the porridge looked cool enough for Hector to risk a spoonful, which he was lifting to his mouth when Tom let out a snarl and a more than generous amount of moisture. "Looking for some teeth for yourself last night, was you? Find some under my pillow?"

"I'd stick nothing in my mouth that's been anywhere near yours, believe me." Hector tipped the spoon into his mouth and champed the porridge with his gums, only to find that it was still too hot for them. The ache blazed through them and pierced his brain, and he leaned across the table, spitting porridge into Tom's face. "Want to search me? Want to stick your fingers up my arse to see if I've hidden them there, is that your style?"

The priest hurried over, pulling at his polo-neck as if he'd only just discovered that he'd forgotten to wear his clerical collar. "Some disagreement here, chaps? Can I take an overview? I'm sure it should prove helpful."

"Someone nicked my teeth while I was asleep," Tom said more sullenly than distinctly, wiping his face.

Hector subsided onto the bench and loaded his mouth with a spoonful of porridge from the edge of the bowl. If his gums had been able to flinch, they would have. He sucked in a breath to lower the temperature, then he swallowed the searing mouthful and threw the spoon on top of the pasty mass. "Want a poke round in my bag to see if there's any teeth in it?"

"I'm sure that won't be necessary. I'm sure Tom—"

"I've got a voice in my head, padre, thanks ever so buggering much. It's teeth I haven't got, and as long as he's saying we can look in his bag—"

"That's it. I'm not staying here to be called a thief. Thanks for the bed and the prayer meeting, and you're welcome to this slop."

"Hang on, please. Do please hang on, what's his name, Bert? Bert, please don't fly off, I'm sure between the three of us we can—"

That was all Hector heard before he was out of earshot. As he tramped along the corridor and up the stone stairs he mouthed his thanks to Tom, who had given him an excuse to leave so ostentatiously that nobody would suspect him of having anything to hide. When the steps brought him into the sunlight beside the cathedral, he shrugged off his rucksack and dug among the few clothes it contained as he limped into the enormous porch. Having retrieved both sets of Tom's teeth, he dunked them in the font and sloshed them about in the holy water until he considered them clean enough for his mouth.

They didn't fit. Tom's mouth had appeared to be the same size as his, but the teeth were more curved than Hector's gums, if only slightly. When he tried to force them into place, first with his hands and then by closing his jaws with the teeth jammed between them, he felt as though he was grinding his gums raw all the way to the bone. "If I chuck them back in your water," he mumbled, relaxing his jaws, "will you make them fit? That wouldn't be much of a miracle, would it?" The teeth chattered while he spoke as if they were urging him to make the act of faith, and for an instant he contemplated it, until he realised that then he would be as deranged as the worst of Adele's residents. Adele . . . He spat the teeth and several crimson blots into the font and trudged away from the cathedral.

It didn't take his feet long to remind him they were capable of aching as badly as his gums. He couldn't go on like this. He was out in the open again, beneath a sky as bright as any child's room. Wherever he walked he would encounter children sooner or later—the world was crawling with them—and what might he have to do if he wasn't able to make them laugh? He couldn't hide from himself, but at least he could try to hide from them. And however long it took him to get there, however painful the journey might be, he'd thought where he could hide.

FOURTEEN

Ian was so disappointed not to be home from school to help their new tenant move in that Jack let him assist with the unpacking instead. When Leslie returned from work that Friday, she found the Nova parked outside the house and heard two pitches of male laughter in the back bedroom. Jack was transferring the last few shirts into the wardrobe from one of a pair of large suitcases while Ian lifted books out of a carton with a thoughtfulness she'd never previously seen him show for books. "Mom, can I read this one?" he said.

These days his asking permission for anything was exceptional. "Better ask Mr. Lamb."

"Jack," Jack said to both of them. "Your mom mightn't be too happy with you reading that, Ian, or trying to sound like me either."

"I don't mind if you don't," Leslie said, having leaned across the bed, the quilt yielding beneath her hand, to glance at the apparently unillustrated black cover on which the title and his name were composed of bones. "*The Old Monster* isn't for children, then."

"Is that what it sounds like? Could be that's why it didn't do so well."

"We'll let Ian give you his opinion. At least it's a book, not a video."

"Great," Ian said, and hugged the fat book.

"Maybe not that great," Jack told him. "The scariest part is the author photograph."

As Ian turned the book over, the front caught the light and flashed Leslie a glimpse of a malevolent old face grinning like a skull. She preferred the image on the back, of the author with hair streaming over his shoulders, with a smile that looked close to having been held a moment too long. From the youthfulness of the photograph, not least its hint of vanished brashness, she guessed the book to be five or six years old. She pushed herself up from the bed and smoothed the quilt as Ian lifted a hand to stifle his mirth. "It's okay to laugh, trust me," Jack said.

"Okay then, I won't."

Leslie didn't know whether he was so ready to please Jack because he was American, or from Hollywood, or a writer, or even just a man, and she was content not to care. "Let's let Jack settle in for a while."

"I was going to show him some tricks with my word processor," Jack said.

"In that case I'll leave you men to entertain each other while I get on with dinner."

"Do you need to fix it?"

"It won't take long. It isn't too elaborate a welcome, I'm afraid. I didn't know what you liked."

"Can it wait until tomorrow? Then why don't you save it and I'll buy you both dinner. I feel like celebrating where I've ended up."

Ian was pretending to read the blurb of the novel and imperfectly concealing an expression not unlike the one Melinda would have worn if she'd observed the situation. "Did you have anywhere special in mind?" Leslie said.

"I don't know this part of town too well yet. If you have a favourite I can drive wherever you like."

"And not drink."

"You have to get used to that in Angel City. That and having to tell the same story over and over until it doesn't feel like a story any more."

"Sorry, telling a story . . ."

"To movie producers, in case they're the one who buys what you're offering."

"Someone still could even though you're over here, do you

think? If you want to share a bottle there's a good Chinese restaurant down on the main road we could walk to."

"Sounds fine to me if it does to Ian."

Ian was reading the first page of *The Old Monster*. "It's good," he said without looking up.

She steered him, still reading, out of the room. She watched him make his slow way downstairs, turning another page as he reached the hall, before she went into her room to choose an outfit. Her favourites all had something to do with Roger. For months that hadn't bothered her, but now, inexplicably and so even more annoyingly, it did. The black dress she'd worn for clubbing with him in the West End, the ankle-length cream silk he'd bought for her last birthday, the pert red one to which she'd treated herself for their second honeymoon, a weekend spent in Paris while eleven-year-old Ian had given her mother plenty to criticise once she'd handed Leslie a brimming cup of boiling tea to keep her seated . . . She was only going out for a Chinese meal, for heaven's sake. Eventually, after a session of holding clothes in front of herself as though she were the sort of cardboard figure she used to dress when she was little, she put on the white silk blouse and pinstriped skirt and jacket she'd worn for the opening of the shop, a costume that had certainly pleased Melinda. She hooked silver stars into her earlobes and dabbed perfume behind her ears, and stepped out of the bedroom to meet Ian on his way upstairs. "Will I do?" she said.

"More than that," Jack said, emerging from his room.

He was wearing a white linen jacket, pale grey knife-edged slacks, a dark grey shirt and slim back tie. "You will too," she was able to say without blushing, for which she was far too old, and walked lightly downstairs to let them all out of the house.

Janet from next door and Mrs. Lancing were in conversation halfway along Jericho Close. They turned as Jack, having held the gate for both the Ameses, closed it with a snap of the latch. "Hello, Leslie and Ian," Janet said, "and hello . . ."

"Jack," Ian said with a proprietary air.

"Jack Lamb," said Jack.

"I'm Leslie's neighbour Janet Hargreaves. Welcome to Wembley."

Mrs. Lancing had kept her gaze on him but swung her head aside as if attending to a commentary. "Aren't you quite a long way from home?" she not so much asked as informed him.

"Not any more."

"It's the kind of place you'd live, is it, in America?"

"It's the kind of hospitality I'd hope for, sure enough."

"And have you and Mrs. Ames known each other long?"

"Feels like it."

Leslie hardly hesitated. "I'd say that too."

"You'll have met here, I suppose, since Ian and his parents never managed a trip to America."

"Last week. The day you watched me arriving," Jack said. "I saw Leslie had a room to let. Turned out it was just the place for me to work on my new book."

"So do we take it that you work from home?"

"That's how I'd like to think of it, sure."

"I imagine it will do no harm to have another adult in the house to keep a check on things."

Leslie opened her mouth, but Jack was faster. "Seems to me Mrs. Ames is doing, you'll forgive me if you need to, goddamned fine under all the circumstances, and Ian's shaping up pretty well too if people give him the chance."

"Well—"

"Which is how it is with most of us, I was going to say."

"And I was about to say we're all entitled to our opinion."

"You bet, only maybe some—"

"I can tell one of us is starving," Leslie said, steering Ian away with an arm around his shoulders. "See you, Janet. Come for coffee soon."

Leslie's party was at the corner of Jericho Close when Jack said "Sorry if I said too much back there. Full of words, that's my problem."

"I don't think either of us was complaining, were we, Ian?" She might have taken Jack's arm if that wouldn't have seemed too forward, not to mention the risk of embarrassing Ian. Instead she was doubly, if silently, appreciative of being doubly escorted to the main road.

They were nearly at the restaurant when a boy who was emerging from a newsagent's stood and stared at them. He was about Ian's age, wearing leather and chains, and had a dull somewhat pudgy face that Leslie took to be the product of depression and too much junk food. He gripped his thighs, digging his thumbs into them, and scowled after Ian. "Friend of yours?" Jack murmured.

"Rupe Duke? He's nobody's friend much."

"Good Lord, that's who he is, of course." When Jack had closed the door of the restaurant behind them Leslie explained "He's the brother of the little girl . . . you know, the little girl . . ."

"Should anybody talk to him right now?"

"I think it's best left, Jack, if that isn't too English of me. Do you ever speak to him at school, Ian?"

"He isn't in my class."

That was presumably as much of an answer as Ian wanted to give, and Leslie was afraid that insisting might make him revert to his previous taciturn self. She followed the waiter to the table, where Jack told her and Ian more than once to order whatever they liked, after which he nearly deceived her by pretending to be the kind of American who ordered a meal and then asked the kitchen to hold the sauce, and succeeded in persuading Ian that there was a Cantonese delicacy called Butterfly Wing Soup, consisting of water in which the wings of butterflies were soaked until they vanished, and produced two lines of a limerick for Leslie—

"When he's writing his music, Ry Cooder
Shouts out words that are ruder and ruder . . ."

—before desisting with a droll apologetic look. He challenged Ian to pick up the smallest amount of rice with chopsticks, though it looked as if Leslie would beat both of them until Jack lifted a single grain of rice to his apologetically smiling mouth. By this time Leslie had seen off more of the second bottle of Chablis than he had, thanks to his refilling her glass whenever it was on the way to being empty, as he told Ian tales of his boyhood, trout fishing with his grandfather who could trail his fingers in a stream to call a fish, helping in the auto repair shop Jack's three uncles and his father owned, his mother teaching him to play basketball at midnight in a floodlit cage, the years of Thanksgiving dinners where all the aunts told him he wouldn't be a man until he could carry the twenty-pound bird by himself to the table . . . By now Leslie felt mellow from head to foot, even a shade unsteady when at last they abandoned the remains of dinner, so that outside the restaurant she had no hesitation in accepting the support of Jack's arm.

Ian didn't mind, or only to the extent of walking ahead, which struck her as having more to do with encouragement than embarrassment, not that she intended anything other than a leisurely stroll. The quiet suburban houses glowed from within, the streetlamps seemed to be lighting the way to the future. She squeezed Jack's arm and relinquished it as they came to their gate.

She saw Ian unlock the front door and step into the house. A moment later the hall fitted a carpet of light to the path. Ian had halted at the foot of the stairs and was gazing toward the kitchen—into the kitchen. She'd closed all the doors before leaving the house, yet the kitchen door was wide open.

A shiver chased away her mellowness as she ventured into the house. A chill had come down the hall to meet her, and something else was wrong with the kitchen. The view beyond the back door was too clear—she was no longer seeing it through glass. A glistening of crimson drew her attention upward. With a cry of dismay and rage that left her throat raw, she sprinted up the stairs to read the words that were dripping from the door of her room and Ian's and Jack's.

FIFTEEN

It was only a bit of paint sprayed on the doors and spattering the carpet in front of them, Leslie kept telling herself. Whatever people said, being broken into couldn't be as bad as being raped, though the sense of being invaded had lodged deep in her body, the sense that someone had delighted in the mess they'd left. Jack brought her a coffee Ian had made, a bubble that looked full of brown earth bursting on its surface, and then he loitered by the stairs, visibly wishing he could do more to help. The coffee only lent the dullness that was her delayed shock a harsh edge. "At least you can't say your first night wasn't memorable," she said.

His lips twitched as if he didn't feel entitled to smile. "It already was."

"For us too. Thanks again."

"Gee, I wish you wouldn't say that."

"Why ever not?"

"Because if I hadn't insisted on buying you guys dinner your house would be fine now."

"It's still going to be. We'll make sure it is, won't we?" Ian had emerged from the kitchen, allowing her to turn to him and let Jack choose whether he wanted to be included in her pronouncement. She sensed he was about to respond when they heard a car door slam, echoed instantly by its twin.

She pulled the front door open just not soon enough to head off the doorbell. The unnecessary trill sounded more piercing than usual, and she hoped the pair of policemen didn't assume she'd stiffened at the sight of them, their thin faces younger than hers and looking as though they had recently been scrubbed by their mothers, their chins blue as litmus from the hours they must already have worked. "Mrs. Ames?" the foremost, whose sharp quick eyes were almost exactly the colour of his chin, said.

"Come in."

He gazed at her as if he was waiting for his question to be answered, then he planted one foot in the hall. "Did we ask you not to touch anything?"

"No, but we haven't."

"That'll do," he said, both feet in the hall now, and emitted a sniff that she thought was referring to the vandalism until he added "You'll have had a drink to help you cope, will you?"

"Just some wine with dinner. We were dining out when whoever broke in broke in."

"Somewhere local, was it?"

"Close enough that we all walked to it, if that's what you're getting at."

"I was trying to establish how long you were out of the house."

"Three hours at least," she told him and his brown-eyed colleague, whose face immediately toned down the little expression it had. "We were back by half past ten and I rang you it couldn't have been more than five minutes later."

"It's been a full night," the policeman with the chin-blue eyes said, presumably explaining the hour's delay. "So where's the damage?"

"They broke in at the back, and what they did is upstairs."

"Are you saying they because you think you can identify the perpetrators?"

"No, I'm saying it because I don't."

His gaze flickered at that, then raised itself above her. "I'll deal with upstairs."

He was speaking mostly to his colleague, who headed for the kitchen. "Good excuse for staying up late, is it, son?" Leslie heard him say, and Ian barely answer, while blue-eyes halted on the stairs. "This is about your house," he said.

Leslie saw the graffiti swell up like red weals on the wood. KILLER LOVER, they said on her door, and KILLERS FRIEND on Ian's. The wielder of the aerosol must have run out of ideas or paint or time in front of Jack's door, on which there was either too much of a word—KILLE—or not enough. A sudden prickling of her eyes made her blurt "Why, do you think it should be?"

"It's not my job to have opinions like that, Mrs. Ames."

There was little doubt in Leslie's mind that he meant yes. She was struggling not to retort when he said "Were these doors open?"

"No," Leslie admitted, the paint on the carpet having betrayed as much. "We needed to look in the rooms."

"Pity. Knobs are favourite for prints," he said, surveying the chaos in the rooms—not so different from usual in Ian's, but clothes strewn on her floor and Jack's, drawers pulled out, wardrobes gaping, quilts thrown or kicked to the floor. "Have you missed anything?"

"Nothing's been taken that we can see, can't see, if you see what I mean."

"Let's see if there's any joy downstairs."

She trudged after him in time to hear his colleague say "And where are you from, sir?"

"Hollywood," Ian responded with some pride on Jack's behalf.

"Does this look like a professional job to you?" Jack said.

"In what way, sir?"

Jack was indicating the old sink plunger that had apparently been used to hold the pane in the back door steady while the edge of the glass had been carefully smashed. "More likely they got the idea from a film," the policeman said with a brown-eyed glance at him, so blank it was meaningful.

"I'll do the paperwork if you want to take a look around," his colleague said and sat on a kitchen bench.

He asked Leslie questions about herself and Ian followed by questions about Jack while the other policeman prowled the back garden toward the alley gate Leslie'd locked last night, no longer locked. Before the questions ceased she was having to close her eyes, because the floor kept twitching like a sheet about to be thrown off a sleeper. She could have imagined the night was half over when she heard "Was there anything you'd like to add?"

It was a mutter from Ian, not quite a word, that made her open her eyes. "Sorry," she said for more than one reason. "No."

"We'll get out of your way," the other policeman offered, locking the door with her key and lifting the sink plunger in a plastic bag, and then the doorbell contradicted him. "That'll be fingers," he said.

The newcomer was a short man in a gray suit rather too ample for him. His freckled dome was striped with half a dozen lines of faded black hair. His expression as he spread dust on various surfaces suggested that he was unable to shift an unpleasant taste from his mouth. He seemed especially to dislike being watched at work by Ian, though Leslie didn't see why he should object to someone following him around their own house and into their own bedroom. Eventually the fingerprint man tramped downstairs, looking dissatisfied. "Are you through?" Jack said.

The man sucked in his lips as if he'd swallowed some of the dust. "We'll want your prints."

At first Leslie thought only Jack was going to be fingerprinted, presumably for being a foreigner. Once that was finished it was Ian's turn, however, and then hers to be made to feel like a criminal, having ink rolled onto her fingertips before they were pressed one by one against an official sheet of paper. By the time the last of her fingers had been pinched in his finicky grip she felt manhandled and grubby. As she held her blackened hands away from herself Jack said "That's going to help, right? You had to eliminate us."

"I doubt that'll be called for."

"By which you mean . . ." Leslie prompted.

He didn't answer until he'd snapped the locks shut on his briefcase. "Anyone who takes that much care breaking in isn't likely to leave prints."

Leslie felt more than ever like a victim, and not just of the break-in. She let Jack and Ian see him out while she used a nailbrush in the bathroom, then hurried downstairs to clear away the broken glass, only to find Jack busy with dustpan and brush, and Ian on his hands and knees in search of stray fragments. "Can you get the window fixed tonight?" Jack said.

"It'll wait until tomorrow so long as nobody can get in."

He helped her upend the table against the door and wedge it with the benches. She switched off the fluorescent tube, though a trace of its glare appeared to linger in the concrete, and led the way upstairs, bracing herself for the sight of the raw words on the doors. "I should try and get some sleep, Ian," she said. "You'll have all tomorrow to tidy your room."

Perhaps that sounded too much like her frequent rebuke. "Won't need it," he muttered.

"Will it bother anybody if I make a start on my room now?" Jack said. "Just thump on the wall if I keep you awake."

Once Leslie had closed her door she had to restrain herself to tidying only the bed. She lay naked beneath the quilt, all her skin tender with her sense of the invasion of the house. Every so often she heard faint sounds through the wall she shared with Jack, the metallic whisper of a coat hanger, the hushed creak of a board. She found herself waiting at the edge of sleep for a cry that would mean he'd discovered his research or however much of his new book he'd written had been tampered with or destroyed. But his room stayed almost as quiet as the suburb, and eventually she deduced that he must have crept into bed.

For the first time in months she felt alone in hers. She stretched one arm across the mattress and turned her empty hand palm upward, and squeezed a fistful of the quilt. The thoughts she began to entertain, if a little guiltily, resembled a better dream than she would have expected of herself just now, and in time her awareness of being less alone in the house than yesterday allowed her to sleep.

She was wakened by smells of coffee and bacon and toast, and Jack's and Ian's voices downstairs. All that made the sight of the sunlit mess around the bed more bearable than she would have dared hope, and she was letting herself bask for a few seconds in a sense of unexpected rightness, when it occurred to her that the kitchen staff might be planning to serve her breakfast in bed. She kicked off the quilt and grabbed her bathrobe from the hook on the door, and was tying the cord around herself when the doorbell rang. "I'll get it," Jack said.

She heard his footsteps, which already seemed part of the house, tramp along the hall. She heard the front door open, and Jack's surprised voice, and then Ian's. "Don't let her in," he shouted.

SIXTEEN

Ian had almost finished cramming socks and shorts into the top drawer when he heard Jack go downstairs. He would have called out to him except for not wanting to wake his mother. She must be the worst upset of anyone about last night, and she was getting old—she'd be forty in just a few years. He leaned his weight on the stuffed drawer to close it, then he went down to find Jack.

He was in the kitchen doorway, gazing into the room. He didn't notice when Ian paced along the hall and stared past him. "What's wrong?" Ian said.

"God *damn*." That was all the surprise Jack betrayed as he turned to grin. "I thought I'd fix breakfast for your mom after her evening was ruined. Just trying to decide what to put together for her."

"Oh, right," Ian said, though it was evident to him that Jack's thoughts had been on more than breakfast—he guessed, with some amusement he managed to keep to himself, that they had been focused on his mother. "Want some help?"

"How are you at scrambling eggs?"

"Don't know."

"Better leave the little guys to me, then, and you can be the toast and bacon chef."

"No problemo," Ian said, which he thought was the kind of thing Americans said or liked to hear.

As he laid rashers of bacon on the grill and tried to judge how crisp they ought to be before they were joined by slices of bread, he felt increasingly American himself, a cook in a diner. He liked having someone new in the house whom he could sense there was plenty to learn about yet, unlike his father, who had become less and less of himself in the months before he and Ian's mother had split up, and whose efforts to regain himself since he'd moved in with Hilene were too obvious and strenuous. Ian no longer resented him so much for having moved out—could even be grateful to him for taking the tension out of the house. If Ian's mother carried on growing happier, that was fine too—would have been if last night hadn't been wrecked. Was he alone in having identified the culprit? Once he'd discharged his duties as short order cook he meant to ask if Jack had solved the case too. But he was standing guard over the last slices of toast when the doorbell rang.

"I'll get it," Jack said, so swiftly that Ian supposed he must be expecting some post—some mail, as he determined to call it from now on. He watched Jack transfer the scrambled eggs in a single uninterrupted movement from the pan to the plate with a spatula and slide the plate into the oven on the way to consigning pan and spatula to the sink as a preamble to striding down the hall to open the front door. "Excuse me," he said, adding with a brightness that seemed meant to apologise for his apology "Hi. Are you looking for Mrs. Ames?"

"Whom else?"

Ian recognised both the voice and the grammar before he saw the reporter from the *Advertiser* sitting in her wheelchair on the path. "Don't let her in," he shouted, imagining how little his mother would want to find her in the house.

The reporter scarcely even blinked at him on the way to raising her appraisal to Jack's face. "And you'll be . . ."

"Jack Lamb. I'm the lodger. How about you?"

Ian heard his mother's footsteps, anything but gentle, and the thud of her doorknob against the wall. He grabbed a plate and loaded it with the contents of the grill and shut the plate in the oven as his mother marched rapidly downstairs to confront the reporter, who said "I represent the press" and then "I understand you've had some further trouble, Mrs. Ames."

"May I ask who told you that?"

"An anonymous call to the paper. My colleague who took it

thought the voice was disguised and couldn't tell the age or gender."

"When?"

"Close to midnight, I believe. It was thought best not to trouble you that late."

"And what did your friend say?"

"My colleague? The caller. Just that your house had been broken into and vandalised as a result of its reputation."

" 'The Ames house has been broken into and vandalised as a result of its reputation.' "

"Words to that effect," the reporter said blankly, "yes."

"Well, they were right, and you don't need me to tell you it must have been one of your readers, except of course it might have been more than one."

"Mrs. Ames," the reporter said, though she was looking at Jack, "I really don't think you can blame—"

"Can't I? Watch me." Ian's mother darted into the front room to fetch a copy of the *Advertiser*. "I ought to introduce you, Jack. This is Verity Drew, and here's the kind of thing she writes: MOTHER AND SON TO STAY IN MURDER HOUSE. Mrs. Ames claimed she had overcome her feelings about the house's history of horror, and her thirteen-year-old son agreed with her. 'It's my favourite house' is something else it says I said."

"I assure you I'm not given to misquotation, Mrs. Ames, but if you have any specific complaints you'd care to put in writing to my editor—"

"I'd rather not join your happy band of letter-writers, thanks. I'd just like you to see what someone did, only you can't, can you? It's upstairs."

She would never have made such a remark if she wasn't almost uncontrollably furious. Whatever reaction the journalist might have displayed was precluded by the slam of a door of a car that had parked behind hers. She peered around her chair as a man festooned with camera equipment opened the gate. "Perhaps you'll permit my photographer to view the scene instead."

"He won't be scared to come in? He won't be tainted by his visit? He can wait until I'm dressed." Ian's mother held the lapels of her shaggy white bathrobe together as she padded upstairs, then she leaned over the banisters. "No, someone bring him up if he wants a picture of the doors. I've said enough."

"Let me," Jack called, and climbed the stairs ahead of the photographer. "No need to have me in it," he protested when the camera began to whir and click, and Ian wished he'd gone up instead of Jack, because he wouldn't have minded being shown as the custodian of the graffiti. The photographer scampered downstairs with a rattle of equipment and out of the house, and Verity Drew gazed up at Ian and Jack. "One further matter I'd like to raise," she said.

"Would you care to come in and sit down?" Jack suggested.

"Sitting in the sunlight suits me, thank you. I understand some little girls have been terrorised here recently."

Though she'd turned most of her attention on Ian, it was Jack who said "Did you get another anonymous call?"

"You wouldn't expect us to dismiss anybody's genuine concern just because of how it might be expressed," the reporter informed him, and stared wholly at Ian. "What can you tell me about these little girls?"

"Excuse me, I think at least you'd better wait—"

"It's okay, Jack, I don't mind telling. One was my dad's girlfriend's who got scared when he came in the house, and the other was my friend's little sister. She did come in with me and our lot, then she got scared and ran off."

"Scared of what exactly?"

"We were pretending there was a ghost or something." He was growing increasingly conscious of being heard by Jack. "We never thought there was really," he said, struggling not to lie in case that made Jack more rather than less dissatisfied with him, "and I dunno if she did either."

"You quite enjoyed the game, did you?"

"Suppose."

"Frightening people younger than yourself."

"Hold on, ma'am, don't try to make him into something he isn't. Didn't you ever throw a scare into a younger kid? Sounds as if maybe it got a tad out of hand, but he's sorry for it. I shouldn't think an incident as small as that is worth reporting even in a local paper."

"May I ask why you would want it suppressed, Mr. Lamb?"

"I don't hold with censorship. I couldn't very well when I've written horror books. I just think these guys have been harassed enough."

"Are you suggesting I'm harassing them?"

"If he's not," Ian's mother said, "I am."

She was wearing a T-shirt and shorts, and Ian had to straighten a grin at Jack's admiring glance as she moved between him and the reporter, saying "I apologise for what I said about not being able to handle the stairs."

"I accept your apology," Verity Drew said stiff-faced.

"But now we've had enough of you. I don't think there's anything more to be said."

"Well, Mrs. Ames, I must say it's a change for you to want to keep me out of your house. As I recall, last time you and your son did your best to keep me in it."

"Then your memory wants fixing. All I did was try and help you down the step because you seemed to need help."

"You'll forgive my wondering what policy you have as regards the alternatively able where you work."

"Anyone can come into the shop straight off the pavement, can't they, Jack, only you'd call it the sidewalk. As far as employment goes there's just me and my partner Melinda, and we're both, how can I put it, what you see."

"I've seen all I require, thank you," the reporter said, and performed a rapid three-point turn on the path before glancing back. Ian was tempted to run after her and at least push her out of the gate, and he'd taken a step when his mother planted a hand on his chest as she closed the door. "We can't stop her saying whatever she's going to say. Maybe her editor won't let her indulge herself too much."

"She'll get round that. She knows how to say things so you can't prove she did."

"Not like us straightforward Yanks." Observing that his remark made Ian no happier, Jack said "There's one good thing about all this publicity."

"What?"

"Yes, what's that?" Ian's mother said.

"It—it finishes. It ends. Mine surely did for my books. Say, am I the only one that's hungry here? That breakfast smells like it wants to be eaten."

"I think that's the best idea anybody's had this morning."

Ian thought he had a better one that it was time to share. He waited until he and Jack had served his mother breakfast and he was seated in front of his own, his bare feet resting on concrete almost as warm as sunlit earth, and then he said "If she's going to write stuff about us we should have told her who messed up the place."

His mother opened her mouth before she'd quite finished her mouthful. "Why, who do you think it was?"

"Mom, I mean mum, you saw him. You know who it's got to be, don't you, Jack?"

"You mean the guy we saw last night near the restaurant?"

"That's him. Rupe Duke. Did you know it was before I said? You could have told the paper woman. She'd have believed you more than me."

"I only figured he was who you had to mean. I guess I'd need more evidence before I shot my mouth off."

"And there isn't any, is there, Ian? We can't go accusing someone just because of how they looked at us. I'm afraid on that basis it could have been a good few people."

"We don't have any reason to assume that lady would have bought it from an old storyteller like me," Jack said, and loaded his mouth.

"If you wanted to be really helpful, Ian, you could go down to the shops after breakfast and buy something to clean off the paint while I see who'll fix the window, and then I'll go to work."

He took this as a way of dismissing his suspicions, though he thought Jack might have believed him. Once he'd downed his breakfast and offered to wash up, only to have Jack say he would, he pocketed the money his mother gave him and went upstairs to fish some footwear out of the disorder in his room. From the hall he saw Jack and his mother at the sink, standing so close to each other they were bound to touch soon. He grinned and let himself out of the house.

The Homeneeds store occupied most of a block of the main road. An assistant in an overall red as a brick and with bristling orange hair that stopped short an inch above his outsize ears sold him a can of paint remover and a brush. The lumpy plastic carrier practiced bruising Ian's thigh as he emerged into the sunlight, more of which the front of a bus to Pinner threw at him. He closed his eyes to clear them of blindness, and opened them to see Rupe Duke swaggering toward him.

Though the pavement was crowded with shoppers, Ian saw

only him. He was wearing more leather than ever, much of it displaying a rash of studs. He held his fists at his sides and jerked his face higher and shaped his mouth into an inverted grin, and stood in Ian's path. "Fixing your house?" he said, so monotonously it was barely a question.

Ian didn't swing the heavy can at the other boy's face or at his crotch, he simply came to a halt. "What's it look like?"

"Something need doing?"

"You should know."

"Who says?"

"I do. You were there."

"Who says I was?"

His eyes were flat, and their dullness hoped to be kindled with violence, but it struck Ian that the question could mean one or more of the neighbours had seen Rupe breaking in. If they'd intended to tell Ian's mother they would have done so by now, and so they must think she wasn't worth telling. "You and me know," he said into Rupe's face, "and I'm going to make you know I do."

"Try it. Go ahead, try it now. Don't dare, do you? I'm not some little girl you like scaring." When Ian walked past him, Rupe dodged around him and backed ahead of him, butting his head at him as though to invite the first punch. This wasn't the place, and so Ian was glad to encounter Janet from next door, wheeling a heaped Frugo trolley home and looking to him for help. He saw Rupe fall behind, sending a gob of spit down the side street after him, but he was more aware of the crowd through which Rupe had stayed with him—of all the faces that had seemed to be expecting him to maim Rupe, to live up to the reputation they were creating for him. He'd deal with Rupe all right, but he'd choose the time and place. Even Jack couldn't stop him from doing what so many people expected of him.

SEVENTEEN

"Adele, don't scream or anything. It's me. It's your dad."

"Daddy, how can it be you? You're dead. You've been dead for years."

"Not your real dad. Hush and look closer."

"My God, it's you, Hector. You poor thing, what have they done to you?"

"Wipe your eyes now. No need to feel sorry for me when I've come home. Nobody's had hold of me, don't fret. I did this."

"How could you hurt yourself like that, Hector? How could you bear it?"

"Because I knew I was only doing what I had to, just like always. It was worth it to be safe. None of the neighbours know your father's dead. Once they've got used to him living with you, he'll be able to go out of the house when he wants and lead a normal life."

"You make sure you're careful, Hector. I thought I'd lost you when you fell out of that boat. I don't want to be losing you again."

"I won't be going that far again, promise. Maybe you'll get tired of having me around the house."

"Not as long as I live. You've been too many surprises for me ever to get tired of you."

"I hope this one wasn't too much of a shock, old girl."

"I couldn't ever be shocked by my old Hector."

"Not even when he's this old? An old rag with too much hair

and no teeth that nobody but you would want to look at twice, no, make that once. A scarecrow that's got loose, that's prattling away to itself and nobody wants to look it in the eye . . ."

He was indeed talking to himself as he limped into Cricklewood. Shoot Up Hill had turned into the Broadway, where a pavementload of shoppers were doing their best to ignore him while children giggled and pointed at him. "That's all right," he cried, "let's have a laugh," too late to prevent one woman from yanking at her daughter's arm and cuffing her so violently about the head that the little girl's pigtails began to unravel. He jabbed his thinnest fingers deep into his ears, but even when the ears began to blaze with pain he couldn't quite shut out the child's howls, and so he dodged faster through the crowd, his lowered forehead driving at the heat and the wavering fumes of the traffic, his unwashed hair snatching at his cheeks, the rucksack jerking his undernourished shoulders at every step. He had to slow down or he would be home too soon—he would be home before he knew what to say to Adele.

He couldn't believe she would refuse to take him back, but he still owed her an explanation. He'd never given her so much as a hint of the secret tasks he'd had to perform; she'd had enough on her mind with running the Haven. As he turned toward Childs Hill he managed to check his momentum and unplug his ears, whose throbbing had spread to his jaws. He didn't want to feel closed in with his voice, which had recommenced chattering to itself like a senile old man's—it could, since he wasn't one. "Adele?"

"Hector?"

"Don't look like that. I know it must have been a shock when you heard about the children, but I only kept it from you to protect you."

"Like you were trying to protect them."

"That's me. I knew you'd understand."

"I'm not sure I do, Hector. You'll have to help me."

"It started with Biff and how he suffered till he died, and then there was your sister."

"Pamela? What's anything to do with her?"

"It was her got you into caring, for a kickoff, her being a social worker and telling you how much was wrong."

"She affected me right enough, but—"

"You never realised how much she affected me, did you? You had to cover your ears sometimes when she talked about the little ones she saw, but I heard it all. I remember the first one I couldn't stand hearing about, the little boy with cigarette burns all over—"

"Don't say it, Hector. I keep telling her I don't want to know when I can't do anything."

"You see how it still gets to you even though he's at peace. He was my first, and I'm proud he was. You know, I hoped he'd be the only one I'd have to help, but Pamela kept talking about others that were as bad or sounded like they'd end up that way. I just wish the parents, not that most of them were even that, the bad lots that were arrested on suspicion could have stayed locked up after the police found out about me. That's the one thing I do regret."

"Those people should never have been in charge of children, Hector."

"Maybe nobody should, not even people like us. We ended up wishing we never had, didn't we? Think of all the people you have to look after—they used to be children. I'll bet all our money in the bank the ones I took care of would have grown up like them or worse. Children suffer too much, only nobody wants to know, and it takes a bit of courage to put a stop to it, let me tell you."

"It must. I understand even if nobody else does, Hector. You needn't talk about it any more unless you want to. You're safe now. You're with me."

He wouldn't be quite yet, however. Adele mightn't return from the Haven for hours. He could let himself into the house and make himself presentable. By now he'd passed under the railway bridge, and several men who'd alighted at the station were giving him rear views of their suits and hostile backward glances, obviously wondering what business anyone who looked like him had in their suburb. He mumbled incoherently at them and touched his forehead with two long-nailed fingers, and dawdled so as to watch the men out of sight before he dodged into the treelined street that led home.

The links of an enormous chain clanked in the sky—trucks on the railway line—but otherwise there was only a fluttering of wings and a shrill chattering from the round leafy heads of the trees. In less than two minutes he'd made his way down the self-satisfied street to his gate, from which a narrow path wound away from the concrete drive and between tall thick rhododendrons to the wide pebble-dashed house. Once he sidled between the bushes he was hidden from the road and the neighbouring houses, but he crouched low as he extracted his keys from the rucksack. He limped into the spacious oak porch he'd built and thrust the front door key into the lock. It wouldn't turn.

He had been anticipating so vividly how he would feel to be back in his own home that he almost twisted the key out of shape before he managed to relax his grip. He pulled the key out of the crooked slit and eased it in again, and jiggled it with a gentleness meant to persuade it to work. It still didn't, not even when he slid it out a fraction in case that lined it up more precisely with the internal mechanism. His grubby skin was beginning to prickle and sweat, but he mustn't lose control—perhaps Adele was home and had bolted the lock for some reason. He was reaching for the bell push when his hand cramped itself into a fist that clawed at its palm. There were voices beyond the front door. There were children in his house.

He shoved the keys into a clammy pocket of his trousers and backed away from the door. The voices had halted near the stairs. "You tell me where you put her right now, Baxter," a girl was demanding, to which a boy who could only be her brother said "Or what, Philippa?" Hector didn't want to listen—was afraid that any moment the girl might start to wail—but he had only just stumbled out of the porch when he faltered, having caught sight of the front room.

It was no longer his or Adele's. The antique suite he'd bought from a customer at a fraction of its value had been ousted by some modern chairs, starved almost down to the wood. The reproductions of old London maps had gone, replaced on the walls by pastel landscapes that looked as though they had been left in the rain. The oak mantelpiece above the glassed-in coke fire had been occupied by photographs of a brother and sister, babies turning by stages into children as old as the scarcely teenage voices in the hall. The lock had been not jammed but changed. Adele had sold the house.

He was shuffling backward fast when a bush snagged his rucksack. It felt as though he'd been arrested, not by the law but by his own mind. However much Adele had taken with her, there was no reason to assume she'd found his photographs. They must still be hidden under the floor.

He couldn't leave them when he'd gone to so much trouble to

produce them, fitting out a darkroom he'd told Adele was for Before and After pictures of his building work. He'd thought of an excuse. There was no point in pretending that he hadn't been looking forward to seeing them again, and besides, suppose the children in the house found them? They might be too young to appreciate the peace in them. The thought awakened the skills he'd learned, and he freed himself from the bush and limped swiftly to the corner of the house.

The children were running upstairs, and arguing harder than ever. Any adult in the building would have intervened by now. On the back lawn a swing was swaying itself to a halt, and Hector was sure that whichever child had just left it for the house wouldn't have bothered to lock the back door.

Hector made for it as fast as stealth would let him. Nobody was watching from any of the windows above the ten-foot hedge alongside the house. His kitchen was deserted and almost familiar; only the pans resting their mouths on the draining board weren't white but a cartoonish red. He grasped the handle of the back door and pushed it down just enough. The door yielded, and the next moment he was in the house.

As he eased the door shut he heard the children chasing from room to room upstairs, the boy taunting his sister, who sounded dangerously close to tears. The threat of her distress snagged deep inside Hector, but he couldn't do anything about it except clench his face. He added to his fingerprints on several surfaces as he crossed the spacious sunlit kitchen—he almost laughed aloud at leaving traces of himself that nobody would ever know were there. He tiptoed into the wide hall, so carefully he didn't even limp, and used both hands to muffle the sly squeak of the knob as he inched open the door in the side of the staircase, then flattened one palm against the light switch to hush its click.

The high broad space under the stairs was no longer the darkroom. The shelves he'd built were full of cloths and dusters and sprays, the scent of one of which caught in his throat. Coiled pythonlike on the lowest shelf was the detachable tube of a vacuum cleaner that was lounging in a corner along with two brushes and a mop, its grey tendrils glistening in a bucket. The mop and its companions were resting on the floorboard farthest from the door—the board he had to raise. He sidled into the room and coaxed the door after him, leaving it just sufficiently ajar to let him hear the children. He lifted a brush in each hand to move them to the corner nearest the door, and the plug of the vacuum cleaner toppled off one of them and struck the bucket with a loud clank.

There was silence for an instant, and then a rush of footsteps upstairs. He was going to have to deal with the children—with both of them. It dismayed him to think that one would have to wait until he finished with the other, but he mustn't let that deter him. He'd taken a breath and was about to dash to the foot of the stairs when he realised that the voices had veered into a bedroom. They had been too busy arguing to hear him.

He had to contort himself almost back to front to shift the brushes out of his way, and then the bucket with the mop lolling in it, and then the vacuum cleaner. The manoeuvre spread an ache from the base of his spine that made him grind his gums together. As he lowered himself to his knees, pain shot through his legs all the way to his creaking hips. He inserted a finger in the knotholes he'd enlarged at either end of the floorboard. The board rose from its niche with the faintest wooden groan, and he ducked forward, his shadow plunging into the dark beneath the floor. The treasure wrapped in cellophane was still there.

He propped the board against the wall and lay full length on the floor, the toes of his shoes digging into the angle of the underside of the staircase. He stretched an arm down, the edge of the gap scraping his armpit, and hooked his fingertips beneath the album not much bigger than his hand. Soil gritted under his nails, and the cellophane felt as cold as any child's face he remembered touching. He was closing his thumb over the package when he heard the voices emerge from a bedroom. "Want a clue?" the boy said.

"You tell me where she is this instant, Baxter, or when mum and dad come back I'm telling them."

"Think of a fairy story I used to read you."

Hector didn't know why he held his breath—held it harder as the girl let out a wail. "You've never put her in the oven. The timer's on," she cried, and bolted for the stairs.

Hector made himself breathe out and in again, smelling earth. He lifted the album from the hole and dragged himself into a crouch. His hand felt energised by the cold and stillness of all the children's faces in the album; the energy was spreading through him like ice in his blood. A sobbing wail and a clatter of childish footsteps passed over his head and raced down past him to the hall.

He stowed the album on a shelf and took hold of the edge of the door. She sounded as if she might never stop crying, but in a very few heartbeats she would. Once he had snatched her into his hiding place, she would know nothing while he went to find her brother, and Hector couldn't help a toothless grin at the thought that the boy might glimpse his sister vanishing under the stairs. He would come down to find out why, and—

The boy raised his voice. "Don't be wet, Philippa. Sleeping Beauty was the one you always made me read. Your doll's in your bed. I can't believe you're such a prune you didn't see."

The girl's footsteps left the stairs and took two paces toward the kitchen. It was too late for her, Hector thought: she must have seen his fingertips on the door. He was tensing himself to leap the moment she came abreast of him when she sprinted back upstairs. "She was never there before," she cried. "You put her in just now."

Hector thrust the album into his trousers pocket, which was clammier than ever. When he heard the children race into the bedroom that used to be his son's, he tiptoed into the hall and through the kitchen onto the patio. He left the garden as speedily as he could, and headed for the park, eager to revisit the photographs that were rubbing against his thigh. Looking at them ought to comfort and restrain him, but he didn't know for how long. There were so many children in the world.

EIGHTEEN

The photograph showed Jack waving at the lens and grinning. He'd been trying to wave the camera away until he was out of the shot, but it looked as though he were happily indicating the graffiti on the doors. It was a picture of "Horror writer in murder house," and the headline said MURDER SCENE DAUBED. Less than half the text consisted of what seemed to Leslie a grudging admission that her house, "a site of terror for children of the neighbourhood," had been vandalised, but then the reporter apparently thought the writer of violent horror novels who'd moved in was called Jack Lamp. "So may I know what your objection is?" Leslie's mother said.

It occurred to Leslie that the question could at least as well have been addressed to Jack, who was perched somewhat awkwardly on the edge of the sofa. "Do you want this back?" she countered.

"I've digested it, thank you."

"You must be better at swallowing than me. Where did you find it? It doesn't cover your area."

"We took out a subscription after you told us how unfairly you felt it was treating you. I hope that won't be another source of disagreement. I hope I'm allowed to care, since I can't stop being your mother."

"I don't want you to."

"Am I to get any help with understanding what's so wrong with the piece in the paper? Mr. Lamb, do you think it's untrue?"

"Jack by all means, ma'am. I'd have to say it's kind of true, but it's like Ian said when the lady who wrote that was here, it ain't the words so much as what's behind them."

Leslie's mother frowned at Ian, who was watching American wrestling with the sound turned low. "Ain't?"

"That's my word, ma'am, not his. I don't really use it either. What he got hold of, though, this lady has a talent for meaning more than you can prove she said."

"You speak as a writer yourself. I would still like to know—" She shook her head in Ian's direction and squeezed its features small. "Could you be an awfully good boy for me and turn that down? Or off, for preference. I should have thought there had been quite enough mayhem in this house."

Leslie had to exert a good deal of restraint to say only "Maybe you should get your things, Ian, so you'll be ready."

"Why, is it father's day? Away you scamper then, Ian, and do turn that off."

He killed the television and sprawled out of his chair, slinging the remote control on top of the newspaper Leslie had dropped on the floor. He hadn't reached the hall when her mother said "I still don't understand why you think this journalist should have taken a personal dislike to you."

"Because we won't let her say stuff just because she's a whee-lie," Ian said.

"I beg your pardon? A what?"

"A wheelie," he repeated, sitting on the air while he spun imaginary wheels beside him.

"Well, I never would have dreamed my grandson would have turned out such a nasty little boy," Leslie's mother announced, and even more to Leslie "Especially when you were brought up to re-spect people no matter what their race or other disadvantages."

Jack cleared his throat. "I think you'd need to meet the lady in the chair."

Leslie was about to speak when the doorbell intervened. "I should answer that if I were you," she told Ian, and gazed after him rather than risk saying anything else.

"How's life, big feller? As bad as that? I'll be socialising while you assemble your overnight gear." Having started heartily enough to be addressing several people, Roger stuck out a hand as he strode into the front room. "You'll be the famous chap," he either asked

Jack or informed him. "I wasn't expecting to see you here, Ivy."

"I rather think you weren't alone in that."

Jack used the handshake to pull himself to his feet, and Leslie had the impression that he was testing Roger's strength as he appraised him, the broad square face Roger had passed on to his son, the suede jacket and slyly expensive slacks and the white silk polo neck Leslie knew had been Hilene's first present to him. "Jack Lamb. Don't know about famous," Jack said. "You have to be Roger."

"That's me, just the ex." Roger let go of Jack's hand but didn't otherwise move. "How's the room for you? Made yourself comfortable?"

"At least that, thanks."

Roger swung his half-closed hands toward him. "You sound like there's more."

"It's my workroom also. I'm hoping to start my new book soon in it."

"You're for using a place for all it's worth, are you?"

"That's about the size of it, sure."

"Are you two going to sit down?" Leslie said, and watched the men lounge against opposite arms of the sofa, planting a block of silence between themselves. She was searching for some not too obviously neutral remark to make when her mother picked up the paper. "May I ask what you make of this, Roger? Don't be shy of stating your opinion."

He spent less time on the text than on the photograph. "Good publicity for you, is it, Mr.—you said your name was Lamb?"

"I don't need it right now, and more to the point, Leslie and your son don't need that kind."

"What kind are you saying it is?" Leslie's mother enquired.

"Gee, I may dig myself deeper into an argument here, but from what I saw of the lady who wrote that and likely picked the photograph, she trades on her condition just like Ian said."

"Well, Ian," Leslie's mother said as his footsteps heavier with luggage reached the hall, "you must be pleased, having a grownup to encourage you."

"I'm glad he knows how that feels," Leslie said.

Roger strewed the newspaper in the no man's land on the sofa and slapped his thighs with some force to stand himself up. "Time for the men to be moving, those of us who've got somewhere else to go."

One of the first doubts she'd had about him concerned how fast he absented himself whenever she and her mother seemed likely to argue. She watched him stretch an arm around Ian's shoulders to steer him out of the room. "Have a good time, Ian," she called along the path, "we'll see you back here for dinner tomorrow," and returned to the front room, where Jack was tidying the newspaper while her mother gazed at the air above him. "I expect you'll want me out of the way too," her mother immediately said.

"Why should you expect that?"

The gaze found Leslie, but seemed unhappy that it had. "I should like us to talk in the very near future."

"What's wrong with now?"

When her mother swung her face toward Jack while holding Leslie with her gaze, he said "If I'm the problem . . ."

"I don't think you're one at all, Jack."

Her mother's gaze acknowledged him at last. "How would you say Ian and his father were getting on, Mr. Lamb?"

"Pretty well, I'd say. I'd hope."

"I'm glad we have that in common. A child ought to be shaped by both its parents, would you agree?"

"Sounds ideal."

Leslie was reflecting that her father hadn't been allowed much influence, but said "Are you driving at anything, mother?"

"Since you press me, just that it's a pity you didn't feel able to continue living with Ian's father."

"I should have rolled over with my legs in the air when I found out about Hilene, you mean."

"I shouldn't be surprised if he had a similar impression."

She meant now and Jack. Leslie might have laughed if she hadn't been furious. "You make me wonder sometimes if there's anything you wouldn't say to put me down."

"I think that's most unfair, and may I remind you we have an audience."

"All right then, I wonder if you remember half of what you say. You gave me a lecture about everything you thought was wrong with Roger when you met him, and you liked him even less once you found out Ian was on the way when we got married, and when you heard about Hilene you said I should have known, but now suddenly he's the prize I ought to have hung onto."

"I won't utter another word, since everything I say is mistaken." Leslie's mother remained seated, however, until it became evident that she wasn't going to be contradicted, at which point she dug her nails into the arms of the chair to raise herself with such an apparent effort that Jack sprang up and supported her by an elbow. "Thank you," she said so crisply that the words were barely distinguishable as separate, and no more as Leslie saw her to her car, even when Leslie offered "Give my best to dad and look after each other." She doled Leslie a dry pursed wrinkled kiss and readied herself to drive, then she slitted her window. "If I'm permitted to say this," she said, "take care. I don't want you to feel betrayed again."

"Mother . . ." Leslie wasn't sure what to add to that, and so she only watched the Jaguar purr out of Jericho Close. Her thoughts slowed her down as she returned to the house, and Jack came to find her. "Hey, I'm sorry," he said.

"For what, Jack?"

"For getting you accused of all that stuff."

"What are you assuming isn't true?"

"Well, gee, I—all of it, I should think. Aren't I right?"

"Do you want to be?"

"Not necessarily," he said, matching her look.

Too much might be happening too fast. "I'd better see to dinner," Leslie said.

He gave her more than enough room to pass, then seemed uncertain where to go. "Need help?"

"Thanks, but let me display my talents."

"Just a fraction of them, you mean."

"Better wait until you've tasted what I'm offering."

"Glad to," he said, and with a swiftness that suggested he found the conversation as perilous as she did, "I'll be upstairs working."

"Bring your work down here if you need more space."

"What you gave me is fine."

Maybe he preferred not to be too close to her just now, she thought as she sprinkled coriander on the ceviche, her best Mexican dish. She'd intended a Mexican dinner to help him feel at home, but now she wondered if her version might have the opposite effect. She put a compact disc of Purcell songs on the player in the dining room, then switched it off before the countertenor's pure sexless voice had sung a second bar, in case the noise interfered with Jack's work. Now and then she heard him pacing as if he were enacting her nervousness, and each bout of pacing ended with a creak of his bed. She set the dining table and thought of lighting a candle, but it wasn't even dusk yet. When the spicy odour of burritos reached her from the kitchen, she went to the foot of the stairs. "It's ready, Jack."

"Then I am," he responded, and ran down eagerly as a boy years younger than Ian. He sat opposite her as she pulled the cork out of a perspiring bottle of Californian Chardonnay and poured him nearly a glassful. She watched while he took a sip and then a forkful of her marinated raw fish. "Any good?" she asked.

"A whole lot better than that, and the wine too. I've never had it before."

"I hear they keep the best for export."

"Not including me," he said, and looked abashed for having invited a compliment until she gave him a frown of amused reproof.

He insisted on clearing away the plates from the first course and carrying the baking dish full of burritos from the oven to the table, not allowing his face to show any pain even when he'd set the dish on the protective mat and snatched off her old worn two-handed oven glove. Once he'd enthused about the main course he set about recounting weekends he'd spent in Ensenada: the pelicans that swooped through the fish market, the hawkers who sold plaster figures of Christ and Elvis at the border, the children crowding around tourists to sell single sticks of chewing gum for pesos and begging for food if you ate at a sidewalk cafe. . . . She could tell how much their plight affected him, and she felt instantly closer to him, so that she reached for his hand. The last thing she would have wanted to happen then was that the phone should ring.

"Damn." She'd caught Jack's glass with her knuckles and spilled a half inch. "I'll mop up if you'll answer that," she said.

As she returned with a handful of paper towels from the roller above the sink, he was saying "Hello? Someone there?"

She slipped the fat paper under the wet tablecloth. "What are you hearing?"

"Not sure," Jack said, having covered the mouthpiece.

"Is he singing?"

"Is—" Jack began, then addressed the receiver. "Say what? I don't think you want me, you want—Hey, same to you, friend, and good—" With a look that suggested he didn't expect such language from an English phone, he hung up. "He went," he said.

"Any message?"

"He wished me on my way in not so many words. He was just a kid."

"Could it have been a wrong number?"

"I'd say not," Jack said, and took a step toward her. "What did you ask me about singing?"

"It was a call I had before I advertised your room. Whoever it was didn't speak, they just sang. It sounded like a lullaby to me. I suppose it was meant to remind me of the little girl who was murdered, you know, her going to sleep for ever."

"Jesus."

"I didn't get much sleep myself that night, I'll admit."

"Christ. How could . . . My God."

"It's a good job you didn't take that call if even hearing about it makes you inarticulate for once. Don't let it bother you too much, all right? I've survived."

"Okay. Okay, I will too," he said, and closed both hands around the one she'd extended toward him.

They stood there, she in the doorway and Jack in the hall, for longer than she would normally have held a breath. She didn't want to make a mistake—wanted to be certain whether he was holding onto her for companionship or a need for reassurance or more than either. All the same, she couldn't help being disappointed when he glanced past her at the dining table, until he said "Are we finished there?"

"Would you like dessert?"

"You bet," he said, not by any means slackening his warm firm grasp.

"Are we talking about the same thing?"

"I believe so," he said, and leaned forward.

Their mouths met and simultaneously opened. Their tongues found each other. She disengaged her hand and gripped his shoulders and pressed herself against him, feeling him swell. When after some time she opened her eyes, she saw a bedroom light up beyond the back fence, presumably signalling that someone was about to appear. "I think we'd better continue elsewhere," she murmured.

"Sure enough," he said, but didn't presume to admit knowing what she meant until she led him upstairs.

The doors were pale where the graffiti had been scrubbed off, but the irregular patches and what they meant had lost their power to anger her. She patted Jack's chest to stay him on the landing while she drew her bedroom curtains, then felt ashamed of having been secretive about him. She atoned for it by pulling him into the room and undressing him almost as swiftly as he undressed her. He was impressively ready for her, and her body let her know how delighted it was, so that she had to restrain herself in order to take from the back of the drawer of the table that had accompanied the bed from her previous house the half empty pocket of Roger's condoms she'd kept meaning for months to throw out. "Marital leftovers," she explained.

Perhaps Jack thought that might include some disparaging reference to herself, because he held her gaze with his and stroked her face. She pushed him gently back and sheathed him, then straddled him and lowered herself onto him. The sensation of being entered streamed up her arched spine and out of her uptilted face in a long soft gasp. She felt as if the whole of her was being renewed, forgotten aspects of herself revived. She moved slowly and luxuriously around him until he drew her to him and rolled her over in his embrace. Then they were panting in the rhythm they'd discovered they shared, and when it reached its peak the explosion of pleasure spread to the roots of the nails she was trying not to dig too hard into his shoulders. "Well, gee," he said when he'd regained his breath, and settled his mouth over hers.

"Mm," said Leslie, agreeing with and appreciating him. In time they would have to return to the larger world, but she was in no hurry to leave the drowsy contentment of their embrace. She felt grateful to Melinda for having had the notice in their window, to Ian for leaving her and Jack alone, even to Roger for having taken Ian. She rested her cheek on Jack's chest and listened to the calming of his heartbeat, and enjoyed her growing sense of him. She was sure that in some way—maybe it was part of his being a writer who could no longer write what he liked—he needed caring for.

NINETEEN

"Daddy," Jonquil sobbed, and two tears crimson with the sunset streamed out of her eyes, but he saw that she was giving him the best smile she could manage with her fangs. He tried to raise himself to her, but the heads of the nails her brother had driven through his hands felt larger than his palms. As his feet shoved helplessly at the oak table, his legs began to jerk as if he was trying to sire an invisible child in the air, a child that would be his salvation. He saw Jonquil lift the lump hammer and the sharpened

"Ian, why are you looking like that?"
"Because I'm reading. I've nearly finished."
"Mummy wants you to take me down to the river to see the boats."
"Let me finish this, then. I'm on the last page."

a child that would be his salvation. He saw Jonquil lift the lump hammer and the sharpened piece of wood. Behind her the sunset was creeping out of the cellar window, driven out by darkness. "Do it, for God's

"Is it by the man who's living in your house?"
"What? Yeah, him. Let me read the end."

"My mummy says he writes nasty books. She says—"
"Sure. Okay. Tell me when I've finished."

driven out by darkness. "Do it, for God's sake," he moaned, arch-
ing his back to offer his chest to the stake.

He felt the point dig between his ribs and break the skin. The
pain was sharp and warm, as if the wound was letting the last
of the sunlight into him. He saw Jonquil steadying the stake with
one hand while she struggled to hoist the hammer above her head.
"You can do it," he cried through his clenched fangs, and saw
the last thin beam of sunlight

"My mummy says if you read nasty things you'll end up nasty
too."

"She talks a lot of crap sometimes. Just shut up and let me
read."

"Mummy, mummy," Charlotte cried and ran into the house.

"Piss off and good riddance," Ian murmured to himself. He sat
forward, having heightened the recliner a notch, away from all her
things on the back lawn of the house on Richmond Hill—her
swing, her climbing frame, her Wendy house, her swing-ball dangling from its pole. He'd played with her on or in them all that
morning, and now he wanted to finish Jack's book.

"You can do it," he cried through his clenched fangs, and saw
the last thin beam of sunlight shrink as it retreated up the wall.
The darkness that was filling his body with power was too much
for the sun. In a moment he would be able to tear the nails out
of his hands and thrust them deep into her eyes to put out the
pity she'd dared to feel for him. He'd almost let his love for her
overcome him, but he was still a creature of the dark, and that
was her destiny too.
  Then

"Ian, may I have a word with you?"
"Only got a paragraph, just a paragraph."
"Very well, if it's so important to you, I'll wait here till you've
finished."

Then the weight of the hammer pulled Jonquil's arm down.
The metal head struck the stake full on, splintering his ribs asun-

der. He felt it burst his heart. Agony shuddered through every inch of his body and out of him, and darkness rushed in to take its place, darkness that had the greatest power of all, the power of peace. In the moment before it took his sight and the rest of him away, he saw her fangs begin to turn back into the small neat teeth of his beautiful daughter, hardly more than a child's. The last thing he ever saw was her tearful smile.

"Is that a very long paragraph, Ian?"

"What? No."

"I ask because it's taking you such a long time to finish it. Is it hard to read?"

"No." Rather than dab at the moisture that had somehow escaped from the corner of his right eye, Ian scratched his cheek there. "I've read it now," he said, and turned to Charlotte's mother.

She was sitting on an elaborately curly garden chair beside the Wendy house, her thin ankle-length white muslin dress not quite obscuring what she called her body that Ian thought of, whenever he couldn't help noticing it, as a basque. Her upturned hands were folded loosely in the cleft of her skirt, an area he could have done with ignoring, and her head was slightly lowered as though to frame her patience with the glossy blonde hair that curved toward her chin. Her almost invisible eyebrows were raised, enlarging her big blue eyes—he suspected her brows had been raised ever since she'd sat down—and her pink lips were pressed together in a straight line, denying they were shaped like a sexy kiss. "May we speak, then?" she said.

She was doing her measured best to be reasonable, and he might have been receptive if the question hadn't included Charlotte, who'd perched on Hilene's knee and was regarding him with at least a show of nervousness. "Let's keep our heads and put them together," Hilene said "and sort out the squabble I hear you had. We don't like squabbles polluting the air in our house, do we?"

"No, mummy," Charlotte said, twisting around in her white-frilled yellow dress. "Mummy—"

"Let Ian have his turn now. What do you say happened, Ian?"

"She kept on at me to play when I was trying to read."

"Did you do that, Charlotte?"

"Spose."

"It's a bigger word than that, now, isn't it? Words aren't insects, so we don't squash them."

"Suppose. But mummy—"

"Give Ian his chance. We don't want him to think he has to be polite to a rude little girl."

Charlotte sat resentfully straighter, looking not unlike a ventriloquist's doll. "I played with her all morning," Ian said.

"Nearly all, would that be closer to it? A couple of hours if we're going to be absolutely fair. That was kind of Ian when he was wanting to read, wasn't it, Charlotte? I hope you said thank you. We shouldn't stop people reading, unless of course what they're reading isn't good for them."

Charlotte glanced at her mother so as to copy the expression that went with the remark, and Ian felt outnumbered before Hilene said "All the same, Charlotte says you swore at her."

"That's crap. I never."

"Mummy, he did it again. Mummy—"

"All right, Charlotte, I heard perfectly well. Even if that isn't strictly swearing, Ian, it certainly isn't a welcome guest in our house or in the garden either. We don't want to be breathing blue air, do we, Charlotte?" When the little girl had finished shaking her head so vigorously it loosened her yellow bow, Hilene said "Is there that kind of language in your book, Ian?"

There was spectacularly worse, just one of the many things he was coming to think Americans did better than the English. "Some," he admitted.

"May I see it?"

He didn't know whether she meant the book or just the bits she was sure to object to, and he wasn't about to care. As he passed her *Blood Count* she lifted Charlotte off her knee. The eight-year-old shrank away from the cover with its reddened eyes using part of the topmost embossed silver word for sockets. "It's nasty," she complained.

"It's not just nasty," Ian said, caring after all.

"Go and play in your room now, Charlotte, or watch television if you must. I'll call you when we've finished discussing the book."

"But mummy—"

"Let's see those little feet tripping inside or they won't be going to dancing class."

Charlotte stamped once before flouncing in slow motion into

the house. Her mother gazed hard at the door until it shut reluctantly, then she lowered her attention to the book. She flicked the pages and emitted sounds, not much more than short breaths and some hardly even that, on her way to taking a few seconds over the last page. She laid the book on the threshold of the Wendy house and found Ian with her frown. "What good are books like that meant to do?"

"What good is taking her down to the boats?"

"That's a question, not an answer."

"That's not a question," Ian said as Jonquil's brother in the book would have.

"It isn't clever to be clever, Ian. Can't you say how the book affected you?"

It had made him even happier that Jack was living in his house—even more admiring of how real a writer Jack was—but those weren't things you said. "I liked it. It was good."

"Did it excite you? Frighten you? Improve your vocabulary? Give you ideas?"

"Sure."

"That's what I'd be afraid of." She picked up the book, so urgently that the breeze of it caused the Wendy house to shrink away like Charlotte. "Aren't you old enough to see it doesn't make sense?"

"It did to Jack, and you only read the last bit."

"Which is all I had to read. A good book ties up all the loose ends, Ian. This has a brother who isn't even there, and the father wanting to be killed one moment and the next—I'd rather forget what it says he wants to do to his daughter."

"That's because being a vampire takes over when it gets dark. He tried not to turn her into one, but then he couldn't stop. She didn't die of it, that's why she can stand the sunlight, but she has to kill him or she'll always be a vampire. Her mother sent Jonquil's brother away to be adopted when he was little, that's why he isn't one. He came back and nailed their father down so he couldn't get away, then their father's slave, who wasn't a vampire, and the brother killed each other."

"Can't you hear how senseless all that is?" When Ian shrugged, meaning not that it didn't matter but that her opinion didn't, she shook the paperback at him. "Is this actually yours?"

"It's Jack's. Careful," he said, and grabbed the book.

"I must say if I were your mother you wouldn't have access to language or violence like that. Isn't there enough nastiness already in your life?"

He felt as though she were trying to replace on top of his mind the slab Jack's presence in his life had lifted. He repeated his shrug and met the eyes on the cover until Hilene called Charlotte, who came out of the house so promptly he would have expected her mother to be suspicious. "Correction over," Hilene said. "Now if he's kind Ian will take you down to the river."

"Don't want to go now. The boats have gone."

"They haven't, Charlotte. Look, you can see them," her mother said, pointing to the multicoloured sails on the glittering bend of the Thames half a mile away below the sunlit roofs of Richmond Hill.

"They're going. They'll be gone if we go."

"I'm sure Ian didn't mean them to be, did you, Ian?"

Ian almost let the slab on his mind keep his answer unspoken, but she raised her eyebrows a notch, and another. "Did you?" she said.

"No," he said.

"I really don't think you can compare reading, I suppose the gentleman who wrote it would call it schlock, compare reading an item like that with a grown-up remedying a situation."

It wasn't just her patronising him that made him stand up, it was how reasonable she expected him to think she was being. "Okay, I'm going home," he said.

"Charlotte won't look up to you if you go off in a sulk whenever you're criticised."

"She can do what she likes. I want to talk to Jack about his book."

"Your father said he'd take you and Charlotte to McDonald's when he gets back from golf. You don't want Ian to go yet, do you, Charlotte?"

Charlotte had flung herself on the recliner, both to claim it and to remind them she'd been disappointed. "If he gives me a hundred, if he gives me two hundred pushes on the swing."

"Half that, shall we say, Ian?"

Ian peered at Hilene to convince himself she wasn't joking. "Tell Roger I went home," he said.

"If you're really determined to go early I should phone first."

"Why?" He knew at once, which was all the more reason for saying "What for?"

"I just should." Having observed that Charlotte was listening, she pushed herself out of her chair. "I'll do it myself."

Intrigued by the prospect of her speaking to his mother or Jack, Ian followed her through the pale pine kitchen into the hall that seemed to smell of the flowers of the wallpaper. He watched her dial and then stroke her cheek with that fingertip, and gaze roofward as though there might be something she would need to ignore, and lean her head toward the wire in case that gave the answer less of a distance to travel, and very eventually replace the receiver. Before it touched its cradle he was on his way upstairs to throw his things into his overnight bag. As he expected, Hilene waylaid him in the hall. "I really think you should wait for your father," she said.

Ian might have retorted that his father shouldn't have gone off to play golf, though admittedly he'd invited Ian to join him in however many hours of tedium would have been involved. "I'll see him next time," Ian said, retreating down the cobbled path under several trellises of roses and out of the toothy white wooden gate.

He felt as if he were leaving the slab from his mind on the hill. He was sure he would like whatever he found at home, even if it was Jack and his mother hurriedly emerging from some part of the house together or pretending not to be. He didn't want to embarrass them. What he mostly wanted was to write a story Jack would like.

Church bells were competing across the width of the river as he caught the train to Willesden. North of the Thames the roofs of Acton swarmed by with churches sticking up among them. By the time he changed trains he'd thought up a little girl called Carlotta whose father wasn't really dead, he was a vampire that was hiding in the cellar. When her mother came home one day to their farmhouse near Los Angeles she scraped her hand on a point of the gate in the white picket fence, and when she went into the bedroom where Carlotta had been sleeping all day and her mother had gone to the chemist's, the pharmacy, the drugstore for medicine, the little girl smelled the blood and . . . He didn't know what happened then. Perhaps he could ask Jack's advice.

He didn't even consider turning toward Shaun's when he emerged from the station at Stonebridge Park. He was glad not to encounter anyone he knew as he walked home, his head feeling like a writer's, full of ideas that led in all directions to ends that wouldn't come clear. Gardens whirred with mowers, cars streamed with soapy water, but all that was irrelevant to the ideas he wanted to share in case Jack could tell him where they should lead—except that Jack's car wasn't outside the house.

Ian did his best not to feel disappointed as he let himself in. Jack might be somewhere researching his book or, since the house was empty, helping Ian's mother shop. Ian paced toward the kitchen as if he weren't certain what he would find there, and stood on the secretive concrete in case that might put him in more of a mood to write.

It didn't, but as he lingered, trying to bring some of his thoughts to a conclusion, he knew what would. Jack surely wouldn't mind if Ian borrowed his word processor to write a story for him to read, not when the machine helped Jack work. Of course Ian would have asked permission if Jack had been there to ask. He ran upstairs and into Jack's room.

Sunlight with a spicy tang of aftershave was reaching for the small desk Jack had bought and assembled, on which the word processor sat in the window. Ian left the door open and, having plugged in the machine, switched it on as he sat writerlike in Jack's secondhand swivel chair. The screen welcomed him and showed him its icons, from which he selected the writer's friend. The screen filled with tiny sketches of files bearing names, and he was trying to think of a title for his when the name of a file caught his eye. It was PROGRESS.

He'd heard Jack refer to his book in progress. The notion of reading a book that was still being written seemed irresistible, and he clicked on the file, which opened in front of him. It wasn't a book, it was only the notes for one. He read the first, and didn't know what shape his mouth had taken—felt as if he had forgotten how to blink.

HW's builder's yard on Blackbird Hill, edge of Wembley/ Kingsbury. Sign says "Specialist in Property Renovation." HW uses empty buildings for burials.

David Baxter (7) disappears March 1974 in Kingsbury. HW's first victim. Remains found under floor of house 300 yards from home.

Julie Oakley (8), November 1976, Dollis Hill. Under new conservatory by Gladstone Park.

Stephen Mullins (6), December 1977, Hendon. Basement of house beside M1 motorway.

(Some victims not yet identified?)

Vincent Wearing (6), June 1980, Willesden. Extension, Kensal Rise . . .

At that moment Ian heard his mother's voice. Much of the rush of guilt he experienced was on Jack's behalf. The swivel chair rumbled away from him on its castors as he craned over the desk. His mother was in Janet's garden next door. Before he could move, she vanished into Janet's house.

He was pressing one ear against the party wall, straining to hear whether she was staying at Janet's, when he heard the front door open. The footsteps it let in were Jack's. Ian might have had time to unplug the word processor and dart into his room, but he shrugged off the idea. He pulled the chair to him and sat on it, resting his folded arms on the back, and was facing the door when Jack strode whistling into the room.

TWENTY

"Are you lost, you poor old thing? Where are you looking for?"

"I can't go home. They've stolen my home."

"Try not to distress yourself. Try and think where it is."

"I know where. Someone's living in it. My wife sold it while I was away and I don't even know where she's moved to."

"Poor thing, have you nobody at all to care for you?"

"My wife might if she knew I was alive, but they told her I was dead."

"Then you must stay here till you find her. We've room. Some of our residents had to go back to hospital because they weren't up to something my husband got them involved in."

"Did he mean to harm them?"

"I don't know if he meant to harm anyone. It doesn't matter now. He isn't here, you are. I just need your details and then I'll show you your room and you can have a nice long peaceful bath."

"Suppose I had to tell you something about me you mightn't like?"

"It wouldn't matter. I'm meant to care for people, not judge them. Whatever it was, you'll get over it if you stay here."

"Promise you won't slam the door in my face if I tell you my secret."

"I never slam doors, it upsets my residents. You're dying to tell me. Go on."

"It's me, Adele. I had to let everyone think I was dead. I wanted to tell you, you don't know how much I did, and now I have."

He was nearly there. Walking from Cricklewood to Sudbury had taken a couple of hours, hardly worth mentioning compared to all the walking he'd done since his death, but he'd had enough of trudging and aching and starving with only the fruit and raw potatoes he'd snatched from outside shops to eat. He'd had to pull the potatoes to bits before his gums could deal with them, and he could still taste the soil from their skins, like the taste of a kiss he might have given children before he covered up their faces. In fact he couldn't kiss children, not since he'd been unable to kiss Biff. Just now he couldn't stand their noises either, couldn't distinguish cries of woe from those of pleasure. He hadn't managed since he'd found that his house was no longer his. Any high-pitched childish sound sent him crouching away from it for fear that he would be compelled to intervene. He didn't know how much time that had added to his journey, but now he was almost in sight of the single place where he could be himself, the solitary person who would let him. He was going to be calm, he told himself. Adele's residents wouldn't miss a little of their medication each, and he needed it as much as they did—he'd done a lot more to deserve it, after all.

The Haven Care Home was a wide white three-storey house beyond a curve in a side road hushed by trees. Branches toyed with branches over the solid eight-foot fence. He limped alongside the fence and made to swing into the drive. Instead he continued past, his legs trembling with the effort not to run and attract attention to himself. A police car was parked on the expanse of concrete outside the house.

It seemed more likely that one of her residents had misbehaved than that Hector was the reason the police were there. He swivelled, sending an ache up his body from his bruised feet to his gums, and crept into the drive. He assumed Adele and the police would be in the office, their discussion veiled by net curtains nervous with a breeze, and if he stood between the front door and the window he ought to be able to hear. He'd sneaked to the corner of the building so as to edge along the front when he heard the hall door squeak open.

He darted around the corner and pressed his back against the house. The rucksack hunched him forward as if the warm bricks were fending him off. He heard the front door and a voice that had to be a policewoman's. "We may need to speak to you again, particularly if any more of your husband's victims come to light."

"I want you to find them if there are any, poor little mites, but I hope to God I can be left alone soon to try and forget about him."

As soon as the car door slammed the front door shut too. When the police car backed into the road he felt as if it were withdrawing the house from him. Even more than her words, Adele's tone had made it clear how unwelcome he would be—so unwelcome she was bound to call the police. His aching gaze found the waste bin to the rear of the house, and he paced toward it in case it contained anything he could bear to eat. He only wished Adele could see the state to which she'd reduced him.

He raised the plastic lid and rested it against the house. Under a newspaper he found a mushy mass of leftovers spilling out of an imperfectly sealed bin-bag. A sick bitter taste filled his mouth, and he was about to lurch away when he read two words of a headline in the paper Adele must have brought from wherever she was living now. MURDER HOUSE, they said.

The underside of the paper was sodden with rot. He wiped his hand on the house and tore off the front page. A photograph showed a man on the stairs of the house where Hector had come closest to bringing a child peace. Above the man doors were dripping with graffiti, and perhaps he'd been chosen to point them out because he was a horror writer as well as the new lodger.

Hector folded the page small and pressed it against his heart until he was able to fit it into the album, where it joined the other newspaper photograph. He listened to be sure there were no sounds from the front of the Haven, then he limped fast and stealthily down the drive and went in search of a phone booth.

He found one on Whitton Avenue. As he looked up the address of the nearest overnight refuge, a couple of pensioners taking their extravagantly long-haired dog for a walk stared at him and murmured and stared over their shoulders as well. Apparently people who looked like him weren't supposed to use phone directories, or perhaps the couple thought he was planning to rob the coin box. He shouldn't have to suffer their contempt or another night in a refuge; he deserved better—he'd earned a little of the peace he had brought to all the children he'd taken responsibility for, the kind of responsibility no one else dared take. The word on all the doors in the photograph was supposed to mean him, and however unfair it was, it made him part of the house. It made him feel as though the man in the picture was trying to take his place.

TWENTY-ONE

Janet had just called her in from the back garden when Leslie saw Jack's car in the road. She made herself sip coffee that seemed unusually and unhelpfully hot while she chatted to Janet about how Ian was doing better at school, showing more interest in studying English, not seeing so much of his friends she disapproved of. Of course she was really talking about Jack, and hoping that he didn't regret last night any more than she did.

They'd slept in their own rooms overnight, and confined themselves to smiles and pleasantries this morning, and been wary of touching each other too much. Before he'd gone out, supposedly to research his new book, she had sensed there was something he wanted to tell her. She sipped Janet's coffee and eventually saw off enough to feel justified in abandoning it. "Will you have another?" Janet immediately said.

"Thanks, but I'd better start seeing to the things one does on Sundays."

"I understand. You've another hungry chap to take care of."

As Leslie let herself out of Janet's house, sunlight on the driver's window of Jack's Nova caught her like a flashbulb, and she heard a shiver pass through a series of trucks on the distant railway; otherwise the suburb might have been holding its breath on her behalf. She unlocked her door, all her keys jangling, and stepped across the threshold. "I'm—"

It was the sight of Ian that caused her to falter. Despite all her problems with him she had never wished him away, but at that moment she almost did. "Want some coffee?" he said along the hall.

Before she could wonder aloud if he shouldn't be somewhere else, at least getting some fresh air, Jack came out of his room. His face was so guarded that her own stiffened in response. "Ian?" she called.

"Want some?"

"Not right now. I forgot to get a Sunday paper. Could you run down to the shops, no need to run, I shouldn't think?"

"Leslie?"

"Just a second, Jack," she said, but his expression wouldn't let her wait that long. "What is it?"

"Can we talk?"

"That's what I—if you can just let me—"

"I should talk to both of you."

"Should you?" The proposal seemed so unrelated to anything she had tried to prepare herself for that she didn't know how to feel. "Well, if you think . . ."

As he left the stairs he stretched out a hand but didn't quite touch her, instead indicating the front room. "Care to join us, Ian?"

"Anybody having coffee?"

"Go on since you've made some," Leslie said, apparently the quickest way to move him.

"In that case I'll take some too," Jack said.

She could tell he wanted it no more than she did. They both glanced at the couch before taking a chair each. Having taken turns to risk a smile, they concentrated on the doorway. By the time Ian appeared in it, bearing two mugs of coffee and a glass of the cranberry juice he'd taken to liking since Jack had arrived, she'd begun to feel coated with static. She took yet another sip of coffee, one that tasted like a preamble to bitterness. "So, Jack."

"Sure." The word seemed to imply anything but certainty, and he took a gulp of coffee that must have hurt. "I wish I knew how bad . . ."

When he pressed his lips together hard enough to pull up the flesh of his chin she said "However bad it is we're used to coping, aren't we, Ian?"

Ian shrugged and thought better of it. "Sure."

"So give us a chance, Jack. If we can help, tell us how."

"You already have. That's kind of the problem. You've helped with my book."

"Which—" Leslie said, and realised aloud "Your next one."

"You got it, the one I want to write next. I think—okay, I think it ought to be about this guy Hector Woollie and what he did."

"Including here."

"I couldn't very well not deal with that, I guess. Tell me, or maybe you'll need time to study it, would that be a problem?"

"I imagine you'd get closer to the truth than the paper bothered to."

"I could include something about how the paper treated you if you like."

"I think we might, do you, Ian?"

"Reckon so," he said as if he wanted to sound even more American than Jack.

"Then if you've been waiting for permission you can stop, Jack."

"Well, okay. Thanks. Only . . ." He raised the mug toward his face but lowered it, refusing its concealment. "I have to say I didn't wait. I already started researching."

"We forgive you." She gathered that was what he wanted, so much that she had to say "When did you begin to plan it?"

"Maybe the first time I saw your house."

So this was the secret that had been making him anxious, or his fear that she would feel betrayed had. "I suppose that comes with what you are," she said.

"You're saying I'm . . ."

"A writer, what else? You have to take ideas where you find them, I can understand that. You can't feel as guilty about that day as I do, or you shouldn't. I wouldn't expect you to have told me as soon as you got the idea for a book, but I should have told you the kind of place I was bringing you to."

"The kind of place that may change my career, and I never felt more at home."

If Ian hadn't been present she would at the very least have taken Jack's hands. Instead she ensured there wasn't too awkward a pause by saying "What would you have written otherwise?"

"More horror, I guess. That's how I used to get the dark stuff out of me. True crime is a whole different area. I don't know yet how it's going to work."

"I'm just a reader, but if there's anything I can do . . ."

"One thing maybe you both can. Did you ever meet the guy?"

"Mr. Woollie, you mean."

"Hector Woollie, right. Did you meet him?"

"A few times. Most of the time we were staying with my parents," Leslie said, and was ambushed by a shiver.

"Don't talk about it unless you want to."

"I'm not sure I can tell you anything useful. He seemed just like a builder. He took me in, and I wouldn't say I'm stupid. I did think he was a bit too eager to make you laugh."

"How about you, Ian? What did you make of him?"

"Never met him. I was at mum's parents' or at school."

"Hey, no need to be disappointed. I guarantee you wouldn't want to meet him. Listen, Leslie, if you figure I'll be reviving anything I shouldn't, I can still back off."

"I wouldn't want to be the girl who killed a book."

Perhaps that was too coy for Ian, who grabbed his glass and the empty mugs. Once he'd escaped to the kitchen Leslie held Jack's gaze with hers. "Was last night another kind of research?"

"Are you serious?" he murmured, even quieter than her. "Only the best kind. Only finding out how good we were together."

"We were, weren't we." She leaned forward and squeezed his hands. "I'll try and remember more to tell you," she said. "I'll just have to keep reminding myself Woollie's dead and can't touch us."

"I'll vote for that," said Jack.

TWENTY-TWO

"It is you, isn't it, son? You've been so quiet I thought you'd gone for good."

"It's me and nobody else, dad."

"Where have you been all this time?"

"Far away. Maybe I should take you there. Maybe that's where we both ought to go."

"Are you content, son? Are you happy?"

"If I was any happier I'd burst."

"We wouldn't want that, would we, son? Your mother wouldn't like the mess. It'd be a laugh though, wouldn't it?"

"There's nothing like a laugh to make things right, dad. You taught me that and a lot more."

"So long as things are right for you, son. That's all I ever wanted. I always had you in mind."

"I know, dad. You mightn't have been so bothered for those children if you'd been happier with me."

"We shouldn't blame ourselves for the past. It's what you are now that counts. You've been reborn, is that it?"

"You don't mind, do you?"

"How could I when you've come back to me? I feel born again myself. I did when I came out of the sea, and now here I am lying in the sand again."

"You oughtn't to stay here much longer, dad. You don't want people hearing you talking to me."

"Where am I supposed to go tonight? I can't sleep at the shelter again, not when that woman left her handbag open with a bag of change in it. She looked like she had plenty, and she's there for the benefit of folk like I'm having to pretend I am, but she mightn't see it that way."

"There must be other shelters you can walk to in a day, aren't there? Now you've got some money you don't even need to walk."

"They don't let anyone who looks like me on public transport. Do you reckon they would if I told them I was an actor made up for a film? I'm a celebrity right enough. Maybe I should tell them."

"That'd be a laugh, except remember you don't want to draw attention to—"

A sound like the whoosh of an arrow followed by an impact silenced him. He thought a child was playing at archery somewhere nearby until he recalled where he was. He squirmed his arms through the straps of the rucksack and inched his head over the top of the bunker, feeling as though the early sunlight were a lid he had to raise. He was in time to see a second tweedy female golfer take a stroke before they strolled away from him across the grass. He scrambled out of the bunker and limped as fast as his stiff aching legs would carry him after his shrinking shadow across the deserted greens to the road.

Last night he'd been unable to think of anywhere else to sleep. He was sick of shelters full of people he had to keep reminding himself he wasn't like, but he'd allowed himself to be distracted by Adele's rejection of him. If it hadn't been for the miracle of their son's rebirth, a miracle she deserved never to learn of, Hector might have turned into the vagrant he'd been forced to play. Now that he was no longer alone—no longer the outcast his wife, his own wife, had tried to make of him—he was going to be able to restore himself.

He headed southwest into Barnet, keeping to the parks and open spaces wherever he could, restraining himself from baring his gums at the people he skirted, all of whom clearly felt they had more of a right to be there than he had. Dogs being taken for walks yapped at him, and once he had to give a wide berth to party of schoolchildren led by a teacher: though not a wail or a complaint was to be heard from them, he didn't want to risk imagining there might be. He heard the children laugh at the spectacle of him, of the shabby unshaven lank-maned old man with his tortoise neck poking up beyond his shell of a rucksack, and nearly spun around in case a toothless grin might earn him more laughter. Then he heard the teacher rebuking them, and did his best to hasten out of sight before he could feel responsible for having caused them any grief.

A length of road posted with pensioners leaning on wheeled baskets while they deplored the world, including him, eventually let him into a park that greeted him with an increasingly less muted roar—the noise of the motorway that stood above the foot of Mill Hill. As he plodded lopsidedly down a slope patched with grass, past a selection of the unemployed using cans of lager to ensure they didn't grow dehydrated, he felt as if he were descending into a medium that could drown any sound he would rather not hear. He was beginning to trust the promise of calm when he heard a child's wail behind him.

Pain flared from his left shoulder to his right ear as he twisted his head around. A woman so obese he couldn't judge if she was pregnant was dragging a boy about six years old down the path. The large flowers printed on her dress were half the size of her breasts, which were sagging nearly to her stomach. "Right, that's done it," she was vowing. "No Burger King for you today, you little brat."

The boy's wail faltered while he took in her words, then it doubled in volume and piteousness. Hector fled toward the motorway, but its noise couldn't blot out the child's woe, and Hector was unable to outdistance him and his mother. Hector was yards short of the foot of the slope, and maddened not just by the wailing but by the jerky dance of the rucksack on his spine, when she shouted "You make one more sound and I'm selling your bike."

Hector held his breath as if that might silence the boy. When the cry renewed itself, more despairing than ever, he raised his hands toward his ears, then swung around in a crouch. The boy's face was red and distorted and streaked with all its fluids. "That's the finish," the woman yelled. "You're not having your mates round tomorrow."

Hector had made things worse by looking. His hands closed on the air and hauled him upright. "Stop it now, son," he blurted. "She just wants you not to cry. Give us a laugh instead. See, here's a worm coming out of its hole, a big worm, look."

He would have thought the boy incapable of producing a worse or louder noise, but that was the child's response to the sight of Hector's tongue squeezing itself between his gums. The woman jerked the boy's thin arm so hard he almost fell over. "Get a move on, you. No cartoons for you today and no MTV. The moment we get home you're going to bed."

A convulsion widened the boy's mouth, and Hector held up his hands that wouldn't quite stop being claws. "Pardon me, madam, but you're just upsetting him. He'll never stop if you keep saying things like that."

The woman stared at him as though he had revealed himself to be even worse than his appearance, then she stumped at him, her flesh from her swollen ankles to the pouches of her face wobbling at every step. "Piss off out of it, you smelly old tramp. What do you think you are, a social worker?" she demanded, yanking the boy past him. "As for you, just wait till I get you home. I'll teach you to make a show of me."

Hector limped after her, extending his crooked fingers. "Madam, please don't take it out of him because of me. Poor little soul, he hasn't done anything to deserve—"

She turned on him, dragging the boy on the toes of his sandals. "If you don't piss off right now," she warned, so loudly that several of the drinkers on the grass laughed and applauded, "I'll get the police to you and we'll see what you deserve."

He'd already drawn too much attention, and he didn't want to begin to imagine what he might have brought upon the helpless miserable child. He watched the woman march out of the park and turn the corner of a narrow nondescript street, the boy at the end of her flaccid balloon of an arm having to scamper and stumble and scamper again to keep up, and then he lurched under the motorway. Its roar trailed over him and rose above him to wait on the far side of the pedestrian tunnel, so that he felt as if he couldn't shake it off—as if it were adding itself to the weight of his rucksack, which might have been his guilt rendered solid.

He'd fled at least a mile through a tangle of streets before he felt sufficiently unobserved to give himself some reassurance. He limped under a railway and heard the lines squeal at him, and dodged into a park where he could sit on the banks of a stream. Nobody was watching as he took out the photograph album. The stream carried on its introverted monologue while he gazed at the picture until he was sure of it and himself. "I know you're there, son," he murmured. "I'll be with you soon. I'm not mad, am I? I'm not going mad."

TWENTY-THREE

Wembley, England.
An average day in an average suburb.
Small neat houses, small neat lives.
Bright summer sunlight. Children playing; children visiting
one another's homes.
But there's one house where a child came to visit and

"Yeah, right," Jack muttered, and needed little more reflection to add "Crap." Having deleted the sentences, he raised his eyes so that his mind wouldn't be deadened by the blank screen. Beyond the back gardens separated by a narrow alley, the roofs and their dormant chimneys dovetailed with a sunned blue sky. Miles above them the silver brooch of an airliner slipped off the wadding of a cloud, and from the main road he heard the rattle of the rear door of a truck. Otherwise the streets outside his open window were as silent as the airliner; there wasn't a child to be heard—not because the children of the suburb were afraid to make a sound within earshot of Leslie's house, but because they were at school.

Wembley, England. An early afternoon in summer. The
small, neat suburban houses doze in the heat and stillness. Soon
the children will be home from school to wake them up. But one
child

"Useless," Jack told himself, and sent the fragment of a paragraph back into the nothingness that had produced it. He knew he didn't have to keep his opening lines in the final version—they could just be his route to the material he would keep—but these seemed less meaningful than the hollow clatter of the keyboard, they felt like an absolute failure to grasp what he ought to be writing. Did he need to rid himself of habits he'd learned from years of writing fiction as distanced from reality as possible? Or was his problem simply that there was no point in struggling with the first lines when he'd yet to come up with a title he liked?

At least selecting a title would let him feel he was writing. He opened a file for titles and gazed at the sky, which had taken its clouds off. He managed to ignore the faint impatient hum of the word processor until he had a thought worth typing, and it was followed by another that brought its close relative along.

THE HOUSE THAT CAN'T FORGET
THE LEGACIES OF MURDER
INHERITORS OF MURDER

They were pretty good titles, but not for this book. It wasn't just about Leslie and her house, not even mostly. No wonder he was having trouble with the book if he couldn't keep his mind on its theme. Maybe he needed a title to remind him:

CHILD KILLER
THE MAN WHO BURIED CHILDREN
SILENCED CRIES

They were enough. Just because the book had to deal with the man behind it all, Jack didn't have to start with him. He still wanted to begin with Leslie and her house, with the way she'd been identified with a history she had never been part of, as if because the public needed somebody alive to blame, she would have to do. Once he'd written that chapter he could show it to publishers while he continued his research. He wanted the chapter to represent his best work.

There were things he couldn't write. He would have to leave out how Leslie felt in bed—her soft firm breasts, her cool lips and inventively responsive tongue that tasted faintly of toothpaste, her

long legs squeezing his waist—and he didn't think he would even
be able to include how she'd made him feel more accepted than
he would have dared hope. Nevertheless he had let her believe he'd
revealed his plans for the book without being prompted, and he'd
implicated Ian in the deception as well. Perhaps he wouldn't be
able to write honestly until he was open with Leslie—until he admitted that his visit to her shop had been no coincidence.

He'd been in England for just a few days, a writer abandoned
by public taste and searching for a way of renewing himself, when
he'd learned about her house from a piece in the *Evening Standard*
and known at once that it was where he had to go. He'd been
studying it to form a first impression before he ventured closer
when Leslie and Ian had come out together. When they'd separated
at the main road, Ian dodging a kiss, Jack had followed her to work.
Once she'd disappeared into the staff room at the rear of the shop
he'd strolled past the window, only to be halted by her notice. He'd
walked through the secretive alleys of Soho while he came to terms
with his luck, and then he'd veered back to the shop.

How would she react when she discovered he'd been schem-
ing? Perhaps she might think it was only as odd as writers were
supposed to be, but she was entitled to feel deceived, used, even
betrayed. He ought to meet her for lunch, if only so that Ian's presence wouldn't inhibit him from saying too much, and he was about
to head for the phone when it rang.

He felt as though she'd sensed his need. He swung himself out
of the swivel chair and ran downstairs. Whyever she was calling,
he wouldn't let her go until they had a date. He held onto the
banister and leaned off the stairs to snatch the receiver. "Hi," he
said, followed by "Hello?"

This brought him no response either. "Hello," he repeated less
invitingly. "This is—"

"I know."

The voice was a man's, and he had to be drunk; it wasn't just
blurred but inexplicably affectionate. "Excuse me, what number do
you think you called?" Jack said.

"Yours, son. Yours and the lady's with the teenage boy."

"I guess there are a whole lot of families like that. Do you have
a name?"

"For her?" Jack was awaiting some insult to identify the caller as deploring Leslie's presence in the house when the man said "Leslie Ames."

"Okay, that's right, this is her place." Nevertheless the man's tone—fond or sympathetic or both—had started to confuse Jack, who could only assume it was meant to be ironic. "Did you want to talk to her?"

"Just you, son. Couldn't be anyone else with her at work and him at school."

"Sure, so excuse me, who are you and what do you want?"

"Don't you know yet, son? Do you really not know?"

When a dull ache spread up Jack's arm, he realised his fist had clenched around the banister. "I don't, so if you'd like to cut the bullshit—"

"It's me, son. I'm alive. It's your father."

Jack's body was a burden he had to lower onto the stairs. As it sank he heard himself protest "I've no idea who you are."

"I understand, son. Take your time. It must be a bit of a surprise."

"Will you stop calling me son?" Jack bowed forward to prevent the taut cord from hauling the base of the phone off the table. "I can't imagine who you think you're speaking to, so maybe you should—"

"Don't be like that, John." All at once, despite the mushiness of some of its consonants, the voice was sharper and firmer. "I know it's you. I saw your picture in the paper. I wasn't sure at first, but I am now. It's you all right. I'm not mad."

Jack straightened up, and the plastic base flew off the table at him. He slammed the receiver into its housing and crouched over it as if that might keep it silent while he struggled to recover. "No. Come on. No," he said, and even tried to laugh.

TWENTY-FOUR

"And now I expect you're all panting to hear what I thought of your stories," Mr. Cardigan announced, loudly even for him. "I'd stake a month's salary that there are a few boys in this classroom wishing they'd sprayed their armpits a lot harder this morning."

Ian joined in the chorus of dutiful laughter. He wasn't sweating, but he was certainly eager. Mr. Cardigan had told them to write a story about anything they liked so long as it was told in the first person, and Ian was sure the story was his best work, good enough to show both his mother and Jack. He'd imagined Carla's viewpoint so vividly that for whole paragraphs he'd come close to feeling like her, lying bound and gagged beneath the cellar floor that a psychotic serial killer in a mask had nailed down, and utterly unable to respond to her mother's calls in the house overhead. He waited while Mr. Cardigan prolonged the suspense, hooking his thumbs under the gold chain of his steel-grey waistcoat and drumming his fingertips on his tautly buttoned stomach, before he began to fling exercise books off the pile on his desk, and comments after them.

"Very careless, Hobbs." That didn't surprise Ian, since Baz had boasted of smoking two joints in the course of writing his story. "Too slick to be convincing, Sheeney," the teacher declared, presumably unaware that Stu had copied most of the story out of a crime magazine, substituting English names that didn't go with the Chicago location. "Starts off well, Nolan," Mr. Cardigan told Shaun, "so what truncated your inspiration? Was it a girlfriend or just a video?" By now practically the whole class had been dealt with, and Ian couldn't help feeling the teacher was saving the best until last. He was getting ready to allow himself a grin when the lunchtime bell shrilled. "Bayliss. Fong. Choudhury. Davison. Davidson," Mr. Cardigan rattled off, lobbing some of the books the length of the room, then tucked his thumbs in his waistcoat pockets and wagged his fingers upward to indicate the class should rise. "Time for your airing, gentlemen. Do try not to mangle the language too grievously while you compete at being up to date."

A solitary exercise book remained on his desk, and Ian was hurrying forward when the teacher took him to be trying to escape. "Linger, Ames, if you will," he bellowed.

Ian's friends glanced at him with as much sympathy as their age and gender allowed, but he didn't feel in need of it. Once he was the only boy in the room, Mr. Cardigan marched to the door and shut it with almost a slam, then he rubbed his neat moustache between finger and thumb before transferring them to his chin-sized beard. At last, having barely lowered his voice, he said "Have we a touch of the pos?"

That was what Ian heard him say, at any rate, and wondered if he was being asked about his intestinal health. "Sorry, sir?"

"Edgar Allan Poe. Have you been reading that old horror?"

"No, sir."

"Or watching a film of a premature burial, perhaps."

"Didn't know there was one."

Mr. Cardigan frowned at the answer or at the lack of sirring. "Is this story all your own work?"

"Sure is, sir."

"I'm not suggesting it was written by an adult, but I wonder if you were advised by one."

"Like who?"

"I understand you have a writer boarding in your house."

"Jack," Ian said to demonstrate how close they were. "Jack Lamb. Have you heard of him, sir?"

"I should think his reputation is at least as widespread locally as he could wish. Did he have a hand in your composition?"

"He doesn't even know about it yet."

"So I'm to understand this came out of your own head."

Ian felt safe in sounding a little proud, perhaps even a little like a writer. "It did, sir."

The teacher glanced at the last page of the story, where the cellar light became visible through the floorboards only for Carla to see it go out because her eyes and her brain had. "I think you should speak to someone else about this."

"You mean try and get it published, sir?"

"I mean very much the opposite. I should hope your mother would prefer it to be kept as quiet as possible."

"You said we could write anything we liked."

"Within reason, Ames, reason, heaven preserve us. I would never have expected you to exploit a tragedy to prove how horrid you can be."

"It's not about my house," Ian protested, perfectly sincerely. "It's just an idea I got."

"Then I would strongly recommend your mother takes you to see someone who can rid you of such ideas."

That was preceded by a disbelieving look, which was why Ian insisted "I wouldn't write about my house. Jack is."

"Not an occasion to celebrate." The teacher was shaking the exercise book at him as if that might scatter the words out of it. "Please show this to your mother and inform her I should be happy to discuss it further."

Ian idled back to his desk, giving Mr. Cardigan time to vanish in the direction of the staff room, and then he read the comment that resembled crimson scratches on the page. *Sufficiently well written that one hopes these skills will be put to more wholesome use,* Mr. Cardigan had scribbled, followed by a C in the circle he always drew around his marks, presumably not realising this one looked like the symbol you saw in published books—Jack's, for instance. Ian's resentment of the criticism faded as he thought of Jack; his was the opinion that counted, and Ian felt all the closer to him since they'd let Ian's mother believe that telling her about the book had been purely Jack's choice, nothing to do with his having been found out. She might have over-reacted and asked him to leave, and Ian thought Jack had been afraid she would. Jack owed him a little secrecy, and part of that might cover the teacher's comments.

He was opening his desk to put away the book when he heard Shaun's voice under the open window. "Ian? Has he gone?"

"You'd hear if he hadn't."

"What was he bitching about?"

"Just the stuff I wrote. He thought it was about, you know, Duke's sister."

"Was it?"

"What do you think? I'm not that sick."

"Bring it out and let's have a look."

"See it later," Ian said, and sat down to open the exercise book. He hadn't finished reading the first page when Shaun called "Are you coming out?"

"In a bit." Since not only the teacher but also Shaun had assumed he could have been writing about Harmony Duke, Ian wanted to reassure himself they were wrong: he didn't think his mother would like the story otherwise, and that might be true of Jack as well. Ian hadn't had their house in mind while he was writing; there had been nothing in his head except the story itself. The house was nothing like theirs, it was American and had a cellar, and if Carla was anybody real she was Charlotte, though she used as many American words as he'd been able to fit in. Now that he'd reread the story he could see bits he would like to improve, but he was certain nobody at home would share the teacher's disapproval. He was resolving to ask if he could borrow Jack's word processor so that he would have a copy to be prouder of when someone opened the classroom door.

"I was just checking my homework," Ian began to say, having guessed that the incomer was a teacher, all of whom were devoted to chasing boys out of the school at lunchtime. But the intruder, who came in fast and heeled the door shut, was Rupe Duke.

He took one heavy step forward, swinging his arms like a boxer or a bouncer, and gave his head a vicious jerk that might have been intended to shake some of the dullness out of his eyes and his uncared-for face. "What've you been writing about my sister?"

Ian leaned his fists on the book. "Nothing."

"Not what I heard."

"Shouldn't have been listening then, should you? Better piss off before a teacher comes. You're not allowed in this room."

Duke advanced two steps that Ian thought were even stupider and less impressive than the first. "I want to see."

"Like you wanted to see in my house, right?"

"Maybe."

Ian gripped the sides of the desk. "Here's how it goes, Duke. I'll let you read it if you say you broke into my house."

"You know I did."

"And wrote all that shit on the doors."

"You know it."

Since he'd overheard Ian in the classroom, he must be audible to Ian's friends outside. Ian had witnesses, and felt so pleased with himself that he pushed the book across the desk. "Go on then, read it. It's not about her."

Duke trudged forward and grabbed the book. As he flipped the cover open his face closed around his feelings to ensure not a hint of them escaped, and Ian was taken off guard by a surge of unexpected sympathy. After all, how was Duke supposed to feel when his little sister had been murdered? If Charlotte had been the victim Ian could imagine being more upset than he wanted to admit. His understanding didn't change the fact that Duke had vandalised his house, but at that moment he decided to let adults deal with the other boy. He watched Duke turn the page with a slowness that suggested respect and read to the end. Duke glared at the teacher's comment, and then the glare found Ian. "You cunt. You lousy cunt," Duke said.

"Yeah, well, that's your opinion. Give my homework back."

"No fucking chance," Duke said, and retreated around a desk.

"It's got nothing to do with you. Give it back."

"You're not doing that to my sister. You can have your book all right."

Ian grasped the threat at once, too late. Before he could retrieve the book, Duke had flapped it open and torn out the story. He let the book fall and ripped the pages swiftly in half, in quarters, eighths, sixteenths. "There's your book," he said, "and you can have this when I've finished."

The slab was pressing Ian's mind small. He felt as though everything he'd put into the story, his hopes for it and his sense that he could be someone better than he'd taken himself for, had raised the weight high only to have it drop back into place. His story was beyond rescuing, and what he saw himself doing seemed pointless, but so did refraining from it—only the rage that turned his mouth dry as paper seemed real. He snatched up the book and used it to slash Duke across the face.

The boy stumbled backward, scattering fragments of paper as his hands leapt to his face and he collided with a desk. Before Ian could see how badly he was injured—surely less than the muffled sound behind his hands was claiming—an assortment of footsteps in the corridor reached the classroom. Shaun was first in, followed by Stu and Baz. "Did you hear him?" Ian demanded. "Did you all hear what he said?"

"Said when?" Shaun asked as if he didn't want to know, and stared at Duke. "Shit, what have you done to him?"

"Just hit him. He'll live. But listen, you heard him say he broke into my house, right?"

"No."

"You must have. You heard me and Cardy before."

"We heard it was Duke in here. That's why we came, in case he needed sorting. Look at him, Ian, it looks like you've—"

Ian turned away from him, from the pointlessness he seemed to be embodying. Could Ian really have handed Duke his story to destroy and gained nothing by it? "You heard Duke say he was in my house, didn't you, Baz?" he pleaded. "Stu, you did."

Both of them shook their heads. He couldn't reassure himself they hadn't understood, even though they were gazing in dismay at Duke. "We'd say if we had," Stu said, and grimaced as if he found it hard to swallow. "But Christ, look what you've done. You've blinded him."

TWENTY-FIVE

When the phone rang Jack's hand clenched on the coffee mug. He managed to relax his fingers, which felt capable of shattering the stout baked clay. He was sitting at the end of the back garden in the hope that strong black coffee and the open air might help him think. Neither had, and he'd barely sampled the coffee, which had only intensified the ache that was his absence of thoughts. It had taken him minutes of staring at the phone to realise the call might be traceable, but when he'd dialled 1471 a recorded voice had told him with more cheerfulness than seemed appropriate that the caller had withheld their number. He'd retreated upstairs to switch off the word processor, on whose screen the words *Child Killer* and *The Man Who Buried Children* and *Silenced Cries* had appeared to brighten before they were extinguished, leaving marks on his eyes. The words seemed both entirely beside the point—at least the effort he'd put into manufacturing the phrases did—and inescapably relevant. He was trying to clear them out of his mind, which was using them to fend off things he was afraid to think or feel or remember or admit were possible, when the phone rang.

It repeated itself twice before he set down the mug with a clunk that spilled tepid liquid over the back of his hand. The sensation felt as if someone had licked him. As the phone shrilled again he swung his legs off the bench and sprinted up the garden, towards pairs of sunlit facades that might have been standing together to cast him and his secrets out. He had to deal with the call, even if it was the one he was afraid of—especially if it was that call.

The kitchen floor felt ominously harsh after the softness of the lawn. He was halfway along the hall before he ceased to feel he was still running over concrete, as though his sense of what had been hidden beneath that surface was pursuing him. The phone fell silent, and he closed a fist around the receiver, willing the bell just to have paused between rings. "Hello?" he gasped, and with the rest of the breath his lungs could spare "Hello?"

"All right, John, no need to panic. Only me. Had time to think?"

Jack wasn't as prepared as he had convinced himself he was. He sat quickly on the stairs and moved the base of the phone to his lap, and felt as if he were cradling a toy for comfort. "About what?"

"Nothing if you don't need to. I just reckoned you might want time to get used to having your old dad when you thought you'd lost him."

"I still am getting used, if I've even started." Part of Jack's mind was desperate to hang on to the life he'd invented for the biography on his book jackets and had elaborated for the Ameses, but it was deserting him like a series of ideas that failed to hold up when he tried to write about them; no grandfather who'd taken him fishing, no auto repair shop, no midnight basketball, only the childhood their departure was uncovering. "Never mind me," he said with all the conviction left to him. "We have to talk—"

"I'll vote for that. It's been too long. Only don't ask me not to mind you when I'm your dad. You've got on well, haven't you? You've made a name for yourself."

"I did my best."

"That's my boy. We brought you up right, didn't we, me and her?"

Jack knew he had to sustain the conversation until his father trusted him, but the only response he could manufacture was a wordless mutter. Apparently it was enough for his father, who chortled as though he had just seen a joke. "Jack Lamb, eh? Woollie Lamb. That's a laugh. Shows you're a joker like your dad. We had a few laughs when you were living at home, didn't we?"

"Guess so."

"I remember we did. Maybe my memory's better than yours. You've never been far from my mind. Did you think of me sometimes?"

"How couldn't I?"

"Good thoughts, were they? Good memories?"

"Some."

"And the other sort too, is that what you're saying, John?"

"Dad . . ." Uttering the syllable disturbed him even more than being addressed by his old first name. "What do you want? Why are you calling?"

"That hurts, that does, you asking that. It really hurts." Jack heard an indrawn breath so wet it made the receiver against his face feel moist as his father said "It makes no odds how long it's been, you're still my lad. You know you are, or you'd have changed your name more. Just because your mother did her best to part us doesn't stop you being my son."

"I don't think she was trying to separate us. I was allergic to some stuff you used at work you couldn't help bringing home on your skin."

"That's what her and the doctor made out all right."

"I had an allergy for sure."

"More like she got you thinking you were allergic to me so she could send you to Pamela's."

"Say, dad . . ." Jack thought he glimpsed a chance. "I'm finding this hard, you know."

"Fair enough, let's leave your mother out of it. She's had her time. She saw a lot more of you when you were at her sister's than I did."

"You don't blame me for that, do you?"

"Don't you reckon you were old enough to tell them what you wanted? You were the same age as the lad where you're living now."

Perhaps only Jack's nervousness made that sound like a threat aimed at Ian, but it was another reason for him to say "Look, I said this is hard. I've never been good on the phone."

"You sound as if you're doing pretty well to me."

"I'd rather we were face to face though, wouldn't you?"

"You mightn't think much of my dial now, the way it's ended up. It'd take even more recognising than yours did."

"You don't think I'd let that matter, do you? As you say, you're still my dad." Jack managed to follow that with "You want us to meet, don't you? Isn't that why you rang?"

"Maybe."

"We can't very well meet here. Even if the people I'm living with didn't see you, the neighbours might. I guess that's one thing you don't need."

"Why's that, John?"

Jack had a grotesque vision of his father, a clownish figure with a grin as wide as a horse's and large hands pale with concrete dust and boots thick with dried mud, his elbows on the table as he dined with Leslie and Ian and Jack. "I just thought," he said carefully, "you'd like to avoid it."

"You'd get embarrassed if your friends and neighbours saw you with your old dad, eh?"

"Not that, no. Why would I? I thought you mightn't want to be seen around here in case you were recognised, however you look."

"Cheer up, son, or you'll have me crying. Don't you know a joke when you hear one? Let's have a laugh or I'll think I've lost my touch."

"Got you." Jack produced a stuttering series of grunts he hoped could be taken as evidence of mirth, and was rewarded by a prolonged sound like the panting of a dog but moister. "That's the spirit," his father said. "It's laughing that keeps us alive, am I right?"

Jack's innards shrank from a sudden memory. "Something else must be."

"True enough, I'm having to fend for myself."

"Well, now you needn't. That's what this is about, isn't it? Tell me where to come if you want looking after."

"You'd like to find me, would you, John?"

"Meet you, sure. I figured that was the point. If you don't want me to know where you've been hiding—I mean, there's no reason you should be afraid of that, only—"

"Bit eager to track me down, aren't you? I'd better give it a think."

"Go ahead. I can wait. If there's anything you need to ask—" Jack was anxious to compensate for whatever he'd said that had roused his father's distrust, but it seemed he shouldn't have tried. A click interrupted him, and then the line hummed smugly to itself.

"Asshole," he snarled, not at his father. "Stupid ass." He dialled 1471, but of course the other number had been blocked. He brought the receiver and its stand together and abandoned them to the table so as to crouch over himself. He felt as though a knot at his centre were pulling him smaller, reducing him to the child he'd been—the child his father had recalled by speaking to Jack.

"Let's have a laugh." When had he first heard that? The first time Jack had cried, perhaps, or complained, or appeared to be ill or injured or miserable or simply not happy enough? And his father had always required a laugh of him immediately after finding any kind of fault with him, after "Sit up straight at the table, nothing wrong with your back" or "No need to hold your knife and fork like that, you've been shown how" or "Walk properly, be glad you can" or "Hold your pen like your teachers told you or they won't be able to read your writing" . . . Jack's mother had told him about his father's little brother who'd died, and eventually that the brother had suffered years of agony from having been born with an exposed spinal cord, but the explanation hadn't helped Jack— it had made him feel that his father kept accusing him of imitating the dead child, of poking fun at him. On top of that pervasive guilt had been not only the exhortations to laugh but how his father watched him while he did, a scrutiny which had seemed to caution him not to laugh too loud or long or high or wildly and which had relented only when he'd produced as much mirth as he'd thought safe.

Could all this have led his mother to concoct a reason to send him to his aunt's in Ruislip? Could she have been aware, at least instinctively, of worse? Jack didn't know if he was only imagining he remembered an impression that requiring him to laugh had been his father's mode of restraining himself from some other behavior. Just now his definite memories were enough to cope with: the way Aunt Pamela had cared for him as if he was another subject of her social work; his Sunday visits home, which he'd grown to dread, because his father's attitude to him had become mechanical, a parody of itself, as though—or was Jack inventing this in retrospect?—his mind had been on somebody elsewhere. As Jack had struggled through adolescence his aunt's solicitude had oppressed him, so that his mother's sister who returned to tour Britain with her American husband had personified a promise of release from Jack's father and Aunt Pamela as well. Jack had befriended his by then American aunt, he'd got himself invited to stay in San Francisco, and the second time he'd stayed he had been old enough to apply for papers to allow him to work. A variety of menial jobs had enabled him to move into a small apartment, and it had been his mounting sense of freedom that had impelled him to try writing the kind of book for which he'd acquired a taste from the thousands of dog-eared paperbacks his American aunt hoarded. He'd sold the first novel within months of stuffing the typescript in an envelope. John Woollie had struck him as no byline for a writer, and so—

His American memories were letting him feel more like the person he wanted to be, and he had straightened up when the phone rang. He lurched forward, renewing his crouch, and fumbled the receiver toward him. "Hello?" he called as soon as it was close enough.

"Waiting for me, were you? Hoping I'd ring back?"

Jack planted the base of the phone beside him on the stair and forced his body upright to convince himself he would do better this time. "Sure," he said.

"Why?"

"I don't believe you mean that. You're the one who keeps reminding me you're my father."

"Have a go at this, then. Shouldn't be too hard for you at your age, seeing as how you're so clever with words."

"I'm not trying to be."

"Not so sure about that, son. It's your job, isn't it? I'll tell you what I've been wondering. Why did you come back?"

"Because I heard you were dead and what you'd been doing, and I figured I'd write about it." Those were truths Jack thought better of telling, but he couldn't pause long. "To see how my mother was surviving," he blurted.

"You've been to visit her, have you?"

Suppose his father knew Jack hadn't—perhaps was even hiding at her house? "Not yet," Jack admitted.

"Shall I let you into a secret, son? That doesn't surprise me at all."

"How come?"

"Because you'll be wondering how much she knew."

"Nothing, I should think. I can't imagine you'd have told her."

"More like you hope I never did. All right, John, I won't keep you in suspense. Your secret's safe with me."

"My . . ." Jack did his best to laugh, then had another try at speaking. "What do you mean, my . . ."

"No need to pretend with me. Remember it's your dad you're speaking to."

"That doesn't mean I've any idea what you're talking about."

"Does it not, John?" Underlying his father's apparent disappointment was more than a hint of worse. "Remember this?" he said, and began to sing.

"Now I lay you down to sleep,
Close your eyes good night.
Angels come your soul to keep,
Close your eyes good night . . ."

He was halfway through repeating the verse when he broke off. "Remember when I used to sing that?"

"Yes," Jack said, but that didn't get rid of the question. "When I was small and you wanted me to go to sleep."

"Like my mother used to sing to me. It's a good memory, isn't it?"

"Sure."

Perhaps Jack's answer was too quick or too suspiciously unspecific, because his father made a moist rude sound. "That isn't all you remember though, is it? Remember where else I'd sing?"

Jack felt as though the personality he'd taken for his adult self was about to disintegrate. "What if I do?"

"Just don't be so keen to find me if you're thinking of telling anybody where I am. You wouldn't expect even your dad to protect you if you shopped him. If I were you I'd be thinking how to look after my old dad and make sure nobody else knew he was alive."

"Nobody does as far as I know, I can promise you that, but what are you saying I need protection from?"

"Oh, John. I just hope for your sake nobody's listening to us. If I got caught I'd have to say you helped me."

"Why would you?"

"Because there'd be no reason for me not to tell the truth."

"What truth?"

"Do me a favour, son. You were never that thick. Even if you'd forgotten about it, it must have come back to you now, helping me to flatten the earth down in those houses. What did you think I was singing about then? You must have thought something."

"I was young," Jack protested, almost pleading.

"You weren't that young. Or if you were to start with it must have affected you more, mustn't it? I wonder how much like your dad you really are deep down. I reckon if anybody found out who you are they'd have some ideas about why you're living in that house."

Jack's mouth worked, but all that emerged was a shaky breath. "I'll leave you to have another think," his father said. "I'll be in touch."

When the phone reverted to humming, Jack found he had to think which hand to use for replacing the receiver. Sunlight was leaning through the glass above the front door and wedging itself into the hall, but he felt as though its brightness couldn't reach him; it was too dark inside his head—dark as the underside of earth. He was remembering how he'd helped his father.

Though he'd done it only twice—the properties had needed to be close enough for him to visit on his way to school—it felt far worse than twice too often. In one case he'd been almost Ian's age, but it was the other that was restaging itself in his mind. He'd been no more than eight years old, yet he remembered how the morning had tasted of fog, how a spider's web that resembled spun glass had been swaying in a breeze outside the kitchen window of the vacated house, how the kitchen had smelled of the earth where the floor should have been. "Make sure there's no irregularities, son," he could hear his father saying as he'd handed Jack—no, John— a brush. He could feel the soil gritting beneath his feet, could hear the repetitive scrape of the brush, but surely he was only imagining in retrospect that he'd sensed anything under the earth; he'd thought his father was behaving no more oddly than grown-ups often did when he'd started singing in little more than a whisper "Now I lay you down to sleep . . ." But he couldn't dismiss the memory, not when his research had enabled him to put a name and an age to the victims he'd helped bury. Billie short for Wilhelmena Carter, six years old, not much younger than Jack had been at the time. Martin Hawthorn, also six.

What had his father been expecting of him on those occasions? Some kind of unknowing encouragement, some reassurance that he himself was acting properly, or could he have hoped Jack would inherit his behaviour? The question seemed to pervade everything Jack was and his surroundings too, so that when the phone rang he couldn't help wishing it had brought him his father again. "Yes," he said into the mouthpiece, so sharply his breath chilled his teeth.

"May I speak to Mrs. Ames?"

It was a woman's voice, and he had to make an effort to respond. "She's at work."

"I've been trying her there, but it's engaged. I'll try again." Instead of ringing off, however, the woman paused. "Are you the writer?"

Jack had little sense of who he was any more. "I guess."

Perhaps that seemed unworthy of a reply, or perhaps she felt she was responding to it when she spoke. As if she thought he was accountable for the state of affairs and unworthy to be told the details, she cut him off once she'd finished saying "If you happen to speak to her, please ask her to contact her son's school urgently. I'm afraid he's in grave trouble."

TWENTY-SIX

"Fix Duke's eye for him."

Leslie swung round to stare at the group of boys who were passing her and Ian. Any of them might have been pretending not to have spoken. "There's been quite enough of that," she said in a voice that rang on the concrete of the schoolyard, but as the boys vanished behind an annexe that resembled a temporary office on a building site, she heard them start to joke.

The brown bricks of the school, half a two-storey H with its middle bar facing the gates, looked sandy with mid-morning light. Dozens of windows leaned out as though to scoop heat into the classrooms, which were emitting a selection of the noises schools made. As Ian opened a side door for Leslie, she said "Don't let anyone start thinking you're a hero."

"I didn't mean to get his eye."

"You've told me that and I believe you. You aren't a monster, but you aren't a hero either. You're more or less who you've always been, so try not to let what people say about you affect you. Except what your headmaster says is going to have to count, and we'd better hope it isn't too bad."

The door closed behind her and her awkwardly overgrown son with more of a slam than she could think was encouraged. A classful of boys laughed and thought about whatever they were laughing at and laughed again, a master's voice echoed down the corridor whose walls looked slippery with paint. She felt as though she'd been sent back to school, and uneasier for knowing that some of the pupils thought the Duke boy's injury was a joke. How could they want him to be hurt when he'd lost his little sister? Perhaps they disliked how that had changed him, but why couldn't they see past their dislike? Now she was at the doors that gave onto the corridor inhabited by the headmaster, and when Ian pushed one open she saw Mrs. Duke and her son.

Four straight chairs had been placed with their backs to the headmaster's office, two on each side of the door. The Dukes were sitting on the farther pair, and turned just their heads toward the newcomers. The boy's movement might have been intended to reveal the right side of his face, the eye covered with a wad of gauze held by a cross of adhesive plaster. His mother let her dull gaze weigh on the Ameses as they took the remaining chairs, and Leslie tried not to imagine that she was comparing her grey suit and white blouse with Leslie's more expensive version of the outfit. When eventually she felt Mrs. Duke's stare lift itself from her she glanced at her wristwatch, and had another look a minute later. It was past time for the appointment, and so she wondered aloud "Should we tell anyone we're here?"

She had to turn and gaze at Mrs. Duke, then cock her head and raise her eyebrows, before the woman said tonelessly "He knows we are."

Either that or Leslie's question brought Mr. Brand to his door. He was a tall chubby man who smelled of sweetish shower gel and whose blond hair persisted in flopping over his brow. He extended his hands on either side of him, so slowly that he might have been offering a dual handshake or advising the women to remain seated or even inviting them to inspect his small neatly manicured nails. "Is everyone present?" he said.

Since Mrs. Duke only shrugged, Leslie risked trying to lighten the mood. "Looks like it, or there wouldn't be enough seats."

"One or both of the gentlemen would have given theirs up, I trust," the headmaster said, and with a residue of admonition "So it's just mothers and sons."

"Has been," Mrs. Duke declared, "since they took my man in because they thought he'd done something to Harmony."

"There's no chance of a reconciliation?"

"Not after what I said to him when I thought he had."

"I'm certain everybody sympathises with your tragic situation."

Mr. Brand held a respectful pause before saying "Shall we continue in my room? The ladies will need seats."

"I'll bring them," Ian said.

"Rupert can carry mine," Mrs. Duke told everyone.

The headmaster made a sound not unlike that of a machine gun with his throat and led the way into his office, a wide bright room slitting its blinds at a view of the outstretched legs of the building. Ian planted a chair well away from its twin before the broad oak desk, and Leslie sat while he stood beside her. She remembered when she would have lifted him onto her lap; she sensed the vulnerable little boy hiding inside him and imagined one inside Rupert too, and willed Mr. Brand to be quick with the interview. Instead he reached or at least mimed reaching for the phone. "Will the ladies have a coffee?"

"Not with my nerves," Mrs. Duke said.

"Tea, then."

"You won't want me gurgling when you're talking to them."

The heat that the blinds were failing to exclude was parching Leslie's mouth, but she shook her head at Mr. Brand. "I'm fine," she lied.

"In that event let me hear the accounts. Duke, you may begin."

"Ames cut my eye with his book."

"I think that's common knowledge. How is it presently feeling?"

"Hurts."

"I fancy it must," Mr. Brand said dabbing at both of his own. "What word from the hospital, Mrs. Duke?"

"His corny whatever they call it is ripped."

"The cornea. The horny membrane, from the Latin," Mr. Brand told Rupert in case the knowledge came in useful. "How will it affect his sight, can that be told yet?"

"He won't lose it, the doctor said."

"That's cheering. Meanwhile I understand it tends to aggravate Rupert's problems with his schoolwork."

"It would, wouldn't it?"

"Anything else you would like to place on the record, Duke? What do you say led to the incident?"

"Ames wrote a horror thing about putting a girl under the floor."

"So Mr. Cardigan informs me, but I wonder what it has to do with you."

"You're joking. It's like using what that bastard did to our Harmony."

"I didn't mean her. I wasn't thinking of her."

"No polyphony, if you please. One voice at a time. I must say, Ames, if you weren't thinking about her then perhaps you should have been."

"He shouldn't have wrecked it. He won't be able to wreck the book Jack's writing about all the stuff Hector Woollie did."

"He's what?" Mrs. Duke demanded.

Mr. Brand showed her a palm. "Anything further, Duke? Anything that doesn't involve language we don't expect from our boys. Intemperateness only leads to the sort of incident we're having to discuss." When some or all of that left Rupert speechless, Mr. Brand said "Ames's version, then. Speak as freely as you wish within the limits of politeness and accuracy."

"It's like I said, Duke heard Mr. Cardigan talking about my story and he came and tore it up. I was going to show my mother and Jack. Duke made me mad, that's all."

"Are you saying you were temporarily insane?"

"Just mad."

"Angry, you're trying to say. Furious."

"Right."

"There's no merit in a usage that blurs meaning." Having led a silence to mourn the loss, Mr. Brand said "The destruction of another boy's schoolwork is a serious matter, but I think we may accept that Duke has paid for the infraction. On the other hand—"

"Sir." Ian waited to be sure he would be heard, and then he said "That isn't all he did."

"I see," Mr. Brand said, though Leslie was certain he had no more sense of what was coming than she had. "Continue."

"He broke into our house and sprayed stuff on the doors."

"That's a rotten lie," Mrs. Duke cried, grabbing her knees with her silver-nailed hands as if to launch herself at him, and Leslie was readying herself to intervene, breathing as deliberately as she could to slow her pulse that felt like the shakes, when the headmaster brandished a hand. "What evidence have you of that, Ames?"

"Duke said."

"Is that true, Duke?"

Rupert dragged his glare, intensified by its confinement to one eye, away from Ian and neutralised his look before it reached the headmaster. "Can't remember what I said."

"In other words, you might have."

"He got me so furious angry I could've said any—anything, sir."

"That would hardly have improved the situation, would it? I appreciate you must have felt aggrieved, Ames. Nevertheless—"

"Hold on." Leslie's throat was so dry she had to clear it with a cough. "Can we stay with what we just heard? Can we establish if he broke into my house?"

"He just said he did," Mrs. Duke informed her as if addressing a backward child.

"No, he only admitted he said it. Was it true?" Leslie asked him.

His tight lips twitched, and she saw Mrs. Duke open her mouth to talk over anything he said, but it was Mr. Brand who spoke. "Forgive my interrupting, but I think we must confine ourselves to school matters. If you've reason to believe Duke was responsible for any damage to your property you should contact the police."

"It's us that ought," Mrs. Duke protested. "We'll be sending them after her boy for what he did to mine if you don't give him what he deserves."

"I assure you I shall be taking all the relevant factors into consideration." The headmaster raised his chin an inch as if to render his unruly hair less prominent or his solemn expression more so. "However provoked you may have felt," he told Ian, "you could very easily have blinded him."

"I know." Ian grimaced with regret or to steel himself to add "Sorry, sir."

"Easy said and not enough," Mrs. Duke objected.

"When it becomes necessary to expel a boy," Mr. Brand said, "I feel the school has failed."

Leslie held her breath and found she couldn't look at Ian. By the time Mr. Brand went on, her eyes had begun to sting. "Given everything I've heard here today, and bearing in mind the need to send a signal to the students, I shall with immediate effect be excluding Ames for the remainder of the term."

"That's not nearly enough," Mrs. Duke said at once. "You heard what I said about the police."

"I hope you wouldn't expect that to alter my decision, Mrs. Duke. If your son weren't injured I should have to consider excluding him for destroying Ames's work. As far as recourse to the police is concerned, I gathered that if either you or Mrs. Ames were to involve them, the other would reciprocate."

Mrs. Duke gave him a long dull stare before saying "Have you finished with us?"

"Unless there was anything further you wished to say. Thank you for attending."

"Come on, Rupert. Can you see where you're going all right?" Mrs. Duke said, and as a parting shot "Time you were in your class if it doesn't hurt too much to work."

Leslie supposed the headmaster's decision was just, but she wished he could have stopped short of making her feel helpless over the break-in at her house. It was like so much of life, she thought: a mess of motives and emotions that couldn't be brought to a satisfactory conclusion, that would simply linger until the passage of time let the frustration of it dissipate. "What will Ian do about his schoolwork?" she said.

"Arrangements will need to be made with his teachers. Perhaps you could telephone the staff room at lunchtime." Mr. Brand stood up, and as a further sign that the interview was over, used his fingertips to clear his forehead of hair. "I hope to see a continuing improvement in your work, Ames," he said. "I hear your teachers had been happy with your progress."

Leslie tried not to feel ostracised as she left the building for the deserted schoolyard. "It's good that they're pleased with your work, isn't it?"

"Guess so," he said, not much more than a shrug.

"It is, Ian. The bad stuff's been dealt with, so let's concentrate on the good. If you have time and you want to, you could try writing your story again for me and Jack to read."

He turned his back on the suggestion and walked ahead, and she kept the rest of her thoughts to herself along the North Circular Road. Most of the journey across the recreation ground was accompanied by a terrier that was determined to see her and Ian off, to the amusement of its slowly jogging rotund owner, and some of the people in the streets nearer Jericho Close were visibly of the opinion that Ian should be at school. At least the sight of her house was welcome, not least because the Nova in front of it meant Jack was in.

She didn't call to him as she stepped into the hall. He'd been preoccupied of late, no doubt with his book. She filled the percolator in the kitchen and sent Ian to fetch a mug from the garden table. When she saw him wave at Jack's window and at Janet's, she went out herself.

Jack was at his desk, and gazing either into the distance or at the screen of his word processor. It took him a few seconds to notice her, at which point he raised a thumb and then its fist, though not far. Rather than distract him further, she only smiled and turned to Janet, who was leaning out of her bedroom window. "Just finishing the packing," Janet said, "and then it's the time-share for three weeks. Do I see someone else on holiday?"

"Just studying until the end of term because of the fight he was in."

"Boys." Having summed up a great deal in the syllable, Janet presented Ian with a grin as compensation. "Still," she said, "I'll sleep better knowing there's two men at home to keep an eye on the house."

TWENTY-SEVEN

HORROR MAN WRITES BOOK ABOUT MURDER HOUSE

"Bitch."

"Now, Ian, there's no need for that."

"Well, she is. I bet Jack thinks she is."

"I'm sure Jack is too well brought up to say so even if he thinks it. That's right, isn't it, Jack?"

"I—I didn't catch who we're talking about, to tell you the truth."

"Rupe's mom. She must have told the paper you were writing your book. I shouldn't have said at school you were."

"Hey, it's okay. No harm done that I know of."

"No such thing as bad publicity, don't they say?"

"I guess."

Perhaps Leslie should have kept the observation to herself. He was obviously more bothered than he wanted her and Ian to know. She folded the newspaper on the kitchen table to conceal the headline and the reappearance of the picture of Jack on the stairs. "At least it won't have spoiled your book, will it?"

"I figure it's still safe in here," he said, knuckling his forehead so sharply that she winced. "That's where I live."

"With us too, I hope."

"See, Rupe's mother didn't care if she wrecked your book. That makes her a bitch, and the wheelie woman's one as well."

"Ian, I do think you could put away some of your vocabulary for a while if not for good. It doesn't hurt to choose your words even if it takes more time, does it, Jack? I'm sure that's part of being a writer."

"It's helped me so far."

"There, Ian, advice from a professional."

"If you can use a tad more, try writing that story you wrote again before you forget it. It'll be a second draft, and real writers do those. Want to promise me you will?"

"I'll try."

"If anyone's to blame for the lady in the wheelchair keeping after us, I must be. I didn't handle her too well the time we met."

"Stop feeling guilty, Jack. You've no reason I can see."

"It's sweet of you to say so." Looking as though he might have reached for her if Ian hadn't been there, Jack stood up. "Guess I'll take a shower and try to wash away my sins."

That was so deadpan it hardly sounded like a joke. He'd already been preoccupied when he had come downstairs in his dressing gown—his robe, she supposed he would call it—for a cup of the English breakfast tea he'd grown fond of, and she wished she hadn't left the newspaper in sight, though he would have had to deal with the report sooner or later. She hoped he had now. She was clearing away her and Ian's breakfast plates—Jack hadn't wanted anything to eat—when the phone rang.

Ian sprinted to it, but his eagerness lasted only until he'd answered it. "Some man for Jack."

"Run up and tell him."

She hadn't meant quite so immediately that he didn't take time to ask the caller to hold on. She dumped the plates and utensils in the sink and hurried to pick up the receiver. "Hello?"

"You'll be what's your name again?"

It wasn't only how blurred the slow male voice was that threw her, it was its resentment of having to turn its answer into a question. "You tell me," she said.

"Doesn't matter. Is Jack Lamb there?"

"There's some man on the phone," Ian was shouting over the cloudburst of the shower as Leslie made an effort to meet rudeness with politeness. "My son's just letting him know you're calling."

"Knows who I am then, does he?"

"My son? He does if you told him."

"Then he doesn't."

"Phone," Ian yelled, "some man," and before Leslie had time to word a retort to the person referred to, the bathroom door flew open, revealing Jack in the process of wrapping himself in a towel. "Who is it?" he demanded.

"No idea, and frankly I can do without knowing. He doesn't seem to want anyone except maybe you to know. He's all yours, or I can cut him off."

"No," Jack said, "no, don't do that." Having secured the towel around himself, he ran down to her, leaving a moist footstep on each stair. "Jack Lamb," he said, turning the receiver and his head toward the wall.

Leslie returned to the kitchen while Ian took the chance to brush his teeth. "What name is that?" she heard Jack say, and "Right" and "Not yet" and "Not one of those either" and "Working on it" and "Sure, if you want." She saw him scribbling on the pad beside the phone before he said "I'll be in touch."

"Anything good?" she risked asking.

"Nothing bad, I guess." He tore the page off the pad and found nowhere to put it. "I wouldn't know how much to trust the guy, though, if he's as drunk as he sounded this early."

"But it wasn't as bad as you thought it was going to be."

"I don't—how do you mean?"

"He wasn't as bad as I made him sound."

"Got you. Maybe not. He was an agent wanting to know if I had one in Britain and if I had a publisher yet. For, you know, the book he heard I'm working on, though don't ask me where he heard I was."

"It's got to be encouraging to find you're in demand, hasn't it? It could be the start of a revival. We can hope."

"You think?" For a moment he seemed about to say more, and then a shiver brought his knees together. The hall didn't strike her as cold or draughty, though of course she wasn't wearing only a towel. "I'd better get my shower," he said.

"Tell Ian I'm just nipping next door," Leslie called after him and, having watched his increasingly—not to say enticingly—bare legs ascend the stairs, let herself out of the house.

The *Advertiser* was protruding from Janet's and Vern's letter-box. She dragged the paper out and stooped to peer through the slot. The hall and the stairs and the three closed doors were as they should be. She released the metal flap and heard an echo of its clank somewhere within. As she straightened up she became aware that a woman who'd parked a red Volkswagen halfway along Jericho Close had halted at her gate.

She was wearing a long autumnally brown dress too voluminous for her thin neck and thinner limbs. Beneath sparse curls the colours of metal beginning to rust, her small face looked drawn together by concern. She came to some decision and advanced, sandals clacking beneath her heels, toward the door Leslie had left open. "Excuse me, can I help?" Leslie called over the fence.

"Don't trouble. I know where I'm going."

"So do I," Leslie said, mildly enough. "To my house."

Even when Leslie strode down the path and up her own, the woman seemed less than convinced. "Tell me what you want by all means," Leslie said, "and who you are would be nice."

"Are you sure you live here?"

"I'm sure of a few things, and that's one of them." Leslie was running out of patience, having expended too much on the man who'd phoned Jack. "Now it's my turn to get some answers, so if you'd like—"

"You're Mrs. Ames."

"That's me, but I knew it already, believe it or not. What I'm asking you—"

"You wouldn't say you were unless you really were." The woman held out her hands and then curled her fingers toward herself, and Leslie couldn't tell if they were recoiling or indicating their owner until the woman said with no more than a hint of defensiveness "I'm Adele Woollie."

Leslie didn't quite gasp, but she had to press her lips together. Harder to deal with than the revelation was the way Mrs. Woollie seemed to be implying Leslie would be sympathetic to her because they had something in common. Even if that was only notoriety, Leslie wasn't anxious to admit sharing it with her. "So what do you want?" she said.

Mrs. Woollie tried to square her thin shoulders, a gesture that gave her the appearance of being manipulated like a puppet. "My son."

For a headachy moment Leslie thought she was referring to the child who'd been buried under the kitchen, and had to remind herself that victim hadn't been a boy. "Well, you aren't going to find—"

It wasn't Jack who cut her off, because he was only calling to Ian "I'm through with the bathroom"; it was how Mrs. Woollie's face changed as she heard his voice. Don't say it, Leslie willed her. I won't believe you if you do. It's ridiculous. It's impossible. It's too much.

"That's him," Mrs. Woollie said.

TWENTY-EIGHT

As Jack withdrew his face from the cone of hot water his thoughts came clear. He had to tell Leslie who he was. Even once he'd turned off the shower and stepped out of the bath his skin was still crawling, not with trickles of water but with the memory of his dread that the man who'd phoned a few minutes ago would prove to be his father. Any caller might be, and suppose Leslie guessed? However she might take the truth when Jack revealed it, having it betrayed would be worse. He'd hidden it for fear of harming their relationship, but he valued her so much that he wouldn't feel deserving of her if he failed to tell.

His novels had been attempts to deal with his past, though he hadn't known they were while writing them. The book he planned to write could have been a bolder step in the process or a way of persuading himself that his father had nothing to do with him. Telling Leslie was the key to admitting the truth to himself, and so inevitable it calmed him.

"I'm through with the bathroom," he called as he made for his room, and wondered how Ian would react to his confession. He heard the front door shut as Leslie returned to the house. He dressed himself quickly and lightly, and was halfway down the stairs before his eagerness allowed him to hear another woman's voice. As he hesitated, less than prepared to chat to a stranger, Leslie looked out of the front room. "Jack, can you come in here?"

"Sure."

His response sounded more willing than he was, particularly since her face was as good as blank. He hadn't begun to interpret it when she turned her back. If her visitor was unwelcome, perhaps Leslie wanted help. He ran down and was nearly in the room when he faltered, one foot in the hall.

A thin woman in a large brown dress, her reddish curls interwoven with grey and close to baring glimpses of her scalp, was sitting in the farther armchair. He almost knew her, and then he did, when her small face seemed to expand with happiness as she jumped up and held out her arms. "John, it *is* you," she cried. "I should have known the first time you were in the paper."

He couldn't step forward, he couldn't retreat. His hands rose as though they were being hauled toward her, then found nothing to do while she rushed to him. He had to put his arms around her and accept her protracted wizened kiss as he saw how much care had settled on her face and grasped how much weight she'd lost. She hugged him as if she might never let go, and eventually stood back so as to appraise him. "Hi," he said.

"Is that all you can say to your mother?" She looked ready to deal him at least a playful slap. "He sounds just like an American, doesn't he," she declared instead, and held him at arm's length as a preamble to an augmented hug and kiss. When those were over she said "All done. They're all the same, boys, aren't they, however old they are. Sit down before you fall down if your mother's such a shock."

He hadn't sat when Leslie said in a voice as expressionless as her face "Would you like me to leave you alone?"

"No," Jack blurted. "No need."

"I don't know if Mrs. Ames wanted me to see you. I hope she doesn't think I'm the least bit like you know who."

"I shouldn't wonder," Leslie said. "That's what you're suggesting."

"Of course you should, you wouldn't be human if you didn't, but I hope you'll see I'm not. Do you know what I'll never forgive Woollie for? What he did to those kiddies, obviously that, but on top of that the way he used my residents, pretending he was helping them when he was banking nobody'd believe them if they saw anything. And when some of them did, it set them right back after all the care I'd taken of them."

"So to sum up, you're glad he's gone."

"That's as true for me as I'm positive it is for this big chap."

"In that case you really must sit down, both of you."

Jack had to sit in the middle of the couch, feeling isolated and scrutinised. He was trying to find words for at least some of the explanation Leslie deserved when his mother clapped her hands, either calling for attention or applauding in advance. "Well, John, you've certainly done all right for yourself."

Even if she didn't mean Leslie, Leslie might assume she did. He attempted a deprecating laugh as his mother said "I always knew he would. He's been good with words ever since he was at school."

"I've noticed," Leslie said.

"Have you read him?"

"I've been doing that, oh yes."

When his apologetic look brought no response from Leslie, he said to his mother "How about you? What are you up to these days?"

"The same as I'll be till I have to be put in a home myself. Looking after people who need it because they haven't got a hospital to go to. You'd know that if you'd been to see me."

"I would have soon."

"You didn't come to find me at home, then."

The question disguised as a statement sounded unsettlingly like a trap his father might have set for him. "No," Jack admitted.

"You wouldn't have found me, because I've only got a flat now. More than enough for a widow living by herself."

Presumably her pause was intended as another gentle rebuke, but it reminded Jack that only he knew his father was alive. The truth was searching for a way out of his mouth when his mother said "I'm still running the same place, though. They let me after all my residents vouched for me."

"You'd expect them to," Leslie said.

"Nobody knows me better except Woollie and maybe John, or he will if he wants to. You haven't said how long you've been home, John."

"Not too long. Here, only a few weeks."

"I got that from the paper. Where were you before Mrs. Ames took you in?"

He'd done all the taking in, Jack thought, but said "Staying with friends."

"For quite a while, was that?"

"Couple of months."

"They must be good friends to have you that long. Should I know them?"

"No," Jack said, wishing he hadn't persisted with the story. "Some guys I met stateside."

He sensed that Leslie realised how careful he was being with his words. He felt as if both women were interrogating him, and he couldn't help yearning for just about anything that would give him a break. "You could have stayed with me, you know," his mother said. "There's room even for a big lump like you."

"Right," Jack said, though not at once. He'd heard Ian emerge from the bathroom. When his chest began to ache, he became aware of holding his breath while Ian let his weight drop from one stair to the next all the way down. The boy wandered into the room and halted with a quick shy grin. "No need to be frightened, son," he was told. "I'm just his mother."

Ian stepped forward and held out his hand. "Pleased to meet you, Mrs. Lamb."

"Mrs. Woollie."

"Mrs.—" Ian's mouth opened wide and seemed unable to find itself a shape as he turned to stare at Jack. "You're—"

"That's who I am. I'm sorry. Yes, that's me."

"Oh, John, don't say I've—I have, haven't I?"

"No reason for you to apologise," Leslie said.

Ian was regarding Jack with something like awe. "You're his son."

"And mine," Jack's mother said. "Mrs. Ames, you can under- stand why he mightn't have wanted to say who he was."

"I do indeed."

"He's always been a good boy, even if he didn't come and see his mother. Even if he went off without telling his family where and changed his name," she said, having directed her voice at Jack. "He mustn't have wanted Woollie to know where he was, Mrs. Ames. He must have sensed there was something not right about Woollie before the rest of us knew. He was always a sensitive soul, our John." As if some of what she'd just said needed contradicting she added "They never had anything but good to say about him at school."

"Mrs. Woollie, I'm a mother too."

"I see you are. So you'll know us mothers know all about our children."

"We like to think we do."

"He's a credit to you," Jack's mother said, and for a moment that let him grasp how confused he was, Jack thought she was referring to him. "We could do with a few more as polite as your boy."

"As long as they're honest as well."

This time there was no question that Leslie meant Jack. "I think I've trespassed long enough," his mother said, though she stood up so gradually she might have been hoping to have it contested. "You'll be wanting my address, will you, John?"

"Sure."

"You must have something I can put it on, you being a writer."

Even if he had, Jack would have taken the opportunity to escape from the room. He fetched the pad and pencil from beside the phone for his mother to write down a Northolt address. She tore off the page and clasped his hands as she returned everything to him. "Just you remember how welcome you'll be. I hope I haven't made trouble for you with your landlady, but if I have . . ."

Jack felt his face stiffen. His mother's gaze veered to Leslie and back to him. "Oh, I see," she murmured. "Oh dear. Oh double dear."

"Let me walk you to your car."

"I'd like that," his mother said, then stooped toward Leslie. "If I can say one more thing—"

"Please don't," Leslie said, and raised herself from the chair until the other woman had to move out of her way. "If you'll excuse me, I'd like to get back to where I was before."

Jack let his mother out of the house and opened the gate for her. "I know I should have been to visit you."

"I shouldn't have come here, you mean. You'd have been better off without me."

"I didn't say that, and you shouldn't think I meant it either."

She bent her head toward him as though to peer behind his words and said "I'll tell you this even if you don't thank me. If she doesn't understand she can't be much good for you, John. You've had to try and understand more than that, you poor boy."

"I have to ask you a question."

"Let's be hearing it, then."

"Did you ever—" Jack had lowered his voice, which made it seem to be shrinking back into his mouth. "Did you have any idea, any at all, what my father was doing?"

She walked rapidly to the Volkswagen, her loose sandals scolding the pavement, and shoved the key into the door with a loud rasp before she turned her saddened gaze on him. "How can you ask such a thing of your own mother?"

"Because I need to be sure. You said I had to try to understand."

"Don't you think if I'd had the least suspicion he was up to something I'd have kept on at him till I thought I'd got the truth out of him?"

"I'd have figured you would."

"Don't you know if I had I'd have told even though he was the man I married? There's too many people keeping quiet in the world."

"Okay."

"You don't have to keep sounding American. I know who you are." She gave him a hug and kiss not quite so assured as their predecessors, then ducked into the car. He watched her take time to settle herself in the seat and draw the belt across herself, and perhaps he appeared to be waiting for reassurance, because she wound the window down. "Do you think I'd have let him anywhere near my residents if I'd had even a glimmer how he was using them?"

"I guess—I don't suppose so."

"I should hope not." She reached for him, but her hand stopped short of emerging and his stayed outside. "Can I look forward to seeing you again soon?" she said.

"I imagine," Jack told her, the best he could manage when she'd left him feeling more alone than ever with aspects of his childhood he kept trying to convince himself he'd faced. He waved as the car chugged away, and saw his mother vanish round the corner with a smile that could, given more time, have looked both encouraging and brave. Its implications followed him back to the house.

Leslie was in the kitchen, and kept her back to him as he ventured along the hall. "Do you think I'd better speak to Ian?" he said.

"No."

Since she hadn't moved, Jack didn't feel he could go closer. His heartbeat had begun to grow uncomfortable when he heard Ian running downstairs. Leslie turned and called past Jack as if he wasn't there "Make sure you get all the ingredients on my list or I won't be able to make your favourite."

"See you, J."

"I hope," Jack said.

As the front door slammed, she let her determinedly neutral gaze find him. "Do me one favour, and if you need to think about it, think after you've done it."

"If that's what you need," Jack said, and heard his pulse.

"Leave us alone. He's my son, he's all that's left. Don't be here when he gets home."

Jack couldn't argue—he didn't feel entitled—but when she held out a hand he thought she'd taken some pity on him. He was imagining the softness and warmth of her clasp as she said "You won't be wanting my keys any more," and he could only fish them out of his trousers pocket and drop them on her outstretched palm. Until she said "Thanks" he had never realised how final the word could sound.

TWENTY-NINE

There was another way to tell the story, Ian thought. Part of it could be about how Carla's mother felt. She would have left Carla alone in the house for an hour while she drove to the next farm to borrow some milk because the contents of their own cows had run out, milk for Carla who was ill in bed. On the way back the mother would hear on the car radio, except she would be driving a truck, that the maniac wearing a mark had been sighted in their area, their state. She would send the truck screeching into their yard and stamp on the brakes and run through the cloud of dust into the farmhouse. "Momma's home," she would call, and maybe even think she heard a feeble answer from upstairs, if farmhouses in California had one, but when she hurried into Carla's room the bed would be empty except for the patchwork quilt they'd made together. She would run through the house in a panic, crying for her daughter, and Carla would hear her from beneath the cellar floor—she would hear her mother's frantic footsteps on the boards that were nailed down over her, would feel the vibrations and the dust sifting down onto her face. And then—maybe then her father would come home from the, from the slaughterhouse where he worked, and Carla's mother would run to him for help, and he would search for Carla everywhere—under the hay in the barn, in the pigsty, in the wardrobes—and end up standing right on top of where she was. Then—"Yes!" Ian gasped—as he climbed the rickety steps his pocket would catch on a nail, and out would fall the mask.

The new version of the story had made itself up like a dream, and now its aspiration to be written wakened him. Should he try to scribble it all down while it filled his head? He kicked the quilt aside and sat up, and as sunlight hit him in the face, his sense of the story began to retreat from him. Creating it had let him feel like Jack, but had also caused him to forget Jack was no longer there to tell him whether it was any good.

Surely he ought to be able to contact Jack, otherwise the slab might fall on his mind. He'd had weeks of being rid of it nearly all the time, and he didn't want it back. It had threatened to return while the headmaster was judging him, but being excluded from school had shown him he worked better without the distractions of Stu and Baz and Shaun. He'd vowed to show everyone what he was capable of, only now he realised he'd wanted mostly to show Jack.

He would. He had to. He grabbed his English exercise book and turned to the middle, past the pages he'd written on since Duke had torn his story out. *Carla's momma drives for milk*, he wrote, and *Maniac on radio*, before he dropped the book on the introverted tangle of the quilt. The notes seemed as good as meaningless; they wouldn't come alive for him until he was sure of contacting Jack. He hurried to the bathroom, then he buttoned his shorts and padded downstairs to find his mother.

She was in the front room with a piece of music for company, either quiet in itself or turned down so as not to waken him. The four bearded men on the compact disc box were demonstrating a variety of ways to hold stringed instruments and trying to outdo the music, which Ian saw with no interest was by either Shostakovich or Tschaikovsky, in lugubriousness. Perhaps that was his mother's mood too, because he thought she continued rubbing the window with a dissonant wash-leather to give herself time to raise her lips at least to horizontal before she faced him. "Hungry?" she said.

"Some."

"I thought you might be when you hardly touched your dinner last night." She draped the leather over the rim of a plastic bucket standing on a copy of the *Advertiser* and let the corners of her mouth stray up. "I know you miss him. I know it's hard for you. Try and make do with me again for a while if you can."

"How much of a while?"

"I meant until someone—Look, I just meant we're the whole of the team. You shouldn't think I was talking about whatever he wants to call himself."

"Jack."

"That's the name he made up, right enough."

"Lots of writers do that, don't they? He couldn't help who had him. His mother seemed okay."

"Oh, Ian . . ."

"Why did you send him away?"

"Because I couldn't trust him."

"He never did anything to hurt us. The Dukes and Mr. Brand and the wheelie woman did, but Jack wouldn't have."

"I'm not saying he did you any harm. Maybe he was even good for you, and I hope you can hang on to the good."

For the moment he was more aware what she was leaving unsaid about herself and Jack, which suggested that adult lives might be as messy and as difficult to make sense of as his own. "Did you get his address?" he blurted.

"Why would I have done that, Ian?"

"For me."

"I'm afraid not. It didn't occur to me, and I have to say it seems not to have to him either."

"I bet he'd have given it to me if you hadn't sent me to the store."

"We'll never know. And please, Ian, you aren't an American. There's no need to keep trying to sound like one."

She was determined to erase every trace of Jack, he thought, but she wouldn't take Jack out of him. The lugubrious quartet, having finished being slow, struck up a dance so inappropriate to the situation that he saw her think about switching it off. Instead she retrieved the leather, only to say "Better get dressed. We're about to be visited."

His father's Peugeot was drawing up at the gate. A trickle of water on the front room pane made Charlotte appear to shiver and squirm in the passenger seat. Anger and frustration sent Ian up to his room, from which he heard his mother keep his father waiting once the doorbell rang, and eventually her voice. "Here's a surprise."

"Not too bad a one, I hope."

"Short of unbearable."

"Sorry, then. I should have rung. Call me impulsive."

"We'll see. What's the occasion?"

"Before we talk, can I ask who else is here?"

"Ian."

"Just Ian?"

"That's who I said."

"Is he available?"

"He's meant to be getting dressed."

"You don't mind, do you?" Apparently Ian's father was asking for permission to enter the house, because his voice advanced to the foot of the stairs. "Ian?"

Ian hesitated long enough not to seem to have been eavesdropping when he emerged from his room. "What?"

"Hello, Dad, or hi, Dad would have been nice, or even what a great surprise on a sunny Sunday morning. When you've a few more clothes on than that, would you like to take Charlotte to the park?"

"Don't know. Would I?"

"She asked to come and see you, which means quite a lot when she's still scared of this house. She thinks of you as a big brother, you know. She was hoping she could have a walk to make up for the one you didn't have last time you stayed with us."

"Where is she? Why can't she come and ask?"

"She's by the car. I've persuaded her I won't come to harm in here, but that's as close as she'll venture herself. Do us all a favour and don't keep her waiting long. Nobody wants another bout of hysterics."

Ian tried to tell himself he couldn't care less, except if he were American he would say he could and mean the same thing, but he knew he would be blamed for any row Charlotte made. He picked his way across the floor strewn with clothes and schoolwork to the window. Charlotte was fingering the bonnet of the car to judge whether the vehicle was clean enough to perch on. She stepped away from it with a jerk of the blue bows on either side of her head and a flounce of her blue silk dress, and peered nervously at the house. "Don't fret, Charlotte," Ian's father called. "Ian's just making himself decent for you."

"When will he come? I don't like waiting here."

"He'll be there before you know it, sweet."

"Can't you tell him to hurry? I don't like seeing the nasty house. I won't be able to sleep tonight if we don't go soon. I'll have horrible dreams."

All this and his father's shout for him to get a move on would have caused Ian to dawdle if he hadn't already determined to prevent her from making a scene. He dressed in yesterday's clothes with a sloppiness meant to display his anger and tramped downstairs, his shoelaces snapping at the air. "Thanks," his father said. "Don't be less than an hour, will you? Help her trot off some of her chub."

Whatever his father was here for, Ian suspected he was out of luck—was pretty certain, though annoyingly not quite, that he hoped it. He grinned to himself as he shut the door behind him, and didn't bother to lose the grin as he reached the gate. "What's funny?" Charlotte demanded as if it might be her.

"Lots of stuff."

"Didn't think you'd got much to laugh at."

"You don't know dick about me."

She glanced at the house as though she might raise a complaint about his language, then she took hold of his hand. The unexpected gesture seemed so trusting he felt bound to respond. Keeping hold of her small plump sticky hand however much it squirmed became rather a task, but he felt more like the person Jack had shown him he could be. At least he didn't need to talk as she tugged him in the direction of the recreation ground, and he was trying to remember all his ideas for the story so as to write them down later when two women with small dogs panting in their arms turned to observe him across the road. He saw them recognise him and begin to murmur about him above the yapping of the flat-faced dogs. "What do you want to do in the park?" he said so loudly the dogs snarled at him.

"We can play if you aren't rough."

"You can choose."

By the look of the women, that sounded sinister. Maybe that was how people who wrote his kind of story ought to sound. The yapping followed him, and he grinned at the notion that the women were making the noise like a pair of Pekingese werewolves. He would have to remember to carry a notebook so that his ideas didn't escape.

There wasn't much to the park. Some girls were dangling their feet in the river that he would have called a stream, and some boys were playing football using their wadded shirts for goalposts. Down in Willesden, beneath a sky that was nothing but blue, the bells of at least two churches were toppling over one another. Ian had more than finished noticing all this when Charlotte touched his arm and immediately flinched away from him. "What's up with you?" he said, amused so far.

"You're it."

That was how he began to feel, especially once he tired of letting her dodge him when he could have caught her every time. No sooner had he made to tag her than she released a squeal that carried across the park to the women who had let their Pekingese loose on the grass. Had they followed him to keep an eye on him? He hoped they noted that Charlotte also squealed whenever he dodged her, though before he'd had much of a chance she slumped into a sulk. "Not fair. You've got longer legs."

"Can't do much about that unless I chop them off."

The dogs yapped and the women stared as if they'd heard the worst of his suggestion. "Let's sit now," Charlotte pleaded.

"Thought I had to take you for a walk."

"We've had one," she said, then grew a scowl so fierce it pulled her whole face out of shape. "What do you mean had? Who said I need one?"

"It wouldn't have been my mother, would it? She's got no reason to care about you."

He hadn't meant that as an insult, but Charlotte looked vengeful. "Do you know why Roger wanted us to go out really?" she said.

"Looks like you're going to tell."

"You can't stop me. He's talking to your mummy and the horror man about you."

"Dream about it when you dream about my house."

"He is. I heard him say to mummy he was going to."

"Then he's had a big surprise."

Her smugness wobbled. "What kind of surprise?"

The dogs yapped at her shrillness, and Ian said "Let's go. I've had the park."

Charlotte plumped her bottom on the grass at once. "Not going, not till you say what's happening to Roger."

"Then you won't know till you get back to my house," Ian said, pacing away from her. "He said we had to be an hour."

He'd retreated perhaps a hundred yards before she jumped up and bolted after him, crying "I'll come. Tell me. You have to."

Ian said nothing until she was alongside, running intermittently to keep up with him. "What do you think's happening at my house right now?"

"Nothing. You're making it up like the horror man does."

"Keep telling yourself that till we get back, or maybe you want to go on your own and see."

"You said you'd tell," Charlotte wailed, dragging at his arm.

He hadn't, but he was bored with the game. "Do you know where Jack is?"

"Yes." More shrilly: "No." More desperately: "Where?"

"I don't know either. Gone."

She hung onto his arm while smugness settled on her face again. "Good," she said.

"Who says?"

"Roger and my mummy, and I'll bet yours does too. Did she tell him to go away? Roger and my mummy say he's a bad influence."

"Yeah, like they'd know."

"See, he even made you talk like him. My mummy says he's as bad as the man who put the little girl under the floor."

"That's what she says when she never met him, right? More of her crap." Nevertheless Ian was experiencing more than anger— something akin to a secret delight waiting to be discovered. "What's she think they've got in common, Jack and old Hector?"

"She says the horror man's as bad if not worse because he's"— Charlotte screwed up her face until she managed to produce the phrase—"exploiting the situation."

"Gee, I thought he just wanted to write a book because that's his job."

"He must be as nasty as his books, my mummy says, and that would be the nastiest."

Anger and imminent delight weren't just mixed up in Ian's

mind; they seemed to be pressing it smaller, more intense. "It's a good job he isn't here or you'd be scared I'd do stuff you think he'd make me do."

"What?"

"You tell me."

They were at the pinned-back gates onto the North Circular Road. An open lorry piled with bundles of rubbish roared by, trailing scraps of litter and fumes that made Charlotte cough rather than answer. The women with the dogs were watching him across the park. Maybe deep down Charlotte felt like they did about him, and now he saw that the back of her dress was damp where she'd sat on the grass. The stain looked as though it was betraying a fear of him she was doing her best not to acknowledge. "Come on then," he said.

"Where?"

"Wait and see," Ian told her, and immediately knew. Before the plan left no room for any other notions in his mind, he tried to retrieve the ideas he'd neglected to write down. All that was left was the image of Carla under the floor, unable to cry out or move. If his father hadn't burdened him with Charlotte he might have been writing the story at that very moment: he would have been able to hold onto it except for her. The idea seemed to feed his delight that was growing darkly brighter for being hidden. He took Charlotte's hand, which he was pleased to find didn't resist his grasp, and led her out of the park. "We've plenty of time before they start wanting you back," he said.

THIRTY

At least Roger had the grace to look uncomfortable, Leslie saw. He must be assuming or at any rate suspecting that he'd been supplanted by Jack. She wasn't going to be the first to speak. She rubbed the last pane so hard her fingertips tingled and her forearm throbbed, then she turned to leave the dining room. He stepped out of the doorway at once, not just to ensure that she needn't come too close to him but to pick up her bucket. "Where to?" he said.

His broad square face was almost neutral. Less than an inch of the right side of his mouth was hinting at a grin, perhaps a wry acknowledgement of his never having helped like this while they'd been married. "Kitchen, thank you," she told him and strode down the hall, refusing to let the sound of his footsteps behind her waken any memories of him or Jack. She faced the window and drowned his reflection in white froth, then rubbed the glass clean as if that might erase his image. When it only grew clearer she stooped to move the bucket. "Sorry," he said.

"For what?"

"I should have put the paper under."

Perhaps he hadn't brought the *Advertiser* through because he resented carrying its picture of Jack. "It doesn't matter," Leslie said. The wet ring would fade into the concrete, she thought, because she'd yet to have the floor tiled. She had been leaving it bare as a reminder of what the floor had concealed, but how did that help anyone? Sometimes you had to stop remembering so as to get on with your life. She straightened up, feeling as though she'd dropped a burden she hadn't realised she was bearing, and Roger said "Anything else I can do for you?"

She'd delayed talking long enough. She draped the leather over the side of the bucket and sat at the end of a kitchen bench, and indicated that he should sit at the far end of its twin. "We've got rid of the children, so what's it about, Roger?"

He interlocked his fingers and rested his chin between two of them, propping it with his elbows on the table to render his gaze even steadier. "I should think you'd know."

"Let's see if I do."

"It's not like you to be defensive."

"It still isn't, believe me, so don't you be. What's the problem?"

"What else do you think it could be except Ian?"

"Maybe I don't automatically think of him as a problem."

"Maybe you should a bit more than you do, and then he mightn't be in the situation he's in now."

"Playing the big brother, you mean. Trying to come up with ways to keep her quiet, I shouldn't wonder."

"I'd say having to look after someone younger ought to do him good, especially when she cares as much about him as Charlotte does. But no, that wasn't what I meant and you know it. I meant being chucked out of school."

"Why do I get the feeling I'm expected to take all the blame?"

"You aren't, not all of it. I think it's at least as much—"

"Yours for making him feel less wanted than the family you shacked up with?"

"I've done my best to see he doesn't feel that way. I suppose you could have too."

"Believe it or not, I tried to help him understand what you did. For his sake, not yours."

"Thanks. Sorry if I'm not allowed to say that. I won't deny I must be responsible to some extent, but as well as us—"

"There's the Duke boy."

"Hang on, Les. That's going too far, blaming the victim."

"One of the victims. I'm saying this to you, I wouldn't say it to Ian however true I think it is, but don't you think he must have felt like one when something he'd taken care with and was proud of was destroyed before anybody he wanted to read it could read it?"

"I wonder if you're including me in that privileged group."

"I'm not including you or leaving you out. That would have been up to Ian, and I should imagine he'd have liked you to read it if you weren't put off by the idea behind it."

"That's quite a big if by the sound of what you said the story was about, but I don't take that to be the point. Whatever Ian may have written isn't worth a boy's sight."

"I told you on the phone the Duke boy hasn't lost his. We've been through all this, and I can't see why you've come here if you're just going to repeat—"

"There's more that needs saying. No piece of writing, and you can include all your music in that, is worth having if it harms even one person, and that needn't mean physically, it could be psychologically."

"That's an argument I don't think we have to get into. Ian didn't want anyone to be upset. It's not as if he set out to show the Duke boy what he'd written."

"Maybe not, but he'd been encouraged not to care."

At that moment the Tschaikovsky quartet in the front room ended with a flourish, and there was silence except for a whisper like the faintest breath from close to the kitchen floor. Leslie glanced down to identify the source of the noise—bubbles on the surface of the liquid in the bucket giving up their air one by one—and then she met Roger's eyes as if she hadn't looked away. "Who are you accusing?"

"Don't tell me you're going to defend him as well, your friend who seems to have made himself scarce. Did he see me coming?"

"What difference do you think that should have made to him?"

"Doesn't anything? Not even the effect he might have had on Ian?"

"You'd have to ask him that."

"You don't know him so well, then."

"About as well as I found out I knew you."

"Not as well as you'd like."

Roger had to hesitate before he said that, and Leslie almost laughed, though it wouldn't have involved much humour. "Maybe I should have learned by now. One mistake ought to have been enough."

"That's a bit harsh, would you say? You don't think everything we had was a mistake. You aren't suggesting Ian was any kind of one."

"No, not Ian."

"And if we made any mistakes with him we want to be careful not to make any more, don't we?"

"I'd reached that conclusion all by myself."

"Well, good. I just wanted to be sure. You won't hold it against me that I care as much about our son as you do, will you?" When Leslie shook her head and closed her eyes until she'd done so, Roger said "So is Mr. Lamb likely to put in an appearance before the children do?"

"What if he should?"

"You said before I ought to have a word with him."

"You and your tricks, Roger. You could give him lessons on how to play with words. No, he won't be here before the children are, so you've sent them out for nothing."

"I'd hardly call encouraging their relationship nothing, would you?" To break her silence he said "When are you expecting Mr. Lamb?"

"I'm not."

"Look, I'm not going to touch him. I hope at least you know I'm not that sort, so there's no need for you to protect him."

"I don't care what you do, or him either, but if you ever talk to him again it won't be here."

"What's wrong with here?"

"Nothing at all. It's my home and Ian's and nobody else's."

"You mean your Mr. Lamb—"

"Isn't mine and doesn't live here any more."

"I follow." Deciding that it was inadvisable to look sympathetic, Roger restrained himself to pointing all his interwoven fingers at her. "Do you mind if I ask where he's gone?"

"It doesn't matter if I mind, because I've no idea."

"Well, that's—" Whatever Roger might have said was overtaken by a thought. "Presumably Ian hasn't either."

"No, and he isn't thanking me for not getting an address." She was about to conclude she'd told Roger enough when she realised he was likely to learn the rest from Ian, or at least not so unlikely that she could be sure she wouldn't be accused of keeping it from him. "He might need a name as well," she said.

"A name for what? Whose name?"

"Whoever Jack Lamb's calling himself now."

"Why would he use a false name?"

For as long as it took her to answer she was tempted to enjoy giving someone else the shock. "Because his real name is John Woollie."

"You're saying he sounds—you're saying people would think he must be—"

"I'm saying he's Hector Woollie's son."

"Good God. Christ." Roger looked ready to invoke the third person as well, but instead demanded "When did you know?"

"Not long at all before I asked him to go away."

"I should hope not. I always knew there was something about him I didn't like. How did you find out?"

"His mother came looking for him."

"That's one solitary thing we can thank the Woollies for, then. What did the swine want? Him, not his mother, though personally I'd wonder about her too."

"Calm down, Roger. It's over. He's gone. Maybe he wanted to come to terms with whose son he was. You can't blame him for not being anxious to advertise it. Look how people have tried to make me and Ian feel just for living here."

"Don't compare either of you with somebody like that. No wonder he writes the kind of, Ian's word will do for once, the kind of crap he writes. I'll tell you what he wanted—to make his fortune out of what his father did, and he didn't care how much he used you and Ian to do it. Ten to one when his book comes out he'll say who he is to jack up the sales."

"We can't know that, Roger."

"My God, as if writing about here wasn't bad enough. That was what I was going to confront him over." Roger drew back to focus on her or to put some extra distance between them. "You seem rather eager to defend him."

"I simply don't see the point of portraying him as worse than he is."

"And how bad are you saying he is?"

"He's the son, not the father."

"Which just means you have to wonder how much he might have had to do with what his father did."

"I've no reason to suppose he had anything to do with it, and

I should imagine you'd hope people survived their childhoods."

"If you still think so much of him, why did you get rid of him?"

This no longer had enough to do with concern for Ian, Leslie thought, and she wasn't letting Roger think he was entitled to worry about her. "I don't want to talk about him any more."

"All I hope is he didn't get too close to you or Ian."

"You can ask Ian that yourself if you want to upset him," she said, and pushed the bench away from the table, making the concrete screech. "I'm going to have the bath I was meaning to have and then I won't feel so grubby. You might ask Ian to come up and tell me he's home when he brings Charlotte back."

THIRTY-ONE

The hotel where Jack had previously stayed was full. He had to phone three others before he found one with room for him. A Pimlico location sounded promising, especially once he learned it was close to Buckingham Palace Road, which made the room rate seem all the more reasonable. The reddish four-storey facade looked impressive enough, even if the stained pavement beneath the awning lacked both a doorman and a porter. The Iranian receptionist was so effusively welcoming that he almost made up for the sign requiring payment in advance. Not too long after Jack had paid for a night to be going on with, a porter in some of a uniform revealed his presence by exhaling a last puff on a cigarette and loaded Jack's bags into the solitary lift, leaving barely enough space for himself and Jack. The scratched grey box took its time about creaking to the top floor, where the porter struggled with the luggage down a narrow corridor not quite dim enough to hide how several patches of the furry chocolate wallpaper were worn down nearly to the plaster. He unlocked a door whose pair of digits leaned away from each other and, having manhandled the luggage into the room, loitered as though waiting for Jack to share the joke of it. "Everything all right?" he eventually said.

Very little if anything was, but abruptly Jack felt he deserved no better. He gave the man a pound, which failed to convince him Jack was satisfied, perhaps because he thought Jack was riding the lift down with him in order to complain. "Everything fine?" the receptionist not so much asked as declared, and Jack felt compelled to assure him it was.

Ten minutes' driving around the crowded side streets brought him to a dauntingly expensive car park, from which he walked through Westminster and Belgravia, seeing nothing he wanted to see, feeling far too much. When he found himself in Pimlico he bought more of an Indian meal than his stomach welcomed, and once he'd finished reassuring the staff of the otherwise empty restaurant that the food couldn't have been better he retreated to the hotel.

Having confirmed that the armchair squeezed between the wardrobe and the bed was quite as lumpily uncomfortable as it looked, he lay on the bed that was barely wider than himself to watch the dwarfish television. The swarming pointillist pictures gave him no reports of missing children; nor, when he managed to reinsert its insecure knob, did the boxy radio on the wall. His father had to realise that abducting any children risked betraying he was alive. That was clearly the last thing he wanted, Jack told himself, and tried to sleep.

He'd had to force the token window open, since the air-conditioning only raised the temperature and emitted a relentless rattle while it did. Now he had the uproar of a riotous Saturday night for company, and the sounds of both a coach station and a railway terminus to go with them. The continuing activities of his Indian dinner ensured he never dozed for long. The night was far from over when he started wishing he'd phoned Leslie before it was too late to call.

He ought to tell her everything. Suppose his father tried to contact Jack at her house or even went to find him? He had to tell her that his father was alive and that he himself had been an accomplice, however inadvertent. Once he'd told her he would be able to tell anyone, which meant the police, but he should tell her first so that she would be forewarned in case the media saw the truth about him as the basis of yet another accusation to fling at her. He mustn't care what she and Ian would think of the truth about him—he had to protect them if he could.

The streets outside the window had settled into an uneasy slumber broken by the occasional shout or scream and the whoops of police cars giving chase. He dozed, only to be wakened by a succession of glimpses, increasingly bright and detailed, of the unnecessarily elaborate pattern of the wallpaper that was almost touching the end of his nose. Then he was telling someone who'd knocked on the door to go away, which despite how it felt must have been hours later than his previous awakening, because the knocker shouted in approximate English that unless he planned to stay another night he would have to vacate the room. When he succeeded in rolling his almost immovably ponderous body over in far less space than it wanted to use, he had to strive to fumble his watch off the shelf that by no means compensated for the absence of a bedside table. It was twenty-five to twelve, and checkout time was noon.

He dragged himself to the edge of the bed to grab the phone from a corner of the dressing table. The outer curve of the flimsy receiver that had started its life white was cracked, and the digits of the keypad were discolored with portions of fingerprints. The 9 was the grubbiest, but he had to tap it to obtain an outside line. As he dialed he had an unpleasant sense that traces of someone else's prints were adhering to his fingertips. He'd hardly roused Leslie's phone when the ringing was snatched away, and there was silence at his ear.

Someone was waiting for him to speak. For a moment that proved he wasn't as awake as he presumed, he wondered if it could somehow be his father. "Who's there?" that made him exclaim. "Hello?"

The silence seemed to intensify before it produced a voice. "Do I know you?"

It was more an accusation than a question, and threw Jack so badly that he had to speak while he tried to think. "That's Roger, isn't it?"

"Nobody else but. And you'll have to be—what am I supposed to call you?"

"Jack."

"Of course, Jack. We've been introduced. Pity we didn't have time for more of a chat. How's it looking for you now, Jack?"

"How's what looking?"

"Why, the thing that means most to you, I should think. The book you said you were going to write here."

"Oh, that. I—"

"You shouldn't make light of what you do, Jack. It isn't just how you earn your living and your reputation, is it? Haven't we got to assume it's what you are?"

"I guess. Not too much of a living in it right now. Anyway, listen, could—"

"Not doing too well at what you chose to be? This new book of yours is bound to change that, isn't it?"

"I don't know. It could if I write it. Anyway, could you let me—"

"You aren't having second thoughts, surely, Jack. Wasn't it your reason for coming here?"

"Where?"

"To this country. To a foreign land. Didn't you hear about all the things Hector Woollie had been found out for and decide what they needed was an American to write the story?"

"I see how it looks, but it wasn't as simple as that. Now could—"

"I appreciate that, Jack, of course I do. I know it's hard for an innocent like me to understand how a writer works. You won't think less of me for trying, will you?"

"Sure, go ahead, only maybe we could leave this for another time. I wanted—"

"You won't think it odd of me to be concerned. Once upon a time this was my family."

"Are they there?"

"Forgive me. We've been having such a fascinating conversation I forgot you wouldn't have rung to speak to me. I expect you were quite taken aback to find me picking you up."

"You bet. I thought you'd moved out."

"That makes two of us, doesn't it, Jack?"

"I'm gone. I just want—"

This time it wasn't Roger who interrupted, it was a repetition of the knocking at the door. "How long are you now, please?" the chambermaid called.

"I'll be out by twelve," Jack shouted away from the mouthpiece, and was making to speak into it when Roger said "Why did you leave, Jack? Did you find something not to your taste?"

"Ask Leslie why," Jack was desperate enough to say. "Look, I haven't much time, and I need to speak to her. Is she there?"

"I'll take a message."

"No, I have to speak to her personally. It's something I ought to have told her while I had the chance."

"Tell me and I'll let you know if you should."

"I don't believe she'd want you to ask that or me to tell you."

"Then let me guess."

"I can't stop you doing that, but while you are can you bring—"

"You're going to say you're nothing like your father."

For several seconds Jack's pulse was as loud in his ears as the chambermaid's knock had been. "She told you," he said, not quite inaudibly enough.

"Better goddamn well believe it, as you might say if you were pretending to be American. Les and I are still closer than you hoped."

"I don't care about that right now. It isn't about me, what I have to say to her. Just tell her I'm on the phone, will you? You have to respect her enough to let her decide if she wants to talk to me."

"I said I'd take a message, Mr. Woollie. That's the best I can do for you, John. She's gone for a walk with Ian. Maybe you should wonder what she's having to explain to him about you."

"I'm sorry. I wish—" Jack wished he'd had a chance to speak to Ian before leaving, but it seemed inadvisable to tell Roger so. "Do you know how long they're likely to be?" he said.

"Hours, the way Ian's been made to feel." Roger sounded resigned as he added "I'll do this much. I'll take your number."

"And give it to Leslie when she comes back?"

"That would seem to be the idea, wouldn't it?"

"I'm out of here in a few minutes. I'll give you two numbers, and I'll be at one or the other this afternoon, say in a couple of hours."

"Sounds as if you're in demand."

Jack let that pass and read out the numbers from his notebook. "I can trust you, right?" he said.

"As much as she can you."

"Then I can."

"If you don't hear from her that means she wants nothing to do with you. Got that?"

"So long as you tell her it's very urgent. It's something she'll want to know, and it's not about me."

"I've no excuse not to tell her then, have I?"

Jack could think of nothing else to say that mightn't undermine the hold he appeared to have established. "Thanks," he said. The receiver was scarcely back on its stand when he was struggling past the chair toward the cupboard the hotel called a bathroom. He had to be swift, not just to check out. He needed to be at one of the numbers by the time Leslie tried to contact him.

THIRTY-TWO

As Leslie raised her face into a shower so fierce it drove away all thoughts, the phone rang downstairs. She was fumbling to turn off the taps when she heard the back door slam and Roger sprint into the hall. She twisted the taps hard and, having practically vaulted out of the bath, padded wetly to unbolt the door. "Who is it?" she shouted through a gap of no more than an inch.

"Wrong number."

Presumably having to pick up a call that wasn't even for her or Ian made him feel more out of place than ever. She bolted the door and treated herself to a shower that came close to overwhelming all her senses. When at last she emerged into the foggy bathroom, she had to extract water from her ears with a corner of the towel before she was able to hear. She rubbed herself pinker and wrapped herself in the towel, and opened the door just far enough to call "Where are you?"

"Where you left me. Can I do anything?"

"Nothing I can think of, thank you," she told him, and dodged into her room.

Once she'd covered up her crucial bits with underwear, she was frustrated to discover that she wasn't sure how else to dress. She was inclined to put on something shabby and shapeless to demonstrate how comfortable she felt in her own house, or how uncompelled to impress Roger she was, but since all her old clothes dated from their marriage, wouldn't they suggest an attempt to revive memories she had no desire to share? She slid back one of the mirrors that were doors, slimming her reflection in the process, then immediately closed the wardrobe, shutting up the sight of the elegant black number she'd bought to wear next time she went out for dinner with Jack. She was going to dress for herself, and if Roger dared so much as hint he wondered whether she'd done so for him . . . She pulled on a baggy T-shirt and tighter denim shorts, and when she caught herself reconsidering the latter she grabbed the towel that was looking woebegone on the double bed and stormed onto the landing to fling it into the laundry bin. She was trying to prepare to pick her way through another dialogue with Roger when she heard the scrape of a key in the front door lock.

Some seconds passed before Ian eased the door open and stepped into the hall, pushing his face forward and turning it from side to side. His expression looked uncertain what to be. Leslie was waiting for Charlotte to make her appearance as part of the game the youngsters were playing when Ian began to inch the door shut. "Don't do that," she said.

His arm jerked, the door slammed, and she saw he had been too preoccupied to notice her. As he raised his face, his eyelids drooped. "What?"

"Don't snarl at me like that, and don't shut poor Charlotte out if she wants to come in."

That was something of an if, she realised, and so she was confused when Ian said "Hasn't she?"

"What's wrong?" Roger said from the kitchen, and from the hall "Where's Charlotte?"

"Isn't she here?"

Leslie had forgotten how much longer family conversations took than any other kind, how much more strewn with repetitions they were. "What would she be doing here the way she feels about it?" Roger said not far short of Ian's face. "Why isn't she with you?"

"She was. She ran off. I thought she'd have come back."

"You were meant to be taking care of her, Ian," Leslie said, and before she'd finished Roger was demanding "Why did she—"

"Maybe she hid in the car. I'll look."

Ian was turning his back with, Leslie sensed, a good deal of relief when his father said "She can't be there, it's locked. You haven't told us why she ran away. Open the door while you're at it, will you."

Ian pulled the door wide. From the third stair up Leslie could see all the way along Jericho Close, which the sunlight emphasised was deserted. Either this or the continuing spectacle of Ian's back put an edge on Roger's voice. "You're supposed to be answering my question."

Ian's shoulders moved as if considering a shrug, but he said "We got bored in the park. I was taking her to see someone, only she made a scene. You know how she goes."

"Talk to our faces, Ian. Nobody out there wants to hear you." Before Ian had progressed much further than starting to obey, his father snapped "Who?"

"Who what?"

"I don't know whose time you think you're wasting or why. Who were you trying to make her see?"

"I didn't think I'd have to make her. I thought she'd want to go."

Leslie wondered if he might be more responsive to a hint of gentleness, and so that was how she said "Who would it have been?"

"Crys Nolan."

"Shaun Nolan's sister?" Roger said in a tone that was determined to be answered. When it failed he tried "What was the idea of getting Charlotte mixed up with your gang?"

"She's the only girl I knew for Charlotte to play with."

"So what was the problem?" Leslie felt the need to learn.

"Her. Charlotte. Her not thinking I could know any girls."

"I can imagine," Roger said. "Thank God at least you didn't involve her with Shaun and the rest of that bunch. I'd have had some explaining to do to Hilene." His voice hadn't softened much, and now it sharpened. "How long is it since you let Charlotte run away?"

"Don't know what you mean by let."

"I'm wondering, believe me," Roger said, and with all the fury he'd been withholding "Never mind playing word games with me, Ian. That's one of the things you can do without having picked up from your friend who was no kind of a friend. How long has it been since you last saw Charlotte?"

"However long it takes to come through the park."

"Were you running? Were you anxious for her?"

Ian's response might as well have been a shrug. "What do you think?"

Leslie was afraid his father might lash out at him for the first time in their lives, but as she moved close in case she had to intervene, Roger only said "Where did you lose sight of her?"

"On the North Circular by Shaun's."

"Which way was she going?"

"Didn't see. She ran into the traffic."

"Well, I hope you're happy with yourself. You're asked to take care of a child for an hour and you're incapable of even doing that. Try looking at me now and then when you're being spoken to. You can't make a situation go away by pretending you're somewhere else."

"Roger."

"All right, I know this isn't bringing Charlotte back any sooner. Tell me what will if you can."

"I was just going to ask you if you thought that call could have been her."

"Which?"

"The one you said was a wrong number."

"That's what it was, a wrong number."

"Who was it?"

"How should I know? It was a wrong number."

"It couldn't have been Charlotte trying to get through?"

"How, when she's got no money on her?"

"Then you wouldn't have heard her and known it was her."

"It wasn't."

"You're sure. You heard someone that wasn't Charlotte."

"Obviously," Roger said with a stare of disbelief that she'd pursued the subject this far.

"So there won't be any point in seeing if the phone can tell us where the call came from."

"If you think there's a reason to do that despite everything I've said I can't stop you, can I? It's your phone in your house."

Leslie rested her fingertips on the phone and knew at once there was a better reason to use it. "We aren't thinking, are we? There's only one place she'll be."

"Where?" Roger said, and she saw Ian swallow the same question.

"On her way to her mother's, of course."

"Didn't I just tell you she hasn't got a penny on her? What are you saying would make her try to go all that way on foot?"

"She might have called Hilene to pick her up, do you think? Called her and reversed the charges. Should you check?"

"If there's any need," Roger said, and strode to the gate and then to the end of Jericho Close. Having stood in the middle of the junction and used one hand as an eyeshade, he set off in the direction of the park. He was out of sight for so long that dismay tugged at Leslie's mouth when he reappeared without Charlotte. He trudged back along Jericho Close, rubbing his forehead with his knuckles and glancing over his shoulder more than once, to halt by his car. "Do you want to drive and see if you can find her?" Leslie suggested.

"And what would the rest of us be doing?"

"Someone could walk and look for her while the other stays here in case she comes back."

Roger pushed himself away from the car and tramped up the path. "Hilene was going to do the garden. That's how she calms herself down," he said, and less dolefully "If she's out that'll mean Charlotte called."

"If you say so."

"You're right, she'll be fetching Charlotte," he said, though Leslie was unaware of having made any such claim. "I remember now, she told her once how to reverse the charges if she ever needed to."

He used three fingers on the keypad to demonstrate his skill or to get the task finished. His head began to tilt to one side as though the receiver were weighing it down, but when enough time had passed he raised both. He was allowing a look of relief to emerge onto his face when his eyes switched toward the receiver. "Oh, hello," he said.

Leslie experienced a wrench of the disappointment he hadn't managed to keep out of his voice. She glanced along the hall at Ian, who was concentrating on his feet or on the kitchen floor. "Sorry if I brought you in," Roger murmured. "Having a productive time? We'll be seeing more flowers soon, will we?" All this said, and Hilene's answer listened to, it was clear he wished he could say something other than "You won't, I don't suppose you'll have heard from Charlotte?"

Leslie saw expressions she remembered from the beginning of the end of their marriage accompany his words and the pauses when his mouth got ready for another try. "I'm afraid she seems to have toddled off on her own . . . A bit of a tiff with Ian . . . No more than, not much more than half an hour . . . The park, and I shouldn't be at all surprised if that's where she is now on a day like this . . . I only thought she might have rung you. She isn't likely to ring here the way she feels . . . I will. Of course I will . . . I will, of course . . . That's what I'll do now, and you could keep an ear out just in case."

He planted the receiver on its stand and sent a look of disfavour along the hall. "I don't know when you'll be coming to visit again, Ian," he said, and to Leslie without bothering to change his tone "I'm going to drive and look for her. You'd better both stay here in case she comes looking for me."

Did he think Charlotte would bolt if she saw Ian by himself? Would she have any reason? Leslie tried to think not, but found she didn't want to speak to Ian. She sat on the front doorstep and leafed through her Sunday paper, which contained too much about children in peril all over the world. Dozens if not hundreds of glances away from it kept showing her how deserted the road was. Far too eventually the Peugeot reappeared, containing only Roger, who gave her an interrogative stare that didn't want to own up to being a plea. She was wondering what she could offer him except her empty hands when the phone shrilled.

He was even faster than she was. By the time she lifted the receiver he was almost in the house. Before she could speak she heard "Is Roger there?"

"He is, Hilene, but I'm afraid—"

"May I have him, please."

"All yours," Leslie said briskly as he stepped over the strewn newspaper.

"She hasn't turned up here, Hilene. I've been—" Though the blood didn't drain from his face, the expression did. "Are you sure? You don't think—No, of course I wouldn't want—All right, please go ahead . . . I appreciate you don't need my permission . . . I'll wait, shall I? . . . I'll wait, then."

His fingers appeared not to be working too well as he fumbled the receiver into place. "I'll stay for a little longer if you don't mind," he said, so unsurely and apologetically that Leslie might have thought he was asking for refuge. "I think she's being premature, but if it puts her mind at rest . . ." He raised his voice for Ian to hear, and Leslie wished it didn't sound so much like an accusation. "Hilene is calling the police."

THIRTY-THREE

"Are you looking for someone?" Melinda said.

Leslie turned from watching a man in an elegant summer suit walk past all the offices of film companies he might have dressed up for and vanish along Wardour Street into Soho, perhaps for another kind of meeting. "I was just remembering," she said.

"Poor Leslie."

"Not so poor. I was only thinking about the day Jack Lamb appeared."

"That's what I said, poor Leslie."

"Well, don't keep saying it. I don't feel anything like you think I'm feeling. It's gone. Deleted. No longer in demand. All I'm remembering is how I had the notion somebody had followed me from the house."

"You told me. So now you think . . ."

"It was him. He already knew about the house. He was pretending he didn't when he saw my notice about the room. That was something else he managed to fool me about for as long as I had him on the premises."

"You wonder how it's possible to be so wrong about somebody you're close to. I don't mean just you, Leslie. Everyone is sometimes."

"Thanks, Mel, but I think I wish you hadn't said that. Maybe I shouldn't have come into work today. It isn't taking my mind off much."

"Leslie, I'm sorry. Come here."

Despite the invitation, Melinda didn't wait for her, instead bustling along the space behind the counter and taking Leslie in her arms. She pressed her cheek against Leslie's and stroked her back just below her shoulders. Leslie felt surrounded by perfume and warmth, and though she was a little uncomfortable with the closeness of both, she returned the hug. She was wondering how long she ought to keep it up when she and Melinda grew aware of being ogled through the window by three wiry youths dressed in singlets and football shorts, who were making sounds and gestures they might have used to encourage a live sex show. "Piss off," the women chorused, and held each other until the youths wandered off, at which point Leslie intensified her hug before letting go. "I feel better for that," she was able to say without lying.

"I'm glad," Melinda said, but held her at arm's length to read her eyes. "Don't you dare start feeling guilty when you've done everything you could."

"Which wasn't much."

"You'd have told the police more if you could."

"More than just about nothing, you mean."

"It wasn't your fault if that was all you knew. I'm sure Ian did his best to help them."

"He told them more of the truth than he'd told me."

Melinda took time to peel the adhesive tape off a carton of compact discs with as little noise as possible, and then she said "What did he say?"

"Apparently after he'd had enough of her, not that he told the police he had but he didn't need to tell me, he was taking her to play with one of his friends' sisters, one of the friends I was hoping he'd grown out of, and Charlotte started prattling on about how bad, let's call him Jack because that's the way I can't stop thinking of him, how bad Jack must be to write his books, so Ian told her who he was."

"You would though, wouldn't you? So . . ."

"According to Ian she refused to believe him at first, and when he made her she panicked and ran off."

"Made her how?"

"Told her. What else could it have been? They were on a street full of people."

"That has to be right, that's right. If it had been anything else someone would have remembered and come forward by now."

"Why can't we notice things when it's important to? Two of the neighbours say they heard Ian and Charlotte arguing in the park, and another one saw him coming back by himself. For once I wish she'd made a bit more noise, drawn more attention to herself. She's not the kind to go unnoticed when she's upset, and if nobody's seen she is by now, what's keeping her quiet?"

"Maybe nothing you have to worry about."

"You mustn't think that, Mel. It doesn't matter whose child she is, she's a child and I care what happens to her."

"You wouldn't be you if you didn't. I just meant she might be feeling guilty about running off when she was meant to stay with Ian, so guilty she's afraid to go home."

"So afraid she'd stay out overnight?"

"It was pretty sultry, wasn't it? A good night for sleeping in the open if she found somewhere. Kids have done stranger things, I believe. Or couldn't she have stayed with a friend?"

"Not without Roger and Hilene hearing."

"And he'd have called you if she'd turned up."

"Even Hilene would."

"At least there's one thing to be thankful for."

Leslie could only hope not to be able to see through this latest reason for optimism. "What's that?"

"You don't need to worry about the Woollie man." Apparently feeling this might be ambiguous, Melinda added "The father."

"No, but we don't know how many others there may be like him."

"None that bad, surely."

"I wish I could think so."

"Then think about her probably making her way home right now if she isn't already there and they haven't got round to phoning you. And remember the police are looking for her. They'll have ways to trace people we wouldn't think of."

"Thanks, Mel. Don't say any more, thanks."

Just then a businessman came in, loosening his tie as a preamble to deploring the existence of Birtwistle and Maxwell Davies and seeking tuneful British composers he hadn't heard of. Leslie played him examples of Finzi and Dyson and was able to sell him discs by both, after which the task of locating distributors for a pageful of obscure Eastern European symphonies listed by a customer helped her get through the rest of the afternoon. "You head off home to Ian," Melinda said as the hands of the clock met on the way to closing time. "I'll lock up."

"See you tomorrow, unless—I can't think why I wouldn't see you tomorrow."

"And you know I'm as close as the end of your phone if you need to talk."

Leslie gave her a smile she hoped was only grateful, not expressive of the doubts their conversation had raised, and struggled through the crowds to Oxford Circus. She had to stand and sway and be bumped into nearly all the way to Stonebridge Park, and when she escaped the heat that was coagulating on the train the spacious suburban evening offered little relief. She kept hearing cries of children in the streets—children at play—but that didn't render the sounds less capable of troubling her; they made her retreat from imagining what kind of cry Charlotte might have, or want, to utter.

As soon as she opened the front door she saw Ian beyond the house. The sight of him behind the table at the end of the garden seemed to transform the hall into an optical instrument with the kitchen window for a lens. The unreality passed as she strode toward him. She was at the back door when he looked up from writing. He screwed up his face and shook his head to tell her there was no news of Charlotte, and Leslie wished his wordless answer had been intended for the other question she had to ask. She felt as if the question were driving her forward, off the unyielding concrete onto the soft springy grass. She was halfway along the lawn when his face began to dull in readiness for the interrogation he must have seen bearing down on him, but she didn't speak until she was seated opposite him. "Is there anything else you haven't told me?" she said.

THIRTY-FOUR

"Hush now, Charlotte," Hector said, and began to sing under his breath.

THIRTY-FIVE

"Mr. Woollie?"

"He wants you, Mr. Woollie."

"Mr. Woollie, I'm Terence, remember."

"And I'm Hughie, remember too."

"Are you here to get some help, Mr. Woollie?"

Each of them paused before speaking, and left quite a few gaps between words too, presumably as a result of the medication they were on. Their intent faces were waiting for Jack's answer, Terence repeating a smile of encouragement that jerked his oval face and pressed lips high, Hughie maintaining a wide-eyed frown that sent its ridges up his broad balding pinkish skull. Jack glanced around the lounge of the Haven Care Home, but there was little hope of an interruption: several of the residents sitting in assorted chairs around the room bright with nursery colors seemed to want him to respond, and his mother was conversing with a small inaccurately dressed old woman in a voice whose increasing quietness was meant to persuade the listener to reduce her volume to an indoor level. "What kind of help?" Jack said.

"With your book, Mr. Woollie," Terence told him. "Aren't you writing a book?"

"I may be. I may have to."

"About Mr. Woollie?"

"I wish I could," Hughie said. "Write a book. I wish I could put things out of my head like that."

"About Mr. Woollie?"

"That's what I figured. Seemed like I might know stuff about him other writers wouldn't know."

"We do too. That's how we'll help."

"I'm Terence, remember."

"And I'm—"

"I got that. You introduced yourselves when I came in."

"No, what he means is, and me too, what we both mean is he's Terence and I'm Hughie that used to help Mr. Woollie. And Vern did, and Chas, and Arthur and the other Arthur, but what we mean is we saw the little finger, didn't we, Terence."

"And then Mr. Woollie took me to the sea because he saw I'd seen. He made out it was a treat for being his best worker, but really and truly he wanted to drown me, only he got drowned himself instead."

"Don't upset Mr. Woollie telling him about Mr. Woollie. Are you upset, Mr. Woollie?"

"I guess so if that's how I look. Just let me say you don't need to call—"

"I've finished about how he got drowned, except how the police asked me about it and when I was telling them about him I said about the finger. Then I had to take them where it was, the house some man gave to a woman and a boy. I don't suppose they liked it so much when they knew he'd given them a little girl under the floor, what do you think, Mr. Woollie?"

"Watch, Terence. Watch out, I mean. Mr. Woollie looks upset again."

"I'm not saying about Mr. Woollie being drowned any more, Mr. Woollie."

"That's okay. No need to watch out for me, I can take the truth. Only if you could stop—"

"Everyone shipshape here? Having a nice chat?"

Jack's mother had succeeded in toning down the rowdy oldster and was standing behind him. The way he felt, he thought at first her concern was all for him. "Sure," he said, mostly to get rid of the questions.

"It's good to chat," said Terence.

"Best to laugh," Hughie said.

"And if you can't laugh—"

Either Terence forgot the rest or Jack's panic at the echo of his father's catchphrase communicated itself to him. He looked confused until Jack's mother said "It's kind of John to come and see us, isn't it?"

"Has he come all the way from America?"

"He's living here now, Terence."

"Here like us?"

"Not here in the Haven. He's staying at my flat till he finds somewhere else if that's what he insists on doing, though he knows he's welcome to stay with me as long as he wants."

"Did you go away to get away from Mr. Woollie, Mr. Woollie?" Hughie said.

"You went to make something of yourself, didn't you, John?"

Jack sensed his mother craved more reassurance than she was admitting. "That's me," he said.

"I'll leave you three to get on, then, while I see that everybody is fit. Just shout me or one of my carers, John, if there's anything you need."

There was plenty, but Jack was growing less and less convinced that he would find it at the Haven. His mother moved away to talk to a crouched man whose face was turning purple over the task of inverting every second page of a large newspaper, and as Jack struggled to dredge more conversation out of himself, Terence said "Did Mr. Woollie ever try to bury you when you were little, Mr. Woollie?"

"Christ, no. Don't you think Mrs., my mother would have gone to the police? And listen, can you call me Jack."

"Mrs. Woollie says you're John."

"Yes, well, I was when I was living with her and my father. Now it's Jack."

"You're living with her again," Hughie objected, "so you ought to be John."

"My father called me that. It was the name of his brother that died when he was little, only my father had a nickname for him. I'd have thought she'd want me to be Jack."

"Maybe she wants you to be you again," Terence said.

"That me is gone. Gone like my father."

"Don't you want to keep any of him, Mr. . . . ?"

The way Hughie's question trailed off, he might have been asking all over again what Jack's real name was. "Keep what?" Jack said, he hoped not too harshly. "Keep it how?"

"In you."

"That's where it's got to be," Terence assured him.

Jack shoved himself out of the armchair so violently that both men flinched away from him, a reaction that dismayed him. "Good talking to you," he made himself say.

"We can tell you more about him if you like," Hughie said.

"Maybe another time."

"He gave us work when nobody else would."

"And he gave us treats except the time he wanted to drown me."

It was the way Terence said that, as if it weren't worthy of more than a casual remark, that troubled Jack most of all. He crossed the large room, gaining himself a loose askew smile from one woman and an obscure body movement from another, then stooped to his mother, who was on one knee beside the rearranger of the newspaper, retrieving pages he'd decided were best on the linoleum. "Can I use the phone in the office?" Jack said.

"Anyone special?"

"An agent who was interested in my stuff."

In fact Jack had no intention of contacting the agent, who had sounded likely to forget his enthusiasm as soon as he'd sobered up. Jack withdrew into the hall, which had been more spacious before his father had built an enclosed staircase for the safety of the residents and an office just inside the entrance. His father, his father . . . Jack hardly knew why he'd come to the Haven today—perhaps to judge how the men employed by his father had survived the experience, perhaps to discover what they thought of Jack—but it was one more failure to take action. He closed himself in the boxy office twice the size of the cloakroom it had once been and sat behind the desk.

He had to warn Leslie about his father, no matter whether it was an excuse to delay informing the police or a step in that direction. He hoisted a directory off the pile by the desk and leafed through the pages, which smelled hot with the sunlight through the netted window, until he found the number of Classical Discount. It was busy. It was engaged.

It was again after he'd given it most of a minute not to be, and after more than another minute's wait too. He cut off the rapid high-pitched nervous tone and dialed Leslie's home number. Ian ought to make certain she called back. This time the phone did ring: it rang and rang until a woman's officious voice told him to try later and immediately repeated itself. Jack quelled the repetition and was waiting to redial when his mother stepped into the office to hang a clipboard on a hook. "In business?" she said.

Jack let the receiver slump into place. "No. No luck."

"You'll have some soon, I can feel it. I expect these agents are out most of the time seeing editors and publishers and whatever else they do."

"I guess some are."

"Try not to worry. Worry never made anything come." She pushed a scattering of official forms together on the desk and perched in the space she'd cleared. "Do what you can and be patient and the best that can happen will happen," she said.

"So I remember you saying when I was a kid. Mom, I mean mother . . ."

"I used to be mummy. Some of the people I care for think I still am."

"I figured that. Listen, I was going to say . . ."

"Say it then, John. Mother's listening."

He'd tried to leave himself no choice, but he still had to force it. "That wasn't an agent I was trying to call just now."

"Never mind, John. I know you'll have one soon if you need one." Even more forgivingly, she said "I knew it wasn't when you told me. I haven't stopped knowing you just because you went away. Parents don't, you see."

That ought to be his cue, but instead it silenced him as she said "You were always making up stories, pretty well as soon as you could talk. I'd have been surprised if you'd stopped."

"What kind of stories?"

"All kinds about who you were or who you were going to be. I remember you went to see a Roy Rogers once and you were a cowboy for weeks. Lawman John, you were, and me and you know who were supposed to own a ranch. What was the name if it? Hush while I think. The Crazy, the Crazy—I've got it, the Crazy Bull."

Jack had opened his mouth more than once during all this. The further the conversation strayed from the subject he was determined to leave himself no chance to avoid, the harder it would be to broach. "Could have been. Must have been if you say so," he gabbled. "Anyway, about the call I tried to make . . ."

"Don't tell me if you didn't want me to know."

"I do. I need you to." He took a breath that sounded too loud between the close walls, and said "It was about my father."

"What about him, John?"

"He isn't dead."

The breath Jack held while he awaited her reaction emphasised how dry his mouth had grown. He wasn't prepared to have her frown reprovingly and say "That's cruel."

"Cruel. You mean . . ."

"Maybe I don't know you as well as I wanted to think."

"I'm still not clear . . ."

"That's not the kind of story I was saying you used to tell. You made up things I liked to hear. Save it for your book if you really have to, though I hope you won't, but I'd have expected you to have enough tact not to try it out on your own mother."

"I'm sorry if you're upset. I mean, of course you'd have to be, but—"

"I'm not upset, I'm disappointed. I'd convinced myself I'd brought you up better than that."

"To tell the truth."

"You always did except when you were telling stories we knew were stories."

"I still am."

"All right if that's how you meant it, but can we be done with it? You were right, it does upset me. It isn't necessary, and it brings back too much I'm having to live with."

"Okay, I shouldn't have bothered you with it. I didn't think enough."

"So long as you're doing that now, John. Would you say I might be able to look forward to not hearing any more about it ever again?"

"I don't know if I can promise that."

"And who do you think is going to believe you if your own mother doesn't?" She swung herself heavily off the desk and stood in front of it, fists on hips, elbows straining to point at him. "Go on then, convince me. Where is he supposed to be?"

"I don't know. I—"

"How's he managing to hide when his face was in half the papers?"

"I didn't know it had been. I guess—"

"How come, that's what you Americans say, isn't it, how come nobody's recognised him? What's he made himself look like?"

"I haven't seen him."

"Oh, you haven't. You're going to though, are you? Is he coming to show you his face so you can describe him?"

"I can't say. That would be—"

"I won't say what I think it would be, I'm not that rude. Is he invisible? Ghosts are meant to be, aren't they?"

"He's no ghost. He—"

"I'm glad you've admitted that at least. That's the kind of story you've been selling though, isn't it? It's how you made your name."

"Not as much of one as maybe you believe. But this isn't—"

"So you're trying to make yourself more of one with a new kind of story. John, I don't blame you for that. Just think a bit more about how it will affect me if you carry on with that part of it. I'll be able to stand the rest of it because it'll be true, but not you saying he's alive."

"Suppose he is, mother. Suppose for someone else's sake."

Her eyes hardened, and Jack saw she'd already had to admit too much about his father. "All right," she said, "you tell me how he managed not to be drowned."

"I don't know that yet."

"You haven't made it up yet, you mean."

"They haven't found the body, have they?"

She looked ready to grab Jack and shake him. "So that's where you got your idea, is it? I hope they do before your book comes out if you dare to say he's alive in it. Serve you right if your book's a flop."

He was in the path of all the grief and rage that made her say so. He felt like the child he'd been. "It isn't for the book," he said.

Either his words enraged her further or she hadn't time to listen to them. "You'd better have more to show or everyone will see through you. And I'll tell you what, if they find out you were calling from here they'll think I've had to take you in. Yes, Karen."

The greeting was addressed more gently to an overalled young woman who had ventured to knock on the open door. "Big Arthur doesn't want to take his medicine," Karen said.

"You'll excuse me, John, won't you? I've got to attend to somebody less fortunate than you." Her tone denied that anyone had heard her lose her temper. "Will you have finished in here?" she said, but it wasn't a question.

Jack followed her out of the office. When she glanced at him, her expression poised to forgive, he responded "I guess I can use a stroll round the block."

"That never does any harm." Her expression hadn't declared more of itself when she said "Don't do anything that would make me not want to have you stay with me."

He had to, despite any consequences of that kind. It was some help that the nearest public phone was out of sight of the Haven. Nevertheless, when the Classical Discount number proved to be engaged and Leslie's home number only rang, he had to own up to some relief. The task of convincing anyone his father was alive seemed not just well-nigh impossible until he had some evidence but also less urgent when he recalled how unmenacing his father had rendered himself. The man no longer had his business to conceal him or his activities, and it was clear that he knew he wouldn't be safe unless he continued to hide. If he tried to return to his old ways he would only betray his existence. He couldn't be that mad.

THIRTY-SIX

"Do you want your mouth undone, Charlotte? Will you keep quiet if it is?"

Eyes.

"See yourself in the mirror there. You look like a doll, don't you? A big doll they forgot to put the mouth on. See the funny doll that looks just like you."

Big eyes.

"All right, maybe you're not funny. Even if you are you can't laugh. That's no good, is it? You should always be able to laugh. Do you know what makes the world go round? Of course you do. It's laughter."

Eyes blinking.

"Careful now. You're not scared, are you? You don't want to be scared. You know you needn't be scared of me. There's no call for it. It only makes trouble."

Eyes and lids trying to keep still.

"That's the style. No, it's not. I don't like that. Maybe it's not having any mouth that's making you look scared. See? Am I right?"

Eyes blinking at the mirror.

"You want to say yes, don't you? You want to talk. If I let you undo your mouth you mustn't speak any louder than I'm speaking. Can you promise that? If you're sure you can, just nod."

Head moving stiffly up and down twice, eyes watching Hector.

"Go on then, you undo it. It might hurt if I pull it. You'll know how hard to pull."

Hands trembling toward mouth, flinching away.

"It won't hurt much. You won't have to scream. You're not a baby. You don't scream at your age unless you're like Biff. You'd better pinch your lips together if you think you're going to, mm mm, like that. You can do it better than me, you've got teeth. Never mind, when you haven't got any you can make funny faces like this. I expect you'd laugh at it if you could. I'll show you again if you undo your mouth."

Hands lifting, eyes wanting to retreat from them.

"Go on. Don't think about it, do it. Give a big pull and don't stop till it's off. Right this minute or I'll have to do it for you."

Hands flying to corners of mouth. Eyes widening. Fingers and thumbs closing, tugging, tearing mouth free. Exposed lips quivering, raw as new flesh.

"There, it's over. You'll be fine. Just quieten yourself. Don't even think about making a row or I'll have to do you up again. You wouldn't like that, would you?"

Head shaking, eyes wobbling.

"Let's see a bit of a smile, then, now you've got a mouth. Oh, more than that, come on. A corpse could do better than that. Let the ends go up and the rest will have to follow. Is it stiff from being done up? Give it a try, then it won't be so stiff. Lift the ends like this, look. Up, up, up."

Corners of mouth twitching, trying to twitch higher.

"That's the way. Bit more. Bit more. Bit more even than that. There's nothing in your eyes, is there? I say, you haven't got anything in your eyes. Give them a dab if you want. If they carry on looking like that you'll have me thinking you're going to make a row, and you wouldn't want that, would you?"

Head shaking, hands jerking up to eyes as though to hold them still.

"That's better. You can talk, you know, I told you. Just make sure it's no louder than this, in fact even a bit quieter to be safe. Have a try so I can hear you can. You aren't scared, are you? I say you aren't scared."

Head shaking as though moved back and forth by the hands on the cheeks.

"Speak up for yourself, then. Smile when you do it, that'll

make it easier. Is there anything you want that'll let you give me a real smile instead of that shaky item? Look in the mirror and see if it doesn't make you laugh. Don't start that with your eyes again. What are you going to say that'll make you smile? What do you want? Anything within reason. Just don't go mad."

"I w . . . I w . . ."

"Take your time. Don't force it if that's going to make it come out too loud. A little bit quieter than that, all right? And remember it's got to be something that'll make you smile. Get the smile going first and that'll help you say it. Off you go. You want . . ."

"I want to go home."

"You don't really. Give it a bit of a think. You can't want to go back to those people. You sounded more scared when they were about than you're sounding now. You said you were going to have nightmares. You wouldn't want to have them and be screaming half the night like Biff."

"I won't. I promise."

"Aren't you listening? I didn't say you'd do it here. I'll be making sure of that. I said you would if you went back to those people."

"I want to go home to my mummy."

"She can't be much of one or you wouldn't be here, would you? Better give those eyes another dab. We don't want them spoiling that smile. You're not having such a bad time with me, are you? Just don't think about going home and then you won't mind being here."

"I want to. I want to see her."

"Then you shouldn't have made me care about you, should you? You were glad enough to come to me when you didn't know what to do with yourself because you were scared to go near that house. You oughtn't to have been so anxious to hide in here with me if you didn't want to stay."

"I want to go now. I want mummy."

"That's dealt with. Finished. We're not talking about it any more. You sound as if you've used all your voice up saying that so much. What do you want instead? I know, you want a laugh. Here's a face to make you laugh."

Hector sucked in his lips, then turned them inside out as far as they would go and let his tongue steal between them. It ought to amuse her—it was painful enough to produce—but when he looked in the mirror to examine his face before presenting it to the little girl, he saw her pushing herself away up the bed, leaving ripples in the quilt, and when he turned to her she shrank against the padded headboard. He tried lolling his head from side to side and bulging his eyes while his tongue appeared and disappeared between his exposed gums, but that didn't earn him a smile either, never mind a laugh. "You've got to have no teeth to make that face," he whispered, "I pulled all my teeth out myself for it," but that didn't improve her response; nor did his crouching at the foot of the bed and ducking out of sight before poking his head over the edge of the mattress and doing his best to grimace even more comically as a preamble to saying "Peep." When two more performances of this routine went down as badly, he desisted. "You're no fun," he muttered. "All right, you tell me what'll make you laugh."

It seemed to Hector that he couldn't be more reasonable, and the girl could surely do better in the way of an answer than moving her lips from side to side, as though whatever expression they were struggling to form kept slipping off. He stared around the room in growing desperation. What was there to amuse her? He could borrow a comb from the dressing table and stick out his upper lip to prop it up—if the comb fell off while he was talking in a Hitler voice, that might be even funnier—but she might be too young to know who Hitler was and besides, a Hitler voice would have to be louder than he ought to risk. He didn't think a Hitler whisper would be funny enough, though he wasn't sure that he needed to whisper, having heard the phone next door stay lengthily unanswered a few minutes ago. He turned to the chest of drawers and exposed the contents: a few pairs of socks and tights left at home by their owners, two drawerfuls of fat squashed sweaters awaiting winter, a scattering of male and female underwear. He supposed he could wear some knickers on his head and be Old Nick—he could pant at her, and she might laugh if she understood the joke—and then he knew what she ought to enjoy as much as he'd enjoyed it at her age. "Have you been to any shows?" he whispered eagerly. "Does your dad take you to the theatre?"

He would have grown frustrated with the wordless shaking of her head if he hadn't realised the sound she'd released was a word. "Mum."

"Which show did she take you to?"

"A pantomime."

"I never know why they call them that, do you? Pantomime means when you act without any voice. It's not supposed to mean a fairy tale show with all that song and dance and laughs and the rest of it put in. So which one did you get taken to?"

"Riding Hood."

"The little red one, eh?" There must be a joke for Hector to make about that, and he was annoyed not to be able to think of it. "Her and her old wolf," he said. "Did you like him?"

If she hadn't she must think it would please Hector if she pretended she had. She nodded and almost managed to smile at the memory of the wolf. The hint of a smile came apart, however, when Hector strained his head up and thrust out his lower lip as far as it would go and uttered a muted howl. He was beginning to resent how hard she was to amuse. "What else did you like?"

"Snow White."

She was barely able to speak for apprehensiveness. She must be afraid he would show her the wicked queen, Hector thought. Even though his face was perfect for the old crone the queen became, he resolved to be the dwarfs instead. He lowered himself into an aching crouch and trotted back and forth, holding his upper third visible over the end of the bed. "See if you can guess which dwarf I am. See which you think is funniest," he said.

He was baffled to find that the answer was none of them. Each character he laboured to produce only caused her face to tighten—he might as well not have allowed her to undo her mouth. The one with his squashed-together lips stuck out and his frown so exaggerated that it nearly shut Hector's eyes proved unpopular, and it occurred to Hector that he looked too fierce, but what was her objection to the daft one with his wagging head and his tongue groping for the corner of his mouth, and the other little fellow with his rolling eyes and his hopeful grin that kept collapsing whenever he met her gaze? Had she no sense of humour? It wouldn't do her any harm to make a little effort to be appreciative; Hector was certainly making an effort himself, enough of one that he was determined to see more of a reaction than he was earning so far. How could she fail to like the jolly dwarf, his eyes stinging with enormousness, his smile so wide that Hector's bared gums tingled? At least the fifth midget brought a response—a jerk of the little girl's body and a creak of the headboard against which it pressed harder each time he let fly another sneeze he'd screwed his face up for.

Having to sneeze in a whisper was aggravating his frustration, and so was his inability to think how to portray the one with spectacles. He was stumbling back and forth in his crouch while he prepared to play the dozy dwarf, and reflecting that he would settle for her being asleep, when he had an idea that jerked him to his feet. Her eyes seemed to tug her head up as she watched him dance away the pain of having left his crouch. He wondered if she thought he was still performing, and told himself to keep his temper if she laughed. When the agony in his legs subsided enough for him to stand still he said "Did she ever take you to *Hansel and Gretel*, no, what did they call it, *Babes in the Wood*?"

Charlotte's head shook, or she shook her head. "Do you want to see it now?" he urged. "Do you want to see the dame?"

"Where?"

"Where do you think?"

"In a theatre?"

"If you call this a theatre. We aren't going anywhere if that's what you were hoping. Don't try to be funny, that's my job. The dame's already here. You watch."

He was pleased to find she couldn't take her eyes off him. He opened the wardrobe and glanced away from her just long enough to select a voluminous bright yellow dress with pink cartoon fish grinning all over it, which told him that it was meant for the beach. He thought of pointing out that the fish were laughing, but it was no longer his ambition to make her laugh. He unbuttoned the top of the dress and pulled it over his head, to see Charlotte hadn't dared move while he couldn't see her. He needed a hat to help him be the dame, and there was a black straw one on a shelf above the hangers in the wardrobe. Wasn't it judges who used to wear black hats? She wouldn't know that, and he needn't dwell on it himself. He buttoned the dress and forced the hat onto his head with a creak of straw, then bowed to his audience. "Do you know what happened to the babes?" he said.

He couldn't see why she should be afraid to answer that, but it took some time for her eyes, which were fixed on him, to let her head deliver a reluctant nod. "They got lost, didn't they?" he said. "Got lost in the woods and went on walking till they were so tired they lay down under a tree. And then the dame—no, it wasn't the dame, come to think. It was the good fairy. You'll like her."

He needed a wand. He'd glimpsed something glittering on the

floor of the wardrobe—a pair of mauve shoes with sparkles on them. He picked one up and shut the wardrobe to give himself more room to perform. He pirouetted on his aching legs and waved the twinkling shoe at Charlotte, and was less than pleased when she flinched against the headboard. "See, it's magic," he said—might have said through his teeth if he'd had any, she was starting to perplex him so much. "It's got magic in it to help you sleep. Settle down now like a babe in the wood. Close your eyes and the good fairy will sing you to sleep."

He waltzed slowly back and forth and waved the shoe and beckoned to her with his other hand until she slid down the quilt as though dragged by a magnet, her head ending up on the pillow. "Close them now," he said, not least because the way her eyes protruded so as to watch him over her face was making his own eyes smart. "You haven't slept since you came. You must be sleepy. Your eyes must be heavy. Close them and I'll sing."

Fairies mightn't talk like that, but hypnotists did, and whenever you saw them on television it worked. She had to go to sleep so that Hector could think what to do with her. He'd taken her in because she'd seemed so lonely and frightened, he'd been unable to resist when she had strayed so near his hiding place, but he'd forgotten until it was too late that he would have to prevent her from betraying he was still alive. "Time to sleep now. Time to go to sleep. Close your eyes now. They're so heavy. Let them close," he droned, none of which earned him even a blink. Maybe she was waiting for the song he'd promised her, and so he began to sing in a whisper, beating time with the shoe.

"Now I lay you down to sleep,
Close your eyes good night.
Angels come your soul to keep,
Close your eyes good night . . ."

What was the matter with her? She was going to have to sleep sooner or later—why couldn't it be now? It looked as though she was determined to defy him, refusing to be anything but scared after he'd expended so much energy on finding ways that ought to have amused her. What did he have to do in order to make the lullaby work? Adele and the police had cut off his access to pills.

"Now I lay you down to sleep . . ."

Whatever happened ought to be as swift and gentle as he could manage. If instead of her face being on the pillow their positions were reversed—

"Close your eyes good night . . ."

If that was the only action he could take, there was no point in delaying. He wouldn't need pills, he reassured himself. She must be so exhausted that once she was unable to resist falling asleep she wouldn't even notice what was happening.

"Angels come your soul to keep . . ."

They would take her away from whatever was making her so afraid. That wasn't only him—not even mainly him. If she hadn't already been afraid she wouldn't have needed him to give her a refuge. Even if he never learned what he was saving her from, it would be enough for him to know he'd brought it to an end.

"Close your—"

As though to demonstrate how completely he was wasting his breath, her eyes widened. At once they tried to pretend they hadn't, but they couldn't fool him. He'd heard the same noise she had heard. He was beside her in a second, and as she tried to sidle out of reach he snatched the pillow from beneath her head and pressed it over her mouth—just her mouth. For the moment holding her quiet and still was sufficient. Downstairs the front door had opened and shut, and somebody else was in the house.

THIRTY-SEVEN

Ian was returning across the park when he caught sight of a blue ribbon peeking over the bank of the river. He felt worthwhile at once, and glad he'd gone out to look for Charlotte. If she wasn't hiding down the bank, afraid to be found after having worried everybody overnight, at least the ribbon was a clue for him to show the police. That ought to prove they had no reason to suspect him, but more important—though he would never admit it to her, and probably not to anyone else either—was finding Charlotte safe. He ran across the patchy turf as quietly as he could, hoping that the scrap of blue material would be snatched into hiding as Charlotte attempted to take cover. It didn't stir, although something appeared to be moving on it—not only crawling but also growing bigger. He was nearly on top of it before he saw that the object he'd assumed to be a ribbon was the largest fragment of a pocket mirror, the rest of which was scattered down the bank, one shard winking at him as it snagged the river. The blue had been the colour of the bright sky, and the creature he'd taken for an insect was himself.

He wouldn't have believed he could be so disappointed not to find Charlotte. He felt as small and useless as the bit of mirror, and guilty all over again. Maybe she would have bolted if he'd introduced her to Shaun's little sister—if she'd heard about Crystal's experience at Ian's house—but they hadn't got as far as Shaun's. However often Ian told himself that Charlotte shouldn't have run away, that it was her fault for provoking him by going on about

Jack until he'd told her who Jack was, it didn't make him feel any less responsible. He should at least have run after her, and then he would have seen where she went. Now he felt as though he'd wished worse to happen to her than he wanted to imagine—felt almost as bad as he might have if he'd done it to her himself—and so guilty that when he glanced across the park from the gate nearest home, pathetically hoping to find Charlotte sneaking after him, and saw that a police car had halted at the far entrance, he dodged out of sight at once.

He wouldn't have if his mother hadn't suspected him. Anyone else could—even his father since he'd left them for Hilene and Charlotte—and Ian would have managed not to care, but being distrusted by his mother was too much. Even if he'd succeeded in convincing her that he'd told her everything he knew about Charlotte's disappearance, she shouldn't have had to ask. He'd thought at least she would never wonder if he was the kind of person the Dukes and the wheelie woman and half of Wembley seemed to want him to be.

He had no idea how to spend the rest of the day now that he'd searched. He hadn't much enthusiasm for schoolwork just now, or trying to write another story or rewriting the same one, or even rereading Jack's book uninterrupted, since that would only remind him of having wished Charlotte away so that he could finish it. He unlocked the front door and stepped into less sunlight, and was about to give the door his habitual slam when he grew aware of the phone in the hall.

Suppose someone had called about Charlotte while he was out—perhaps even Charlotte herself? He eased the door shut with a gentleness that felt like an unspoken wish, one that stayed with him as he dialled 1471. Samples of a female voice informed him that an outer London number he didn't recognise had called less than twenty minutes ago. "To return the call press 3," the voice advised him as he did.

The distant phone had barely had a chance to ring when a man interrupted. "Haven," he said, sounding proud of it and of himself.

"What?" In an attempt to be more polite and perhaps more accurate, Ian added, "Who?"

"Haven Home." After a pause that might have implied he was having to remember his own name the man said "Arthur."

"Right. What . . ."

"Don't tell me you don't know what a home is, and I expect you know what a haven is, what is it, one of them, like a place to hide, a refuge, so is it me you want to know about?"

As if all this wasn't sufficiently distracting, Ian could hear sounds that suggested the man was dancing as he talked. He had to hold the receiver away from his face before he grasped that the thudding of feet was somewhere near the house. "Sure, if you called here," he said. "Did you call?"

"Me call?"

"You, right. Was it you calling before?"

"Me calling?" the man said, and in case that was insufficiently frustrating, expended several seconds on a laugh. "I never called. You're worse than me. You did."

"Not just now. Twenty minutes back. Someone called from your number."

"Wasn't me," the man declared with a finality that threatened to end the conversation, then only took his voice some way off. "Someone says I called when I never."

"Thanks, Arthur, I'll have it now. Arthur, could you take Arthur back to the lounge? Thanks. Thanks for answering the phone, Arthur." Throughout this the woman's voice had been approaching Ian, and now it addressed him. "Who do you want, please?"

"I don't know. Somebody called from there before."

"Who am I speaking to?"

"Can't you tell me that? The phone says you called us."

"This is the Haven Care Home and I'm Adele Woollie the proprietor. Do you know enough now?"

He wasn't sure how much he knew. "It's Ian, Mrs. Woollie."

"Ian who?"

"Ian Ames. You came to our house."

"Oh, the young boy. I remember. How are you now?"

"I'm okay. But listen, did you try and call my mother?"

"Not this lady, I'm afraid. If any of my residents have been bothering you I can assure you they don't mean any harm, but I'll see they don't trouble you again."

He had to ask the question, however impolite it seemed. "Was it Jack?"

"Didn't you understand me? I was talking about my residents. He's not one."

"I guess not, but was it him that phoned?"

"Why should you think that? You'll have to let me go now. Someone needs me."

"Wait," Ian said, feeling uncomfortable and rude but determined. "Will you tell him to phone again now I'm home?"

"How can I do that if it wasn't him?"

"If it was, will you tell him?"

"I'm coming now, Arthur," Mrs. Woollie said, to which there was such a lack of response that Ian deduced she was speaking to nobody. Nevertheless her voice moved closer to the phone before she said "I shouldn't think your mother would want you having anything to do with John."

"Why, what's wrong with him?"

"Not as much as some people have tried to make out. Not as much as he'd be entitled to have wrong, in fact not much at all," Mrs. Woollie said, and with anger Ian thought was directed at least partly at herself, "That's not the point. I can't be going against your mother, and she wanted him out of your lives."

"She won't want me getting depressed like I get. I never had a chance to say good-bye to him."

Mrs. Woollie released a long unsteady breath. "If I happen to see him I'll think about saying you called."

Though that didn't seem much of an undertaking, persistence was liable to turn it into less of one. "I need to talk to him," Ian risked saying, only to discover that he wouldn't have been able to provide a reason, so that he was glad when Mrs. Woollie's silence let him hang up. He might have wondered why Jack had called if there hadn't been a more immediate problem. Had the thump of feet he'd heard while he was on the phone come from the house next door?

He ought to check the house in any case—it was more than a day since he had. He scribbled Mrs. Woollie's number on the top leaf of the pad and wrote JACK even larger than the digits as if that could repudiate the name Jack's mother insisted on calling him, then he slipped the page into his shirt pocket and took Janet's spare keys from the drawer of the hall table. Even if nothing was amiss, it was more diverting to pretend something was, and so he slid a kitchen knife into his hip pocket once he'd caught the sunlight on the blade all the way to the front door.

He needn't have bothered concealing the knife unless any of the netted windows of Jericho Close weren't as blind as they

feigned to be. The suburb appeared to be enjoying a siesta while
using an unseen lawnmower to keep up a gentle snore. He opened
the gate and its neighbour without making any noise he could hear,
and hurried not much less quietly than a dream along the path
parallel to his. He inched the key into the lock and turned it almost
as slowly as the ticking of the seconds on his wristwatch, and set
about creeping the door inward. It had moved nearly a foot when
the phone rang in his house.

His reaction jerked the key out of the lock. The door swung
toward him, and he had to block it with the toe of his shoe. He
fumbled the keys into the hip pocket that wasn't heavy with the
knife. The phone was still ringing, robbing him of thoughts while
it demanded he think what to do. It surely couldn't be Jack so soon,
and if by any chance it was he would certainly call back. If it was
anyone else they would have to do that too, besides which Ian
would be able to find out their number unless they withheld it, in
which case it wouldn't be worth having. He edged the door open
and sidled through the gap. He was releasing the latch when the
phone, almost inaudible now through the wall, gave up.

Perhaps it was the intensified silence that made the house seem
abruptly unreal, as though it had become more of a mirror image
of his than it was affecting to be. The hall was pale blue with large
vague pinkish flowers, suggesting to him that the wallpaper was
betraying the presence of a hidden chemical. Some of the flowers
were partly concealed by framed photographs, a hobby of Janet's
husband Vern: photographs of sunsets with silhouettes against
them, an Indian palace with its colors reduced to black, a Chinese
pagoda that might have been carved out of ebony, a castle like the
outline of a fairy-tale illustration waiting to be coloured. All of this
was diverting his attention from the very element that rendered it
so vivid. Was that the silence, which felt like a breath held for too
long? He was starting to think he might be imagining most if not
all of this, fun though it was—perhaps the feet he'd heard had
belonged to a bird on the roof. He paced forward, letting himself
feel like the daughter in Jack's book as she searched for her father,
and pushed open the door to the front room.

As far as he could tell, the room was as it ought to be. The
chairs and sofa draped with white lace were keeping the television
company, and the only movement was the palpitation of the colon
between the digits of the clock beneath the screen. He had to re-

mind himself not to play xylophone with the banisters as he passed them on his way to the dining room, where six chairs faced one another across a walnut table glossy as a windless pond. A blanket that made him think of Westerns in which gunfighters had stubble and no names was nailed to the far wall. Nothing owned up to being wrong here either, and he advanced to the kitchen.

Apart from a hint of imported spice in the unventilated air, and the view of the garden leading to the fence and its bolted gate, the fitted kitchen might still have been on display in the showroom. Ian shook the back door to confirm it was locked, not bothering about the noise now he'd abandoned the idea that there was an intruder in the house. He was heading for the stairs when he swivelled round. What had he almost noticed?

The tall refrigerator emitted a loud click that gave way to a muted hum like an apology for having distracted him. The digits of the microwave announced a new minute, and less than a second later the digits on the hood of the oven did. The wall-cupboard to the immediate left of the window was slightly ajar, but it wasn't big enough to contain even a tiny child. The door to the garden: the rectangle of glass didn't look quite straight, because the putty that framed it wasn't. He crossed the room and touched the putty, and his nail sank in. The substance was very new.

He was gazing at the bits of fingerprints in the putty all around the new pane when a glint on the floor caught his eye. A solitary fragment of glass had lodged against the table, and he felt stupid for not having noticed it sooner. He went to the kitchen bin, which was drooping a lip of white plastic liner, and trod on the pedal. The bin was indeed full of broken glass, and he was lowering the lid very gradually when he heard a faint creak.

It was overhead in the back bedroom—the creaking of a bed, immediately suppressed. He pulled out the knife as he lowered the lid into place with a rustle of plastic. The kitchen seemed twice as bright and several degrees hotter, and he wiped his forehead with the fist that held the knife while he made for the stairs as swiftly as stealth would allow. The blade flared like a flashbulb, then dulled as he tiptoed upstairs, leaving much of the sunlight in the hall. As he stepped off the stairs, resting some of his weight on the ball of his foot and then more on his heel before relinquishing the banister, he felt as though the knife were guiding him toward the back bedroom.

Two careful breathless paces brought him close enough to grasp the doorknob. At once it was slippery with sweat, and increasingly difficult to hold while he turned it fraction after fraction of an inch. Suppose the door was snatched out of his hand? He raised the knife above his head and kept it there, even when his arm began to ache. Nobody pulled the door away from him, and he had to advance it several fragmented inches before he could peer into the room.

It was darker than the rest he'd seen of the house, because the curtains were drawn. You weren't meant to leave curtains shut when you were away—it only gave the hint to burglars—and he knew Janet and her husband never would have. Besides, he could see what the curtains were intended to hide. Someone was lying under the quilt on the double bed.

He'd lowered the knife, but he lifted it again as he approached the bed, his feet barely advancing in front of each other with each measured step. He was almost close enough to grab the quilt when he heard a muffled whimper. It was a girl's voice—it was Charlotte's. He felt as if he'd tracked her down in the longest game of hide-and-seek he'd ever had to play. How she would scream if she saw him brandishing the knife! He was slipping the knife into his pocket as he took hold of a corner of the quilt and threw it back.

The head it revealed wasn't Charlotte's. It was an old man's, lying on a ragged wad of long grey hair. It greeted him with a wide grin, exposing toothless gums notched with purple and red. A large hand with grimy unpared nails appeared beside it and reached out to fold back more of the quilt, revealing the other arm in a yellow sleeve decorated with pink fish and what was at the end of it—the hand tightening over the little girl's face. "Shut the door and give us the knife and don't even think of making a sound," the man whispered, still grinning with some kind of delight. "Here's company for you, Charlotte, look," he said, and pulled her eyes wider with two fingers. "It's the other babe in the wood."

THIRTY-EIGHT

As soon as Jack reached a decision he went back to the Haven. He wouldn't try to call Leslie again, he would go to the shop. At least then she ought to be able to see truth in his eyes. If Melinda heard him—he could hardly expect her to leave them alone unless Leslie asked her to—he would just have to be persuasive enough to convince both of them, after which they would be certain to insist he contact the police. As if to demonstrate that his mind had focused itself, a limerick he'd tried to invent for Leslie's entertainment while he was living at her house put itself together in his head.

> While composing his music, Ry Cooder
> Utters curses progressively ruder.
> Should a phrase fail to fit,
> He'll be heard to shout 'Shit!'
> Like (in German, of course) Buxtehude.

He mustn't expect to be given a chance to regale her with that, but surely there was no harm in imagining her reaction—maybe a laugh, maybe the kind of gasp that sounded like one, maybe a comically pained look that couldn't quite and wasn't intended to conceal how pleased she was, would have been, to have even such a piece of ramshackle doggerel invented for her. He hid his smile inside himself as he strode into the driveway of the Haven, not wanting his mother to ask his thoughts. He planned to tell her enough of the truth, that he was going to the West End, and he continued to resolve that when he saw her watching for him from the office window as though he had yet to grow up.

He hadn't reached the front door when she opened it. "Come in," she said, so urgently that she might have been anxious to hide him. She repeated the words and the urgency once he was inside, and only her retreating into the office showed what she meant. He'd hardly followed her in when she said "Shut the door, for heaven's sake," and was seated behind the desk by the time he had. "What did you want with that young boy?" she demanded.

"Which young boy?"

"Which do you think? How many of them are there, John?"

She was making Jack feel as if he deserved to be accused of somehow resembling his father. "I can't understand you," he said.

"You're saying that to me? It should be me that's saying it to you. I thought if you respected someone you were supposed to respect their wishes."

"I'm still lost."

"That's what I'm afraid of, John," she said, rubbing her forehead with three fingers that failed to erase her frown. "Don't parents have rights where you've been? Aren't they allowed to decide what's best for their children even if you wish they weren't?"

"Which parent?"

"Oh, John, don't try and make out I'm talking like one of my residents. You know who you had a go at calling before you went out for your walk."

"How do you know?"

"How would you think?"

"Are you saying he called back?"

"Somebody did, and I hope now you'll leave him alone. His mother doesn't want you bothering him worse than he is already."

"Leslie called? How long ago?"

"Don't torture yourself about that. I'm sorry, she wouldn't have wanted to speak to you even if I'd caught you, John."

"But she called. You're telling me she called."

"You said it, as you'd say," Jack's mother told him, and rammed her fingers between one another before planting her elbows on the desk with an angry thump that made her wince. "That's what I'm trying to get you to understand."

"And said . . . She said . . ."

"Have I got to spell that out for you? She thought she'd heard the last of you. Maybe not of you but from you. She hoped she had."

"Did she ask why I'd tried to contact her?"

"She didn't, no." His mother seemed relieved the question had come up. "But I'll guarantee you this, John, she'd have been even less happy if I'd mentioned what you'd have told her, never mind her son."

"You can't know that."

"Oh, but I can. For all sorts of reasons I can. Now if you won't leave them alone because I ask, will you for her? You would if you still cared about her, and if you don't there's no excuse at all for you to pester her."

"It isn't an excuse. I tried to tell you—"

"John." His mother was rubbing her elbows as if she'd only just noticed they were hurting. "She wants to forget you, and the last thing she'd want to hear from you is that tale you told me."

It wasn't only his mother's words that swayed him at last, it was the sight of her having needed to injure herself in the heat of her determination to persuade him, as though her work weren't taxing enough. He stepped back and opened the door for both of them. "I'll see you at the apartment," he said.

"Are you going there now?"

"I guess."

He saw her consider asking him to promise not to phone from there. She knew he'd seen, and must have decided her insistence would be more powerful if unspoken. She watched him from the front porch as he crossed the parking area, and he felt as if her notion of the right course for him to take was gripping the nape of his neck.

Nevertheless he wasn't sure what he was going to do as he drove out of the streets hushed by trees. He would have to pass the station on the way to the apartment, and he couldn't help feeling that would give him one last chance. If Leslie turned out to believe his story despite all the doubts his mother had loaded onto him, he would feel confident in telling the police, but otherwise how could he expect them to credit him if even Leslie didn't? It didn't help to realise he was trying to project the responsibility for his indecision onto her; the sort of insight that would have been crucial to writing about a character was far harder and apparently far less useful to apply to himself. Maybe, he thought, writing was a substitute for changing himself, but knowing that didn't help either. Perhaps the compulsion to write rendered you even less capable than other people of changing. Perhaps you couldn't both change and write.

He was in the midst of these reflections as the bridge over the main road beside the station came into view. Beyond the bridge the reversing lights of a parked car brightened the shadow of the arch, and then the brake lights flared. The car was backing out of a bay, and the traffic would halt it until Jack was close enough to occupy the space. He felt as if he wasn't merely being offered an opportunity, he was being exhorted to use it, and he would.

He was nearly at the bridge, and two vehicles short of the parking space, when a small dusty bus flashed its headlamps at the car, which backed halfway out and then swung resolutely in. It hadn't been leaving, only lining itself up with the kerb. How could Leslie believe him when he'd already caused her not to trust him? What would she think his motives were? He almost laughed—there seemed nothing else for him to do—as he drove out from under the bridge, away from the line that would have carried him to the West End.

THIRTY-NINE

"Ian . . ."

"Is that his name, Charlotte? Tell me all about him. Whisper it to me."

"He's Ian."

"I worked that bit out for myself, love. Were you trying to make me laugh? Let's have the rest of it. Where does he live?"

"Next door."

"Just checking you're a good girl that tells the truth. Good girls haven't got anything to be frightened of, have they? Who is he then, your Ian from next door?"

"Roger's son."

"Is he that very thing? You'll have to say who Roger is, won't you?"

"My new dad."

"Did a swap, did you? Bet you think you're the lucky girl. This new dad Roger of yours, does he live next door too?"

"At home with me and mummy."

"Ian's too young to live all by himself though, isn't he? Who's he got?"

"Just his mummy."

"That's like the boy with the beanstalk, isn't it? Maybe we can play that later. I'll give you a bit of wisdom to be going on with, there'd be less trouble in the world if families stuck together like they used to. Do you think that's why Ian's bad, because he's given you his father and got none of his own? Don't let him scare you. Does he scare you?"

"Sometimes."

"He did with that knife, didn't he, waving it about like that. Don't worry, I've got it safe. Nobody's going to be using it for anything, I hope. It was bad of him to scare you with it, but shall we let him play all the same?"

"What?"

"We'll have to think of a game that ought to be fun for everyone, won't we? You want him to stay, that's what I'm getting at. You'd be upset if he left you with nobody except your new grandad who's forgotten how to make you laugh. You tell him."

"Ian . . ."

"See, that's what she was asking you in the first place, son. Look how upset she's getting just to think you might go off and leave her like your dad left you. She wants you to stay and not make any row, and then we'll find a nice quiet game we can all play to take her mind off things. You can see that's what she's crying out for, can't you?"

Ian saw. From the stool on which he'd been directed to sit in front of the dressing table he saw both Charlotte and her captor. She was seated on the quilt and leaning against the headboard of the double bed: she was propped up immobile as a doll except for her mouth, which kept not quite opening and then pinching its lips together for fear that too much of a noise might escape, and her eyes, which kept straining leftward before renewing their plea to Ian. She mustn't be able to see much of the old tramp, who was resting his shoulders against the closed door, the fingers of his large hands splayed on his thighs and covering two of the jovial pink fish on the yellow dress that reached halfway down his baggy trousers, his gums baring themselves in a raw moist smile that was impatient at being alone with itself, his face a caricature of how Jack might look when he was old. The stale heat of the room, the smell of the man's sweat and shabby clothes, the faint trace of Janet's scents, all seemed to gather in Ian's throat and drive out words like spit. "You're him. You're alive."

"Careful. Don't scare your playmate."

"You—" Ian almost blabbed what the man had done, but no longer wanted to frighten Charlotte. Instead he thought of another offence the man was responsible for. "You made people think I'd done something to her."

"That's people for you, son. They've always got to have someone to blame. Who thought that, then?"

"My mother."

"Don't go raising your voice round here. Keep your temper. Think of your playmate," Woollie said with a smile at her that made her mouth wince like a wound. "There's no accounting for women, son, no joy in trying to predict them. You'll find that out when you're a bit older." He ran his tongue around his lips as though to check their shape before murmuring "Will she wonder where you've got to?"

"Better believe it. I'm supposed to be home since they chucked me out of school because they thought I was like you."

"Then you'd best tell her where you've gone."

"Sure enough. She won't have left work yet. I'll give her a phone from downstairs."

"And tell her what? Tell her you've got your playmate?"

"Sure, if that's what you want her to think, only she won't if she doesn't hear Charlotte. I'll have to take her down with me."

"You reckon that'll solve things, do you?"

"Should."

"He's a laugh, isn't he, Charlotte? Wants to start you chattering to people and making all sorts of a racket, I shouldn't wonder, after all the trouble I've been taking to get you to hush."

Ian had been hoping Woollie was as mad as his appearance suggested—mad enough to be persuaded by the first trick Ian could think of. His own aching disappointment was bad enough, but the way a version of it flickered over Charlotte's face was close to unbearable. "Don't expect my mother to believe me, then," he protested in a whisper that was growing intolerable too. "She knows I didn't know where Charlotte was."

"He must think I'm as senile as I look, mustn't he, Charlotte? He must reckon I've forgotten he just said she thought he'd made you vanish."

"She did till I showed her different."

"Better start thinking what to say to change her mind, then. And don't bother getting any more ideas about the phone. You'll be writing her a note."

"What with?"

"Try that bit of paper in your pocket there."

Ian grabbed his shirt pocket as he tried to think whether it was best to keep Jack's number or give it to his mother on whatever note he might be forced to send her. "I've got nothing to write with," he said.

"Better find something."

"I saw a pencil by the phone."

"He's eager to get there, isn't he, Charlotte? What do you reckon he's thinking? We'll go down with him so he doesn't forget he's meant to be helping look after you. Are you going to be able to stay quiet or will I need to do up your mouth?"

Charlotte's hands flew to her lips but shrank from touching them. Her teary gaze lurched toward the floor between the bed and the window, and Ian noticed for the first time what was there—a roll of insulating tape. Even if he'd imagined worse treatment for Charlotte in the months his father had lived with her, the reality was another matter. Woollie must have seen his fury at it, because he sat on the edge of the bed and hugged Charlotte to him. "You know how to hush, don't you? You were being nice and quiet before he came and spoiled things," he whispered in her ear, and rubbed his stubbly chin over her tangled hair as he turned his face to Ian. "Concentrate on what you have to write, son. Never mind anything else."

Ian struggled to produce a voice that wouldn't rise out of control. "Let me go and write it, then."

"We'll be quick all right, but don't you try being too quick. You haven't said yet what you're going to write."

"You tell me."

"Surprised you need to ask when you were wanting to say it on the phone before. Just tell your mother you've taken your playmate away for some fun. There's enough boys who do that these days," Woollie said, and rubbed his lips together in disgust.

"I'm not saying that."

"Don't start being difficult, you're worrying your playmate. You ought to feel how tense she's getting. We don't want her being nervy. Never know what might happen then and be your fault."

"Maybe you can make me say it, but you can't make my mother think it. She'd never believe I'd do that kind of stuff to you, would she, Charlotte?"

Charlotte's name was hardly beyond taking back when he

wished he hadn't brought her into it—hadn't made Woollie even more aware of her while she was afraid to speak, afraid once she'd done it of having given her head a solitary shake. He saw Woollie's free hand finish digging its knuckles into the pillow and reach for her. He was preparing to fly at Woollie, to save her however he had to, when the hand set about stroking her hair. "Good enough, son," Woollie muttered. "You've changed my mind."

Ian couldn't take much pride in that as he saw Charlotte stiffen so as not to flinch away from the soft slow prolonged movements of the hand the size of her face. The heat was parching his throat, the smells of the room were massing like nausea, by the time Woollie let his hand drop to the pillow and murmured "I know what you want to write."

Ian had to swallow hard. "What?" he said, almost too low to be heard.

"You can tell your mother you've gone off by yourself because she thought you were up to something with your playmate."

She oughtn't to believe that either, which surely meant she would have to do her best to figure out where he really was, if he hadn't succeeded in rescuing Charlotte by then. "I could have too," he said.

"Time to play follow the leader, Charlotte. We don't want him writing anything that might cause an upset, do we? I expect he knows to be a good boy now, but no harm in making sure." Woollie patted her head and rested his hand there while he reached for the doorknob. "You lead, son. We'll follow," he said with none of the archness he was using on Charlotte.

Ian was furious with his legs for developing an intermittent tremor as he crossed the room. He was nearly at the stairs, and struggling to devise a plan, when he heard Woollie and his captive behind him. "Walk soft, son," Woollie murmured. "I know there's nobody in your house, but it'll do you no harm to practice not being heard."

Ian felt as though the man had seized him by the ankles, hindering his steps. The empty hall and the sunlight it led to looked like a joke at the expense of his inability to escape with Charlotte. The way the banister filled his grasp made him wish he were holding a weapon. If only he hadn't been so anxious for Charlotte that he'd given up the knife! Now it was the reason why he had to pretend to be doing as he was told. He placed one foot on the top stair, then lowered his weight gradually onto the next. He was re-peating the performance from there when Woollie muttered "No need to take all day, son. I hope you aren't trying to be funny. That's not the sort of laugh we're after."

Ian hadn't just been following instructions—he was attempting to buy himself time to think. Each step brought him closer to the table with the phone on it, the message pad with its stubby pencil, and the problem of his having failed to memorise Jack's number. He ought to give it to his mother—at least it would be truer than the lie he was being forced to tell—but he mustn't write on the same side of the paper when Woollie was bound to examine the message. He descended a step and sneaked his free hand across his body, stepped down again and pressed his elbow against his side in case that helped conceal how his hand was creeping to his pocket. Another step, and two fingers nipped the edge of the paper, and Woollie said "What are you after, son? Everything you want is down there."

"I see it," Ian said, gripping the banister so hard his whole hand ached, and eased the page out of his pocket. He was straining his eyes downward and glimpsing a hint of the digits when Woollie said "What do we reckon he's hiding, Charlotte? Do we think it's something he oughtn't to have?"

Another inch would show Ian enough for him to identify the digits, but the high muffled sound Charlotte emitted made him screw his head round. She and Woollie were three steps above him, Woollie's left hand enclosing her right and her wrist. She had let go of the banister so as to cover her mouth. "It's nothing," Ian said, groping with his foot for the next stair down.

"Must be a job to take nothing out of your pocket, mustn't it, Charlotte? What you call a fuss about nothing. That's a joke." No louder but more harshly Woollie said "Give us a gander, son. Think of your playmate."

Ian snatched out the page and swung toward him, brandishing it upside down, the used side facing himself. "It's a bit of paper. Satisfied?"

"It nearly looks like nothing, doesn't it, Charlotte? Except what's that name I'm seeing through it? Something something cee kay. Blimey, it's Jack that's really John, and half of him the wrong way up. Give it here so we can see how you do that trick."

Ian felt his hand begin to clench. He could crumple the page and swallow it, but what might Woollie do to Charlotte then? Besides, if Woollie rang Jack he would be revealing he wasn't dead after all. Ian sent himself far enough up the stairs to drop the page into the outthrust hand, and memorised the digits as Woollie stared at them, his lips and then his gums parting. "I know this number," he whispered. "So that's where he's hiding from his dad now."

His stare rose like two drowned objects breaking the surface and settled on Ian, who didn't think he was being seen. "I should have known, shouldn't I?" Woollie muttered, though not to him. "I'd like to know what stopped me thinking."

The possibility that he meant or was on the way to meaning Charlotte rendered Ian as incapable of action as he saw she was. He had to fight not to look directly at her while Woollie folded the page and slipped it into the pink and yellow pocket that contained the knife, where his hand lingered as he focused on Ian. "Write to your mother," he said with what sounded like the end of any patience. "We're watching."

Ian went quickly down to the hall, forgetting to be quiet about it, and took hold of the pencil. He was thinking of moving to block Woollie's view when the man said in a whisper that seemed to fill the hall "Let's see what you're doing, son."

Ian paced around the table and was almost within reach of the front door. He could be out of the house in seconds and yelling for help—but a glance showed him Charlotte in the man's grasp and her captor's other hand bulging the pocket in which he was holding the knife. Ian gripped the pencil so hard it started to bend, and dragged the pad toward him, and tried to keep his mind on words he would be allowed to write. He imagined scribbling draft after draft and never managing to satisfy the smelly old tramp who hid children under floors. A sentence that might have been his desperation speaking formed in his head, and he wrote it. "Fast as a rabbit, wasn't he, Charlotte?" Woollie said. "Hold it up."

Ian forced his fingers to relinquish the pencil so that he could display the pad. He saw Charlotte read the message and not dare to react—he felt as if she were showing him how obvious a trick it was. Then Woollie said "It'll do. You can take it home."

Ian nearly peered at the message to confirm he'd written what he'd intended to write. I'VE GONE BECAUSE YOU SAID I TOOK CHARLOTTE. His mother had said no such thing, and surely she would know that he meant her to realise. He tore off the page and dropped

the pad on the table, and had taken a step toward the front door
when Woollie said "Not quite so hasty, son. What are you planning
on doing?"

"Sticking this through my door."

"And then you'll be straight back to see nothing's happened to
your playmate, will you?"

Ian found himself hoping Charlotte didn't understand the
threat and unable to look at her in case she did. "Right," he said.

"That'll take care of everything, do you reckon, Charlotte?"

When she didn't speak Ian had to look as she realised more
than a nod was required for an answer. "Yes," she said like a plea.

"What's it going to take care of? Don't be scared to tell the
truth. Good girls sleep best, and I know you'd give all your teeth
for a sleep."

Her face worked as though it was afraid even to appear afraid,
and that was too much for Ian. "Lay off her," he blurted, "or I'm
not going."

"Why are you trying to shut her up, son? What don't you want
her to say?"

Ian could think of no reply that mightn't put her more at risk,
including the truth that he hadn't been aiming to hush her at all.
He saw Woollie lose patience again, and was tensing himself to dash
up the stairs before the knife could emerge from the pocket when
Woollie said "Did you think she'd spotted you weren't going to put
your keys to here back next door?"

Charlotte frowned, then understanding smoothed her forehead and her eyes gleamed with dismay. She might have been
enacting Ian's realisation that the absence of the keys could have
told his mother where he was. He felt his ability to think begin to
dwindle under the weight that was lowering itself onto his mind.
"Where d'you keep them?" Woollie said.

Lying seemed both dangerous and pointless, as everything did
now. "Same place as they keep ours," Ian said, pointing at the
drawer of the hall table.

"That's lucky, isn't it, Charlotte? He'll just be on the other side
of this wall, and we'll know exactly how long it should take him.
We'll play a game till he gets back, shall we? Shall we play one
that'll bring him back? Say yes for him to hear."

"Yes."

"That's a good girl. You keep your voice like that. You nearly had me thinking you didn't want him to come back when you didn't answer. You're not that scared of him, are you?"

"No."

"Why are you talking like that, then? You'll be fine once we play our game so long as your playmate joins in. You'll play for her sake, won't you, son?"

"What?"

"Keep your temper. I told you that before. You can make a bit of noise in a minute. That'll be part of the game. Boys make more noise than girls, don't they? Don't they, Charlotte?"

"Yes."

"We'll listen for the noises he makes, shall we? We'll hear him with the gate and his one, and if we listen hard we'll hear him opening his door. But you know what we'll want to hear most of all, don't you?"

"No?"

"Don't sound like that, I'm going to tell you. Him throwing the keys in the drawer and coming straight back. You'll remember to play by the rules, won't you, son? When the keys drop that's the halfway mark."

"Halfway to what?"

"Your playmate knows, don't you, Charlotte? I hope he's not trying to be the wrong kind of funny. I hope he's not thinking of playing a game we wouldn't like. You're going to help him play, aren't you?"

"Yes?"

"See how good she is, saying that when she doesn't know what she'll have to do. The moment he opens that door, Charlotte, you start counting. No, hang on—the moment he walks away from that table, then we'll know how long it has to take him to get to the one next door."

At that moment a plan Ian had begun to conceive was crushed by the slab in his mind. "Don't worry, Charlotte," he nevertheless said, and for the first time in his life gave her an affectionate look, not even having to pretend much. "I'll come back."

"Of course he will. He knows he has to. He's off, look. Start counting. Count his steps."

Ian heard her as he took his second step. Her voice was small and tight and even higher than usual. Each number sounded like a hint of the panic she was doing her best to suppress. That dismayed him and confused him, so that he wasn't sure if he was walking fast to be out of earshot or to convince Woollie that he wouldn't try to trick him or simply because he couldn't stop himself. Three paces brought him to the front door. "Close it and carry on like that," Woollie said, and then Ian was out of the house.

The sight of the quiet street beneath the overexposed sky propped up by wattled red roofs beyond roofs came as little less than a shock. He felt as though he'd forgotten anything was real outside the house, not that anything appeared usefully to be. The street was empty of people, even of parked cars, though what would he have done if he'd seen anyone? The murmur of the suburb was keeping its distance; the loudest sound in his ears was Charlotte's clenched voice. "Five," it wailed urgently, "six," growing fainter as it forced him to keep pace with its counting. By the time he reached the gate he couldn't hear it. It began to grow audible again as he tramped rapidly along his path, having clanged both gates, but he could hear only its pleading tone, not its words. He shoved the key into the lock and dodged inside his house.

The safety of the place felt like an exhortation to rescue Charlotte somehow while Woollie couldn't see him. The phone was demanding to be used to call Ian's mother or Jack, and the pad and pencil beside it were at least as anxious for him to scribble a note. He hadn't reached the table, however, when he heard a sharp knock through the wall beside it, and Charlotte's trapped voice rose in pitch. "You should be there now, son," Woollie said. "Let's hear those keys drop."

He sounded as though he were muttering inside the wall—as though his influence had invaded the whole house, not just the earth under the kitchen. An impatient repetition of the knocking demonstrated that he was using the handle of the knife. The thought closed over Ian's mind. He hauled the table drawer open and placed the note to his mother in it, then threw next door's keys on top with a clatter. He was about to close the drawer when he managed to think. At once he was heading for the front door. By trying to ensure Ian had no time to trick him, hadn't Woollie tricked himself?

Ian's gate clanged, and one hasty step later the gate next to it echoed the sound slightly higher. Charlotte's counting, audible once more as the only other individual sound in the suburb besides his tread, was tugging him by his legs along the path, but he'd done

something Woollie didn't know about, and it had to work. He was
a single pace from Janet's door when it was snatched open, showing him Charlotte where he'd abandoned her on the stairs. "Thirty-
one," she seemed compelled to wail, "thirty—"

"Game's over, love. You can stop now," Woollie said, his dress
flapping as he closed the door and showed Ian the knife in his hand.
"He was a good boy this time, wasn't he? We'll all be fine so long
as you're both good."

Ian glimpsed uncertainty in the eyes that were red and bright
with sleeplessness. Deep in himself Woollie must know his optimism wasn't genuine—couldn't be. It took far too long—almost
longer than Ian was able to hold the breath he'd sucked stealthily
in—for Woollie to finish scrutinising him and transfer his attention
to Charlotte. "Take her up then, son," he muttered. "I'll be right
behind you with the jabber."

Ian risked a smile at Charlotte that was supposed to reassure
her all would be well—would soon start to be. Her face only began
to crumple before she remembered not to look upset and turned
unsteadily to climb the stairs. He caught up with her and gave her
small clammy hand a squeeze, and it closed trustfully on his. He
was leading her to the cell of a bedroom, but he had to believe it
wouldn't be for long. Surely when his mother saw he'd left the
drawer open, displaying the keys as well as the message, she would
figure out where he was. In a couple of hours—as unbearably long
as that—she would be home.

FORTY

Though Leslie had never allowed herself to believe that Ian could have done Charlotte any real harm, she'd let him feel she might consider the possibility, and that was almost as bad. It was nearly as insistent in its nagging at her mind as Charlotte's disappearance. The more she thought of having left him alone at home to brood over her suspicions of him, the more she blamed herself. She would have phoned him if she hadn't thought the matter was best discussed face to face. When there was a lull in the gratifyingly busy afternoon, she left Melinda womanning the shop while she hurried along Oxford Street to the HMV store and bought a tape of Persistent Vegetables, one of Ian's favourite bands and one she disliked so much that hearing them anywhere in the house would be a penance. The floor devoted to pop music was loud as a disco, and she had to conduct the transaction at the counter in sign language. She ventured upstairs to the video section, knowing Hilene hadn't worked since the Ameses had sold their house, but Roger was off too, and so she couldn't ask if there was any news of Charlotte.

"Hope everything's all right soon," Melinda said as they locked up, and Leslie wasn't sure if she was expressing a wish or advising her to hope. On the train home she was provided with a seat by a little girl of about Charlotte's age who perched on her mother's knee, and she found herself close to praying that Hilene's daughter would be returned safely to her. Maybe Leslie and her son could figure out together where Charlotte might have gone: maybe there was some insight he didn't realise he had, if Leslie could approach it in a way that showed she trusted him. By now she understood one reason for his secretiveness was that he was more worried about Charlotte than he wanted anyone to see, but surely she could let him realise she knew.

She took her keys and the tape out of her bag as she reached her gate. At least there was nobody at Janet's to suffer Ian's musical taste, though in any case few sounds penetrated the shared wall. Not for the first time she found herself wishing it hadn't afforded Woollie so much cover when he'd been working in the house. She unlocked the front door and stepped into the hall. "Ian," she called. "Come and see what—"

A resigned grimace cut her voice off. He'd found yet another way to be an untidy teenager: he'd left the drawer of the telephone table protruding like a tongue. "Ian, can you hear me? The least you could do . . ."

Was answer so that she didn't feel she'd driven him out of the house, and maybe leave fewer things for her to clear away or otherwise deal with on his behalf. She retrieved her key and gave the door an elbow, and by the time it slammed she was pushing the drawer shut. "Ian, would you like to answer? Just a syllable would—"

She stopped to listen, because she thought she heard him somewhere—a rustle of movement apart from the shifting of keys. The sound came from the drawer, however. She tugged at it, having to jiggle it when it stuck, and blinked at the square of paper she had belatedly realised she'd glimpsed. Most of the words on it were hidden by the keys. YOU, she saw, and CHARL, and almost tore it on the keys as she snatched it out to read.

It glared whiter in the sunlight through the kitchen, and the pencilled writing seemed to wobble like a cheap superimposition in a film. I'VE GONE BECAUSE YOU SAID I TOOK CHARLOTTE. "Oh, Ian," she said helplessly, "I didn't," but she was in no doubt that as far as he was concerned she might as well have done so. She stood the Persistent Vegetables tape by the phone and stalked to the front door, only to feel she was both blaming the suburb and displaying her own guilty self. She heard footsteps taking their time on the cross street and eventually demonstrating that they hadn't been worth waiting for, since they belonged to a boy she'd never seen before, however much like Ian's his teenage emblems were. Of course, Ian would be with his friends—the ones she disapproved of.

She left the door open as she stooped to the directory on the shelf under the table and saw that she'd left his tape where magnetism from the phone might spoil it. That would serve him right, she thought, but moved it to the stairs before her failure to take care of it could seem ominous. Nolan, Nolan—what looked to her like a whole clan staking out its territory in the middle of a page. There was just one address on the North Circular Road, printed in thinner type as though it were trying to hide from her. "Be there," she said.

The phone seemed to have given anyone who might be at Shaun's quite enough time to answer it when the ringing relented, to be succeeded by a burst of mirthful coughing. This withdrew into the background, having turned most of itself into laughter, as a voice not unlike Ian's but not his said "Shut up a minute. Hello? Shut up, you'll make me start. Hello?"

"Is that Shaun?"

"Hang on, I'll look." The boy aimed an explosion of merriment away from the phone and said "She wants to know if I'm you." To a question that must have been mouthed he replied "She didn't say" and brought his amusement back to the mouthpiece. "He wants to know—"

"This is Ian Ames's mother. Is Ian there?"

"It's Ian's mother asking if he's here."

"Hello," Leslie said in a tone that made clear how much more than enough she'd had. "Will you tell me if he's with you or I'll come and find out for myself."

There was sudden consternation, which she thought she'd caused until she heard what Shaun was shouting. "Shit, it's my mother and Crys. They weren't supposed to come back yet. Open the window and get rid of that and give us something to—" and presumably more that the phone cut off.

Leslie released a gasp as loud and short and almost as coarse as the word she would otherwise have uttered, and jabbed the redial key. The phone rang longer than it had the first time, and she imagined the boys willing her and perhaps yelling at her to go away or words to that effect. All at once the receiver emitted a violent clatter and Mrs. Nolan's voice. "Just what have you three been smoking? Go up, Crys, keep out of the way," she cried, and not much more softly to the phone, "Yes? Who is it?"

"It's Ian's mother, Mrs. Nolan. Is—"

"I'm dealing with something. What do you want?"

"I was going to ask if Ian was there."

"Not that I've noticed. Just the usual hooligans. Have you had Ian Ames round, Shaun, on top of everything else?" After no answer that Leslie could hear, and barely sufficient pause for one, Mrs. Nolan said "He's not been, no."

"You're sure."

"Shaun won't do what he's been told not do. Finds other things as bad to do instead, that's his trick." Having turned on him, Mrs. Nolan's voice found the phone again. "And he's been told not to have your Ian round after that business with Crys and then nearly blinding a boy at school."

Leslie restrained herself. "Did Ian know?"

"You do now, so you can tell him. Anyway, I've got to deal with some delinquents. I expect you know what that's like."

"I should think you've had more experience," Leslie retorted, but she was talking to an empty line. At least Ian wasn't with Shaun and his cronies; Jack had helped divert him away from them—and at once she knew where Ian might be.

Except that she didn't know where Jack was. If anyone could tell her, it was his mother. There was no Adele Woollie in the directory, not even an initial A, but the Haven Care Home in Sudbury was listed. Two and a half pairs of rings caught her a woman's voice. "Which Arthur is it? Tell him I'll be two shakes," it said, and in much the same maternal manner "Haven Home."

"Am I speaking to Mrs. Woollie?" Leslie thought it best to ask.

"You are."

"Would John be there?"

"Which John?"

"Jack." When Leslie heard no response to that she said "Your son."

"I'm sorry, who is this?"

"Leslie Ames, Mrs. Woollie. You came to see Jack at my house."

"So I did. I can't remember if I complimented you on how much you'd made of it. That must have taken some strength."

"Thanks. So is Jack . . ."

"Why should he be here? Why do you want to know?"

"Because Ian, you met Ian, my son, he's gone missing."

"Why should that have anything to do with John? What are you trying to make out?"

"Just that they were friends and Ian might have gone to him if he wanted someone to talk to."

"About what?"

"Being blamed too much."

"I can't imagine what you think John would know about that." Before Leslie could decide whether that was meant as an accusation or a denial, Mrs. Woollie said "How do you think he would have got in touch with him?"

"I suppose he would have had to call you to ask where Jack was."

"I hope you don't think I'd have told him. I got the impression you wanted rid of John, and I presume that includes your son."

Leslie had to reassure herself that Mrs. Woollie meant she wanted to keep Ian away from Jack, not get rid of him. "And if he calls to ask where he can find John," Mrs. Woollie said, "you've my word as a mother I won't tell him."

"If he does, could you tell him to call me instead? I just want him back."

"I understand. As long as I'm respecting your wishes, can I ask you to respect ours?"

Leslie couldn't help growing wary. "Which are . . . ?"

"Just that John would like to choose his own time to let the world know who he is. They know here because one of them recognised he was my son, they can be sharp like that sometimes, but you and of course your boy are the only others who do."

"I've no reason to tell anyone. Jack's been there, then."

"He couldn't stay away from his mother. I'm sure your boy won't be able to either. Things are never as bad as they seem, that's my experience."

Leslie had to assume Mrs. Woollie was putting her husband out of her mind. "Jack isn't there, I don't suppose," she heard herself admit to wanting to know.

"He's not. Now I must go and see what one of my residents needs. If you're worried about your boy, I should call the police."

"Thanks," Leslie said, even less sure than before why she was saying so, especially since Mrs. Woollie hadn't hung on long enough to hear. She wasn't ready to contact the police—she had to make another call that would be at least as fraught. Beyond the front door the houses were losing some of their colour, and three parked cars had taken their places along Jericho Close, but otherwise nothing had changed. The evening hush made her feel overheard as she took a deep breath before hefting the receiver.

The phone had hardly rung when it was answered. "Yes?"

"Hilene?"

"Yes, who is it?"

"Leslie Ames."

"I thought so."

This was so toneless that the only rejoinder Leslie could think of was "How are you?"

"Feeling like I'd never want anybody in the world to feel."

"I'm really sorry. There's been no news, then."

"No."

Leslie had the grotesque notion that one of them was about to be compelled to quote the old saying about no news. Instead Hilene demanded "Have you got something to tell me?"

"What do you mean? What could I have?"

"Anything that would help."

Leslie experienced a rush of sympathy for the other woman. She'd let herself speak sharply because she'd been too quick to feel Hilene was accusing her on Ian's behalf. "I wish I had, honestly I do," she said. "I just called—"

"I'll give you Roger."

"I only—" But Leslie was talking only to herself. She had plenty of time to reflect how distressed Hilene must be to have used the words she just had while a muttered conversation, mostly in Roger's voice, eventually delivered him to the phone. "Leslie," he said.

"Is—"

"What did you say to Hilene?" he said, more reproachfully still.

"Just asked her how she was."

"That would do it. I'd have thought you would have known."

"How could I when I didn't know if you'd heard anything?"

"I'd have called you."

"You might have been trying to get through." Feeling encumbered by too much needless argument, Leslie said "I'm sorry if I upset her. Tell her if you like I'm a bit upset myself."

"Oh." That was close to a rebuke, and so was the pause before he said "By whom?"

"Not by Hilene, if that's what you think I meant. By Ian. He's run off and I don't know where."

"You surely weren't thinking he'd come here."

"I had to check. Why, are you saying he couldn't have?"

"I shouldn't think—" Roger lowered his voice, presumably below Hilene's hearing. "He'd hardly want to be around us when we can do nothing but worry."

"I do see that. Sorry," Leslie said, this time for having heard another accusation aimed at Ian where there had been none. "I'll have to try and think straighter, won't I? All I've got to go on is a note."

"From Ian, you mean."

"There's nobody else to leave me one, is there?" Angry with herself for having said that, Leslie blurted "Do you want to hear what it says?"

"I should."

Leslie knew it by heart, but blinked at it anyway. It must be the withdrawal of the sunlight that made the large untidy capitals look already faded, writing from the past. "It says 'I've gone because you said I took Charlotte.' "

"When did I ever say that to him? You were there. I didn't and I wouldn't have."

"Not you. He means me," Leslie said, and with rather less conviction "I didn't either."

"I'm sure you never would. He'll be feeling guilty for what he did do, that's all, and trying to load some of the guilt onto you. How long has he been gone?"

"There's no time on the note, Roger. Maybe as long as I've been out at work."

"Very likely not that long then, would you say? Just long enough to make sure you feel as bad as he thinks you ought to feel, or maybe now he's staying away because he feels guilty about that."

"You don't think I should call the police yet."

Roger was silent, and she had time to wonder if he thought she was trying to compete with Hilene. At last he said "I think you should call them when you feel you have to."

If she let herself, she already did. Roger promised to contact her if he should hear from Ian, and then he said goodbye with an abruptness that might mean Hilene was wanting him to finish, unless he was giving Ian a chance to call. The receiver had no more to say to her, however. When she found herself wondering if she should ring her parents, she knew whom she indeed ought to call. Nevertheless it was dark, and she'd found several ways of pretending to use her time—making dinner for herself and Ian and even managing to eat a mouthful, tidying his room so that she could confront him with having failed to do so, sitting on his bed and leafing slowly through Jack's novel, staring out of Ian's window as the twilight drained colour from the streetlamps and blurred their outlines until they resembled sculptures constructed of fog and finally touched their lights off—before she called the police for advice.

FORTY-ONE

"They're noisy, aren't they, Charlotte? Noisy neighbours that don't care about a little girl who wants to go to sleep. You try anyway. Look, he's trying, the other babe in the wood, the big babe. You try as well and when they stop their row next door I'll sing to you. I'll sing you my song for babes that are going to sleep."

Woollie pushed himself up on the bed, resting his back against the headboard, and laid his pink and yellow left arm across Ian's chest, his right across Charlotte's. The shaggy head loomed, not much less blurred than a chunk of dust, above Ian in the dimness that was almost dark, and a smell of stale cloth and sour sweat descended on him. He willed Charlotte to give in to her exhaustion so that she would be less of a problem and less at risk. He tried to quell his awareness of the arms that were pinning him and Charlotte down, and strove to lie absolutely still, hardly even moving his chest when he breathed, in the hope that Woollie would conclude he had no need to wonder what Ian was thinking or planning. The trouble was that while Woollie kept hold of Charlotte, Ian was unable to plan and not much more able to think. For the moment he was reduced to listening, and as close as he had ever come to praying—wishing fervently that whatever happened next door would do him and Charlotte some good.

The noisy neighbours Woollie was deploring were Ian's mother and someone who had come to visit her—surely the police. Ian had heard the slam of a car door and a louder slam from his front door, which his mother must have opened before her visitor had had time to ring the bell. Then, so faint it had almost been destroyed by the throbbing of his pulse as he'd strained his ears, Ian had made out the sound, agonisingly close yet impossible to reach, of his mother's voice.

Almost at once it moved out of earshot, taking a male voice with it, presumably into the front room. There was silence except for Woollie's breaths, each of which caught in his throat with a sound like the start of a snore, so that Ian wondered if the man might be the first of them to fall asleep. He tried to send the thought across to Charlotte that both of them should keep still to lull Woollie to sleep, an attempt at telepathy that showed him how desperate he was. Woollie's breaths were growing slower and deeper, and Ian found himself counting them mentally in the yet more absurd hope that he might be exerting some kind of mute hypnosis over the man. He was in the thousands when he heard his mother's voice again—not her words, not even her tone. Her visitor said something Ian guessed was meant as reassurance, followed by an elongated silence that was brought to an end by the microscopic clang of Ian's gate and two slams, one of metal, one of wood. "And don't come back," Woollie muttered.

Ian tried to relax so as not to betray his panic at discovering the man was awake. Through his slitted eyelids he saw the blur of a head turn to him. "One of you's off, anyway," it said in its throat. "Time the other one was."

Ian couldn't tell which of them Woollie was addressing, nor which he took to be asleep. The gaping smile lowered itself toward him, and its smell found him, a reek like old raw meat. He did his best to close his nostrils and keep a shudder to himself, but his shoulders writhed. "Thought as much. Just playing, eh?" Woollie whispered into his face. "Stay shut up, son. She's gone at last."

Far too much time passed before he raised his head, grasping the quilt beside Ian and not letting go, and Ian had to take a breath while the smell of the mouth hovered over him. "You're a bit old to be sung to sleep," Woollie said, quieter than ever. "I should try and get some all the same."

Ian's body yearned to do so but felt as though it might never be able to rest again. "What'll you be doing?" he had to ask.

"Don't you fret about me. I'll be seeing you don't get any ideas."

Though sleep had to overpower him at some point—it struck

Ian as unlikely that he'd slept since he'd trapped Charlotte—keeping watch on two captives might render him more sleepless in the meantime, hence more dangerous. "But what are you going to do?" Ian whispered. "We can't stay here."

"Can we not, son? Who'll be chucking us out, you?"

"The people who live here. They're nearly back."

"Are they now? When are we expecting them?"

Ian almost said the next day, but then Woollie might decide to take Charlotte out at once, giving her no chance to rest and so making her more of an unpredictable threat to him. "The day after tomorrow," Ian said.

"Cut their holiday short, did they? Got too much sun?"

"Don't know what you mean. They were always coming back then."

"Well, there's a laugh. I'd have sworn the woman said they wouldn't be back for three weeks. What a joke, eh?" Woollie said, and emitted a satisfied grunt that perhaps was intended as mirth. "Any more tricks?" he enquired, aiming a raw breath at Ian's face.

"Don't suppose."

"Better be surer than that, son. Think of your playmate. You don't want her upset, do you?"

"No," Ian said, and nothing more until the head, whose presence felt like the slab in his mind, raised itself. He had to talk to Woollie—had to find a way of reaching him. "What are you going to do with her?" he dared to ask.

"I've done it. I've put her down."

"What about when she wakes up?"

"Let's hope that's none too soon. We can all do with a bit of peace."

"But when she does . . ."

"You've known her longer than me. You'd better come up with some games to take her mind off things."

"What things?" Ian almost demanded. Was Woollie determined to pretend there was nothing wrong or odd about his having captured Charlotte, or did he believe it? "Suppose I can't?" Ian said.

"Then nobody's going to be very happy, are they, son?"

The fist at the end of the arm that was pinning Ian down took a firmer grip on the quilt, and Ian guessed the other hand was doing so beside Charlotte, or was it grasping the knife? "How long do you think you can keep her?" he whispered.

"As long as it takes. Her and you both, mind. Don't leave yourself out."

As long as what took? Ian swallowed the question and a stale taste of panic, and thought of an approach that seemed worth trying—had to be. "Why don't you just keep me?"

"How's that again?"

"When she wakes up let her go and I'll stay, all right? It's her you're afraid will make a fuss. I won't, and she won't dare to say you're here when you've got me. Then I'll come with you and help you hide somewhere else she won't even know about. That's what you want, isn't it? That's what you'll have to do."

The lump of dimness leaned down to peer at him in the gloom that was all of the glow of the suburb the curtains admitted. The impression of a mouth widened and hitched up its corners before it spoke. "Good try, son, but you're not on."

"Why not?"

"I told you before about how loud to talk. We don't want her back with us yet, do we?"

"Okay," Ian said urgently in a voice that was little more than a breath with syllables in it, "but why not? I can make her promise not to tell."

"Oh, she'd do that for you. There's not much doubt of that, I reckon."

"She'd mean it. I'd make her. She would."

"Maybe so."

"And then you could get out of here before anyone finds you."

"We'll all be doing that, so you may as well get used to it."

"Why?" Ian pleaded. "Why all of us?"

"Because I don't care what you try and say, she wouldn't be able to keep her trap shut once she went. I've heard the kind of fuss she makes."

Ian saw the truth of that, but would have done his utmost to persuade Woollie otherwise if the man hadn't said "That's it now. Do her and you a favour and stay quiet like she is. I want a chance to think."

He snapped the last word so harshly it was clear he was close to some edge. His agitation might be capable of wakening Charlotte, and Ian saw it was best not to aggravate it—not to seem to be there at all. He closed his eyes and tried to do without all his senses except for hearing. It took some time for his awareness of the head looming above him to fade, but eventually his awareness of the arm that was pinning him down relented too: it was just a weight he mustn't disturb or think about. Listening for his mother was more important, although knowing she was nearby gave him strength only if he focused on that, otherwise it kept reminding him of his inability to reach her or to rescue Charlotte. The trouble was that he couldn't hear his mother for the pounding of his blood—hadn't heard her since the visitor had left, and might have thought she'd left the house if the sound of the gate hadn't preceded that of the front door. Any noises she was making must be inaudible through the wall, which suggested that for her to over-hear anything from Janet's house, it would need to be louder than Woollie imagined, but Ian didn't know if that was reassuring or the opposite. Was she downstairs or had she gone up to her room? She couldn't have guessed why he'd left the keys on display in the drawer, but suppose she belatedly understood? The prospect of her entering the house to check if Ian was there no longer seemed desirable, given how near Charlotte was to the knife. He found himself willing nothing to happen until daylight, when Charlotte would at least have slept and he would be able to plan or see a chance. Then, in the darkness that was far short of dawn, he heard her whimper, and her side of the mattress creaked.

She was only dreaming, Ian thought so fiercely his head throbbed. The dream must go away before it wakened her, so that there was no need for Woollie's hands to drag at the quilt, scraping it over the mattress. But she whimpered again, and as Ian's eyes sneaked open he glimpsed the blurred head ducking toward her. "What's the squeaking for?" Woollie said with a heartiness all the more menacing for being restrained to a murmur. "Think you're a mouse?"

"Want to go."

Charlotte sounded by no means fully awake or in control of her voice, and Ian was suddenly very afraid for her. "We're going nowhere till I've thought," Woollie muttered, "so stop making a row about it."

"I've got to. I need to."

At least her words were growing clearer, and Ian had to hope her sense of the situation was. "Plumbing problem, is it?" Woollie said. "Then we'll have to come with you. You're still awake, aren't you, son? Stop pretending."

Had he known all the time or was he trying to convince Ian he had? Ian thought of attempting to persuade him he'd been wrong and still was, but that wouldn't help Charlotte. "Now I'm awake," he mumbled.

"He's a laugh, isn't he?" Woollie said, hitching himself down the bed, his knuckles bumping along Ian's side and presumably along Charlotte's. The movements of his indistinct bulk grew less jerky as it left the bed and moved to the doorway, where its face was no more discernible in a faint glow. "Come on if you're desperate," it said. "You know the drill. Walk quiet and don't touch anything. This way, straight across the bed. Make yourself useful, son, and get her hand."

Ian found one of Charlotte's hands. It was limp with disuse and clammy as fever, but responded by clutching his so gratefully he felt like an older brother. He helped her off the bed and escorted her toward the doorway, and was almost close enough to touch the hulking silhouette when it retreated. In the glow that the glass above the front door admitted to the hall, features appeared to float up from the murk within the outline of Woollie's face: a glint of watchful eyes, a glistening crescent of mouth. "You know what you have to do if you want to go, don't you?" the mouth muttered.

Charlotte took a firmer hold of Ian's hand. Perhaps that was intended to signify assent as well as distress, because she was silent until the mouth insisted "Say it then, love. Let's be sure."

"Leave the door open and don't pull the chain," Charlotte said, barely audibly.

"That's the routine. We want to see you aren't tempted to get up to any kind of mischief in there, don't we? And we can't have you making a noise for the neighbours to hear." The silhouette moved to block the stairs, resting one hand on the top of the banister, the other on the pocket containing the knife. "Tiptoe in, then. Get it done," the mouth urged.

If Ian shoved their captor hard and unexpectedly, might he lose his balance? Falling had to injure him—but that would leave him in the way, either on the stairs or at the foot of them, and probably not unconscious. Ian let go of Charlotte and was trying to know what to do by the time she opened the bathroom door when the mouth renewed its moist grin. "Go with her, son, so I can see you both."

"You dirty shit." Ian was so furious he could hardly force his voice out. "I'm not doing that," he said, and tensed himself to throw all his weight at their captor—even if they both fell downstairs, that would give Charlotte a chance to escape. Then her hand fumbled into his and squeezed it clumsily. "It's all right," she whispered. "I don't mind."

At that moment he admired her courage as much as he hated their captor. He couldn't exert any less control than she was having to use, and the sight of Woollie's fist clenching around the banister showed how useless an attempt to dislodge him would be. Ian had to bide his time, and so he allowed Charlotte to lead him to the bathroom.

The snout of the bath taps announced itself with a hollow drip as she pushed open the door. A crumpled shower curtain dangled inside the bath and glimmered in the mirror. A scent of soap and talcum powder tried to disguise another smell. Ian turned his back as Charlotte reached the unlidded toilet, and then he stood between her and the watchful silhouette. He didn't care what the man said, he wasn't giving him a view of Charlotte. He stared fiercely at the silhouette as if that might stop his own face growing hotter at the various sounds she made. Eventually the final trickle trailed away, but he didn't move his eyes until she touched his arm. "Are you going as well?" she murmured.

"Better do what she says, son."

He meant so that he wouldn't be disturbed again, Ian deduced. All at once Ian's bladder was urging him. As he ventured into the bathroom he cupped a hand over his mouth and nose, and tried to hold his breath until he'd finished jetting into the mercifully invisible pool urned by the porcelain. He didn't quite succeed, and had to press the hand to the lower half of his face while he zipped himself up before turning to find Charlotte with her back to him. The spectacle of her braving their captor so as to spare Ian embarrassment made him all the more determined to prevent her from being harmed. "I'm coming now, Charlotte," he told her.

"It's back to the woods for the babes."

Charlotte raised a hand as if she were at school, then shook it and her head. "Thirsty."

"That's a bit of a laugh, isn't it? You've just let it out and now you want to put more in."

"I'm thirsty. It hurts."

"Oh, for God's sake let her past if it'll keep her quiet, son."

"Not water. A proper drink."

She wasn't wailing as Ian would have feared—she sounded more in control of herself than he would have dared hope. Could she have figured out a way for them to escape? At least her insistence would take them downstairs, closer to freedom. "There's stuff in the fridge," he said.

"How would you know that, son? This isn't your house."

"More mine than yours," Ian had to struggle not to retort. "I got a drink when I came in," he lied. "There's some juice."

"What kind?" Charlotte said eagerly.

Though she was trying to be positive, her question seemed to have ruined everything until, surely in time for his silence not to have exposed his lie, he thought of an answer. "The kind you like."

Woollie didn't move. Only his eyes did, dark wet bulges whose gleam flickered toward Ian and then back to Charlotte. When Woollie leaned at her to scrutinise her face she didn't flinch. "It'll be a chance, I reckon," he said.

That sounded as if it might be supposed to lead to a joke, but Ian couldn't ask the question either he or Charlotte was obviously meant to ask. When she stayed mute too Woollie said in a tiny shrill voice "Chance for what?"

His eyes searched for an audience reaction, then his mouth drooped like a clown's. "A chance to stretch our legs," he said in his ordinary mutter. "You follow me, love, quiet as that mouse you were making a noise like before, quieter than that, and the big babe can be right behind you."

He hadn't let go of the banister. His fist slithered down the curve of it as he edged backward. His foot wavered in the air, feeling for the top step, and that was when Ian should have pushed him, but Charlotte was in the way. Then the silhouette jerked several inches lower, and again, and no more until Charlotte followed it onto the stairs with Ian at her heels. "This is a funny way for me to go, isn't it?" Woollie said. "Worth a grin at least. Save your laughs for when we're back upstairs."

His face was gathering more detail at each step, and Ian realised the same must be true of his and Charlotte's. The eyes within the silhouette were intent on their reactions, the mouth kept closing only to reopen in another expectant smirk. Woollie's hand slipped down the banister with a series of squeaks like the cries of a small terrified animal, and Ian heard the man's feet brush the carpet each time they groped for a foothold. Every one of the sounds made him wish he'd gone for Woollie at the top of the stairs. But the man was at the bottom now, retreating just enough to give his captives space to pass. "All the way along," he whispered, "and sit yourselves down for your midnight treat."

Charlotte sidled hastily past him and fled down the hall. She was out of his reach, and Ian was close enough to go for him. He tried to appear to be thinking of nothing whatsoever, which might have been why Woollie's hand darted to the knife and slid it out just far enough to produce a glint. "Keep up with your playmate," he murmured. "There's been enough fuss."

That couldn't stop Ian, not while Charlotte was out of danger, even if he got hurt himself. He was taking a breath that would help launch him at Woollie as he shouted at Charlotte to escape past them, when Woollie strode swiftly yet noiselessly after her. In a second he was patting her on the head while his other hand stroked the outline of the knife. "Come and join us, son. They're slow-coaches, these teenage boys, aren't they, Charlotte?"

He continued to pat her as far as the kitchen, a performance that dragged Ian's arms down stiffly at his sides and drew his hands into claws, their fingers aching, the nails tingling. Woollie reached past her and nudged the kitchen door wide, releasing the token glow of the room. He took hold of Charlotte's shoulders to place her on the low bench closer to the hall. "Sit the other side, son, and we'll see what you were talking about."

"We weren't talking," Charlotte blurted rather too loud.

Ian heard his heart thump several times before Woollie finished staring at her and said "What he was saying was in the fridge."

"She knew you meant that. She was just trying to make you laugh."

"I told you we don't want to be laughing down here."

"We promise," Ian said, and would have said anything necessary to prevent Woollie from deciding against opening the refrigerator. That would be Charlotte's solitary chance—she would have a clear run to the front door, and Ian would ensure she wasn't chased, whatever that took. He willed her not to speak except to promise too. When she didn't even do that, Woollie paced to the refrigerator as tall as himself and opened the upper door. "Surprise," he muttered.

"What is?" Charlotte pleaded.

"Your playmate hasn't let you down."

The light from the refrigerator spilled into the kitchen, turning her face pale. It couldn't be long before Woollie noticed that the light was rendering the three of them more visible than he wanted. Ian touched Charlotte's foot with his under the table and nodded at the hall. "Go. Go," he mouthed, and saw her shake her head.

"I'll fix him." He was grimacing now, and mouthing so violently he heard the movement of his lips. She had to shift at once or it would be too late. He jammed a fist against his chest and jerked its forefinger to point behind her. "Go. You've got to," he said, nearly audibly.

"What kind of a drink are you after, love?" Woollie said, and leaned into the refrigerator. "There's orange and there's lime."

If Ian jumped up he was almost certain that he could trap the man with the refrigerator door. "Charlotte," he said, desperately, aloud.

"You as well," she told him, and pinched her lips together.

She meant she wouldn't flee without him. He'd made her run away when he didn't want her to, and now he couldn't make her when he did. He was trying to think past the tangle of his admiration and frustration when Woollie swung toward her. "Let's be hearing from you, love. It's not much of a choice."

"Orange," she said, and with a politeness Ian found dismayingly grotesque, "please."

"That's what I'd have given you," Woollie said, and stood the carton with its gaping beak in front of her. "We don't want you crying the other stuff's too sour."

"Please may I have a glass?"

"Better do without. Could be dangerous." He shut the refrigerator and paced to stand between her and the hall. "Get it down you, only not so fast you start coughing. Remember we don't want a row."

He was staring a warning at Ian, who could only watch as Charlotte raised the carton to her lips and swallowed twice, and once more. She released a small terse gasp before planting the carton on the table with a thud. Though it wasn't loud, it was why Woollie's voice grew harsh. "Take your turn, son. Nobody wants you deciding you'd like a drink after we're back upstairs."

Ian took hold of the frigid carton. A glass would have been a weapon, but so was the juice—it could sting Woollie's eyes, it might even blind him long enough for both his captives to escape. As if sensing Ian's thought, Woollie stepped close behind Charlotte and began to run his fingertips up and down the outline of the knife. "Knock it back, son. Can't be much for you to finish."

There was little more than a mouthful, but Ian took less than that while he strained to think. If he opened the refrigerator and left it open, might Woollie head for it? He was halfway to standing up when Woollie said "What do you reckon he's thinking of doing, Charlotte?"

"Putting this away," Ian told him.

"Nothing to put, we both know that. There's been too much light around here as it is. Chuck it in the bin."

The bin was full of glass. Ian didn't know how he would use it, he didn't want to think about it yet—he had to ensure Woollie neither saw nor heard him conceal a piece in his fist. He moved in front of the bin and was resting his toe on the pedal—holding his breath as if to show the contents of the bin how silent they must be—when Woollie said in a voice like a protracted mirthless laugh "Just stick it on top of the lid, son. Bin's full, and we don't want anybody getting hurt on all that glass."

Ian let the lid drop, jarring a muffled tinkle out of the bin. He dumped the carton on the lid and turned on Woollie with no kind of plan, only rage that felt as though it might somehow be enough. The man was already in the hall, and leading Charlotte backward with one hand on her shoulder, the other tracing the shape of the knife. "Get a move on, son," he murmured. "Your playmate doesn't like you being all that way away."

The sight of Charlotte being led into the dimness that closed around her face and wiped it out returned the slab to Ian's mind. Woollie held onto her as he retreated beyond the stairs. "You go first, son. Back to the woods."

If there was anything Ian could do except obey, his mind was unable to grasp it. He felt chances falling out of reach behind him— the front door, the telephone, the weapons he'd failed to use—as he trudged upstairs. He sensed rather than heard Charlotte start after him: all he could hear was Woollie's mutter that sounded as though he were thinking aloud. "You won't be here much longer. Thanks for helping me see that, son."

FORTY-TWO

Ian:

> I've gone to work. PLEASE RING to let me know you're back.

Leslie stared at that and saw it was no good. What was it supposed to be expressing? Impatience, anger, self-righteousness? Certainly none of the feelings she wanted him to know she had—none of the love that, however much he worried her, made her want him back. She had plenty of time to write before she had to go out; the dawn was only starting to renew the colours of the roofs beyond Jericho Close. Soon the streetlamps would acknowledge that one more night was dealt with, and the street would brighten like a stage awaiting an entrance—a stage as empty as the street was now. She took a harsh gulp of coffee in case that reduced her need for the most of a night's worth of sleep she'd missed, and retrieved the message pad from the low table in front of the sofa. She crumpled the top sheet and stared at the blank page, and thought of putting on some music to help her think or rather find words for her state. It was too early, even though there was nobody next door to be disturbed, and besides, it would seem too much like taking advantage of Ian's absence to listen without having her pleasure impaired by her sense of his dislike of the music. She gave the deserted street another imploring glance and crouched over the pad.

Dear Ian,

 Please read all of this.

 I'm sorry for letting you think I could say what you thought I did. I never would have, but maybe I almost considered it, and I know that's bad enough. Try and understand it wasn't because I was suspicious of you—it was me being so anxious to know what's happened to Charlotte I couldn't think. She's still gone. I know you care about her however much of a pain she can be, so do you blame me for trying every way I could to figure out what's happened to her? Maybe you have too—maybe you've been looking for her, that's what I hope. When I asked you if there was anything you hadn't mentioned I ought to have said anything you might have forgotten that could help the police.

The police had questioned her last night, less than an hour after she'd called them. They'd been represented by one stout red-faced avuncular constable with hair only below the rim of his monochrome helmet. Perhaps his age and slowness were supposed to be reassuring, but she'd wondered how skilled he could be at his job not to have risen to a higher rank. He'd asked her questions she had already asked herself—whom Ian could spend the night with, whether he had friends she wasn't aware of, as though the raising of that possibility would somehow furnish her with their names— and one she hadn't entertained: whether he might have taken refuge with her parents. The policeman had needed almost more convincing than she had energy for that Ian never would have—that if, incredibly, he had, her mother would have let her know at once. Perhaps the constable had allowed himself to be persuaded there was no point in troubling Leslie's parents only once he'd grasped how reluctant she was to phone them. He'd borrowed last year's school photograph of Ian and promised to circulate a description, and had taken some time to assure her that in his experience most children who ran away from home after an argument showed up shamefaced or defensive or determined to swagger the next day. That meant there were some who didn't, Leslie had reflected as she'd watched him drive away, and that was the start of the rest of the night—of Ian's night somewhere.

 Now it was over, and soon, if not sooner, it would be time for him to come back. Maybe the thought of breakfast would tempt him. If it did, he'd better be quick—she hoped he wasn't assuming she would stay home for him. She'd had a shower and was dressed, and once she'd finished writing to him she would head for work. She aimed her ballpoint at her last words, and enlarged the bulb of the p of "help" to engulf the full stop, and coaxed the t of "the" not to be a capital, and leaned on a dot after "police." Doing all that helped her think of more to write.

But I care about you more than I care about her, just in case you were wondering. If you've stayed away to make me see that, you didn't need to. Just so long as you've come back, and obviously you have since you're reading this, that's all I care about. Better be ready for me to raise my voice a bit when I see you, though. PLEASE STAY, THAT'S ALL. Don't go away again. Phone me at the shop to let me know you're there, then I can tell your father we know where you are so he can stop worrying about you when he's already got someone to worry about. You've made your point, all right? If you love us, and I know you do, you'll put us out of our misery.
Lots of love, you know how much if you let yourself,
Mum

She considered adding kisses, but her message might embarrass him more than enough without them. When she read it through she found it almost too much herself. She could rewrite it if she was quick, she thought, and then she clicked the nib into the pen and stood up. She'd written what she felt. She pinned the three small square pages down with the phone on the hall table and made for the kitchen to wash her coffee mug. When she became aware of gazing through the window above the sink in search of anything she could watch to keep her at home at least a few moments longer, she took herself out of the house.

Car alarms were greeting their owners as the houses sent forth a selection of the people weekday mornings sent forth. In the park, beneath an increasingly translucent blue sky, boys of about Ian's age were demonstrating ways they behaved: smoking, arguing, walking with girls and perhaps even holding their hands, laughing as loud as they could. They made her want to hurry home to see if Ian was back. Once she was on the train, trapped on a seat by more and more people who also had to go to work whatever else might be happening in their lives, she wanted to be already at the shop, to be close to the phone if it rang—when it did.

Under Oxford Circus a violinist was performing a jaunty piece by Saint-Saëns, which might have cheered her if it hadn't been so distant it sounded deep in the earth. It sank away, and before she stepped off the highest escalator she couldn't hear it. She let herself be crowded up into the sunlight, where she felt as though she were leading half the crowd to the shop, outside which she halted and sucked in a breath that was bitter with a stench of petrol. Melinda was replacing the phone on the counter, and whatever she'd just heard had left her close to tears.

Leslie managed not to speak until she'd shut the door behind her. "What is it? Is it Ian?" she heard herself demanding, and perhaps worse still "Is it about him?"

"Why should it be?"

That was too harsh to be anything but a denial. "I'm sorry," Leslie said, rediscovering some gentleness. "What, then?"

"Sally's leaving me. I think there's someone else."

"Oh, Melinda. You too? Us and our partners." Leslie gave her an awkward hug that came near to squeezing out Melinda's tears, and dared to say "I'd move in with you to help you get over her if I was at all that way inclined."

"You stay how you are. I don't want to be one of the people who tried to screw up your life. I'd rather have you straight as you are. Take that how you like." Melinda raised a smile that left her eyes moist, and blinked. "Why were you looking like that about Ian? What's he been up to now?"

"Stayed out overnight because I made him feel I thought he might have done something to Charlotte."

"Anyone would have wondered that if they were you. It's the kind of thing we think even if we don't want to," Melinda said, and renewed her brave smile. "I shouldn't have bothered you with my love life when you've got your own worries."

"Don't fart at the mouth, Mel. I know we'll be hearing from him any time now. I left a note saying he had to call."

"I'm sure you'll see him before I see Sally," Melinda said, which dislodged two large slow tears. Leslie gave her another hug and had to dab at her own eyes, and then she and Melinda stared at passersby to make them stop spectating. Leslie's tears were mostly at the realisation that secretly she hoped Melinda had spoken the truth. There would be plenty of time for the women to share a real weep once they knew Ian was safe.

FORTY-THREE

"This is Haven Home. Hello? Haven Home here. It's the Haven Home."

"Say, boy, who's this I'm talking to?"

"It's Terence."

"You the head honcho there, Teerence? You in charge?"

"I just live here. It's Mrs. Woollie's, but she never comes till ten. Mark's in charge till she comes. He's looking at something in the kitchen. Shall I get him?"

"Tell you who you get for me, Teerence. You know John?"

"Which John?"

"Hey, you said a mouthful. He ain't called John no more, right? Rub that out. The guy I need is calling himself Jack."

"Mr. Woollie?"

"What's that, boy? What the—what you saying?"

"You mean Mr. Woollie? That Jack. Mrs. Woollie's son."

"That's the guy, sure enough. Hold a moment. Hush now, little lady. Save it, okay?"

Hector accompanied the latter part of this with a smile wide enough to expose his gums and a stare that peeled the skin back from his eyes, but Charlotte carried on emitting sounds not far short of mirth at the voice he was having to use. Any other time he would be happy to make her laugh; why had she withheld it until she might be overheard? Didn't she understand how she was endangering herself, or did she expect to be saved if she revealed she was there? She was sitting on the fourth stair up, more than close enough for him to grab, but he didn't want any upset when he had another way of solving the problem of her, or at least of postponing the solution. He let the fingertips of the hand that wasn't holding the knife outline the knife for her playmate, who was sitting as he'd been told to sit with his legs on either side of her, to see. "Quieten her down, son," Hector whispered, pressing the mouthpiece against his heart. "You know there's nothing to laugh at right now."

Ian learned forward and clasped the girl's shoulders. "No point in pissing him off," he murmured.

Her face convulsed at the bad word, and then appeared to begin to relax. Either he'd impressed her by wording it like that or the message conveyed more to her than it had to Hector. For the moment Hector couldn't ponder that, not when he'd come near to betraying himself on thinking Terence had identified him. He stared at Charlotte until her mouth sank inward, and then he raised the phone. "You still there, Teerence?"

"I've been here all the time. What was I hearing?"

He'd overheard Charlotte's stutters of hilarity or Ian's voice, Hector thought, glaring at his charges. "I dunno, boy. What you reckon you heard?"

"Some machine going bumper bumper bump."

"Must have been in your own head. I guess you need to see the doc to check you ain't got too much blood pressure."

"Is that what it was? Thanks. I will."

Terence was as suggestible as ever, Hector saw. He might have enjoyed amusing himself at Terence's expense, but Charlotte looked in danger of another fit of mirth. "So you got Jack Woollie there?" he said.

"He doesn't live here."

"Guess I never said he did. Hangs out there, though, ain't that the truth?"

"Sometimes."

"Like right now, boy?"

"Not yet. I expect he's still at Mrs. Woollie's, being a writer and not having to get up."

"When you looking to see him?"

"Not today. He said he was going to try and do a bit of a book."

"Gonna stay at his momma's, is he? Why don't you give me her number."

"It's up here on the board."

It sounded as if Terence assumed that was all he needed to say, and Hector felt his limbs growing stiff with frustration, not least because Charlotte was clutching her mouth with a hand that looked less than capable of restraining whatever it was doing its best to hold in. He was reminding himself not to raise his voice by the time Terence read him the number. He was in the midst of scribbling it on the pad with the pencil when Terence said "Who do you want me to say you were if he comes?"

"Hold everything while I get this written down. Matter of fact, why don't you tell me again to make sure." While Terence repeated the number Hector finished transcribing it and thought of a name for himself. "Tell him Mr. Dadd was asking for him."

"Dadd."

"That's the tag, sure enough. Hush her up now, boy. Give her a hand if hers ain't enough."

"I didn't catch that."

"Be glad you didn't, Teerence. Just tell Jack Woollie Mr. Dadd that he's been speaking to is gonna be in touch. Tell him it's a proposition we gotta keep between ourselves."

"Is it about his book?"

"Mebbe so. Hey, Teerence, didn't I just get through saying it's between me and him? Tell you what, you give him the message if you see him and we won't stop you thinking you helped with the book. Mebbe you'll see your name in print if you do like I say."

"I've been in the paper," Terence said, with some pride but also a hint of unease that showed Hector it was time to end the conversation. He put an end to Terence without moving his gaze from the pair on the stairs. Ian hadn't helped Charlotte cover up her mouth, but if Jack should hear her, surely that would impress on him the importance of obeying his father. Hector dialled the digits that masked his number and then rang the one Terence had given him. "That ole magic coach is gonna be here 'fore you know it to carry you away," he told Charlotte in the voice he seemed unable for the moment to abandon. He stared at her to warn her not to laugh so loudly she would be audible outside the house, but she took her hands away from her mouth without releasing a sound. Perhaps his words had silenced her. Only the ringing of Adele's phone was to be heard: no voice, neither the one he wanted nor the one he was glad not to hear.

"Guess that ole coachman jest stepped out. Guess mebbe he's watering them hosses." He saw Charlotte's face writhe, trying to fix on the reaction she thought he wanted, and above it the boy gazing so blankly at him that Hector came close to fearing he'd lost the power to make anyone laugh. The boy was attempting to undermine his confidence, that was all.

Everything had been going right for Hector until the children had turned up. He'd been watching for John from the alley behind the houses when he'd heard the woman calling from her window that she and her husband would be away for weeks. Hector's keys had still fitted the locks at Woollie's yard, and better yet, he'd found a pane of glass already cut to the size the woman's kitchen door took, standard as it was. He'd had to hide just twice from nocturnal strollers on his way with the pane from the yard to the house, but it seemed he'd hardly secured his refuge when he'd heard Charlotte crying out for peace.

He leaned against the wall beside the phone, wishing he'd thought to bring a chair while it had been dark enough for him to risk fetching it. He would have if the boy's presence hadn't given him too much to be aware of. He stared at the children until the boy's expressionlessness spread to the girl's face, and then he picked up the receiver and poked the redial key. The bell was waiting all by itself.

He let it ring until a robot woman cut it off and told him to try later. She was there next time he rang too. He was giving John a chance to return from wherever he'd gone and get rid of her when he saw Charlotte's mouth begin to work. "You itching to whisper something to me, babe?" he said.

Her mouth wavered open, and the tip of her tongue risked venturing around it as though seeking the shape of a word. Perhaps it was remembering a taste, because she admitted "I'm hungry."

"No remedy for that right now, babe. Gonna have to wait just like the rest of us."

"There's stuff in the fridge," Ian said, not nearly quietly enough.

"You already told me that once, boy. Guess you better make sure I hear less of you. I saw in there, babe, and it ain't much. Anyway, you should have asked when we were there."

"But I'm hungry *now*."

"Can't do anything about that now it's light. Reckon you'll survive. I've gone longer without rations, and look at me," Hector told her, cocking his head and giving her a wide-eyed smile. Despite his efforts she seemed determined not to cheer up—he thought the boy wasn't letting her—and so he said "Wait till the coach comes to take you out of the woods. You won't be hungry once you get where you're going."

In fact he had no idea where he would have John take them— time enough to decide that once he made sure John would come when he was called. He watched Charlotte's face sink into a resignation unsteadier than he would have preferred, and then he redialled. The bell . . . the robot woman. He slammed the receiver down and saw Charlotte think better of pleading. Maybe it was the toilet this time, but could she really want to go again or was the boy causing her to think she did? She'd become far more trouble since the boy had intruded—Hector had been on the very edge of singing her to sleep when the boy had disturbed her, and because of the boy he'd had no sleep himself. Could the boy have devised a means of communicating silently with her? Was that why she was threatening to grow restless? Maybe his legs were exerting pressure on her sides, conveying a coded message to her or just ensuring she didn't nod off. Hector took hold of the receiver and jabbed the button, pretending to be intent on the phone while he watched for the slightest secret movement of the boy's legs. The intolerably familiar bell rang twice, twice more, and Hector's prickly eyes had just glimpsed a minute shifting of the boy's left leg when John's voice said "Hello?"

"John Woollie."

"Excuse me, who is this?"

Hector had failed to relinquish his American accent, to his own amusement now. "You mean you or me, boy? Who you figure you're talking to?"

"That's what I asked."

"Try Mr. Dadd. Know me now?"

"Mr. . . ."

"Your dad," Hector would have said through his teeth if he'd had any, his lack of all the sleep Charlotte's playmate had stolen from him leaving him very little patience. "What's wrong, boy? Forget I was alive?"

"I was wondering where you'd got to. Are you going to want to speak to my mother?"

"No way. You and me, that's the whole team."

"Are you saying you don't want her to know about you?"

"She ain't gonna be no help to us. Got her hands full with folks that are mad enough to need her."

"Then you'd better give me your number. She could be back any minute and I'll have to ring off."

"Cute, boy. Very cute. Don't try to be no cuter," Hector said, glaring at the children. "If you have to cut me off you wait there till I call back."

"Suppose she answers?"

"Then she ain't got no reason to think she's stopped being a widow, right? Nobody knows except you, ain't that the truth?"

"Sure."

The word was heavy with resignation, and at once Hector knew why. "You been trying to tell folks about me, ain't you, boy."

"After you said I hadn't to?"

"Guess you figured you didn't have to do what your dad says since you left home and tried to kid everyone you weren't my son. Only you found out nobody believed you, right? Nobody believes I ain't dead, and I reckon if you tried to tell anyone they thought it was one of your stories. Thought you'd run out of bogeymen to make up."

"You're your own invention, sure enough."

"Didn't I just say not to be cute?" Hector found himself as unable to stop glaring at the children as he was to abandon the accent, but they deserved to feel he was warning them—the boy especially did. "Best keep me to yourself from now on in," Hector said. "You've a good reason, better believe it."

John wasn't so quick with an answer this time. After quite a pause he said "What's that?"

"You'll see when you get here."

"You want me to come to you."

"Sounded like I said that to me."

"Sure I will. Just tell me where."

"Not right now, boy. Not till I need you to pick me up and a couple of babes."

"Babes," John said, and even more incredulously "Women, you mean."

"Ain't none of them things here, no. Not that kind of babe."

John was silent long enough for his voice to fill with dread. "What in Christ do you mean, then?"

"Hey, boy, no need for that talk. Never raised you to make free with the Lord's name. Mebbe writing them books of yours got you too fond of the devil. I'll let you hear what kind of babe," Hector said, and pointed at Charlotte. "Seeing as how you're itching to talk, say a word for John. Just one word."

Her teeth squashed her lips together, and he thought she was so confused she would only cry, which would do fine as long as she stopped when she was told. This time there was no doubt, however, that he saw the boy send her a message, pressing his legs against her sides as if to squeeze out the word she released. "We—"

"That's perfect. Hush now," Hector said, covering the mouthpiece and scowling at the boy to ensure he helped to quieten her. Only when she pinched her mouth shut with a finger and thumb did he speak into the receiver. "Hear that, did you, boy? Hear the little pig going wee? She'd like to go wee, wee, wee all the way home."

"I don't know if I heard anyone. Let me again."

"Not so cute as you think you are. You heard sure enough. Don't want her upset, do you? You know how that upsets me."

"Don't harm her. Give me your word you won't and I'll do whatever you ask."

"Just remind me, boy. You ever give me your word when you were younger you wouldn't leave me and your momma?"

"I never said that. I know I never did."

Hector didn't think he had, but was simply guaranteeing that John would be desperate to please him, a prospect so appealing it bared his gums. "How you gonna make me believe that?" he said.

"Any way I can. By doing what you want. How couldn't I? Who is she?"

"Nobody that means anything to you, boy."

"She does. That's why you've got my word."

"You sure you ain't trying to be cute again?"

"Christ no. Sorry, but I mean, how can you think that? Do I sound as if I am?"

Hector had to trust him: there was nobody else. "Mebbe not. You got a coach there, right?"

"A what?"

"A coach. A car." Sleeplessness, aggravated by his difficulty in choosing his words or his voice, was crawling beneath Hector's scalp. "You got one of those to bring."

"As soon as you like. You said you want to take her home."

"You hear me say that, boy? Better listen closer. Wouldn't want you getting your instructions wrong. That wouldn't do her no good at all."

"I'm listening, but wait. You said a couple, not just one. Who—"

"You'll see soon enough. Keep that on your mind while you're waiting for me to call. You got no reason to go out till I do, that a fact? Somebody's hoping you ain't."

"I'll wait here for you, that's a promise, but how long—"

"You'll find out when it happens, and where to come too. Just be ready. When I want you I'll want you fast."

"You've got me. Only I could use some idea how far—"

Hector burst out laughing. Not only could he hear John attempting yet another ruse, he could see Charlotte's playmate opening his mouth. "Jack," the boy called, his voice so high it must have embarrassed him, as Hector slammed the receiver down and Charlotte shrank into the refuge of the boy's legs. "Don't bother trying, son," Hector whispered, his false accent deserting him at last. "He'll know where we are when I want him to know."

"Where's he going to take us?"

"Where he's told."

"Where?"

"That's enough row, son. You're upsetting your playmate."

"No he isn't," Charlotte said.

It was the boy's fault, Hector thought in a rage that made his scalp feel as raw as his gums. The boy was encouraging her to rebel. When Hector took a step toward him the boy crouched protectively over her, more like the babes in the wood than Hector welcomed. "You don't know, do you?" Charlotte said.

"I know everything worth knowing, love. Grown-ups do."

"You don't know where you want him to take us."

She wasn't far from laughing at him. She wouldn't laugh or even smile when he wanted her to, only when it would confuse him. Didn't she and her accomplice realise they were simply enraging him? "You'll find out I do when John does," Hector muttered, and wiped his chin with the hand that wasn't reminding him of the knife. "Go on now. Back up to the woods to wait for the coach."

Her face dared to turn pitying. "There aren't any woods and there isn't a coach."

"A car, then. Settle down. Better get used to waiting till I say it's time. Let her up, son. She knows where to go."

Neither child moved. Hector planted a foot on the bottom stair with more of a thud than made sense, another indication of how they were blurring his concentration. He was clutching the knife in his pocket when Charlotte blurted "I will if you promise he'll take me home like you said."

John had accused him of saying that too. For a moment Hector thought the children were somehow managing to conspire with his son, and then he grasped that the girl's assumption should help him quieten her. "I'll do what you heard me say."

"And you have to let Ian go too."

"Don't worry, I'll have no use for him once you're gone."

She rested her hands on Ian's knees and rose unsteadily, and was sidling past him when she halted and peered over her shoulder at Hector. "You haven't promised."

"Thought you said you heard me. All right, don't start creating. I promise."

"You have to say what."

Beside her the boy was staring as if he had the right to judge someone of Hector's age, and Hector had to restrain himself: it was best to keep them as calm as he could while he thought how to deal with them. "I promise you'll be going home," he muttered.

"Why can't we now?"

"Not till I'm going somewhere too."

That appeared to satisfy her. She turned and had climbed three stairs not too intolerably slowly when the boy, who'd remained seated, said "Where?"

"Never you mind. You've got what you wanted. You've got my promise."

The boy gripped the stair he was sitting on, rendering himself more of a barrier between Hector and the girl. His face was dull with stubbornness and incredulity, though Hector wasn't sure what he disbelieved—the promise or that Hector had a plan. Hector saw him opening his mouth to make even more of a nuisance of himself, and interrupted before the boy could speak. "Let's have a bit of quiet now. Your playmate wants you to follow her so she can have a rest."

It was clear that not much would be needed to bring her down the stairs, encouraged by the boy's refusal to move. The sense that the situation was turning against him flared like a short circuit under Hector's scalp, and he snatched the knife out of the pocket of the beach dress he was hardly conscious of wearing. The boy's face hardened, doing its best to pretend not to care, but the girl's rebelliousness collapsed at once. "Don't hurt him," she wailed. "I'm going up, look. Come on, Ian, you come too." With that she bolted, almost tripping over the top stair, and vanished into the back bedroom.

The boy grimaced after her as though she'd failed to carry out a plan they'd concocted together. He stared at the knife in an attempt to appear unimpressed before he retreated upstairs, Hector close behind him, sliding the flat of the blade over the banister. "Look what you've done now," Hector whispered. "Upset your playmate for no reason. Better find a way to take her mind off things." Once that was achieved he would be able to determine how to bring John without revealing their whereabouts. Just now he was unsure of far too much. Having given a promise he had no intention of keeping, how could he know John would keep his? Doubts swarmed beneath his scalp, and he needed peace so as to think—needed the boy to calm his playmate down and cease being any kind of a distraction himself. That struck Hector as increasingly unlikely, but if he wasn't able to think because of the children and his own sleeplessness, he didn't like to imagine what he might do instead.

FORTY-FOUR

Each time Jack compelled himself to wait he became convinced all over again that there was more he could do. He'd heard a child's voice, for Christ's sake. His father had a child with him. She hadn't sounded frightened or aware of any danger, as far as Jack had been able to tell before his father had blocked the mouthpiece, but what could he allow that to prove? His father had seemed to imply that she wasn't alone with him, but Jack didn't see how that could be reassuring either. Call the police, his mind urged yet again, do it now. That was what people did in situations such as this—call the police.

Except that he was more convinced than ever they wouldn't believe his father was alive, and even if Jack succeeded in persuading them, what then? He had no idea where his father was, and any search might send the man deeper into hiding—might mean he wouldn't contact Jack. While Jack was trying to win over the police, suppose his father attempted to get through and realised why the line was busy? Any approach Jack made to the police might very well put the child or children at greater risk.

His thoughts did their best to settle on that before renewing their chase around the hollow brittle inside of his head. They sent him roaming the apartment, the very little of it there was to roam. In the perfumed pink bathroom with its frilly toilet seat and a joke on a wall plaque waiting to be re-encountered by anyone who sat down, he flung cold water in his eyes and let it drip into the sink the colour of healing flesh. In the kitchen overlooking a schoolyard for the moment empty of children, a coffee jar turned out to contain only a coating of brown dust, and he had to make do with tea out of a bag. He tried switching on the radio to help him wait, and found it was tuned to a wartime comedy show, the laughter of voices that might well be dead by now, laughter determined to fend off the state of the world. Even news seemed preferable, but tuning across the dial found none, and so he took his untouched mug of tea into the only other room besides his mother's bedroom, the large space that functioned as a dining room and television lounge and, when the sofa was unfolded, his temporary bedroom. The tea grew cold and stagnant as he sat on the sofa by the phone and fished for cable channels with the remote control, which brought him a good deal of dismaying news but none about a missing little girl. The lack wasn't reassuring: it simply reminded him how he'd failed to do even the least he could have. He ought to have made his father promise not to harm the child.

It wouldn't make any sense for him to hurt her, not when he wanted Jack to side with him, but that was assuming his father made sense. As soon as he called again Jack was going to extract the promise, and he'd insist on hearing the little girl speak. Those resolutions involved waiting, and pacing through the apartment that felt as though it shrank with each wander he took, and having his thoughts repeat themselves over and over and drag him through all the emotions attached to them, and worse still, hearing the children in the schoolyard at lunchtime. Their cries and laughter drove him back into the main room, but even with all the doors and windows shut tight they were audible. He was staring at the phone, willing it to ring or himself either to act or to resist acting, when he wondered how his father had known where to reach him.

Perhaps he hadn't known: perhaps he had only guessed, but he'd seemed not at all surprised to hear Jack answer the phone—he'd sounded absolutely sure of finding him. Did he still know Jack well enough to realise he would have to take refuge with his mother? The notion that his father could predict his behaviour made Jack feel not just too close to his own childhood but in danger of being controlled, reached deeper into than he himself could reach and influenced. His father must have looked up the number of the woman who believed she was his widow, and Jack found himself consulting the directory as if confirming his suspicion could be any possible use. Wi, Wo, Woo, and here was a block of Wool-lies. The name dragged him down into his old buried self, but only until he saw his mother's number was unlisted.

It had to be too new. Just to check, and willing his father not to call while he did, Jack phoned Directory Enquiries. But the operator refused to give the number even when Jack assured her he was calling from it, and he had to restrain himself from starting an argument while his thoughts began to chatter. Had his mother lied to him when he'd attempted to convince her that his father was alive? Had she known then, or only when his father had managed to learn Jack's whereabouts from her? What could have persuaded her to tell? Far more important, might she have some idea where his father was?

Jack forced himself to wait some minutes in case his father had decided on whatever basis he might have that it was time to call, and then he dialled the Haven, hoping to speak only to his mother. It was indeed her breathless voice that eventually said "Haven Care Home."

"It's me. It's Jack."

"Is it very urgent? Only I'm in the middle of trying to be tactful about telling people not to just wander into the office when there aren't staff in it."

"It's pretty urgent, yes."

"Tell me then, but quickly if you can."

It wasn't only his sense of interrupting her work that made it impossible for Jack to accuse her of having lied to him. "Did you let someone know where to find me?" he said.

"Who, John?"

"Anyone."

"I wouldn't, not without asking you first, not unless you said I could. All right?"

"Not even someone we know?"

"Particularly not anyone like that, I should think. They'd know who you were, and I thought you didn't want people knowing till you said."

"But who knows where I am besides you?"

"Some of them here do, don't they?"

His thoughts had been so narrowed he'd forgotten that. He'd heard nothing other than honesty in her voice, and had to accept she hadn't spoken to his father. "Would any of them have given out your number, do you think?" he said.

"They might have, the way some of them are in and out of this office. Do you want me to ask?"

Jack wasn't sure what use he could make of the information, but said "If you wouldn't mind."

"Hold on then."

"Why don't I—"

Before he could propose to call her back, the phone clattered on her desk. She was gone for so long that he was about to break the connection when he heard the squeak of the office door and, after more of a pause than struck him as warranted, her voice. "Nobody who's here knows anything about a call for you, but Terence and the Arthurs have gone out for a walk. If it was any of them I'll get him to ring you."

"Any idea when?"

"Late this afternoon. Should be before I start back."

There was another problem to join the chase inside Jack's head: that his father mightn't call until his mother was home. Even more than previously, he could find nothing to do except prowl the apartment and keep returning to the news channels, none of which had any news for him, and repeat thoughts that felt like being unable to think, and wait for the phone to ring. He had to listen to the children in the schoolyard twice, during their afternoon break and at the end of the day, before it did.

"Hello?"

"Hey there, Mr. Woollie."

Someone was trying to sound American. All that Jack could risk in the way of an answer was "Yes?"

"How ya doin'? What's goin' on?"

"I'm not sure. What is?"

"You sayin' you don't know who you's a-talkin' to?"

"Put me out of my misery," Jack said through what felt like a grin only in terms of the shape of his mouth.

"It's Terence, Mr. Woollie. Terence from the Haven, the Haven Home. Terence that you were talking to the other day."

"I got you, Terence. Why were you speaking like that?"

"Like what? I can't remember how I did."

"Just now, I mean. Were you trying to sound like someone?"

"Lak theeyuss, you sayin'? That was just meant for a laugh."

"You weren't imitating anyone."

"Sorry, Mr. Woollie."

Jack was beginning to feel the conversation would never get started, never mind come to an end. "Sorry, for what? Sorry for what?"

"I wouldn't imitate you ever. Sorry if you thought I was. I was only trying to be like the man who was going to help you with your book."

"Which man?"

"What was his name? A funny name, it was. Made me laugh. What was it?" Terence said, not far short of demanding the answer of Jack, and then preceded it with a giggle. "Mr. Dadd."

Jack felt his mouth wrench itself out of shape. "What's funny about that?"

"Sorry, is he a mate of yours? He must be if he's helping you, mustn't he. Sorry." Terence sounded close to retreating inside himself to avoid giving any further offence, but dared to add "It was a bit funny how he talked."

"How was that?"

"More American than you, even more than, but you're not a real one." Some or all of that seemed meant as an apology, though not one Jack grasped. "Did he catch you, then? Did he track you down all right?" Terence said, and allowed himself another giggle. "I thought he thought you were one of us."

"How come?" Jack said, harshly enough for his breath to rebound from the mouthpiece.

"He must have thought you were working here really. He took a lot of telling you weren't here."

"You're saying he expected me to be."

"I thought he thought I was trying to hide you at first, only why would you want to hide from him? How's he going to help you with your book?"

"Is that what he said he wanted?"

"I thought he did." Terence's enthusiasm slumped while he said that, then roused itself. "Does he make films? Is there going to be one of your book?"

"Right now I don't know what there's going to be." That was all their conversation seemed to have told Jack, and it might be getting in the way of a call his father was trying to make. "Thanks for phoning, Terence," he said, "I have to go now," and kept his hand on the receiver in case it was about to spring his father on him—in the hope that it would. He listened to the silence that was the absence of children and felt his thoughts preparing to swarm around the inside of his skull. He needed to catch hold of one before they did—whichever of them would explain his sense of having learned more from Terence than he understood. The impression made him feel as though he had heard a sound he had yet to realise he'd heard.

FORTY-FIVE

"I know a game that'll be fun for you both. It used to make John laugh when he was your age, Charlotte. Laugh till he cried, he would. He'd laugh till he tired himself out with it and had to go to bed. That's what you both want, a bit of a giggle. It's easier to rest when you've had a laugh."

It might work for Woollie, Ian thought. If they were lucky it might put him to sleep. Then—if Woollie didn't wake himself up by falling off the stool on which he was sitting against the door— Ian would be able to creep around the bed and retrieve the knife. "What game?" he murmured across Charlotte next to him on the bed.

"I never thought of a name for it, son. I made it up once when he wouldn't stop creating over some toy that got broken or wore out, I forget which. Tell you what, that can be part of the game, thinking what to call it. You see if you can think of a better name than your playmate, Charlotte, will you?"

He seemed placid, close to sleepy, but anything unwelcome was bound to jar him out of that state, not least having to wait too long for an answer. All the games he'd insisted on playing in a whisper—I Spy and Twenty Questions and Who Am I?—had visibly aggravated Charlotte's exhaustion, and it was clear to Ian that she was too tired to fall asleep, perhaps even to respond with any enthusiasm. He was about to answer for her in the hope of rousing her when she mumbled "What for?"

"For a bit of extra fun."

She shook her head impatiently, tapping the headboard against the wall. "What's the name for?"

"Keep that still. Get your head on the pillow. You too, son. Right on it so you're not tempted to try and send messages next door when there's somebody to hear. And I told you what for once, love. It's an extra part of our game."

He was wide awake now, and closer than ever to losing control. Ian had to lie on one side and watch him over the back of Charlotte's untypically tousled head. With an effort that sent a brittle shudder through him he contained his frustration at the way Charlotte and their captor were scraping each other's nerves. "She means what game is it going to be," he intervened.

"That's what I've been trying to tell you if I'm given the chance. Somebody says a word and the next one has to rhyme with it, and the winner is the one that makes someone else laugh. Sound good? Sound like fun?"

"I guess," Ian said with all the conviction he could fake.

"I'm asking your playmate."

Ian was having to restrain himself from nudging an answer out of her by the time she whispered "Yes."

"That's the girl. Cheering up already, are you? You start, then. Ladies first as usual."

She was silent even longer, and Ian was beginning to hope she'd fallen asleep so that Woollie might too when she thumped the bed with a fist. He thought she was overcome by frustration, and would have started the game himself if she hadn't muttered "Bed."

"That's a good one," Woollie said as if he were greeting a joke. "Your turn, son. That's the order."

"Bread."

"Careful," Woollie warned, presumably because Ian had referred to food, and gaped with inspiration. "Fed."

"Led," Charlotte made herself say, or a word that sounded like it.

"Zed."

"You'd say zee if you were an American, wouldn't you? Or pretending like some people try. Ned," Woollie offered, and flapped his hands behind his ears. "That's what they call donkeys, did you know? Eeyore. Eeyore," he brayed in a murmur, punctuating the noises with a wide slack grin.

He was expecting a laugh, but Ian could tell that Charlotte managed not to shrink back from the spectacle only by tensing herself. "Fred," he blurted to bring it to an end.

Woollie's mouth drooped as his hands sank, the right one settling on a pink fish that hid the knife. "People used to laugh at that name. Can't think why," he said peevishly. "Go on, love, you have another go."

"I don't know," Charlotte complained until his raw stare told her she better had. "Dead," she gave him with almost no breath.

"Not much fun in that, is there? It's nice and quiet, though. Just like going off to sleep, really. You'd be surprised." Woollie's gaze withdrew into his eyes, taking their expression with it, and Ian willed Charlotte to make herself as unnoticeable as he was trying to be in case the man reminisced himself to sleep. Then the eyes bulged at him as though Woollie had guessed or even overheard his thoughts. "Speak up, son. Just remember you're meant to be trying to make us laugh."

"Ted."

"That's not even as funny as Fred, that. I reckon you're not trying. Head," Woollie muttered, planting the tips of his forefingers on his temples and poking his thumbs under his flabby jaw so as to wag his head back and forth like a wide-mouthed big-eyed mask. "I've seen a few of them gone to sleep," he said, and returned his hand to the knife. "Your go, love."

Charlotte must have been preparing her turn. "Said," she hissed at once.

"That's cute. That's quite witty. Said's what you said, eh? You said said. I'd call that a laugh." Apparently content to say so rather than utter one, he directed an upturned grimace at Ian. "That makes her the winner, don't you reckon, son?"

"Sure."

"He sounds a bit jealous to me, love. It's you to go for winning. See if you can think of one that'll start off a few laughs."

Charlotte lifted a fist as if to punch the bed but clenched it on the quilt. "Don't want to."

"I know what you'd rather do. Think of a name for our game."

"Can't."

"Try or you won't be able to stop trying when you want to

sleep. How about Riotous Rhymes? Or Pitiful Poetry, that's not bad, is it? Here's a good one, Wormy Words," Woollie said, his voice growing lower and more intense with each suggestion, and leaned forward in a crouch that might have been about to launch him at the bed. "You say one now as long as mine don't make you laugh."

"Don't know any."

"I didn't either till I thought of them, and I've been up longer than you." They were competing at peevishness again, and Ian was searching under the slab in his brain for a way to intervene when Woollie appeared to recall what he was meant to be doing. "Right enough, you need your beauty sleep at your age. Get your head down and shut those eyes, then, and you'll be gone in no time."

"Can't."

"Of course you can, love. Just shut them. Just let them shut like they want to."

"Can't," Charlotte wailed. "I'm too tired."

"That doesn't make sense, love. Think about it and you'll see it doesn't. When you're tired you sleep, don't you? That's what children do."

"Can't."

"Calm it down. Don't go upsetting yourself or you'll have the rest of us in a state. Your nerves are all itchy because you want to go to sleep, see? Do you want me to sing you to sleep like I nearly did when we were on our own?"

"No."

Woollie's gaze submerged as his mouth tried out a series of increasingly less reassuring grimaces, and Ian saw he had to save the situation while it was only dangerous. He couldn't just ask Woollie to sing—he didn't know how Charlotte might react to his request—but if she looked at him, surely he could make her understand that they had to put up with the ordeal. He reached out to finger her tense back, hoping she wouldn't flinch or cry out, and Woollie said "I know what you can see to help you go off."

Not much expression had resurfaced in his eyes, and it was clear to Ian that Charlotte would have preferred not to respond. Somebody had to. He was parting his dry lips with his dry tongue when a word that sounded as though it had had to struggle for release escaped her. "What?"

"I'll show you someone else asleep."

His gaze remained somewhere behind his eyes as he raised

himself an inch from the stool to haul up his pink and yellow dress. He reached in his trousers pocket, and the top of an object like a wallet crept into view. Ian imagined Woollie carrying photographs of his victims in his wallet to display to strangers, the way parents showed pictures of their children. The object—a photograph album the size of Woollie's hand—emerged from the pocket, and Woollie settled himself, tugging his dress down. "Here you are, love," he murmured, and laid the album next to her clenched fist. "Take a glance at these. They're restful, you'll see."

His gaze was ready to come out of hiding if she didn't do as she was told, and Ian was afraid of how it might look. He watched her hand very gradually relinquish its grip on the quilt and stray toward the album. Barely in time to delay her, he touched her shoulder. "Let me look too," he said.

At least that made her turn toward him. She was fighting to keep her eyes and mouth steady, and he focused all his energy in projecting reassurance at her while she groped behind her for the album. He saw Woollie lean over to place the album in her hand, a contact Ian could imagine sending her panic out of control and then Woollie too. But her hand found the album before the man's reached it. She lifted it over herself and dropped it between herself and Ian.

It was fattened with at least a dozen photographs. It smelled of stale leather and, unless Ian was as mistaken as he hoped he was, of earth. He inserted a fingertip under the cover, which felt damp and chill as the earth under a house must feel. He did his best to smile at Charlotte as Woollie crouched closer to watch—close enough to touch her. With a nonchalance that failed even before the gesture was completed, Ian flipped the album open.

His nail caught a plastic sheath, and the album opened at two photographs. He heard Charlotte's teeth click as she trapped a cry, and his own body turned cold as the leather. The children in the photographs—a boy in the left-hand picture, a girl opposite him, both of them about Charlotte's age—might almost have been nothing but asleep. Though each photograph was framed to contain the child's whole body, only the face was visible; the earth in which they lay was drawn up to their chins like sheets. Each face was pale with a flashbulb glare that glistened on the moist black soil. A sprinkling of earth on the boy's eyelids helped them resemble the blank eyes of a stone statue, and there was a trickle of mud at one corner of the girl's slack mouth that suggested to Ian she might be stuffed with earth. He was trying to crush the notion when Woollie whispered eagerly "They're peaceful, aren't they? Don't they make you feel like them?"

In that moment he grasped how much worse the man might be capable of where Charlotte was concerned than Ian had let himself think. Her lips trembled, and he was so afraid of her being unable to restrain a cry that he answered for her. "No," he blurted.

"Studying to be a ventriloquist, are you, son? I was asking your playmate."

"She doesn't either. You're upsetting her and you keep saying not to."

"She wasn't upset till you wandered in." Woollie seemed undecided whether to glare at him or search for something inside himself. "All right, love, if you can't go to sleep just looking at them you can play with them for a bit till you do."

Ian saw Charlotte shrink back from the proposal. "Play what?" he demanded.

"Anything that doesn't spoil them. Use your imaginations for a change. You could cut out some paper clothes to put on them, love. Girls your age like dressing things, don't they? Only we can't have you playing with scissors." His eyes fixed on Ian and grew larger and redder. "Tell you what, son, why don't you make an effort for a change and think of something you can do instead of leaving it all to me."

The slab closed down on Ian's mind so heavily it seemed to darken the room. "Like what?" he could hear himself demanding, except that might push Woollie over whatever edge he was swaying on. He was struggling to think of at least a temporary answer when Woollie said "Here's what you do. You tell us a bedtime story about the girl in the picture."

"She's . . ." It was like being asked a question in class but far worse, because he couldn't just stay silent or say he didn't know: he had to produce something Woollie wanted to hear that wouldn't distress Charlotte too much. "She looks happy, doesn't she?" he said desperately.

He was afraid that Charlotte would be unable to keep her disagreement to herself, but she only bit her lip. "She is happy," he risked saying. "She's happy because . . . Because she's where she wants to be."

That was in the earth under a house, he thought, and waiting for more earth to be thrown on her face. Even Woollie looked less than convinced by Ian's assertion. The slab on Ian's mind let another lie crawl out, all he could find to say. "She's with someone she wants to be with," he muttered.

Woollie leaned his shoulders against the door and gave a slow nod that might have been hinged on his unwavering stare. "That's more like it. Carry on."

"Her name, her name's Carla." All at once Ian knew a story, and if he took long enough to tell it, perhaps it could even put Woollie to sleep. "And she had a grandmother who was the person she was fondest of in the world, even fonder of than she was fond of her mother and father. Then one day the grandmother had to go into hospital because she, because she had something wrong with her the doctors had to look at. And Carla went to see her every day and took her flowers and candy, sweets, and read stories to her like her grandmother used to read to her. Only one day she went in and her grandmother wasn't there, and when she asked her mother and father where her grandmother had gone they said she'd see her again after she'd grown up . . ."

Woollie was nodding; his eyes appeared to have relaxed. Could Ian's tale be soothing him to sleep? "Only Carla knew she wasn't going to be able to wait that long to see her grandmother when she'd been so fond of her," Ian murmured, "they'd been so fond of each other. And just when she thought she was going to start being so sad she'd never stop being it she remembered something her grandmother had told her once when she was sad about something else. Her grandmother used to say if there was a dream you wanted to have you had to think about it as hard as you could while you were going to sleep, only not so hard it woke you up . . ."

Woollie's eyes were vanishing. The upper lids settled toward the lower and fluttered apart, but nobody was looking out between them. "So when Carla went to bed that night," Ian murmured just loud enough for Woollie to hear, "she thought of the best time she'd ever had with her grandmother, and she kept thinking of it as she went to sleep, the best time she'd ever had in her life . . ." The lids tried to part again, but gave up, and he was almost certain it wasn't a trick—certain enough to close the album and push it toward the foot of the bed, away from Charlotte. "And the moment she fell asleep she saw her grandmother coming to her with her arms held out, and they just stood and hugged, and Carla never wanted to wake up . . ."

He paused for a breath, then dared to pause longer, but the lids didn't stir. "Never wanted to wake up," he repeated. If Woollie had been less than thoroughly asleep, surely the repetition would have roused him. In the twilight that was all of the late afternoon light the curtains admitted to the room, the man looked dwindled, fallen inward now that his vigilance and the effort it required had collapsed—he would have looked like an old woman sleeping in a cardboard box except for the beard. "And so she never did," he whispered in case Charlotte wanted to know, and put a finger to his lips. He rolled gradually onto his back and was easing himself toward the far side of the bed, resting his fingertips on the quilt at the edge of the mattress, when she grabbed his free arm, shaking her head so hard the pillow flapped.

He let go of the mattress and placed his hand over hers, which felt smaller and clammier than ever. "Don't wake him," he mouthed. "I'm getting the knife."

Fear glistened in her eyes. Her fingers squirmed under his palm, and he was afraid she might pull away before she realised how much noise that would make. He pressed her hand against his arm and mouthed "I have to. It's our only chance."

He felt as though he were telling her another story, but he was going to have to enact this one. When he risked letting go of her hand it jerked away from him, but only to jam its knuckles into her mouth. She kept it there, and he saw she was using it to cover any sounds of panic. He flashed her a smile that almost made him feel courageous and resumed crawling on his back toward the edge of the bed. His feet reached off it, and too many seconds later his legs up to the knees did. He raised himself onto his elbow to push himself up from the mattress, and the bed gave a loud creak.

He froze in that position, his body aching and shivering with strain. It took him the duration of several short harsh breaths to twist his head round far enough to see Woollie clear. Charlotte had the knuckles of both hands against her mouth, but the man hadn't wakened. His chin was resting on his chest, his back against the door. "All right," Ian mouthed, nodding hard at Woollie until Charlotte ventured to turn her shaky eyes in that direction, and eased himself off the bed.

This time it didn't make a noise, but at least one floorboard had creaked when Woollie had sent him to lie on the bed. Even if that didn't rouse the man, the sound might aggravate Charlotte's fears beyond bearing. Ian mimed dropping to all fours so as to creep past the end of the bed. Once he saw that she understood and was controlling her apprehension, he lowered himself onto his hands and knees.

A smell of carpet shampoo caught the back of his throat. He had to swallow fast and hard and dryly before the sensation could provoke a cough. Worse still was his inability to see what Charlotte and their captor were doing. He lumbered forward a pace, then another, and felt a board start to bend under his clenched fists. He shifted his weight to the board ahead of it, which contented itself with a squeak surely too muffled for Woollie to hear, though sufficiently loud to drive out sweat from the bends of Ian's elbows and behind his knees. Another stumbling pace that nearly planted his knees on the loose board, and he had a view along the side of the bed.

Woollie hadn't moved. Yes, he had: the hand that had been fingering the knife was resting palm upward on the stool. Charlotte was craning over the edge of the bed to watch for Ian. As he came in sight her grimace of concern began to slacken, then intensified at the thought of his aim. "Okay," he mouthed. "Nearly there."

Almost an inch of the handle of the knife was protruding from the pocket, which the hand must have dragged down as it slipped onto the stool. Ian drew as much of a breath as he dared, anxious for the smell of shampoo not to lodge in his throat again, and shuffled forward on his knees. He stretched out a hand above Woollie's on the stool, toward the grinning fish on their sunny background. At that moment a phone began to ring.

It wasn't downstairs, it was in Ian's house, and further muffled by the bedroom door. Nevertheless Woollie opened his eyes and saw him.

FORTY-SIX

He shouldn't have known, Jack thought. His father oughtn't to have had any idea where to find him. The last time his father had spoken to him at Leslie's he'd said that he wasn't surprised Jack hadn't visited his mother, but Terence had insisted that the man who'd phoned the Haven hadn't just expected Jack to be there, he'd had to be convinced he wasn't. It made no sense unless Jack's father had spoken to someone else between the two calls. The innocent source had to be Leslie, since she'd picked up on the fact that Jack had phoned her from the Haven. That much he was sure of, because his mother had told him Leslie had called back to warn him to leave Ian alone. Might Leslie have some insight that might lead him to his father even if she didn't realise she had?

It seemed unlikely. It reminded him of the sort of plot development he would find himself considering when a book was going badly—the kind of desperate contrivance he would struggle to elaborate in the hope that a better idea would suggest itself—but as long as it was his only lead, surely he ought to follow it up. Letting himself grow apprehensive that his father might try to call while the line was busy was just a way of putting off the task: it was clear to Jack by now that his father didn't plan to summon him before dark. He grabbed the phone and dialled Leslie's number.

It rang at once, but that was all it did, and the same proved true of the phone at her store. When he'd had enough of the relentless trilling of the bell he reverted to what he did best: pacing the apartment at the end of a tether that was the sound of the twenty-four-hour television news. He let half an hour plod by before he tried Leslie's home number again, but it had the same answer for him. Soon his mother would be home, and the thought of this additional complication made him dial Leslie's number one last time as the hem of the sky began to blacken.

He was pacing back and forth as far as the cord of the phone would stretch when the bell was interrupted halfway through its third pair of rings. "Yes?" Leslie said breathlessly.

She sounded so eager that for an instant he gave into the wish that she could have been expecting him. "Hi," he said.

"Yes, who is it?"

"Sorry. Just Jack Woollie."

"Yes, Jack. Why are you calling?"

He'd assumed her enthusiasm would vanish once she recognised him, but it hadn't flagged yet. "I guess first I want to tell you I haven't been in touch with Ian," he said.

"Oh."

The syllable appeared to mean so much yet conveyed so little to him that he felt bound to add "Because you told me twice not to."

"Did I? Right now I wish you were calling to tell me you had."

He would have been encouraged to hear that if the animation hadn't deserted her voice. "Why," he said, "what . . ."

"He stayed out overnight and I don't know where he is."

"I guess people do that kind of stuff at his age."

"Did you?"

"You could say I did worse when I wasn't much older. I went to the States and figured out that was where I ought to be. Hey, but I'm sure Ian wouldn't do that."

"You don't think so."

"I don't see how he could have got the idea from me. I never talked to him about it. If I had I'd have done my best to put him off. I know you need each other."

"Jack . . ."

"I haven't gone anywhere."

"This is hard for me to say, especially just now, but I think I was wrong about you."

"Well, okay. I mean, that's . . . Wrong how?"

"Ian trusted you, I'm sure he still does, and that should have meant more to me. And I know you never tried to do him anything but good. I'm the one who screwed him up."

"I can't let you say that if you're counting me as a friend or even if you aren't. I saw you doing your best to keep him together."

"And failing. Once is enough if it's bad enough."

"Tell me what's so bad it could cancel all the rest you've done for him."

"I made him feel suspected. That's what his note says."

"Suspected of what?"

"Of doing something to Charlotte, but I know he didn't now it's too—" She found an excuse to interrupt herself that came as an audible relief. "Charlotte, she's Hilene's daughter, that's the woman Roger moved in with. She ran off, Charlotte, the day before yesterday while Ian was meant to be taking her in the park, and she hasn't been seen since."

The cause of the shiver that passed through Jack was surely nothing, he thought, but evidence of the way a writer's mind worked, trying to tidy up reality and force it to make more sense than it did. "How far from your place was she when she took off?" he hardly knew why he asked.

"The far side of the park."

"That's the one with the river in it."

"If you can call it a river. Too shallow to be much of a danger if that's what you had in mind. Anyway," she said, having regained some vigour by the sound of it, "this can't be why you called."

"Well—"

"Before you tell me, let me tell you I wish now I hadn't shown you the door."

"I wish that too."

"If you were phoning to talk about that . . ."

"I wouldn't have presumed to."

"Still, you see you can. If it's something you'd rather not talk about over the phone . . ."

"I'd love to see you. I hope I can soon. Only right now I need to stay here and wait for a call."

"You should have told me to stop interrupting."

"You aren't, and I called you, remember. This other business isn't due for hours yet," Jack said, because the sky appeared to be renewing its multicoloured glow. "Keep talking. Sounds like you can use it as much as I can."

"Where have you ended up, Jack?"

"At my mother's. Do you want the number? It isn't in the book."

"I'd like it."

She asked him to repeat it, she read it back to him, and then she said "There's something I don't understand."

"Tell me."

"You said I asked you twice not to contact Ian. When did I?"

"Once when, you know, when I was having to leave, and then you gave my mother the message."

"When I rang last night, you mean?"

"Last night? Is that the only time you spoke with her?"

"Except when she came to find you at my house. I rang in case you'd heard from Ian."

"Jesus."

"Why, what did she say I'd said?"

"That I shouldn't try to reach either of you."

"It was more her assuming that was what I wanted, Jack. She oughtn't to have told you I said it."

"So long as I know the truth now," Jack said, and tried to disentangle one more thread of the confusion that had begun to reveal itself. "I don't suppose anyone tried to call me at your number that you're aware of."

"That's so. Was that why you rang?"

"Originally, but I'm glad we had this chance to talk."

"Me too. I feel as much better as I can just now."

"Shall I get out of the way in case someone else is trying to reach you? You could give me a quick call if you hear any news of Ian, if it's not too late."

"Poor Jack, I've given you my worries. I'll say good-bye, then." In a moment her voice returned, closer to the mouthpiece. "For now," she said.

"You bet," Jack responded, but his thoughts were already elsewhere. He had to put aside whatever he and Leslie might have regained, so that he could attempt to work out the other implications of their talk. He laid down the receiver and kept his hand on the phone in case it was about to ring, but that didn't help him think. He had just let go of it when the street door slammed.

It was his mother. He heard her tramping up the hollow stairs and her weary key scratching at the lock. She leaned against the door to shut it, deflating her cheeks with a long loud puff, before trudging to dump herself and her bag on the sofa as though she was too fatigued to locate her own chair. Nevertheless she said "Have you had something to eat?"

"Not yet."

"We'll have something brought in, shall we? The Chinky by the station does if you ask. Are you feeling like a dear?"

"What kind?"

"The kind who'd bring his poor old fagged-out mum a cup of tea."

Jack paced into the kitchen yet again and dangled tea bags in two mugs. He was resting his hand on the electric kettle while it lost its chill, and watching colours withdraw almost imperceptibly from the sky, when his mother called "What have you been doing today?"

"I'll tell you when I'm there."

He felt the metal achieve body temperature like someone assumed to be dead who was reviving. Soon it was nearly unbearable to touch, then more than nearly, and then it lost itself in contemplation for minutes before emitting a sneeze of steam. Jack splashed the water into the mugs and arranged them together with a half-full carton of milk on a tray like a framed photograph of children at play in a fifties schoolyard, a photograph tipped onto its back to turn their faces upward. "What did you say you'd been up to?" his mother said as he bore it into the main room.

He watched her add milk to her tea and fish the bag almost to the surface only to return it to drowning. When she looked inquisitively at him he said "I just got through speaking to Leslie Ames."

His mother's face stiffened and squeezed its lips outward, rather as they used to invite a kiss when he'd been a child. She stared at her mug and began to jerk the string of the tea bag as though teasing it with the notion of rescue. "Are you going to tell me what Mrs. Ames said?"

She was trying so hard to make him feel guilty he almost laughed. "She says she didn't speak to you yesterday when you said she did."

"Who are you going to believe, a woman you hardly know or your own mother?"

"Whoever's telling the truth."

She hauled the bag out of the muddy liquid and dropped it on the tray, where it lost shape in the midst of an expanding stain, then fed herself a sip from the mug. "That's made too strong," she said, and as if this were part of the same complaint "Perhaps someday you'll know what it's like to have a child turn on you after you've done your best for them."

"You aren't saying you were lying on my behalf."

"I won't, then."

"How were you? How was it supposed to help me?"

"Do you want more of the kind of publicity you got while you were, while you were staying with her? That won't do your career any good, John."

"That's—Hold on. It was Ian you'd spoken to when you told me Leslie called, wasn't it?"

"And if it was?"

"Let's stop fencing. What did he want, did he say?"

"I've absolutely no idea. Presumably to speak to you. Perhaps he missed having a man about the house. I know how that feels myself."

"So what did you tell him?"

"I said I didn't think his mother would want him speaking to you after she'd turned you out. And as long as what she says is so important to you I may tell you she didn't contradict me when I spoke to her last night."

"You won't like me asking this, but what did it have to do with you whether I talked to him?"

"Oh, John, for heaven's sake. Try and think straight. You've the intelligence. He's just a boy. If you'd spun him that tale about your father not being dead there's no knowing who he might have told, and you just tell me if you can what good that could have done you."

Jack wished he'd never tried to persuade her that his father was alive, not by any means the only thing he'd said or done recently that he yearned to take back. His defeat must have looked like the end of the conversation, because his mother stood up. "I'm going to make a fresh one," she announced, picking up her mug, "and while I am perhaps you can get some use out of the phone."

"How do you mean?"

"Call the Chinky," she said with an incredulous glance at him.

"The menu's in the drawer of the phone table. I hope you're starving. I am."

It showed how trapped by pressure his thoughts were when for as long as he'd taken to ask the question he'd been unable to think what the answer could be. He seemed to have spent the last half hour in learning nothing useful, in confusing himself further and worsening the prospect of speaking to his father while his mother was in earshot. Surely now she couldn't suspect his father wasn't dead. One wrong word from her for his father to overhear—one hint that she knew about him, even if she didn't . . . Jack's imagination was so eager to foresee the worst that he found himself wishing he'd never inflamed it by writing books.

FORTY-SEVEN

"What are you playing at now, son? What's the game?"

Ian felt as if he'd left his breath somewhere in front of him. The hand that had been reaching for the knife had darted to the floor and helped push him backward a stumbling pace, but he didn't know if he'd been swift enough for Woollie not to have glimpsed his intention, and Woollie's expression wasn't telling. The toothless mouth lolled in a grin that looked near to idiotic, the eyes might have been watching a dream. Next door the phone continued to ring, interrupting Ian's thoughts as they struggled to put themselves together. He could find nothing to say except the truth, and suddenly he didn't care—but Charlotte, who was gazing in paralysed dismay at him over the edge of the bed, opened her mouth with such an effort he heard her lips part. "He's being a horse."

As Woollie's head jerked sideways his gaze stuck to Ian. "What's that, love?"

"He was being a horse pulling the coach."

"What are you babbling on about? Not talking in your sleep, are you? My eyes aren't past it yet, and I can't see any coach."

"The one you said was coming to get us."

"That'll be coming all right. It better had for everyone's sake." Woollie's gaze twitched closer to the surface and turned to her. "He was trying to entertain you, are you saying?"

"He was funny."

"That so, son? Were you putting on a show?"

Ian didn't respond until Woollie's raw gaze swam round to him, and then he made himself nod. As the phone in his house fell silent he realized he was moving his head not unlike a horse's, and succeeded in producing a whispered neigh followed by one somewhat louder. "All right, no need to carry on," Woollie said, and slid his hand off the stool to pat the knife as if he'd only now remembered it was there. "What are we going to do with him, love?"

"Don't know," Charlotte mumbled, and her arms shrank against her sides. "Nothing," she begged.

"Can't do that, can we? We'll have to do something with a horse that's got itself into a bedroom."

Both the mattress and the loose board emitted creaks as Ian rested his hands on the end of the bed and shoved himself to his feet. "Too late," Woollie muttered. "He doesn't want anyone thinking he's a horse any more."

He might have been addressing the room rather than his captives. When his gaze acknowledged them it alighted none too favourably on Charlotte. "Have you finished, love?"

"What?" she hardly more than mouthed.

"The sleepy children," Woollie said with little patience, jabbing a finger at the album on the bed. "Have you done with them?"

"Yes."

Ian understood why that sounded so much like a prayer, and could only hope Woollie hadn't noticed. The man thrust out a hand for the album, but Charlotte pressed her arms harder against her sides. As Woollie's mouth began to droop into a clown's exaggerated grimace, Ian grabbed the album and paced around the bed to plant it in the outstretched hand. He was on the point of doing so when he grew intensely aware of being close enough to struggle with their captor—to launch all his weight at Woollie and knock him off the stool before he could pull out the knife, and keep him clear of Charlotte long enough for her to escape. But the stool would be in the way of the door, and probably their struggle would be too, and all he would achieve would be to infuriate Woollie and terrify Charlotte. Or was he simply finding excuses not to take the risk, not to put himself in danger of being cut or stabbed? As he tried to draw enough of a stealthy breath to lend his bravery some oxygen, Woollie stretched his forefinger along the blade and raised the handle far enough to grasp. Ian had lost any chance to surprise him. He dropped the album on the man's intimidating palm with a slap that smelled of earthy leather, and backed away feeling hopelessly useless, trapped under the slab in his mind. "That didn't work, did it, son?" Woollie said.

Ian had a nightmarish sense of being unable to conceal any of his thoughts. "What?" he tried to say as if he didn't know.

"What do you reckon we're talking about? Your story and nothing else."

"Which story?" Ian had to ask.

"The one that was going to put your playmate to sleep."

The realisation that he'd strayed close to betraying himself even though Woollie hadn't been suspicious of him caused Ian to sway against the bedroom wall. Sleeplessness was catching up with him, sneaking nightmares in among his thoughts. He watched uneasily as Woollie laid the album in his lap beside the eager knife and gazed at one or the other of them. "So what's the plan now?" Woollie said.

It was only to save Charlotte from feeling expected to respond that Ian mumbled "Don't have one."

"Not good for much but telling stories, are you? You take after someone else we know." Woollie squeezed his eyes and mouth shut, possibly intending to mime slumber but looking more like a displeased corpse, then his eyes came out of hiding to check that Ian hadn't dared to move. "Tell you what you do. Give your playmate a cuddle and see if that helps her go off."

Charlotte's unhappy gaze followed Ian as he retreated to the far side of the bed. He guessed she would rather he placed himself between her and their captor, but he wanted to be able to watch the man. He swung his legs onto the rumpled quilt and lowered his head to the misshapen wrinkled pillow, his skin crawling with the stifled heat of the unventilated room. He stretched one tentative embarrassed hand toward Charlotte, and she turned to face him, hunching up her shoulders at Woollie's presence behind her. As Ian's hand settled over the small of her back, Woollie said "That's more like it. That's how the babes should be. Shut those eyes now and I'll sing you to sleep."

A shudder passed through Charlotte, then her body grew so stiff that Ian found himself stroking her back. "Don't worry," he murmured, all that he could think of to risk saying, by no means enough in itself.

"You can listen to him for once, love. Those eyes aren't shut, are they? I'll know if they're not. Yours as well, son. Set your play-mate a good example for once."

"We'll be okay," Ian whispered, and rubbed her spine harder. Her thin dress began to ride up, and she tugged it down furiously and sent him a scowl he might have expected from someone his age or even older. When he moderated his touch she let down her eyelids as though acknowledging his thoughtfulness and, with a final nervous blink at him, squashed them shut. That was Ian's cue to close his own until her face was no more than a glimmer and their captor's shape a flickery silhouette. He continued to massage the taut ridged wire of her spine, which felt in danger of snapping with tension, as Woollie began to sing.

> "Now I lay you down to sleep,
> Close your eyes good night.
> Angels come your soul to keep,
> Close your eyes good night . . ."

Ian wasn't confident of being able to stand much of this him-self, especially while he was aware how it appalled Charlotte. No sooner had Woollie croaked the lullaby in an almost tuneless mur-mur than he recommenced, and Ian grew desperate for a way to soothe her. As her eyelids shivered, unwilling to imprison her with whatever she might be seeing in her own dark, his hand found the nape of her neck and began to manipulate it gently as he remem-bered his mother once treating his when he'd been nightmarish with a fever. Her shoulders worked, suggesting that they wanted to dislodge his clasp, and then, despite the drone of yet another repetition of the lullaby, they started to relax. Her eyelids slackened into restfulness, her forehead became smooth, her breathing adopted the rhythm of his fingers on her neck. When her body curled toward him he knew she was asleep.

Woollie knew as well. He had been leaning sideways off the stool to observe her, but subsided against the door, letting Ian glimpse the movements of the hand in the man's lap, a regular movement that kept pace with his song. The notion of what he might be doing now that he was unaware of being watched came close to making Ian laugh, although there would have been no humour in it. Instead he widened the slit between his eyelids.

The album was spread open, and Woollie was running his fingers over and over a photograph as he might have stroked a child's head. It wasn't just this spectacle that horrified Ian—it was the recognition that his own hand on Charlotte's neck was following the rhythm of the lullaby. He felt implicated with their captor. He ran his hand down to the small of Charlotte's back and rested it there and closed his eyes to keep out the sight of the fingers caressing the dead picture. As long as the man kept repeating the song Ian would know where he was.

The lullaby blurred into little more than a monotonous sound. When Charlotte snuggled against him, the rise and fall of her chest was unexpectedly calming. He stroked her upper back to keep her breaths steady, then remembered he shouldn't be taking his pace from the lullaby but carried on stroking until he had to be reminded to continue by the song he'd grown unaware of hearing. If he breathed in time with Charlotte that would show him exactly how fast to rub her back, which he thought he was still doing somewhere in the distance near the song. Much further away a phone was ringing, but it seemed to have nothing to do with him, not while he felt as safe in her arms as she was in his, at the end of some old story he used to know. His breathing settled into her slow placid rhythm, and then he couldn't hear the song or the phone or feel his hand or any other part of himself.

FORTY-EIGHT

"Are you asleep, love?"

"She isn't really."

"He isn't either."

"Never mind trying to have a laugh with me. We haven't got time for that now."

"He's not."

"Nor's she."

"Trying another of your games, are you? Having one more go at confusing me?"

"You won't know he has till he's done it."

"Nor her, 'cos she's as sly as me."

"Only because you're making her like you," Hector snarled, lurching off the stool that was wedged between the half-open door and its frame. For a second, perhaps quite a few of them, he couldn't shake off the conviction that he had indeed heard the children talking—if not their actual voices, at least their thoughts— and he didn't know what he was about to do with the knife that had found its way into his hand. Just in time he recognised that he'd been voicing his suspicions of the children: as yet he hadn't any evidence that they were pretending to be asleep. He mustn't let himself be rushed into causing any unnecessary upset or mess, not when he was so close to summoning John's help. Though his legs felt as brittle with insomnia as the rest of him, he managed not to make a noise as he approached the bed. Flattening his free hand against the wall above the headboard, he leaned down to peer at the dim faces that were turned to each other on the pillows.

They might be asleep. When he aimed a long slow hot breath at each of them, they didn't stir. He lowered the blade toward the boy's face and twisted the point no more than half an inch from the entrance to the ear. That failed to provoke a response, although surely the girl would have been unable to restrain herself if she were able to see him apparently torturing her playmate. He repeated the trick on her ear with as little effect, then drew the duller edge of the knife across her throat and did so rather less gently to the boy. He watched the dark lines fade from both throats, then pushed himself away from the bed. A growl at the medley of aches the movement brought with it escaped through the gap where his teeth should have been, but the children didn't stir. For the moment they were thoroughly asleep, and he needn't waste time wondering if they were about to have another try at tricking him.

They thought they'd persuaded him that the boy had been imitating a horse. If they believed he'd been too quick for Hector to have seen him reaching for the knife they must be desperate, which meant they were dangerous. That was how the boy was affecting his playmate, him being too old and too spoiled by his life to value the peace she deserved—too narrowed by his own self-centred adolescence to let her enjoy a stillness he couldn't understand. Soon Hector was going to have to deal with him, but first he had to phone John. He eased the door wider and propped it with the stool and padded softly out of the room.

He'd spent hours listening for sounds of the boy's mother. He'd heard her come home just in time to answer the phone as the boy had followed his playmate to sleep. Her voice had been barely audible enough for him to tell she was having a long conversation, undoubtedly about her son. Once it was over he'd heard so little for so long that he'd begun to wonder if she could have sneaked out of the house, but the night that had darkened the room before it was dark outside had emphasised sounds her house wasn't quite able to contain. At last he'd succeeded in hearing her slow ascent of the stairs and a selection of bathroom noises followed by three muffled clicks, the latter pair in the same location toward the front of the house—her bedroom light being switched on and eventually, no doubt reluctantly, off. Since then he'd waited until the children had begun speaking in his head, unless he'd been speaking aloud on their behalf, and surely that was more than long enough for her to have fallen asleep. He slid the knife into his pocket and placed one foot on the dimmest of the stairs, and heard a stealthy movement in the room behind him.

"I hear you, son," he muttered. It occurred to him to put some kind of face around the door on the chance that the girl was awake too, but she never seemed to appreciate Hector's efforts to amuse her, and in any case he was tired of playing games. Instead he sidled noiselessly into the room.

His eyes had to adjust to the dimness again. Though they took only a couple of seconds, that was longer than he ought to have to wait. His gums clamped his tongue, his hand groped for the knife, which was ready in his grasp by the time he distinguished the figures on the bed. He thought they were pretending not to have moved until he saw that the boy's hand had slid off the girl's back and was lying on the quilt between them.

Perhaps he was indeed as asleep as he must want Hector to think, but he was less so than the girl, who hadn't shifted at all. He was the threat, not her. Things had started to go wrong once he'd intruded. If he wakened while Hector was on the phone, there was no telling what tricks he might play. Hector dodged around the bed and in one swift movement returned the knife to his pocket, sat on the boy's legs, gathered his wrists in one hand and used the other to press the boy's mouth shut, his thumb and fingers digging into the bony cheeks, as he turned the boy's head to face him.

The boy emitted a snore that in less fraught circumstances Hector would have made the basis of a joke, and his eyes stuttered open. In a wink they were as wide and protruding as they could go. "Keep very still, son," Hector said, gripping the wrists harder and leaning more of his weight on the legs as his captive's struggles began to shake the bed. "Wake your playmate and it's all over. Settle down or there'll be no coach."

At first the boy seemed not to understand. If he carried on struggling, Hector might as well finish him off. He would struggle just as much, but not for long. When all at once the boy went limp Hector grew hot with frustration. He could still rid himself of the trouble, he didn't need an excuse—but if the boy breasted too much trouble while he was being put to sleep for good he was bound to awaken the girl. "You and me are going down to the phone," Hector muttered instead. "Don't make a sound when I let go of your face."

The boy's lips moved under his palm as if they were preparing to cry out, and Hector only had to bring his thumb and forefinger together to pinch the boy's nose shut for as long as it took. He wouldn't have known what else to do if he hadn't remembered the knife. No sooner had he released the boy's mouth than he snatched out the knife and jabbed it at his captive's face, so fast that he managed to halt it scarcely a couple of inches short of the rapidly blinking right eye. "Just seeing you keep quiet," he murmured. "I'm going to get up off you now. Don't you move a muscle till you're told."

He freed the boy's wrists and planted his hand between the children, and waited. Even when Hector raised the knife an inch, then several, the boy's wrists stayed crossed on his chest. All the children Hector had brought peace had lain that way as he'd covered them up for the night, and he couldn't help feeling that the boy yearned for the same peace even if he didn't know he did. The impression was so powerful he had to remind himself that he was supposed to be phoning John. He lifted himself from the bed, and as Hector's weight left him the boy uttered a grunt of pain, but nothing more. "I'll let you have that," Hector whispered. "It's all the noise you're going to make. Worm yourself over here, slow as you like."

The boy took him at his word. He spent so long over inching himself down the bed that Hector began to suspect him of stalling. By the time the boy eased himself off the corner of the mattress Hector was having difficulty in keeping the knife to himself. "Quiet out of the room," he muttered, and saw the boy step over the board that would have creaked. Though it looked like obedience, it could be the start of some trick, and so Hector followed close enough to find the boy's face with the knife the instant there was any need. As the boy sidled past the stool, however, Hector thought of another way to deal with him. "Wait out there," he whispered, and groped under the stool.

He'd straightened up before the boy peered warily at him. Perhaps he suspected Hector of being about to harm the girl, which showed how little he knew about Hector. "Turn yourself round, son. Never mind looking at me," Hector said. "Let's have your hands behind your back. Let's see you cross your wrists since you're so good at it."

The boy didn't move except for clenching his fists at his sides. "What for?"

He'd spoken far too loud. For a moment Hector didn't know which hand he was about to use on him. He glanced back to see the girl hadn't been disturbed, then he poked at the air immediately in front of the boy's face with the knife in his left hand, holding the other and its contents out of sight behind the door. "Can't have you trying to run out of the house, can we?" he whispered. "Can't have you getting hold of the phone either. Your playmate doesn't want you spoiling things for her now, so better do as you're told."

"Come away from her, then."

"I will as soon as you turn round, that's a promise. Keep me waiting any longer and maybe she'll wake up and start making a fuss, and then I won't be able to call John, so you figure out for yourself what I'll have to do."

The trouble was that the threat made Hector feel threatened himself, less in control of the situation than he ought to be, in danger of having to finish things off because his plans weren't as complete as he should have ensured they were. The boy's eyes glinted in the dimness as if he realised some or all of this, and insomnia surged through Hector's hot raw grimy brittle skull, urging him to give up his efforts to think ahead, just to act and assuage his frustration. Then the boy's shoulders drooped, and his fists opened as he turned, crossing his wrists behind his back.

Hector was on him at once, using a fingernail to scratch the end of the insulating tape loose from the roll. In a second he'd wrapped it tight around the boy's wrists. He bound them again and a third time for luck before cutting the tape off the roll. "That's the way," he murmured, watching the fingers wriggle in the murk like undersea creatures eager for food. "No point struggling, that won't help your playmate. Don't struggle now either."

The boy's head swung toward him, just what Hector wanted. It was still turning when he stretched the tape across the mouth. The boy jerked his head away, which only stuck the tape to his right cheek. He tried to retreat, giving Hector space to dance around him thrice on tiptoe, unspooling the tape around the parcel of a head, over and over the mouth. "Done up properly now, aren't you?" he muttered, slashing at the end of the gag with the knife.

"No need to flinch. I've done what I'm doing for now. Careful as you go down. We don't want you breaking your neck."

Or did he? The boy would be able to make even less noise if that happened, and not much while it did—but there would have to be the sound of his fall, which was more than Hector needed to risk. Silencing the boy had revived Hector's ability to think. As he followed one step behind his captive, who swayed like a drunk as he lowered his weight onto each stair so gingerly it was comical, Hector's plan completed itself in his head. He restrained himself from laughing aloud, but he stretched his mouth wide in a grin that felt like a wound, nearly healed. He knew how to bring John to them without revealing their whereabouts, and once the call was finished he knew what the boy's fate would be.

FORTY-NINE

Just when Jack thought his mother had finally left him alone she reappeared in her pink dressing gown. "Let me make up the couch for you at least. You look as if you're never going to bed."

"Don't worry, I'll do it. You need your sleep."

"So do you, John. We've both got jobs that take a lot out of us." She tramped to the sofa, her footfalls and indeed her whole body expressing dissatisfaction, and yanked at the cushions until they unfolded into a segmented mattress. She stooped to lift the heap of bedclothes from beside the sofa and rose red-faced with sudden anger. "It's ridiculous, these people expecting you to wait up all hours till they get around to phoning. Who do they think they are? You're important too. More important, because you're the one that writes the books."

"You wouldn't expect publishers to see it that way."

"Then they should. You tell them your mother said so." She shook a pillow hard as if to make it see sense and flung it on the couch. "What time is it supposed to be where they are?"

"It's eight hours earlier in California."

"So they should be well back from their lunch even if it's on expenses, shouldn't they? What are they making you wait for?"

"I won't be the only—"

"They won't have many writers over here, will they? They ought to deal with you first. *I* know," she declared, and let go of the sheet he was helping her to spread. "Why don't *you* call *them*?"

Jack was well into wishing he hadn't told her the story, but it had been the only explanation he could invent for staying up. "It isn't done," he had to tell her now.

"Who says so?"

"You don't ever pester a publisher. It can turn them right off you and your work. And it makes you look desperate, so you can't negotiate when they come up with an offer."

"That isn't pestering, ringing them so you can get to bed. You tell them your mother's seen how not sleeping can affect people. You say she knows what she's talking about because she has to look after people with that kind of problem."

Jack took the quilt from her and flapped it across the sheeted mattress. Now he wasn't only worried that his father might call before she was out of earshot, he was afraid how much more dangerous his father might have grown for lack of sleep. "I don't think that's going to help," he said.

"Well, I'm sure I'm not qualified to advise you about your business. I'm just your mother." She pulled the quilt straight and stalked out of the room. She had one foot in the hallway when she glanced forgivingly at him. "Shall I make you a bedtime drink?"

"I never use them, thanks."

"You did when you were little."

"Yeah, well, I grew up. I know more about myself."

To his dismay, she turned back to him, looking no more persuaded by his claim than he was. "I don't like to think of you sitting up all by yourself," she said. "I won't be able to sleep."

"Sure you will."

"You may know a lot, John, but there are things you don't know about me." She paused long enough for him to grow nervous of what revelation she might have decided to share with him at last, and of how she could hardly have chosen a worse time for it, before she said "Most likely you've forgotten, but there was one night when you were twelve and the trains were stopped so you were hours late home from going to the West End for some silly thing or other, and even after you got in I didn't sleep a wink all night."

"Why, what did you figure I'd been doing?"

"Just what you said you had. You never gave me any reason to doubt anything you said." That felt to Jack uncomfortably like an accusation, especially when she paused before saying "It was what could have been done to you I was afraid of."

"Well, you don't have to worry any more," he said, his thoughts chasing one another around the dark hollow inside his skull as he tried to find a way to bring the conversation to an end. "I can handle myself."

"I'll have to keep remembering that then, won't I?" The look she sent him was as heavy as her words. It might have been her silence that was weighing her down, trapping her in the doorway, and he was searching desperately for another parting shot when she shook her head. "Good night," she sighed and turned away slowly, letting him see a few more dissatisfied headshakes. He heard her plod to her bedroom and close the door, and the creak of her bed, and the sound of a cord snapping the light off. "Good night," he called, but there was no response.

He mustn't assume she was unable to hear. He hurried to the door and shut it as fast as he could without making a noise, then he sat by the phone. He was reaching for the remote control, to put the television news on low, when the phone rang.

He couldn't help feeling that his father had been awaiting the exact moment—that he'd been watching every move Jack made. Jack dislodged the receiver with a clatter before he managed to capture it and raise it to his face. "Yes," he whispered.

The only answer was a crackle of static, and he wondered if his whisper might not be identifiable enough. "Yes," he said more urgently and louder.

"You're sounding very positive, John. Hope that's how you're feeling."

The whisper was so close and so like his it might almost have been his own. "If I can," he said, turning away from the door and crouching over the receiver as he lowered his voice.

"Keeping a secret, John?"

"Not that I'm aware of. How do you mean?"

"You'd think you were, talking like that. Or are you trying to sound like me for a laugh?"

"I shouldn't think we've any time for that. I'm just—"

"You haven't got much time, you're right there, and you're not the only one that hasn't." Nevertheless his father added "Feeling like me, is that why you're sounding like me? Having to admit you're my son?"

"I'm just keeping it quiet because my mother's in the next room. She'd hardly gone to bed when you rang."

"What have you told her?"

The question felt like chill spit in Jack's ear. "Nothing," he said with all the conviction he could put into a whisper.

"Then who's she going to think is ringing this late if she's still awake? You're meant to be intelligent, aren't you?"

"I mean I didn't tell her anything about you. I said a publisher was calling from the States."

"I'm your publisher now, eh? I'll be helping you with a book."

The short laugh his father released seemed less amused than bitter, and Jack felt it best to move them on. "You said we didn't have much time. Where do you want—"

"Stay right where you are, son."

"I don't understand. If you don't want me to—"

The laugh that greeted this was wilder—dangerously so, since Jack couldn't imagine what had provoked it. "Only till I say where to come," his father said. "I'll tell you this, though. You can be here in ten minutes from when you hang up, and if you aren't I'd start getting nervous."

"I'll be out of here as soon as you say, but I want something in return."

"Think you're haggling with that publisher, do you? Let's have it, then. Maybe it'll be a laugh."

"I want to know the little girl's all right."

"Never better. I've been taking care of her."

"No, I mean I want to hear."

"You just did. I'm not talking that soft."

"I want to hear her speak."

"Not asking me to wake her and upset her, are you? She's asleep. She's a sleepy child. That ought to show you how happy she's been to have me looking after her."

Jack could scarcely bear to consider the alternatives, but he was about to repeat his insistence when his father whispered "If you got here and she'd come to any harm you wouldn't help me, would you?"

That had to make sense—Jack prayed it did. "Okay, let me hear the other one."

"Which?"

"Whoever else you've got there," Jack said, his whisper

cramping his parched mouth. "Last time you said there were two."

"I never said that."

"You said there was more than one babe."

"I did, right enough."

"So where—" Jack tried to find some moisture in his mouth to let him speak again. "What—"

"Just a doll. Girls have them, you know. Nothing for you to worry about at all."

Jack yearned to believe that but wasn't sure he could. He was searching his mind for a way to proceed when he heard footsteps in the hall. As he twisted in the chair, chafing his neck with the cord of the phone, the door swung wide. "For heaven's sake stop whispering, John," his mother protested. "You don't need to for my sake. You're only making it harder for them to hear you all that way away."

"Who's speaking?" Jack's father hissed with something like savage delight. "Is it who I think?"

"Yes," Jack admitted, and had to remind himself how to talk above a whisper. "All right, mother," he said too loud. "I'm nearly through here. You can go back to bed."

When she only folded her arms he was afraid she might be capable of stalking across the room to remonstrate with the caller. "Can she hear me?" his father muttered in his ear.

"Not yet."

"What's that supposed to mean?"

Jack saw his mother shift her weight in his direction, and pressed the receiver against his face with both hands. "Maybe if you wait much longer."

"I won't be waiting long. I told you that."

"So, so give me the details while you can, for Christ's sake."

"You sure it's only you that's listening?"

"Yes," Jack pleaded, then reverted to a whisper in case that somehow helped convince his father. "Yes."

"Better be telling the truth for the sake of you know who. Except I forgot, you don't know who yet, do you? Shall I tell you her name?"

"No need now," Jack said, only to fear he'd antagonised his father. "Sure, if you want."

"It's Charlotte. That's a good name for a babe in the wood, don't you reckon? A good old-fashioned name."

"Sure." Jack's head was throbbing with his sense of who the girl might be, and with seeing his mother take a purposeful step into the room. He would have said almost anything to urge his father out of whatever perversity was making him delay. "So where—"

"You'll laugh. At your lady friend's house."

Jack's gasp might have sounded like a laugh for all he knew. "My—"

"The woman you moved in with in Wembley. Don't say you've forgotten her already. You're good at that, aren't you, leaving people and forgetting them."

Jack could hardly think for wondering where and how Leslie was, and watching his mother halt too close to him, and realising his father was so out of control he was either not aware of squandering time or indifferent whether he did. "No," Jack blurted.

"Glad you remember. Better get going, then. I'll see you in ten minutes or less. Have a guess what'll be happening if you're late. Hope your car starts," his father whispered, and was gone.

Jack's fingers were so stiff with tension he almost couldn't find the cradle with the receiver. He used the phone to shove himself to his feet and dodged around his mother. "I'm just going out," he said, which wasn't enough. "For a drive," he added, but that was too much. "To think."

"John."

She must have thought her tone would stop him; he was nearly in the hall before she caught his arm. "Not now," he managed to resist exclaiming, and said "I need to go."

She didn't say a word until he had to look and see her reproachfulness. "I thought there was one man in the family I could trust," she said.

"You can." Rather than wrench his arm out of her grasp he murmured "Sorry, okay?"

Her fingers moved, but they were only taking a firmer grip on him. "So where are you really going?"

"I can't say now. When I get back."

"It won't take long just to put your mother's mind at rest and let me know where you're going and who you're going to see, will it?"

"Too long. Too complicated. I'll give you the whole story soon as I can, promise."

"What sort of person can you be going to at this time of night, John? Call me out of date, but I don't believe it can be anyone decent, not when you won't even say who they are."

"Mother, let go. I don't have the time. If you knew what you were doing—"

"I've still got all my wits, and don't you dare suggest otherwise. It's my job to care for those who aren't so capable in case that had slipped your mind." She'd snatched her hand away from him, but as he retreated toward the hall she upturned her fingers and flattened them at him. "If you want me lying awake half out of my wits with worry because you've lied to me and made me feel I can't rely on you for anything, then off you go and good riddance."

"I'm sorry, honestly." He was in the hall at last. "As soon as I come home—"

"If you go out now after everything I've said this won't be your home any more, so don't bother coming back."

She surely couldn't believe that would hold him. It must be her way of relinquishing power over him while making him feel as guilty as possible about the loss. As he jerked the chain of the apartment door out of its socket he glanced along the hall, halfway down which she was clutching her shoulders with her crossed hands, but she turned her back on him. "Nothing bad is going to happen," he called, at least as much for his own reassurance as hers.

He missed every second stair, and nearly a third one too, as he sprinted down without using the reluctant time-switch. Beyond the stone steps that led from the house to the sidewalk, his car looked iced by the white glare of a streetlamp. He thought he felt a premonition of chill in the air, though perhaps it was only in him. His argument with his mother couldn't have lasted more than a minute, two at the outside, and surely he could make up that time on the road. He unlocked the van and slammed the door and twisted the key in the ignition as he threw himself into the driver's seat. The engine gave no more than an irritable cough.

He'd begun to fear that his father's last words to him had been disastrously prophetic when he thought to tread on the accelerator while he turned the key again. This time the engine snarled, then roared, and he sent the car forward as fast as the street halved by parked vehicles would allow. Surely the police car that turned on its siren somewhere close had nothing to do with him.

FIFTY

"Hope your car starts. I should have said his coach, shouldn't I? Should have told him to crack the whip and get the horses going."

"Neigh."

"They say cars have horsepower, did you know that? I remember when I heard my dad say his did and I thought there'd be horses pulling it. We were innocent back then, us children. People let us be. Maybe John's wishing he had you to pull his car, do you reckon? If he had an extra horse he'd be quicker."

"Neigh. Nei-ei-eigh."

"Is that all you can say, son? It's not much of a laugh. It's not doing much for my nerves, to tell you the truth."

"What do you want me to say?"

"Not a lot, now you ask. Don't worry, you won't need to be quiet for very much longer. John's already had a minute. He'd better be on his way. Do you know how I can tell how long he's had?"

"Neigh."

"That means no, does it? Should have known. You're never happy unless you're disagreeing, are you, son? Disagreeing or being disagreeable or trying to make your playmate act like you."

"Neigh."

"Never mind arguing when we all know the truth. You'd try anything and hope I wouldn't notice, wouldn't you? You've made me forget what I was telling you. Hang on, I remember—how I know how long he's had. See through there, in the front room? The telly's got a clock on it, about all a telly's good for. So can you guess where we're going now?"

Ian didn't say a word, not that he had so far. Having Woollie answer for him and utter noises on his behalf was almost worse than being gagged. The tape was wound so tightly that the flesh beneath it felt like a single ache that encircled his head, starting at his squashed lips. The palms of his hands were trapped against a stair, his bound wrists were caught in the small of his back. His ankles pressed against a lower stair while one midway dug into his buttocks, but none of that prevented him from swaying every few seconds as if he was about to lose his balance. Apart from that, he hadn't moved since he'd shifted his feet apart halfway through the phone call, when Woollie had told him to stay right where he was—he'd hoped Jack might realise whom his father was addressing then, but he hadn't dared make a noise. Now he forced a grunt past the tape under his nostrils and shook his head from side to side twice.

"You can answer when you want to after all, can you, son? Had me thinking you were too scared for a moment there. Heave yourself up, then. Hang on, here comes some help."

It was too soon for that to be Jack, and whatever else Woollie might mean by it seemed more ominous than reassuring, especially when he lurched at Ian, his pink and yellow dress flapping, his face a featureless blur against the light from Jericho Close. As he rested one hand on the banister, metal rapped wood as a reminder that he was holding the knife. He closed a fist on the front of Ian's T-shirt to haul him to his feet and walk him down to the hall, his knuckles bruising Ian's chest at each step. "Can't have a horse trying to walk upstairs, can we? That'd be a laugh," Woollie muttered, sliding the knife along the banister as he released him. "We're staying down and going in the front. Less chance of your playmate being woken up that way, and we can watch the clock and keep a look out for your coachman."

At least that would place Charlotte out of immediate danger, and perhaps his not having to worry quite so much about her might let some plan lift the slab from Ian's mind. He walked into the front room as fast as his awkwardness allowed: he didn't want to antagonise Woollie if he didn't have to, not when the man was clearly on the brink of losing control. Though the room wasn't even half as bright as the street outside, which in any case was deserted, Woollie flew after him and clamped his fingers on Ian's scalp to force him into a painful crouch. "Sit down quick, out of sight. Sit where you can see the time."

Ian landed on the sofa that faced the television and the street. Most of his weight was thrown on his left elbow, discovering extra pain in his bound wrists. Worse than feeling crippled was the possibility that Woollie might sit next to him, and so he dragged his legs onto the sofa and pressed his left shoulder against its back. "Hard to get comfortable, is it?" Woollie enquired, leaving his grin open as if that might elicit a response. "Shouldn't be for long. He's already had more than two minutes."

In a moment he seemed to forget he was supposed to be grinning. There wasn't much sign of him in his eyes or the shape of his mouth as he swung, bent almost double, toward the window. When he planted his clawed fingers on the sill and sank to his knees so that only his head was visible from outside through the lower left-hand corner of the pane—he must resemble an ornament if he resembled anything at all—Ian risked turning his back to the sofa and planting his feet wide apart on the floor. "Sit still now, son," Woollie muttered at his breath on the glass. "You don't want to get me more on edge. John's doing that without you joining in."

Ian's lips fought to wrench themselves apart behind the tape. The powerful adhesive clung to his skin, stretching it raw, but he succeeded in thrusting his tongue just far enough for its tip to recoil from a taste that nobody was ever intended to have in their mouth. It made all the trapped heat of the room rush at him and swim up through him to the top of his head as he tried to scrape his tongue clean against his teeth. If he'd been able to speak he would have said almost anything to persuade Woollie to calm down, but he could only listen while the man started mumbling as if wholly unaware of being overheard.

"Can't do much he's meant to, can he? Couldn't even keep Adele away while he was talking to me. I'd like to know what he said to her after I got off. Better have told her he was talking to the feller who was going to do his book for him. Hang on though, did it sound like he was?" His voice sank lower as if he were talking in his sleep while he dreamed of being American, to judge by the accent he more or less adopted. "Maybe if you wait much longer . . .

Give me the details while you can, for Christ's sake . . ." Then his voice was his own once more, a whisper as sharp as the knife beneath his fingertips on the windowsill. "You don't talk like that to a publisher, I don't care who you are, and I reckon even Adele would have to notice. How long has he got left, son?"

It took Ian more than a moment to grasp that Woollie couldn't see the luminous red digits in the rectangle under the screen. They'd shown twenty-eight past midnight when Woollie had declared that Jack had had a minute, and now the zero of the thirty shrank into a one. The red flare swelled into Ian's eyes, stinging them, and he was trying desperately to think how he could answer—how he could persuade Woollie that less time had passed than he saw—when the man released a laugh so fierce the window blanched.

"That's a joke, isn't it? I forgot horses can't talk. Must have been dreaming I was in that fairy tale with the babes in the wood. The things you imagine when you're her age upstairs, eh? The things you can take for granted." His voice was drifting inward, but it roused itself. "Wait, though, I remember something. When I was her age my dad was going to take me to see a horse that could count. You asked it a sum and it stamped its hoof to tell you the answer. Want to try, son? Want to be the horse that knows all the answers?"

How could Ian respond if the man wasn't looking at him? When Woollie turned it was with such impatience that he almost lost his grip on the sill. As Ian nodded fast and hard, the knife fell to the carpet with a muffled thud. Woollie groped in search of it, keeping his eyes on Ian. "Go on then, horsey," he muttered. "Let's see your trick."

Ian lifted his right foot an inch or so—far enough for his leg to reveal how shivery it was—and let it drop. When his captor only stared Ian repeated the action and tramped on the carpet a third time before pressing his heels against it. Woollie kept up his unblinking stare, his eyes glinting like lumps of coal, as he found the knife and raised it, and Ian's legs began to tremble with resisting the temptation to count the fourth minute. Then Woollie murmured "Not so loud next time I ask you" and faced the street again.

It was still deserted. Far too soon Ian saw the clock display a two. His legs were uncertain whether to grow stiff or to shiver with anticipation of his being asked to count, but seconds pulsed by, the colons between the digits throbbing like holes in an artery, and Woollie didn't speak. If his sense of time was slowing down, perhaps Ian could double or more than double the extra he was claiming on Jack's behalf. If the man was as intent on watching for Jack as he appeared to be, Ian could risk trying to free his wrists. He inched forward so that his hands weren't trapped against the sofa. Then a police car made itself heard in the distance, and Woollie's forehead nudged the window.

"He's never got himself arrested, has he? He's supposed not to be attracting attention. Too fond of publicity for his own good or anyone else's. It's not as if nobody ever showed him how to keep things quiet. That's the way, carry on, you'll have her upstairs awake in a minute."

The exhortation was pronounced in such a vicious whisper that his spittle glistened on the pane, but Ian thought his savageness might be an attempt to keep him awake, because his mutter sank into itself as the siren sped closer. "Meant to keep the peace, aren't they, the law? Not doing much of a job. Maybe he's had to tell them where he's coming and they're so excited they've forgotten to switch their row off. Maybe he called them or his mother did."

He must be talking in his sleep or close to it, otherwise surely the ideas he was considering would have infuriated him more than they seemed to be doing. The police car sounded as though it was at least as close as the park. Ian was willing it not to disturb Woollie further when the siren began to dwindle, and shortly there was no question that it was speeding out of earshot. "That's more like. Leave us alone. Let her have some peace," Woollie murmured, and then his head wobbled round. "How long's it been now?"

His voice was blurred, his eyes were losing the energy to keep their lids up. If Ian could avoid rousing him, he might nod off. Ian drummed a heel on the carpet, exerting all the control he could find in himself not to make more noise than Woollie wanted nor so little that the man would have to strain to hear. One muted thump, two, three, and as he performed the fourth the final digit of the clock increased. It might be safe to ignore the latest minute, but suppose Woollie had noticed that Ian's foot was hesitating in the air? He dealt the floor a last dull reluctant blow and took the opportunity to sit forward another inch. "He's had half his allowance then, hasn't he? He'd better be halfway here," Woollie mumbled, and leaned his forehead against the glass.

His voice was nearly gone. His face was so close to the pane that each breath swelled up before his eyes like fog. Surely he couldn't have borne that if he were awake. Ian bowed forward and dug the knuckles of his left hand into the side of his right forearm and levered at his wrists with all his strength.

The tape didn't give even a fraction. When he succeeded in jamming both hands against each other's forearms, all his efforts achieved was to pierce his arms and shoulders with an ache. He barely managed to swallow a gasp of frustration that might have roused Woollie. As the inflamed three transformed itself into a four, he tried to screw his wrists free of the adhesive, but they were bound too tight for that—only the bones ground back and forth inside the flesh. In films whenever captives had to release themselves from their bonds there was always a sharp object somewhere within reach, but the sole item of that kind in sight was the knife under Woollie's fingers on the windowsill.

Ian couldn't use that, and the knowledge lent the slab in his mind more weight and substance. Woollie might as well not be asleep for all the advantage it gave Ian—and then Ian saw it had. He could sneak out of the open door and upstairs to waken Charlotte, and, if they were swift and silent enough, they could steal out of the house. He only had to get off the couch.

He pressed the hot prickly backs of his knees against the edge of it and tried to ease himself to his feet. He hadn't begun to imagine how painful this would be. All his weight was dragging at the muscles of his calves, and he'd risen no more than a few inches from the sofa when the awkward posture gave way. The pain in his calves brought tears to his eyes as he managed to lower himself rather than sprawl on the couch.

He took several deep breaths while the pain subsided and his vision grew less moist and blurred, then inched himself forward until he was perched on the edge of the sofa. He had to stand up this time or he never would. The heat surged through him, locating all the places it could make him sweat, and his arms began to ache and shiver like his legs. The red scratches that composed the four rearranged themselves into a five, putting him in mind of the count at the beginning of a race. He threw his weight onto his calves in a last effort, and the knife slipped from Woollie's fingers. It skittered down the wall and clanged against the skirting-board and stood on the end of its handle for at least a second before toppling over with a thud.

When none of this appeared to have roused Woollie, Ian let out an unsteady breath. He'd frozen in mid-air, supported only by his shaking calves which, having suffered as much as they could bear, deposited him on the couch. A cushion muffled his fall, and he was gathering himself for a renewed bid for freedom when Woollie's fingers that had been resting on the knife began to slide off the sill.

They did their best to retain their hold. The fingertips scrabbled back onto their resting place twice, nails scratching at the wood. Then they strayed off it and down the wall, and the knuckles grazed the skirting-board before the hand slumped on its side. Even this failed to disturb Woollie, but the fingers and thumb opened and closed in search of the knife. They had no success until his head wobbled round to peer at them. They closed on the handle as he twisted away from the window. "How'd that happen?" he demanded. "Was it you?"

Ian could barely find the energy to shake his head. Beyond Woollie's silhouette the street exhibited Jack's nonappearance while the silent pounding of the colon of the clock urged the final digit to increase. It was by no means reassuring that Woollie seemed not to know what to do with the knife or with himself. Ian felt as if the throbbing of the colon was his pulse rendered visible by the time Woollie decided to return the knife and his hand to the windowsill. "Is he coming?" he muttered. "Is that him?"

At first Ian couldn't hear anything. He'd begun to suspect Woollie's mind was having fun with its owner when he heard a car, so distant that the sound might have been a breath. It wasn't fading, it was staying constant: perhaps it was even approaching, if that wasn't just the effect of his straining his ears. Then the noise sank into the night, and in a few throbs of the colon it was gone.

"It wasn't him. What's keeping him? Does he think I'm just having a laugh?" Woollie rubbed his forehead against the pane as if that would enliven his mind, and apparently thought it did. "By God, I know what's keeping him. It's her. It's his mother, the interfering cow."

As he clenched his fists on the sill the knife jerked in his right hand, its point inscribing a scribble like a secret message in his fog on the glass with a small excruciating screech. "She wouldn't let

him come alone. She'd want to know where he was off to so late,"
he snarled, no longer in a whisper. "She'll give us no peace. I
wouldn't care, she was never much good with children. She'll be
telling him to slow down, don't drive so fast or someone's going to
be killed. She won't know she's got that the wrong way round, will
she? What a laugh. How long have they had?"

He hadn't finished speaking when the five on the clock added
a line to itself. That wasn't the only reason why Ian hesitated: he
was trying to decide how much better or worse things would be if
Jack's mother had indeed accompanied him. "It doesn't need any
thinking about," Woollie whispered, turning an impatient ear to
him. "How long?"

Ian hitched himself forward before starting to count. Even now
Woollie was awake, there was still a way for Ian to intervene between him and Charlotte while he had the chance. The imminence
of it drew his stomach into itself. He had to delay Woollie until Jack
came, alone or otherwise. He began to drum his heel on the carpet
as slowly as he dared. Seven thumps, and he thought of stopping—
one more, and he did.

Woollie was silent for two beats of the clock, and then he let a
moist disgusted noise trail out of the side of his mouth toward Ian.
"And the rest," he muttered. "They've had it, haven't they?"

Ian pressed his feet against the floor so hard he was afraid it
might creak and betray him. He'd regained enough strength to
launch himself off the sofa, he was sure he must have, and he had
to bear however much pain the effort took. He could reach the
door ahead of Woollie and kick it shut and hold it closed: Woollie
wouldn't dare injure him too badly when Jack would be here any
moment. Ian leaned his torso backward, preparing to throw himself
forward so hard it would carry him all the way to the door. Then
Woollie crouched away from the window and came at him, licking
his lips as though shaping his wet grin. "Let's see how clever the
horse was."

He ducked his head toward the clock and then at Ian, and
pointed at him with the knife. "Not such a good horse after all, eh?
Not so well trained. Can't even count. I've still got all my wits.
You've been having a laugh, haven't you, son?"

Ian wouldn't have known how to answer. He might be able to
knock the man off balance if he flung himself at him, but what
would that achieve? He was certain to be brought down before he

succeeded in crossing the room. "We both have," Woollie murmured. "You didn't know that, did you? You thought you'd made
me think you were being a horse."

His eyes and his loose smile glistened as he spun round in his
crouch to survey the deserted road. "You've had long enough," he
whispered to Jack or to Ian. "Time I—"

His movement had taken him almost out of Ian's way. Ian
hurled himself forward onto his calves and staggered to his feet,
and swung himself away from Woollie, toward the door. Woollie
grabbed at his legs and missed. He sprawled on the carpet, and the
knife flew out of his grasp, clattering against an angle of the
skirting-board. Ian was already close enough to the door to hook
it with one foot and slam it. He fell against it and fumbled for the
doorknob.

He had to squat awkwardly before his right hand found it and
clenched on it. Pain reawakened in his calves, and then his shoulders set about aching, and his wrists that were pinned against the
door. He mustn't let any of that distract him when there was more
he could do. He clung to the doorknob and began to kick it with
his right heel. The noise had to awaken Charlotte, and it might
bring his mother too.

He'd accomplished two loud kicks when Woollie sprang at him
amid a flapping of jolly pink fish and pried at his grip on the doorknob, but Ian held on until fingertips began to peel his nails away
from the flesh. He aimed another kick at the door and missed as
his captor whirled him round and threw him on the sofa. The backs
of Ian's knees struck the upholstered arm. The cushions softened
his fall, but his fingers blazed with pain as they took most of his
weight before they could flatten themselves against him.

He saw Woollie glance toward the knife as he came after him.
"No need for mess," Woollie muttered, "let's have all the peace we
can have," and snatched a cushion from a chair. Before Ian could
squirm off the couch or even suck in a breath, the cushion was
over his face. In a moment Woollie was sitting on it and had
wrapped his arms around the backs of Ian's calves to haul them
toward him.

Ian couldn't move or breathe. His legs were pinned together
above his stomach, and the agony in them seemed to have cut their
muscles off from his brain. His hands were trapped beneath him,
his head was sandwiched in a soft place in which there was no air,

only a choking smell of faintly scented cloth. Above him he could just hear Woollie singing "Now I lay you down to sleep . . ." His thighs struggled to jerk him free, but the grip on his legs increased, grinding them together. For a moment the weight on his face lessened as though Woollie had raised himself to watch something, and then the cushion refitted itself to Ian's face without having allowed him to find any breath, and there was only the agony of waiting for the pounding blackness inside his head to burst its shell. At last it did, flooding his eyes with a blindness so solid it swept away everything he was or had ever been.

FIFTY-ONE

Leslie didn't know what wakened her. Until it did she hadn't realized she was asleep. She was lying on top of the quilt because of the heat that was stuffing itself under the raised sash of the window, but the shock of remembering that she had no idea of Ian's whereabouts sent a chill through her from her brain that was crawling with half-formed thoughts all the way down to her clammy feet. Could she have heard him sneaking into the house, too ashamed of having worried her to want her to know he was there? She pushed herself up on her elbows and lifted her head and held her breath.

The house was as quiet as a sleeping child. The silence made her ears feel exposed and empty and cold. She was beginning to think she remembered what she'd heard as she'd wakened—a knocking somewhere near the house. Perhaps she'd dreamed it, and in any case it had stopped. The only sound outside was the speeding of a car, and that wasn't in Jericho Close. She was lowering her head to the pillow, though she'd little chance of resting now that all her fears were jostling to be first to take shape in her head, when she wondered if it could have been the phone she'd almost heard.

Surely it would still have been ringing when she awoke—the way she was feeling she would have almost at once—unless it had been Ian and he'd panicked at the prospect of having to speak to her. He ought to know she couldn't be anything except relieved, but the idea wasn't going to leave her alone until she checked when she had last been called. She snatched at the light with the dangling cord and swung her legs off the bed, and came face to face with Ian's note she'd pinned down with the bedside clock.

Twenty-three minutes to one in the morning. I'VE GONE BE-CAUSE YOU SAID I TOOK CHARLOTTE. The time and the note seemed as unreasonable as each other—indeed, she felt as if they were encouraging each other to aggravate her frustration at not having a phone she could keep by the bed at night—but there seemed to be some insight buried in the midst of her feelings, some perception that her half-awake state might be capable of allowing her to reach. She dug her feet into her slippers and retrieved her dressing gown from the hook on the door, and turned back to the room as she tied the cord about her waist. Neither the clock nor the piece of paper seemed to have anything fresh to tell her, except perhaps that she ought to know better than to trust hunches she had when she wasn't fully awake. Nevertheless the impression was as reluctant to vanish as it was to make itself clear, and so she gazed at the note in her hand all the way down to the phone, where she dropped it on the pad as she picked up the receiver. A pieced-together female voice reminded her of the call she'd taken far too many hours ago. She was silencing the unhelpful machine when the receiver and everything around her took on weight and substance in an instant. She'd seen what she'd missed seeing.

She used a forefinger that was all at once steady as a ruler to slide the note off the pad. The sheets of paper were almost the same: the pad was square, the loose page was more rectangular by less than half an inch, yet that made all the difference. Ian had brought the note into the house from somewhere else, but why? She remembered finding it in the open drawer with next door's keys on top. The sounds she'd seemed to hear as she awoke could have been in Janet's house.

She pulled the drawer out and grabbed the keys and strode to the front door. It was less than half open when she halted it and the spread of the light from the hall onto the path. A car was switching off its headlamps as it coasted to a hushed stop outside her gate. It was Jack's.

He caught sight of her as he eased the door shut. He looked as taken aback by her advancing down the path as she was bewildered to see him. "I'm coming," he said, so quietly that she had to tell herself he could only be speaking to her.

She had an abrupt sense of knowing less than she thought she did. As she unlatched the gate he frowned past her at the lit hall. "What are you—" he murmured with an urgency she understood no more than his next question. "Why have you come out?"

"I was going to ask you something rather like that myself."

"You . . ." His frown dug itself deeper, and turned from her to the house, and pulled his eyes wide. "Isn't there anyone . . ."

"You're going to have to finish a few more of your sentences if I'm expected to understand what you want."

He stepped onto the path and ducked toward her as if the frown was tugging his head lower. "Are we alone?"

"I can't see anyone but us, can you? That isn't to say we aren't being watched, meeting in the middle of the night like this and me not dressed for it."

"Watched from your house, you mean."

"I wish I did."

His gaze flickered toward it, and his frown seemed not to know what to do with itself. "You aren't just having to say that."

"Why on earth would I, Jack? What's all this about?"

"Christ." Louder, but still not to her, he said "Christ, it was a trick."

"I'm glad you told me that or I'd have no idea what's going on."

"Leslie, I've none either." He met her eyes, and his frown cleared. "Wait though, maybe I have. Did someone phone you? Is that why you're up?"

"Nobody's called me since yesterday."

"He will, though. That has to be it. He's going to call me at your house."

"Is everything meant to be obvious to me now?"

"Sorry. It's only just getting that way for me." He held out his hands and risked touching hers. "Do you mind if we do this inside? There may be a call any second."

"Do what, Jack?"

"I'll try to tell you the truth."

"What sort of problem are you saying that will be?"

"For you to believe it, mostly, I guess."

"Another instalment, you mean?" She was having to deal with

too much all at once, not least with her uncertainty how she felt about his reappearance, when she was supposed to be finding Ian. "I've got to go next door first," she said, and stepped around Jack. "Just tell me who'll be calling you on my phone."

He was already making for it, and she was about to enquire what was so important that he'd neglected to ask her permission when he stopped and waited for her to lock gazes with him. "The truth?" he said.

"What else, and nothing but."

"My father."

It was his expression—hoping much more than expecting she would believe him, but resigned to either—that made her unable to laugh at his words. The night grew intensely present around her—the dark and all it might hide. Jack saw her fail to dismiss what he'd said, and backed toward her hall. "Do you mind if I . . ."

Though his belated politeness was almost comical, it still wasn't in her to laugh. She had to go after him, not just to learn everything but to hear it before Ian could. "We both will. Next door can wait. Hurry," she said.

She didn't know whose urgency she was expressing, his or her own. She was at his heels by the time he reached the threshold. She held onto the latch so as not to slam the door behind them in her haste. As Jack stood by the phone she dropped Janet's keys in her pocket and leaned against the door, though her wakefulness and the situation were reluctant to let her stay in one place. "Your father," she urged.

"He isn't dead. He faked it when he knew he was going to be found out, I figure. He must have thought one of my mother's residents would make a great witness to persuade everyone he was dead because he'd be taken in himself."

"But you've been in touch with your father."

"He called me, that's right. If you were going to say it could have been some joker pretending to be him, I wish—"

"I wasn't. I was wondering why he would contact you if he wanted everyone believing he was dead."

"Seems like he read I would be writing about him. Maybe he wanted to make sure I got it right. Only now he—"

"Tell me something. Did he get in touch with you while you were living here?"

"He called me a couple of times. That was the first I heard from him after he was meant to have drowned. It was before you knew who I was."

"Which was why you didn't bother telling anyone a killer was still alive, you mean."

"I know. I'm sorry, believe me. I've no excuse. I just didn't think he would be dangerous any longer, not when he was having to hide and he'd let me know he was." Jack dragged at his frown with his fingertips. "Why doesn't he call? He said I had to be here by now. He must have been meaning to contact me here, and he'd only do that by phone, wouldn't he? It doesn't make any other kind of sense."

"Look, let's say I believe he's alive. What sense can you see that I can't in him calling you at my house when he's supposed to be pretending he's dead?"

"Maybe this is the only place he could think of to phone me except at my mother's. That's where he sent me here from, but he said he was here. I'm certain that's what he told me," Jack insisted, and she saw him shake off the notion that she might have been forced to conceal his father. "Unless he doesn't know where he is any more. Christ, I hope that's not it, that his mind—"

"Slow down. There's another question to sort out. Why is he calling you at all?"

"He needs me to drive him somewhere. He mustn't feel safe wherever he's hiding. That's some of it, but . . ."

"Go on. Jack. Nothing but the truth, remember."

"It won't just be him I'm driving."

That was more than Leslie's nerves would let her stay still for. She darted forward and made her hands drop for fear of how painfully she would have grabbed Jack. "What are you saying?"

"He's got a child with him. I'm sure he took her so I wouldn't be able to give him away, and that has to mean he won't harm her. Only . . ."

"Finish it. Don't do that, don't keep stopping."

"I guess it isn't so uncommon a name, is it, but he said she's called Charlotte."

"How long have you known that?" Leslie said once she was able to move her stiff lips.

"Since maybe ten minutes ago. Since I last spoke to him. It's been longer than that now, it's been too—" Jack's eyes widened, and then the gap between his lips did. "Hold it," he gasped.

"What, Jack? What?"

"He said he'd see me in ten minutes. I don't believe his mind's that far gone yet. When he said see he meant it. He's somewhere close by. Where?"

Leslie pulled out the keys as she spoke. "They're away on holiday next door, but I'm sure I heard someone in there just before. I thought it was Ian. He could have used these to get in."

"Suppose it was Ian as well?"

Leslie took a breath to retort, only to discover she wasn't sure what to say. "That's it," Jack declared. "I couldn't figure how my father knew where to call me, but if Ian found out and then—"

He sucked in whatever his next word might have been and twisted round to glare at the wall the houses had in common. Leslie clutched at the keys with her free hand, because otherwise they would have fallen from her shocked grasp. The next moment she and Jack were sprinting for the front door. They'd heard a man's shout through the wall—a shout of triumph. Though it had done without words, there was no mistaking its significance. It was the cry of the victor in a game of hide-and-seek.

FIFTY-TWO

It was the boy's fault as usual, Hector thought, but all the same he sang to him. He used his hands that were locked behind the boy's knees to bend his captive's body almost double, and leaned his weight on the cushion that covered the boy's face. He resisted an urge to sing louder as if that might help him overcome the struggles the boy was straining to perform, because the point was to stifle any row that might waken the boy's playmate upstairs. Perhaps he was singing to give himself some peace, some patience that would help him wait for the boy to give up attempting to resist the inevitable. But the stubborn body was still sweating to unbend itself when a car appeared at the end of the road.

Hector craned to peer over the net curtain that obscured the lower half of the window. The headlamps died as the car halted outside the house next door, and John climbed out to gaze toward that house. Though he was late, Hector no longer resented that: it had given him time to deal with the boy, after all—but the trouble was that he hadn't finished. As he sat harder on the cushion over the boy's face he saw John open the neighbouring gate. Hector could catch his attention, he only had to find something within reach that he could throw at the window—and then the boy's mother appeared on her path.

So the boy had managed to ruin Hector's plan. Hector hauled the legs toward himself in a rage and pressed all his weight down on the boy's face while he sang the lullaby softer and sweeter than ever. He saw John and the woman walk around each other on the path, exchanging words he couldn't hear. The woman glanced towards Hector more than once, but he had to believe she couldn't see him for the net curtains and the dimness. Then John vanished in the direction of her house, followed by the woman, and the boy's legs jerked and went limp.

Hector wasn't to be fooled. He held onto the boy's legs while he raised himself very tentatively from the cushion. When the body under him didn't betray any movement, he crooked one arm behind the knees and snatched the cushion off the face. The eyes were closed, but there was no telling what the mouth might be up to behind the gag: suppose the tape was hiding a grin at Hector's credulousness? He found the end of the tape to unwrap the head—he almost fell for that temptation. Instead he pinched the lashes of the right eye between fingers and thumbs and leaned close.

He saw the lower lid twitch as his grip plucked out a hair. Surely the boy couldn't stand that without flinching unless he was at peace, but Hector continued tugging until the upper lid peeled back. The eye was blank white, more like a marble that had been inserted in the socket. He found the spectacle unexpectedly dismaying. "Close your eyes good night," he murmured, releasing the eyelid, which stayed ajar over a glistening crescent of white until he pulled it down. He tiptoed in a crouch across the room to retrieve the knife before heading swiftly for the hall. He wanted to hear what was being said next door—not, if John had any sense, about him.

He'd stepped into the hall and was lifting his smile toward the silence upstairs—at least there was one babe in the wood that knew she was meant to stay asleep—when the woman's voice beyond the wall grew clear as a radio that had just been tuned in. "He's supposed to be pretending he's dead."

For a moment Hector was so thrown he thought she was referring to her son, and peered at the body on the sofa to reassure himself it hadn't moved—and then he heard John say "Maybe this is the only place he could think of to phone me except at my mother's."

He'd betrayed Hector. He wasn't able to keep quiet about him, which showed he couldn't be trusted at all. The knife in Hector's fist swung to point toward his betrayer, but as he restrained himself from jabbing at the wall with it, John's next words reached him.

"That's where he sent me here from, but he said he was here. I'm certain that's what he told me."

Hector covered his mouth to suppress a laugh. The knife touched his lips and his delighted outthrust tongue like a kiss that tasted metallic as blood. John was having to explain his presence to the woman, and he was at such a dead loss he could think of nothing to tell her except the truth. They didn't know where Hector was, and he wouldn't be there much longer. He only had to ensure that he wouldn't be leaving anyone capable of raising the alarm while he made himself scarce. He couldn't risk staying or even just stealing away when at any moment the girl might waken and find she was alone and start a fuss that might be heard next door. He felt as if the boy's body were urging him to be far away before it was found—as if the boy were having a last try at making it harder for him to think.

He didn't want to use the knife. It might be quick, but he was afraid that its effect wouldn't be peaceful—wouldn't look that way to him, at any rate. He slipped it into his pocket and ran on tiptoe into the front room to snatch the cushion from beside the couch. It was wet with the boy's saliva, which seemed to promise that the babes would be going to sleep together as they should. He'd nothing against the girl, after all—he just wanted her to be peaceful, and if having a companion with her would help, that was her choice to make. "He needs me to drive him somewhere," John was saying through the wall, and Hector was able to grin at him. He didn't need John's help any longer, he was safest by himself, as he always had been. He hugged the cushion and stroked it as he ran upstairs on his toes, singing under his breath.

> "Now I lay you down to sleep,
> Close your eyes good night.
> Angels come your soul to keep,
> Close your eyes good night . . ."

It had often occurred to him at these moments, but never so intensely as now: he was one of the angels himself—the angel that brought peace into the lives of children who were crying out for it. What he was about to do was inevitable, not to mention desirable, and he found himself wondering why it had taken him so long until he recalled how the boy had interrupted him. The interruption was done with, and even the boy turned out to have his uses. "Your playmate's waiting for you," he murmured at the door propped open with the stool. "Him and the other sleepy children."

He hugged the cushion harder as he left the stairs and felt he was hugging the peace he'd given to the boy. John's voice and the woman's had stayed downstairs, incomprehensible now. Closer to him, beyond the open door, was a silence that embodied a peace he only had to prolong to make it perfect. He held the cushion in front of him and sidled into the room, reserving a deep breath for a lullaby once the cushion was in place. Then he closed his eyes to do away with the trick the dimness was playing, and opened them at once, and grimaced so hard that a trickle of saliva ran down his chin. His eyes hadn't been mistaken. There was nobody on the bed.

His mind went out like a television whose power had been cut, and then it came back. He would have seen her through the doorway of the front room if she had sneaked downstairs while he was busy with her playmate. Even if she'd realised there were people next door all too ready to run to her aid, she hadn't called out—perhaps she didn't dare. He mustn't lose patience with her when that might give him away to John and the boy's mother. "Where are you, love?" he murmured. "You ought to be in bed. It's past your bedtime. Just tell me where you are and I'll put you where you ought to be."

There was no reply, but he sensed he wasn't alone in holding his breath. "Whisper to me where you are or you won't see your playmate. He's waiting for the coach to come and take you both away. You don't want to bother him, do you? He'd want you to know you needn't hide from me. Just think about it, love. He wouldn't have left you by yourself otherwise, would he?"

Surely that was a question she would feel bound to answer, even if to disagree, but she must be doing so in her wilful little head. She hadn't been like that until the boy came. Downstairs the muffled voices were carrying on at each other, and the threat of discovery they represented made the inside of Hector's skull feel scraped. "Come on, love, you've had your bit of a laugh with me," he coaxed. "Stop your game now or you'll miss the coach. We've got to get you ready for it like your playmate is."

She was either on the floor beyond the bed, he thought, or in the wardrobe. Without warning, but silently, he lurched around the bed. The carpet was bare apart from the black straw hat he'd discarded after his first efforts to amuse the girl. He dropped the cushion on the bed and slid the wardrobe door back, just slowly enough not to make a sound. "Who's in here?" he whispered, leaning into the cell that wasn't so dark his eyes couldn't deal with it, and saw a long black dress flinch in front of him. "Who's hiding in the house where the flat people live? All of them flat as pancakes except the one who's called Charlotte."

He didn't grab her. He only closed his hands around the flat breasts of the dress, just about where her neck ought to be. When his hands met on nothing except the slippery material he thought she'd contrived to slide out from under the dress. He clawed at it before realising she had never been there: only his whisper had stirred the dress. He stretched his arms wide and planted a hand on the clothes at either end of the rack, and heard a frightened squeak as he brought them together—the squeak of the hooks on the runner. The clothes were empty, and so was the rest of the wardrobe except for the shoes on its floor. He ducked out of the enclosure before he could give in to the rage that tasted hot and raw in his mouth, then retreated to the corner furthest from the door so as to survey the room. At once he saw what he'd overlooked. Under the window the quilt hung off the bed almost to the carpet, except for an indentation like a rumpled archway where someone had crawled underneath.

"Whose burrow's this?" He only mouthed that as he dodged on tiptoe around the bed so that he was between it and the door, then he dived onto all fours. "Which little animal's made its nest under—"

His voice was rising when it failed. There wasn't space for anyone under the bed: hardly even room for him to shove his hand beneath. The shape of the quilt must have been meant as a trick. He reared up in a fury that turned his surroundings black as buried earth, and groped almost blindly for the cushion, but then gathered up the pillows instead. They were softer, and nobody could say he was cruel, no more so than he ever had to be. He padded onto the landing only just audibly and heard a drop of liquid strike the bath.

"That's where you are, is it, love? Can't control yourself? I keep telling you there's nothing to be scared of." His words of reassurance took his head around the door, but he thought they'd had the opposite effect to the one he'd intended when a gush of liquid spattered the bath. Then he saw that the solitary spout of the taps had released it into the dim trough. He could see nowhere else in the room for the girl to hide, and he was backing out past the ajar door when he glimpsed her shoes in the mirror.

They were behind the door—she was. "Now I lay you down," he mouthed, and sprang around the door, a pillow poised in each hand. They met with a soft thump where her head ought to have been. Only her shoes were hiding behind the door. Had they been meant to delay him? She'd tricked him twice: how far had that got her? His gums ground each other raw at the thought of her having slipped out of the house—and then, closer than the maddeningly incomprehensible bricked-up voices, he heard her sob. She was in the front room.

She must have found her playmate. He'd been some use after all. Hector tiptoed down so quickly and deftly he was scarcely aware of touching the stairs. She didn't notice him as he reached the hall and saw her kneeling by the sofa, trying to locate the end of the tape around the boy's head with the fingernails of one hand while she lifted his head with the other. "Wake up, Ian," she pleaded. "You can. Just wake up."

She either heard or glimpsed Hector scampering across the room and turned as though to offer him her face. In a moment it and the rest of her head were sandwiched between the pillows, and he had no idea how loud his cry of triumph might be. At once his voice was under control and he was. The nails clawing at his hand on the pillow over the girl's face, the small shoeless feet drumming on his shins, were no more than minor irritations of which he was hardly even conscious as he began to sing.

FIFTY-THREE

Jack felt as though his father's shout were directed at him—as though it were saying that he hadn't needed Jack or, far worse, that he'd done what he wanted despite him. Jack almost pushed past Leslie as she threw her front door open, and he groaned when he saw that the fence between the gardens was too high to vault. She had the keys to the next house, and so he could only sprint after her down the path, through the gate and U-turning through its neighbour, up the path that felt like retracing the steps he'd just taken while he sucked in altogether too many harsh, short, desk-bound breaths. Now Leslie was at the door, surely only a few seconds after they'd heard the shout, and driving a key into the lock. She was twisting it when he saw movement in the room beside it and peered through the curtains that netted much of the light from the street. The material seemed to grow less substantial—everything around him did—as he saw what was happening in the room.

A figure had swung round to stare toward the hall. Though it had an old man's shrunken face, its grey hair straggled over its shoulders, and it wore a pink and yellow dress as though it were trying to be more than one parent or to portray some childhood nightmare. For a moment Jack thought, or perhaps only yearned to think, that it was playing with a blue doll the size of a child, holding it by the pale featureless head that was much too large for the body. But the caved-in lips were moving, pronouncing a message to the toy that had been lifted high off the floor, and Jack heard the song as though it were being murmured in his ear. If that hadn't sent him dashing after Leslie as she flung the door wide, the victim's struggles would have. "Let her go," he roared.

He was nearly in the room when Leslie halted in the doorway. "Oh," she said, so quietly that it sounded as though all emotion had been shocked out of her.

Ian was sprawled on a sofa facing the television. His legs hung limply over the end of the sofa nearest the door, his arms were pinned beneath him. His face was turned up to the ceiling, but whatever expression it might bear was wrapped around with tape. Jack was afraid that grief at the sight had paralysed Leslie, and he was about to move her aside as gently as swiftness permitted when she slapped the light-switch with a force that propelled her into the room. "Put her down," she said.

The hulking toothless stooped old man in the yellow dress strewn with pink fish recoiled a step, squeezing his eyes shut so furiously that they leaked and pressing the pillows together harder to compensate. The next moment his eyes opened with a flutter of their lashes that looked as if it were meant to go with the dress, but he didn't relax his grip on the pillows. "I'll deal with him," Jack said, knowing Leslie would understand whom he meant, since she couldn't feel he was entitled to do anything for Ian after all he'd been responsible for. He was dodging around her when he heard a snort and a choke and as much of a cough as the gag would allow.

It was Ian. His legs moved vaguely, trying to discover where they were, only to drop against the end of the sofa with a feeble thump as he fought to breathe. "There you are, missus," the old derelict croaked. "He isn't even dead. The girl's not your concern, fair enough? See to your lad."

That was when Jack realised how far beyond anything he could imagine his father's mind had gone. He sent himself toward that unknown as Leslie fell on her knees by the sofa and lifted Ian's head with one hand while she searched for the end of the tape with the other. In a second she had it and was peeling it round and round his head. Jack saw his father's gaze flicker, considering whether he could reach the door, and grasp that there were too many obstacles—furniture and Jack. "Give her to me," Jack said.

"Don't interfere, John. That's what he did, and look what happened to him. Promise you'll do what you said you'd do, take me somewhere I won't be bothered any more."

The little girl's feet began to kick more desperately as her nails scraped skin off the bulging veins on the back of the hand on the pillow. Jack's father seemed to find none of this worth noticing as he pressed the back of her head against him with the pillow and snatched a knife out of his pink and yellow pocket. "Stay back. We don't want a mess," he said.

"Let her go and we'll talk about where I can take you. Let her go now."

His father gave him a smile whose ends drooped as soon as they'd twitched up, and felt around his lips with his tongue while the knife probed under the foremost pillow. "You aren't expecting me to fall for that, are you? I'd have nothing to bargain with then. Just get yourself out to your car and I'll bring her. The quicker you are the happier she'll be."

A ripping sound made Jack wince as Leslie yanked the last of the tape off Ian's mouth. The boy coughed and almost rolled off the sofa as he struggled to push himself to his feet, desperate to be outside before he vomited. He was too weakened and too late. "Good God," Jack's father protested, "can't he keep that to himself? I hope he'll be cleaning it up."

That overcame whatever reservations Jack had, too deep in him for definition, about grappling with his father—but before Jack could make a move his father rested the point of the knife against the inch of the little girl's throat that was visible below the pillow. "You aren't going to touch me, John," he wheedled. "I'm your—"

Jack grabbed the wrist of the hand that held the knife and wrenched it higher than his father's head, and was rewarded by kicks on his shins from the girl. He took hold of the fingers that were digging into the pillow and bent them back, feeling as though he were fighting dirty in a schoolyard. He felt the knuckles start to crack before his father released the pillows, his raw eyes watering. "That's not the way to treat your dad," he complained as the little girl dropped to the floor, crying out as her feet struck it, and wobbled across the room like someone barely able to see or walk.

Leslie saved her from falling, and she gave another kind of cry. "Ian's all right. He's all right, isn't he?"

"He will be," Leslie said fiercely. "Both of you."

Jack took that as partly a plea addressed to him. He let go of his father's fingers so as to pry the knife loose from the other hand, and gave his father a shove that dumped him in the chair furthest from the hall. "Don't move," he warned. "Leslie, can you take them next door? I'll keep him here for the police. Call them and whoever else you need."

"Can you stand up, Ian? I'll get your hands free as soon as we're home." Leslie helped him up while supporting Charlotte, who did her best to help him too. They were progressing toward the hall, avoiding Ian's accident and Jack's father as if these were much the same sort of thing, when Leslie said "Shall I take that with me?"

She meant the knife Jack was holding. "No," he said.

Whatever she took that to mean didn't detain her. Jack listened as she led the children out of the house. When he heard the door of her house shut he moved a chair between his father and the hall and sat in it, holding the knife in his lap. His father was rubbing his injured fingers and flexing them, and only when he'd finished inspecting them for damage did he lift his gaze to Jack. Having produced a reproachful look that his toothlessness helped appear pathetic, he turned it to the knife. "What's the plan, John?" he said in a tone of being nearly ready to forgive him.

"You heard it."

"I heard what you told her to get rid of them, but you're talking to your family now."

Jack was trying not to feel he was. Despite the grotesque dress, the long-haired unshaven man wasn't quite unrecognisable, though he would have been if Jack had passed him in the street, but the only memories Jack had just now of times they'd spent together were the ones he'd done his best to bury. He closed both hands around the handle of the knife as his father adjusted a tentative grin with his tongue. "Have a heart, John. Those kids are going to be all right, she said so. She won't notice if we slip off while she's busy with them. I reckon she's so happy for them she won't care what we do."

Jack was unable to silence his response. "She won't care if she never sees me again, sure enough."

"Couldn't have been worth having then, could she? I expect she's only interested in people she can look after, like your mother is. Anyway, let's talk when we're on our way, shall we? We'll have lots of news to tell each other," Jack's father said, and took hold of the arms of the chair.

"Don't try it. I told you, don't move."

"Who do you think you are, speaking like that to your father?

You've read too many of the kind of books you write." When that had no effect he pulled his lower lip down with a forefinger and gave Jack a knowing look. "If you hang on much longer the police are going to be here and then I'll have to tell them what you used to do."

Jack's memory sharpened and came absolutely clear. "I hope you will," he said.

"You're admitting it at last, are you?"

"I'm seeing the truth if that's what you mean. You know I never realised what you were making me do. You'd never have been able to make me if I had."

"That's what you'd love to believe, you mean." He searched Jack's eyes as if to convince them or himself that they were hiding some unsureness, and then his mouth drooped further open as he scowled at the knife. "I notice you didn't tell your lady friend what you want that for."

"Whatever has to be done."

"You're no different from me then, are you? You just wish you were. What are you going to tell everyone about me? Going to try and turn me into one of your horrors? Maybe you think I'm something you made up."

"I know you aren't." It was as much as Jack could produce in the way of sympathy to add "I know some of why you're how you are."

"You don't know the half of it. If you knew everything you'd save me if you care at all for your own flesh and blood."

"I'll say what I can when I'm asked to."

"It won't be enough. Listen, I know what we can do. Let's go for a drive while I tell you the rest of it and if it doesn't change your mind you can bring me straight back."

"No need. We're here. You can tell them yourself whatever you want them to know."

"They won't understand, can't you see that? They won't like you ought to, and it won't be only them. Don't you know how the villains would be after me in prison if they heard I'd done something to kids? They have to find someone they can reckon is lower than them. You wouldn't want to think of that happening to your own father, John."

That was true, especially given how aged and exhausted he looked. Jack's grasp slackened on the knife until he saw his father pretending not to notice. "There's a lot I don't want to think of about you," he said. "If you manage to persuade them you had enough excuses maybe they'll just put you away somewhere you can't harm anyone else."

"I can't now, John. Take a good look at me and tell me if you think I could."

"That's why you're dangerous, because someone might think you aren't."

"Are you still fretting about those kids next door even though they're going to be fine? They're the last. I'd have no more opportunities. I'd just want to keep myself to myself." He risked letting Jack see his hopefulness, and when all this failed to make a difference he said resentfully "I wouldn't have bothered with her except she was upset, and then he wandered in and got me all confused."

"Are you through yet? You've said a lot more than too much, and it's making me feel kind of sick."

"Won't it be good for your book, me talking to you? I'd like to think I helped." He started a laugh that didn't get far, then attempted a grin that sagged with disgust. "I know why you feel sick, it's the stink in here. You get that round kids. You wouldn't know, never having had to deal with them. Let's go and sit somewhere you'll feel better."

"I can put up with it where I am."

"Is there nothing that'll move you, John?" his father complained, glaring at him with eyes that looked ready to weep. That wasn't about to affect Jack, who met his gaze, vowing not to blink before his father did. His eyes were beginning to sting, and he was gripping the knife harder and telling himself it couldn't matter less who blinked first—he would rather lose the contest than appear close to tears—when he heard the whoop of a siren behind him.

It sounded near—perhaps at the end of the street. When he glanced over his shoulder, however, Jericho Close was deserted. He turned back to the room and found his father standing over him. "Last laugh, John," his father said.

He closed his clammy hands around Jack's on the knife and leaned his face toward him, grinning so gleefully his gums dripped. Jack's nostrils filled with smells of cloth and breath and unwashed flesh that merged into a choking staleness. As he tried to heave himself out of the trap of the chair and drag his hands free, his father's grin collapsed into a grimace at Jack's attempts to escape him, or at the situation where they'd ended up, or at himself. "Like horror, do you? I'll show you some horror," he muttered into Jack's face, and jerked the knife upward as he ducked and brought the underside of his chin down hard.

Jack felt the knife snag and cut through the obstruction. He saw his father's tongue flinch as the point of the blade found it from beneath. His father's mouth gaped in a silent cry and fought to raise its shaky ends into a smile as he reared up so violently the handle was wrenched from Jack's grasp. "Tell me to shut up," his father mumbled, his eyes wincing as his tongue caught on the knife. "Let's have some peace at last." He fell back with a flurry of pink fish into the chair he'd vacated, and the impact drove the blade through his tongue, which turned crimson in his gaping mouth. His eyes clouded, but he peered past Jack through the window. An ambulance had swung into Jericho Close.

He stared at Jack and managed to shake his head an inch from side to side, and again. In case that failed to make his wishes sufficiently clear, he used his reddened hands to haul at the knife, almost splitting his tongue in half. Jack had to turn away from the spectacle of the blade wagging like some kind of silent joke in the wound of a mouth. Leslie was helping Ian and Charlotte down her path as the attendants came to meet them.

The children were in the ambulance, and she was about to climb into it, when she glanced in Jack's direction. His hand lifted itself before he knew what it meant to communicate, and then he did. He mustn't delay any treatment the children might need, and he needn't imagine how the sight of his father's condition could affect them in their present state, but perhaps these were reasons he was giving himself not to acknowledge how he didn't want to be responsible for prolonging his father's life. How would that benefit anyone? He showed Leslie his open palm and waved her away, and glimpsed the beginning of a puzzled frown as she followed the children into the ambulance. He watched the vehicle leave Jericho Close before he turned to face his father.

He wasn't quite dead. His chin was leaning on the handle that was propped against his collarbone while he gazed at a photograph album in his lap. Jack couldn't distinguish the photographs for the red fingerprints on them, but he guessed what they were, and when he heard the sounds his father's mouth was producing along with a great deal of blood—a bubbling murmur that Jack was just able to hear had the tune of a lullaby—he wanted to snatch the album out of his father's clutches. Instead he sat back with some weariness and waited. Soon the vague humming lost its hold on the melody and subsided into a gurgle, and the album slipped from the limp fingers, and the eyes grew dull as pebbles above the slack, raw, disappointed grimace that had helped the pink and yellow dress acquire a crimson bib.

Jack leaned forward to close the eyes. Apart from a shudder when the lids proved reluctant to descend over the swollen eyeballs, which felt rather too firm to be lifeless, he experienced only relief. Before long even that gave way to a crushing sense that he had nothing left to do, since the police would want him to leave the scene untouched. The few minutes it took them to arrive felt to him more like an entire sleepless night. He went to the front door as two uniformed officers strode up the path. Curtains were stirring at several bedroom windows in Jericho Close. "He's in here," Jack said, loud enough for whoever was watching to hear. "Hector Woollie. I'm his son."

EPILOGUE

Ian had never met anyone at a restaurant before, but since the girl who showed him to a table seemed not much older than him and less dressed he didn't mind. She handed him a menu bigger than the table and shouted "I'll be back" as though she were quoting one of the films for which there were posters all over the walls and pillars of the huge crowded high-ceilinged room. She hadn't returned when a neighbouring foursome—noisy even by the standards of the restaurant, presumably as a result of all the bottles of beer they'd lined up like trophies—was joined by a friend. Like them, he was in his twenties and in black—boots, jeans, T-shirt, cap on backwards—though their resemblance to an American street gang stopped short of their accents. He slouched over and took hold of the chair opposite Ian with the hand that was empty of a Budweiser. "Anyone using this, mate?"

"They will be in a minute."

It seemed that mightn't be enough to dissuade the thin-faced customer, who wore a grin meant to announce that nothing had better upset him, from commandeering the chair, but then the waitress came swiftly back. "Get us a chair over here, love," the man said.

"I'll be with you when I've looked after him." To Ian she said "Can I bring you anything till your friend comes? Something to drink?"

Ian was tempted to try for a beer or to call her Sophie after her name-tag, not least since the black-capped five were watching. Instead he asked and felt childish for asking "Can I have a Zingo?"

"Course you can." She flashed him a smile that could have advertised toothpaste and was on her way again before the standing man had a chance to yell "What happened to my chair, love?"

"I'll see what we can fix you up with," she called, not as loud but more distinctly, and consulted with a waiter as she dodged around him.

The man returned to his friends and made a comment with her name in it that raised a raucous laugh. They better hadn't give her a hard time when she'd been so friendly with Ian—he'd faced worse than them. They hadn't noticed his disapproval by the time their mirth subsided, and he began to feel rather at a loss, even in danger of learning that he'd been the victim of a change of mind. The only person to approach him in the next five minutes was Sophie, bearing his Zingo in a tall glass on a tray. "Want to order now, or are you saving yourself?" she said.

"Okay if I wait another five?"

"Just call me when you want me. Your date won't stand you up if they've any sense."

The compliment turned his face not entirely unpleasantly hot, and he was trying to think of a suitable response, too late for this time but designed to greet her next appearance, when the man with no chair shouted "Where's my seat, love?"

"Somebody's working on it."

"Fucking building it, more like."

Either she didn't hear or object to his language or decided nobody else would for the uproar. As she headed for the kitchen yet again he stalked across to Ian's table and seized the unoccupied chair. "I'm having this, all right," he declared.

"You can't. I'm keeping it for someone."

"So you can tell them I got to it first, can't you, mate."

Ian was about to argue when a voice cut through the hubbub. "That'll be mine, I guess."

"Hey, Jack."

The man in the cap didn't move as Jack gave Ian a quick handshake and stretched out a hand for the chair, but then the waiter Sophie had approached brought a stool from the bar. "Can you make do with this, sir, till you and your party are ready to eat?"

The man took the stool and pointed at Jack with its legs. "You look like you think you're somebody."

"I've tried to be."

The man perched above his cronies and drew sniggers from them with a comment, while Jack ordered a Miller and a burger and Ian made his twice the burger. "So," Jack said to him with a tentativeness that went with his expression, then raised his eyebrows and the corners of his mouth. "How's everyone?"

"Who?"

"You, for instance."

"Okay."

"Back at school, yes? How's that now?"

"It's school."

"But you're doing how well at it? Well?"

"I guess. They like some of the stuff I've written. Shit, I was going to show you a story I wrote, but I've left it at home."

"What was it about?"

"Mostly Charlotte. How she is really, not like the story I had the fight over. That was crap. Maybe this one's a bit less crap."

"You're starting to sound like a writer, so keep writing. How is Charlotte?"

"She isn't such a pain now she's older. I go there every week. My dad likes me to since she said it wasn't my fault she ran away, only I don't think Hilene likes me there too much. She puts up with it because she doesn't want to upset Charlotte. Christ, you know what my dad told me Charlotte said? She wants to marry me when she grows up."

"She'll be someone else by then. Anyway, there are worse things than being wanted." Jack seemed to welcome Sophie's reappearance, either just the interruption or his drink as well. He took a swig before saying "She's over the worst, then."

"She had to take stuff to help her sleep. I think maybe she still does." Ian felt suddenly restless with guilt, not least because he'd brought away no nightmares from being trapped by Jack's father, only dreams every night as he was falling asleep of all the chances he ought to have taken to save Charlotte. "Did you see what the wheelie woman put about us in the paper?" he said.

"I saw a lot of papers. Saw a bunch of reporters first, same as I expect you did. What did that one say?"

"Said we were all HEROES OF TWIN HOUSES OF HORROR," Ian told him, mocking the headline as much as he could.

"I did see that. It ought to have meant you and Charlotte. I hope it impressed your neighbours at least."

"They've been okay with us, most of them have. I think some of them don't know what's true, or maybe they don't want to know. Tell you who thinks now she was wrong about me—my gran. You know, my mum's mother."

"But just when you've got all these people on your side you were saying on the phone you're going to move."

"I don't mind now. Mum wants to, and Janet and Vern can't stand it at theirs. Some company's buying the houses and leaving just the outsides and turning them into flats. Anyway," Ian said to rid himself of a sense of being obscurely accused, "you've moved."

"Had enough of the spotlight for a while. That's great, thanks."

His enthusiasm was aimed at Sophie and their lunch. She gave them a smile and turned a version of it on the five at the nearby table. "Are you guys planning to order some food soon? You can't really sit there if you're only drinking."

The man on the stool jumped up, knocking it over with a clatter, and threw back his head to drain the bottle as a preamble to gasping "Then let's fuck off somewhere we can."

Until the rest of the party stood up, Jack didn't even glance in his direction, but that was apparently sufficient excuse for the man to take more of a dislike to him. "You still look like you want us to think you're someone."

Jack shrugged, which was no longer enough of a response for Ian. "He's Jack Lamb."

"Never heard of him."

"He's a writer. He writes books."

"Don't read them," the man said with some pride.

"I'll tell you something else he is. Hector Woollie was his dad."

"Don't know him either."

"That's how I'd like it to be," Jack said.

The man looked primed to take his bafflement out on someone when his friends yelled they were off for that drink. He swaggered after them, and then the only confusion was Ian's. "Aren't you going to write your book?"

"It wasn't such a good idea."

"But if you don't write about your dad someone else will."

"That's okay. I don't mind. Maybe you should try and write something if it bothers you that much."

"How about you? How are you going to make a living?"

"I'll have to do what I'm good at, won't I? Thought I'd have a go at a crime novel while I wait for the stuff I really like to write to come back. It always does, you know."

Ian had no sense of whether that was true—couldn't tell if Jack was simply trying to be positive to cheer them both up. Like the encounter with the gang in black, his meeting with Jack seemed to be ending up nowhere in particular. The venue had been Ian's choice, but now it was proving too noisy to let him think, and the things he still wanted to say struck him as hardly for shouting. He busied himself with his burger instead, and had finished it and its accompaniments by the time Jack abandoned the remains of his. Jack insisted on paying for him, which was the last he saw of Sophie, and it felt as if that might be the case with Jack too as Ian followed him into Leicester Square.

Out here the noise was less enclosed, but that didn't help Ian much. He was gazing about at the cinema hoardings and a couple of trees that appeared to be intended to remind the crowds it was autumn when Jack said "What's your plan for the rest of the day?"

"I was going to my mum's and Melinda's shop. Walk along with me if you want."

"How far did you have in mind?"

"All the way if you like."

"Nice try, Ian, but I guess not. I don't think I'd be . . ." Jack took the opportunity to fall silent while he moved out of the way of a troop of American tourists, and then he said "Tell me the truth here. Did your mom know we were meeting?"

"Sure."

"And her attitude was . . ."

"She said I had to make my own choices."

"That sounds like her, sure enough." Jack suppressed a reminiscent smile before it could become too public. "Tell her hello from me if you think you should. I'll say good-bye to you now, okay? Going to head back and try to work up some notes for a novel."

"Good luck," Ian said, all he could think of to say.

"Double that to you and your mom." Jack gave him a protracted handshake and appeared to think of hugging him, but let go instead. He was stepping into the entrance to the underground when he looked back at Ian. "If you write anything you'd like me to read you can always call my mother again to find out where I've ended up."

Ian watched him vanish down the white steps, and then he made his way into Soho, through the narrow streets and narrower alleys that looked determined to be brighter than the afternoon light. He'd grown used to being propositioned by girls in the area, in fact quite enjoyed it, but just now he had to remind himself to be polite in his refusals, because he was trying to ensure the slab didn't settle on his mind. Why wasn't he as disappointed by his meeting with Jack as it seemed he should have been? Why did he have the impression it had given him a reason to feel good? He was close to figuring it out as he reached the end of Wardour Street and saw, beyond a slow parade of buses, his mother's and Melinda's shop.

They were behind the counter, facing the street, smiling side-long at each other with their arms around each other's shoulders. His mother had been out at night a few times with Melinda since Jack had left the Ames house. Ian wasn't sure what this implied, but it was his mother's choice and he could live with it. That thought and his meeting with Jack came together in his head, and the threat of the slab withdrew.

He'd been looking for endings where there weren't any. Life wasn't a story unless you made it into one. Jack's father had come to an end, but nobody else whom Ian knew had. His mother might be on the way to becoming someone else—no, someone more— and so was he, and he hoped the same for Jack. He looked over his shoulder, suddenly wondering if Jack might have decided to follow him after all. But there were no faces he recognised behind him, only ahead.

The women saw him as the traffic let him cross Oxford Street. They didn't move apart or release each other, and kept their smiles as they turned toward him. Rapid high-pitched music wove patterns above him as he closed the door, and he was surprised to realise he didn't mind it too much. "You look pleased with things," said his mother.

"Been somewhere special?" Melinda asked him.

"Yes," Ian said.

the Viper & the Urchin

NO. 1

the
BLOODLESS
ASSASSIN

CELINE JEANJEAN

http://celinejeanjean.com

ISBN: 9782492523175

Requests to publish work from this book should be sent to: celine@celinejeanjean.com

**Cover design by
bonobobookcovers.com**

CHAPTER

1

Rory congratulated herself on her timing. She and Jake had just reached the end of the lane, and peering around the corner, she could see the mark a few yards away. He was a trader with a belly that hung over his belt and a self-satisfied air. She could already tell how pleased with himself he would look when he stepped in to save the poor, scrawny urchin girl from a beating.

Moron.

She counted down silently with her fingers. *Three, two, one.*

Rory launched herself into the trader's path with a shriek. Startled, the man jumped back just as Jake burst into the street, his face contorted into a perfectly fearsome mask. He grabbed Rory with his paddle-sized hands, lifting her off the ground.

"Help!" she screamed, kicking her legs in the air, careful to miss Jake.

Jake drew back a meaty hand as though to strike her. She screeched again, waiting for the mark to react. Any moment now, he would step forward, his face a sneer, his rapier drawn, and he would tell Jake to 'let the girl go.'

Jake snarled and raised his hand farther behind him. Rory cowered in his grasp.

"Please not again, please no, please…" she gabbled.

The target stood aside, gawking, as though seagulls had pecked out his brains.

"Teach you to try and run away," Jake grunted.

Still nothing.

Crap.

Rory had picked a dud.

Nothing for it, Jake was going to have to follow through and hit her or the game would be up.

Jake's hand came down in a wide arc, just catching her cheek. Rory let her head snap to one side, howling to make it seem more painful than it was. Still the merchant stood watching. She cursed under her breath. If he was going to be cowardly, the least he could do was leave and be cowardly somewhere else so they could end this charade.

Jake raised his hand again.

"Not so fast now."

At last, the melodious sound of a rapier being pulled out of its scabbard. The trader pointed his blade at Jake.

"Put the girl down."

"Not your goddamned business," Jake grunted.

"I've just made it my business. Put her down."

Jake glowered ever so convincingly at the man, and he let Rory drop to the ground. She made a show of collapsing onto the cobblestones before scrambling up towards the trader.

"Now go." The man raised his chin haughtily behind his rapier.

Jake grunted again and skulked off down the lane from which they had come, making it look all the more narrow as he squeezed his massive frame through it.

"Thank you, sir, oh thank you!" Rory grabbed the trader's distended waistcoat as she pulled herself up. "I been trying to escape for months, sir, months!" She squeezed out a few tears for good measure and sniffled loudly.

"Now see here—" the trader began.

"I got no one, sir," Rory interrupted, still clinging to him as though she was drowning, and he was the last plank of wood left in the world. "I'm an orphan and all alone, my family died." At this, she began to wail loudly.

The trader extricated himself from her clutching fingers, his philanthropic aspirations rapidly vanishing. "There, there…I'm sorry but, er, I can't do anything for you. I'm only passing through Damsport, you see."

That was a lie—he was clearly a Damsian.

"Please, sir!" She wailed louder, clutching at him faster than he could remove her hands. Her fingers felt his purse, and she was delighted to find that it was as fat as he was.

"Now see here," said the trader. "I have to leave… My ship… Will you just…get off!"

He gave her a shove, and she staggered back, the purse vanishing into one of her pockets. She gave the trader a forlorn look, cutting a pathetic figure in her rags, mess of rope-like hair, and snotty nose — the gods be thanked for her ability to sniffle on demand.

The trader hurried away without looking back.

When he had turned the corner, Rory spat once on the cobblestones.

"Hypocrite."

Saving the girl always worked, but no one wanted to actually *save* the girl. They only wanted that brief moment of glory when they pointed their rapier at Jake. That was fine by Rory. They just had to pay the price of their purse for the privilege of feeling like a hero for a few minutes.

She hurried after Jake, grinning. He was waiting for her at the rendezvous point.

With an exaggerated flourish, she pulled out the purse she had lifted and dangled it next to her ear.

"It speaks to me… It says…half coins inside!"

Jake grinned. "Give it here."

She threw it at him and he hefted it appreciatively as they walked. "That's got a good few coin bits in it." He felt the purse between his fingers. "I think I feel a couple of whole 'uns too."

"Yeah, a good taking."

"Aye. Plenty more than you need."

Rory nodded and her stomach briefly knotted with excitement and nerves. It had been two years of scrimping and saving, and despite getting robbed twice by muggers in the rare moments she worked without Jake, she could finally meet Master Xian's price with a little to spare.

Jake threw her the purse, and she squirrelled it away in one of her many pockets, surprised at how nervous she was now that her lifelong ambition was about to become reality. She would leave with Master Xian, the most famed sword preceptor in Damsport and travel with him as his pupil and assistant. It was so close she could almost taste the salty spray that would spatter her face once they were out at sea.

"What time's the steam galley again?" asked Jake.

"I'm to meet Master Xian at six at the Starry Inn."

"Plenty of time. What say you to a celebratory pint?"

"Don't think I could drink right now," she said. "Stomach's doing all sorts of flipping."

"Suit yourself."

They continued walking in a comfortable silence, punctuated only by the tinkle of the talismans that hung around Rory's neck, a hangover from her days of begging at the temples.

"You sure you want to leave?" asked Jake. "We got a good thing going here."

"Yeah, I'm sure."

"You never told me what the big deal is with learning to fight with swords, you know."

Rory shrugged with all the nonchalance she could muster. It had been ten years since she had met the Scarred Woman, and she had never breathed a word of it to anyone. Not even to Jake. The years had washed the woman's features from her memory, but to this day Rory could still picture how her rapier had gleamed, how smooth and fast her movements had been, and how easily she had despatched that giant of a man. Rare was the night when Rory didn't dream she was the Scarred Woman.

"Just something I've always wanted to do, that's all." She kicked a piece of unidentifiable rotten fruit out of the way.

The truth was that it consumed her. She thought of little else — all she wanted was to be a warrior, a hero, like the Scarred Woman. She was also well aware of how ridiculous that ambition was, coming from her. She had been sixteen for about two years now — not knowing exactly how old she was, she picked whatever age suited her — and although she knew her real age was probably around eighteen, she was still small enough to pass for fourteen. And a scrawny fourteen-year-old at that.

The reaction of the last sword preceptor she had approached before Master Xian was still as fresh as ever in her mind. The woman had laughed. A big belly laugh, as though Rory's dreams were a joke. Rory clenched her fists at the memory. The sword preceptor had shooed her away like all the others, and her apprentice had given Rory a good kick up the arse that had sent her sprawling out the door and into the gutter.

"Gutter rats don't wield rapiers," the lad had said before slamming the door.

Master Xian hadn't laughed. He had simply named an eye-watering price.

"You still gonna be a cobbler?" she asked Jake, to change the subject.

"I reckon so," he replied. "My Da was a damned good cobbler, and I remember some."

"Well, when I'm a famous hero, I'll come to you and only you to fix my boots."

Jake grinned. "Aye, and I'll only rip you off by half."

Rory punched him on the arm. "Yeah right. You'd be rob me blind if I let you."

"Fair."

They reached the chaotic warren of lanes that was the Rookery, and the air became thicker, full of the cloying stench of mould and decay. Banyan trees poked out randomly from streets and houses, their roots crawling through the cobblestones, their dead leaves and inedible fruits covered in guano, rotting on the ground. Shacks were built resting against their trunks, some turned into little stalls from which cobblers, minor-repair machinists, and other small tradesmen operated. Men, women, and children milled about the streets, calling, shouting, fighting, hawking wares, and arguing, their voices louder than the seagulls.

Rory and Jake walked past houses that sagged on rain-saturated wooden frames; only a few had been able to afford the conversion to steelwood beams. Some covered their beams with tar, and the rest made do with houses that sweated and rotted under the weight of the humidity.

Rory waved and called out greetings while Jake stayed silent, only pushing the low-hanging laundry lines out of his way. He had never been one for social niceties. Rory, on the other hand, understood the importance of having friends. The kind of friends who, if you asked after her, would say, 'Rory? Never 'eard of her. Not seen anyone like that in these parts. You must be thinking of some other girl.' Those kinds of friends were invaluable, especially when you were in the business of relieving people of their belongings.

Rory and Jake reached a deserted lane that was more rotten than the rest, and they made their way to a solitary house, its neighbours little more than a pile of rubble overtaken by banyan trees. One side of the house had caved in so that it looked lopsided, like an old man after a stroke. A banyan tree had sprouted on what was left of the roof, its web of roots stretching down what remained of the house's front like a caul.

Rory went in first. Inside, there was no first floor to speak of — only a few beams remained. She found the familiar footholds on the wall and began to climb towards the yawning hole in the roof.

When she reached the top, she walked carefully along an exposed beam until she reached a single black steelwood pillar that stuck out of the house's side like a finger. A thick coil of rope was tied to it, and she threw it down to Jake.

Jake lifted himself up the rope easily, the muscles on his bare arms bulging under his brown skin. Rory left him to it, making her way over to their little shelter by the banyan tree. It had taken them a couple of years to build something that could withstand the summer storms, and while the current effort didn't look like much, it kept out wind and water.

Rory walked past the shelter and lifted up a couple of tiles, uncovering a niche that held two bulging purses. She took them out, checked their weight, and sat down cross-legged with the purses between her legs to keep them from rolling away. Jake heaved himself up, pulled the rope with him, and came to sit next to her. He picked up his purse, hefted it with one hand, and his normally ugly features broke into a delighted grin.

"That's a good bit of coinage, that is."

Rory began counting out the day's takings. Some silver bits, a couple of half coppers and half silvers, five full coppers, and a single, beautifully whole and shiny silver. Rory held it up with an appreciative whistle. It was almost perfectly round, if you squinted and ignored where the edges had been shaved or clipped.

The process of sharing out the loot began. They each carefully weighed the coins, gradually creating two equal shares. So many currencies flowed through Damsport that Damsians had resorted to using coin weights for their currency, weighing copper, silver and gold, and cutting coins into smaller pieces when making change. Jake and Rory didn't waste money on coin scales, instead estimating coin weights with their fingers. It worked well enough, since they both always checked every weight, never trusting each other. They argued over the splitting of the loot until they both agreed the weights of silver and copper felt equal.

"Coming to the Old Girl's Arms, then?" Jake asked, carefully putting his coin pieces away.

"Nah, told you, don't have the stomach for it. Gonna wait here until it's time."

"Come on, don't be boring, come for a drink. My treat. Old time's sake and all that."

Rory hesitated. She knew it would be fun to go to the Old Girl's Arms and chew the fat with Jake, but she couldn't risk being late and missing the steam galley. With Jake it was never just the one drink.

"Not gonna risk it," she replied. "You could wait with me, though. Escort me to the docks, make the most of my sparkling conversation while you can, and all that." She winked.

"Your conversation would be a hell of a lot more sparkly if I could experience it with a pint of cider in my hand." Jake stood up, pocketed the purse, and stretched, his back cracking like the knees of an old supplicant. "Gods' breath, that feels good!"

"The purse or the stretch?"

"Both." He grinned. "Come on —" He nudged Rory with his boot. "Come to the Old Girl's Arms. Just one, and that's a promise."

Rory was tempted — if anything, it would steady her nerves before her adventures began.

"Well…alright. Maybe one."

"Atta girl! Reckon you'll see something real special, too. I feel a lucky streak coming on."

"Hold on — you're going gambling?"

"Just a little flutter. I got plenty to spare" — Jake patted the pocket containing the purse — "and I'm pretty sure today's gonna be my day."

"Seriously? Jake, how many times you got to lose everything for it to register in your thick head that nobody's ever lucky with cards? Anyone would think you wanted to be poor for the rest of your life."

A chill settled despite the sweltering midday heat. Jake didn't reply, looking sulkily at the ground. Rory looked away, frustrated with his stubbornness and annoyed at herself for lecturing him when she was about to leave.

The silence stretched on, heavy and uncomfortable.

"Well, I guess that means you're not coming," Jake said at last, breaking the silence, "so I'll see you when I see you."

He patted her awkwardly on the shoulder and turned away. Rory's stomach lurched. This wasn't how she had wanted to part ways. She tried to think of something to say, but no words came to her. Jake disappeared down into the ruined house.

She stared at the space where he had been for a moment, a tight feeling in her chest. Of course she was still excited to leave and become an adventurer. Of course. But dammit if she wasn't sad now, too.

CHAPTER 2

A few hours later, the five-o'clock cacophony began with the clatter of bells, as usual. It was quickly followed by a swelling of drums, steam trumpets, gongs, water chimes, and whatever other instruments the temples used to mark the hour. Timekeeping was as fluid a notion in Damsport as Rory's age: each of the myriad of temples had its own concept of time so that every hour the o'clock was sounded for a good fifteen minutes.

When silence returned, indicating that it was some time after five, Rory got up and stretched. Time to go. The Starry Inn wasn't far, but she wouldn't take any chances. She kissed a couple of her talismans at random, not caring who she prayed to as long as whoever it was listened and brought her luck.

She gathered her meagre possessions: a silk line and grappling hook, which she wrapped around her waist, and a Talegian steel dagger. The dagger was unusual, fashioned out of a single piece of steel, the handle curved to look like a peacock's head, the blade itself like the sweep of tail feathers. It was small, the blade thin, but it was as sharp as a razor, and Rory loved it more than anything in the world.

She was about to take her purse when she heard the whistle that meant Jake was outside. Grinning, she hurried over to lower the rope.

"Well, I'm flattered that you've interrupted your drinking to come say goodbye," she called as she went back to pocket the purse, carefully making sure the bulge wasn't visible through her tunic. She tucked as much of her threadbare trousers as she could into her boots, a token effort at looking respectable. "Or is it that you've come to escort me to the docks? I think an escort would be fitting for the — stone the gulls, what happened to your face?"

Jake hauled himself onto the roof with a grunt. His lip and nose were bleeding, as was a nasty gash on his eyebrow. An angry swelling shut his eye, and another bruise bloomed on his jaw like an ugly flower. He moved gingerly, in obvious pain.

"I'm sorry, Rory. I'm sorry."

"What happened?"

Her stomach relocated to her boots when a second head poked out from the hole in the roof.

"Jake, who is that?"

Jake shook his head, not meeting her eye. The man came and stood next to him, and it was like a boulder settling into place. Jake and the man were as tall as each other, but the newcomer was even beefier, with no neck to speak of, so that his head seemed to be skewered directly onto his shoulders. Rory took a step back.

"I'm sorry, Rory, I really am," Jake said. "I just need a little. Maybe half. You'll still have plenty to go on with. I'll pay you back, I promise."

Rory shook her head. "You ain't getting nothing from me. I can't pay for the steamer if you take half, and you know it. This is your shit, you deal with it."

As she spoke, another man climbed up to the roof, and then a third. They looked like copies of the first: neckless wonders with scowling faces.

"Alright," said the first. "I didn't come here to listen to a domestic with your girlfriend. She got the money?"

When Jake didn't answer, the man swung a fist into his kidneys, and he groaned in pain.

"I don't like silences," said the man. "She got the money?"

Jake nodded miserably.

"You boys stay away from me, alright," said Rory. "I ain't got nothing to do with this. This ain't my man, and this ain't my business." She stepped farther back, all too aware that she was cornered. There was nowhere for her to climb from where she was. She pulled out her dagger.

"Well, well, seems we have ourselves a kitten with a claw," said the second.

"Rory, don't make things worse than they are," Jake pleaded. "I'll make it up to you one way or another, I promise. Just give them what they want so they'll leave."

Two of the men advanced on Rory, the third standing menacingly next to Jake. When they were close enough to her, Rory lashed out at the first thug with her dagger. He dodged easily, moving his bulk with surprising speed. The other grabbed hold of her, pinning her arms to her sides. She squirmed and kicked uselessly.

"Get off me, you fish-brained cretin!"

The first thug patted her down, found the purse, and took it.

"Hey," protested Jake, "you only need half of that."

"Half of the purse is to pay my employer, the other half is my fee for inconveniencing me. Time's a precious commodity, and I don't like mine wasted."

The thug released Rory with a shove, sending her staggering dangerously close to the edge.

"There now," he said with a grin full of broken teeth, "that wasn't so hard, was it?"

The two men turned back towards Jake, the third already making his exit. Rory felt a blinding flash of hot rage, and before she could consider what she was doing, she ran after them with her dagger at the ready. The man nearest to her didn't even flinch. He turned just as she reached him, his backhand catching her jaw, sending her flying back. She rolled once heels over head on the sloping tiles, dropping her knife, and pitched over the side.

"Rory!" Jake rushed over.

Rory had caught a stray banyan root, and she dangled, her legs swinging beneath her, but all she could think of was her dagger. Had it fallen over the side, too? She craned her head to try and catch sight of it. Jake grabbed her arms and hauled her back up.

"Rory, you alright?" he asked in a shaky voice.

The thugs had gone, and so had her purse, but her dagger was there, resting on the tiles. She snatched it up, weak with relief, running her finger along it. Even though it was only a simple piece of steel, it was her first blade, and she couldn't bear to be parted from it.

"Rory?" Jake touched her shoulder and she threw a punch, knuckles cracking against his already bruised jaw. She sucked in air between her teeth, shaking her hand against the pain.

"Stay away from me," she spat.

"Look I'll find a way —"

"I want nothing from you."

"I know I messed up, I know. But I'll make —"

"You'll do nothing!" she yelled.

Jake stopped, startled.

"You'll do nothing," she whispered. "We're done."

She sheathed her blade and slipped it through her belt. Without another word or look at Jake, she left.

***

Rory sped through the streets, the wind streaming in her face. She wiped her cheeks angrily. Tears were pointless if there was no one to take advantage of. As she ran, her hand kept returning to the hilt of her dagger to make sure it was still tucked into her belt. Losing it on the roof earlier, even temporarily, had been an atrocious feeling.

She made for Six, the thoroughfare that led straight to Tinsbury Dock.

Six was busy as always, a steady flow of bodies, horses, and carts heading from the enclosed docks to the Great Bazaar. One of those new-fangled steam trolleys rolled past, ferrying traders and merchants. A boy banged the bell at its front to signal for people to get out of the way. Rory watched the trolley glide past, eyeing its passengers.

This wasn't a suicidal affair like the traversal steam coaches that clattered by so fast it made your teeth rattle. No, the steam trolleys on Six and Twelve moved slowly, safely, with a kind of stuck-up, stately importance. She felt an overwhelming urge to jump aboard and hold them all at knifepoint for their money. They would have what she needed and then some. But she knew that Six crawled with guards, and any sort of hit here would mean a guaranteed trip to the galleys.

Rory continued down Six. The traffic was still oozing slow as mud, and even for one as tiny as her, it was slow going weaving through the throng. Cursing, she turned off into a side street. The lanes twisted and turned back on themselves so that there was no straight way anywhere, but here at least she was free to run. And right now she needed to feel like she was moving.

She ran faster and faster, until her legs felt like they were pumping independently from her, and her lungs burned. She almost careened straight into a cart as she reached Tinsbury Dock.

"Watch where you're going!" the driver shouted.

An enormous four-masted galleon was disgorging its cargo, its crew swarming around it, crawling through the rigging like an efficient colony of ants. Next to it, hard and gleaming in the afternoon sun, a steam galley made its final preparations. The steam galley that she should be getting ready to board. Its articulated steam-powered oars hovered just above the water, bent midway so that they looked like the legs of an enormous metal insect.

She pushed her way through the crowd on the wharf, towards the Starry Inn. It was one of the nicer inns that fronted the docks: mouth-watering smells wafted from it, rather than the piss, rancid wine, and vomit that were the norm for dockside establishments.

She ran through the main room and bounded up the stairs at the back.

"Hey! Where d'you think you're going?" shouted the innkeep.

"To see Master Xian," she yelled back over her shoulder as she took the steps two at a time.

She ran to his room. The door was open, and he was slowly, methodically, folding up a tunic.

"No need to rush," he said with his smooth, level voice. "We have plenty of time."

"I ain't… I ain't got the money," she panted.

"Ah. Then we have a problem."

"It weren't my fault, my partner screwed me over and —"

"That great lumbering idiot you were dragging around last time?"

"Yes — Jake."

"Can't say I'm surprised."

"Look, I know we had an arrangement and all that. But I can earn my way, right. I can work for free for however long you need. I'll do anything. Anything. If you take me with you."

Master Xian looked at her with a frown.

"Rory, do I look like a nurse? Or like one of the good sisters of the Exalted Consciousness? Hmm?"

"No."

"Exactly. I've not been put on this earth to look after little girls. I don't do charity. You want to come with me, fine. But you can't get on a steam galley without paying and they're expensive. You can't hit the road without supplies, and for supplies you need money. So, if you don't have money, you can't leave Damsport. It's very straightforward. Not only that, but you gave me that speech about wanting to be a warrior, about wanting to see the world. I was impressed by your ambition, and now look at what you've shown me. I gave you a simple task two years ago, when I was last at Damsport. I told you to beg, borrow, or steal the money to pay for your way. That's it. That was all you had to do in exchange for my expertise and training. If you can't even do that, then what exactly makes you think you're ready for a life on the road, hmm? Better you find yourself a sword preceptor here in Damsport."

"I tried, no one else will take me on account of me being a street urchin and all."

"Stop your whining. What are you, a child? If they won't take you of their own will, then make them! Gods, Rory, I have no time for this snivelling. I set you a challenge and you bring me excuses. You want to be a fighter, then fight! Don't come to me crying about your problems. Now get out, I have to finish packing, and then I have a galley to catch. You can look out for me when I'm next back, which should be in two or three years. Price will stay the same, but if you're still crying over people not taking you seriously, then don't bother."

He turned his back on her and went back to meticulously packing his bag.

Rory stared at his back for a while, and then without a word, she turned and walked away.

CHAPTER

3

Longinus smiled in anticipation as he skirted the warehouses that fronted Tinsbury Dock. It was always a pleasure to kill, and never more so than when death was brought about elegantly.

The dockworkers, as expected, paid him no attention. Dressed head to toe in black, his brow hidden under the wide brim of a hat, his chin and mouth covered with a black silk handkerchief, he blended perfectly with the night's shadows.

Blissful are the dim-witted. If only they knew how close they are to Damsport's deadliest assassin.

All the same, he wished they had at least enough sense to shiver with quiet dread as he passed.

Is it really too much to ask that the common dockworker experience a faint malaise in my presence? Obviously.

Tinsbury Dock was full of activity despite the late hour. Shouts and curses echoed across the still water, steam hissed, and metal grated against metal as great steel arms swung overhead, unloading cargo from waiting ships. Vapour lamps, hanging from poles along the quay, bathed the enclosed dock in an otherworldly orange glow, creating shadows in the hollows of the dockworkers' faces so that they looked like animated skulls. Beyond, the night bristled with the naked masts of a hundred ships, stretching to the moon like skeletal fingers.

As Longinus reached the end of the dock, he cast a wistful glance over his shoulder. It would provide such a delightfully macabre backdrop to his art — a shame tonight's job was to take place in the neighbouring marina. Smaller boats docked in Smallport Marina, and it would be quiet at this time. That would, of course, make the job easier, but as Damsport's most elegant assassin, Longinus didn't care about ease; the art of assassination was all about theatrics. Killing someone on a dark and empty dock was as banal as rain in summer. Luckily, he had just finished creating a poison that had such panache it should offset the mundanity of the night's work.

The noise from Tinsbury Dock faded away as he entered the marina, the silence now only broken by the creaking of ships as they swayed on their moorings. Longinus lowered his handkerchief. The air was cooler and fresher here with only a hint of brackish water and salt. It was bearable, even to his delicate nose.

Longinus' target for the night — a sailor — sat at the other end of the marina. No one else was there. Longinus smiled wolfishly.

The stone walkway along the marina was narrow but lined with shaggy banyan trees, their aerial roots dangling towards the ground. Longinus walked behind them, hidden in their shadows, keeping a careful eye on the target.

The sailor threw his head back, his mouth clamped on a bottle's neck, attempting to coax out its last remaining drops. Longinus recognised the bottle as Smithy's Gold, a cheap, nasty rum. Sailors were so predictably devoid of class. And taste.

He crept closer, until he was level with the sailor, and he stopped behind a banyan tree, peering around its trunk. The sailor had made himself at home, with a second stool in front of him on which he had set out a bowl, a spoon, and a flatbread. He put down the bottle and tore off a piece of bread.

A noise sounding suspiciously like a boot against cobblestones startled Longinus. The sailor heard it too, and he looked about him, but thankfully away from Longinus.

A ship's hull groaned as the wood contracted in the cooler temperature. Nothing stirred.

The sailor relaxed and sat back down, but Longinus continued scanning the darkened marina. Was someone else out there? Still nothing moved.

Longinus glanced back at the sailor to find that he was spooning a dark mixture from the bowl and into his mouth. He ate messily, and a little had dripped on his chin and tunic. Whatever it was, it gleamed as black as blood in moonlight. At the thought, Longinus paled and staggered back.

It isn't blood, it isn't blood.

He took a deep, ragged breath, waiting for the rising nausea to pass. He focused on his newest poison instead. Alchemy had always been a great source of comfort.

There was a flare of light, and Longinus peered once more around the trunk. The sailor had stuffed tobacco in a long-stemmed pipe, and he puffed away, letting out flat plumes of smoke from the side of his mouth.

Longinus rubbed his hands. The target's night vision would be destroyed. Now was the perfect time to strike.

He pulled on thin leather gloves, overlaid with a fine but watertight mesh made from mineral fibres. One could never be too careful when dealing with poison, especially this newest one, and besides, they looked devilishly stylish in the moonlight.

He then produced an oblong box inlaid with the same mesh, inside which was a Talegian steel stylus and a tiny glass vial. He screwed the vial into the base of the stylus and slipped out from behind the banyan tree, his stylus at the ready. He only needed to write a period on the man's skin to paralyse him. A little more, such as a comma, would bring about death — thus providing punctuation with the fearsome respect it so deserved.

The stylus is mightier than the sword.

Longinus drew out the moment, savouring the anticipation as he slowly crept towards the sailor. The unsuspecting mark blew smoke rings at the star-punctured night.

Longinus struck.

24

With his free hand, he grabbed the sailor's collar and yanked him to the ground, knocking his head in the process. His right hand brought the stylus to the man's temple, resting its pointy tip on the skin.

"Don't move," he hissed.

The sailor froze, feeling the cold touch of sharp steel so close to his eye. A fatal hesitation. People always assumed that blades were the most fearsome weapon. Fools! As if any assassin worth his kills would allow a job to be marred by something so crude as a blade piercing skin.

The sailor's hesitation allowed just enough time for the poison to travel along the stylus' nib, and it dropped onto the skin, creating a perfect circle, a period, at the corner of his eye. Paralysis immediately began its inevitable course. The sailor made a garbled noise and jerked his head convulsively. His legs twitched, as though a puppeteer was pulling the strings attached to them. He tried to move his arms, but they were no longer his to command, and his face twisted with panic.

Longinus released the man and cocked his head, admiring his work and debating whether to turn the period into a semicolon. He went with a period but couldn't resist adding a touch of his natural flamboyance. With a flourish, he signed 'The Viper' on the sailor's forehead. That done, he stepped back to examine his work.

Beautiful.

A vague gurgling marked the sailor's last breath.

Longinus returned the stylus and vial to the box and pulled out a card, which he carefully pinned onto the body's shirt. It looked like an ordinary playing card, but where an ace of spades would have been, a black viper was coiled, ready to strike. Tiny knives were drawn at each corner, with gleaming silver blades. Longinus took great pride in his cards, designing them himself. He had tried to use cards with vials of poisons at the corners, but he had been mistaken for an exotic perfumer. This was, of course, unacceptable, and he had been forced to put knives instead, to drive the meaning home.

Crude, inelegant weapons. They lack all the refinement of poison.

It was tiresome to have to lower his standards, but it was necessary — he couldn't have his artistry go unnoticed, or worse, misunderstood. He blew at the card to make sure the wind couldn't dislodge it. It wouldn't do for some (lesser) assassin to try and take credit for his work, either. Like any artist, Longinus signed each and every one of his masterpieces, and this was one he was particularly proud of.

A small sound, like a light cough, broke the silence. Longinus froze. He scanned the marina.

The water lapped gently against the floating docks. His mind playing tricks on him, perhaps? And yet the sailor had heard something too, earlier.

When still nothing more stirred, Longinus prepared to leave. He glanced at the body, and his stomach contracted at the sight. He had stayed too long. The eyes had turned a pale, milky blue, and the veins on the man's face stood out, dark and inflamed, fanning out from the writing on the forehead.

Longinus staggered back, knocking over the stool. He fancied he could smell it, all that blood encased in a thin sack of skin. So easily spilled.

He clamped a hand over his mouth against the nausea rising in his throat and ran away on shaky legs, his black cloak flapping behind him.

***

Longinus sat at a corner table in the Hand and Tankard, surveying the room. He had swapped the black silks he wore as the Viper for simple leathers, the better to blend in with the crowd. He found it best to tone down his natural elegance when mixing with common folk. That said, he was unable to compromise on the cut of his clothes, and he had had his leathers tailored to within an inch of their lives. A shame that he was sitting down, really; they showed off his figure so exquisitely he should have stood at the bar, the better to be admired.

He listened to the talk around him, waiting for the gossip on the Viper's exploits. He had spent the rest of the previous night writing pamphlets about his most recent kill, and he had left them at the docks first thing that morning for a lucky few to find and read. He liked to think that his prose did more than inform the wider public of the Viper's actions — it elevated their minds, too.

Which was why he was growing rapidly annoyed with the direction the conversations were taking: the weather, the upcoming Revels, and speculation as to whether the Old Girl, the Marchioness of Damsport, was going to pass the torch to her daughter. All of it without interest. It was incredible what mundane banalities the small-minded could find interesting.

Unfortunately, he had to rely on them to spread his reputation about town. His reputation was improving, but it was nowhere near what it ought to be. Notoriety helped him get commissions, but most importantly, one could only be an artist if one was spoken of. There was nothing worse for an assassin than obscurity.

At last, a woman he knew by sight on account of her starched white apron arrived. Mistress White Apron sat down and regarded the others around her table with the kind of smugness particular to a woman about to unveil a fresh piece of gossip.

"Have you heard the latest on the Smallport Marina killing?"

At last! Longinus smiled. Mistress White Apron could always be counted on. Maybe he should find out where she lived and distribute his pamphlets directly to her door.

"Yeah, I hear it were that Viper character again," said a sailor.

"Everyone knows that," said the woman with contempt. "He leaves a card behind. But have you heard the particulars? Hmm?" She looked at the faces of her audience, so puffed up with self-satisfaction she almost seemed to be expanding. Longinus beamed. The saintly woman was about to unveil his new poison.

Mistress White Apron leaned forward. "I have it on good authority that he skinned his victim. Slipped the skin right off, like you do with a rabbit."

Longinus almost fell off his stool. Skinned? *Skinned?* Had that idiot even read his pamphlet?

What is the point of me writing them if these simpletons blithely ignore them?

"Oh really? I heard it were poison," said another woman.

"Not this time," said Mistress White Apron. "I heard it from my cousin's sister-in-law's nephew. He works with the guards." She lowered her voice. "I hear the Viper even drinks the blood of his victims, like a vampire."

Longinus felt himself go green at the thought.

Ridiculous, this is ridiculous…

But there was nothing ridiculous about the image that was now firmly imprinted in his mind.

"You're making it up," said the sailor, obviously disgusted.

"I am not," sniffed Mistress White Apron. "Just because you can't handle —"

"If I might interrupt," said a small pinched man at a table next to them. "I saw the body myself and…"

Longinus couldn't listen to any more. The butchery of his art was almost as unbearable as the thought of the Viper drinking blood. He fumbled into his purse and produced two coins, which he threw on the counter before hurrying out.

"Hey, I haven't weighed them," shouted the barkeep.

Longinus ignored him, pushing the door open with trembling hands. Once out, he leaned against the wall, taking deep gulps of air. The barkeep hadn't run out after him, and he guessed that his coins had been heavy enough for his meal and drink. Not that it was a surprise: Longinus' fingers were unrivalled in their ability to estimate a coin's weight.

When he felt steadier, he peeled himself from the wall. He needed to get home to rest before the night's job, and tomorrow he would address this gross misunderstanding of his art. He couldn't have all these ridiculous rumours circulating about the Viper. He would simply have to increase the volume of pamphlets and distribute them more widely.

The propensity of the common man's mind to turn to the violent and bloody really was intolerable.

Interlude

Ten Years Ago…

Rory sat on the edge of a flat roof, her legs dangling over the edge, cradling a bunch of unripe cherries in her hands. They were crunchy and sharp enough to make the lower corners of her mouth tingle. Up ahead, across one row of houses, she could see Tinsbury Dock, and she watched as a boat that looked like a mountain of wood ploughed slowly through the water, guided by steamers at either end.

Farther down the dock, she saw a small patrol of Varanguards — the Marchioness' bodyguards — escorting a fat man. She leaned forward in her eagerness to observe them. She had seen them plenty of times guarding the Old Girl's mansion, but it was something else to see them in action. They moved like dancers, their burnished helmets winking in the sun. Long black horsehair ponytails sprouted from each helmet, skimming the backs of their thighs and swishing with each step. The knives concealed within the horsehair glinted here and there, as they caught the sunlight.

The creation of the Varanguards was her favourite story of the Three Day Battle. They were named after Varan, a dancer who was famed for her long black ponytail and what she could do with it. On the final day of the Three Day Battle, she had tied knives to strands of her long hair and thrown herself amongst the Airnian soldiers, killing with great flicks of her ponytail and dancing in the sprays of blood. The Marchioness had created the Varanguards after the victory, calling Varan a symbol of the Damsian spirit.

The Varanguards delivered their escort to a ship and, to Rory's disappointment, turned as one and left the dock. Rory spat out her cherry stone, hitting the roof across the lane. She grinned and picked another cherry, the talismans given to her by the temples tinkling softly. Her right forearm still bore the scar the Two Billies had given her for fighting back when they had taken her money. It was back to stealing and begging at the temples for her until her hand was nimble enough to pick pockets again. She wiggled her fingers, feeling the stiffness in her forearm.

She hoped it wouldn't be too long before she was back to normal.

The cherries finished, she climbed down from the wall into the shaded lane below. As she headed towards the mouth of the lane, she heard footsteps, and quickly dove behind a rotting crate. She peeked through the slats and saw a man in black fighting leathers turning into the lane. He wore a wide-brimmed leather hat with a blood-red feather that kept most of his face hidden. A rapier gleamed at his left hip and a long dagger at his right. He had barely entered the lane when two shadows fell into step behind him. Rory held her breath. She didn't need to see their faces to recognise them.

The Two Billies moved with surprising stealth, considering how oafish they were. One of them pulled out the iron blade that had torn Rory's forearm, and she winced at the sight. The other produced a thin, unusual-looking dagger that was just a single piece of steel.

Three more lads joined the Two Billies, each pulling out their own weapon. The five of them crept up to the man as Rory looked on.

"Careful!"

Rory clamped both hands over her mouth, shocked that she had been stupid enough to call attention to herself. One of the Two Billies, the one with the iron blade, turned back and caught sight of her behind her crate. Before she could get far, he pounced on her and lifted her off the ground with a malevolent smile.

"Well, well, what have we got here?" said a raspy voice over his shoulder.

Rory's eyebrows shot up to her rope hair, and Billy turned around in surprise. The voice belonging to the man in black was raspy, but it was unmistakably a woman's. She had drawn her rapier and dagger and faced her four attackers, her face still hidden by her hat so that only her chin was visible.

"Five of us lads and one of you," said the other Billy. "And you're a woman. That's what we got here."

The woman laughed. "I'm so glad you lads are here to inform me of my gender."

"Give us your purse and we'll let you live. We don't mind killing women."

"What a coincidence, I don't mind killing boys."

There was a brief pause, like a heartbeat, and all four lads threw themselves forward in perfect unison. Rory thrashed and squirmed for all she was worth, hoping that the lad holding her would be distracted enough to fumble his grip, but he merely laughed and hit her across the face with his spare hand.

"You think you can rat on us," he whispered. "I'm gonna —"

There was the grating of metal on metal, and then the wet tearing of blade meeting flesh followed by a gurgled scream. A moment later, the woman was surrounded by four bodies oozing blood so dark it was almost black.

Billy dropped Rory.

"Now, you stay back," he warned the woman as she advanced on him. His voice quivered, betraying his fear.

A brief flurry of movement, and he collapsed to the floor, his blood mingling with the rest.

"Thanks, kid." The woman touched the brim of her hat and walked away without a second glance.

Rory stood dumbstruck for a moment, still processing what had happened. It wasn't until the woman had disappeared out the other end of the lane she galvanised herself into action. She scampered over to grab the steel dagger she had noticed in one of the Billy's hands.

The handle was shaped like a peacock's head, and it was small enough to suit her nicely. She slipped it in the string that she used as a belt as she hurried after the woman. The string fell apart, cut neatly in two.

"Crap."

She kept the dagger in one hand, breaking into a run and holding her trousers up with her other hand. She didn't bother searching any of the bodies for money. Bad enough that she was carrying a dagger; if she attracted more attention to herself with the tinkling of coins as she ran, she was guaranteed a shakedown.

Rory caught up with the woman quickly. She didn't seem to be in any hurry, as though she hadn't just killed five strong lads. Rory marvelled at the ease and confidence with which she walked, at the power in each of her movements, like a great jungle cat poised to strike. She followed, careful to stay far enough behind that she couldn't be mistaken for a threat. Not that a girl as scrawny as she, no more than six to eight years old, could be seen as a threat by a woman like that.

Eventually the woman found her way to Bayog, an area that Rory stayed clear of. She knew enough stories of what could happen to girls who got caught up in the tangle of Bayog at night, even girls as young as her. A swollen belly was the least of it.

The streets were quiet now, grey and washed out in the daylight, the air thick with stale alcohol, tobacco, and other foreign smells Rory didn't recognise. The silence was occasionally broken when the woman ahead nudged an empty bottle with a boot.

Nightingales peered out from darkened doorways, their faces pale, their makeup greasy and smeared, their eyes suspicious. Rory made herself as little and pathetic looking as possible. Nightingales could be incredibly vicious if they felt their territory was being encroached on. The woman didn't seem to notice or care about the looks she was eliciting. Then again, if Rory could despatch five armed lads as easily as the woman had, she wouldn't be afraid of Nightingales either.

Eventually they reached the Slaughtered Kraken, a dingy drinking house. The woman pushed the door and disappeared inside. The door swung slowly back on stiff hinges, allowing a tentacle of smoke to unfurl towards Rory as though trying to lure her in. She gulped, gripping the handle of her newfound dagger tighter for reassurance, and after a brief hesitation, she pushed the door back. She wasn't sure why she was following the woman, but the impulse was so strong that she couldn't ignore it.

Inside, the smoke was so heavy it made her eyes water. Old-fashioned gas lamps sputtered from sconces, their smoke leaving a thick, tar-like substance on the walls. Tables were strewn about the room, some upright, some on their sides, as though they had been scattered by a giant hand. A few dark forms stared into steins as they hunched over the upright tables, elbows leaning on the rotting wood. At the back of the room, Rory could just make out the shadowy contours of a bar counter. Nobody paid her any attention.

The woman had reached a man sitting at a table to the far right. He was dark and skinny, with a hooked nose. They nodded to each other silently, and the woman sat down, carelessly throwing her hat on the table. Rory saw her face clearly for the first time. An old scar fanned from her temple and over her left eye, partially hooding it, extending all the way down to her jaw.

Rory sidled over, hugging the wall, still clinging to her dagger. When she reached the corner, she stopped, realising that she had no idea what to do now.

"So rumour has it you're leaving?" said the man.

The Scarred Woman nodded, gesturing imperiously for a drink. Rory wondered how the barkeep could see through the smoke, but sure enough a little man with yellow skin and yellower teeth appeared at the woman's elbow with a stein. He peered at Rory briefly, licked his obscenely red lips, and returned to his counter. Rory shuddered.

"You coming, Raynard?" The Scarred Woman took a sip from her stein.

The man shook his head. "Nah, not for me."

"Coward."

"Maybe."

They drank in silence. Rory felt a lightning bolt of certainty: she wanted to go with the Scarred Woman. This was what she wanted to be when she grew up. Powerful, in control. A warrior. A real hero. She gathered her courage and prepared herself to step forward, when the door slammed open.

An enormous man stooped through the doorway, bristling with steel and leather. His face, neck, and hands were patterned with scars. He stared balefully at the thin crowd.

"You." He pointed at the Scarred Woman. "You killed my brother."

"Not now, Traeon," said the Scarred Woman with an irritated sigh. "Unless you want to join him, I suggest you leave."

Traeon pulled out a mean-looking broadsword. "Oh, you'll be the one leaving alright, but not by the door."

"You really want to do this now? Fine, it's your funeral."

The Scarred Woman stood up and pulled out her matched rapier and dagger.

Rory pressed herself into the wall, wishing she could disappear into it. Being in the drinking house suddenly seemed incredibly stupid — and incredibly dangerous.

The barkeep made some strangled plea for them to fight outside, but he was interrupted when, with a grunt, Traeon swung his massive sword and brought it crashing down on the Scarred Woman. She dodged nimbly, rolling forward and springing up to the man's right. His sword buried itself into a mouldy table. He wrenched it out and swung for her again. She deflected the blow with her dagger and retaliated with a jab of her rapier that cut a gash in his forearm.

The few patrons cleared the room or retreated behind the bar counter to watch. A few went as far as moving tables out of the way. Woman and giant circled each other, thrusting and parrying, the Scarred Woman jumping this way and that, the man's hands and arms soon covered with a myriad of small cuts, as though he was being attacked by an insect with razor-sharp claws. Traeon was visibly losing his patience, his thrusts growing in intensity but lacking the deadly precision of the Scarred Woman.

A particularly strong blow sent her careening all the way back to the wall. Rory frowned. It looked like she had continued staggering back even after she had regained her balance.

With a shout, she pushed herself from the wall and sprinted towards the giant, who roared and raised his broadsword. At the last moment, she threw herself legs first to the ground, skidding forward so that her momentum propelled her between the man's legs, his sword missing her by a hair's breadth. She slashed out twice with her rapier and dagger, and he pitched forward, blood gushing from the back of his heels.

The Scarred Woman stood up. "See, that's the thing with tendons, once they're cut, even a giant like you becomes as useless as a baby."

She sheathed the rapier and swung her dagger lazily so that it cut swirls out of the thick smoke.

Traeon pushed himself back up to his knees, his feet trailing uselessly behind him. He picked up his broadsword, making a valiant effort to try and fight, but he couldn't hold himself up.

"Oh, well," she said with a shrug, and she slit his throat. It was done quickly and matter-of-factly, as if she was just wringing the neck of a chicken. She wiped her dagger on

Traeon's tunic and returned to her friend, taking a sip from her stein as she sat down.

Nobody in the tavern moved. A low moan rose up from behind the counter, along with whimpers about mess and guards and cleaning.

Rory realised that she had been clutching her dagger so tight her knuckles were white and her hand ached. She relaxed her grip a little. The few patrons returned to their table, ignoring the enormous body and quickly spreading pool of blood.

Rory mustered all her courage and stepped forward, her eyes never leaving the Scarred Woman.

"Take me with you."

The Scarred Woman looked up, surprised. "Pardon me? Oh, you're that kid from the lane. Very kind of you to warn me."

"Aye, it was. And since I saved your life, taking me with you's the least you can do."

The Scarred Woman laughed. "You didn't save anything, kid. You think I can't handle a few boys? And anyway, seems to me that if anyone saved anything, it was *me* who saved *you*."

"I could be your assistant," said Rory, trying a different tack. "I'd work real hard and I'm dead handy at things."

"By that you mean I'd have to act as your nursemaid."

"I don't —"

"What makes you think I need or want to drag a child around with me?"

"I would work, I'd earn my way. I could… I'd look after your weapons."

"Any warrior worth her kills looks after her own weapons."

"I could cook."

"Cook my own food." The Scarred Woman took a sip of beer.

"I'll do anything, whatever you want. I'd be useful, I really would."

"And if we got into a fight like this one, what would you do? Come crying to me for help? I didn't see you step in with your little dagger."

"I don't cry," said Rory, jutting her chin forward.

"Really?" The blow came before Rory could duck, catching her temple, throwing her to the floor. Her head cracked painfully against the stinking floorboards.

"Gods, girl, you weigh even less than you look," muttered the Scarred Woman.

She picked Rory up from the floor, setting her on her feet. She picked up the dagger too and put it back in Rory's hand. Rory's legs swayed, her head dizzy from the blow and the fall. She blinked a few times to clear the spots that danced in front of her eyes.

"See, I don't cry. And my name ain't 'girl,' it's Rory," she said.

"Well, Rory, you've got nerve, I'll give you that. More nerve than some men," the woman added with a sigh.

"So you'll take me?"

"Of course not. I don't take anything with me that will slow me down. Go back to where you came from. Get some meat on your bones. Eat well. Grow big, grow strong; learn to fight. Learn to kill. If you become a decent fighter, and if we meet again in the land of the living, then maybe I'll take you with me."

Rory nodded but she stayed where she was, worried that she would fall over if she tried to walk.

"Are you alright, kid? Can you walk?"

" 's alright, I been hit plenty of times before," Rory replied. "I'll be fine. But you watch out for me because one day I'm going to be as good a fighter as you are."

The Scarred Woman laughed. "Well, when you are, you and I can become partners."

Rory grinned, elated at the idea.

"Alright, now get out of here," said the Scarred Woman.

"Aye aye."

Rory headed towards the door on uneasy legs. She felt as though she was on board a lurching ship.

"Oh, and Rory? Never drop your blade again."

Rory reached the end of Tinsbury Dock and stepped into a derelict house. It stank of piss, sweat, and the ripeness of unwashed bodies. In the gloom she could make out shapes on the ground: beggars and others of the homeless persuasion were catching a little shut eye before the nightshift of begging and stealing began. She had slept amongst them too, once upon a time. Before Jake.

Rory picked her way up the stairs, nimbly avoiding the rotten planks. The house was a low, squat, two-storey affair. The first floor was practically rotted through, and there was very little to be found there other than a speedy return to the ground floor. Few bothered going up the stairs: the ground floor required no climbing and presented no risk of falling.

She continued up, all the way to the roof through a hole that may have once been a skylight. The city stretched out in front of her, its thoroughfares crawling with people beneath the low sun that hung like a great bronze gong in the sky.

Damsport occupied a peninsula, only attached to the mainland by a narrow strip of land aptly called the Bottleneck. In the centre was the Great Bazaar, and from it twelve straight wide roads ran out, arranged and numbered after the hours on a clock face. Squeezed in between Twelve and One was Thirteen, the road that led up to the cemetery.

Traversals connected the thoroughfares, tracing concentric circles around the Great Bazaar. Rory liked to imagine that if she could fly as high as the seagulls, Damsport would look like a huge spider's web. The key to the survival game in Damsport was to be a spider, not a fly. And right now she was definitely a fly, and Jake had ripped off her wings.

"Bastard," she whispered.

She turned around and climbed up the roof, towards the chimney against which she liked to sit and watch the activity of the enclosed docks. It was a comforting place, safe and familiar, and exactly what she needed after the day's events.

Which was why she was less than impressed to find someone sitting in her very spot, nonchalantly leaning back against the chimney. Rory pulled out her dagger. She had no intention of getting into a fight, but she was going to let the lad know that he wasn't welcome here.

Approaching from his right, she could see that he was young, somewhere around twenty. His clothes didn't look like five people had died in them, he was clean, and his dark hair was neat enough to suggest the presence of a comb not too long ago. Although he had the dark skin of a Damsian, his was a few shades lighter than hers, indicating that he didn't spend his days outdoors. That meant money. Probably the son of a merchant going through the requisite rebellious phase the wealthy young always seemed to indulge in. She had seen plenty of them slumming it in the poorer areas of Damsport for fun — until they got robbed and beaten, that was.

Rory crept forward carefully. If she was lucky, she might be able to loosen his purse as she kicked him off her roof.

She was about three arm's lengths away when he turned and faced her. His face had an arrogance that begged to be slapped.

"Well, well. What have we got here?"

His hands moved with speed, and he produced a rapier, its blade gleaming in the sun. If it hadn't been pointing at her, Rory would have found it beautiful. Then again, she thought that about every blade she clapped eyes on.

"Not very neighbourly to try and kill a man when he is in the middle of deep contemplation."

"Who said anything about trying to kill you? I just want you off my roof is all."

"Your roof? Forgive me, I thought this was a run-down rat hole beggars slept in. From your immaculate clothing, I gather that you are a wealthy property magnate? Delighted to meet you. Rafe's the name, Mistress Magnate."

Rory scowled.

"In fact," continued Rafe, "unlike you, I have some knowledge of this place. The owner died a number of years ago, and he had no next of kin. That means the house is now public property. Do you understand what I'm saying? Public property," he repeated slowly and loudly.

"I'm not deaf."

"I don't doubt your hearing for a second. It's the comprehension part I'm dubious about."

"I understand you fine. And this roof belongs to me, right, because I'm the only one who comes up here."

"Evidence to the contrary, since I'm here too. But the roof is large enough for two, so why don't we leave the blades out of it? You sit at one end, me at the other, and everybody's happy." As he spoke, Rafe sheathed his rapier, although he kept his hand on the hilt. "I'm not in the mood for a fight, although by the looks of you, it wouldn't be a fight so much as me beating you bloody, which I have to admit isn't something I'm particularly fond of doing. Especially not when my opponent is a scrawny girl. I hear it's ungentlemanly."

Rory ground her teeth. She was completely and infuriatingly outmatched now that she had lost the element of surprise.

"The roof may be big enough for two, but you're in my spot." And now, to top it all, she sounded like a child whining after a stolen toy.

"Ah, then I refer you to the ancient rule of finders keepers. If you want to keep your spot, you have to get there before everyone else. But feel free to come and sit next to me if this spot is so important to you. No need to fear me, my preferences run towards girls of the less…fragrant variety."

He patted the space next to him, raising an eyebrow. For the second time that day, Rory saw red. Before she knew what she was doing, she was hurtling at him, blade cutting through the air.

Unfortunately, air was all it cut.

He caught her wrist with one hand, her throat with the other. He crushed her wrist and she let go of her dagger with a squeal of pain. It clattered on the tiles and slid along the roof, landing on the stones below with a faint clang. She felt it in her bones as clearly as if she herself had fallen off the roof, and she gasped.

Rafe released her. "Well, that was uncalled for. I was being so polite, too. If I wasn't a gentleman, what a good thrashing I'd give you. Now, if I were you, I'd run along and fetch that dagger of yours. Talegian steel, if I'm not mistaken. Nice blade, for an urchin. You obviously take good care of it, and it would be a shame to lose it." A lazy smile spread across his face.

Rory didn't answer, shaking from anger and humiliation and from worry for her dagger below. She hurried down, feeling a rush of relief when she spotted it, reflecting the late afternoon sun.

She picked it up, carefully inspecting the blade for any sign that the fall had damaged it, but it was fine. She tenderly ran a finger along it and returned it to her belt, where it belonged.

What little adrenaline she had left evaporated, and she sagged, drained. Everything was going wrong. Everything. She wanted to crawl into a hole and sleep until it was all behind her. But she'd be damned if she would sleep with the beggars, where that smug bastard could see her. Nor would she return to the shack she had shared with Jake.

She turned to the lanes between Six and Seven and walked listlessly until she found a house that was derelict enough for her to climb up to its roof. Damsport's rooftops were her domain — no one knew them as well as she. Up on the rooftops, she was as powerful as the Marchioness herself, or at least she liked to think so.

By the time the sun began to set, she had found a place to spend the night, above a narrow and obviously rarely frequented lane. She made herself comfortable, leaning against a chimneystack, and watched the iron-grey clouds in the distance, the fading sunlight turning them pretty and pink. She wasn't fooled — she knew what the arrival of the clouds meant. Summer storm was brewing, and no mistake about it.

CHAPTER

5

The night was hot and still, pregnant with anticipation, as it awaited the Viper's next kill. Longinus felt the soup-like air part on either side of his face as he moved forward, as though the air was thick with invisible spider's threads.

Summer storm won't be long.

He pulled his silk handkerchief over his mouth and nose, the vial of poison topped with a small atomiser ready in his other hand. The target had been most uncooperative in sticking to the thoroughfares and busier roads, but at last he had turned into a narrow and deserted lane. Houses loomed up on either side, four or five storeys high, with narrow shuttered windows.

Tonight's target was a man with a neck wider than his head. He walked with a swagger, overly confident in the power of his guard's uniform. The sword at his side clinked against his left leg, making his gait sound uneven. Longinus held back at the lane's entrance at first, and then he saw the guard's purpose. He had wandered halfway into the lane and was now leaning a hand against the wall as he contributed to the alleyway's stink of urine.

There really is nothing as inelegant as a guard.

Longinus hurried forward silently, hugging the opposite wall. The poison he had prepared for tonight's job was fast acting so that a spray in the vicinity of the man's face was enough for him to drop dead after a few breaths. Tonight was not about theatrics, it was about getting the job done. He was looking forward to returning home so he could work on his pamphlets.

As he got closer, he was startled to find that the guard had a red handkerchief around the base of his neck. It brought to mind the terrible, bloody picture Mistress White Apron had painted and, distracted, Longinus stepped into something soft.

It squelched.

The guard swung around, spraying an arc of urine. He smacked the vial out of Longinus' hand and sent it crashing against the wall. Not bothering to put his tackle away, the guard pulled out his sword, the scratching sound of the blade against the scabbard setting Longinus' teeth on edge. His sword was wide and heavy looking — a mean, crude weapon.

Longinus opened his mouth to suggest the guard take a minute to put himself away before they crossed blades, but the man lunged at him before he could utter a word. Longinus ducked just in time, his reflexes slowed by his bewilderment at being attacked by a man hanging out loose like that.

Realising that the code of gentlemanly conduct was of no importance to his opponent, Longinus was left with no alternative but to draw his own rapier, the leather-lined scabbard making little more than a whisper. The two blades clashed, screeching into the night.

Longinus immediately launched into Ayre's attack, footwork precise, movements a blur of speed. A good assassin should be versed in every method of killing, even something as distasteful as sword fighting, and Longinus was unrivalled with a rapier. All the same, he wished he had worn his boiled leather armour to protect himself from any cuts. He knew he was at a serious disadvantage: should first blood be drawn, he would be unable to continue fighting. He needed to disarm his opponent, and fast.

The guard traced a vicious arc with his blade and Longinus used Sandercock's defence to parry, the force of the impact vibrating in his arm.

Lithe as a snake, nimble as a fly, lithe as a snake, nimble as a fly.

The guard's tendons stood out on his neck as he hacked with his sword, but Longinus danced around him, dodging and parrying every attack. His hand and wrist were already aching from absorbing the impact of his opponent's formidable strength. He kept this up until he noticed that the guard's thrusts were becoming clumsy.

Time to use my signature envelopment, and his sword will be mine.

Longinus didn't have time to launch into the attack. The guard locked blades, closing in quickly, and punched him square in the face. Longinus staggered back, dizzy from the pain, and he tripped on a loose cobblestone. He fell flat on his back, and the guard charged with a roar. Longinus' reflexes kicked in. He stabbed out with his rapier.

The roar abruptly turned to a gurgle that wasn't enough to hide a wet, tearing sound, and the guard's sword fell to the floor with a clang. Longinus released his rapier at once, leaving it protruding from the guard's belly, and he scrambled away. The guard swayed on his feet, his mouth an 'O' of surprise. A dark stain spread out where the blade was embedded in his abdomen, and Longinus' stomach contracted at the sight.

He vomited.

Gods alive, the blood, the blood!

From the corner of his eye, he saw the guard stagger towards him. The fabric of his uniform was saturated with blood, and some of it dripped to the ground, the sound impossibly loud in Longinus' ringing ears. He could smell it, sickly and salty.

He vomited again. His head swam and sick dribbled on his chin.

The guard put a heavy hand on Longinus' shoulder and spun him around, smacking a fist into his temple. Pain exploded in Longinus' head. He tried to retaliate, throwing a clumsy punch, but he couldn't focus. He missed, and the momentum had him lurching forward against the guard. His hand felt something wet through his silk glove.

Longinus made a strangled sound and froze, unable to react as the guard's hands closed around his throat, crushing his windpipe. Longinus could feel pressure building up in his head, his eyes bulging as though they wanted to abandon their sockets before things got worse.

Suddenly the guard fell to the ground, dragging Longinus down with him. A little shadow rose up, picked up the loose cobblestone, and brought it crashing into the guard's skull.

Longinus fainted.

CHAPTER 6

Well, that was a bit of a mess. Rory had acted on instinct, and now she wished she had stayed up on the roof. Nothing good ever came out of meddling in other people's business, but she hated seeing an underdog get beaten up, especially by a guard. And that man, with his obvious fear of blood, was an underdog and no mistake about it.

"Us runts gotta stick together," she murmured.

Still, she wasn't sure what to do now, so she decided that, as with everything, it was best to go back to basics.

She checked the guard's pockets.

No point letting a nice purse go to waste after all, and a very nice purse it was. She pulled the rapier out from the guard's stomach and wiped the blade on his uniform. The sword was beautiful, more beautiful than anything she had ever seen. The basket was black and of an intricate design, more delicate than lace.

She held it up so that the moonlight could gleam off the blade, and her throat constricted a little at the feel of it in her hand. This was what she was meant for. It felt like coming home, like falling in love — or at least what she expected falling in love was like. It was one thing to have a dagger, it was another to wield a rapier. Warriors and heroes like the Scarred Woman had rapiers, and now Rory was one step closer to her dream.

She slipped the rapier into her belt, a small, very reasonable fee for saving the unconscious man's life. You couldn't put a price on being alive after all.

She searched the unconscious man — not to take anything, mind you, just out of curiosity. She located his purse, a nice fat one, and was surprised to find she wasn't even tempted to take it. The rapier was one thing, but stealing an underdog's money, well, it felt like what Jake had done to her. As she returned the purse, something about him caught her attention. The handkerchief over his mouth and nose had fallen during the fight, and there was something...odd about his face.

He was in his thirties with the brown skin of a Damsian, but his features called to Rory in a way that suggested they were familiar. She groped through her memory for any recognition, when her fingers brushed against something, distracting her.

It was a set of cards, like playing cards but with a black snake in the middle and knives on the corners. She had heard of those cards; she had even seen one.

She looked back at the man on the ground. *That* was the Viper? That man who had thrown up and fainted after killing the guard? How was that possible? And yet there was no denying it: he carried the Viper's calling cards.

Now that was a turn for the books, and no mistake about it. She fiddled with the cards as she thought. There was an opportunity in this, if only she could be smart enough to work it out properly. She could sell the rapier, of course, but to what end? Master Xian was long gone, and money on its own wouldn't buy her a spot as an apprentice with the sword preceptors of Damsport. She had already tried.

Maybe the Viper could act as some kind of reference to recommend her to a sword preceptor? No, that would probably end with her getting arrested for being associated with an assassin.

What if he took her on himself and trained her? She knew enough to recognise that he was a very good swordsman.

He was bound to be grateful — she had saved his life after all. Training her was the least he could do as thanks for saving his life. On top of her modest fee of the rapier, that was.

And yet…

She thought of Jake, her partner for all those years, and of how completely he had screwed her over. You couldn't rely on people— that much she had learned. The Viper might not be grateful; he might not care that she had saved his life. He might laugh her away as that sword preceptor had laughed, and then what? She'd be left high and dry again, that's what. No, you couldn't rely on people.

Now, if she blackmailed him, he'd have no choice. An assassin with a fear of blood could only be a laughingstock: his reputation would be ruined, and he'd never work again. That was some pretty powerful leverage.

Her heart hammered in her chest at the thought. Could she do it? Blackmail an assassin? A trained killer? Rory was a master at the game of survival, but this might be too dangerous a game, even for her. She returned the cards to the Viper's pocket and kissed a number of her medals for luck.

"Aim small, win small," she whispered to herself. "Aim big, win big."

This was probably stupid, very, very stupid. She would no doubt regret it, if the dead could regret anything. But if she could pull it off…

CHAPTER 7

When Longinus came to, he found an urchin sitting cross-legged opposite him, running a rag carefully along his rapier's blade. He could make her out quite clearly in the moonlight. She was a scrawny thing, wearing rags that were so big for her she looked more like a coathanger than a kid. Her tiny face was dwarfed by an odd mass of rope-like hair that hung in thick segments down to the small of her back. Her skin was so dark it looked almost black in the night, and her eyes gleamed like those of a fox, watching him.

Longinus moved, catching the smell of blood and vomit on himself, and he thought he might faint again. He tried to push himself up, but his hand sank into something cold and congealed that seeped through the thin silk of his glove. He pulled away with a yelp.

"You had carrots today," said the urchin, as conversationally as if she was discussing the weather. "I saw it in your sick."

Longinus' stomach lurched in response, as though offering to give her a second specimen to examine.

"Help me up," he croaked, extending a hand. His legs felt so weak he wasn't sure they'd be able to support him.

"No," said the urchin. She got up and pointed Longinus' own rapier at him. "Here's how it's going to go. I just saved your life, right? I know you're the Viper, and I know you're afraid of blood. Now how do you think people are gonna react when they find out, eh? An assassin afraid of blood?"

"Please," said Longinus weakly. "Not that, not that." He felt the old familiar shame rise to the surface. He thought he had gotten rid of it a long time ago, but it seemed to be alive and well, and so very close to the surface. A suffocating feeling crowded his chest.

"Also," continued the girl, "I have you at the tip of *my* rapier."

Longinus clenched his teeth, gathering himself. "What do you want?"

"To be your apprentice, to learn how to fight. You're handy with a sword, you are. Surprising given that you're afraid of blood, but I don't care about that. Teach me and I'll take your secret to the grave."

"And if I refuse?"

"I'll tell everyone in Damsport about you, see if I don't." She touched Longinus' chin with the tip of the rapier. Longinus swallowed down a whimper, hating how weak and vulnerable he was.

"Alright," he said in a strangled voice. "Alright. Step back and let me get up."

"Not so fast. I ain't stupid. I'm gonna need some sort of assurance that you ain't gonna kill me the second I look away. I know what you assassins are like. Swear it."

Longinus hesitated, but the touch of the rapier made his mind up.

"By my honour —"

"Screw honour. Swear on the Old Girl."

"Ah, I swear on the Old Girl that I won't hurt you or try to kill you while you are my apprentice."

"Good." The girl took a step back, and Longinus sagged with relief as the blade retreated. "Although I don't trust promises as far as I can throw them. That is to say, I don't trust them at all since I can't touch them. I'll be leaving the rapier with a friend. Talegian steel, right? Very beautiful design on the basket. Very unusual."

Longinus gritted his teeth. *It isn't beautiful, it's exquisite.*

"I reckon," continued the urchin, "that whoever made this sword will remember who bought it. And if I had the word 'viper' engraved on it, well that would be enough to convince people it belongs to the Viper. People can be stupid, you know, they believe whatever they want to see."

Longinus couldn't disagree with that. He understood the importance of appearances better than most.

"So if anything happens to me, right, that friend will spread word of what happened here tonight along with the rapier as her proof."

"You said you wouldn't tell anyone."

"This is someone I can trust."

All of a sudden a wave of exhaustion crashed over Longinus and what little fight he had left disappeared. He felt weak, he was covered with blood, vomit, and who knew what else… He wanted to wash, pour himself a glass of port, and forget all about this blasted evening.

"Fine," he said. "Fine." He extended a hand. "Help me up."

"I ain't stupid enough to do that. What, so you can try and overpower me? Pull the other one."

"I wouldn't… I gave you my word."

"Yeah, well people got a habit of letting me down, so I ain't trusting your word. We're going to your house so I can know where you live, right, and then I'm taking the rapier to my friend. I'll come back first thing in the morning so you can start training me. Alright?"

"You're… You're coming to my house?"

"Obviously, where else you gonna train me?"

Longinus could find no answer. He nodded weakly and inched up to a standing position, his legs shaking from the nausea and the dizziness. He had to get home and regain his strength and composure. He would deal with the urchin and this mess tomorrow.

He could see the dark outline of the corpse out of the corner of his eye, and he walked away from it, propping himself up with one hand against the wall, not wanting to risk another fainting spell. The urchin followed behind him as he made the slow journey home.

CHAPTER

8

Rory had dropped the Viper off at his house, watching him enter the back door. He had looked so exhausted and pathetic that she had felt a twinge of guilt at what she was doing. She hadn't expected him to be so easily defeated.

It could be an act, she reminded herself. She was going to have to keep her wits about her. Assassins were masters of disguise and trickery after all — she couldn't afford to be taken in by this little show. She wasn't sure if leaving him alone where he could recoup was a good idea, but if she didn't at least look like she was following through on her claim that someone had her back, there would be nothing to stop the Viper from overpowering her, promise or not.

The truth was that she couldn't work out who to trust with the rapier. Jake would normally have been her go-to person, but that was now out of the question. It was disorientating, having to work out a plan without him. It felt awkward, foreign, like lifting a purse with her left hand.

Her acquaintances at the Rookery could be counted on to help with the blackmail, but the rapier would get sold faster than you could say Talegian steel.

Rory's hand returned to the rapier's hilt. Every time she felt the grip in her hand, it was as though a small bolt of lightning ran through her. A girl could take on the world with a sword like that. By all the gods, she would never whine or snivel again, not now she had a rapier at her side.

Her first rapier. Her first step towards becoming a swordfighter like the Scarred Woman — a hero.

She knew she would never allow it be sold, so anyone from the Rookery was out. That only left Cruikshank. Rory frowned. Cruikshank was far too honest to be trustworthy. She would keep the rapier, that was for sure, but if she knew about the blackmail, she would probably try to return it to the Viper. Maybe even tell the guards. There was no telling with an honest person. That was the trouble with them: they were far too unpredictable. Maybe if Rory made up a story, she could —

She became aware of a presence behind her and cursed inwardly. She had been so distracted by the rapier that she had broken her cardinal rule: when alone at night, never stay on ground level. She could feel a shift in the air behind her, the smell of alcohol on breath. She spun around and pulled out the rapier.

Jake swayed back, surprise painted comically on his features.

"Stay back," ordered Rory.

"You got a sword?" He slurred heavily.

63

"Yeah, I got a sword, so stay back."

"Look, I know you're mad." He made some indistinct gesture. "You've every right."

"Damn right, I do."

"But partners are partners. And we're still partners."

Rory felt a faint tremor of temptation. Being partners with Jake was familiar, comfortable, like old boots moulded to her feet.

"You screwed me over, Jake," she said.

"Now see here, I'm trying to apologise and you're throwing it back in my face. Gods damn you, I said I'd make it up. First, I got this." He produced a small purse that tinkled with the sound of coin bits. "I drunk some of it, been a long day and all that, but it's something."

At the mention of his drinking, Rory's face darkened and all temptation evaporated.

"I don't want your making up, Jake. I don't want nothing from you."

"You're pissing me off, Rory. I said I'm sorry, so take the damned purse."

"No."

"I *said* take the damned *purse!*" He thrust it at her, startling her. The rapier moved, nothing more than a flick, but its tip sliced a thin red line in Jake's chest. He looked down with a frown.

"What the — you cut me?"

"It was an accident. Look, just leave me alone, Jake. I don't want your money, I don't want your making up. Just…leave me be."

But Jake wasn't paying attention.

"The hell? You *cut* me?"

"I told you to stay back and you weren't listening, so yeah," she replied, with more bravado than she felt.

"I come to apologise, to give you money, and you cut me? You ungrateful little *bitch*!"

As he spoke, Jake grabbed the tip of the rapier with his left hand, not noticing as the blade bit into his palm. He wrenched it out of Rory's hand and sent it clattering to the ground, while his right fist caught her by the eye. It all happened so fast she barely had the time to register the rapier leaving her hand before pain exploded in the left side of her face, and she crumpled to the ground.

She picked herself up slowly, her head swimming. Jake looked down at his hands with dumb surprise, as though they had acted without his consent. Blood dripped from the cut in his left palm. He mumbled something, still staring at his hands.

Rory felt strangely detached, as though she was floating high above the scene like a seagull and all of this was happening to someone else. She looked for the rapier.

"I'm sorry, Rory, I…I dunno what happened…"

She walked past him to retrieve the rapier and slipped it into her belt.

"Rory?"

Jake put a hand on her shoulder, and what was left of her dizziness cleared at once, as though his hand had conducted a lightning bolt. She lashed out with her right foot, catching him straight in the crotch. He groaned and fell to his knees, his hands covering his groin. She kicked again, catching his ribs with the end of her boot, which was tipped with iron.

"Don't come near me again," she said.

She didn't wait for an answer, walking away.

The detachment slowly cleared, and to her annoyance, her eyes began to water. She wiped them with her sleeve, wincing as she touched the rapidly swelling bruise around her left eye. That would be swollen shut tomorrow, and no mistake about it. She walked away as quick as she could, anxious to leave the scene behind her.

Jake had never hit her like that before. Sure, they had fought like cats and dogs as kids, and he had hit her plenty of times when they were conning marks, but that was different. She wiped her eyes again. What did it matter, anyway? She had decided that their partnership was over, so what if he had hit her? That just confirmed she had made the right decision.

Still her eyes watered.

"Focus on the future," she muttered.

She held onto the rapier's grip tightly, but the magic had gone. It was just a piece of metal in her hand now.

***

Rory reached Medlion Traversal and heard the distant rumbling that announced the arrival of Crazy Willy. Finally some luck. Nobody else worked as late as Crazy Willy did, and nothing in Damsport went as fast as his steamcoach. She would be at Cruikshank's in no time.

Grateful for the distraction, she fumbled through the guard's purse until she found a half copper. It was a bit on the small side — she probably could have gotten a proper half copper from the purse Jake had, but nothing could have convinced her to take his money. The small half copper would have to do, and Crazy Willy wasn't too fussy about weights anyway. Sometimes he got a little more, sometimes a little less. All came out in the wash was what he said. She kissed three of her talismans for luck, clamped the half coin between her teeth, and waited.

Rory liked to imagine that catching and mounting a wild beast mid-flight would be a little like climbing on board Crazy Willy's steamcoach. She kept her knees bent, hands at the ready, head turned to the right as she waited for it to arrive.

The noise grew louder: the mad clatter of wheels, the rattle of the coach, the whine of springs, the grating of metal on metal — and just audible over the commotion, Crazy Willy's crazy laughter.

It appeared like something out of a nightmare, screeching around the corner, the metal wheels sending sprays of sparks on either side. Two wheels lifted from the ground, tilting the whole coach sideways, and Crazy Willy laughed louder. He turned the steering wheel slightly, and the coach crashed back to the pavement.

The steamcoach rushed towards Rory, huge and dark, bristling all over with metal rungs that gleamed in the moonlight. The engine's chimney poured out smoke as thick as tar, and fire roared, glaring out of air holes like the burning eyes of a beast.

She leapt.

And nearly missed.

Maybe it was the pain in her face, or maybe it was all that had happened that evening, but she didn't quite extend her left hand far enough. Her right hand caught a rung, but she was off-balance, and the coach's speed sent her crashing into its side, the back of her head smacking painfully into another rung, her feet dangling in the air.

Keeping a vicelike grip on the rung, she sought the little ledge at the bottom of the coach with her feet, digging her heels into it. Before she could try to turn, Crazy Willy's monkey appeared at her shoulder. It wore a red jacket with a little fez that was secured by a piece of string under his chin. It extended a small, hairy hand, holding onto the coach with its feet and tail. Rory knew better than to try and bat it away — that battle could only end with her rolling on the road and breaking several limbs, if she was lucky. She extended her neck, showing the monkey the piece of coin between her teeth. It snatched it from her.

"Eight!" she shouted over the noise. She had no idea how Crazy Willy had taught the monkey numbers, but damn if that creature didn't know every number from one to twelve. Never thirteen, though. Crazy Willy didn't stop for the dead. The monkey ran back to the driver, leaving her dangling on the side of the coach. Now that she had paid, it didn't matter whether she could hold on until her destination.

She swung herself around with her right hand and grabbed a rung with her left, moving her feet so that the tips of her boots were on the ledge, rather than her heels. She climbed up slowly until she reached the flat roof. Two other people were there already, and neither gave her so much as a glance. She sat down with her knees against her chest and grabbed a rung on either side of her. The speed made her eyes water some more and she closed them, letting the wind stream through her hair.

The Scarred Woman wouldn't have missed that rung.

When they reached Eight, Crazy Willy pulled the coach to such an abrupt stop that if she hadn't been holding on, Rory would have flown straight over his head.

"Eight!" he shouted.

Rory scrambled down as quickly as she could. She had barely touched the ground when the coach sped forward once more, swallowed by the night in a shower of sparks.

CHAPTER

9

Now that he was as clean as he could get without visiting the baths, Longinus was beginning to feel like himself again. He had burned that night's silks and was now wearing a burgundy brocade waistcoat inwrought with thread of gold over matching trousers and with a fine silk smoking jacket. He didn't smoke, but no assassin should be caught dead at home without a smoking jacket.

He leaned back in his chair, allowing his eyes to drift across the bottles of poison that lined his shelves. The soft glow from the vapour lamp glanced off the curve of the bottles, and they almost looked like a hundred benevolent eyes, watching over him. The thought comforted him, gave him strength. He was going to need it to deal with that devil child. Blackmailing him like that. No shame, no shame at all. He clenched his fists at the thought. His anger was a comfort too, and infinitely preferable to the paralysing and all-too-familiar shame.

He went over a number of plans. However, no matter which way he turned, he was confronted with two problems. The first was that she knew who he was, and she knew his secret. The second was that he had sworn not to kill her, at least while she was his apprentice, and Longinus was a man of his word. So in good faith that meant he could do nothing for a few months, at least.

He got up and paced the room, stopping only to pour himself two fingers of port in a crystal tumbler. It was infernal to find himself in this position, but there was nothing for it: he was going to have to keep the girl close. He took a deep draught. He must be crafty, calculating.

He returned to the problem at hand. He would have to keep the girl happy. Make her feel as though they had some sort of teacher-pupil bond. And then when the time came and her apprenticeship finished… He would have to find the friend, too.

Longinus didn't like the idea of killing a young girl — there were rules after all, but some things (such as his reputation) were more important than morals. Until then she would be a chore, one he would have to contend with as well as he could. Probably starting with a bath, because he didn't know how long he'd be able to put up with the stench of her.

Another idea came to him then. The Viper, as a generous benefactor. A picture painted itself in his mind. The girl looking up at him admiringly, as he (wearing the most divine emerald silk shirt with a lace cravat, like a froth of foam at his throat) taught her the mysteries of poisoning. None of his secret formulae, of course, but the basics. The girl, trying (and failing) to replicate the complicated manipulations. He, again, demonstrating the importance of long, slender fingers when handling rare and dangerous compounds.

He spread his hands to admire them. Artist's hands, with long, elegant fingers. He should maybe wear a ring when he was teaching. Maybe the sapphire to contrast with the shirt? No, too many different colours. Change the shirt, then? Maybe even order a new one? Yes, a new shirt, some trousers too, and a waistcoat to match.

He would do that in the morning before the girl arrived.

CHAPTER

10

Rory made her way down Eight, skirting Spirepass, the area wedged between Seven and Eight. Farther on, towards the sea edge, was Machinist Crescent. It hugged the shore from the enclosed docks up to the end of Nine.

Spirepass was an area of domes and spires, of gold leaf and mosaic, and Rory could see its many curves in the distance, gleaming in the moonlight.

Along Eight, porticoes kept the now-shuttered jewellery shops in the shadows. The thoroughfare was deserted, save for the street sweeps. They swayed their long-handled brooms side to side in a semicircle, keeping to a slow rhythm, pushing the day's rubbish to the street's edge. Later they'd sift through it and keep anything that could be sold or made into something else, leaving the rest for the rubbish collectors.

The sweeps had rods down the backs of their shirts from which dangled a blue vapour lamp, just above their heads. The light was pale and sickly, and it cast long shadows over their wrinkled faces. In the distance, they looked almost like ghosts, the rhythm of their broom bristles and the tinkle of their lamp chains taking on an otherworldly quality in the silent night. They reminded Rory of the game she and Jake had played as children, hopping over the broom handles to see who would miss first. Rory had always won. Her melancholy deepened as she replayed the awful surprise when Jake had struck her.

Rory turned off Eight, plunging into Spirepass proper. She wound her way through a procession of smaller streets and courtyards until she came out into the wide plaza that hosted the Spirepass baths, a great domelike structure cornered with four tall spires. She trotted past the baths, knowing full well what kind of transactions took place within their walls at this time of night. As she reached the end of the plaza, she went to turn into a lane and crashed into something.

A hand stopped her from falling back.

"You alright, girl? I didn't see you there."

The man she had crashed into was middle-aged and balding, and an odd smell emanated from him. He shook a vapour lamp to light and caught sight of her face.

"What happened to you?"

Rory shrugged and stepped back into the shadows. "Not your business."

"Here." He searched his pockets and produced a small glass jar. "I always keep some of this handy — I bruise easily. Here." He thrust it at her. "It will help with the pain."

Rory hesitated, and the man pushed the jar into her hand. She took it and retreated, still feeling too raw after her encounter with Jake to face the stranger properly.

"Put it on your eye," said the man.

She nodded, and the man regarded her for a moment. There was sadness to him, to the slump of his shoulders.

"Alright then," he said, and he continued the way he had been walking, towards the baths. Rory heard him mutter "Not entirely useless" to himself. He entered the baths and disappeared from sight.

Rory remained where she was, wishing she had at least thanked him. She opened the jar and sniffed its content. It had a medical smell, eucalyptus maybe or camphor. She smeared a little of the paste on her eye. At first it burned, making her draw in a startled breath, but then the sensation cooled and it soothed the hot throbbing under her skin to a tingle.

She squirrelled the jar away and headed off, committing the man's face to memory. If she saw him again, she would be sure to do something to pay him back for the jar.

Soon enough she reached Machinist Crescent, a maze of warehouses and stark, functional buildings without any kind of street system to give it order. The buildings had been erected as and where required, leaving only gaps to allow people and machines to pass through. Warehouses loomed on either side of Rory as she walked, the moonlight not quite able to penetrate the narrow gaps between the buildings, so it was like navigating through the depths of a canyon.

The warehouse she was after was right in the centre of Machinist Crescent. It was older than the rest, rusty in parts, the red bricks of its walls chipped and dull. As she got close, the smell of smoke and tar and hot metal filled her nostrils.

Just as she reached the door, she heard voices within, and a metallic clunk indicated that the door was being unlocked. Rory melted back into the shadows. Two women and a man, all tall and sinewy and wearing fighting leathers, stepped out. They wore the burnished helmets of the Varanguards with their distinctive long black ponytails. Rory could see glimmers of silver from the hidden knives. She was so busy admiring the Varanguards that she didn't immediately notice the smaller, older woman who followed them out.

Rory's stomach tied itself into knots of excitement when she recognised the Marchioness of Damsport. She had never seen the Old Girl so close before. Her brown skin was heavily lined, her hair was grey and pulled back in intricate braids, and she wore simple leathers. There was an air of power and iron-like strength to her, and yet she was completely dwarfed when Cruikshank appeared in the doorway. Although short, Cruikshank's musculature was impressive, silhouetted as it was by the orange light of the furnace within.

"Thank you for seeing me, Eleanore," said the Old Girl. "I know I seem paranoid, but I can't be too careful around the anniversary of the Three Day Battle."

"No need to explain, Elspeth," replied Cruikshank, and Rory gaped at the familiar use of the Old Girl's first name. "I'm always there to help."

The two women shook hands, and Rory half-expected to hear the cracking of bones.

At a nod from the Old Girl, her bodyguards formed an escort around her, and the party walked away. Rory slunk back to a crouch as they passed, not wanting to risk the Varanguards mistaking her for a threat. She knew they would be particularly jumpy this time of year: it was widely whispered that the Airnian Emperor had never forgiven the Marchioness for the humiliation of the Three Day Battle and that he plotted her death so he could take Damsport back.

He had let Damsport go willingly enough when it was little more than a rotting pustule clinging to his empire like an unwanted barnacle. Without the Empire's support, the city would wither and die, he predicted. The Marchioness, at twenty-five, was too young to know what she was doing, he told her when she asked for Damsport's independence.

She had pushed on nonetheless, and he had granted her request.

The Marchioness had then negotiated defence alliances with neighbouring kingdoms, to the amusement of the world, who laughed at the young girl trying to play at politics. One older, kindly king took her aside to explain that nobody in their right mind would ever care enough about Damsport to want it as part of their territory, let alone engage funds, resources, and soldiers to take it by force. Rumour had it that she had smiled and batted her eyelashes and asked him to indulge a young girl's fancy. The old king had agreed.

Rory liked to think that everyone had laughed at the Old Girl back then just like the sword preceptors laughed at her own ambitions now. Well, the Old Girl had shown them.

Damsport's independence and alliance treaties in place, the Old Girl had poured what remained of her family's fortune into creating the first enclosed dock — Tinsbury Dock. Only a narrow stretch of Damsport's coast south of the city could be approached by sea — the rest was all cliffs and jagged rocks. Before the enclosed docks, there had been space enough for a couple of small fishing boats to berth, at most. Although a peninsula, Damsport had never been a real port.

The enclosed docks finished, the Old Girl abolished all trade taxes, and this permanently. It didn't take long for merchants to come take advantage of the tax break, bringing money and produce to trade with them. Within a few years, Damsport rose from the cesspit of its previous self like a phoenix from its ashes, transforming into a thriving city.

The Airnian Emperor was furious, claiming he had been tricked and demanding that Damsport be returned to him. The Old Girl — to the joy and pride of her people— sent his envoys packing. The Emperor retaliated by sending his army to the Bottleneck Wall, forcing the Marchioness' allies to send their own troops. They were no doubt more interested in preventing the Emperor from controlling what was fast becoming an important centre of trade than in displaying loyalty to the Marchioness, but the result was the same.

The allied forces took three days to arrive — three days during which the men and women of Damsport, led by the Old Girl, held back the world's largest and best appointed army. Thousands died, but they fought tooth and nail for each and every inch of the Bottleneck Wall, and when the allied armies arrived, it still hadn't been breached.

It had been a resounding victory for the Old Girl and a humiliating defeat for the Emperor — one he had yet to forget or forgive.

As Rory watched the Varanguards and the Old Girl walk away, she felt ashamed of her earlier despondency. The Old Girl had faced mocking from the entire world; she had faced an attack from the Airnian army, and there was Rory moping because Jake had struck her. Rory made a promise to herself there and then never to mope again. Whatever the future brought, she would face each obstacle like the Old Girl had.

Would the Scarred Woman have let the betrayal of a friend get to her? Of course not. And neither would the Old Girl have. Heroes and warriors never felt low or dejected — they didn't know the meaning of those words.

Rory stood up as tall as she could manage and placed a hand on the rapier's hilt. Full of newfound confidence, she approached Cruikshank's door with a kind of swagger. It felt a bit awkward — she would have to practice.

The door wasn't locked, and she let herself in.

CHAPTER

11

"You know the Old Girl?" Rory said from the entrance.

Cruikshank started and turned around, lifting the goggles from her face. They left owl-like circles around her eyes where the skin had been protected from the soot, smoke, and metal shavings. The rest of her face was caked with dirt, which accentuated every line, making her look older than she was. She wore a leather vest and leggings covered with more cuts and lashes than a whipped back. Her curly russet hair was piled high atop her head, making an odd contrast with her dark brown skin.

"Rory! You startled me, lovey. What are you doing here? Come in, come in."

Cruikshank ushered her into her workshop. It was a single large room dotted throughout with pillars to support the roof. Hooks were welded to them, supporting heavy chains and large cogs, some as big as cart wheels. A metal walkway hung overhead along the walls, housing Cruikshank's office at one end. Beneath the walkway, the walls were covered with a scaffolding of shelves full of small pieces of clockwork, bits of unfinished machinery, tools, sketches, and notebooks. The whole room was covered in a film of soot and bathed by the molten orange glow of the furnace.

"Why are you here?" asked Cruikshank. "Not that I'm not happy to see you, lovey, of course I am, but I thought you'd be on a steam galley by now, off to begin your adventures with Master Xian."

As she spoke, Cruikshank picked up an enormous sledgehammer, the muscles on her bare arms rippling beneath the skin. Her right arm was covered with an intricate cog tattoo that came to life as she moved.

"That ain't happening no more," said Rory.

"Why not?"

"Had a disagreement with Jake. He thought my money could be used for his gambling debts. I didn't agree."

"Oh, lovey, I can guess how that went. Is that what happened to your face?"

Rory didn't answer. That was between her and Jake, and she didn't want to talk about it.

"Will you *please* sleep here tonight," said Cruikshank. "It's not charity —"

"It *is* charity, alright? I'm just fine sleeping on the roofs, and I make my own way, thanking you very much."

As she spoke, Rory felt the weight of the jar the man had given her, and she made another promise to herself to find him and pay him back for it. Heroes didn't accept charity from anyone, even well-meaning strangers.

"You're a difficult one, lovey, you know that?"

Rory grinned and then winced from the pain in her swollen eye. She would need to apply more of that paste. "I'll take that as a compliment," she said. "Why was the Old Girl here, by the way?"

"She came to inspect the machine I'll be unveiling at the Revels." Cruikshank gestured at the huge shape that skulked in a corner beneath a tarp. "Her Varanguards are visiting every act that will be performing at the Revels to check for weapons or anything that could be used to attack the Marchioness."

"Yeah, but why did she come to see you personally?"

"She did it as a courtesy to me since I'm her Head Machinist."

"What? You are? I had no idea. Why don't you —"

"Put on airs and wear some ridiculous chain or brooch to proclaim my status? You know me better than that. Anyway, the only reason I'm her Head Machinist is because I was the only one who knew her arse from her elbow back when we started work on the enclosed docks. We go way back, me and the Marchioness. I knew her when she was too young to be called 'Old Girl.'"

Rory gave Cruikshank a newly impressed glance. She knew Cruikshank's modesty well enough to realise that she would have had a much larger role in the creation of the docks than she admitted to.

"So tell me, lovey," said Cruikshank. "Since you're not here to take me up on my offer to stay with me, to what do I owe the pleasure of this impromptu visit?"

"I came to ask you a favour. I got something of value, right, and I ain't got nowhere to keep it."

"If you think I'm going to help you with whatever you stole with Jake —"

"It ain't like that, I got me a new sword preceptor."

Cruikshank looked at her dubiously. "Really?"

"Yeah. He's a bit, um, different. Eccentric. Doesn't get out much. He gave me this." Rory pulled out the rapier.

"You expect me to believe that he just gave you a sword?"

"I saved his life. He got attacked and, um, I got him out of it."

Rory didn't want to give Cruikshank any more details than strictly necessary. The best lies were always the simplest.

"Aren't you the little saviour, lovey. You gonna hang it over his head for the next five years, too?"

"Eh, you can't put a price on being alive," said Rory with a grin.

"I would have lived," replied Cruikshank.

"Course you would, but Charlie Little Fingers would have kicked the living crap out of you."

"True. And as thanks, you should let me put you up in my workshop," said Cruikshank. "The roofs are no place for a girl to live."

"You taught me to read. That's plenty."

Cruikshank lit a cigar, the matches incongruously small in her thick jointed hands, and blew a plume of blue smoke.

She examined Rory through the smoke as though debating whether to press the issue. Rory hoped she wouldn't.

"So what is it you want me to do with this rapier?" Cruikshank said at last.

"Well I can't hold onto it —"

"Why not?"

"You know how it is. I walk around with something like that and it'll get taken from me before you can blink. I don't got Jake to protect me no more."

"You know I can tell when you're lying," said Cruikshank.

"I ain't lying, why you gotta be so suspicious of me?"

"Hmm."

Cruikshank took a long drag of her cigar and gestured for the rapier. Rory handed it to her with more than a little trepidation. Cruikshank examined it with a critical eye, cigar clamped between her teeth.

"So what you're telling me is that my workshop is good enough for your sword to sleep in, but not for you?"

"Come on, you know it ain't like that."

Cruikshank took another drag of her cigar.

"Tell you what, lovey, I'll keep your sword for you. I find out there's anything dodgy going on, and that's the last you'll see of it. If everything is above board, though, you can come and take it as you please. Deal?"

Rory swallowed. This was not how she had planned the conversation going, but backing out now would be admitting that she was lying.

"Sure. Whatever you say. You're a right cynical one, Cruikshank. Sometimes a girl does something nice and is rewarded."

"With a rapier that's worth more than most people make in a year?"

"Must be my charm."

Cruikshank gave a short laugh full of smoke.

"And you're sure you won't sleep here tonight, lovey?" she said. "Summer storm's brewing, it won't be nice up on the roofs."

"I'll be fine. Anyway, I need to get back to my sword preceptor."

Rory left Cruikshank's workshop unsure if she had made a good move in leaving the rapier or a big mistake. She cursed softly under her breath. Damn honesty, it was always so complicated.

CHAPTER 12

The storm broke just as she reached the street the Viper lived on, the skies opening with the suddenness of a bucket of water being tipped from up high. Within seconds, Rory was drenched to the bone, squinting through rivulets of water that ran down her face and into her eyes. She sought shelter under one of the trees that lined the street, wiping her face and wringing out her hair. Around her, the rain hissed against the cobblestones, making it hard to see, but it barely penetrated the thick foliage overhead.

She peered at the Viper's house. It was dark and quiet, like all the others on the street. In fact, there was nothing to distinguish it from the rest, but Rory wouldn't be taken in by a veneer of respectability. This was the lair of an assassin — who knew what would be waiting for her inside. She'd have to be insane or utterly stupid to breeze through the back door come morning, as they had agreed before she'd left.

On the way over, she had decided that she would climb to the roof and find a way to break into the house. Catching the Viper unawares in the middle of the night would be the best way to keep the upper hand, allowing her to see what he had planned and whether he intended to keep his promise. She would begin as soon as the storm had passed — climbing in the pouring rain could be tricky, but thankfully, summer storms were almost always short-lived.

Soon enough the rain reduced to a light patter and Rory set off. She reached the house and slipped down the narrow space that separated it from its neighbour, unwinding her silk line and grappling hook from around her waist. A few swings of the hook to gather momentum, and she loosed it towards the roof, where it found purchase. Rory grinned. Few could match her with a grappling hook and line. A few tugs of the silk line confirmed that the hook was secure, and she began to climb.

The wall was slick with rainwater, and she moved slowly, checking each hand and foothold carefully to make sure it wasn't too slippery for use. When she reached the roof, she was pleasantly surprised to find a skylight. As expected, it was locked, but a look through the glass revealed that the room below contained discarded furniture covered with white sheets. Rory smiled at her luck: beneath the window was something in the shape of a chaise longue, which should be soft enough to absorb the noise of falling glass.

A quick kick with her heel broke a hole large enough for her to stick her hand through, and she opened the window. She stuck her head in and checked the room over to make sure there wasn't anything or anyone waiting for her. The air was stale and dusty — no one had breathed in there for a long time. Once she was satisfied that the room was safe, she secured her grappling hook and lowered herself down. She returned the grappling hook back to her waist and made for the door, letting herself into the house.

She found herself at one end of a long, carpeted corridor. The house was dark and silent, save for the ticking of a clock somewhere. At the other end of the corridor, a sliver of light filtered out beneath a door. The room occupied by the Viper?

Rory crept towards it slowly.

About halfway down the hallway, she came across a door with a deadbolt across it. She paused, glancing towards the light at the end of the passage. Once she had made herself known to the Viper, she would no longer be free to look around, and a room with a deadbolt could mean something of interest. Something she could use.

She hesitated only a fraction longer before her fingers found the deadbolt. It was rusty. She inched it backwards as slowly as she could, making a faint scraping noise.

The door swung open silently. Rory stepped across the threshold, peering into the gloom. She frowned.

It was a child's room. Did the Viper have a child? And why would he have the room dead-bolted?

The curtains were open, but very little light made it through the window. Rory could just make out a small bed and what must have been a canopy over it at one end of the room. There a little desk, there a chest of drawers, and that shadow in the corner had to be a rocking horse.

The clouds parted at that moment, and the room was briefly illuminated with moonlight. The rocking horse was old, its paint chipped, its leather saddle cracked and eaten in places by time and moths. Atop the chest of drawers was a collection of dolls that looked at her with beady black eyes, their clothing greyed and full of holes. Everything was covered in a thick layer of dust.

The floor was covered in an intricately patterned rug — Kushanian design and no doubt expensive — and in the middle of the rug was a large, dark stain. The stain was a little bigger than a child, and it made Rory shudder. She had seen enough corpses in the night to know when she was looking at dried blood. The rug and stain were covered with as much dust as the rest of the room.

She looked up again to find the dolls' eyes still on her. Suddenly she felt uncomfortable. Her skin crawled, and it was all she could do not to slam the door shut on the dolls, the dust, the bloodstain. She maintained composure, closing the door carefully and drawing the bolt back across it. Then she hurried down the passage, only glancing back once at the locked room.

Once she reached the door with the light, she pressed her ear against it, but she heard nothing. A little beyond the door was a set of stairs, leading down to the ground floor. No sound there, either.

She grasped the doorknob and turned it back as far as it would go. Then, taking a deep breath, she burst forth into the room.

It was empty.

Opposite the doorway was a four-poster bed, still made, and to the left a set of double doors had been thrown open, leading to a vast wardrobe full of brightly coloured, expensive-looking clothes. To the right was a desk on which papers were perfectly stacked, and above it was a painting that depicted a very beautiful and proud-looking woman. Clutching her legs was a small boy, looking fearfully back over his shoulder at the painter. The resemblance to the Viper was unmistakable. Next to him, the rest of the painting had been cut out, all the way to the frame. The only sign that there had once been a person in that gap was a bit of fabric painted to overlap one of the boy's arms. It looked like the hem of a girl's skirt.

Rory thought of the room with the stain.

A sibling then, perhaps? She briefly considered looking through the Viper's papers and wardrobe, but the thought made her feel ill at ease. Except for the cut-out painting, the room was so ordinary, so harmless. This wasn't the dark lair she had expected of an assassin, and she felt like she had trespassed into something very personal.

A faint sound came to her from the stairway, and Rory spun on her heels, drawing her dagger, heart hammering. The ticking of the clock marked the passing seconds.

Nothing stirred.

She closed the door and slowly headed down the stairs. She took each step carefully, hugging the wall and testing each one with her toes to ensure it wouldn't creak beneath her weight. She kept her dagger at the ready.

When she reached the bottom, she found another door under which filtered a little light. Again, she pressed her ear to the wood, and this time, she heard something: a rustling sound and a deep sigh.

"Got you," she mouthed.

Once she had turned back the doorknob, she opened the door abruptly, intending to startle the Viper.

He was not startled.

In fact, he didn't even stir, sound asleep as he was, sitting in a blue velvet chair. His head was in one of those awkward angles heads always found when you slept sitting up, and a little drool oozed out of the corner of his mouth, dribbling down his chin and onto his waistcoat.

Rory let out a low, incredulous laugh. Weren't assassins supposed to be cunning? Careful? Masters of survival? She had always imagined that they slept with an eye open and a dagger at the ready. Obviously not this one. Then again, she reminded herself, most assassins weren't afraid of blood. All her concerns for safety melted away like butter in the sun. It was hard to feel threatened by a man who drooled in his sleep.

She crept closer, until her face was inches from his, but still he didn't wake. Rory gave herself a satisfied nod. She would definitely be able to stay in control of him. She felt a little sorry for him: the man was obviously pretty useless as an assassin, but that wasn't her problem. Her focus was only on learning to sword fight. Having seen him in action, she felt confident he'd be able to teach her that — or at least enough that she would be worthy of the Scarred Woman's respect when they next met.

She remembered how odd his face had seemed earlier, and again something about it niggled at her. It was a weird face, to be sure. Too long, his cheekbones too prominent, his lips too curved. The overall impression that emanated from him was one of neatness: his brown skin was smooth and devoid of scars, his chin clean-shaven — although in Rory's opinion that ridiculous little moustache should have been shaved off with the rest — and his shoulder-length hair was neatly combed. But there was something else... Rory shook her head. It would come to her.

Behind him was an array of bottles arranged over floor-to-ceiling shelves. Some of the bottles were of clear glass, filled with liquids so brightly coloured they gleamed like gems. There were little vials full of smoke, dark glass bottles with long elegant necks and ornate stoppers, enamel jars topped with iron handles, and copper flasks, some simple and utilitarian, some engraved with complicated swirling patterns. She had to admit that as a collection, they looked rather impressive. She assumed they were the poisons the Viper worked with.

The other side of the room was taken up by a wide alchemy bench, in the middle of which was a small furnace with a few embers still smouldering inside. The bench was so clean, it looked like nobody had ever worked on it. Glass bottles and beakers were lined up in perfect rows and metal tools she didn't recognise were painstakingly laid out so that the distance between each was the same. All of it rested on a pristine white table runner.

But what really caught Rory's attention was a set of glass cabinets containing an astonishing collection of weapons, from elegant stiletto knives and curved scimitars to leather-wrapped garrottes, no doubt to prevent the skin from breaking. Some bordered on the bizarre, like a dagger with a tiny clock in its hilt and a fan with needles protruding from its top.

And then there were the rapiers. Set out in their own cabinet, each one had an ornate basket similar to that of the one Rory had taken. She was surprised to feel a weight lift, and she realised she had been feeling a little guilty over taking the Viper's sword. Well, now there was no need, since he had so many of them.

She sidled over and put her hands up against the glass, like a child peering into a toyshop. The blades shone like mirrors, sharp and deadly. Rory sighed. One day she would own a collection of swords, too. One day, girls would dream of being her like she dreamt of being the Scarred Woman.

When she removed her hands, she was dismayed to find she had left a grubby mark on the glass. She tried to wipe it off with her sleeve but only succeeded in smearing more filth. For the first time in a long time, she became aware of how dirty she was, and she felt a little ashamed.

She was about to turn away when she spotted something that gave her pause. It was a brass box, odd and out of place amongst the weapons. It was delicately engraved with the initials LP in one corner. She took out her picks and set to work on the cabinet lock; it gave way easily. She picked up the box and lifted the lid. Inside were tubes and parts, some that looked like they telescoped into something longer. It reminded her of a machine taken apart.

A slurping noise startled her, and she spun around, the box still in her hands.

CHAPTER

13

Longinus awoke with a start and a slurp, horrified to find he had been dribbling on himself. He blinked a few times and wiped his chin with a handkerchief. He didn't remember falling asleep. Light tinged with pink filtered through the window, announcing dawn. Longinus stretched, his neck aching. It was unusual for him to fall asleep in a chair like this. He should go rouse his tailor and get the clothing ordered before the blasted urchin girl arrived. What colour had he decided on in the end? Was it green?

He was about to get up, when a voice interrupted him.

"Don't get up on my account."

Longinus cried out in surprise, tumbling back into his chair.

The urchin was skulking by his cabinets, and she had left a visible smear of filth on the glass. Her left eye was like a study in purple and swollen to a slit. Surprisingly, the other eye was bright blue, making a startling contrast with her dark brown skin. There were also unusual hints of red about her weird rope-like hair that he hadn't noticed in the dark.

"What in all hells are you doing here?" asked Longinus, gathering himself and standing. "And why have you got my crossbow out of the cabinet?"

"Crossbow?"

"Yes." He marched over and snatched it from her, returning it to its rightful place after checking that she hadn't removed any parts. "It's a folding crossbow and it — good lord, what is that smell?"

He clamped a hand over his mouth and nose. Now that there wasn't the stench of blood and vomit to cover it, the stink of her was overwhelming. The girl's face crumpled for a second before she composed herself, her good eye flashing at him haughtily from beneath her mass of hair.

"Yeah, well, you try living on the streets and then we'll see how good *you* smell."

Longinus almost came back with a cutting remark of his own, but he had to concede the girl had a point. Instead, he glared at her. "How did you get in, anyway?"

"Ah, well." The girl had the decency to look a little sheepish. "You know…"

"No, I *don't* know."

"Well, I broke in, didn't I?"

"What? Unacceptable."

"That ain't gonna change the fact that it's true."

"Listen here. I gave you my word to train you in the art of killing —"

"Of sword fighting."

"Excuse me?"

"I want to learn to fight with swords."

Longinus glared at her again. "To train you in the art of *killing*," he repeated, "but that doesn't mean you can break into my house, open my cabinets, and walk about as you please. Have you no shame? No manners?"

"Shame and manners are in short supply where I come from. Look, I'm sorry for breaking in, alright? I wanted to make sure you didn't have no trap waiting for me."

"I gave you my word," replied Longinus stiffly, offended that she might doubt the strength of his promise. "A gentleman's word is his bond."

"Yeah, well I ain't met much in the way of gentlemen so far, so I don't know much about their word. And anyway, waiting around outside ain't the safest for me right now," she said, gesturing at her face.

Longinus felt a brief pang of guilt, but he checked himself. It wasn't his job to look after the urchins of Damsport after all, nor was it his problem if the girl got into scrapes. And she was irritating enough that she no doubt deserved whatever she got. Still, Longinus was a gentleman as well as an assassin, and it didn't sit well with him to see a girl beaten up like that.

He cleared his throat.

"Well, in any case you're to give me your picks."

"No."

"Yes. Give me your picks or I'll develop a case of amnesia."

"Alright, then I'll get real verbal about your fear of blood."

At the mention of his secret, Longinus looked away, unable to hold her gaze.

"Fine," he said, too ashamed to look back at her. "Keep the picks, but the first lesson of the day will be the baths."

"Unless that's a sword fighting move, I ain't got no interest."

His outrage at her refusal to get clean was soothing. Easier to bear than his shame. He focused on the outrage, rousing himself to his full height, the better to look down at her.

"Young lady —"

"I ain't a lady."

"Evidently. Forgive me, I don't know what I was thinking. As I was saying, young…er… What is your name?"

"Rory."

"Fine. Rory. Yes, that will do."

"It ain't like you're choosing it for me, that's my name."

"Yes, yes," Longinus snapped. "Now, although you know me as the Viper, I would prefer you to call me Longinus."

"Long genius? Really?"

"Lon-gee-nus," he clarified. "With a soft 'g'. Although some have indeed referred to my intellect as genius-like," he added with a modest smile. "My skill with poisons and alchemy is second to none. Of course, it is vastly underappreciated, since I operate in the shadows. For example, see this?" He picked up a bottle full of a bright orange liquid, with a large stopper that was securely tied to its neck. "This is an olfactory poison. *Not* to be confused with a nasal poison. Olfactory poisons simply need to be smelled to be effective. Nasal poisons are best applied with the use of a syringe."

Rory snorted. "When would anyone allow you to stick a syringe up their nose?"

"If the target is asleep, and on their back, obviously. An assassin, young...er, Rory, must be prepared for *any* eventuality. The skill of an assassin isn't just in the killing, it is in the variety and complexity of the methods used. Auricular poisons, for example, are applied to the ear using a funnel. Also useful for sleeping targets, but best if they are on their side."

"Look, I ain't here to learn about poisons. I want to learn about swords."

"Yes, yes, all in good time." Longinus picked up a pretty blue bottle, displaying it proudly. "Deafly Silence is one of my most delicate poisons."

Rory failed to complete the tableau he had in mind by providing the awestruck pupil to his wise and noble teacher.

"That's a stupid name," she said. "Look, can we start? I *am* blackmailing you, so you got to do what I say, right? And I say we start with the rapier."

Longinus returned the bottle to the shelf.

"You don't have to keep reminding me," he said. "How long is this, ah, arrangement, supposed to last?"

"The blackmail? As long as it takes for me to learn how to fight with a rapier. The sooner you start, the sooner it's gonna finish."

A very good point.

"Fine, then let's get started," he said aloud.

He retrieved a blunt training rapier and a pair of gloves. He was about to give her the gloves when he remembered the smear on the cabinet. It gave him an idea.

"You're sure I can't persuade you to take a bath first?"

"Positive."

"You'll have to train without gloves on, then," he informed her with a smirk. "I can't have you ruining them."

"Makes no difference to me," she replied with a shrug.

Longinus' face fell.

"What? It doesn't bother you to train without gloves?"

"Course not. I ain't never worn gloves, and you can't miss what you never had."

"Poverty is not an excuse to be bandied about at every turn. Now, take this."

He handed her the training rapier. She slashed the blade through the air a couple of times, grinning at him idiotically. Longinus closed his eyes and pinched the bridge of his nose.

"The gods help me, this is going to take forever."

CHAPTER

14

By the afternoon, Rory was exhausted. Longinus had had her lifting weights, stretching, and sprinting back and forth in the weapons room for hours. He now had her standing with her arm outstretched, holding the rapier.

"Alright," he said as her arm spasmed from the effort of keeping it up. "I think it's time for a break. To the baths."

"I told you, I don't want a bath. When's the *real* training gonna begin?"

"This is real training, Rory."

"Standing around holding out my rapier like a lemon? When am I ever gonna need that?"

"You'll need *stamina*. You'll need *strength*. And you are sorely lacking in both. Why, at your age I would have lasted twice as long."

Rory ground her teeth and lifted her arm once more. She'd be damned if she'd let Longinus mock her. Her arm spasmed so badly she dropped the rapier. Longinus put down his glass of port.

"We're going to the baths now," he said.

"I don't need no bath."

"You do. There are rats in the city with more grooming than you. Speaking of which, you don't have any hidden in your hair, do you?" Longinus let out a short laugh.

"Anyone told you it's poor form to laugh at your own jokes?" said Rory.

He ignored her and went to the bench, where he scribbled something down, still smiling. Rory followed, trailing the rapier behind her.

"Really, you're writing *that* down?"

"Mind your business," snapped Longinus.

"That's better. I'm not sure I like it when you make jokes."

***

Much to Rory's consternation, Longinus took her to the baths in Spirepass, between Seven and Eight. They were dangerously close to Cruikshank's warehouse, but for all her pleading and arguing, Longinus wouldn't hear of going anywhere else.

"But why?" she said. "Baths are just water and soap. Water is the same everywhere, and so is soap."

"My dear, you are so naive. Soap and water is the least important part of a bath, and the Spirepass baths are the only ones worthy of the name."

Rory looked up at him, confused. What else was there to a bath? She followed Longinus inside, glancing uneasily about her. If Cruikshank came to the baths, this could be a disaster. She had a pretty good idea of how things would go if Cruikshank and Longinus met. She'd make some comment about his generosity in giving Rory the rapier, and the truth would come out. The rapier would get returned, and Rory would be in for a world of trouble.

Inside the baths, it was surprisingly cool. Rory looked up and gasped. The domed ceiling was so high, and covered in mosaic of so deep a blue, that it almost looked like the sky on a sunny day. Gilded grapevines ran down the pillars that circled the dome, and in the middle was a huge but shallow pool with a fountain that gurgled water. The light from the vapour lamps played with the water, casting dancing shapes on the walls and ceiling.

"Is that the bath?" asked Rory, looking at the pool dubiously. She had no intention of washing in there for everyone to see.

"Are you going to this effort for me?" called a vaguely familiar voice behind her. "You really shouldn't have. I'm touched."

Rory turned and was dismayed to find Rafe regarding her with a mocking expression.

"Who is this?" asked Longinus.

"Nobody," answered Rory through gritted teeth.

"Just one of her property contacts. Rafe, at your service." He bowed with excessive formality. When he came back up, his gaze flickered to her black eye, to Longinus, back to her. "Seems I'm not the only one you managed to rub up the wrong way. Everything —"

"Mind your own business," said Rory hotly.

Rafe lifted an amused eyebrow. "Is that so? Well then, I won't keep you, Mistress Magnate. A bath will do you wonders anyway. That way next time you try and attack me, your stink won't give you away." He winked and headed for a door across the room.

"What did that mean?" asked Longinus.

"Nothing." To her annoyance, Rory could feel her face turning red.

It had never mattered how she smelled when she and Jake worked together. In fact, it had probably helped with the whole helpless urchin act. Now she was almost looking forward to getting clean.

Almost.

"Ah," said Longinus, "there we are."

A beautiful woman clad in a simple white tunic and wide, flowing trousers padded towards them. As she drew near, she bowed and murmured a welcome.

"A full clean for the girl, please," said Longinus, producing a few coins. "It's her first time in the baths, so have one of your matrons guide her."

The woman gave a knowing smile and pulled out a tiny set of portable scales from her pocket. She weighed the coins, then clapped her hands smartly twice. Another door opened, and a woman with thick ruddy forearms and legs like tree trunks appeared.

"I'll see you here when you are done," said Longinus, paying for his own bath.

"I don't think this is a good idea," said Rory, as the matron dragged her none too gently towards another door.

"Come on now," said the matron. "Or I'll carry you."

Rory tried to resist, but the matron manhandled her as easily as she would have a small child.

"Longinus?" she called. "I changed my mind. I ain't taking no bath, and I'm in charge, remember?"

He ignored her, already heading towards the door that Rafe had disappeared through.

"Longinus?"

***

Taking a bath turned out to be far more complicated than Rory had imagined. The matron stripped her of her clothing, wrapped her in a large white towel, and dragged her from one bath to the other.

There were warm baths, scalding hot baths, icy plunge pools, scented baths, baths full of fish to eat dead skin, baths full of leeches to clean the blood, baths of mud, of clay, of seaweed, and many more. Rory was dunked, scrubbed, and scoured to within an inch of her life.

The matron went as far as to clean inside her ears and between her toes, making her squeal and squirm. Rory had no idea why she bothered since nobody would be looking that closely, but any attempt to explain this was ignored. The only part of her that remained impervious to all the washing was her hair. It resisted all combing attempts, much to Rory's delight, and the best the matron could do was rub each segment with soap.

Once she had finished with Rory's hair, the matron told her to stay put, leaving her alone in the hot and steamy marble room. No sooner had the door swung shut behind her than Rory pushed it open once more, feeling the blessedly cool air of the corridor. She could see the matron to the right, and she slipped out the door to the left, hurrying down the hallway, hugging her towel to her. She had no desire to find out what other delights the matron had planned — there was only so much cleaning a girl could put up with, after all.

When she reached stairs that led farther underground, Rory hesitated. She was about to turn back when she heard the matron's voice.

"Have you seen a girl go by? Scrawny kid with hair like rope."

The reply was indistinct, but the echo of the matron's tread made it clear she was headed this way. Rory ran down the stairs.

They led to a chamber with a huge pool that mirrored the entrance room above. A quick glance confirmed that this was a dead end — no doors, no more corridors. To her left was a small alcove, only about chest height, in which was a large decorative urn. Rory crouched down and crawled to the space behind it.

No sooner had she gathered her knees to her than the matron's solid legs appeared in her line of sight. The matron walked past the alcove, looking around the chamber, hands on hips. She muttered something under her breath, and then, at last, turned and climbed back up the stairs.

Rory waited a little while longer, just to be safe, and then came out from her hiding place. Now that she could take in her surroundings, she saw that the chamber was really quite beautiful. The mosaic on the domed ceiling traced geometric patterns in red, orange, and gold. One of the chamber walls was a rock face, and water trickled down from a wide opening at the top, where the wall should have met the ceiling. At the base of the rock was a deep pool that was linked to the main bath by a narrow channel. The water flowed lazily down the channel, mixing along the way with almond milk that poured out from two marble cornucopias.

Women lounged about the bath in various states of undress, laughing and talking confidentially, their voices tinkling against the marble pillars. Rory couldn't help but stare at them.

They were gorgeous.

Their bodies were soft and full of curves, their smooth skin like unctuous caramel. Rory felt acutely aware of her elbows and knees, of her ribs so obvious under her skin, of her tiny breasts. She felt sure the women were looking at her, maybe even laughing at her. She hugged her towel tighter and sat as far away from them as she could, right by the rock, letting her feet dangle in the water.

She watched the water cascading down the rock and noticed that it flowed irregularly, as if something was blocking its progress. Rory peered into the gap from which it flowed. She could just make out something darker within the shadows. It was moving, slowly dragged forward by the flowing water.

As she watched, the blockage reached the edge, hovered for a moment as though undecided, and crashed down into the pool below. The women screamed, and Rory sucked in a breath. Floating face up in the pool was a bloated, waxy corpse. Rory stared at it, and then stared at it again, recognition setting in. It was the man who had given her the jar of paste the previous night.

His eyes were cloudy and a milky, pale blue. Dark veins stood out on his face and neck. Nowhere was this more pronounced than on his forehead, where they spread out like a spider's web from a single word: *Viper.*

"And you're sure it said 'Viper'?" asked Longinus for the umpteenth time, visibly agitated.

They were walking rapidly away from the baths, which now crawled with guards. Rory had quickly clambered up the wet rock face after having found the body, but all she had found in the space above it was darkness, rock, and a tiny gap through which the water flowed. Whoever had killed the man must have deposited the body up there by coming in through the baths. There was no way the body would have fit through that gap.

"Yeah, I'm positive. I can read, you know."

"Well, your hair suggests otherwise, so forgive me for being sceptical."

"My hair?"

"Yes, the sure sign of a thinking man is in the neatness of his chin and the grooming of his hair. With the state you're in, I'm surprised you can even string a sentence together."

"Oh, really? Well, you just remember that *I'm* the one blackmailing *you*, so if I'm an idiot, what does that make you, eh?"

The vein on Longinus' forehead looked dangerously close to bursting. He walked stiffly ahead and then stopped abruptly again.

"And you're sure the eyes were pale blue all over? Maybe the lighting made them seem that way, or —"

"Yeah, definitely. They were all cloudy and pale blue, like…like blue milk. And it definitely wasn't you who killed him?"

"Don't be ridiculous, do you really think I'd be so crude as to leave a body in water to grow…" he finished the statement with a hand gesture, obviously not comfortable elaborating on what water could do to a corpse.

Rory hadn't quite decided how she felt about finding her benefactor dead, but knowing that Longinus wasn't the one who had killed him was definitely a relief. It would have made things far too complicated otherwise.

Longinus sped off again, muttering to himself, so Rory had to trot behind to keep up with him. She hadn't yet revealed that she had met the dead man, and she decided to keep that to herself until she had a better idea of what was going on.

"Do you think someone is trying to impersonate the Viper?" she asked.

"*Obviously*. Unless you read the message on the forehead wrong. I can't believe I'm relying on someone like you to confirm such an important piece of information."

"Sod off, I can read perfectly well. Why would someone want to impersonate you, though — or the Viper?"

"What a stupid question. It was inevitable that someone would try. Men want to be the Viper, women want to be *with* the Viper. It can be a terrible burden to be so admired, you know. Fame and adulation can be a double-edged —"

Rory snorted.

"What was that?" Longinus glared at her.

"What?"

"That noise."

"I just had something in my nose."

"Then blow your nose and be quiet when I talk."

Rory blew her nose in her fingers and wiped them on her tunic, watching with glee the shock and disgust on Longinus' face.

"What?" she said innocently. "That's what you asked me to do."

"I meant in a *handkerchief*!"

"Ah. Well, next time be more specific," she replied. "And maybe think twice before ordering me around. Oh, and buy me a handkerchief."

They reached Seven, the traffic flowing like cold molasses as people tried to avoid Six to get to the Great Bazaar. In the middle of the thoroughfare, a man had erected a platform like an island in the middle of the flow of traffic, and standing on top of his makeshift podium, he shouted a sermon at the passing throng. Rory kept her head down and followed Longinus closely. As an urchin, she was always a prime target for religious zealotry. Why everyone kept trying to save her soul was beyond her — last she had checked, her soul was fine. It was her stomach that was in need of saving.

Longinus crossed Seven in a long diagonal with Rory in tow, and they dived off into a quieter side street.

"And you're sure the eyes were clouded and blue?" Longinus asked.

"Yes! How many times am I gonna have to tell you? What's the big deal with them being blue, anyway?"

"It's a very specific side effect of one of my poisons. In fact, it is my new signature poison, my most recent and most deadly creation. I call it The Writing on the Wall. No one has the formula. No one. But what you're describing sounds exactly like the effect of my poison. Do you understand, Rory? Someone might have stolen my work." He gasped and grabbed her arm. "What if whoever this is has stolen more of my poisons? My work, my life's work! Oh…" He looked down at her arm, only now realising that he was holding it. He released it as one might something foul, fingers recoiling in disgust. He fished for a handkerchief to wipe his hand on and then let it fall to the ground.

"I have just had several sodding baths, you know," Rory said, annoyed.

"Yes, and it's quite impressive that you still manage to smell this bad."

"Must be my clothes," she replied, trying to look like she didn't care.

The truth was that she had shuddered with disgust as she had gotten dressed. The fabric of her tunic and trousers had been slimy from the heat and steam, the stench almost overpowering now that she was clean. The fabric was itchy, but it was a travelling itch that moved from one part of her body to the next. She wondered what Longinus would say if he knew she had fleas.

"I have to go home and make sure nobody has tried to access the formulae for my poisons," said Longinus. "This could be a disaster. A *disaster*."

"What about me?"

"What about you?"

"I'm blackmailing you? You're supposed to train me?"

"Yes, yes, that can wait. Come back tomorrow."

Rory watched him hurry off, nonplussed. She wondered if any other blackmailer had ever been told by her target to 'come back tomorrow.' Longinus was turning out to be more difficult to control than she had expected, although she was grateful for the time alone. She wanted to think things over, work out what her next move should be.

***

Night had fallen by the time Rory decided to head to the docks. She had ambled aimlessly up on the rooftops since leaving Longinus, and she was no closer to working out what she should do. It was an odd feeling to find herself in the debt of a dead man. She knew that she was possibly the last person to have spoken to him before he had died, and the thought made her shudder.

Part of her wanted to find out what had happened to him, to bring him justice. He was one of the few people who had shown her kindness without being condescending or pitying. And yet she was worried that to do so would take her off course. It had been hard enough to get this far while being utterly single-minded; if her focus shifted, would it endanger her chances of meeting the Scarred Woman again?

She had just reached Tinsbury Dock, busy as it always was ahead of the Revels, when she smelled something familiar.

"Jake," she said, not turning around.

"Aye aye."

Rory faced him, giving him a dark look. Adrenaline pumped through her, her skin tingling with awareness. If he was going to try anything, she would be ready for him this time. Her hand hovered by the handle of her dagger.

Jake looked and smelled like he hadn't stopped drinking since they had last met.

"What do you want now?" she asked, voice cold.

"No need for that, I ain't gonna hurt you," said Jake with a sad note to his words. "I need to talk to you. I knew you'd come back here eventually. There somewhere quiet we can go?"

"What, so you can give me a right eye to match the left? Sod off."

"Hey, you started that. You're the one that cut me after I tried to give you money."

"Right," Rory replied, voice dripping with sarcasm. "It's all my fault."

"I swear I ain't gonna hurt you or nothing," said Jake. "I got to talk to you, got an offer for you. That's all."

Rory fiddled with her medals.

"Fine," she said. "We go down that lane, there. And I'm keeping my blade out," she added, unsheathing her dagger.

Jake nodded, and they stepped into the lane's gloom.

"So what's this all about?" asked Rory.

"I come to make you an offer. See, some man approached me last night after you'd left, and he made me a deal. He paid me to convince you to come back and be partners again."

"He what? Why?"

"Dunno why. But he wants you to stop what you're doing at the moment."

"What am I doing?"

"Don't you know?"

Rory shook her head. "What if I refuse?" she asked.

Jake hesitated and looked down at his hands. "Then I'm to kill you."

Rory's blood ran cold.

"Course I'd never do that," Jake added hurriedly. "But he looked proper serious. If it ain't me, it'll be another. I think it'd be best if you came back. It's a win-win, really. I'll share what he paid me, and we'd be set up for a good long time. I never got why you wanted to leave, anyway. We had something good going, we can just go back to that, pretend the last few days didn't happen. Look what he paid me and all."

With a grin, Jake produced a coin from his pocket that made Rory's jaw drop. A Damsian golden guinea. Currencies from all parts of the world flowed through Damsport, which was why Damsians used coin weights for their currency, to make conversions easier. The only coins that were created in Damsport were the golden guineas. They were thick coins of pure gold stamped with the Old Girl's likeness. No piece was worth as much as a Damsian golden guinea.

"He paid you all that, because of me?" murmured Rory, unable to take her eyes off the gold. "Why?"

"Dunno. Guess you must have pissed some people off." Jake pocketed the coin. "So, shall we head back to the shelter? Although we could afford to get a room somewhere with that, you know. That would buy us a year in a decent joint, for sure. Beds, roof, the works."

"I ain't coming, Jake," whispered Rory, still staring at the place where the coin had been. She could see a dark spot in the shape of the guinea, as if it had imprinted itself on her eyes.

"Maybe we could do the cobbler thing on the side, too," continued Jake, not listening to her. "Be a good way to get potential marks in, you know? I fix their boots, you steal their purse. Could work well."

"Jake, you ain't listening to me. I ain't coming."

"What? You have to."

"Or what, you gonna kill me?"

An awkward silence hung between them for a heartbeat too long.

"Don't be daft," Jake said at last.

"I ain't coming with you, Jake. You betrayed me twice. I meant it when I said we're over." As soon as she said it, Rory realised how true that was. She felt a brief pang of crushing sadness, and then it was gone.

"Look, don't be silly about this," said Jake. "I get that you're mad at me, but you know it makes sense. I dunno what you did this last day, but you've obviously stepped on some toes, so best to do as the man says. Sleep on it, think things through, and then tomorrow we can decide what the plan is."

Rory didn't reply. No point if he wasn't listening to her.

"Alright then," said Jake, "I'll see you tomorrow."

As he walked away, Rory called after him.

"What did he look like, the man who paid you?"

"Very tall and skinny. Taller than me, even. Ain't used to looking up at people. And a big nose, like a hook. Why, you gonna go look for him? Don't be stupid, Rory."

"Did he tell you his name?"

Jake laughed. "What do you think? Doesn't matter anyway, he only wants you to come back and work with me. He won't be no bother, and if he is, I'll see to him. See you at the shelter tomorrow morning."

After Jake left, Rory made her way to the beggar-house roof. She sat against the chimney, watching but not seeing the activity in Tinsbury Dock.

The last trace of sadness had vanished, and for good. It occurred to her that her partnership with Jake had reached the end of its life a while ago, and she just hadn't noticed. The realisation was liberating. She took a deep breath.

What he had said about the tall man was disturbing, though. Why would someone pay all that money because of her? She was nobody; she was nothing. What was she doing that he wanted her to stop? She thought of the man who had been kind to her, of his body at the baths. Now someone had killed him, and Jake had been offered a small fortune to get her out of the picture. Why?

Was it something she and the dead man had talked about? They had barely said two words to each other. Something he had seen, maybe? But what?

Rory froze.

The tall man had obviously been following her to find Jake. What if he had continued following her after, somehow, and seen her go to Cruikshank? She felt as though her breath had been snatched away. What if he had done something to Cruikshank?

Rory broke into a run down the roof slope and leapt across the gap to the next house. She landed on soft knees, quickly climbing up that roof, ready to jump onto the next one.

If that bastard had gotten to Cruikshank, oh, there would be hell to pay.

***

The windows of the workshop were dark. The usual smell of tar and hot metal was absent, as was the usual rhythmic banging. Rory ground her teeth. If the tall man had so much as touched a hair on Cruikshank's head, she was going to exact such a vengeance on him, he was going to wish he'd never heard of Rory, and no mistake about it.

She picked the lock open and let herself in, silently closing the door behind her. The workshop was dark with only a faint glow from the furnace to provide a little light, although not enough to see properly.

"Cruikshank," she called in a whisper, as she felt her way around the workshop. "Cruikshank."

Everything looked normal — except for the fact that Cruikshank, who Rory had never known not to be working at night, wasn't there.

Near the furnace was the large shape hidden by a tarp that she had seen before. Rory headed towards it, skin tingling with nerves. She lifted a corner of the tarp gingerly, but it was too dark for her to make out anything. With a wide arc of the arm, she threw the tarp off. Before she could take in what was in front of her, two hands grabbed her and threw her back. She went crashing into a set of shelves, setting off a deluge of small machine parts.

Rory rolled to the side, pulling out her dagger as she did. In the gloom, she could make out a thickset man with long hair. She picked up one of the fallen machine parts and threw it at him, catching him square in the face.

"Oh, you're going to regret that," he growled, and he charged at her. She ducked, but not fast enough, and he sent her sprawling on her back.

"What the hell's going on here?"

Rory blinked as a vapour lamp was shaken to life. Behind the lamp, looking none too pleased, was Cruikshank.

"Caught her breaking in to spy on the spider," said the lad, picking Rory up by an arm. He was about Rory's real age — eighteen or so — with dark hair, thick features, and a face spotted with acne.

"It's fine, Norman, that's just Rory. What you doing here this time of night, lovey? And how many times am I going to have to remind you to use the damned doorbell? You can't keep breaking in here."

Rory yanked her arm away from Norman, throwing him a dirty look.

"Who's he?" she pointed at Norman.

"The son of a friend of mine. He's helping me get ready for the Revels. Lovey, what's going on?"

"Nothing, I just got worried, alright? The workshop was dark…" Rory let her voice trail off as she realised how lame she sounded.

"You broke in because the workshop was dark?" said Norman. "You do realise people sleep at night?"

"Hey, don't talk to me like that," snapped Rory. "Cruikshank normally works all the time, alright?"

"Lovey, it's very kind of you to worry about me, but I'm fine."

"So no one's been causing you trouble?"

"Why would anyone cause me trouble?" asked Cruikshank. "What's with you tonight?"

"Nothing, nothing. Just being a bit pecked in the head, that's all."

"You got that right," said Norman.

In the light from the vapour lamp, Rory could now see clearly what had been skulking beneath the tarp. It was an enormous copper spider big enough for a woman to ride it. She pretended to examine the spider to give herself time to collect her thoughts. Maybe whoever had followed her had stopped at Jake and hadn't seen her go to Cruikshank's.

"You sure you're alright, lovey?" asked Cruikshank.

Rory pointed to the spider. "Is that what you're bringing to the Revels?" she asked to change the subject. The spider's abdomen had been polished to a mirror shine so that it showed a distended reflection of the workshop.

"Yes," replied Cruikshank. "I made the Marchioness a spider to go with the spiderweb layout of Damsport. You'll see on the day, should be a pretty good show. But don't change the subject — why would someone be causing me trouble?"

"Jake's been hassling me, and I was worried he might have followed me here last night, that's all."

Cruikshank frowned. "What's he doing? I'll go to the guards if he —"

"Whoa, easy on the mention of the guards, Cruikshank." There it was, that damned unpredictable honesty. Why complicate things further by bringing the guards in? To anyone with sense, that would be the last thing to do. "I ain't on the best of terms with them myself, remember. It's fine, I'm handling Jake. You ain't got to worry about nothing, alright."

"Want me to rough him up a bit for you?" asked Norman. "I'll only charge you friends' rates."

"You changed your tune. You was gonna thump the crap out of me a few minutes ago," replied Rory.

"If Cruikshank says you're alright, that's enough for me."

Rory turned to Cruikshank. "Look, I got to go, but I'll see you real soon."

Cruikshank watched her leave with narrowed eyes. "You look after yourself, lovey, you hear?"

"Of course. I always look after number one, don't I?"

Rory stepped outside, back in the cool night air. The relief that the tall man hadn't gone after Cruikshank was palpable. Still, she didn't want to take any chances. A warehouse roof was just as good as any other to spend the night on. She circled the building to the back, where the wall was exposed to the sea air. The mortar was looser there, nibbled away by the salty wind. She had climbed up it often enough to know exactly where the footholds were, and in no time she sat atop Cruikshank's roof.

She positioned herself near the entrance so she could keep an eye out for anyone attempting to come in. She made herself comfortable and settled for a long, sleepless night. She didn't think the tall man would come to see Cruikshank now, but better safe than sorry.

As she replayed the events of the last couple of days, she let her talismans tinkle through her fingers. She had obviously stumbled on something, but what? The corpse? But then if the tall man wanted her out of the way because of that, why approach Jake before she found it? There was no way he'd know she'd be in the baths when it was found. And why copy the Viper?

She remembered the sadness in the dead man's face, and she knew that if she didn't at least try to find out what had happened to him, she'd feel guilty. Very guilty. Then there was Longinus. From what little she knew of him, he was going to be impossible to deal with until he had found the man who was trying to impersonate him. She might as well help. It would keep him on side, and that wouldn't hurt as far as getting him to train her.

She sighed. Why did nothing ever happen according to plan?

CHAPTER

16

Longinus' notes, the gods be thanked, hadn't been tampered with. His secret formulae were still safe. In spite of this reassurance, he had spent a fitful night's sleep, which was very unlike him. Longinus always did everything properly, and this philosophy extended to sleeping. So on the morning after the baths, he was feeling less than his usual, composed self.

He poured himself a generous measure of port (there was no ailment that couldn't be cured with a little port), and threw himself down on the blue velvet chair in the weapons room. He sipped his port and observed his poisons. The thought that they might somehow have been compromised was simply intolerable, but his sleepless night had brought him to a very disturbing conclusion.

Provided that the girl was correct in her description of the body (and that was a stretch in itself, given the girl was filthy and uneducated), the poison had to be an approximation of his. For the umpteenth time, Longinus railed against having to rely on the observation of an urchin. The ramifications of those observations were larger than the girl could possibly have comprehended, and what might have seemed insignificant to her could be an essential piece of the puzzle.

But there was no denying that if the body looked as she had described, either someone had found a way to replicate his work, or worse, there was an alchemist who had come to this result independently. That would mean an alchemist to rival him.

Unthinkable.

Of course, there could be some thrill in the idea of pitting his intellect and skill against a worthy opponent, but too much was at stake for Longinus to relish the challenge. Whoever this was clearly wanted to supplant him as the Viper, and Longinus would die before he let that happen.

He would have to get to the body and obtain a sample of the poison to analyse. All these conjectures were useless without the hard evidence of alchemy to clear a path through the fog. He took a sip of port, mulling over how to gain access to the corpse, which by now would be under heavy guard. He had a handy little device that would allow him to suction some poison from the skin, so that aspect would be no trouble.

The thought reminded him of the sailor he had killed out in Smallport Marina, and of the ridiculous account Mistress White Apron had given of the state of the body. He put the port aside at the reminder — she had said the corpse had been *skinned*. He put a hand over his mouth as a wave of nausea came over him.

What if she hadn't been lying? What if the sailor had been found with some of his skin missing? A skilled alchemist might be able to replicate the poison from a sample closely enough for its effects to appear the same. Especially to an untrained eye.

Longinus leapt to his feet, propelled by a bolt of nervous energy. That had to be it. The odds of another alchemist creating the same poison, and this days after he'd first unveiled it, were simply too small. Longinus was a man of alchemy, after all; he did not believe in coincidence.

It was more imperative than ever that he get that poison sample. He had to know how close this other alchemist had come.

He paced up and down the room, cobbling together a plan. The guards wouldn't allow anyone to see the body at this stage, save for relatives. There was, however, no way to pose as a relative without knowing who the deceased was. He would be able to obtain the name of the deceased one way or another, but that then destroyed his opportunity to pass himself off as a family member.

Longinus stopped abruptly. The girl. That filthy urchin could finally make herself useful and be the second prong to the brilliant plan of attack already forming in his mind. He smiled and resumed his pacing.

Nothing like a little intellectual challenge to kick off the day.

The door opened, and Rory stepped in, her mouth set in a grim line.

"Ah, there you are," exclaimed Longinus, "and not a moment too soon, either."

"You're waiting for me?"

"Well, of course. You do realise what's at stake here, don't you? I have put together a strategy that will allow us to discover the composition of the poison used, and therefore will give us a good idea of who is trying to replace me. I have a role for you to play, so you can finally make yourself useful. Why are you looking at me with those dead fish eyes?"

"My eyes ain't like a dead fish's, and you can't just assume that I'll be doing as you say. I'm blackmailing you — I ain't your assistant."

"Enough with the blackmail already, this is bigger than your silly sword fighting."

"Yeah, it is, but not for the reasons you think." Rory told him about her meeting with Jake.

"Why would someone care about you?" asked Longinus.

"Plenty of reasons," she replied, clearly miffed. "I'd met the man from the baths the previous night too, after I left you."

"You did? Well, why didn't you say so right away?"

"I didn't know if I could trust you."

"You what? I'm a *gentleman*. I gave you my word."

"Yeah, but I didn't know whether you'd killed him."

"For the last time, I am not entirely devoid of manners and feeling. To throw someone's corpse in the water is not only base, it's —"

"Alright, alright, I get the point."

"Good. Now, since you know the man, that will make things far easier. I will pose as a member of his family and gain access to the body."

"I don't know how you'll do that, I don't even know his name."

For some reason (that Longinus cared little about) the girl looked guilty.

Longinus sighed. *Useless. A good thing I already had a plan in place.*

"We'll have to stick to my original plan, then," he said. "I have a role for you to play, but first I have to change."

"You gotta be joking," she replied. "What's wrong with what you're wearing now?"

Longinus waved a hand. "Please. I won't be long, and then we're off to the barbers. I can't go to my regular man, so it might take us a while to find a suitable establishment."

He paused in the doorway. "Don't touch anything. You touch the wrong vial and you could die a rather unpleasant death."

"Yes, yes, I won't touch anything. More to the point, someone wants to kill me and take your place as the Viper, right, so do you really think the state of your moustache is important right now?"

"You have a lot to learn about the world," he called back as he climbed the stairs. "The state of my moustache has never been more important."

CHAPTER

17

Rory followed Longinus through the streets, glancing about uneasily. He was dressed so extravagantly, he might as well have had a sign tacked to his back asking someone to rob him. He had on wide ochre pantaloons in the fashion of Kushania and a matching open vest that was richly embroidered. His fingers were covered in heavy rings, and the decorative scimitar at his hip was crusted with gems.

"Ain't you afraid someone's going to attack you for the jewels?" asked Rory, pointing at the scimitar.

"Anyone can see that they're fakes. As if anyone would waste jewels on a sword."

"I dunno… They look pretty real to me. I ain't getting involved if someone tries to rob you."

"Thank you, Rory, but I am not in the habit of trusting my security to tiny girls anyway."

Rory skewered him with a look, but he didn't seem to care as he fussed with his pantaloons.

"Damned ridiculous things. What are the Kushanians thinking of?"

"Why are we going to the barber?"

"I need a bigger moustache."

"And why do you need a bigger moustache? I'm working with you on this, right, I need to know the plan."

"To find out who the deceased is."

"Can you be a bit less specific please? The details are overwhelming me."

Longinus ignored her, instead entering a small barbershop with a sign above the door that read Gamp & Son. Rory was left with the choice of scowling outside or inside. She chose inside.

A small man with a congenial smile hurried towards them, bowing as he walked.

"Welcome to my humble establishment! I am Gamp, at your service." He sketched another little bow. "What can I do for you today?"

"Do you do alchemical enhancements?" asked Longinus.

"I do indeed! What will you be needing? Thicker, or longer hair?"

"My hair needs no alterations."

"No, no, of course it doesn't." Gamp bowed again. "What I meant was —"

"My moustache. I am after something with more body, something in the Kushanian fashion."

"Absolutely, absolutely. Please step this way."

Gamp gestured towards a shaving chair with a deep bow.

"While you're at it, I'll also be needing a shave," added Longinus, stroking his chin. "I'm a little dishevelled this morning."

Gamp looked as confused by this as Rory: other than his moustache, Longinus' face was as smooth as a baby's bottom. The barber complied nonetheless, lathering up Longinus' cheeks and chin and stropping his cutthroat razor. After Gamp had scraped the first lot of lather, Longinus inspected it with a critical eye and nodded with a satisfied air, as if seeing some microscopic hair in the foam.

"Good, good," he said. "I already feel neater. Keep going. With the grain, Gamp, always with the grain. By the way, I noticed it said 'son' on your sign. Is he available to comb my assistant's hair?"

Gamp looked over at Rory, paled a little at the sight of her hair, but quickly recovered.

"Junior!" he called. "In here now! It would be our pleasure, sir. We are always ready for a challenge at Gamp & Son."

A lad walked in, a sulky version of his father.

"Junior, please comb this, er, lady's hair."

Junior and Rory looked at each other with equal displeasure, and he gestured at a chair for her to sit. Gamp, meanwhile, continued shaving Longinus.

"And are you going anywhere special, sir?" he asked.

"No talking, Gamp," replied Longinus.

"Yes, quite. Of course, sir." He bowed.

The shave finished, Gamp began applying a foul-smelling, viscous liquid to Longinus' moustache with a little brush. Rory lost sight of them as her head snapped back; Junior had begun attacking her hair with a comb.

"Ow!"

The comb pulled ineffectively at her locks, and she could feel Junior's hand trembling from the effort of trying to rake the comb through one of her rope-hair segments. The comb's teeth snapped off with a dry crack.

"I can't comb her hair, it's broken the comb. I'm gonna have to cut it." He produced a pair of sharp-looking scissors.

Rory leapt out her chair, pulling out her dagger. Junior's expression curdled with fear.

"You crazy? You ain't getting those near my hair! Bad enough that I look like a scrawny boy, you ain't cutting my hair too, you hear me?"

"Rory!" Longinus yelled, startling everyone. "Gentlemen, please excuse us," he continued in a lower tone. "I must have a word with my assistant."

He stood up from his chair, a thick moustache drooping down one side of his mouth. Gamp and Junior hurried out, Gamp throwing a worried glance towards Rory.

"You imbecile!" Longinus hissed once they were alone. "Did someone urinate in your gene pool? You *never* pull out a weapon at the barber's. The gods be damned, girl! It's almost as bad as killing outside your tailor's!"

"He was going to cut my hair, what exactly —"

Rory's eye was drawn by a familiar figure walking past the window. Out of context, it took her a second to recognise him. She froze — Jake. He must have felt her eyes on him because he turned to look at her. He opened his mouth and made to walk towards the shop when he spotted Longinus. He looked back at Rory, caught sight of her drawn dagger, and a quick flicker of hurt passed across his features before his face darkened to anger.

Rory wondered if he had been waiting for her all morning at the shelter. She had completely forgotten about him — not that she'd had any intention of going back to him, but she knew he would be furious at her rejection.

The moment stretched on, Rory and Jake keeping their eyes locked on each other, and she knew that the next time they met it would be trouble.

"Rory, who is that man?" asked Longinus.

Rory didn't reply. Jake clenched his jaw and took another good look at Longinus before skulking off.

Rory sagged with relief, realising that she had been holding her breath.

"Nothing. Nobody. Not your business." She slipped her blade back into her belt. She could have told Longinus that Jake was the man who had been hired to get rid of her, but even now, it seemed wrong to get anyone else involved. This was between her and Jake.

Longinus gave her a weird look, and she realised that he was looking at the bruise on her face. He opened his mouth, then closed it, and shook his head. He returned to his chair.

"Gamp, get back here," he called. The little barber returned, darting nervous looks at Rory. "My assistant won't require your services. We have decided to keep her hair as it is. Now, please finish my moustache."

***

Once Gamp was finished, Longinus was furnished with a luxuriously thick moustache that curled up at the tips thanks to the application of a little wax. Longinus examined himself in the mirror with a satisfied smile.

"Good man," he said to Gamp, who bowed, glowing with pleasure.

Longinus paid, and he and Rory stepped back out onto the street.

"Look," he said, "I…I wanted to say to you… Well, the thing is, um, well there are rules… Yes, there are rules, but then there are rules, you know?" He cleared his throat.

"No, I got no clue what you mean."

"I mean, there are rules, but in your case, of course…I mean, um… you're a girl."

"Yeah, I'm a girl. And?"

"And, um, we're assassins. So there are rules, to each their business…but with girls, it's different. You see?"

"No, I really don't."

Longinus cleared his throat again. "I'm a man, and you're a girl."

"Yeah…"

"And there are rules."

"Alright, and?"

"And your face…"

"My face?"

"Yes. If anyone…um…I mean, well, you know. If anyone tries, er, I'd have to be…um… involved."

"Stone the gulls, Longinus! Are you coming onto me?"

"What? Er, *what?*" Longinus turned beet red. "No! No, no, no! Gods, no!" He glared at her. "You damned idiotic girl, why is everything with you so difficult?"

"Don't call me idiotic, I ain't the one spouting nonsense," replied Rory, more than a little relieved at his answer. She had no desire to see what Longinus being romantic was like — no doubt it would be cringe worthy and unpleasant.

Longinus pinched the bridge of his nose. "The gods help me, women are born to irritate, but you take things to another level."

"I aim to please. You gonna tell me what that was about, then?"

Longinus shook his head. "Forget this conversation happened."

"I ain't even sure there *was* a conversation."

CHAPTER 18

By the time they had reached the guard headquarters, Longinus finally felt in character. He found himself very taken by his new moustache, twirling its tips between his fingers. This was going to be one of his character's tics.

He glanced back over his shoulder to ensure Rory was still out of sight, and he did his best to put her out of his mind. He had to stay in character now, no distractions. Too much was at stake. He walked up to the guard headquarters with the kind of confident swagger that came with wealth.

Although not very large, the building was one of the more impressive in Damsport. Over time it had become an amalgamation of dome-topped turrets, cupolas, and spires, each part reflecting the style of the marquess or marchioness of the time, so that the result was an odd mishmash of architecture that somewhat managed to work as a rather astonishing, cohesive whole.

"Afternoon, gentlemen," Longinus said to the two guards at the gate, putting on an aristocratic Kushanian accent. "I'll be needing to speak to your supervisor. The name's Shakh Sankhrit."

"You got a card to announce you?" asked one of them.

"Unfortunately no, I'm still waiting on the printer. The design was all wrong, had to be remade. But your lieutenant will want to speak to me, so hurry about it. I don't have all day."

The guard who had spoken disappeared within the building, leaving Longinus to wait outside. Longinus twiddled his moustache. It really was a handy tic to have: it kept one's hand busy and gave one an air of superiority. He might have to take that up for himself. Of course, that would mean growing a longer moustache.

Worth considering.

The guard eventually returned. "Lieutenant Grahms will see you. Follow me."

Longinus was led through a succession of twisting corridors, each decorated in its own fashion, mirroring the patchwork effect of the exterior. They finally reached a set of shiny lacquered double doors. The guard knocked.

"Come."

The guard opened the doors and gestured for Longinus to go inside.

Within was an office that was as gaudy as Longinus' costume. Lacquered, gilded screens, brocade upholstered chairs, intricately patterned rugs, all of it clashing, without good taste to guide them into harmony. The lieutenant stood at the window, gazing out onto the Bottleneck. He turned to greet Longinus, who recognised his face from one of the paintings hanging on the office wall.

"How can I help you, Mister…" Lieutenant Grahms pretended to have forgotten the name.

Really? Does he think that is enough to put me out? Laughable.

Longinus threw himself onto a chair without being invited.

"Sankhrit. But you can call me Shakh. I like to use my mother's name for anonymity, but I'm sure you'll have heard of my father's name, Firuz."

Grahms' demeanour changed immediately at the mention of one of the oldest and wealthiest families in Kushania. Longinus smirked. It was so easy.

"Yes, of course, of course! What can I do, how can I be of assistance, Mr, ah, that is, Shakh?" Grahms sat down and called for some refreshments.

"I'm moving to Damsport. Got bored with living on the family estate." Longinus waved a nonchalant hand. "You know how it is. I wanted a little hobby, something fun to fill my days, so I purchased a newspaper. I've always fancied myself a writer, you see, and my prose is second to none. A journalist, mind you, none of that fictional nonsense. So I thought to hell with propriety! I bought the newspaper." Longinus smiled and twiddled his moustache. "And I shall run it, too."

"I see. What newspaper is that?"

"The *Damsport Gazette*. You've heard of it, I'm sure."

Grahms nodded stiffly. "Yes, I've had one or two run-ins with them."

"As I am well aware. I do my research. I was pondering what to do with my newly acquired newspaper yesterday in the baths — your public baths are so delightfully quaint, by the way. There is a *frisson* about slumming it with the common folk, is there not? At any rate, I heard about this ghastly corpse appearing in the women's section." Longinus leaned forward. "Naturally I could not go and investigate this myself, so I came straight to you. This would be a marvellous story for me to start with."

The refreshments arrived and Grahms poured them both a glass of orange wine.

"Your health, sir," he said, raising his glass. Longinus raised his and they both took a long sip. "I'm afraid," continued Grahms, "that I'm not at liberty to discuss —"

"I'd be writing the article myself, you see. And what a joy it would be to describe the lavish, tasteful backdrop to my conversation with the famed Lieutenant Grahms. My father would, of course, be reading all my articles, as would the rest of my family."

"They…they would? I didn't realise the *Gazette* was read in Kushania."

"Oh, it will be now, at least by members of the *right* circles. They are already all talking about it."

Longinus could see the calculating, hungry look on Grahms face. He had him now, hook, line, and sinker.

"Now, I understand you are a professional man," he continued, "and I wouldn't want to put you in a compromising position. Say I held the story back until a time that was suitable for you?"

"Well…that might work."

"I could make you a hero, a noble beacon of justice, Damsport's last virtuous defence, the scourge of the, er…well, you get the gist." Longinus twiddled his moustache again. It really was a fine habit. He leaned back in his chair. "I would very much like to see the body, so I can describe it in all its visceral vividness."

Visceral vividness, nice. Worth remembering—I could use that in the next pamphlet.

Grahms shook his head. "I'm afraid that is impossible. I would gladly help, but no one can see the remains until the family has come. We haven't yet managed to get in touch with any next of kin, so it might be a couple of days."

"Of course," Longinus replied. "I understand."

"But I could let you know once the family has come. You would be welcome to see the remains then."

"My thanks, Lieutenant. Do you happen to have a name for the victim?"

"Yes, that I can give you. It's Doctor Corian, Damsport's most proficient alchemist — after the one who works for us, naturally."

No, he isn't, you dolt! I'm the best alchemist in Damsport.

Longinus produced his writing box and made note of the name. "Splendid! Any suspects?"

"Well, that assassin, the Viper. He signed his name on the victim's forehead."

"Yes, I heard, but any clues as to the man's real identity?"
Grahms shook his head.
Good.

"Marvellous," he said aloud. "That will do for a start. This was…enlightening, Lieutenant."

"My pleasure."

Longinus got up and was nearly at the door when he turned back. "Oh, that reminds me. Wasn't there another killing by that same assassin? Somewhere down at the docks…maybe a week ago?"

"Yes, five days ago. A sailor. Very odd case. The man was poisoned in the same way as Dr Corian, but the skin from his forehead was removed. We're still not sure what to make of it."

So, whoever was behind this must have hired Dr Corian to identify the poison's composition from the sailor's skin. The gods be thanked for the gossip at the Hand and Tankard. Now I need to find out just how close he got to replicating my poison.

"Shakh?"

"Hmm? Yes? Oh yes, well, I have full faith in your abilities, Lieutenant," Longinus replied smoothly. "I'll be back in a week or so to enquire after your investigation. I will be writing to my father on this matter at once, he does love a good mystery. I'll be sure to tell him about our interview."

"I'd be most honoured…Too kind…"

Longinus sketched a small bow and walked out, the lieutenant's simpering thanks following him down the corridor. It was then that it occurred to him that whoever had skinned the sailor had to have been following him that night at the docks. It would be too much of a coincidence for him to have come across the body before the guards got to it. He remembered the noise that both he and the sailor had heard. Unease wormed its way into his chest. This was getting too close for comfort.

"So, what happened?" Rory all but pounced on him as he returned.

"It's just as I expected, he took the skin from the sailor's forehead and used it to re-create the poison. It's difficult but possible. It would take a very skilled alchemist. Coincidentally, that's what the victim at the bath was."

"Really? Who was he?"

"Dr Corian. He was a good alchemist."

Rory thought of the jar he had given her.

"No patch on me, of course," continued Longinus. "No one is — but good enough to do it. He probably got killed as a way to test the poison. An efficient way for his employer to tie up a loose end. Quite elegant, really."

"So what now?"

"Just as expected, I couldn't see the body, but with his name, you can pass yourself off as his niece."

"Won't they know I'm not related to him?"

"They haven't found his family yet, so no, they won't. Anyway, he was well known for being a loner, and he had no family, so they will be searching for a while. Here's the device you can use to extract the poison —"

"Hold your steamers there. I ain't going in there looking like this. The key to a con is in the appearance, right, and while I can do a desperate urchin girl better than anyone, I ain't gonna pass for no doctor's niece, not by a long shot."

"You're right, how could I have overlooked such a detail? We'll get you some clothes."

"I ain't got no money, and anyway this is for you, so you're paying."

"Don't be any more crass than you already are, Rory. A gentleman doesn't speak of money."

"I ain't no gentleman."

"On that we agree, at least. You will, however, have to become one if you're to be my assistant. This way."

Longinus led the way down a lane, and Rory trotted after him.

"I ain't your assistant!"

***

Buying clothes turned out to be even more humiliating than the baths. It wasn't the gasps or the tutting at the state of her clothes that got her, it was the look of pity on the shopkeep's face. It had been a long time since she had come across genuine pity, and she swore to herself there and then that she never would come across it again.

They had to go through a large selection of items in order to find something that would fit her diminutive frame. A sleeveless vest came close enough — it would be a blessing to have bare arms in the heat. The shopkeep sewed three leather straps with buckles along the back, cinching it down to size. Rory tucked her medals beneath the vest, despite Longinus' insistence that she take them off.

He selected some leather gloves and a pair of leather leggings. Although they were the smallest pair available, they were still far too big. Rory lashed them to her waist with her belt so that she looked like she was wearing a brown paper bag around her hips.

"And now for your boots," said Longinus.

"I'm keeping my boots."

"They don't match your belt."

"So you keep saying, but I'm keeping them, alright?" The iron inserts were far too valuable, but Rory didn't want to tell Longinus about them. A girl had to have some secrets.

"I'm the one buying you all this, so I make the decisions."

"I'm the one helping you with"— Rory glanced at the shopkeep — "you know what."

They glared at each other until Longinus closed his eyes and pinched the bridge of his nose.

"You do that a lot," remarked Rory. "It ain't gonna make me any less irritating, you know."

"Oh, I'm well aware — nothing could achieve that. It might just stop me from killing you, though."

"I think you look fine," said the shopkeep, patting her arm with a smile. "If I might suggest one thing…"

She disappeared behind Rory, taking a couple of the smaller hair segments from either side of her face and plaiting them down the back of her head. "It'll keep your hair out of the way," she said, cocking her head to admire the effect.

Rory looked at herself in the mirror and grinned. Despite the ill-fitting clothes, she looked bloody marvellous. Almost warrior like. If she had the rapier at her hip, she might even look fearsome. Her hair looked better, too — it didn't dwarf her face quite as much.

"Thanks," she said to the shopkeep.

"My pleasure. Come back if the straps at the back need adjusting."

"I will."

***

Longinus' moisture extractor went into Rory's new pocket. It was an odd contraption with what looked like a large octopus sucker on one end, a glass vial on the other, and in the middle a little piece of machinery that was activated by a rotating handle. Longinus had gone into extensive detail to explain how the machine created a vacuum, therefore drawing any moisture through the contraption's sucker. Rory had tuned him out as soon as she saw him pedantically raise his index finger.

"So you know what you're doing?" he asked for the umpteenth time. "Don't forget, I need the moisture from the forehead, where the poison has been painted. If you miss, it will all be for nothing."

"Yeah, I heard the last three times you told me," replied Rory.

Longinus fidgeted with his pantaloons. "And you remember how to crank the extractor?"

"Even I can turn a handle. You got my silk line and grappling hook, right? Don't you take your eye off them, they're worth a pretty penny, and there are plenty of people who would want to steal them from me."

"Yes, Rory," Longinus sighed. "I have them. Nobody cares about your rusting grappling hook and grubby line, but yes, I have them and will keep an eye on them. Now will you focus on what's important here?"

"Well, my silk line and grappling hook are as important to me as your poisons are to you, alright?"

They regarded each other for a moment, both uneasy, and then Rory turned away and made for the guard headquarters.

She pulled out a few medals at random, kissed them for luck, and tucked them back into her vest. As she walked, she began to squeeze out a tear or two. Her nose, as always, was primed and ready to sniffle.

"Can we help you?" asked one of the guards.

She made herself as small and pathetic as possible, looking up with tear-filled eyes. "I just heard that my uncle died," she wailed, "at the baths." She sniffled and went to wipe her nose, realising when she left a trail of snot on her forearm that sleeves might have been a better idea after all.

"What's your uncle's name?"

"D-d-doctor Corian," she replied, bursting into big fat tears.

"Ah, yes," said one. "We've been trying to reach out to family and —"

Rory grabbed one of the guards by the sleeve. "I ain't got no fam'ly other than him, sir! I don't know what to do!" She wailed louder.

The men looked at each other in a panic, predictably ill at ease in front of a crying girl.

"There, there," said one of the guards, patting her back awkwardly. The other backed away and ran inside.

"Er, there now," continued the guard, "it's alright. No need to cry. Cairn will be back soon, and er…" He glanced anxiously towards the building. "Everything will be fine. We'll need you to, er, sign something and er…"

The second guard had returned. The two men argued for a brief moment in low voices until they decided who would escort her inside. The man who had just returned gestured for Rory to follow him, looking less than pleased.

Much to her concern, the guard took her down into the basement. Basements were tricky, dangerous places: no windows to climb out of. She continued her pitiful wailing and sniffling, keeping an eye out — the good one. Her swollen eye was leaking quite a lot of water, making it hard to see.

The guard walked quickly, evidently eager to get rid of his charge.

"Through here," he said in a gruff voice, pointing to an open door. He hurried off, leaving Rory alone as she entered a room lit by the brightest vapour lamps she had ever seen. The walls were covered from floor to ceiling with gleaming white tiles that reflected the light, making it appear even brighter. She blinked several times as her eyes adjusted.

The room was stark, only furnished with a desk that heaved under a mound of paper, an alchemy bench much like the one Longinus had, and a marble slab. On the slab was a body covered with a white sheet so that only the face was visible, a spiderweb of black veins spreading out from the word Viper.

Rory didn't have time for anything else before a man wearing an impressive set of optics stepped into the room. The lenses were thick, magnifying his eyes so that they seemed to be as large as the lenses themselves. In front of the right eye, several additional lenses were lowered, further magnifying it and creating the disturbing illusion that one eye was significantly larger than the other. The left lens was set on the end of a telescoping tube with a number of dials on the side to adjust the distance by which it stuck out.

"You are the niece of the deceased?"

"Yes."

"Hmm, good. Hold on." The man adjusted his lenses until they were both the same size. "Ah, there we are, yes. I am Dr Howshinger."

"What happened to my uncle, sir? What happened?" Rory went to Howshinger, bubbling tears and snot, pulling at his sleeve, but he seemed impervious to her unique brand of charm. He pulled his arm away.

"Your uncle was poisoned, and I mean to discover how." He nodded to himself, as if agreeing with his own statement. "Yes, I mean to discover how. A very interesting little riddle. Very interesting. Now, if you would kindly confirm that this *is* Dr Corian, and you do, yes? Good. Then you can sign, er, where has the document gone?" He went to the desk and rooted around in the papers. Rory pulled out the extractor, keeping an eye on him, but he turned back too quickly, and she had to slide it back into her pocket.

"There it is. You can sign here and then be on your way, yes? Plenty to get on with." He nodded and held out the paper, which was covered in some illegible scrawl amongst which the name Dr Corian was visible. She looked up at him as pathetically as she could and burst into fresh tears.

"Come, come," said Dr Howshinger, "this is not the time, nor the place. This is a place of alchemy. Of alchemy! So sign and be gone."

Rory dried her eyes, annoyed that her act wasn't working.

"I don't have a pen," she said sulkily.

Dr Howshinger produced one. Rory made as though she was about to take it, and then she had an idea.

"No!" she shouted, stepping back and putting on a horrified look. "You ain't defiling his body! I know what you're gonna do, you're gonna cut him open, like he was no more than the carcass of a pig, ain't you? The Lord of Consciousness will not allow it."

Dr Howshinger's magnified eyes blinked with dismay.

"You're a member of the Sisterhood of the Exalted Consciousness?"

"Yes, I am," replied Rory, wracking her brains to remember one of the lectures she'd had to listen to when she had begged the sisters for food. The good sisters could preach alright, but they weren't so good on actually practicing charity, so Rory never used to visit them much. "And the Lord of Consciousness sees all," she continued. "He will…er, strike you down if you try and prevent the soul of one of his, er, to prevent my uncle's soul from rising to the…heavens! You ain't ruining the consciousness of his body and condemning his soul to be eaten."

Rory was pretty sure that last part was doctrine from the Huer Priests, but Dr Howshinger didn't seem to notice. Damsport was a smorgasbord of religions, and keeping track of every belief would have been a job in itself — one that few were interested in.

"My dear, that is not my intention at all, no, not at all. I am, on the contrary, seeking to help your uncle, yes, to help him. I seek only to bring him peace, and to you, too. Peace of mind, once we understand what happened to him, and who — yes, more importantly, *who* was behind this ghastly crime."

Rory squeezed out a couple more tears. "That's very good of you, sir."

"But I cannot catch the person who did this to him if I don't know how he died, you see. And for that I need to, er…"

Rory could tell he didn't care a whit about catching anyone. There was a hunger in his eyes every time he looked at the veined forehead of the corpse. He was after the poison, and no mistake about it. Maybe Longinus was as good as he made out to be.

151

"Well…" she said slowly, pretending to think. "My uncle was in fact a follower of the Church of Equilibrium. I suppose if I was allowed to take something from him I could perform the ritual…"

"The ritual? Yes, of course, absolutely! Yes, yes. What do you need?"

"Some of his essence."

"His essence?" Howshinger looked understandably confused, since she had just made that up.

"Yes."

"And then you'll sign?"

"Yes."

"Alright, great, yes. Good."

Rory moved to the body's head.

"Wait, not from there! I mean, er, wouldn't it be better not to deface him?"

"The third eye lives in the middle of the forehead, as everyone knows, Dr Howshinger. And that's what I must take for the ritual."

In truth, she had no idea what the ritual was, or even if there was one. She moved quickly before he could object again, applying the sucker to the forehead, right over the 'P.' She cranked the little handle, and there was a suctioning noise. When she removed the device, there was a perfect red circle where the sucker had been, and the P and part of the neighbouring letters had disappeared.

Dr Howshinger watched her with a frown.

"Now where do I sign?" she asked.

"Why do you have a moisture extractor?"

"I'm a doctor's apprentice," she lied.

"Really? I don't remember a female apprentice registering." He pulled a massive ledger from the desk. "What did you say your name was again?"

"I haven't had a chance to register yet, I only just joined."

"Hmm, then, young lady, you should not, I repeat, should *not,* be passing yourself off as a doctor's apprentice. You are only part of this hallowed profession once you are inscribed within the pages of my ledger, yes, inscribed."

"Sorry, sir."

Rory glanced towards the door, anxious to leave now that she had what she'd come for. Howshinger blinked at her.

"You look awfully young for a doctor's apprentice. How old are you? Which doctor are you apprenticing with?"

Rory backed towards the door. This was not going the way she wanted at all.

"Dr Howshinger, sir," she said coldly, raising herself as tall as she could. "My uncle just died and he were the only family I got, right? This ain't the time to be questioning me. Ain't you got no manners?"

"Yes, yes, of course, you're right. My apologies, miss. Ah, wait. Before you go, I need your signature... There."

Rory took the proffered pen and scribbled something illegible.

"There," she said. "Good day, I got to go perform the final ritual."

She hurried out before Howshinger could think of something else to ask her. As soon as she was out of eyesight, she unscrewed the vial that now contained the poison sample, jammed in its little stopper, and screwed in the spare vial Longinus had given her. The vial of poison she squirrelled away in her vest, just in case Howshinger should try to give her any more trouble about the moisture extractor.

Longinus had explained that the poison would now be harmless, but she still felt a tremor of nerves at the thought of carrying it so close to her. She climbed the stairs as quick as she could without looking suspicious, sniffled a little as she got close to the exit, and murmured a pathetic little "thank you, sirs" as she walked past the guards at the gate, keeping her head down. She was about to walk towards Longinus when she froze. A little farther on, Jake skulked at the mouth of a lane. When he saw her stop, he stepped out and walked towards her, his face grim.

Rory turned abruptly and gave Longinus a slight shake of her head, hoping he'd understand. She walked away as quickly as she could without arousing the guards' suspicion, her mind racing. As soon as she was out of sight, she broke into a run. Almost at once, she heard the rhythmic thud of Jake's boots on the cobblestones as he gave chase.

She was fast, but so was Jake. She knew that to stop and climb a wall would slow her down enough that he'd be able to catch up with her and pull her down. Not only that, but he'd be expecting her to climb, so he'd likely have something on him to throw at her and knock her off. No, she had to stay at ground level. Her best bet would be to head for Twelve, which would be heaving at this time of day, and try to get lost amongst the traffic.

She glanced over her shoulder as she reached the end of a lane and saw that Jake was dangerously close. Before she could turn back to look ahead, something crashed into her, throwing her against the lane wall. Her head smacked into the stone, dizzying her. She barely had time to register the moisture extractor being wrenched from her before an arm had her in a chokehold that threatened to crush her windpipe.

She gasped and spluttered, the pressure immediately building in her head. She desperately tried to scratch her attacker's face, but he was tall, far too tall. The back of her head barely reached his chest, and her hands scratched uselessly against his clothing. Her vision started to darken. A loud buzzing picked up in her ears.

She kicked and thrashed, scratching at the arm around her neck, but the man didn't seem to notice. Her movements lost coordination and strength, her arms flailing uselessly.

Just as everything went dark, she heard a voice.

"What's going on here?"

And then Rory was on the ground, coughing and wheezing.

"You alright, kid? What happened?"

Rory blinked, struggling to focus on the man behind the voice. She could just make out a guard's uniform. She nodded, her breathing ragged.

"Fine," she managed to rasp.

She got up on all fours and the guard pulled her up. She swayed a little on her feet, blinking to steady her vision.

Once it had cleared and she felt a little steadier on her legs, she patted herself down to check that the vial and her dagger were still there. Luckily, she hadn't fallen on top of the vial and it was intact. She had no desire to test Longinus' assertion that the poison was now harmless.

The guard asked her a few more questions and then offered to escort her back home. For the first time in her life, Rory would have been grateful for the presence of a guard, but she shook her head. Even in her current situation, spending too much time with a guard was a bad idea.

He let her hobble away, and Rory soon found a house up which she could climb. She made her way back to Longinus' house via the roofs, taking her time, her legs uneasy, checking nervously over her shoulder every few steps for any sign of Jake or a particularly tall man.

CHAPTER

20

Longinus rubbed his eyes. He was tired but satisfied. After a sleepless night of working on the sample Rory had brought back, he finally held some answers to his questions.

Dr Corian had undoubtedly replicated the poison from the sailor's skin. While this was disturbing, Corian had been unable to replicate the chemical signature that Longinus included in all his poisons. That meant that his art was still uncompromised.

Unfortunately, those answers begged yet more questions, which he was no closer to resolving. How long had Dr Corian been replicating his poisons? Had he done this before? And with how much success? Who had hired him? Had this mysterious assassin executed other copycat kills?

A noise startled Longinus, and he turned away from his alchemy bench. There, in his blue velvet chair, was Rory. She was fast asleep.

Not for the first time, he noticed the red mark around her neck. Rory had been shaken when she finally returned with the vial, but she refused to discuss what had happened. Longinus felt a little guilty for having been too consumed by his poison to really pay attention to her. No doubt about it, someone had tried to strangle her. That lad who had chased after her at the guard headquarters? It was the same lad they had seen outside the barber, and Longinus began to wonder if he wasn't implicated in this unpleasant copycat mess.

Either way, the attack didn't sit well with Longinus. Strangulation was a perfectly acceptable method of killing, of course — a little on the crude side perhaps (it wasn't poison, after all) but acceptable. But strangulation on a young girl? There were rules, after all. No, that didn't sit well with him at all.

He frowned. When he caught up with whoever that man was, he was going to give him a piece or two of his mind. For now, though, he would make something to help with Rory's throat — it would no doubt be sore.

He had just finished when Rory stirred and awoke. She was on her feet at once.

"Why didn't you wake me?" she asked, voice still raspy.

"You're assuming that I want to spend time with you," he replied, turning back to his bench.

"Straight into the pleasantries, I see. You gonna tell me what the results showed?"

Longinus pretended to ignore the question, thrusting a beaker of golden liquid at her. "Drink that for your throat," he muttered.

He had no intention of letting her know how eager he was to discuss his findings and even less that he had been worried about her. After a long pause, he finally looked up.

"It's as I thought," he said. "Dr Corian copied my poison from that sailor I killed a few days ago. But," Longinus raised a finger and smiled, "he missed my chemical signature, so although he got close, he hasn't actually replicated my poison."

"Not sure that matters," replied Rory. "To everyone else, it looks the same as yours. You're the only one who can tell the difference."

Longinus' face fell. He hadn't banked on the obtuse nature of the common man. Of course they would all be too simple to know the difference. A signature saying 'Viper' would be enough for them. Never mind that there was no calling card, that the kill lacked finesse (dumping a body in the water for it to grow ugly and bloated was a crass move), or that the chemical signature was missing.

"We should go to Dr Corian's place if we can," said Rory, interrupting his thoughts. "Try to see if there are any clues there."

"No, first we must establish if this copycat assassin has killed anyone else under my name. Damsport is big, and the guards are forever trying to keep my kills secret — he could have been operating for a while and I wouldn't know."

"Well now, that's something I can help you with."

"How?"

"It'll cost you a few copper bits, and maybe a couple of whole coppers."

"Copper bits? I don't keep currency that small."

"You don't? Then what d'you do when you get change?"

Longinus shrugged, annoyed that she was making him feel like he had been doing something wrong.

"You mean you *throw* them away? Stone the gulls, man! Well then, I guess we'll have to find a smith to make change for us."

They headed out and found a smith easily enough. Longinus watched, a little appalled as the smith cut the coins into eight segments, like the slices of a pie.

"What a waste," he said, shaking his head.

"Ain't a waste, it's smart, is what it is."

The coins taken care of, Rory took him to the Rookery. Longinus was annoyed that she hadn't told him that was where they were going. He had dressed in a manner befitting the visit of a respectable (if only mildly talented) alchemist, and he was utterly out of place in the Rookery slum.

He had done a job at the Rookery a few years ago and had seen no reason to ever return to that gods-forsaken place. It stank, its people were vile, it was… Well, just like Rory when he had first met her, really. Seeing her now against the backdrop of such filth, he realised with pride just what a change he had already worked on the girl. And in such a short time, too. She was clean, and she was clothed almost respectably, a far cry from the rugged urchin he had first come across. No one would be daft enough to call her pretty, but she was now almost pleasant to look at.

It was to be expected, really. His natural elegance couldn't help but rub off on those around him.

They reached the boundary between the Rookery and Tinsbury Dock, and Rory led them to a narrow, reeking alley. It was so narrow the sunlight couldn't squeeze between the buildings, leaving it dark and gloomy.

Rory ruined what faint illusion of respectability hung about her by sticking two fingers into her mouth and letting out a shrill whistle.

"Give me one of your bigger coppers," she asked.

He fished one out for her, and she displayed it at the empty lane.

"Anybody want to earn a good solid Kushanian copper?"

To Longinus' surprise, there was movement in the gloom. Little dark faces appeared like black worms crawling out of the earth. They were filthy faces, caked with dirt, hard and hungry despite their juvenile features. Next to them, Rory with her open face and easy smile was positively radiant, bad hair or not.

The urchins eyed the coin hungrily, gathering around her. More appeared at the lane's mouth, drawn to the coin like moths to a flame. Rory flipped the coin and caught it. The urchins followed its trajectory, never once taking their eyes off it.

"I gots a proper job for ya, so listen up," she said, and Longinus was surprised by her thick dockside accent. It sounded perfectly natural, and he wondered which was her real accent — dockside or the weird mix she normally spoke.

"You 'eard of a cove called the Viper, aye? Well, I'd be needin' ya ter keep an eye out fer 'im, and an ear to the ground. I wants ter know who he's killed recent-like. I already 'eard 'bout the cove they found in the baths, and the sailor on the docks, so you'll 'ave to find something else to earn this." She flashed the coin again.

"'ow do we know yer gonna come through and pay us?" asked one boy with quick eyes, near the front.

"Good question, Pip, although yer should know me better by now. I always does what I says I does. Everyone gets one copper bit now, in exchange for which yer keep yer eye out. You 'ear somethin', you leave word at —"

"Susie's coffeehouse," interrupted Longinus.

Rory frowned. "I don't think that's a good idea," she whispered.

"Susie will know how to handle them, and I trust her." He handed her his purse, keeping a careful eye on her.

"You guys and gals 'eard that?" said Rory. "Susie's coffeehouse. For now you get a copper bit. This"— she displayed the whole copper again — "I'm savin' for the one of you that'll be bringin' me news I wants ter 'ear."

"That's got my name on it, you wait and see," said Pip.

Rory began handing out the little copper pieces they had obtained at the smith, but a couple of the boys decided to get aggressive, pulling at her and trying to get the purse.

She pulled out her dagger at once, and the urchins fluttered away like startled sparrows, hanging back a couple of yards away.

"You try that again wi' me and nobody ain't gettin' nuffin. Got it? I ain't made of charity, and I sure as shit ain't a mark. You're gettin' payment for a job. Do the job and you get a copper. You ain't happy with that you can argue it out wi' my blade."

The two boys looked sheepish, and when they finally came forward for their bit, they took it without trying anything. Each urchin flitted off with their coin piece, clutching it close, hurrying to spend it before someone could try and steal it from them.

The last to hold out her hand was a girl who couldn't have been more than six and who looked like a breath of wind could knock her over.

"I ain't seen you before," said Rory. "What's your name?"

"Alice."

Rory dug a hand into her pocket and produced a small purse. She searched through it carefully.

"Right, Alice, you gonna do something for me," she said, switching back to her normal accent. "You gonna take this half copper here, and you gonna go buy some stew from Big Wendy on Seam Street. You know the place?"

The girl nodded, her huge eyes and hollow face making her look like a little mouse.

"Good. Don't steal from her, but eat whatever you buy in front of her. Someone tries to give you trouble, she'll make a fuss and chase them off. You got that?"

The girl nodded.

"Just remember never to steal from her, and she'll look after you. If you gotta eat elsewhere, eat and run. Always eat and run, only way to ever put weight on, or someone will take your food from you. Got it?"

The girl nodded again, and Rory gave her the half copper. Alice clutched it to her and scampered away. Longinus watched the whole scene with a vague sense of…what? Unease? Guilt? Or maybe it was indigestion.

"Is that something you used to do?" he asked.

"Yeah. It's tough to stay alive when you're so little. You're a target for everyone, even other kids."

"Take a copper from my purse."

"Why?"

"Well, to replace the half you gave the girl."

Rory thrust his purse back at him, face hard. "Don't mistake me for Alice, I don't take charity."

"That wasn't —"

"I pay my own way, and if I chose to give my money away that's my problem, not yours. Now, we going to see Dr Corian's laboratory?"

Longinus put the purse away, unsure if he felt annoyed or embarrassed.

"No, first I need to warn Susie to expect some subpar visitors over the next few days."

"Alright, and then we should get food too, I ain't eaten in a while."

"That's why we're going to Susie's."

"Ain't that a coffeehouse?"

"Correct." Longinus brightened at the thought. As long as there was silk and coffee in the world, everything else would fall into place.

"We're gonna need more than coffee," she replied. "Me especially on account of being a growing lass and all."

She kissed one of her medals and gave the sky a warning look. Longinus wondered how much hassle the heavens would be subjected to when the time came if she didn't grow as she wanted.

"Coffeehouses," he explained, "that is, *quality* coffeehouses, serve some of the best food in Damsport. We're going to have to get one thing straight, now. On the subject of food and drink, you know less than nothing. You know so little, you don't even comprehend the gulf that is your ignorance. Therefore, I'd appreciate it if you kept all opinions to yourself."

"What? I'm perfectly —"

"You know *less* than nothing. Whatever it is you've tasted in the past is possibly as close to coffee as frog spawn is to caviar. I think it's safe to say you have the palate of a stray dog, and nobody asks a stray dog for her opinion on food or drink. Are we clear?"

Rory glared at him and Longinus smiled. That was better. He definitely felt more comfortable when she was being annoying and ignorant. It was, after all, the rightful way of things.

"Now, when we get to Susie's, you must follow my lead," Longinus said as they got near. "I won't have you create a scene or offend anybody."

"I won't offend nobody, relax."

"You offend everybody, Rory. Your mere presence offends my senses. It's a wonder that I've managed to put up with you for as long as I have."

She rolled her eyes. Truth be told, she was intrigued about Susie's. It was known for being the best coffeehouse in Damsport, although she had no idea what could make the coffee there better than the stuff sold on the street stalls. Coffee was coffee, after all. Just water and coffee beans, no matter if it was made in a tin can over a fire or in some fancy coffeehouse.

They turned into a quiet lane that led to Susie's. The coffeehouse fronted a neat square, full of clean cobblestones and well-dressed people.

Inside, the coffeehouse was dark, but of a rich and comfortable darkness, the kind that invited secrets and whispered confessions. The room they stood in was small, with just two tables surrounded by plush velvet chairs.

A woman glided out from behind a polished teak counter.

"Longinus, my dear, what a pleasure to see you," she said in a low voice.

"The pleasure is all mine, Susie, as always."

"Follow me, please."

"First, I have a favour to ask of you, my dear. I'm awaiting word from a few, er, slightly unsavoury characters. Street urchins to be precise. I knew I could count on your discretion should they have a message to leave with me and —"

"Say no more," replied Susie, raising a hand. "I'll be sure to inform you of anyone looking for you."

"Thank you, much obliged."

Susie bobbed her head and led them to an adjacent room. It was long, like a gallery, and in the middle of it were little booths surrounded by high partitions of thick, red-wine-coloured velvet. A few small stained-glass windows allowed a little sunlight to filter in.

The glass was set in a pattern of diamonds, some sections coloured, others plain. All were full of bubbles, so that the world outside was blurred beyond recognition, and the people walking past the windows were little more than light brown shapes that warped and changed as they moved from one pane to the next.

Vapour lamps on tables and in sconces cast a dimmed light over the gallery. As they walked past the booths, Rory glanced at people within talking in low, confidential voices. Deliciously rich smells wafted out from each booth, and her stomach rumbled. Loudly. Much as she was loath to admit it, this coffeehouse smelled nothing like the coffee she had experienced, which was little more than a bitter, muddy-coloured water.

As they sat down, Longinus whispered something to Susie, who nodded and padded off.

"What was that?" whispered Rory.

"I ordered us food and two butterscotch coffees. You're not ready for real coffee yet."

Rory bristled.

"You know less than nothing, remember?" said Longinus. "Besides, butterscotch coffees are amusing."

Susie appeared at the booth once more, bringing with her a little trolley on top of which were two odd-looking contraptions and several dishes covered with vermeil cloches. Rory stopped herself from whistling her appreciation. The cloches would be worth a small fortune.

"You better be paying for this," she whispered to Longinus, hoping Susie didn't hear. "Cos I sure can't."

"Don't be crass."

Susie placed the dishes on the table and lifted the cloches, revealing a dish of duck with chocolate and cherry sauce, fish stuffed with chilli, lemon, and ginger, and a bowl full of little blueberry beignets, generously dusted with confectioner's sugar. Rory's mouth watered.

She then received one of the contraptions and Longinus the other. She peered at it, trying to guess how it worked. It was shaped like an hourglass with an axis through its middle that joined onto a frame, holding the contraption upright. There was a spout at the top of the hourglass, and beneath the lower part was a wide candle with a red, alchemical flame. A little rod poked out from the bottom of the frame, connecting it to a little platform on which was a chiselled vermeil goblet.

Rory picked it up, but Longinus slapped her hand.

"Leave that. Wait 'til the coffee's ready."

They tucked into the food, Rory wolfing hers down with her customary speed. Some habits were hard to let go of.

"Slow down," said Longinus. "Or you'll have nothing left to enjoy with the coffee."

As though it had heard its cue, the hourglass swung slowly around its axis, until it was horizontal. A thick black liquid poured out of the spout and into the goblet. Golden swirls of butterscotch ran through the coffee, and smoke rose up from it. Rory sniffed it. It smelled rich and comforting. It smelled like… She licked her lips, trying to place the scent.

"It smells like stories," she said at last. "Like a book I found on the docks when I were a kid."

Longinus raised an eyebrow. "Not bad. Not bad at all for your first try. There may be hope for you yet. What you are getting is an aroma of leather, wood, and parchment with a rather complex bouquet of library and a hint of tobacco." He raised the goblet to his nose, inhaling deeply as he moved it in circles. "Quite delicious for such a juvenile little coffee."

He took a sip.

Rory tried hers. It was delicious. Rich and buttery, with a slightly bitter note.

"Did you keep the book?" asked Longinus.

"Course not, I sold it to a second-hand book dealer."

He shook his head.

"Yeah, well, reading ain't quite so important as eating when you're living on the street, alright?" bristled Rory.

They finished their food and coffee, and after Longinus profusely thanked Susie and paid the bill, they headed to Dr Corian's laboratory.

***

Dr Corian rented rooms in a shabby-looking house. Being a respected alchemist obviously didn't pay too well. The landlady told them which floor the rooms were on with a mouth empty of teeth but full of rice porridge.

The stairwell was dank and smelled of cabbage. At each floor, Rory could smell the inhabitants beyond the doors. Stale alcohol here, the rich smell of disease there, stew on one floor, cheap tobacco on the next. They climbed up, Longinus keeping his hands and arms against his chest, looking around him with obvious revulsion.

They reached Dr Corian's rooms, but the door was locked.

"Either he left willingly, or someone took his keys," whispered Rory, pulling out her picks. Longinus nodded.

The lock yielded easily and they stepped inside.

Dr Corian's lab was depressing, a far cry from Longinus' anally tidy alchemy bench. Remnants of food on plates, half-covered with mould and mouse droppings, were strewn about the room, as were dirty clothes, books, and mounds of paper. Everything was sprinkled with ash, and Rory recognised the smell of the cheap tobacco leaves some Damsians bought on the docks, rolling them by hand.

Items that Rory recognised from Longinus' alchemy bench were scattered about the room, although it was clear that Dr Corian hadn't worked here in a while. In one corner was a sagging bed, the sheets yellow and rumpled. Rory thought back to the night she met him, how dejected he had seemed.

"Wasn't he supposed to be a famous alchemist?" she asked.

"He was, but he fell into debt."

"Gambling?" asked Rory, thinking of Jake.

"Who cares? The point is, his mind wasn't sharp enough to keep himself in good stead. And that is why, my dear girl, he will never be the alchemist that I am."

"Obviously, 'cause he's dead."

Longinus put on his gloves and picked up a fork from one of the abandoned plates. He wiped it on a handkerchief and threw the handkerchief away.

"Bit unnecessary, ain't it? You're wearing gloves."

"Yes, and I have no interest in soiling them if I can avoid it."

"How many of those handkerchiefs do you throw away?" asked Rory. That handkerchief would fetch a good few coppers at the second-hand market near the Great Bazaar. She would pick it up when Longinus wasn't looking — no sense in passing up on good money, after all.

"As many as needed to keep me from coming into contact with this kind of filth," replied Longinus distractedly. He used the fork to lift papers and peer under mounds of clothing. He sniffed a couple of the glass beakers, peered into a prism that broke the light into a rainbow of colours, and even went as far as to run a finger along a tool with a long, beaklike appendage.

Rory sniffed the air. There was an odd yet vaguely familiar smell — like sulphur but sweeter. She realised she had smelled it on Corian the night she had met him but had been too distracted by what had happened with Jake to pay attention. There was something else about that smell too, something that niggled at her.

"He didn't replicate my poison here," Longinus said at last.

"You sure?"

"Positive. He must have been working elsewhere, probably wherever the man behind all of this is based. If he had —"

Noise coming from below interrupted him. Heavy footsteps were treading up the steps, and voices called to each other.

"His rooms are at the top floor," said a deep voice.

"Sod it, that'll be the guards," said Rory. She marched over to the window, throwing it open.

"No, no, no!" said Longinus. "I am not dressed for a window exit."

"I'm sorry, what?"

"One doesn't scramble around when wearing a cloak," he sniffed, gesturing at the cloak covering his right shoulder. "It is both impractical and unsightly. If I had known there would be a window exit, I'd have dressed completely differently."

"Well, too late for that," replied Rory, uncoiling her grappling hook and silk line. "Some things are more important than fashion, such as not getting caught by the guards."

She swung it and it caught on the gutter, neat as you like. She slipped on the gloves that Longinus had bought her and climbed onto the window-frame edge.

"You coming?"

Longinus looked at her like a cat might, if he were contemplating whether to pounce on a mouse.

"Longinus?"

"I'll see you back at my house," he murmured.

"What, I—"

"Guards!" shouted Longinus, startling her.

"Stone the gulls, are you crazy?" hissed Rory.

"Guards!!" he shouted louder, making shooing gestures at her.

The footsteps on the stairs accelerated. They were at the door by the time Rory galvanised herself into action. Cursing Longinus, she scrambled out, climbing up using the silk line. She heard the guards burst into Dr Corian's lab.

"What's going on?" said someone.

"I caught a girl breaking into Corian's laboratory. A filthy urchin…"

Rory pulled herself up on the roof. An exclamation below told her one of the guards had stuck his head out the window and spotted her.

"I came here to demand Corian settle a debt he owes me," continued Longinus' disembodied voice, "and I found her rooting around in his things. Not that there appears to be anything of value here."

Rory muttered more curses under her breath as she coiled her silk line. Nothing against conning the guards, of course, but still. A little more warning would have been nice.

There were more shouts as other guards poked their heads out of the window, trying to work out a way to get to the roof. The houses had flat roofs in this area, bordered with a low parapet. That meant she couldn't get quite as much acceleration as when the roof was sloped, but she should still be fine to make the jump across the lane. She peered over the parapet edge. Of course, there were more guards down in the streets, and they were all now looking up following the commotion at the window.

She could still hear Longinus' voice wafting up to her as he hassled the guards for the fictitious money Corian owed him, now that they had informed him of the man's death. Rory had to admire his nerve, if not his team spirit. She ran to the other end of the roof to look at the situation below, but no sooner had she stuck her head over the parapet than someone shouted and pointed at her.

She ducked back, cursing. Well, no point dilly-dallying, she was going to be seen jumping no matter which way she went. Might as well get cracking.

Rory leaped. Shouts below told her she had been spotted, as expected. She sprinted to the other side of the roof and jumped again. On and on she jumped, not bothering to map out a route at first. When she saw red-tiled sloping roofs up ahead, she aimed for them. Without the parapets to get in the way, she'd be able to jump far easier.

By the time she reached the red roofs, the guards were trailing behind her. She could still hear their voices but only faintly. Rory crested the first roof. The houses were terraced here, following the long curve of a street, and with the sun gleaming off the red tiles, they looked a little like the vertebrae scales of a dragon. She sprinted along the top of the roofs, dodging around chimneys, laughing as she pretended to climb up an imaginary dragon's back.

chapter 22

Rory made it back to Longinus' house, still annoyed despite the run on the roofs.

"Next time, give me more warning," she told him as she walked through the door.

"Why? You did an excellent job, just as I knew you would. I stopped by Susie's on the way home, by the way."

"And?"

"Nothing yet."

Rory nodded. That wasn't exactly surprising. Urchins were lightning quick, as far as gossip went, but even they needed a bit of time to gather information. She was also disappointed that Dr Corian's rooms hadn't yielded anything of more use.

"Did you notice the smell at Dr Corian's?" she asked.

"Be more specific, I noticed a great deal of smells. Rotten food, unwashed clothing, sweat, sea novelwort sublimate, mediocrity…"

"I don't know," said Rory. "It was a bit like sulphur but kind of sweet, too."

"Hmm, yes, I see what you mean. I have to admit it's not a smell I'm familiar with."

"Really? Because Dr Corian smelled of it when I met him that night. If he was going to the baths to wash it off, it might have something to do with where he's based or what he's been doing. Either way, I think it's an important clue. Also, I think I've come across it before — it's familiar but I can't place it."

"Have you now? Well then, that's something. Let me see if I can't replicate it."

"Alright, but you've also got to train me. Don't think I've forgotten the blackmail just because someone's out to kill me and replace you."

Truth be told, Rory was feeling a lot more threatened by the tall man than she would have cared to admit. When he had attacked her outside the guard headquarters, it had been nothing like what Jake had suggested. No warning to get out of the way, no offer of a bribe or deal. It had been pure, cold, efficient killing — at least it would have been, if it hadn't been for the guard.

She still wanted to solve the mystery of what had happened to Dr Corian, but more than ever now, she wanted to be able to face an adversary with a rapier. She was all too aware that at the moment she was horribly vulnerable to attack, her only paltry defence being to stab with her little dagger.

CHAPTER

23

It had been hours of trying to replicate the smell at Corian's rooms, and they were no closer. Much as Longinus loved tinkering at his alchemy bench, even he was growing tired of the endless manipulations. He presented Rory with yet another beaker. She took a sniff and shook her head.

He nodded, and with a sigh, he turned back to the bench.

"I think we need a break," she said. "My nose ain't barely working no more."

"Yes, you might be right."

"And look, what a coincidence! I have a sword arm here" — she extended her arm — "and it needs training. Perfect way to rest up from all that smelling."

"Alright, but just for a bit, and then we go back to identifying that smell."

"Sure. But it's got to be *proper* training. I ain't standing like no lemon holding out a rapier."

"That *was* proper training."

Rory threw him a glance, and Longinus was astonished to realise it was one that he himself had disseminated on many an occasion. *Oh, please*, it said.

"Fine," he said instead, too taken aback to think of a better answer. Anyway, sometimes it was better to go around an obstacle than to tackle it head on.

Longinus went to his cabinets and retrieved the blunt rapier.

"Put on the gloves that I bought you," he ordered. "You should always wear gloves when handling blades," he added. "You will notice that despite my profession my hands remain smooth, delicate, my fingers long and fine, and devoid of calluses. Of course, in your case, your hands are already ruined." He sighed. "We shall have to make do with what we have. An assassin's hands are just as important as his clothing, you know. Both are the sign of a consummate professional. There is no greater insult than killing someone whilst inappropriately attired, and that extends to the state of one's hands. You see, while these little people are beneath us, we can still grant them the small respect of being impeccably groomed as we witness their final moments."

Rory looked like she was about to say something, thankfully thought better of it, and slipped her gloves on in silence.

"Now. First, footwork," said Longinus.

What followed was again so unlike Longinus' daydream of the Viper as a noble teacher that he not only found himself profoundly disappointed, but he wondered why on earth anyone would want to become a sword preceptor. There was no awe, no wonder on her part, no graceful imparting of his knowledge during which he could display himself at his best advantage.

Instead, for the next few hours, he watched Rory butcher the art of footwork, then hack through the air with her training rapier as though she was trying to clear a path through an invisible jungle, and generally show a complete lack of grace and elegance. All of it punctuated by grunts, intolerable amounts of sweating, and the ridiculous sticking out of her tongue as she concentrated.

Longinus had never known or cared much about women, but he had always been under the impression there was some natural grace to them, some femininity or other that gave them their charm. Not that Rory had any charm, but he had still expected there to be something feminine about her, somewhere.

Evidently not.

Longinus was subjected to several more days of torment as he watched Rory scramble around with the rapier, followed by more endless manipulations to try and re-create the smell from Dr Corian's lab. They had no luck with the smells, and while Rory began to master some fighting techniques, she failed to pick up any kind of grace, no matter how hard Longinus tried.

At least her black eye was fading to little more than a yellowing of the skin (thanks to an ointment of his creation — he had made Rory throw out Dr Corian's paste which was distinctly inferior), and the mark at her neck had completely disappeared. She still looked a disgrace but no longer like a beaten disgrace. It was just as well that they hadn't come across that lumbering character from the barber's, or Longinus would have been hard pressed to resist the temptation of flinging some of his powdered poison in his face.

Unfortunately, they had no luck with the urchins, either. Daily trips to Susie's brought them no word, no messages. It was as though the copycat assassin had decided to disappear, back to where he had come from.

chapter 24

Rory and Longinus were sitting down to another delicious meal at Susie's, accompanied by two butterscotch coffees — fast becoming Rory's favourite drink. Rory had begun to enjoy these daily trips to the coffeehouse almost as much as the training. It wasn't just because of the respite it afforded her aching arms and legs. She and Longinus were settling into a comfortable sort of routine, largely consisting of him hissing at her and poking her in the ribs to remind her of whatever manners he felt she was lacking at the time, while Rory did her best to come up with ever-more-inventive ways to wind him up.

She barely thought of Jake anymore or of the partnership they used to have.

They had just started eating, and Longinus hadn't even had time to start berating her on her table manners, when a commotion at the entrance interrupted them.

Susie appeared at their booth.

"Someone here to see you both," she murmured.

"Thank you, Susie," Longinus replied. "My apologies for the disturbance. Would you be so kind as to add this to my bill?"

He dabbed at the corners of his mouth with his napkin and stood up. Rory followed suit but, not wanting to waste her coffee, she downed it all in one draught. It was still far too hot, and it burned her tongue and the inside of her mouth. As she followed Longinus, she stuck her tongue out, breathing on it, trying to cool the burning sensation.

Back at the reception, she could see Pip and Alice waiting outside. Alice looked timidly about her while Pip's expression was a mixture of outrage and impatience.

"Ah!" he exclaimed as soon as he saw them. "I told 'er and told 'er, I needs to be seeing ya now on urgent bisniss, but she ain't listened to me. Apologies, sir, miss, for the delay, next time inform yer employees of yer important bisniss. Least that's what I'd do."

Longinus and Rory stepped out into the late afternoon light, blinking after the gloom of the coffeehouse.

"What have you got for us?" asked Rory as soon as they had stepped out into the square, before Longinus could begin a lecture on manners or silence.

The urchins both spoke eagerly, Alice raising her voice to be heard above Pip, but the result was so confused that Rory could make no sense of it.

"You first," she said to Alice.

"But —" protested Pip.

"I makes the rules here, alright?" cut in Rory.

"The Viper killed a servant of the Old Girl," said Alice, "by writing on 'er fore'ead."

" 'E killed her last night," interrupted Pip. "I found that out independent of her like, so you 'ave ter pay me."

"How d'you know it was the Viper?" asked Rory.

" 'E left a note," said Alice.

"Aye, and then 'e took all her clothes. Pervert if ya ask me." Pip crossed his arms as though his opinion was the final word on the matter.

Longinus went a grey shade of pale.

"What was the note like?" asked Rory, throwing a worried glance at Longinus. Now was not the time for him to throw a scene.

"Like a playin' card," said Pip

"But with a snake on it," added Alice.

"Alright, that's great. Good work." Rory gestured at Longinus for the purse, and he gave it to her as though in a dream. She handed the urchins their coins.

"And what if we 'ear of more of the Viper's activities?" asked Pip.

"Leave word 'ere, but don't be making a fuss again, or I'll be cuffin' you 'bout the ears, alright?"

"Aye," said the lad.

"Good. One last thing. If yer smart, ya'll work together. Cover more ground that way."

Pip looked at Alice doubtfully. "Dunno…" he said.

Alice looked back at him with her big mouse eyes.

"Trust me," said Rory, "Little 'uns like her can do pretty damn well for themselves."

Pip nodded, understanding the reference to Rory's comparatively tiny frame, but he still seemed wholly unconvinced by Alice.

"See you both soon, no doubt," she said, and seeing Longinus walking away, she waved at the urchins and hurried after him.

"Longinus?"

He turned, seeming startled to find her walking beside him.

"You alright?" she asked.

"No, of course I'm not alright! The Viper is being made out to be a pervert. A *pervert*! You heard the urchin."

"Pip."

"What?"

"His name is Pip."

"Focus, Rory! The name of an urchin is hardly worth our attention at this point! My reputation is at stake. Years of carefully nurturing it and along comes this…this…whoever this is, and he sweeps it away just like that." He snapped his fingers. "A pervert — the Viper. Unthinkable." Longinus was shaking with outrage.

"You thought of why someone would want to do that? Only I was thinking, right, if he wants to be the Viper, why discredit you like that? Makes no sense, he needs the Viper's reputation intact to take your place. And right now your reputation ain't looking too good. It doesn't make sense, we're missing something here."

"I don't know, Rory!" he cried, throwing his hands in the air in frustration. "He doesn't want competition, he wants to be the only worthy assassin in Damsport… Maybe he isn't trying to replace me, just to discredit me. After all, you saw how crass what he did with…" Longinus composed himself and looked around, dropping his voice, "with Dr Corian was. It doesn't matter why he's doing it, what matters is that he's ruining my reputation."

"But then why try to get rid of me? I mean, I ain't exactly here to help your reputation neither, am I? It ain't making sense, I don't get where I fit in. And then there's the issue of how he selects the targets in the first place. Are they random? Why kill the Old Girl's servant? Is he getting commissions from people? Your commissions?"

At this, Longinus seemed to be electrified.

"What?" asked Rory.

She was startled when he turned to her, his face a mask of fury.

"You little…"

"What did I do now?"

"My commissions!" he exploded. "Of course, he's been taking my commissions. I haven't been able to check on them because of you."

"Of me?"

"Yes, you! With your blackmailing, your incessant irritating questions, your —"

"Hey, it ain't my fault if you haven't been doing your job. I haven't been stopping you from doing nothing."

Longinus went silent as they reached his house. He led the way to the back door and, opening it, stepped inside. He left the door open, which Rory took as an invitation to enter.

The weapons room was dark, only partially illuminated by the late afternoon light. Longinus shook the lamps to life, the vapours mixing and producing their orange glow. He finished lighting the last lamp, then he grabbed her by the arm, and dragged her to the door that led into the rest of the house.

"Hey, what —"

He shoved her in through a door immediately to the left of the weapons room and slammed it shut. By the time Rory had reacted and thrown herself at the handle to open it, the sliding deadbolt was already back in position.

"What in all hells is going on?" she shouted, banging a fist on the door.

"There is no way I am letting you anywhere near my commissions. I won't have you getting in my way, either. Because of you, I've let my vigilance slip, and now this man is stealing my jobs. Well, he is in for a rude surprise, let me tell you. But you" — as he spoke, Longinus slapped the door with his hand — "will not get in my head and distract me as you have been doing every day since I met you, you hear me?"

Rory shouted and swore and threw a couple of kicks at the door for good measure as she looked around her. She was in a tiny room with a single, high window. Against the wall was a set of shelves with cloths, rags, bottles, and other cleaning supplies. A couple of brooms were stashed in a corner, along with buckets and scouring brushes.

The window was the only obvious way out, but it was narrow — possibly even too narrow for her. It was also too high for her to get to. Maybe if she climbed the shelves, she could break out of the window that way, although any smashing glass would be easily heard from the weapons room. Still, it was worth a try. If Longinus thought he could keep her locked up in here, he had another thing coming.

Still shouting and swearing to cover any noise she might make, she set to work.

CHAPTER

25

Once Longinus had changed into his black silks, night had fully settled. He went to the cupboard, but Rory had stopped making a racket. He guessed she had gone to sleep.

Good.

He checked the little trap that he had spent the last hour or so preparing. It would fit into the niche where clients normally left him commissions, and if the copycat assassin was stealing his jobs... Well, he would soon find out what it meant to cross the Viper.

Longinus slipped the contraption in his pocket, careful not to knock it against anything. It was designed to burn the hands and arms of anyone who set it off and cover them with blotches of bright purple murex dye, thus making the culprit easier to identify.

He headed out, pleased to finally be alone with his thoughts. He hadn't been able to write or even to think in peace these last few days. The girl was always there, talking, making noise, being herself. It was exhausting. *She* was exhausting. And irritating.

He thought of the pamphlets that needed writing. A small part of him, a very small part of him, yearned to lock himself away in his room and write and write until all of this had blown over.

He took a deep breath, squared his shoulders, and raised his chin haughtily.

The Viper is never defeated. The Viper fights to the end and wins. I will find this mysterious man, I will find him and kill him. I will create a poison so vicious, so deadly, Damsport will shiver with fear at the mere mention of it.

Soon enough he reached Thirteen, at the end of which was the cemetery, on a hilltop by the sea. Although Thirteen was technically a thoroughfare, it was in fact little more than a wide alley between dilapidated houses. Pottersfield was even less desirable an area than the Rookery — nobody wanted to live near the dead.

The streets were dark with no vapour lamps to light the way. Curtain-less windows looked down like black, empty eyes. The few who lived in Pottersfield stayed away from Thirteen, leaving those who visited the dead unobserved. Which suited Longinus just fine, since he had no desire for anyone to see him. Remembering that he had most likely been watched by the docks, he moved carefully, his keen eyes and ears ready to pick up the slightest movement or sound. Something Rory had said earlier nagged at him. Much as he hated to admit it, she had a point. Why was this man doing all this? Why discredit him, and why the interest in getting Rory out of the way?

The houses on either side of the road gave way to gently sloping ground on which grew ragged clumps of trees. Up ahead, Longinus could see the hill on which the cemetery was perched, sticking out of Damsport like the crown of a bald man's head.

Most of the dead were burned at sea, but certain religions still insisted on a ground burial. A few expensive marble crypts dotted the top of the hill, but for the most part, it was a simple cemetery with tombstones protruding from the ground like dragon's teeth.

He paused at his usual spot within the trees, a little way from the wrought-iron fence that circled the cemetery. From there he commanded a view of most of the cemetery, except for the part that backed out onto jagged rocks, against which the sea dashed itself in great sprays of foam.

A white cat, its eyes so pale they look liked moonstones, walked lazily towards him. As it reached the fence, it sat on its haunches, regarding Longinus with obvious antipathy. It opened its mouth, but no sound came out.

Every cat in the Damsport cemetery was voiceless and only appeared at night. Some said they were the spirits of the dead, while others said that they guarded the dead and to touch them meant touching the Other Side. Longinus simply stayed clear of them.

He waited to see if anyone stirred behind the wrought-iron fence, savouring the peace and calm that came with being alone. The thought of having to go through many more days with Rory by his side, with her constant insolence, her irritating questions, her —

"So, why are we here?"

Longinus yelped, nearly jumping out of his skin. Rory stood behind him, regarding him coolly, her eyes pale in the moonlight.

"Quiet," he hissed, heart still pounding from his fright. "Someone might hear you."

"You're talking louder than me," she replied in a whisper.

Longinus pinched his nose and summoned up every ounce of *noblesse oblige*. He hadn't thought it possible for the girl to be any more irritating than she had already been, but there it was.

"How did you even get out?" he asked.

"Please." Rory waved her hand as though the question was beneath her. "I been breaking in and out of places since you were sucking your thumb and crapping yourself."

"Don't try to be a smartarse when you can't even count. You didn't exist when I was a child."

"Oh, I know that, I just assumed you were a slow developer," she replied with a smile. "Now shhh, or someone might hear you."

It was all Longinus could do not to throttle the girl. She was right, though — he couldn't afford a scene now, not when someone might hear. He controlled himself with some difficulty.

"You're going to have to learn to stay locked up when I lock you away," he managed in a low whisper.

"I ain't good at being locked away. Sorry. Why are we at the cemetery, anyway?"

"None of your business. Go back."

"No."

"Then I won't do what I came here to do."

"Fine with me, it's a beautiful night, better to spend it under the stars than in a cupboard if you ask me."

Longinus pinched the bridge of his nose again.

The gods give me strength, but the girl is a she-devil. A harpy, a harridan, a shrew, a termagant.

The outburst of words calmed him a little.

Taking advantage of my generous, trusting nature. I took her in, I fed her, clothed her, taught her, and she won't repay me with any obedience.

He took a couple of deep breaths, reviewing his options. Unfortunately, he was faced only with two: continue on with the girl or return home with the girl. Neither of which was acceptable.

The patience of a saint. I have the patience of a saint.

"Follow me," he whispered to Rory, "and do exactly as I say."

"Alright," she whispered back, her expression irritatingly triumphant.

"And I take back what I said the other day," he added. "If someone attacks you again, I won't be defending you, even if you are a girl. I can't imagine the number of people you've provoked to breaking point."

"Oh, is *that* what that weird conversation was about?"

"Quiet!"

Longinus couldn't believe now that he had ever harboured any delusions that the girl was in need of protection. Even worse, delusions that he should somehow be the one protecting her.

He moved silently towards the fence and followed it around until he reached the gate. It was flanked on either side with vine-covered pillars. A myriad of mythical beasts, grotesques, and various representations of death were carved into the marble, peeking out from between lustrous leaves.

They passed through the gates and weaved their way amongst the tombstones. To the right was the little hut of the grave tenders, but no light shone out of the single window. They crested the hill, passing by impressive crypts, complete with marble statues of the fates, of justice, or of whatever god or goddess the deceased had worshiped. The humid, salty sea air had nibbled away at some of the marble faces so that they resembled hideous lepers with missing eyes or noses.

On the other side of the hill, the tombstones were in much worse condition, exposed as they were to the humid, salt-laden wind. The slope was steeper too, and some of the stones leaned dangerously, as though the sea was trying to drag them in.

Longinus navigated his way with practiced ease down the slope to a particularly runty tombstone. He clucked his tongue with annoyance when he saw how neat it was: the sand and debris from the sea had been swept away, as had the cobwebs and moss that had once covered the stone.

Why can't those damned grave tenders mind their own business? They remove my moss and dead leaves every goddamned time.

He turned to Rory. "Go fetch me some dead leaves and moss over there."

"Why?"

"This tombstone is far too neat."

"Why do you care?"

"Because I need it to look eerie and neglected."

"Why?"

"Enough with your damned questions!" Longinus' voice rose dangerously.

"Shhh," whispered Rory, "you're making a scene. And if you answered me straight, I wouldn't need to ask you so many questions, now would I?"

Longinus pinched the bridge of his nose. "Fine. My clients leave me commissions here, and I need their first experience of working with me to give them chills, or they might not realise that the Viper is a dark and mysterious character. Does that satisfy you?"

"Completely," she replied with a smirk.

"Now can you do as I asked?"

Thankfully, she did, and he was spared any more of her insolence.

CHAPTER

26

Rory was gathering moss when she heard a strangled noise. Looking back, she could see Longinus standing by the little tombstone, holding a piece of paper in his hands. Even in the moonlight, she could see that the colour had drained from his face. She hurried over and as she got near, she spotted something shiny and golden by his feet: three golden guineas.

"What's the matter?" she asked as she reached him. From where she stood, Rory could see a cavity at the top of the tombstone, and she guessed that was where the paper had come from. Longinus was still staring at it with horror.

"Longinus?"

"Nothing," he replied shakily, pocketing the paper.

He produced a small contraption from his pocket with wires sticking out of it and flung it to the sea. There was a tiny explosion when it hit the water.

"We're leaving," he said.

"What about the dead leaves and moss?"

"No need."

He turned and walked away, without waiting for her or picking up the coins. Never one to let good money go to waste, Rory grabbed them and hurried after him.

"What was on the paper?"

He didn't answer.

Rory caught up with him, tripped, and went flying into his back. He righted her distractedly, not even commenting on her clumsiness.

Had to be something serious then.

She unfolded the paper she had lifted from his pocket. Two words were written in very neat letters: Longinus Pendergast.

"That's your name," she said stupidly.

Longinus whipped around, saw the paper, and snatched it from her.

"Why is your name on there?" she asked. "Do you think that means the copycat wants you dead? Surely he must know that you're the Viper, right?"

He continued walking wordlessly and didn't say another word until they reached the house. Once back in the weapons room, Rory tried to engage him again.

"So what's our next move?"

"There is no 'our next move.' We don't do anything. We will not speak of this, of any of this gods-damned business again."

Well, at least he was speaking again. He threw himself down into a chair, covering his eyes with one hand.

"So what, the copycat now wants you dead too, you had to be expecting that. Ain't you gonna do nothing? What's wrong with you? I very much doubt that the Viper —"

"What in all hells do you want from me?" he shouted, taking her aback. "You want training? Fine, I'll give you training. At no point did we agree that you could poke your nose into my affairs. You will leave this alone and never speak of it again, because I am damn well telling you to!"

Rory wiped the spittle from her face, at a loss for a reply. Longinus' features were contorted, the tendons on his neck standing out like cords.

He stood up abruptly and pulled a crystal bottle from a small cabinet, along with a matching crystal tumbler. He poured himself two fingers of port, his hands shaking so that the bottleneck clinked against the glass.

"Go away, Rory," he said, downing the glass in one go. "Go away, and leave me alone."

As he walked out of the room cradling the tumbler and the bottle to his chest, she realised that it wasn't anger contorting his features. It was fear.

***

Rory headed out, closing Longinus' door behind her. She didn't want to stay on her own in his house, and she needed space to put her thoughts in order.

Whatever was going on, it was getting more and more confusing. None of it made sense, least of all Longinus' reaction to seeing his name on the paper. Surely, it was just a message from the copycat, a threat. He had to have been expecting something like that — after all, the copycat assassin had hired Jake to get rid of her. It was only logical that he would want to get rid of Longinus too, if his aim was to replace the Viper.

Which brought her back to the question that she just couldn't answer. Why would he want to be the Viper?

She came across a house with crumbling mortar between the bricks and, almost without thinking, she scaled the wall up to the rooftops. Damsport was bathed in silvery moonlight and from where she was, Rory could see almost all of the thoroughfares, meeting at the Great Bazaar. The streets were quiet in this part of town, the inhabitants turning in for the night, but in the distance, she could see dancing lights and movements. Faint snatches of sound and laughter floated up in the still air. Those areas of Damsport that specialised in night trade would just be getting into the swing of things.

The street she was on was flanked by terraced houses, and she walked from roof to roof easily. The air was thick and moist as exhaled breath, and the tension in the air told her that another summer storm was about to break.

As she walked, her mind kept returning to Longinus' reaction to his name on the paper. He was an assassin, even if he was an eccentric one. He dealt with death. Someone wanting to kill him shouldn't be that terrifying. Shocking maybe, upsetting at a stretch, but terrifying? She had seen how bad his hands were shaking. This wasn't just surprise at having been targeted.

Maybe there had been something on the paper to scare him. Could she have missed a symbol? She was pretty sure it was blank other than the name. Maybe the handwriting? Yes, maybe he recognised it. That would explain the fear. And if he recognised the handwriting, that meant Longinus knew who the copycat was. Maybe all of this was personal. It certainly would explain why the copycat would make the Viper look like a pervert.

It even explained why Jake had at first been hired to get her out of the way and not necessarily kill her. She was just in the wrong place at the wrong time — this wasn't about her and it never had been. She probably had just been an annoyance, one that had to be removed, and it was simply a coincidence that she had met Corian just before his death.

Of course, that didn't change the fact that the attack on her had been very real and very life threatening. Rory touched the spot at her throat where for days she had borne a red mark. If there was one thing she had learned growing up on the streets, it was that if someone threatened you, you had to come back at them with everything you had right away, or you'd be a goner sooner rather than later. Especially if you were as scrawny as she was. The first thing to do would be to get Longinus to tell her who the copycat was. Then they could put together a plan of attack.

Yes, she would go and confront Longinus about it right now. She was halfway back when the storm broke, immediately soaking her to the skin. She skidded back as fast as she could on the slick tiles.

CHAPTER 2

Longinus sat behind his desk, drinking his port. A warm light from the vapour lamp illuminated his room and all the familiar things that normally gave him comfort. His hands were shaking so violently, he kept having to put the tumbler down for fear of spilling port on his papers.

He drained the tumbler in one go and poured himself a second glass, the bottle tinkling against the glass. He drained that and poured himself a third, drained that too, and then poured a fourth for good measure. The port helped, steadying his hands.

It occurred to him that for the first time in a long time, there was someone in the house with him. He wasn't alone. He could go downstairs and talk to Rory.

A stupid idea.

He looked at the painting on the wall, at his mother, proud and beautiful. It was her best painting, although he hated how he had been captured: as a shy toddler, clinging to his mother's legs and looking back at the painter. The cut-out portion of the painting stared back at him, and he shivered. His thoughts wandered to the room farther down the corridor with its deadbolt, and suddenly the urge to speak to Rory was overwhelming. Even putting up with her would be better than being alone.

He ran to the door and yanked it open, rushing to the stairs and taking them two by two.

"Rory!"

The weapons room was empty.

Fool, what exactly did you expect?

He hovered at the doorway, then went to the shelf, and selected a few poisons. The Spraying Mantis, with its atomiser; Throws of Death, enclosed in a fragile glass vial that would break on impact; and his beloved Writing on the Wall, although he handled that last one with particular care. As he returned upstairs cradling the bottles, he fancied he could feel warmth emanating from them, as though they were comforting him.

When he reached his desk, he lined up the poisons along the far edge. Then he pulled out a fresh sheaf of paper, dipped his pen in the inkwell, and began to write.

The house was perfectly silent, save for the scratching of his nib against the page.

***

Longinus was startled to find he had woken up in his bed. He sat up. Something felt odd. The vapour lamp had gone out, and the room was as dark as a tomb. A cool draft blew on his skin, making him shiver, and he understood what was odd. He was naked.

He frowned.

I don't remember getting undressed. Where is my nightshirt?

He pushed the covers back and leaned over the edge of the bed, groping through the dark for the chair on which he normally left his clothes from the previous day. His hands only found empty air. The draft was still blowing, and it was now really quite cold. He looked around for the source of it but could see nothing. The darkness was so absolute he couldn't even see his fingers when he waved them in front of his face.

Part of him wanted nothing more than to rush back to the safety of his covers.

I'm far too old to be afraid of the dark.

He got out of bed, and he heard something that made every hair on his body stand on edge. A tiny scraping sound, like a rusty deadbolt being pulled back. He froze.

The sound stopped.

Maybe I imagined it. Just a trick of the night, the house stretching…

He stood in the dark, waiting. The house stayed silent.

See, just a trick of the night. If you go out, you'll find the door closed as always.

He moved forward, hands stretched blindly ahead of him. It occurred to him that he had no idea what direction he was walking in, and he felt a jolt of irrational panic at the thought of being lost in his own room.

His hands alighted on the reassuring wood of the door. He opened it.

The light in the corridor made him blink, and he shielded his eyes with one hand.

That's odd, I don't remember seeing any light filtering through the bottom of the —

Farther down the hallway, the deadbolt moved, the rust catching and making the same scraping sound he had heard earlier. Longinus stared, transfixed. The deadbolt lurched a little farther back, paused, then moved again.

He watched with horrified fascination as it progressed farther and farther back. It had almost reached the end when Longinus finally galvanised himself into action.

He threw himself down the corridor, hands stretched out towards it, but the deadbolt moved too. Just as he reached the door, it slipped fully back. Longinus came to an abrupt stop, and the door swung open silently.

A sickening buzzing sound started up in his mind, as though a million flies had taken up residence there. In the distance was a little voice: *blood everywhere blood everywhere blood everywhere*

With hypnotising slowness, blood crept out of the room, luridly red, disgustingly shiny. It oozed out into a puddle that widened as it came out the door, spreading into the hallway. Longinus backed away slowly, holding his breath, unable to look away.

The fibres of the carpet soaked the blood up so that a red stain spread through it faster than the blood moved. It spread towards Longinus, ignoring the other side of the hallway as though it had a will of its own. He stepped away from it until his back hit the closed door to his bedroom.

The red, viscous puddle crept after him. Still he couldn't look away. So much blood. Smelling so sickeningly rich.

His hand felt the wood behind him for the door handle, but he found nothing but a smooth, uninterrupted surface. He turned in a panic, both hands frantically searching the door for the handle. It was gone.

Turning back, he saw that the blood had caught up with him. It was inches away, gleaming threateningly. His hands scrambled again at the door, fingernails scratching the wood, searching for something, anything that would open it. The blood reached his toes, oozing around each one.

Longinus screamed.

CHAPTER

28

Rory bounded up the stairs when she heard Longinus crying out.

"Longinus!" she pounded at his door. "You alright?"

Silence.

She pressed her ear to the door. After a while, she heard a faint whimpering sound and she listened harder.

"Longinus?" she repeated, lower this time.

"Don't cut me! Please don't cut me," came Longinus' voice.

The tall man — he had to have broken in somehow. Rory went to open the door, but it was locked. Cursing, she pulled out her picks. Longinus whined and whimpered, and she dropped one. She picked it up, but her normally nimble fingers had turned clumsy from the panic — she was all left thumbs.

At last, the lock gave and she burst into the room. The noise woke Longinus, and he started up from his desk, against which his head had been resting. A sheet of paper was stuck to his cheek. He would have looked comical if it wasn't for the way he looked around him, eyes wild with fear.

"You alright?" asked Rory. "I heard you from downstairs, I thought maybe the man had broken in."

Longinus blinked and looked about him, breathing hard.

"It's fine, it's fine," he muttered, removing the paper from his face. "I was just having a weird dream."

"A dream?" As she spoke, Rory scanned the room, looking for any signs of a break in. Everything looked normal.

"I said I'm fine," said Longinus. "There's nothing for you to concern yourself with."

"You sure?"

"Yes. Now go away, I have work to do."

"I'll be downstairs," she said, heading for the door. She would leave confronting him about the handwriting until morning.

Longinus nodded. As she walked out, Rory saw Longinus grab his pen with a shaking hand.

***

Rory spent a fitful night's sleep. She sat in the weapons room at first, listening out for any noise, jumping up to investigate every creak of the house. She felt sure that the tall man would try something during the night. When the rain had stopped, she decided to head out for the roof so she could keep an eye out on the street should he try to break in.

No one came near the house.

207

After a time the rain started again, making it hard to see anything. She returned inside to wait for Longinus to get up. His nightmare had only confirmed her suspicions: he knew who was after them and he was afraid.

"What a beautiful morning," Longinus announced as he walked in.

He wore an emerald green waistcoat embroidered with gold thread, over a white shirt and ochre trousers, and was wreathed in lace that peeked out from sleeves, collars, and hems like so many clouds of smoke. A decorative rapier hung from his belt, the basket an intricate wisp of golden filigree.

"Good to hear you're in such good spirits," said Rory, "'cause I want to talk to you. Last night I was thinking about all that happened, right, and I worked out that you know who the man is. Don't try to tell me otherwise, alright."

Much to her surprise, Longinus didn't even try to dodge the question.

"Yes, I know exactly who is behind all this."

"Good. Who is it?"

He pulled out the piece of paper from his sleeve cuff and skewered it to the top of the alchemy bench with his index finger. "See here. From the meanness of the 'L' and the sharpness of the 'N's, I can tell that the writer is a petty, small-minded man. And there," he stabbed at a 'T', "look at that. The 'T' of cowardice. Oh, I tell you the man behind all this is a coward. That 'O' shows jealousy. What we are dealing with here is a craven, inconsequential individual, a spiteful little parasite, whose admiration of me has turned to envy and now to this. It is of no more threat to me than a fly is to a lion."

"You really expect me to believe that you're getting all that from his handwriting?"

"Graphology isn't just an art, Rory, it's a *science*. And it tells me that this is not worth my time. The Viper is above that sort of nonsense; it will take more than that to strike fear into his noble heart." As he spoke, he struck his fist on his chest, raising his chin with defiance.

"So why were you so afraid last night? And that doesn't explain why he'd want to get me out of the way, too. What about Dr Corian and the Old Girl's servant? For a coward, he's killing pretty effectively."

"Bore someone else with your complaints, my dear, the Viper has more important fish to fry. Now!" He clasped his hands together. "We have training to do."

"Piss on training, we can't just pretend this ain't happening! You were afraid last night, I saw it. You can't pretend you wasn't. You know who's behind this, I know you do. Tell me, and none of this nonsense about handwriting. I know it's a man, I know he's tall, and I know he has a hooked nose."

Surprise flashed briefly on Longinus' face.

"You see, you know something, I saw it on your face just now," said Rory. "What's going on? Who is he?"

When Longinus didn't answer, she continued.

"Even if you don't tell me who it is, I'll work it out. It might take me longer, but one way or another, I'll get there and —"

"We should get some food before we begin today's training," said Longinus. "Training on an empty stomach should always be avoided. I'll get my hat."

He ran out of the room and Rory rubbed her forehead. What was she missing — why the ridiculous behaviour this morning?

Longinus returned with a matching green hat adorned with a frothy white feather. It was set on his head at a rakish angle. He paused in the doorway, striking a pose. Rory sighed. Someone wanted them dead, and he clearly meant business, and all she had to work with was this: a posing buffoon covered in silk and lace, who had quite possibly lost some of his sanity to the night.

"Let's go," she said, heading for the door.

Maybe food would help.

"What a beautiful day!" Longinus cried as they stepped outside.

Rory looked at him in confusion. Had he lost his sight as well as his mind overnight? Was this some elaborate prank? The sky was still full of roiling clouds, so thick and low they almost touched the taller rooftops.

"It puts me in *such* a poetic mood," continued Longinus. "The shining sun stirs my soul and sets my senses soaring, surpassing all summits to the skies above." He smiled at her, and then his face froze. "I cannot let that line go unwritten. I might forget it." He ran back into the house.

"What are you on about?" she called after him. "There ain't no sodding sun today!"

"Poetic license, Rory, poetic license."

Rory waited, tapping her foot.

When Longinus finally came back out, she did her best to pretend the poetic outburst hadn't happened and tried to engage him again.

"Look, I get that you don't want to talk about who's after us, right, but can you at least tell me what he looks like? Then I can see if it matches the man I saw."

Then she could work out if it was just the tall man or if he had a partner.

"I have a hankering for something a little rustic today," replied Longinus, "so we're going to the Great Bazaar. There's a man there who sells the most divine little pastries made with plantain. Simple but oh so full of flavour. Oh, Rory, the culinary delights you still have to experience! Sometimes I think that being as ignorant and obtuse as you are is in fact a gift, for everything is new and wonderful to your stunted senses."

"Fine, ignore me all you want — I know you're hearing what I'm saying. I'm gonna try again after we've had food."

Longinus didn't reply.

CHAPTER
29

The Great Bazaar spilled beyond the confines of its circus, like a stain spreading out through the weave of the city. The meaner stalls had set up in the shade of the lanes, their owners selling second-hand toys and clothes, only slightly rusted cogs, cracked earthenware and pottery, small clockwork items in need of repair, tools with a few years left in them, and other similar items. Here and there, puddles of rainwater reflected the grey clouds, looking from the distance like huge silver coins dropped from the sky.

The markets were busier than normal, as always in the run up to the Revels. Visitors, merchants, and street performers converged on Damsport this time of year so that the streets around the Great Bazaar were swollen with people, like so many rivers after a flood.

Rory and Longinus walked past the stalls, the sellers calling to them, hawking their wares. Lengthy negotiations took place around them — the farther you were from the Great Bazaar, the more ruthless the negotiating. Out here, the purchase of a piece of dirty yellow linen could take over half an hour as each party tried to squeeze the other for every last coin bit.

Rory and Longinus followed the lanes as they wound towards the Great Bazaar, and the closer they got, the more the noise grew. When they stepped out of the lanes and into the Great Bazaar proper, the noise exploded into a cacophony of sound, no longer kept in check by the walls and houses of the lanes. It was as though they had pierced a membrane. Human and animal voices mingled into an unintelligible roar, interspersed with the sounds of metal being beaten, machines hissing steam, and instruments being played with varying degrees of skill by street performers.

Rory and Longinus had arrived in the book section, where there were no stalls: books were simply piled up in tottering towers over thick rugs to protect them from the filth that flowed out of the Wet Market at the centre of the Bazaar. The towers created a maze through which customers strolled. Each section of the maze was guarded by a bookseller ready to leap out at anyone making more than the briefest of eye contact with his books.

"I know a shortcut," said Longinus.

He navigated the maze briskly, waving away any booksellers that tried to approach him. Rory stuck close to his heels. Once out of the book maze, they passed clockwork merchants, the cloth sellers, skirted around the spice and dried herb quarter with its pungent, brightly coloured mountains of spices, and reached the assault on the senses that was the Wet Market.

The Wet Market was the centre of the Great Bazaar, and therefore the very heart of Damsport. But whereas most hearts pulsate, pumping out life's blood, Damsport's heart dripped.

Live fish and crustaceans dripped seawater onto the cobblestones, and dead fish dripped murky viscera. Blood dripped from meat cleavers, whey from cheesecloths, ale through the cracks of poorly constructed barrels, and piss from table legs, attesting to the passage of a stray dog. Milk dripped from jugs, from udders, from chins; berries dripped juice; makeshift awnings dripped leftover rainwater; priests dripped holy water.

Sweat dripped from the faces of porters, bent under heavy loads, wine dripped down the chins of those checking its quality, and snot dripped from children's and old men's noses.

Fat dripped from sausages, dripping dripped from fried fish, vinegar dripped from prawn dumplings, eaten by hand straight from enormous bamboo steamers. Beer dripped from spilt tankards, mud-coloured tobacco water from water pipes, wine from broken bottles, brandy from over-hurried gulps, fire liquor from glasses dashed onto the cobbles, tea from teapot spouts, and more urine dripped from over-refreshed men.

All of it drip-drip-dripped onto the Wet Market's cobblestones, found its way to the gutters, and trickled off along each of the Twelve, gathering speed thanks to the gentle downward slopes and carrying the lifeblood and stench of the Wet Market out to the rest of Damsport.

Thirteen, however, always remained dry: the cemetery was uphill of the market and appropriately so, for the dead have no need of life, nor blood.

Longinus made his way through the market, pushing through the crowd effortlessly. As Rory followed him, she marvelled at the difference clothes could make. Where once she was regarded with suspicion by all, shooed or even kicked away, now stall owners called out to her, trying to attract her attention.

"Tongue, heart, liver, we got them all," shouted a girl of no more than ten. She sat on the stall table itself, legs swinging from its edge. Around her, offal hung from hooks, already giving off the rich and sickly smell of meat left too long in the heat. An older woman, no doubt the mother and stall owner, had set up a hammock amongst the meat, hanging it from two larger hooks. She was fast asleep in it, her mouth open.

"Eyes," called another girl. "Every kind of eyes you could want. We got sheep, we got camel, we got fish, we got snail, we got — hello, miss, care for an eye or two?"

Rory shook her head.

"Maybe you want to buy some starmole eyes?" asked the girl with a grin.

Starmoles were well known in Damsport for being eyeless. The little creatures had been discovered during the attempted dig of the new underground cistern and had become something of a mascot for the city.

"Aye, I'll buy them on Never's day," Rory replied.

"Shame for me you ain't foreign," replied the girl. "I could do with selling starmole eyes today."

"That so? You selling them for double price to foreigners, I bet."

"Triple price sometimes. Starmole eyes are as rare as they come." The girl winked.

"What kind of eyes do you pass off as starmole eyes?" asked Rory, curious.

The girl turned to grab one of her jars.

"Well, well, haven't we gone up in the world," said a sarcastic voice to Rory's right.

Rafe swaggered towards her.

"Every time I see you," he said, "you change. First a bath, now new clothes. Really, like I said before, you didn't have to go to all this trouble for me. I'm touched, but not interested."

"Oh, go away," replied Rory, annoyed that she couldn't come up with a better response.

"Why? Are you going to claim that the Great Bazaar's yours, too? What a powerful property magnate you must be."

"You think you're so clever, don't you?"

"I don't think, I know." Rafe's smile widened.

"Ever heard of modesty?"

"A waste of time."

Rory looked around for Longinus to tell him they were leaving, but there was no sight of green silk anywhere.

"Dammit," she muttered.

Why couldn't he have waited? She glanced around, craning her head, but she was too short to see very far across the crowd.

"I have to go," she said to Rafe, but he fell into step with her.

"Why, are you on an errand? A quest? An adventurer searching for an adventure? I could be your sidekick, you know. Or your love interest. There's always a sidekick and a love interest in stories."

"Thought you said you weren't interested."

"Well, obviously. But I'd allow *you* to be."

"Ain't you generous."

When she still hadn't caught sight of Longinus, Rory began to worry. Rafe said something, but she paid no attention, her eyes still scanning the crowd for green silk. He stood in front of her, and she tried to walk past him, but he blocked her.

"Not very polite to ignore me like that."

"I have to go, I'm looking for someone. It's serious, alright? I don't have time for you."

"No time for your love interest? You've got your priorities all wrong."

"Dammit, let me go!"

"Fine. Tell me your name first."

"Rory. Happy?"

"Never. What about the name of the person who did that to your face? Was it the man with you at the baths?"

Rory stopped scanning the crowd and gave him a cool look. "That ain't none of your business."

He hesitated over his answer, his face serious for the first time. Then he sketched a mocking bow. "As the lady wishes. You seem to have it all under control, anyhow."

Rory pushed past him and into the crowd, her worry for Longinus quickly turning into panic. She reached the cooked-food section of the Wet Market, and still there was no sign of him. She spotted a half-empty cart that had been left unattended, and she clambered onto it to get a better vantage point. The crowd moved around her, shifting in a myriad of colours, but nowhere could she see Longinus' distinctive green waistcoat.

When she looked to her right, her eyes alighted on a man who stuck head and shoulders above the crowd. His nose was hooked and his features dark. He was staring at her. Rory froze. The man's eyes flicked to a point slightly to her left, and he began to push through the crowd. Rory looked at the direction he was headed and at last saw a flash of emerald green.

Longinus.

She leapt off the cart and dove into the mass of people, scurrying as quickly as she could. When she spotted an upturned crate, she jumped on top of it to reorient herself. Longinus wasn't far, but she could make out the man moving swiftly through the masses towards him, like the shadow of a shark underwater.

She ran hell for leather, not caring who she knocked into.

"Longinus!" she called. "Longinus!"

She could just see him ahead, and she did her best to go faster, shoving and pulling people out of her way. She felt, too late, a hard wooden edge against her thighs, and she flew headfirst into a stall selling curried fish balls. Two very large, very hot, and very full copper pots crashed to the ground, while the stall top fell off its trestles.

People cried and shouted as Rory picked herself up, wincing at the burn on her arm from one of the copper pots.

"You crazy girl," shouted the stall owner. "You pay me for this, you hear?" He made to grab her but Rory ducked, speeding off towards Longinus.

"Come back here!" shouted the stall owner, giving chase.

Rory ducked and weaved through the crowd, narrowly avoiding the stall owner's grasp.

When she finally reached Longinus, the stall owner got a hold of her collar and yanked her back.

"You pay me what you owe me right now!" he roared.

At the same time, Rory saw the tall man break through the crowd. He hesitated as he saw the scene, then turned, and melted back into the crowd.

"What have you done now?" asked Longinus.

"She your daughter?" asked the stall owner. "She knocked my stall over, cost me a day's trading."

"Not a problem," replied Longinus smoothly. "How much do you normally make in a day?"

The stall owner paused, gauging Longinus' clothes.

"Ten jinn in silver," he said.

Rory knew full well that he was lying, but she was more concerned about getting out of the Bazaar. They were far too vulnerable here. In this kind of crowd, a knife between the ribs was an easy thing for a professional.

Longinus paid up, the stall owner pulling out his portable scales to weigh the coins. Satisfied, he left with a final warning look for Rory. She grabbed Longinus' arms.

"Come on, we gotta go," she said, still scanning the crowd nervously. "I just saw the man who's after us. He was going for you, and I think he only stopped because of all the fuss."

Longinus jerked his arm away. "Unhand me. I will not be manhandled by the likes of you."

"Fine, but we got to go, come on."

"You can go, I'm staying right here."

"Longinus," cried Rory in exasperation, "will you stop with whatever this is? I know you know —"

"I told you not to talk about it anymore," he snapped, walking away.

Rory hurried after him. "Oh, so *now* you're listening to me. Took you long enough. So, who is he?"

"Who?"

"Seriously, stop playing dumb with me. The man just now, the man in the crowd."

"I have no idea."

"Oh, pull the other one. You know who he is. Why won't you tell me? You want to get us both killed or something? What's going —"

Longinus spun around and bore down on her with such intensity that she shrank back.

"Shut up!" he yelled. People around them jumped, looking to see what the fuss was about.

He grabbed Rory by the arm and dragged her through the market.

"Hey! What — Longinus, what are you doing? Let me go!"

When they reached a deserted lane, he shoved her forward and released her.

"I told you to stop talking about it. I said you weren't to speak or do anything about any of this business anymore. How else can I make myself clear to you?" His voice shook. "Stop it, stop everything. Leave it alone. And leave me alone while you're at it. Go away and crawl back to whatever hole it is you came from. And do not, and I mean it, do *not* speak of any of this again. You hear me?"

Without waiting for an answer, Longinus marched away.

CHAPTER

30

Rory followed Longinus through the streets, calling after him, but he paid her no attention. Her attempts to apologise fell on deaf ears, as did her reminders of the danger they were both in. She kept an eye out for the man from the Bazaar, but she didn't see anyone following them or paying them any particular interest.

When they reached the house, Longinus let himself in and closed the door behind him, leaving her outside. She heard the sound of a lock turning.

"Longinus," she tried again, banging on the door.

"Leave me be."

"I can break in, you know."

"Harpy, shrew, harridan! Termagant!"

Rory smiled. At least he sounded a little more like himself. Although she had no idea what that last word meant. Nor the second to last, for that matter. Probably not complimentary, though.

"Longinus, come on. I said I'm sorry."

Silence.

"Longinus?"

She hovered by the door, unsure what to do next. Much as Longinus wanted her to leave it alone, she had no interest in waiting for the tall man to attack again. That was a good way to wind up dead in a gutter somewhere. More worryingly, she had recognised him. It had been a fleeting impression, and she hadn't had time to think on it at the Bazaar, but she had definitely seen his face before, and that unsettled her. Try as she might now, she couldn't get any kind of handle on where or when that might have been.

Not knowing what else to do, she eventually walked away and headed to the cemetery. The tall man had to have been there to leave the note for Longinus, and maybe she could find a sign of his passing, a clue to jog her memory. She climbed up to the roofs the first chance she got, moving carefully and glancing frequently around for any sign of someone following her, skin prickling with awareness.

The roofs were as empty as always, and she made it to the cemetery without any trouble.

***

The cemetery had a very different feel in daylight. The voiceless cats were gone, and although the tombstones still protruded from the ground like badly aligned teeth, the crypts and the statues now just looked old and worn, rather than like ghoulish lepers. Two grave tenders, bent old men, moved methodically about the tombs. She stayed clear of them, ready with some story about visiting her uncle's grave, but they paid her no attention.

She climbed the hill and disappeared down the back where the slope was steep and the tombstones were sagging towards the sea. She found Longinus' tombstone quickly enough. First, she examined the hole at the top in which Longinus had found the paper with his name. It was smooth and even, obviously carved by human hands. She could see nothing of interest, and a quick feel with her fingers revealed nothing more. She began to examine the surroundings. She was just about to give up the exercise as futile when she caught a whiff of something. A faint smell, like sulphur but sweeter. She sniffed the air, moving this way and that, trying to find the source of the smell.

A little way away, she spotted an ochre stain on a pale rock. As she approached, the smell got stronger. There it was, the feeling she had smelled it before. The colour of the stain was familiar too, although she couldn't place it, either. She rubbed a finger on it and brought it up to her nose. Whatever it was, it was unpleasant. It evoked a vague memory, somewhere dark, enclosed… She focused on the colour, groping through her memories. Where had she seen that colour before, where…?

She gasped. The underground cistern.

As a child, she had followed some workers back when they were attempting to dig a new cistern into which redirect the flow of an underwater river. There was the Old Cistern, of course, but even back then it had been old — some claimed it was as old as the underground tunnels and that both tunnels and cistern were far older than Damsport.

The Old Girl had ordered the creation of a new, more modern cistern that would better fit the fast-growing city.

The dig, however, had been beset with troubles. The diggers found that the only space beneath Damsport which wasn't taken up by the tunnels was made of an odd, ochre-coloured clay that stank and crumbled. They did the best they could, digging out a large chamber, but in spite of using beams and buttresses to support the walls and ceiling, half of it collapsed. Worse, after a time they discovered that the clay contaminated the water, turning it undrinkable. It was deemed impossible to create a working cistern, and the whole initiative had been abandoned.

Rory had snuck into the digging chamber not long before the project was cancelled. Like every child in Damsport, she was fascinated by the tunnels, and she wanted to see them for herself. There was no shortage of stories describing the monsters that roamed Damsport's underground maze. Every child, even those on the streets, grew up hearing of the tunnels with their traps, their hidden abysses, their otherworldly creatures, and of course, no story was complete without mention of the myriad of ghosts that remained trapped underground, attesting to the lives the tunnels had claimed. Rumour even had it that starmoles were eyeless so as to be blind to the horrors that took place around them.

Rory had wanted to be the first kid to make it to the tunnels, and she planned to bring back more than just stories to prove she had been there. She had imagined that her escapade in the tunnels would make her famous, an adventurer to be reckoned with. Sadly, she only made it to the first digging chamber — far enough to see and smell the odd ochre clay — before someone saw her and dragged her out. For her efforts she got a spanking, a roll of bread, and orders to 'put some meat on her bones.' She had met the Scarred Woman soon after, and she forgot about her fascination with the tunnels.

Rory felt for her medals, letting them tinkle between her fingers as she thought. Of course, she no longer believed the stories. They were just that: stories. But the tunnels were real enough. As was the abandoned cistern. The forgotten chamber would make a perfect hiding place for someone not wanting to be seen, and if her memories were right, it was big enough to easily accommodate an alchemy bench.

The only issue was the smell, distinctive enough for someone to remember. She thought of Dr Corian in the baths. If he had been in league with the tall man and working in the underground chamber, he might have been at the baths to wash off the smell. It would have been easy to kill him there. There was the matter of his body being in the women's section, but Rory knew full well that after a certain time of the night the separation between men and women in the baths was no longer enforced. If he had gone to seek out one of the prostitutes that operated in the baths at night, the tall man could simply have killed him there and hauled his body up into the gap above the rock face.

She let her medals fall back against her chest. There was only one way to see if she was right.

***

The entrance to the now-abandoned cistern wasn't far from the cemetery, a little farther along the rocks that lined the eastern part of the peninsula. They were enormous, some balanced precariously on top of each other so that they looked like an interrupted game started by giant creatures centuries ago.

Rory picked her way over the rocks, looking for a small, natural cave. The dig had started from the back of it. She hadn't yet worked out what she would do if her theory proved to be correct — for now she would simply sneak in, observe whatever there was to observe, and take it from there. She might be wrong, anyway — the underground chamber might hold nothing more than bad smells and a few starmoles, if she could even get inside since it was supposed to be sealed off.

She found the cave easily enough, although its ceiling was lower than she remembered. If she stretched her fingers up, she could easily touch it. She thought of how tall the man from the Bazaar had been. He would have to stoop to come this way.

At the back of the cave, she could see a pile of stones where the tunnel entrance had been. Her stomach sank a little: she was wrong. The chamber was still sealed off. She approached it anyway, and as she stepped to the side, her heart fluttered like a moth in a glass jar. The pile of stones wasn't quite blocking the way: there was a gap to the right, just wide enough for a person to squeeze through. The illusion that the way was sealed off had been carefully maintained, suggesting that whoever had done this wanted it kept a secret.

Rory paused. Should she go back and fetch Longinus? There was no telling what she would find beyond, but it seemed pretty clear that she would find something. Having Longinus with her might prove helpful. Then again, he had been clear enough that he didn't want her to bring up anything more to do with the copycat killer and the tall man — there was nothing to suggest he would have changed his mind in the short interval since she'd seen him last. Maybe if she had a better idea of what they were dealing with, she'd have more luck bringing him around.

She slipped inside.

The ground was even and soft enough that she could walk without making a sound. Ahead of her, the tunnel was perfectly dark, but a little light filtered through the entrance behind. She wished she had brought a vapour lamp with her, although that would alert anyone ahead of her arrival. No use wishing for something she didn't have, anyhow.

She kept her arms stretched ahead of her, progressing cautiously along the downward slope of the tunnel. Voices floated towards her, distorted and warped by the close space. Rory froze and listened, but she couldn't make out what they were saying. She crept forward and almost walked into a wall as the tunnel bent sharply to the right. A ray of light shone out from the end, and the voices cleared enough for her to hear what was being said.

"So, what do you think he'll do after we kill her?"

"I don't know. I don't care, and neither should you."

A pause.

"I think he'll tell Lady Martha to reconsider his offer," said the first voice.

"If he has any sense," replied the second, "he'll get rid of her too, and replace her with someone who'll do as she's told."

Rory's skin crawled. Lady Martha was the Old Girl's daughter.

"Only, I was thinking —"

"You're not paid to think." The second voice was hard. Without knowing why, Rory felt sure this was the tall man from the Bazaar.

"I know, I do it for free." A guffaw. "I was thinking, though. If Damsport is part of the Empire once more, things might be harder for the likes of us. I've heard the Emperor is a difficult one."

"I'm sure he'll make an exception for those who got Damsport back for him."

"True. And with all that money, well, there's no problem in the world that can't be bought. Right? Right?" Another guffaw.

Rory backed away slowly. There was no doubting it, they were talking of assassinating the Old Girl and helping turn Damsport back to the Airnian Empire. Her head swam at the thought. This was bigger than her, or Longinus. Come to think of it, how did Longinus fit in all of this?

A hand fell on her shoulder, making her cry out in surprise. She had time to register bright sparks of pain at the back of her head before the world went dark.

CHAPTER
31

When Rory opened her eyes, the first thing she was aware of was a pounding headache. The second was that her dagger was missing from her side. The third was the smell of the place: sweet sulphur. She sat up with a groan, wincing at the pain at the back of her head.

"She's awake," said a gruff voice, and two big hands lifted her up to her feet. "Don't get any ideas. You pull anything silly and I'll smack you another."

The hands released her, and Rory looked around, blinking. She was in the chamber she remembered from her childhood with its walls and ceiling of ochre clay. Sconces holding vapour lamps were affixed directly into the clay, lighting up the space. At the end of the room, Rory could see where the ceiling had caved, but in this part, the beams and buttresses still held fast.

The items of a rudimentary camp were scattered about the chamber. Sleeping holes had been dug into the clay, covered with rough-spun blankets. In a corner was a bundle of clothes — women's clothing, amongst other things. It looked, in fact, like the kind of thing a servant of the Old Girl's might wear. And to her left was a rudimentary table on top of which were instruments like the ones from Longinus' alchemy bench. In the middle was a sealed glass jar full of a dark liquid.

What little excitement Rory felt at having been right was drowned by the fact that she was trapped, that she was in way over her head, and that she was very possibly looking at a rapid shortening of her life. She continued scanning the room for anything that might help get her out of this mess.

The tall man from the Bazaar sat on an upturned crate, carefully sharpening his rapier. He glanced up at Rory, meeting her eyes steadily. Rory felt another jolt of recognition. She gasped. This time, she knew where she had seen him before. He had been sitting down then too, so she hadn't noticed his height. And anyway, her attention had been completely captivated by —

"Looks like a full house, boys!" The voice was raspy and instantly familiar.

Rory spun around, and her breath caught in her throat.

The Scarred Woman had entered the chamber, moving with the powerful ease that Rory remembered. She was instantly taken ten years back, to the childish awe she had felt then. She didn't notice the man next to the Scarred Woman right away, not until someone shoved him forward and he fell.

A bag was on his head, hiding his features, but Rory would have known that green silk waistcoat anywhere. Behind Longinus was Jake. He greeted her with a scowl.

"Pick him up," ordered the Scarred Woman, and Jake obeyed. She lifted the bag off Longinus' head, and seeing them side by side, the resemblance was unmistakable. Rory realised why Longinus had looked so odd to her at first: time had washed the Scarred Woman's features from her memory, but she had obviously picked up on the similarities without realising it.

"So, brother dear," the Scarred Woman said to Longinus in a mocking tone. "Didn't you get my note?"

To Rory's shock, Longinus nodded meekly, keeping his eyes trained to the ground. Where were the cutting remarks?

"I'm surprised you had the nerve to send your little trained monkey after me. Who knew you'd grow a backbone?"

"The name's Rory," said Rory, "and I'd thank you to use it."

The man who had lifted her up grabbed one of her arms and twisted. "Quiet," he grunted. The Scarred Woman raised an eyebrow.

"Rory? Oh, I remember you. Weren't you that kid who came up to me at the Kraken all those years ago?"

Rory felt an absurd burst of pride that her idol remembered her.

"I don't normally forget a face," continued the Scarred Woman, "but I have to say, I didn't think you'd last another summer."

"Yeah, well, people are always underestimating me."

"Evidently so. I take it that since you couldn't come with me you had to make do with my brother. I dread to think how disappointing that must have been for you. Are you still a disappointment, brother dear? "

Longinus' gaze remained fixed on the ground.

"I bet you're living in Mother's room, aren't you? Of course you are, you pathetic excuse of a man. And to think she threw me out over you."

Silence.

"Can you believe it, Raynard?" The Scarred Woman turned to the tall man from the Bazaar. "My mother, the most talented, the most ruthless of assassins, threw me out over *that*. You," she continued, jabbing Longinus in the chest, "turned Mother *soft*. With your stupid stories, your stupid clothes, your stupid alchemy. We did just fine until you came along, and then it was all about Longinus. You distracted her. You changed her. She would have been great if it wasn't for you — the whole world would have known and feared her name, not just Damsport. You *robbed* her."

Longinus seemed to shrink within himself.

"You robbed me, too," continued the Scarred Woman. "You robbed me of my first kill. If you had bled out quicker, she wouldn't have been able to save you."

Rory shifted uneasily, remembering the door with the deadbolt, the bloodstained rug, the cut-out painting. Her dream of partnering with the Scarred Woman suddenly felt uncomfortable.

"She would have forgiven me," said the Scarred Woman. "She would have, once she saw what life could be like, unburdened by you. Eventually, she would have forgotten you."

Longinus never looked up.

"Let me g-g-g —" He closed his eyes. "Go," he said at last.

Rory's eyes widened. Longinus had a stutter?

The Scarred Woman let out a bark of laughter.

"I would, brother dear, I would. But you see, first you owe me a death. Second, I have business to attend to in Damsport, and would you believe it, I need your help. I really can't thank you enough for your little imaginary friend, the Viper. He's made the perfect cover. I can't believe you're still trailing him around after all these years. 'Don't hurt me, Myran, or the Viper will come get you,'" she said in a high, whiny voice. "Well, I'm about to make your Viper famous. You can thank me for that at least. I'm going to pull off the assassination of the century and the whole world will watch. You'll become famous too, since I need a real person to take the fall for the job — although I imagine your fame will be short-lived."

She turned away from Longinus, facing Rory. "You, kid. You still want to work with me? I could use another pair of hands. If I'd known who you were, I'd have had you working for me from the beginning. Raynard doesn't have my eye for faces, and I can't do much in the open with such a recognisable scar. As it is, I'll extend you the offer you wanted so badly back then."

For a moment, Rory was elated. Her childhood dream had suddenly become reality, and it was magnificent. It must have shown on her face, because Myran laughed.

"I'll take that as a yes, then."

Rory got a handle on herself.

"You want me to help you with what? I won't help kill the Old Girl."

Just saying it out loud made her even more uneasy, and yet this was the Scarred Woman… This was her dream coming true. If she went with Myran, in time she would become a warrior, a hero, to be admired and respected. But there was no way she could be involved in a plot against the Old Girl.

And then there was Longinus. Rory found that she couldn't look at him.

"You're going to k-k-kill the Marchioness?" asked Longinus.

"What's it to you?" said Myran.

"Mother was loyal to her."

"You're wrong." Myran's face was the very picture of triumph. "You know nothing about Mother. I've been speaking to her. That's the thing when you work for the Airnian Emperor: he has connections. He introduced me to a psychic who has been in contact with her. It was Mother's suggestion that I come back to Damsport — it is her wish that the city return to the Airnian Empire."

"Mother's d-d-d-dead," said Longinus, face straining as he pushed out the last word. "The Emperor is p-puh-pl-laying you."

"Ha. The psychic said you'd say that. She knows things, things that only Mother could have told her. She knew of all the plans we had until you came along."

Something flashed across Myran's face, too fleeting for Rory to read it.

"Mother isn't dead," Myran added in a softer voice. "She's trapped in another realm, and if I secure Damsport for the Emperor, he will help me get to her."

"There is no other r-r-realm —"

"Quiet!"

The slap echoed shockingly loud in the silent chamber, Longinus' head snapping sideways. Rory gasped and threw herself forward, but the man behind her only tightened his grip.

"Don't move," he growled.

Longinus lifted his head, an angry red mark on his cheek.

"Tell me something," said Myran with a predatory smile. "Have you finally learned to say my name?"

Longinus didn't reply.

"Go on, say my name. Say Myran so Rory can see how pathetic you are."

Longinus fixed his gaze on the ground once more.

"Say it, say Myran."

The second slap was as loud as the crack of a whip. Rory knew she should say or do something. She knew that she could never partner up with Myran now, not having seen the way she treated Longinus, and yet the full force of her childhood dream, of a life's worth of desire, bore down on her, and she couldn't find her voice.

"Say Myran."

Slap. Longinus remained with his head to one side, his cheek an angry red.

"It's just two syllables."

Slap.

Slap.

Rory could feel what was left of her dream crumbling around her, and it winded her.

"Myran, Myran. Say Myran."

Slap.

This time Longinus looked at Rory. The shame and humiliation on his face were unbearable.

"Stop it!" she shouted.

Myran turned towards her, surprised. "You're siding with him?"

"Looks that way, don't it? And if you don't stop, I'll kick your arse twelve ways from the Bazaar."

Myran snorted. "So, Longinus, adding to your long list of idiocies, you now have a kid defending you. Alright," she said to Rory. "I'll bite. Let's make this a game. Untie his hands," she ordered Jake.

"You sure that's a good idea?" asked Raynard.

"Do you really think I have anything to fear from either of them?"

"True." Raynard returned to his rapier.

"I'll make you a deal, Longinus," continued Myran. "You say my name without stuttering and I'll let you both go. Just like that. I'll find another way to kill the Old Girl, and you can forget you ever had a sister. But if you stutter…" She slowly pulled out a mean-looking dagger, the blade grating against the scabbard.

Longinus made a strangled noise and threw himself backwards. Jake grabbed his arms, holding him in place.

"I'll cut you," finished Myran. "Let's see how well your little monkey defends you then."

Rory squirmed and thrashed for all she was worth, but the man behind her kept her easily pinned in place.

"N-n-n-no," stammered Longinus, eyes wide with terror. "Please m-m-muh-muh —"

"Well, that should count as a stammer, but I'll give you three tries. We are related, after all. That was your first. Now give me your hand."

She yanked his hand forward and held the blade near his palm. Longinus shrieked.

"Careful now, no sudden movements. Are you in such a hurry to see your own blood again? Hmm? Do you remember how shiny and dark it was? I always wondered how such a lily-livered coward could have such red blood. One of nature's little mysteries, I guess."

Rory thrashed harder, kicking back, but her captor only grunted, tightening his grip like a vice around her arms, making her yelp in pain.

"Make your second attempt," said Myran.

"Puh-puh —"

"Puh-puh-puh," she taunted. "You think that will sway me? Say it or get cut."

Longinus closed his eyes, his forehead a knot of concentration.

"Mmmm-m-m —"

"That's two," she cried triumphantly. "You know what they say, third time's a charm."

Longinus looked around desperately, features contorted with fear.

Rory had an idea. She abruptly stopped her squirming and let herself fall limp, as though she had fainted.

"What the —" the man holding her fumbled his grip as he tried to catch her dead weight. She immediately wriggled, throwing herself forward, and she managed to escape his grasp. She sprinted over, and just as Myran looked up, she ploughed into her, head bent forward so that she head butted her right in the stomach.

Someone pounced on Rory, flattening her to the ground, and her lungs emptied themselves.

"Little shit," wheezed Myran. "Hold her up."

Rory was picked up from the floor by two pairs of hands, as she gasped for air.

"You do care for my brother, don't you?" said Myran. "I wonder how much he cares about you. Let's up the stakes. You have one more try, Longinus. You mess it up…" Myran's blade danced a hair's breadth away from Rory's throat. "And it's going to get pretty messy."

CHAPTER

32

"What's going on here?"

Everyone's head snapped towards the room's entrance. Rory never thought she would have been happy to see a guard's uniform, but her heart positively soared at the sight.

"You're late," said Myran.

Rory's heart landed in her boots with an almost audible thud.

"It's not easy getting here unnoticed," the guard replied with a scowl. "So what's going on here? I'm not bringing anyone in if they've been butchered first. The deal was for me to make an arrest. I'm not taking part if they're not in one piece."

"It's just a little cut," said Myran dismissively. "We're playing a game."

"Then find another guard to do your business."

He crossed his arms. Myran glared at him, looking all the more terrifying for her scar, but the guard simply scowled back.

"Fine," she said at last. "Let's get them to the holding area." She patted Longinus on the cheek. "You got lucky, brother. You live to bleed another day."

A bag was stuffed over Rory's head, her arms pulled behind her back, and her hands bound.

"You pull anything funny this time and I'll wring your little neck," growled a voice by her ear.

She was led forward, and she winced as she thought she was about to walk into a wall, but to her surprise they turned and she felt stone beneath her feet. She couldn't work out which way they had gone. She hadn't seen a way out of the chamber other than back out to the sea, but soon her footsteps echoed against stone walls, and she knew they had to be in the tunnels.

She did her best to keep her bearings, to map out a path in her mind, but they twisted and turned, and she quickly felt totally and utterly lost.

"This is a very pleasant stroll," she said through the bag. "Very kind of you to show me around, where are we going exactly?"

A grunt and a cuff to the head were her only response.

Eventually they came to a halt, and the bag was yanked from her head. She gasped and staggered back.

An abyss yawned in front of her just a few feet away. To her right was Longinus, his face a blank mask. He didn't even seem to register the gulf in front of him. Behind him was Jake, but he was pointedly looking away from Rory.

The other side of the chasm was a sheer rock face with a lip sticking out at about the same level as they were now.

"The interesting thing about the tunnels," said Myran, appearing from behind Rory, "is how much there is to discover within them. Did you know, for example, that it was a machine found in the tunnels that gave us the idea for steam engines?"

Myran walked over to a lever that protruded from the edge of the gulf. Beneath it, a rectangular copper block extended three feet over the abyss. She pulled the lever, and with a hiss and the smooth sound of oiled metal, a smaller block pushed itself out, extending further over the abyss, and then another, and another, until a bridge had telescoped out all the way to the lip at the other side.

"Walk," she said, gesturing at the bridge.

"Wait," said the guard. "That's silk. I'll be having that." He ripped Longinus' green silk waistcoat open, popping off all the buttons, and pulled it off his back, leaving him with only his shirt. Longinus didn't protest.

Jake prodded him forward.

"You heard your sister," he growled. "Walk."

Longinus obeyed. His face had the kind of deadened resignation of someone who had lost everything. His boots rang out on the copper bridge, and soon enough he reached the stone platform. Rory also found herself pushed towards the bridge; she didn't put up a fight either, not wanting to risk being thrown over the side. The bridge was wide enough and she had never been afraid of heights, but as she walked across it, she began to find it really quite narrow. She was all too aware that the bridge could get pulled back beneath her at any point, but she resisted the urge to move quicker. The darkness on either side was so thick she could almost feel it on her skin, as if it was calling to her, whispering for her to jump or fall.

At last, her feet stepped onto firm rock, and she exhaled, releasing the breath she had been holding. Immediately, the bridge retracted with a hiss. She turned to see Myran at the lever with her three cronies behind her. The guard was there too, frowning at them with his arms crossed.

"They're all yours," said Myran to the guard. Rory could hear her surprisingly well across the chasm. "Wait for my signal to bring them in."

"And their things?"

Myran nodded to Raynard, who handed over Rory's dagger, her grappling hook and silk line, and her purse. Longinus had obviously not had anything of interest on him when they brought him over. The guard looked this over, obviously disappointed.

"You're getting paid enough for the job," said Myran. "Don't get greedy." There was a low note of threat to her voice.

Myran threw one last look at Longinus before leaving, the three men following her.

The guard pocketed the purse, slung the waistcoat on the back of a chair that was leaning up against the rock wall, and sat down.

He had kept Rory's dagger with him and began to examine it. Rory clenched her fists at the sight of his large hands touching it. It felt like the most personal of violations. He ran a finger along the blade, testing its sharpness, and

Rory felt it as clear as if he had run his finger down her spine.

She wanted to leap across the chasm and wrench the dagger from him, but since she didn't have springs in her feet to make her jump that kind of distance, she was going to have to bear it. She turned away with some effort to look at Longinus.

He had curled up against the rock, drawing his knees in to himself. Rory sat next to him, but he didn't acknowledge her.

"Longinus," she whispered, "you alright?"

He wouldn't meet her eye, staring instead at the rock beneath them. With his right hand, he swept the dust away from its surface. Rory left him to it. Now was not the time to worry about him. First things first: they had to get out. She had no idea how long they had until Myran gave that signal.

She stood up, pretending to stretch as she examined the rock behind her. It was so smooth that climbing it would be difficult, even for her. And anyway, it led nowhere. She walked from one end of the stone platform to the other, which only took her a few strides to achieve.

"What you doing?" called the guard.

"Stretching my legs."

"Well, you better get used to confined spaces." He laughed, as though this had been a particularly sharp display of wit.

"Seagull-pecked cretin," she muttered.

She sat back down. There was no way off that lip other than by having someone pull the lever. They were well and truly trapped.

***

After a while, Rory began pacing again, trying to find something, anything, to get them off the platform.

"You sit back down," called the guard, standing up. Bastard was still holding her dagger.

"What difference does it make?" she called back.

"You sit back down or I'll come over and make you." He pulled out his rapier.

"Sod off," Rory murmured, but too low for the guard to hear. If he came over with his rapier, there wasn't enough space for her to dodge him, and getting punctured with holes wasn't on the day's agenda.

"Longinus, I'm all out of ideas here," she whispered. "You got to help me."

He continued staring at the ground.

"And no talking!" shouted the guard. "In fact, move to the other side. Go!"

Rory glared at him but did as she was told.

For a while, she contented herself with coming up with every imaginable insult for the guard, and that helped somewhat. Unfortunately, not with their situation.

She didn't think she'd have too much trouble provoking him into coming to the platform. The problem was that she couldn't work out what to do then. She couldn't get over the fact that he was armed while she wasn't and that she had no way to get away from him.

What she needed was to get him to extend the bridge but stop him from reaching the platform. She looked around her for any loose stones that she could throw. She shifted towards Longinus and leaned forward.

"Get back to your spot," shouted the guard, standing up. "I said no talking. Don't you make me come over."

Rory was gratified to see that in his annoyance, he had put her dagger down. That was a start.

She shifted back to her spot, having confirmed that there were no rocks for her to throw. She fiddled with her medals and came up with another two insults for the guard.

And with an idea. She took off one of her medals, the largest one she had, kissed it for luck, and held it in her right hand by its leather thong.

"You keep threatening to come over," she said, "but all I can see is a lot of talking and not a lot of doing."

"Shut up," said the guard at once. "Do you want me to come over, is that what you want? Maybe I ought to teach you some manners." He drew his rapier again.

"Ha," replied Rory. "You think waving your blade around over there's gonna scare me? Seems to me you're the one that's scared of *us*, and so you should be, too. You know he's the Viper, right?" she gestured at Longinus. "The real one, I mean. And I'm a famous swordfighter. Ain't nobody too stupid in Damsport to cross blades with me. You're lucky they took my dagger from me, or right now you'd be counting down the last seconds of your life."

"Right, you asked for it. Your friend can get arrested on his own."

The guard pushed the lever and the bridge extended. Before it had even reached the platform, his boots thudded on the metal. Rory's entire body was tense. She waited for him to reach the halfway point of the bridge before she spun her talisman by its leather thong in a circle overhead.

The guard, seeing her purpose, hurried forward, but she loosed the medal in his direction. It hit him square in the face, and he staggered back, one boot slipping at the edge of the bridge…

He regained his balance. A rivulet of blood ran down from his eyebrow where the talisman had hit him.

"You little —" He snarled and ran forward, reaching the platform before Rory had time to take another medal off.

She tried to duck out of his way, but she couldn't move fast or far enough. His rapier sank into her left shoulder. She cried out in pain and wrenched herself away, blinking at the spots that danced in front of her eyes.

The guard marched towards her.

"And now —"

Before he could complete his threat, Longinus crashed into the guard's side and sent him teetering back to the edge. The guard hovered there ,for what seemed like an impossibly long second, before he pitched over with a wail.

"Thank you," Rory said to Longinus, dizzy with relief.

She brought a hand to her shoulder, and it came back red and sticky.

Longinus threw up all over her boots.

"It's already stopped bleeding," Rory called as she tried to tie Longinus' waistcoat around her left shoulder with one hand. She grabbed one end with her teeth, pulling it into a knot with her right hand. On the other side of the clockwork bridge, Longinus huddled against the rock wall, breathing heavily.

Rory pulled the knot as tight as she could around her shoulder. It was a pretty poor job, truth be told, but it was the best she could do. For now, the waistcoat staunched the wound well enough, and she would have to hope they'd get out quick enough for her to get help. Asking Longinus was out of the question.

"There, it's all tied up. There's no more blood," she lied.

She picked up her dagger, and it was like welcoming an old friend. The purse unfortunately had disappeared with the guard, but she still had her grappling hook and line. Those went back around her waist, where they belonged.

"I can smell it, I can smell the blood," said Longinus.

"Alright, I'll step further away, but you have to come. We can't risk Myran finding us here."

Longinus winced at the mention of his sister's name. "Really? I thought you wanted to work with her," he said, not moving from the wall.

"No, I don't."

As soon as she said it, Rory realised how true that was. She felt a dull emptiness now where, for years, the dream of meeting the Scarred Woman again — Myran — had sat within her.

This wasn't the time, she chided herself.

Rory grabbed the guard's vapour lamp and moved away from the bridge, towards the opening from which she and Longinus had arrived. She made sure to stay close enough so that the lamp shed light for Longinus to see the bridge clearly.

"Now come on," she called. "We got to go."

Longinus stood up, his shirt vomit-stained, his face haggard. He looked as though he had aged ten years.

"Go further," he said.

Rory obeyed. At last, he stepped hesitantly onto the bridge. Rory kept an anxious lookout down the tunnel for fear that Myran or one of her cronies might return.

"You go on ahead," said Longinus once he had crossed the abyss, "and I'll follow. I can't be near you with the…with that —"

He dry retched, covering his mouth with a shaky hand.

"Alright then, just follow my light."

Rory walked off down the tunnel, holding the vapour lamp in front of her. The tunnel was made of sandstone, great big blocks of it, arranged so that the tunnel was perfectly square.

When she reached a junction, she closed her eyes and tried to remember which way they had turned on the way over, but her memory was little more than a jumbled mess of confused impressions. She settled for the left, hoping that wasn't leading her back to Myran.

***

Rory moved with more and more difficulty. Her left arm was growing cold and numb, her makeshift bandage soaked with blood. The dizziness was getting worse, and she kept having to blink to focus her vision.

The vapour lamp cast a yellow circle around her, but beyond that, the darkness was absolute. Farther behind, she could hear Longinus moving, following the light.

It was lucky the tunnels were so dark or he would have seen that his blood-saturated waistcoat had begun to drip, leaving a red trail behind Rory that was eagerly sucked up by the sandstone.

When she reached a junction and saw the mark on a stone to the left, Rory made to turn right, but she saw a mark there too. She began to despair. She had been marking her way at each junction for a while now, but no matter which way she went, she always found herself somewhere she had been before.

"I'm going to sit for a moment," she called over her shoulder.

There was a faint noise in the distance as Longinus stopped.

"Is it the blood?" he asked, his voice echoing along the tunnel with a tremor.

"No, no," she lied, "it's completely stopped now. My feet are just tired."

She sat, although it was more of a slump. The movement sent a fresh trickle of blood down her arm. Somewhere in the dark, she heard Longinus sit down too.

"We can't stay too long," she said, more for herself than for him. She could feel herself getting drowsy.

"What does it matter anyway?" echoed Longinus' disembodied voice. "She's already won. She always wins. There's nothing left for me up there."

"That ain't true."

"She's taken everything. She's taken the Viper from me. Even you."

"Me? No, look, I told you, I ain't never working for her, alright?"

Rory wondered what that left her with. Years of dreaming, of aiming towards a single goal, and it had disappeared like smoke on the wind. She no longer knew whether she even wanted to be a warrior now. She didn't know anything anymore — she just felt tired. Tired and cold.

"Why can't you say her name?" she asked, to try and keep herself awake.

There was a long pause.

"Sorry, I shouldn't pry," she said.

"My first memory is of her," Longinus replied in a low voice. "With a knife. At first, it would only be a knick here, a little cut there. I was too scared of what she would do if I told Mother, so I kept it hidden. And then when I was seven…"

Silence fell, and Rory felt her head get heavier. Maybe if she slept just for a little…

She snapped her eyes open.

"We're moving on," she said. That was easier said than done. The cold was spreading to the rest of her body, and her head felt so light it was as though it was no longer attached to the rest of her.

"What's the point?" said Longinus. "There's no way out, we've been going around in circles. If we're going to die down here, we might as well die comfortably."

"Like hell I'm dying in the tunnels. Ain't even any monsters or ghosts," said Rory, trying to drum up some cheek as she pulled herself up to standing. "Right disappointment if you ask me. Starmoles are probably eyeless to stop them from seeing how boring the tunnels are." Her words sounded flat to her ear, like an out-of-tune instrument.

She shivered and swayed dangerously on her feet. In the distance, Longinus didn't move.

"You know," she said, "if you invented the Viper, then Myran can't take him away from you."

"Of course she can. If everyone in Damsport thinks he killed the Marchioness, I can't be the Viper anymore. She'll have soiled him. He's not… He would never do something like that. And please stop saying her name."

"Sorry."

Something flashed in Rory's dozy brain, the edge of an idea, and then it disappeared just as quick. She shook head through the molasses of her dizziness. It had been something about killing, something about the Marchioness. The world was going to be watching, watching…

It disappeared again. Focusing was becoming harder.

"Come on," she said. "There has to be an exit somewhere. Starmoles come and go from the tunnels all the time."

"All the entrances to the tunnels are sealed to stop anyone from getting in and dying down here. There probably isn't a way out," Longinus said bitterly.

"Yes there is, and we'll find it. We're turning right."

Rory picked up the vapour lamp and tripped forward, her feet clumsy.

***

When Rory heard the first squeak, she froze. It came again, a little farther ahead. She lurched forward, pushing past the dizziness. A few more steps, just a few more. She wasn't walking now so much as shuffling. Her mouth was drier than the sandstone around her.

At last, something small and white appeared in the yellow circle of her lamp. The red feelers on its snout, in their star formation, wiggled as it sniffed the air. Behind the snout, the head was perfectly white and perfectly smooth. Starmoles didn't even have eye sockets.

Rory went to it and it tried to escape. Drawing on every last ounce of strength she had left — which really wasn't much — Rory pounced and managed to grab it. She held it in her hands, squealing and squirming, and she could have cried with relief.

"What's going on?" came Longinus' voice.

"I found a starmole," she replied.

She undid her belt, securing her sheathed dagger to the silk line around her waist, and tied one end of the belt around the starmole's neck in an improvised leash. With any luck, it would lead them to a way out.

She returned the creature to the ground. It mewled in protest at first, grabbing at the leash with its little paws, but after a while it fell silent. Rory waited. The starmole sniffed the air with its feelers and then shuffled forward. Rory followed, relieved that it walked slowly enough for her to keep up without any trouble.

It led them down the tunnel and right at the next junction. A few yards after the junction, it got confused and turned left straight into the wall. Rory didn't have the energy to try and correct its path. She watched apathetically, waiting for it to bump into the stone. Maybe this wasn't as good an idea as she had thought. She didn't know how much longer she could go on, but at this rate she —

The starmole disappeared into the wall. Rory could feel it tugging at the leash still, and then it looked as though the starmole was in the stone. Or rather, as though a flat version of it had superimposed itself against the wall.

"What the—"

She stretched out her hand to touch the wall and, to her surprise, only touched air. She stepped forward and saw herself reflected all around.

Mirrors.

Lots of very cleverly arranged mirrors, to create the illusion that the wall was uninterrupted. Rory would have admired the construction if she wasn't so weak, and if it hadn't nearly kept her and Longinus trapped in the tunnels.

"Longinus," she called. "The wall to the left has an opening in it, but mirrors make it look like it's solid."

She moved as far down as she could, until the edge of the light circle was only just touching the tunnel that Longinus was still in.

"Feel your way along the wall and you'll get to a gap," she told him. "Can you see it?"

"Your arm, your —" Longinus retched and heaved.

"Alright, I'll move further on, just follow my voice."

The starmole seemed eager to keep going through this new tunnel. It sloped softly downhill, and the air quickly became cooler. The slight added strain on Rory's legs from the slope was making her head worse. She stopped, leaning a hand against the wall.

"Are you behind me?" she called.

"Yes, I'm in the new tunnel," came the shaky reply.

"Alright then. We're gonna be fine."

Rory peeled herself from the wall and continued after the starmole.

CHAPTER
34

The tunnel eventually opened up into an enormous chamber with high, vaulted ceilings supported by a forest of pillars arranged in perfect rows. Rory gaped. The chamber was filled with water, still and black, reflecting the pillars above so that there appeared to be more pillars beneath them and a vaulted floor.

They were in the old underground cistern.

A pale, silvery light floated about the cistern, bright enough that Rory's vapour lamp wasn't needed, and she turned it off. Without the light from the lamp, the cistern became a still world of black, grey, and silver.

With some difficulty, Rory knelt on the ground and reached a hand towards the dark water. It was cool against her skin, and she cupped her hand to her face, drinking greedily. Ripples spread through the water, shattering the reflection.

The starmole tugged at the lead, making mewling noises. Rory could see that it wanted to climb up into a tunnel to the left, but it was far too small for her and Longinus, and she pulled back on the leash. The starmole whined, but it stayed still. Rory could see a walkway along the edge of the cistern, and she directed the starmole towards it. There had to be some sort of access to the cistern from above where the water was pumped up to the city.

A glance over her shoulder showed her that Longinus had also arrived. Just as she had, he reached down to the water and drank greedily. It was going to be more complicated now that there wasn't the darkness to hide her bleeding from him. At least for now he was far enough back that he wouldn't be able to see her too clearly.

Rory walked past endless rows of pillars, the starmole snuffling in front of her. Eventually, she found what she was looking for: a wooden walkway, ugly and out of place amongst the ethereal beauty around them, stretched out across the water to the middle of the cistern. She could just make out a wide tube that rose from the water, no doubt a pipe to feed the city's water pumps, and welded onto it… Yes! A ladder.

Rory released the starmole, and as she stood up once more, a thicker trickle of blood washed over her arm, dripping audibly onto the ground by her boots. She swayed and almost pitched over into the water.

"Just a little more," she muttered through gritted teeth.

She tried to raise her left arm, but it hung slack by her side. That was going to make climbing the ladder a bit of a challenge.

***

Rory stood as far from the wooden walkway as the silk line tied around her waist would allow. The rest of the line trailed all the way back to the start of the pontoon. Longinus was a few yards farther away, hesitating. To see them both, it would be hard to work out who was in worse shape. Longinus was shaking, and every few minutes, he covered his mouth with his hands as he dry heaved. His skin was grey and there were deep circles under his eyes.

In short, he looked about as good as Rory felt. She clung to the wall with a shivering hand.

"Longinus, we have to move. I'm not in a very good way."

Every time she moved, a fresh wave of blood cascaded down her arm. She fancied she could feel it ebb out of her. The thought almost caused her to faint, and she sagged against the wall. The silk line went taut as Longinus tied the other end around his waist.

He then ripped his right sleeve off and tied it around his mouth and nose, no doubt to try and keep the smell of blood away. Although it was doubtful he could smell anything, covered in vomit as he was.

"I'm ready," he said, his voice muffled.

Slowly, he made his way to the ladder, Rory following at the end of the line. Then he began to climb. Rory inched forward, making sure the line was neither too taut nor too slack. The focus this required felt like the hardest thing she'd ever done. She stared at the rope, blinking at it stupidly, forgetting every so often what she was doing.

Finally, she reached the ladder. Longinus was high up ahead, and the line was taut, yanking her upwards. She put a foot on the first rung and stretched out her right hand to grab another. Her left arm was still useless, hanging at her side. Now was the tricky part. With the line to Longinus pulling her up, she leaned into the ladder, doing her best to keep her balance with her feet on the rung below. Then she let go of her right hand, and as quick as she could, grabbed hold of the rung above. She missed and swung away from the ladder…and grabbed again, this time catching the rung. The metal felt cool beneath her fingers.

The line went taut and it helped pull her up. Then she repeated the process for the next rung.

They made good, if slow, progress. Rory began singing tunelessly to herself.

"The seagull sweeps over the beach,

The beach of Cantaloupe Island he sweeps,

Slow and steady, fast and smooth,

Searching for something of silver and blue."

Suddenly she had the irrepressible urge to giggle. It bubbled up in her throat, coming up into her mouth and nose. It was a crazed giggle, but it wouldn't go away, and she laughed and coughed as she reached for the next rung.

***

Rory came to, swinging through the air on the end of the silk line, with Longinus yelling up ahead.

"Rory, what are you doing? Grab the ladder — I'm going to slip! Rory! Rory!!"

She blinked, looking around her stupidly. Ladder? What ladder? She didn't want to grab a ladder. She wanted to sleep.

"Rory!" screamed Longinus.

Metal rungs materialised in front of her, and she reached for them with both hands but only one worked. That was odd. Both legs worked fine though, and that was good.

"You have the ladder? You have it?"

She slipped as she pulled herself to the ladder, and her forehead banged into the cold metal. That jolted her awake and she remembered where she was.

"Yeah, I got it now," she managed. "Sorry, I think I blacked out."

"It's fine, just keep going. I can see the top. I'll pull you up once we arrive."

After a while, the line pulled at her waist with more insistence, lifting her along. Longinus pulled her out through a round hole by her good arm. She lay on the floor, her head doing all sorts of somersaults.

Longinus crawled off on hands and knees, vomiting violently.

"Just a little more," she whispered.

Only she found that she couldn't get up. She felt like a puppet without strings. Her breathing whistled loudly in her ears.

"I...I think I might have lost too much blood..." she told Longinus. "Can you get...Cruikshank. Machinist Crescent."

Longinus said something, but Rory wasn't paying attention. She felt like she was floating in a warm bath now, although she was strangely cold at the same time. She just wanted to sleep, to sleep…

CHAPTER
35

Longinus had only just managed to get up when Rory passed out.

"Rory? Rory!"

He hovered, then crept forward, and knelt down next to her. His hand touched a little of her blood.

The world went dark.

He awoke on his back with the dreadful stench of blood in his nose. His stomach immediately began its dance, and he turned and crawled away, towards the door. He couldn't think of anything save getting out to the fresh air and away from all that blood. *Blood everywhere, so much blood everywhere, everywhere.*

He reached the door, reached up for the handle, opened it, and flopped out like a dead fish. He lay in the fresh air for a moment, breathing in deep gulps. After a time, he pulled himself up and returned inside. Rory was still where he had left her, lying on her back. Her face was drawn and so pale it looked like not a drop of blood remained inside her. Huge circles surrounded her eyes, and she looked even tinier than normal. Her entire left arm was red and shiny.

Longinus looked away, coughing to try and interrupt another wave of nausea. He needed to cover up the blood, or he wouldn't be able to function enough to get her help. He looked around the room. The gloom made it hard to see, but he could just make out great shapes moving in the shadows with the smoothness of oiled metal. Pistons pumped up and down with only a faint, rhythmic hiss, drawing water from the cistern below.

He headed towards them and finally had some luck. A large tarp was crumpled in a corner. He would be able to use it to wrap Rory up and carry her to Machinist Crescent. He picked up the tarp and returned to Rory, laying it flat next to her.

He tried dragging her limp body onto it, but the proximity to her wound became too much again, and he fainted once more. Again, he came to and crawled outside to grab a few gulps of fresh air before he returned inside. Even the torn-up sleeve over his mouth and nose wasn't enough to keep the smell out, and he gagged.

Again.

This time, he didn't try to move her but first threw the tarp over her. As soon as her wound was covered, he felt better. He tore up more of his shirt and wrapped up his hands so he wouldn't touch any blood and faint again. Then, he grabbed Rory through the tarp and gently turned her onto her front. She was so light, it was like lifting a bird.

Her bloody arm came into view once more, and he turned away, grabbing the edge of the tarp and throwing it back over her. He did the same with the other edge so that she was very crudely wrapped.

It would have to do. He couldn't afford to waste any more time. He picked her up, tarp and all. Was it even possible to be so light? Was it because of all the blood she had lost?

The thought had him swaying on his feet, and he almost dropped her. He headed out, into the early evening light. The sun had almost set and the street was nearly empty. People hurried past when they caught sight of him in his torn-up shirt, covered in vomit, carrying Rory in her tarp.

Longinus quickly got his bearings. They were near Nine, the gods be thanked, and quite close to Machinist Crescent. He moved as quickly as he dared, not wanting to jolt her any more than needed.

They reached Machinist Crescent quickly enough, but once inside, Longinus was utterly lost. This was a part of Damsport he had never had cause to go to, and the lack of streets and organisation made it impossible to get his bearings. He kicked at the first door he came across.

A cross-looking man with enormous optics opened.

"Yes?"

"You know a Crackshank, or Crankshank?"

"You mean Cruikshank. Right in the middle of the crescent. You can't miss her warehouse, great ugly old thing. Red brick."

The door slammed.

Longinus hurried towards what he hoped was the middle of the crescent. He kept imagining that Rory was getting lighter and lighter, and it was all he could do not to think of the blood oozing out of her.

After a few more attempts at finding Cruikshank, and instead coming across various disgruntled machinists, Longinus finally found her warehouse. He could see what the first machinist had meant: it dwarfed the ones around it, and the bricks were dull and chipped, the mortar crumbling, the roof rusting.

Much to his frustration, he had to go to the other side of the building to find the door. He kicked it.

"Open up!"

The door opened a crack, and a boy with a scowl and greasy hair peeked out into the opening.

"What d'you want?"

Longinus burst through the door and into a roasting hot workshop.

"Where is Cruikshank? Now!"

"I'm right here," came a voice over by a roaring furnace.

A small but muscular woman walked up to him, wiping her hands on a cloth.

"What do you mean by bursting into my workshop like —"

"This is Rory, she needs help and bad. She's lost a lot of blood and I just — I don't know what to do. She told me to find you." He thrust his bundle forward.

"Gods alive, Rory? Over here, quick!"

Cruikshank ran over to her workbench, and with a quick sweep of her arms sent its contents crashing to the floor. Longinus put his precious bundle down, and Cruikshank opened the tarp, revealing the bloody mess that was Rory. She sucked in air between her teeth.

"What happened?"

"A rapier... A guard."

When she touched the wound, cutting back the fabric around it, Longinus fainted again.

He awoke to find himself soaked with water, the lad looking down at him with a frown. He had time enough to see Cruikshank's hands moving with impressive speed, her fingers covered with blood, before he passed out again. When he finally came to, this time without the help of the lad, Rory looked much better. Most of the blood had been cleaned off, and Cruikshank was working with a needle and thread to stitch the wound closed. Despite her thick knuckles and wide hands, she worked with astonishing dexterity.

Longinus turned away just as she brought the needle to the skin.

"I have to get some air," he muttered, but no one paid him any attention.

He sat outside next to the front door, drinking in the warm night air, and tried not to think of what was going on inside. Things would be fine now. Rory would get patched up, and if they kept a low profile for a while, things would blow over. If he gave Myran what she wanted — the Viper — maybe she would leave them be. He would simply have to learn to exist without his alter ego. He felt a pang of crushing sadness at the thought, and his eyes welled up as if a real person had just died, but there was no other choice.

The door opened and he looked up to find the lad.

"You can come in now. There's no blood left. You're not so good with it, are you?"

He shook his head.

"What's your name?"

"Longinus."

"I'm Norman."

The lad held the door open, and Longinus followed him back in. Cruikshank looked up as she was wiping her hands.

"Are you the one who's been training Rory?" she asked.

He nodded.

"You're going to tell me what happened, and right now, because if you're responsible for that wound, so help me I will —"

"It wasn't me. I swear it on my honour it wasn't me. Will she be alright?"

"I think so. She's lost a lot of blood, but I think I got there in time."

Rory was still on the bench, laid out on the tarp. She seemed even smaller than usual, shrunken beneath her mass of rope hair. But she was breathing.

"I'm going to move her upstairs to my office," said Cruikshank, gesturing at the wooden box up on the metal runway. "There's very little we can do now but wait."

Longinus nodded. He hoped they wouldn't be waiting for Rory to die.

CHAPTER 36

Rory awoke to the feeling that her saliva had turned to sawdust. She peeled her tongue from the roof of her mouth and looked around. She was in an unknown room. The walls were pale yellow and there was a vase out of which poured a spray of jasmine. The flowers smelled strong and sweet, but beneath there was the smell of hot metal and tar. Through the window at the foot of the bed, she could see that it was the middle of the night.

She turned her head and her neck felt like a stiff hinge — she half-expected to hear it creaking. At the foot of the bed, to the left, was Cruikshank, asleep in a chair. Rory guessed that they were up in her private quarters in her workshop, and it was a relief to be back in familiar, safe surroundings — although she had never been in Cruikshank's private quarters before.

The events of the last day bubbled up in her memory: finding the cavern, hearing of the plot against the Old Girl, Myran…Myran. Guilt as heavy as granite settled on her when she remembered that for a moment she had been ready to take Myran's offer. That she had hesitated before helping Longinus.

Some hero she was.

Something else surfaced, an idea that she had had in the tunnels, too vague and confused for her to grasp it properly. Rory focused on that, finding it far easier than confronting her failings. It had been something about the world watching. Myran had said the whole world would be watching, which had to mean —

"The Revels," she rasped aloud.

Over in her chair, Cruikshank started awake.

"Ah, you're finally up," she said. "You gave us quite a fright, lovey."

She got up and brought a glass of water over. Rory drained it in one go, and Cruikshank poured her another.

"Where's Longinus?" Rory croaked before downing the second glass.

"Downstairs."

Rory moved her left arm a little and winced. It felt stiff, and there was a sharp pain where the wound was, at her shoulder.

"Careful with that, lovey, don't move it too much. I've stitched you up, and you don't want to reopen it."

Rory nodded and let herself relax into the pillows. "How long have I been asleep?"

"Two days."

"What? Someone should have woken me up!"

"Don't be silly. You'd lost a lot of blood, sleep's the best thing for you."

"But that means the Revels are in two days, aren't they?"

"Yes, why?"

"Has Longinus explained anything to you about what happened?"

Cruikshank's face clouded over.

"I don't know how you have been able to put up with him. He has been driving me crazy, trying to tell me how to run my workshop, how to organise my workbenches. He has been up here checking on you constantly, though. But no, he's refusing to talk about what happened, other than to tell me a guard did this to you."

Rory pushed the covers back.

"We have to warn the Marchioness."

"The Marchioness? Why?"

Rory stood up, and she would have fallen right back down if Cruikshank hadn't caught her.

"Easy… Come this way."

She led Rory past the screen and into a very feminine parlour. Rory wasn't sure what she had expected from Cruikshank's quarters, but this certainly wasn't it.

Comfortable-looking chairs faced each other, and next to them on a little round table was an odd plant, like a cross between an orchid and a pitcher plant. Behind one of the chairs, a criss-cross of gleaming copper pipes was fixed to the wall, acting as a bookshelf. Rory was surprised to see that the books crowding the makeshift shelves were all tawdry romances.

"Well don't gape, lovey, just because I'm a machinist don't mean I can't enjoy a little titillating reading." Cruikshank winked and Rory felt herself go red. "Let's get you sat down and then why don't you tell me what is going on, starting from the beginning."

Cruikshank lit a cigar, blowing up a thick plume of blue smoke. Rory recounted everything from the day Jake had screwed her over. She glossed over the blackmail as quickly as she could, earning herself a single dark look from Cruikshank, and she thought it best not to mention that she had broken into Longinus' house too.

As she spoke, Cruikshank picked up a small metal box and began feeding each orchid, taking a wriggling insect from the box with tweezers and dropping it into the flowers' pouches. The flowers shivered in turn as though they were aware that dinner had just been served. Rory leaned back, keeping well clear of them.

When at last she had finished, Cruikshank put down the box.

"Lovey, how do you know Longinus isn't really working with his sister on this? He's an assassin. His expertise is deception."

"He isn't. I was with him when he found out about the killings, right, and when he came face to face with Myran."

"That could all be an act."

"Why would he do that? He could easily have got rid of me before that, and then no need for the act. And would he have saved me after we got out the tunnels? D'you realise how hard it would have been for him to carry me, bleeding and all?"

Cruikshank conceded that she had a point.

"Don't think that makes him innocent, though," she said. "He will still have to answer for his crimes."

"Cruikshank, you're missing the point. Myran is going to kill the Marchioness at the Revels."

"Yes, and I am getting to that. But I won't let you get blindsided by this Longinus. People like him —"

"I can look after myself, thanking you."

Cruikshank looked pointedly at Rory's shoulder.

"That's different, alright?" said Rory. "Longinus ain't getting arrested. He's the only one that knows if there's a way to stop the poison. So you don't say nothing to no one about him, or he and I will disappear and the Old Girl will die, and Damsport will go back to the Empire."

Rory fell silent, a little shocked at how she had spoken to Cruikshank. The older woman looked equally as surprised. She lit another cigar.

"We'll have to tell the Marchioness about him," she said at last. "I've dealt with her enough before, lovey, and she's not an easy woman. She'll need the entire story and all the facts. For starters, is there a way to combat the poison?"

"See, that's why you need Longinus. And if he gets arrested, he might not cooperate."

Rory gave a smug smile. Cruikshank rubbed her forehead, which for once was clean.

"Let's go down. You need food."

"One more thing. Swear on your life you won't say a peep about Longinus' fear of blood or about the fact that Myran's his sister."

Cruikshank opened her mouth to say something, but Rory interrupted. "Swear it. And I know with an honest type like you swearing means something, so you got to say the words."

"Fine, I swear."

"Alright then. Let's go and talk to Longinus."

CHAPTER
37

Rory asked Norman and Cruikshank to give her some privacy with Longinus.

"My answer won't change just because they're out of earshot," said Longinus. "I won't have anything to do with this. You're healed, or at least well enough to function. We can go, leave Damsport maybe, start up somewhere else. I'll keep you as my apprentice, and we can forget about all of this."

"I'm not running away, Longinus." As she spoke Rory bit off a chunk from the strip of cured ostrich meat Cruikshank had given her. It was tough and salty but quite delicious.

"Why, are you still desperate to partner up with my sister?" he asked bitterly.

"No. Look, I'm sorry about that, alright. I was a kid when I met her, and she fought so well… I had no idea who she was. I want nothing to do with her now, and that's the honest truth."

Longinus shrugged and wouldn't look at her.

"I had another idea, too," continued Rory. "A way you can stop her from taking the Viper from you."

He looked up at this. Encouraged, she continued.

"If the Viper saves the Marchioness, he would be a hero. Then Myran's lost twice. Think about it. It's the best way to beat her."

"And how are we supposed to do that? She's unstoppable. She always gets what she wants."

"Well, we know that she plans to use your poison, right? I saw all the uniforms in the cavern. I reckon she means to pass herself off as a member of the Old Girl's staff and get close to her that way. So if you make an antidote —"

"There is no antidote. The poison's too fast. Once it has touched the skin, there is no stopping it."

Longinus' face was a mixture of pride and regret. Rory thought some more.

"What about if you make a pre-antidote, like something the Old Girl would have to take before the Revels that would stop the poison from acting?"

"That wouldn't work either. The best we can hope for is a buffer, something to place between the poison and the skin — like a paste of some kind. It won't be elegant, though, and it won't be very reliable."

"Well, at least that's something. Can you make it?"

"I need my notes and my alchemical equipment. Without my formulae I can't do anything."

Rory called Cruikshank and Norman back over.

"We need alchemical equipment," she told them, explaining Longinus' solution to the poison.

"That's easy," replied Cruikshank. "Tell us what you need, and Norman will go out and get it as soon as the sun comes up."

"Good," said Rory. "Now for the notes… Myran will have discovered our escape by now and she'll be watching the house. If it weren't for my arm, I could climb to the roof and break in, but I don't think I'd be able to climb anything."

"That's something I can help with," said Cruikshank.

She pulled back the tarp that was covering the huge spider in the corner of her workshop. Longinus stumbled back in horror.

"Pretty special, isn't she?" said Norman, who had sidled over.

"She's fast and silent, and she can run the roofs better than you can, lovey," Cruikshank said to Rory, patting one of the spider's forelegs.

She fetched a canvas jacket and two sets of goggles. She passed a pair to Rory.

"The spider's built for two, but Longinus will be too heavy to ride pillion," she said.

"I beg your pardon?" said Longinus.

Rory felt sure he had sucked in his stomach on answering, and she smothered a smile. It was good to see him reverting to his usual self.

"Most people would be too heavy to ride pillion considering how far we have to go," replied Cruikshank. "We might run out of steam on the way back. We should be alright with Rory though, and I'm going to need directions."

"Can you explain where your notes are and what you need?" Rory asked Longinus.

He hesitated. "No one has ever handled my notes except me."

"This ain't the time to be precious," she pointed out. "We got to stop your sister."

Still he looked reluctant. "There's a particular way to get into the compartment where I store them," he said. "I don't know if you'll be able to open it…"

"Longinus, seriously. If you keep wasting time, it'll be Myran getting your notes, not me."

That seemed to decide him, and he explained how to press the marquetry on his desk to open the compartment.

"Can you also take a set of clothing?" he asked. "And then I'll need some of my equipment."

"We can't be loading down the spider too much or she won't jump," replied Cruikshank. "I told you, Norman can go buy the equipment."

"I'm not sure we can trust him with —"

"He's the son of one of my closest friends and a good worker," cut in Cruikshank. "If I say you can trust him, then you can trust him."

Longinus looked as though he was about to reply, but a warning glance from Cruikshank convinced him to keep quiet.

Cruikshank climbed up onto the spider's back, strapping herself into the front harness. Then, both she and Longinus helped Rory get up without making use of her bad arm.

"Strap yourself in, lovey," said the older woman. "We'll be mostly horizontal for this trip, but still, better safe than sorry."

"Horizontal? What d'you mean horizontal?"

***

Once they were both strapped in and ready, Cruikshank pushed a lever and the spider hissed to life beneath them. The legs moved one by one, as though stretching after a long sleep. Cruikshank then grabbed hold of another lever, and the spider scuttled across the workshop with terrible speed, its eight articulated legs making spine-shuddering clicking noises. It reached the opposite wall, put its two front legs up against the brick at Cruikshank's command, and slowly began to climb.

Rory let out a cry of surprise, which was echoed by Longinus. The spider moved up the wall quickly, squeezing through a gap in the metal walkway. Rory held onto the spider with her legs, her good arm around Cruikshank's waist, relieved there was a harness to keep her from slipping off its back.

At the top of the wall was a large window, and Cruikshank guided the spider through it and onto the roof. Dawn was still a way off, but there was enough moonlight to illuminate their path. The spider's legs clicked loudly on the zinc roof.

"She's not made for metal roofs like mine," said Cruikshank. "We'll be quieter once we've left the crescent. She's inspired by your ability to hop around the roofs, you know."

Cruikshank increased the spider's speed, its legs scuttling in a blur of motion. They rushed towards the edge of the roof, and just when it looked like they would pitch over, the spider's legs and abdomen let out a powerful burst of steam that propelled them straight up and over the gap to the next roof.

They landed with a loud clang.

"Landing's a bit shaky," said Cruikshank.

"Still pretty impressive," replied Rory.

They moved quickly from roof to roof, and as Cruikshank predicted, once they left the crescent, the spider no longer made any noise save a soft clicking from its leg joints.

"Can she clear a traversal?" asked Rory.

"She can indeed. And thoroughfares."

Rory whistled softly. Cruikshank would have the run of the roofs now.

"She's a prototype," continued Cruikshank. "I was going to unveil her at the Revels. The unveiling is technically a little early, but on the plus side, it means I can give her a good test run. I've been keeping her locked away in the warehouse — this is her first outing."

When they reached Longinus' street, they slowed to a walking pace, looking out for anyone watching. Cruikshank took the spider to both edges of the roofs so they could look down at the street below, but it was empty.

"There's a broken skylight from when I last broke in," whispered Rory.

"What do you mean *last* broke in?"

"Now's not really the time for a lecture, alright?"

Rory was relieved when Cruikshank didn't press the point. They reached Longinus' roof silent as you like. The skylight was still open, with the hole Rory had kicked in what seemed like a lifetime ago. However, it was far too small for the spider to fit.

"Why don't I go in," whispered Rory. "I know the way. We can use my grappling hook and line to get me out."

"No way," Cruikshank whispered back. "I don't like the idea of you on your own. We don't know who's in there. Can you figure out which window leads into Longinus' room?"

Rory unstrapped her harness and slid down from the spider. She went to the edge of the roof and peered down, immediately retreating.

"It's the left-most window, but we can't do it — there are two of Myran's men out there. The spider's too big, she'll draw attention. It's best for me to go in through the skylight. They won't be expecting us. It's been two days — if we were gonna come, it would have been right after we escaped, right? I'll be fine. Anyway, I'm good at hiding."

Cruikshank looked dubious.

"We ain't got no other option, and we got to get those notes if we are gonna stop Myran from killing the Marchioness."

That decided Cruikshank. She opened a compartment to the side of the spider and pulled out a large coil of rope.

"Easier for me to haul you up with that than your silk line," she said. She also pulled out a tiny vapour lamp that Rory hooked to her belt.

Once the rope was securely fastened around Rory's waist, Cruikshank lowered her through the open window.

"Be careful in there," she whispered.

Rory nodded and turned to look at the room beneath her. It was just as she had left it, with the furniture looming in the gloom under its white sheets. She landed on the chaise and untied the rope from around her waist, giving a thumbs up at Cruikshank. The older woman's face was framed by the window and it was full of anxiety. Rory grinned at her to reassure her, although her palms were sweating.

She made her way to the door and listened. Silence.

She opened it carefully and peeked into the corridor. It all looked normal. Walking as quickly as she dared without making a sound, she headed for Longinus' room. She shuddered as she passed the dead-bolted room, remembering the bloodstain.

Once inside Longinus' room, she closed the door carefully. Even in the dark, she could tell the room had been ransacked. She shook her lamp to life and was grateful Longinus wasn't there to see this.

The bedsheets were torn; stuffing from the pillows and mattress was strewn about the room, as were ripped clothing and broken furniture. The desk rested against the floor, two of its legs broken off, its drawers yawning open. It looked as though every single piece of paper it had contained had been ripped apart, which seemed odd at first

— but then Rory guessed that Myran must have been the one going through the room and she must have taken pleasure in destroying Longinus' precious pamphlets.

Up on the wall, the painting remained untouched, Longinus and Myran's mother looking down on the ruin.

Rory walked over to the desk and pressed the marquetry the way Longinus had explained. Thankfully, it still worked, and with a faint whir of clockwork, a compartment clicked open. Inside was a thick, leather-bound journal, which on inspection contained rows upon rows of odd symbols and complicated-looking formulae.

No doubt, the famous alchemical notes. There were other journals in there too, smaller and simply bound in fabric covers. She flicked through them quickly. The writing was neat but childish.

Myran is so scared she has peed herself like a baby. And she cries like a baby, too. The Viper stands in front of her, tall and terrifying, and she is curled up on the floor.

"Stop your crying!" says the Viper. The words are perfect because the Viper doesn't stutter. "You don't deserve my mercy, but I'm the most powerful man in the world, and I've decided to let you live, but you can never go near Longinus again; in fact I'm taking Longinus away with me so he can learn to become the fiercest assassin in the world, and you will stay behind all alone in the house, and you will think about what you did."

Rory flicked forward to a later part of the diary.

Myran lifted the knife ready to cut Longinus but the Viper appeared, his cape floating behind him, his face terrible to see.

"Get away from the boy!" he thundered, and his voice was so loud that Myran dropped the knife. "You will never cut him again. In fact you will never be able to hold a knife again." The Viper stretched out a hand, and Myran's hands were transformed into cat paws without claws, soft and useless.

She flicked through another journal. Similar stories crowded the pages, the Viper coming to Longinus' rescue over and over again. She wondered when Longinus' imaginary protector had crossed the divide and become an alter ego. She stuffed the journals down the back of her trousers.

Then, she headed over to Longinus' wardrobe. That too had been hacked to pieces, all the silk, lace, and brocade reduced to little more than ribbons. She rooted around in the mess until she found some black silk. She pulled out a black shirt and black trousers that were unscathed. She tied the shirt and trousers around herself like a sash and headed back to the bedroom.

The tinkle of breaking glass made her freeze. She turned the vapour lamp off, listening in the darkness.

Beyond the door, a heavy tread. The sloshing of liquid. Rory returned to the closet and buried herself in the torn fabric. She had just finished covering her head when she heard the bedroom door open. She held her breath.

The sound of liquid sloshing and then spattering against wood or something hard. And then again. A faint grunt, and heavy steps leaving the room. Rory didn't hear the door close and she didn't dare move. She waited in her hideout, straining to hear any more noises. Were both men inside the house?

When she didn't hear anything else, she poked her head out of the pile of ruined clothing. She smelled the smoke a second before she saw the orange flicker coming from the bedroom.

Fire.

She ran out of the closet only to find the doorway to the room obstructed by tall flames. Rory looked about desperately. She spotted the sheets on the bed. Maybe if she wrapped herself up well enough, she'd be able to run back to the room with the skylight.

The fire spread to the desk, greedily eating the rug and wooden floorboards. No time to hesitate. Rory picked up the biggest bit of sheet she could find and wrapped herself as well as she could in it. It barely covered her.

She headed to the doorway and then noticed that the entire corridor beyond was ablaze. She'd never make it. Panic beat against the walls of her chest like a bird trapped in an attic.

The fire reached the closet, and she backed towards the bed.

To her left, the window exploded in a spray of glass. She shielded her face with her arms.

"Get on quick!" Cruikshank gestured from the spider. Down below, shouts erupted as Raynard and the other man spotted the spider.

Rory ran over. The spider was below the window, but with her bad arm, she couldn't climb down to it without slipping right off its smooth abdomen.

"Hold onto me," said Cruikshank, looping a muscular arm around Rory. Rory managed to swing a leg around Cruikshank, clinging to her with her good hand. Cruikshank pushed the spider up the wall, with Rory hanging off the side, until they reached the roof.

"Right, now get on behind me." Cruishank's voice was perfectly calm.

Rory clambered on as best she could, wincing from the pain in her bad arm. She had barely sat down when Raynard appeared at the edge of the roof — he had climbed up the wall.

"Hold on," said Cruikshank, pushing the spider forward.

They made the jump easily, and the spider scuttled off along the next roof, and the next. Holding onto Cruikshank with both legs and her good arm, Rory turned back to look at Raynard. He was giving chase, and although the spider was faster than he was, it was also incredibly easy to spot.

"He's chasing us," she shouted in Cruikshank's ear.

Cruikshank increased the spider's speed, but still when she looked back, Rory could see Raynard chasing after them, arms pumping efficiently, long legs leaping from roof to roof. The man was tireless.

"We're not losing him," she said.

"Dammit," said Cruikshank, "we're running low on fuel."

"What does that mean?"

"It means that soon we won't be able to jump and then we won't be able to move at all."

They were still a long way from Machinist Crescent. Cruikshank slowed right down, and behind them Raynard seemed to speed up.

A few blocks away, Rory could see Medlion Traversal.

"I've got an idea. Get us to the traversal over there."

"Why?" asked Cruikshank.

"You ever ridden with Crazy Willy? I reckon he'd be game for a huge spider on his steamcoach, so long as there ain't anyone already on the top. It's pretty late, so he should be empty. You got coinage on you?"

"And if Crazy Willy doesn't get here in time for us to jump before Raynard catches up with us?"

"Then I guess we're buggered either way. You got any better ideas?"

"No, and that's what worries me."

Cruikshank pushed the spider to top speed until they reached the edge of the traversal. Rory looked over her shoulder. Raynard was hopping from one roof to the next with impressive speed. They didn't have long until he reached them.

When he was only three roofs away, Rory heard the melodious screeching that announced Crazy Willy.

"Here he comes. You ready, Cruikshank?"

The older woman nodded, backing up the spider a little. Seen from the top, Crazy Willy's steamcoach looked even more like a nightmarish beast.

Raynard landed on the roof behind theirs.

"Dammit, he's almost on us."

Crazy Willy's coach screeched around a corner, charging towards them. Raynard sprinted to the end of his roof, leapt, and landed just a few yards behind them.

"Get ready," yelled Cruikshank.

Raynard sprinted towards them, and Rory turned back, dagger out, ready to repel him. He jumped up on the spider's abdomen behind Rory, and she slashed with her blade. He dodged, grabbed her collar, and pulled her back. Rory realised she had forgotten to tie up her harness. She did her best to hold on to the spider with her legs, her left arm dangling uselessly at her side. The surface was too smooth, and she began to slip away as Raynard pulled her back.

"Cruikshank, he's got me!"

Crazy Willy's coach thundered closer.

Rory slashed with her blade, but again Raynard dodged and then threw a punch at her bad shoulder. Rory almost fainted from the pain, and her legs let go. Raynard yanked her backwards, but just as she was slipping off the spider, Cruikshank's hand shot back, catching hold of her belt. Rory hooked one foot under one of the spider's legs, straining to keep herself on. She slashed with her dagger again, and this time she caught something. Raynard grunted. Still he held on. He threw another punch, but this time Rory managed to dodge.

"Now!" shouted Cruikshank. She sent the spider forward, Raynard still holding on at the back.

Rory stabbed immediately behind her neck, and she felt her dagger connect with something. Raynard let out a cry and released her just as they reached the roof's edge. The spider jumped and landed on the back of the coach. Rory was still half off the spider, and her torso and head hung over the side, the street below streaming past at alarming speed. Cruikshank turned and pulled her back up.

"You alright, lovey?"

Rory nodded, shaken. She turned back in time to see Raynard watching them from the rooftop, cradling his right hand, and then the steamcoach turned and he was out of sight.

CHAPTER

38

Cruikshank and Rory returned to the workshop as quick as they could, but the spider was too low on steam to continue on the rooftops for long. They finished their journey at street level, but luckily it was still too early for anyone to be out in the streets, and they made it back without any trouble.

Rory gave Longinus his alchemical notes. When she told him about the fire, he paled, and for a moment, she thought he might faint.

"My poisons," he murmured. "My life's work."

"I'm sorry."

Rory stood awkwardly, knowing there was nothing she could say. She thrust his childhood diaries at him without a word, and Longinus took them in silence.

"We'll get her for that," she murmured. "We'll get Myran and make her pay."

Longinus didn't react. She wasn't sure he had heard her.

"She takes everything," he said at last. "Everything…"

Rory put a hand on his wrist. "You still have the Viper, remember. She can never take him from you."

Cruikshank cleared her throat.

"We have to go to the Marchioness," she said. "The sun's rising. Let me take a quick look at your shoulder, lovey, and then we'll go."

Rory nodded, tearing her eyes from Longinus. Cruikshank peeled back the bandages, examined and prodded the wound at Rory's shoulder, clucked her tongue, and declared herself satisfied.

The two women then headed out, leaving Longinus still in the same spot, looking down at his diaries. Rory set her mouth in a grim line, more determined to get Myran than she had ever been about anything.

The sky was clear enough of clouds for the sun to beat down mercilessly on the city as it awoke. Cruikshank and Rory walked briskly despite the heat, and they soon arrived at the Old Girl's mansion.

It was a simple building, little more than an enormous house really, built in white stone, its roof decorated with green jade tiles. An old-fashioned gate full of curlicues surrounded it, and at its gate, four female Varanguards with hard faces gazed impassively out. Their helmets and ponytails gleamed in the rising sun, and Rory caught a glint from one of the hidden knives. Unlike the Varanguards she had seen back at Cruikshank's workshop, the four women wore the official purple uniform with spiked bracers at their wrists.

"We're here to see the Marchioness," said Cruikshank to one of them. "Eleanore Cruikshank. Urgent business about the Revels."

The Varanguard nodded silently and glanced at Rory.

"This is…my assistant," said Cruikshank.

The Varanguard opened the gate and slipped inside. Behind the gate was a small cabin, just big enough to accommodate one person. Two copper tubes the width of a fist ran along one wall, disappearing into the ground.

"I built that," murmured Cruikshank, gesturing at the copper tubes with pride. "Allows communication with the house without them having to leave their post."

Rory nodded, not paying attention. She shifted restlessly on her feet. The Varanguard reappeared and resumed her post at the gate, face still impassive.

"Well?" asked Rory.

"Wait," said Cruikshank, "someone will come fetch us."

Seconds stretched past. The four Varanguards gazed silently into the distance, pretending they couldn't see the two women standing in front of them. Rory's skin itched with the awkwardness of it.

At last, the door opened, and a small man minced towards them, crossing the distance from mansion to gate in an unhurried manner.

"Didn't he hear this was urgent?" Rory whispered to Cruikshank.

"No point getting angry, lovey, it won't make him go faster."

At last, the little man reached them. He had a fleshy face with feminine lips, and he oozed enough condescension to rival Longinus on a good day.

"Open the gate, if you please," he said in a nasal voice.

The Varanguards obeyed, and Cruikshank and Rory stepped inside.

"I am Brandt. This way, please." He waved towards the mansion and bleated a small laugh.

They followed him, keeping with his slow pace, and Rory wondered what the punishment would be for kicking a member of the Marchioness' household up the arse and running ahead of him. As they walked, Brandt went to great pains to explain just what an honour it was that the Marchioness had deigned to receive them on such short notice, and at such a time in the morning, all the while punctuating his speech with short bursts of nasal laughter. He glanced at Rory frequently, as though to make clear it was particularly an honour for her.

Brandt led them up a sweeping staircase and down a corridor that was panelled with dark wood and bedecked with paintings of the Marchioness' ancestors.

"You must, of course, ha-ha, address the Marchioness as ma'am and wait for her to speak first."

"I've seen her plenty of times, Brandt," said Cruikshank. "You don't need to remind me of the protocol."

"It's, ah, your assistant I'm more worried about, ha-ha. Please note, young lady, that 'Old Girl' is not an appropriate way to address the, ha-ha, Marchioness."

"Really? Gosh, ain't I glad you're here to tell me the way of the world."

"Sarcasm isn't appropriate either," he sniffed.

"Not to worry," replied Rory, patting him on the shoulder. "My sarcasm is all for you."

They finally arrived in front of a set of double doors. Brandt paused and turned to observe the two women.

"This is the Marchioness' study," he said in hushed, reverential tones. "It is from here that she, ha-ha, shapes our fair city, from here that she makes plans that topple empires —"

"Lovey, much as I like to hear about the Marchioness' achievements, you might have noticed the word urgent in our request." Cruikshank went to step around Brandt, ready to push the door open, but he stopped her with a strangled cry.

"I must announce you!"

"Brandt?" called a voice from within. "What in the gods' hair are you doing out there? If Cruikshank is here, let her in, dammit."

Brandt flushed beet red. "Now look what you've done," he hissed.

He fumbled with the latch and pushed open both doors dramatically. "Eleanore Cruik —"

"Marchioness," said Cruikshank, marching past him. The Old Girl sat at a large desk heaped with papers. Behind her was a huge world map, bristling with pins and little flags. The room was panelled with lacquered wood and simply furnished with a couple of chairs in front of the desk, bookshelves in one corner, and a reading armchair.

"Cruikshank, good to see you." The Marchioness stood up and the two women shook hands. She radiated even more power than when Rory had spied her from the shadows outside Cruikshank's workshop. Rory felt like a child, entirely out of her depth.

"Who's this?" asked the Old Girl.

"That's Rory, she has some important information for you."

The Marchioness nodded. "Sit."

Brandt hovered behind them.

"That will be all, Brandt."

"Ma'am." He took a deep bow and scuttled out.

The Marchioness' gaze rested on Rory, waiting for her to begin. Rory felt her saliva traitorously disappear from her mouth, and her vocal cords seemed to forget how to function. She sat with her mouth open, as though she was trying to catch flies. Cruikshank came to the rescue.

"We have reason to believe that someone is planning to make an attempt on your life during the Revels."

"I see. And who is that person?"

Rory galvanised herself into action. She'd be damned if she would make a fool of herself in front of the Old Girl.

"A woman called Myran," she said. "She killed Dr Corian, and your servant, and now she has her uniform. I reckon she means to pass herself off as a servant during the Revels, right, and kill you with the poison she used on Dr Corian, and then she's gonna frame another assassin called the Viper for the assassination, and then she's going to hand Damsport back to the Emperor."

Rory took a deep breath to slow her speech down.

"I see," said the Marchioness.

Rory was surprised by how calm the Old Girl was, as though it was no more than a problem with the steam trolleys.

"And how do you know all this?"

"Well, I was at the baths when Dr Corian fell out, right, and I heard about your servant, but then I overheard men who work for Myran talking about what the Emperor would do after you were dead. And then Myran kidnapped me, and she mentioned about working for the Emperor and how the whole world would see her kill you. So I thought to myself that it had to be the Revels, right, and with your servant's uniform, well, she could get real close to you — close enough to put some of that poison on your skin."

Rory took another deep breath. What was it about the Old Girl's eyes that made her babble like that?

"Is this Myran the Viper?" asked the Marchioness.

"No, she ain't. She's planning to pin it all on him, though."

"Ah. And you work for the Viper."

Before Rory could answer, the Old Girl interrupted.

"Don't lie to me, Rory, you don't rule a city like Damsport without knowing a few things. That and my alchemist, Dr Howshinger, told me a peculiar tale about a girl with hair like rope and a black eye stealing a sample of the poison from Dr Corian's corpse."

Both the Old Girl and Cruikshank stared at Rory. She felt herself shrink beneath their gaze.

"Ain't no law against stealing moisture," she muttered.

"There isn't, no. But to me that says you are involved in this and have been for some time. Which leads me to the conclusion that you are working for this Viper, whoever he is."

"Begging your pardon, Ma'am, but while I been involved, I ain't working for the Viper. I'm blackmailing him."

An amused look crossed the Old Girl's face.

"Unfortunately, that's not much of a guarantee," she replied. "How do I know Myran is even real? The Viper could be the one planning the coup, and you have been sent as a way to distract me from the truth."

"Well, that don't make no sense. If the Viper's behind all this, why bother sending me in the first place to tell you about the assassination?"

"Because we already knew about it. The Viper, or whoever is behind all this, has killed two of my servants, a cook, several guards, and — worse — he got to one of my Varanguards in his home. All of them stripped of their uniforms. Which means that anyone could dress up as a member of my staff to try and get to me." The Old Girl leaned forward. "You might be here to misdirect me, even if you aren't aware of it."

"The Viper is working on a solution right now," said Rory with defiance. "He's trying to help stop Myran."

"So there is an antidote? Howshinger told me it was impossible."

"Not an antidote," said Cruikshank. "Something that can prevent the poison from affecting your skin. Like a buffer. I do think the girl is telling the truth, Marchioness."

"Tell me, Eleanore, what is your role in all this?" The Old Girl trained her iron-grey eyes on Cruikshank and, to her surprise, Rory saw her squirm. "If I was to raid your workshop now, would I find a man called the Viper within?"

"He is at my workshop, yes, but —"

"Eleanore, really. Are you associating with assassins in your old age?"

Cruikshank cleared her throat. "Marchioness, wouldn't it be best to cancel the Revels?"

"But then Myran might try and get to the Marchioness another time that we don't know of and have no control over," pointed out Rory.

"The girl is right," said the Old Girl. "In any case, I will not have my actions dictated by that coward in Airnia. I have another solution."

She leaned back and pulled on a braided cord. Rory heard the double doors open behind her. Boots and spurs rang out on the parquet floor.

"Marchioness," said a voice, which to her dismay was very familiar.

She turned to find Rafe behind them, just coming up from a bow. Rory was shocked to find that he wore the purple uniform of the Varanguards. Their eyes met for a second, and the tiniest flicker of surprise crossed his face.

"You two know each other?" asked the Old Girl.

Damn if that woman didn't miss anything.

"Not really. We had a conversation about property once," replied Rafe.

"Good. Fetch me the Persuader and send a platoon of guards to surround Cruikshank's workshop."

Rory opened her mouth to protest, but Cruikshank squeezed her arm, motioning for her to be quiet.

Rafe bowed again. "Marchioness." He walked out without another look in Rory's direction.

"Assuming you are telling the truth," said the Old Girl to Rory, "I shall want Howshinger to work with this Viper to create a solution before the Revels in two days. I won't trust anything Howshinger hasn't worked on and approved. We will move you all to Cruikshank's old workshop down by the docks, which is smaller and easier to guard. It goes without saying that guards will be keeping an eye on the place at all times."

Rafe returned bearing a tray on which was a bottle and two glasses. The bottle was filled with a clear liquid.

"Now, as to the assumption that you are telling the truth, Rory. This is the Persuader — a poison that your master will no doubt be familiar with. It is odourless, tasteless, and utterly untraceable. It is also very slow acting. This is what I propose. You drink the poison voluntarily. If I survive the Revels, you receive the antidote and survive with me. If I don't, then neither do you. Your friend the Viper will also get a dose."

For the second time that day, Rory found herself unable to speak. Cruikshank began to protest, but the Marchioness held up her hand.

"This is not for debate, Eleanore. You and I go back far enough that I trust you — but this one and the Viper? I can't afford to take chances. This way our fates are intertwined, and there's no stronger will than the will to survive. There's no other way I can make sure they will both work towards my survival."

"But I'm the one who came voluntarily to warn you of Myran's plan!" Rory found her voice at last.

"As I said, I have no guarantee that isn't misdirection."

"Well, what if I'm telling the truth but Myran gets to you anyway?"

"You'll have to make sure that doesn't happen."

The Marchioness fixed her with her steel gaze, holding out one of the glasses, and Rory felt herself grow angry. She wasn't going to be forced into doing anything. She had come here to help from a sense of duty and respect for the Old Girl. Both were rapidly fading, as were any aspirations of becoming a hero.

"And what if I refuse?"

The Old Girl's eyes went cold. "Then I arrest you for treason."

CHAPTER

39

Longinus wasn't happy. Not happy at all. He glared at the little man standing in front of him, blinking through his thick optics. Dr Howshinger licked his lips, eyes darting between the goblet Longinus was holding in one hand and the alchemy formulae he held in the other.

"Hurry up about it," said a guard behind him, "or we'll make you drink it."

Longinus downed the contents of the goblet and slammed it on the bench.

"My dear colleague," said Dr Howshinger, "I really do think that between us —"

"Do not trespass on the territory of familiarity, *sir*," replied Longinus. "I am not your *colleague*. I am here under duress. I have been coerced in the basest of ways. *Colleagues*," he spat the word, sending a spray of spittle on Howshinger's optics, "do not poison one another. *Colleagues,*" he spat again, "do not try to steal one another's secrets. There is an *understanding,* sir, amongst alchemists, and you have grossly violated this most sacred agreement."

Dr Howshinger wiped his optics on a plain handkerchief, which wasn't trimmed with lace or even monogrammed.

Amateur.

"I was not aware," said Howshinger, "that there is any kind of understanding —"

"It is the same kind of understanding that exists between *gentlemen,* a class of individuals to which it is clear from your handkerchief you do not belong, and therefore cannot comprehend. Any gentleman alchemist, such as I am, would understand that to use poison against a fellow alchemist is a most ignoble, unscrupulous, and contemptible act."

Longinus grabbed his notes, turned, and swept away, but of course he couldn't go far since they were all trapped within that dastardly warehouse. Poisoned and trapped, that was his lot now.

They had moved from Cruikshank's normal workshop to an older, smaller, in short, inferior one, as though this would be preferable conditions to work under. Guards patrolled both outside and inside the workshop, so there was no privacy to be had.

"You and Howshinger are getting along well," said Rory, walking up to him.

"I cannot work like this," Longinus said to her in a low whisper. "I cannot be in proximity to such incompetence. He blinks at me every time I open my mouth and cannot finish a sentence to save his life."

"Hey, look, I ain't a fan of Howshinger any more than you, but if you stop interrupting him, maybe he'll finish his sentences."

"You are not helping. Go and tell the Marchioness to remove this aspiring alchemist of hers so I can get on with my art."

"Do you really think the Marchioness will listen to me? She poisoned me, same as you, so she don't trust me neither, and she was pretty clear that Howshinger had to be here. We ain't got a say in this, Longinus."

"Yes, and about that: what exactly made you think that going to her was going to end well for us?"

"I was trying to do the right thing," said Rory bitterly. "I thought we could be heroes and all. Clearly, that was the loss of blood talking. Believe you me, I ain't doing the right thing ever again. This is the problem with honest people, so damned unpredictable, can't trust them with nothing. But we gotta stop Myran, Longinus. I ain't dying because of her."

"Me neither."

"Mr Pendergast?" called Howshinger from the alchemy bench.

Longinus took a deep breath and pinched the bridge of his nose.

"That's got to be the first time you done that and not because of me, right?" said Rory.

"Yes, and what a surprise it is. By the way I, ah, never thanked you for rescuing my journals."

"Don't mention it. But if you could come up with a miracle and save both our arses, that'll be all the thanks I need. Otherwise we might as well have jumped into that abyss."

"Yes, yes, you're right." Longinus took a deep breath, and returned to Dr Howshinger.

"Ah, Mr Pendergast," said Dr Howshinger, looking up. "I came across this very interesting phenomenon. If you would look over here."

Not letting go of his notes in case that devious excuse for an alchemist tried to look through them, Longinus cast his professional gaze on Dr Howshinger's findings.

***

Indecently early on the morning of the Revels, a commotion at the workshop's door startled everyone. Longinus and Howshinger were still hard at work, bleary-eyed and haggard. Rory, Cruikshank, and a couple of the guards not on watch were asleep on whatever approximately comfortable, horizontal surfaces were available.

Two male Varanguards entered, wearing plain clothes. Behind them followed the Marchioness. She wore loose trousers and a simple long-sleeved tunic with a high collar, all made of the mineral mesh Longinus used when he handled his writing poison.

"So how are we doing?" she asked Howshinger and Longinus.

In his befuddled state, Longinus felt the full force of that steel gaze and he momentarily stumbled on his words.

"We have something —" began Howshinger.

"The poison is incredibly fast acting and virulent, as you know," Longinus hastened to interrupt. Nobody was going to discuss his own poison in front of him, least of all that ridiculous little man. "But we have created a paste that can be applied to the skin. It acts as a buffer and neutralises the poison on contact."

"Let me see it."

Howshinger produced the pot containing the paste. It was pale blue, the same colour that the poison turned the eyes of its victims. "There is but one —"

"There is but one flaw," interrupted Longinus again, glaring at Howshinger. "It is affected by water."

"A pretty big flaw," observed the Marchioness, "considering a storm is brewing. I'm assuming it will stop working if in contact with water?"

"Yes. We cannot get around this problem. The very compound that neutralises the poison on contact is the element that is sensitive to water. But we are making enough for you and Lady Martha to continuously reapply it throughout the day, should it rain."

The Marchioness nodded. "It better work, I don't need to remind you what's at stake here. Might I also suggest, Master Viper, that in future you refrain from creating poisons for which you do not possess antidotes. That would save us all a lot of trouble."

One of the Varanguards stepped forward. "Ma'am, it might be wise to cancel the visit to the performers."

"I have visited the performers before every Revels since Damsport became independent. I will *not* change my actions for anyone — not for the Emperor of Airnia, nor for this Myran."

"I don't get my behaviour dictated by anyone neither," piped up Rory, "but getting poisoned has that effect on people. Makes you reconsider things."

Cruikshank cuffed her on the back of the head and Longinus repressed a laugh. Norman, who stood next to them, snickered and earned himself a cuff on the head from Cruikshank, too.

"What? If I'm gonna die tomorrow, who cares if I'm being insolent," muttered Rory.

"There'll be no more talk of cancelling or changing the Revels," said the Old Girl. "The day I start to cower and hide, the Emperor has won. My bodyguards will come to fetch you in three hours," she added to Longinus and Rory, "so make sure you are both ready."

Rory and Longinus made their last preparations. Longinus' rapier, the one Rory had taken from him the night of their meeting, was back at his hip. Rory glanced at it with a pinch of regret, but she couldn't deny that it looked better on him than it ever had on her. A guard had furnished the two of them with weapons of their choosing, and she had been given a rapier of her own. It was too long for her, but she wasn't about to complain and make a fool of herself by drawing attention to her diminutive frame.

Longinus had also selected a dagger, and he had concocted himself a poison to take along. He tucked the vial with its atomiser into a pocket and began fiddling with his baldric.

"This rapier is all wrong with this baldric," he announced. "The balance is off — look, look at how it moves when I walk. It's making me all lopsided. This is just unacceptable. I can't work like this, I am inadequately prepared, I am…"

Rory could see his hands shake as he fussed with the rapier.

"You alright?" she whispered.

He swallowed and didn't meet her eye.

"I don't think I can face her again," he replied in a voice so low she almost didn't hear.

He cleared his throat and looked away.

"It's this baldric," he said louder. "Someone fetch me another, something in black for starters, not this brown monstrosity. Am I the *only* one who notices how badly it clashes with my silks?"

Rory could see a couple of guards by the door laughing at Longinus. She turned away with some difficulty, resisting the urge to draw her rapier and wipe the smirk off their faces. Attacking a guard at this point would do little to improve their situation.

"What if it weren't you facing her?" she whispered. "Can't you be the Viper for today rather than Longinus? The Viper doesn't have a sister, right? Like in them stories you wrote. He ain't afraid of…of her. Right?"

Longinus nodded.

"Plus I'll be there," she added, "and I know enough about swords to do some damage."

"You can't do much, Rory, or you'll reopen your shoulder," he replied. "And anyway, she's a phenomenal swordswoman." He fingered his baldric. "She's unrivalled. I'm a good swordsman, but when it comes down to it, I can't… Well, you know."

There was no time for Rory to answer. An escort of Varanguards arrived to take them to the docks. They deployed around Rory and Longinus, Rafe at their helm. His demeanour was so different, Rory almost didn't recognise him. His eyes were dark and grim, no hint of his usual sardonic humour to be seen. The Varanguards wore ceremonial uniforms: purple with gleaming golden buckles and at their wrists were golden spiked bracers. On their heads were the burnished helmets with their long horsehair ponytails and hidden knives. The helmets' chinstraps were specially designed so that a particular movement of the chin was enough to unsheathe the knives.

The party made their way to Innec Dock, just a short walk away. The Old Girl was already there. The pale blue paste had been applied to her face thickly enough that her brown skin didn't show through, making her look otherworldly. Her lips were painted a red so dark they almost looked black, and her eyes had also been painted dramatically. Her hair was piled high in thick coils held in place with heavy gold combs.

Next to her was another woman, who — other than a different chin and a lighter eye colour — looked like a younger version of her. She was dressed and made up identically, but where the Old Girl's hair was iron grey, hers was shiny black.

"Ah, there you both are. This is my daughter, the Lady Martha. This is Longinus and Rory."

Lady Martha nodded, seemingly as unaffected as the Marchioness at the prospect of an assassination attempt.

Rory couldn't remember what the etiquette was for the Old Girl's daughter so she just nodded back, and nobody seemed to take offence.

"We're going into the performers' area," said the Old Girl. "My bodyguards will keep a perimeter around us at all times. Longinus and Rory, you will walk behind Martha and me. You'll each be paired with one of my Varanguards. If you see anyone that you recognise, or anything remotely suspicious, you are to inform them. I don't need to remind you that your survival depends on me making it through today."

Rory's heart fluttered in her chest like a butterfly in a glass jar. It hadn't quite seemed real earlier, when she had been reassuring Longinus, but now there was no turning back. She would be going head to head against Myran — against the Scarred Woman. She suddenly felt far too small, too weak, too inadequate for the task ahead. It was as though a great boulder had been put into motion, and unless she was quick, she was going to be crushed beneath it as it rolled past.

Overhead, the sky was full of roiling, iron-grey clouds. The atmosphere was thick and tense, as though the very air was waiting for Myran's attack. Rory glanced up at the sky and fingered the talismans at her neck, praying that some god would hold the storm back until after the Revels.

"Move out," called a deep voice.

And the procession set off.

***

Behind the gate was a maelstrom of artists, greasepaint, and feathers. Men and women contorted themselves into mad shapes as they limbered up, people rushed past in a blur of silk and sequins, and above them all rose the din of a hundred voices, louder than even the seagulls.

Rory kept a tight grip on the handle of her dagger, finding the cool, solid feel of it calming. She craned to see every single face they passed, head swivelling left and right like a weathervane. Every so often she glanced at Longinus, who was also scanning the crowd, his face drawn, lips pressed into a line.

When Rory spotted a woman with Myran's height and build wearing black leather, she gasped. Immediately, the Varanguard next to her put a hand to his rapier and said, "Where?" But the woman in the crowd turned, showing a face that was distinctly devoid of scars.

"False alarm," muttered Rory.

She opened her mouth to alert the Varanguard a dozen more times, and a dozen times she closed it as she realised her mind was playing tricks on her. Myran and Raynard danced in front of her eyes and disappeared as soon as she looked at them, blending back into the faces of strangers. So many faces, so many mirages.

The Marchioness and Lady Martha walked leisurely, taking the time to speak to each other, expressing their excitement ahead of the show. There was no rush, no urgency to their movements. No one would have been able to tell the threat they were under. Rory's body, on the other hand, was so taut she felt like she might snap like a twig at any moment.

When they reached Cruikshank, it was a relief to see a familiar face that wasn't an illusion. Rory felt her body relax a fraction. Cruikshank's enormous spider was hidden under a tarp, and she was wrestling with a complicated-looking tool with three telescoping prongs. As soon as Cruikshank spotted the procession, she put the tool aside and went to speak to the Marchioness.

Norman walked past carrying an intricately engraved brass box.

"Hey!" Rory caught him by the arm. "Where you going? You should be helping Cruikshank."

He yanked his arm back. "Got some errands to run. Mind your own business, anyway."

The Varanguard stepped forward at once, hand on his rapier.

"Leave it," called Cruikshank. Behind her, the Marchioness gave a tiny nod. "No need to worry, Rory, he's working for a few different performers today. He'll be coming back to me later. Leave the boy be."

Norman scowled at Rory, but he gave the Varanguard a wide berth as he passed, shooting the man a wary glance.

The Marchioness and Lady Martha moved on, and the retinue followed. Cruikshank stopped Rory as she walked past.

"Here," she said, handing her a pair of binoculars. "This will help when you get to the stadium itself. I'll come give you both a hand as soon as I'm done."

She gave Rory an encouraging smile, and Rory tried to look confident as she took the binoculars. She returned to the procession, and the visit continued undisturbed until they reached the acrobats from Caracka. There was a flurry of panicked activity amongst the performers and stagehands. Beyond the rush of bodies, in the water, was a platform from which protruded five masts with perches along them and rope rigging. No doubt the acrobats would be performing various dives and jumps from the masts. At the top of the tallest, central mast was a long, horizontal beam, like the top of a 'T.'

"What's going on?" asked the Old Girl to a man who was rushing past.

"Begging your pardon, Ma'am," he replied. "We've had to replace our soloist with his understudy, so it's a bit of a rush to get things ready." He sketched a small bow and ran off.

"I'm replacing him," said a pretty woman with a haughty expression. She executed a graceful curtsy.

"How come?" asked the Old Girl.

"He died." The acrobat's face betrayed no emotion.

Rory felt every hair on her skin bristle. She stared and stared at the woman's face, probing her memory for a sign of recognition. Nothing. She glanced at Longinus next to her, but he didn't seem to recognise the woman any more than she did. A man with a swollen belly and short legs hurried over.

"A great honour, Ma'am, truly, a great honour." He bowed deeply to the Marchioness and then to Lady Martha.

"I am Denbar, the manager of this troupe. You heard of our tragedy, our soloist…" He shot the understudy a warning look.

"What happened to him?" asked the Old Girl.

"He was drinking and whoring and he slipped," replied the pretty woman, with careless contempt.

"He was inebriated," said Denbar, stepping in front of her. "A terrible accident…"

The Marchioness turned to Rafe. "Find the whore," she murmured.

"Oh, don't trouble yourself," said the understudy. "She's over there."

She pointed at a stagehand who was making some last-minute adjustment to a costume. Her eyes were red and swollen.

"Fetch her over, please," said the Marchioness.

Denbar bowed and hurried over, bringing the girl back. She walked as though in a dream, letting him drag her along like a rag doll, and only executed a small curtsy when he prodded her. As she watched the scene, Rory felt a few drops on her hands and neck. She looked up worriedly at the sky, which was rapidly growing darker. She touched her talismans again, begging any god who would listen to hold off for long enough to get the Old Girl out of the performer's area.

"We just heard of the terrible tragedy that befell the soloist," said the Old Girl. "My commiserations. Could you please tell us what happened?"

"We were… He was drunk, and when he tried to get out of bed, he got tangled up in the sheets and he fell." She began to cry softly, to the obvious disgust of the understudy.

"A most terrible stroke of bad luck," added Denbar with another bow. "The nightstand was topped with marble, and he hit the corner right on his temple."

The stagehand cried louder, but her voice was lost in a deafening peal of thunder as the heavens opened. People shouted and ran for shelter, pelted by drops the size of pennies. Umbrellas appeared over the Marchioness and Lady Martha's heads, the Varanguards hurrying to protect them from the rain.

"Have someone keep an eye on them," the Marchioness called to Rafe over the din, as her bodyguards began ushering her towards the exit.

Rafe nodded, but before he could move, a man shoved him aside, sprinting towards the Marchioness. Rafe threw himself forward, catching the man by one arm, while two more Varanguards pounced on him. Someone screamed. The Marchioness and Lady Martha were pulled to the ground, and the Varanguards formed a screen in front of them.

It all happened so quickly, Rory and Longinus barely had time to draw their rapiers before the attacker was pinned to the ground and the Marchioness and Lady Martha were no longer visible behind the human wall of bristling weapons and slick black horsehair ponytails. Around them, the crowd had frozen with the stillness of held breath.

Rory noticed that the floor was littered with tiny sheaths. She carefully pointed her rapier towards the ground, knowing that a flick of a Varanguard's ponytail would now be enough to slice her open like a ripe fruit.

Rafe got up, pulling the attacker with him. The man's clothing was filthy and torn, and he smelled like a brewery. He was making vague gargling sounds, his body limp as a rag doll. His eyes rolled to the back of his head, and the noises stopped. In his right hand was a stick with a darkened tip, and on his left hand was a line from which black veins were already spreading. Rory swallowed. He must have touched his own hand with the poisoned stick during the skirmish.

One of the Varanguards who had helped catch him was still lying on the ground, her body twitching, eyes wide with terror. On her breast was the golden crest that identified her as the captain. A tiny mark was on her cheek, smaller even than the one on the murderer's hand. Darkened veins spread out from it.

Rafe let the attacker fall to the ground and knelt next to the captain. He removed the woman's helmet, letting the rain fall on her face. The woman gasped and gurgled, eyes locked with Rafe's. Then the twitching faded and she fell quiet.

Everyone watched in silence. The rain hissed, and water ran in great rivulets from noses and chins. The Old Girl and Lady Martha were still hidden behind their human screen of bodyguards, sheltered by several umbrellas. The

Varanguards breathed heavily, watching for any other signs of attack.

"The paste," said Longinus, startling everyone. "Wasn't the captain carrying it? The rain can't get to it or it will be ruined!"

An umbrella was immediately opened over the body. Rafe peeled back the woman's sodden clothing with febrile hands.

"Shit."

The jar's lid was still strapped on, the fabric swaddled around it to protect it still in place. But one part looked like it had collapsed, no doubt crushed by the woman's weight when she had fallen. It was soaking wet. Rafe hurriedly slipped it beneath his own clothing to keep it from the rain and stood up, staying under the umbrella.

"Move out," he shouted.

Rory watched them push through a silent crowd that parted around them like water. Men picked up the attacker and the captain and followed.

It had all taken little more than a minute, and in that time, the full scope of the attack had crystallised in Rory's mind. Myran didn't have to carry out the attack, or any of her cronies for that matter. Anyone who could be bought could be given a deadly means of attacking the Marchioness.

The attacker hadn't been familiar, he hadn't been at the cistern with Myran and the rest, and yet Rory had seen countless men like him before. Men who looked and smelled desperate. Men who had fallen between the cracks.

The entire crowd could be seething with assassins, each waiting for the right opportunity, and there would be no way to pick them out.

CHAPTER

41

Rory and Longinus hurried after the Marchioness and her bodyguards. The water stadium was a circular marina just off Innec Dock. A narrow channel linked it to the dock, allowing small steamers and barges to bring the performers through to the floating platform in the middle of the water. Tiered rows of benches rose around the water, each row already crawling with spectators, food sellers, palm readers, pickpockets, and street entertainers trying to make a few coins before the Revels.

The rain had begun to slow, and more bodies joined the crush, coming out from whatever shelter they had sought. Excitement seeped from the crowd, laughter and voices echoing against the stone walls that circled the stadium.

Across from the entrance channel, high above the water, was the Old Girl's box. The Marchioness and her daughter were already within, seeking shelter from the rain. The Varanguards covered every possible entry point, but at a nod from Rafe, they let Rory and Longinus through.

Beyond, the box bristled with yet more bodyguards, and there wasn't so much as a cup bearer in sight.

The Old Girl's face was grim beneath her protective makeup, now thickly streaked from the rain.

"Tell me," she said, gesturing at the ceramic jar Rafe had pulled out from his clothing. Rory looked anxiously at Longinus' face as he examined the paste within. He shook his head.

"Can you make more?" asked the Marchioness.

"There isn't enough time for the reaction to take place," he replied.

Rafe stepped forward. "We should postpone —"

"We're postponing nothing," said the Marchioness, interrupting him. "We've had the Revels in the rain often enough, and the winds are calm enough that there isn't any danger to anyone."

"Except to yourself," pointed out Rafe.

"That may be, but if I postpone or cancel, the Emperor has won. I won't be frightened into changing my behaviour. You two," she said, turning to Longinus and Rory. "Find Myran."

"Yes, Ma'am," said Rory.

Longinus returned the broken jar with its useless paste, and they left the box in silence, striding past the grim Varanguards. Rory could see hard glints in their horsehair ponytails from the unsheathed blades. They would be able to hold back hundreds from where they were. But there were thousands in the crowd. How many had Myran armed with the poison? Rory looked at the crush of bodies beneath as they walked down the stairs from the Old Girl's box. What if they were all poised for attack? Her skin crawled as she and Longinus plunged into the throng.

A cheer rose up around them. Looking back, Rory saw that the Marchioness had stepped forward to greet the crowd. The excitement from the people was palpable as they stamped their feet and clapped their hands and called the Old Girl's name.

The Marchioness lifted her arms to signify silence. The noise died down almost at once.

"Damsians!" Her voice echoed across the flat water. "Today marks the fortieth anniversary of Damsport's independence!" A deafening clamour rose up from the stadium in response. She raised her hands once more. "We welcome those of you who have come from abroad to commemorate this important day with us. The Damsian spirit is something to be celebrated. We are small, but we are fierce. No matter what happens, no matter what we face, we will always have our spirit, we will always have our independence!"

The crowd roared its approval. Over the din, the Old Girl called for the Revels to begin. Rory had to admire the woman. If Myran was listening, the Marchioness had told her clear as day that she was absolutely not afraid.

***

Rory and Longinus scanned the crowd as they moved through the spectators near the Old Girl's box. Eager faces looked down at the Revels' first performance, some already reddened by drink.

Music rose up from the musicians beneath the Old Girl's box. Rory caught movement out on the water from the corner of her eye, and she turned to look. Five Stuppaan men and women, their hair so fair it looked almost white, danced on the floating platform. They each held a long tube at the end of which were smouldering globes. They blew on one end of the tubes, twisting and swaying, so that the globes at the end grew and changed as though they were living things.

When the performance finished, five stunning statues of the finest glass were displayed on the floating platforms. In one swoop, the five dancers spun on their heels and smashed their tubes into the statues, shattering them in a tinkle of glass that made the crowd gasp.

This gave Rory an idea. She turned to Longinus.

"What if there's a signal for the attack? Like them performers smashing the glass? Myran don't even need to be here, maybe she's given the poison to hundreds of people in the crowd, and told them to wait for a sign."

Longinus shook his head. "No, she'd never leave something like that to anyone else. This isn't just a normal assassination. This is theatrics: she's putting on a show, and she'll want the eyes of the world on her. She'll be here."

"Yeah, but what about the attack backstage? Clearly she's given the poison to others."

He waved the comment away with one hand. "You saw how clumsy that was. A distraction at most."

"A distraction?"

Rory frowned. A distraction from what? She thought of what the Marchioness had said about misdirection. The Old Girl was only surrounded by Varanguards whose faces she knew, and no one else, uniform or not, would be allowed near the box — Myran had to have expected those measures. So why bother with the uniforms, especially if she had planned to give the poison to strangers in the crowd?

To draw everyone's attention where she wanted it.

Another gasp from the crowd, and Rory turned back to the performance platform. Cruikshank was floating on her clockwork spider, tracing shapes and making the spider dance. With a powerful burst of steam, she brought the spider up to the wall beneath the Marchioness' box and began to climb. An absurd idea occurred to Rory: what if Cruikshank was in league with Myran? It would be the perfect plan. Nobody suspected Cruikshank. She could climb right up to the Marchioness and nobody would stop her.

"That's ridiculous," Rory whispered to herself, watching mesmerised as the spider scuttled up the wall. If Cruikshank had meant to attack the Marchioness, she could have done so back in the performers' area. But Rory remembered Longinus' comment about theatrics. Killing the Marchioness as the entire city watched would make for a much better show.

Rory held her breath as the enormous spider reached the top of the box, praying that she was wrong.

Cruikshank had the spider make an elaborate bow, and the crowd laughed. Rory sagged with relief. What a ridiculous idea anyhow, for Cruikshank to be an assassin. If there was one thing that could be predicted about honest people, it was their honesty. Even if it made everything else unpredictable.

She and Longinus continued their search of the crowd, and Rory returned to her previous line of thought. What if Longinus was right, and the attack in the performers' area had just been a distraction? What could Myran want to distract them from? Was it to get them all back to the box?

The floating platform in the water stadium was pulled away from the centre as the next act approached, tugged along by a small steamer. It was the structure for the acrobats, half submerged in water so that only the tops of the masts protruded. At the apex was the horizontal beam, and in the middle of it was something that caught Rory's eye. She pulled up her binoculars; it was the box that Norman had been carrying. Why was it there? It hadn't been there earlier. Why had he tied it to the top of the mast? And why did she feel sure she had seen it before?

She stared at it though the binoculars. Where had she seen it, where had she —

"Your crossbow," she said to Longinus, handing him the binoculars urgently. "Is that your crossbow, the one I took out of the cabinet?"

He looked. "It looks like it, but —"

"That's how they're going to kill the Marchioness. That haughty acrobat, I *knew* there was something dodgy about her!"

"My poison doesn't work like that. The friction of the air —"

"Don't you get it, Myran doesn't need the poison, she can have that acrobat shoot the Marchioness with the crossbow plain and simple. That's why they burned down your house: so you couldn't see that the crossbow was gone. All the Varanguards are watching the crowd same as us, and no one is looking at the performers, leaving the Marchioness completely exposed!" Rory broke into a run down towards the water. "I'm gonna get the crossbow, you go warn the Marchioness," she shouted over her shoulder.

Longinus caught up with her and grabbed her arm. "I'll get the crossbow. I know how it works if necessary. You go warn the Marchioness."

"Will you be alright?"

"Of course I will," he scoffed, but it sounded like an out-of-tune note.

"Alright. Just remember, *you* are the Viper. Not them. And the Viper ain't afraid of anything, is he?"

"Yes, yes, now go!" He pushed her towards the box and headed for the water.

***

Pushing through the crowd was slow work. The steamer and sunken masts had almost reached the end of the floating platform. Rory ran for a nearby exit and slipped down a narrow lane that led to the disused warehouses behind the stadium. Fishermen typically prepared their catches there before heading to the Bazaar, and it was now empty.

She sprinted as quick as she could, dodging broken crates, careful not to slip on the viscera that was strewn about the floor.

"Rory!"

She screeched to a halt and turned.

Little Alice was poking her head from between two stacks of crates.

"There's someone back here," she said in her little mouse voice.

"Not now."

Rory made to run again when Alice called her back.

"There's one of them cards attached to her."

Rory hesitated — she really didn't have time to spare, but it could give her a clue as to Myran's whereabouts.

"Quick, quick!" she said as she followed Alice through the stacks of crates.

They entered one of the darkened warehouses, and there in the gloom she saw Pip crouching next to something. They hurried over, and Rory was greeted by the sight of the haughty acrobat, a lurid red smile slashed across her throat.

"Shit!"

Myran must have taken the acrobat's place. Longinus was right — she planned to do this with all eyes on her.

Rory spun on her heels and ran out.

"What about our money?" shouted Pip behind her.

When she was out of the warehouse, Rory hesitated. She had to warn Longinus that he was going straight to confront his sister, but she was already too far around the stadium. To turn back now and try to reach him would take too long, and then what? If she was too slow and he didn't manage to stop Myran, they would both die from the poison, not to mention that Damsport would be facing a return to the Airnian Empire.

No, her best shot was to continue as she was. Once she'd warned the Marchioness, she could jump into the water from the box, and swim to the masts and to Longinus. She kissed a handful of talismans as she sprinted off, praying that he would last long enough against Myran for Rory to reach him.

CHAPTER

42

The floating platform had been moved right to the edge of the stadium, opposite the Old Girl's box. The steamer was approaching the platform and began manoeuvring itself so that it could dock at the platform while leaving the sunken masts behind it, near the centre of the stadium.

Around the water were four huts, from which the chains that moved the floating platform could be operated. Longinus hurried towards the one nearest the floating platform. Once the platform had reached the water's edge, he'd be able to get onto it from the hut and then reach the steamer and masts to get the crossbow.

He entered the hut, and immediately his senses were assailed by the loud clanging of machinery and the heat of boilers. The air was full of dancing dust motes. A tall man with his back to him was busy with the platform controls, keeping an eye on it through the window.

"Excuse me," shouted Longinus over the din. "I need to get onto the platform."

The man turned and a smile spread across his face like oil on water. Longinus' stomach sank. Raynard.

He drew his rapier. Longinus drew his too, but his hands were shaking. The acrobat he could handle, but Raynard? That meant Myran was somewhere. Maybe near. Maybe watching.

Raynard saw his fear, and his smile widened. He launched into attack. Longinus parried, but clumsily, allowing Raynard to put him on the back foot. Longinus couldn't focus; Myran had taken a hold in his mind. All he could think about was her taunting smile, the particular kind of terror she awoke in him.

Raynard pressed on, pushing him towards a corner. Longinus could feel the thump of the machinery in his bones, matched by the thump of his pulse in his ears. He fumbled a riposte, and Raynard's rapier slashed a hole in his sleeve, only just missing his arm.

"Guess we'll finally find out how you react to the sight of your own blood," yelled Raynard over the noise.

Focus, focus. Focus, dammit.

Longinus did a passable execution of Pasient's deflection and managed to get himself out of the corner. From his vantage point, he managed a glance out the window. The steamer had docked, and the masts were slowly rising from the water. Was Myran in the audience somewhere, watching it all happen? Was Rory at the box? Could Myran see her?

He didn't have time to look again — Raynard was already on him.

Their swords flew, cutting swirls out of the dust motes, the clash as they met barely audible against the loud clank of the machinery. Longinus tried to close in on Raynard, but before he could execute his pass, Raynard lifted a long leg up and kicked him straight in the stomach. Longinus staggered, crashing back into a metal cog the size of a cart wheel.

Raynard made a mocking gesture, as though he were a gentleman allowing another to pass in front of him. Longinus realised Raynard was so confident in winning that he was happy to let him pick himself up without pressing the advantage. The humiliation of it burned worse than any acid.

"After you," shouted Raynard. "And when I'm done with you, it will be your little girlfriend's turn."

Girlfriend? *Girlfriend?* Longinus was affronted by the suggestion, and he clung to the feeling as he got up. *Focus. Focus on Rory.* Her words echoed in his head. "The Viper ain't afraid of anything."

She's right. The Viper isn't afraid of anything. The Viper is an expert swordsman —

Raynard launched into attack, and Longinus lost his train of thought, his mind filling once more with the image of his sister, her eyes, her scar, bearing down on him.

No! Focus. The Viper is a master assassin.

That was when it occurred to him that this was just a kill, just another kill like all those he had done before. It was just another story that he needed to tell himself.

He spotted a small mistake in Raynard's footwork. Not enough to take advantage of, but enough to elicit contempt. Contempt was good; contempt meant survival.

Amateur. The Viper's movements are swift, precise. No mistakes in his footwork. He is strong as an ox, lithe as a snake, fast as jungle cat, deadly as —

"Poison!"

As he said the word, Longinus remembered the vial in his pocket. Raynard stumbled in surprise at hearing Longinus shout and again made a small mistake. This time, Longinus pressed his advantage. He pushed Raynard towards the machinery.

Raynard's reach was too long for Longinus to get close and spray him with the poison and, besides, doing so would be too risky: Longinus couldn't afford so much as a cut. Instead, he waited until Raynard's head was close to a large metal tube, and then he flung the vial with all his strength, holding his breath as he did. He jumped back immediately, so as not to be close to the poisonous fumes, and covered his mouth and nose with his hand, still holding his breath. Raynard made to follow him, but he stopped in his tracks, confusion imprinted on his face.

He gasped for air, and his hand flew to his throat.

"No… Not fair…" he rasped.

The Viper gives his latest kill a look of contempt. There is no fair in death. And anyway, no assassin worth his name kills with a sword.

Longinus turned away as Raynard's rapier fell to the ground. He hurried towards the door that led out to the platform, lungs burning for air. As he opened it, he had time enough to see Raynard fall to his knees, hands madly clawing at his throat, before he stepped out into the fresh air and slammed the door shut behind him.

He took a deep breath, composing himself. He was the Viper. There was nothing he couldn't do.

Beyond, the masts had almost fully risen from the water. At the base of each was an acrobat, also rising from the water like creatures from the deep. They faced the box and away from him, but he could see the pouches on their back, with the tubes snaking over their shoulders to their faces. Longinus guessed the pouches were alchemically enhanced to provide breathing air.

He turned his attention to the acrobat by the central mast, the one who was, no doubt, supposed to assemble and use his crossbow. He marched down the floating platform towards her.

The Viper has his next kill in his sights. No one can stand between him and his prey; once the Viper has chosen, death is inevitable.

With a final clank, the platform supporting the masts was fully out of the water. The acrobats bowed as one.

CHAPTER 43

Rory re-entered the stadium just in time to see the acrobats bow to the box. They removed the masks that covered their faces, allowing them to breathe underwater, but kept their goggles on. They wore shimmering outfits that shifted between blue and green in the light so that they looked like they were made of water.

Rory lifted her binoculars to her eyes, searching for the one by the tallest mast, the one who would have access to the crossbow. There! Although the woman still had goggles on, there was no mistaking the bit of scar that snaked down to her jaw. Myran.

Rory lowered the binoculars. Behind the acrobats, she could see a dark shape making his way to the steamer. Longinus. He was walking differently than earlier, more self-assured. She prayed that his assurance would hold up to discovering that the acrobat was in fact Myran.

She hurried towards the stairs that led to the box, pushing people out of the way. The crowds had swollen and she made slow progress.

"Move! Move!"

She had to get to the box in time. If she was quick enough, she should be able to tell the Marchioness and Lady Martha to get out of sight, and then jump from the box and into the water, to swim to the masts, and help Longinus. If he could just hold on for long enough…

"Out of my way!"

She had almost reached the stairs, and she could see the Varanguards at the top, black ponytails still wet and gleaming from the rain. When she reached the first step, she let out a cry of victory, but before she could push her way up, two arms picked her up and dragged her away.

Jake moved through the crowd easily, his massive frame cutting through it like a hot knife through butter.

"What are you doing?" said Rory. "Let me go!" She kicked and thrashed, but Jake had her too well pinned. Pain skewered her shoulder, but she ignored it and squirmed and thrashed for all she was worth. Something warm ran down her arm.

"You don't get to tell me what to do no more," said Jake. "I made you a good deal, and you didn't even have the guts to turn me down in person. You chose that fancy man."

"Jake, please. If we were ever friends, please put me down. I got to get —"

"You don't tell me what to do no more," he repeated, voice flat. "I owe you for that money, and I pay my debts.

I'm supposed to kill you, but I won't. I'm taking you away from the stadium, and that will be my debt repaid."

"If you don't let me go now I'm gonna die anyway. Please, Jake, I been poisoned and —"

"Not my problem."

Jake carried her farther and farther from the Old Girl's box. Over on the water, the acrobat was halfway up the mast, while Longinus was just beginning the climb. Right at the top, glinting dully, was the crossbow in its case.

Rory took a deep breath, ready to scream the place down in the hope that if she created a stir the Varanguards would notice her in the crowd. Jake clamped his hand over her mouth before she made a sound.

"Don't even try, I know all your tricks too well."

The Old Girl's box retreated farther from sight.

"Let the girl go," said a familiar voice. Metal flashed at Jake's throat.

Rory never thought she'd one day be genuinely relieved to hear those words. Jake hesitated, and Rafe pressed the tip of the rapier against his skin, drawing a drop of blood. Jake loosened his grasp — just as he had so many times during their cons, and Rory fell awkwardly to the ground. She broke her fall with her bad arm, and for an awful moment, she thought she might pass out from the pain.

"Myran's with the acrobats," she said to Rafe in a weak voice. "She's the one in the middle. There's a crossbow at the top."

She didn't wait for an answer, pushing her way through the crowd and back towards the stairs. Down in the water,

Myran was two-thirds up the mast. On either side of her, the other acrobats were diving off their lower masts and flying through the air from one mast to another.

"Out of the way!" yelled Rafe behind her. "Official business on behalf of the Marchioness!"

The spectators stepped back, responding to the purple and gold of Rafe's uniform, and Rory squirrelled herself through the gaps as fast as she could. Her bad arm was numb and she was starting to see spots dance in front of her eyes. She reached the stairs once more, just in time to see Myran astride atop the beam with her back to the Marchioness. She was hunched over something.

The crossbow.

Longinus was only halfway up.

Rory ran up the steps. The Varanguard at the top acted on reflex, drawing their weapons.

"Let her pass!" shouted Rafe behind her.

They hesitated, but one of them moved a little aside, and she pushed through. She ran into the box, and shouts erupted around her. She heard Rafe's voice, but she didn't stop, sprinting for the Old Girl who had stood up at the commotion.

On the beam, Myran straightened her back. She swung around.

Rory leapt at the same time as Rafe.

The Marchioness and Rafe went crashing to the ground, but Rory was jerked back as the crossbow bolt skewered one of her hair segments to the wooden back of the chair.

She landed awkwardly on her bad shoulder and her vision swam.

"Lady Martha," she gasped. "Myran's reloading the crossbow."

The world went dark.

***

She came to with a start a few seconds later, looking around her in a panic. Someone had released her hair from the crossbow bolt, and both Lady Martha and the Marchioness were protected by a wall of Varanguards. Rory staggered up, feeling lightheaded.

Over on the beam, Myran stood facing Longinus, a long dagger in one hand, the crossbow locked and reloaded in the other.

"Longinus," murmured Rory.

Someone spoke to her, but she paid no attention. She had to get to Longinus. He couldn't face Myran alone. He wouldn't make it. She pulled out her rapier and threw it aside, noticing distractedly as she did that a trail of blood ran down her arm. She lurched to the edge of the box.

"I'm coming," she muttered. "Longinus, I'm coming."

She vaulted over the edge and into the water. Someone shouted her name before the water closed over her head.

Rory tried to swim towards Longinus, but she didn't move forward. She didn't even resurface. Instead, she sank. She kicked and pulled herself with her good arm, but that didn't seem to help. A long stream of red leaked from her shoulder. Rory kicked harder, confused. She had swum fully clothed before but had never sunk so quickly. What was happening?

She remembered the iron in her boots.

The rapidly reddening surface of the water receded farther.

CHAPTER

44

The Viper faces his opponent, drawing out his rapier and matched long dagger.

He didn't wait, launching into attack, keeping the tip of the crossbow pointed away from him with his dagger. With his rapier, he fought Myran's dagger. The world receded until it was just the two of them and the beam. Footwork careful, precise. Moves faster than wind, clearer than glass. No mistake possible.

The Viper knows no fear. He has no sister — he only knows of targets and opponents. Opponents that can be killed. Opponents that can be poisoned.

"Are you silent to keep yourself from stuttering, Longinus?" Myran's voice was like a rusty saw against a nail.

He faltered ever so slightly, made a small mistake.

The crossbow swung to face him. Myran hesitated for a split second, and he slashed at her wrist with his dagger.

The crossbow fell from her hand, hitting the beam and letting loose its bolt towards the water.

"Well played," said Myran. "But now I really am in my element." She grinned wolfishly and drew out her other dagger.

She attacked with a cry, arms slicing through the air with such speed it looked as though there were four, not two.

The Viper parries every blow, increasing his own speed to match hers.

They moved back and forth on the beam with careful, bare feet.

"Shall I cut you again, little brother?"

Their blades flew in a blur of motion.

"Your blood was so pretty, so red. Remember?"

The Viper knows no fear. The Viper has no past, no memories. There is only the present.

"Wouldn't it be a shame if I killed you before you ever learned to say my name? Myran," she taunted with a grin, despite the sweat that poured from her brow. "Myran."

The Viper ignores the taunts, his focus is only on the blades.

Jab, parry, pushing forward, retreating back.

"Myran! Say my name, you no good coward, go on! M-m-m-myran, say it!"

Jab, jab, jab parry, thrust, parry.

"M-m-myran! M-m-myran!"

She made a mistake.

Longinus immediately took the advantage, pushing her on the back foot.

Never again will you torment me, never again will you invade my dreams.

He launched into the Double Knotted Passover (a move of his design), putting her off-balance.

Longinus locked both blades with hers.

You are nothing, nothing. You are a coward. I am not afraid of you. You are only my sister, you are only —

"MYRAN!" he roared, and with a violent twist of both wrists, he sent both her blades flying.

For a heartbeat, she looked at him with fear. And then, from the corner of his eye, Longinus saw a tiny form pulled out of the water.

Rory.

Myran kicked out in an arc, sweeping out his feet from under him. He fell back to the beam, letting go of his rapier, only just catching hold of a piece of rigging with his right hand as he fell. He clung to it, his feet dangling in empty space.

"Good to know I can always count on your weakness, Longinus!"

Myran dove off the beam, pulling her mask over her nose and mouth.

Longinus pulled himself up. He could see the point where Myran had broken the water. If he jumped now, he could get her. But he didn't hesitate for long. He turned away and walked to the other end, towards Rory. He jumped into the water.

***

Moments later, Longinus pulled himself up onto land.

"Out of my way!"

His urgency lending him a force he hadn't known he possessed, he all but lifted the lad who was fussing around Rory, throwing him to the side. She wasn't breathing, her little face still beneath her wet rope-like hair. He knelt down and slammed one fist smartly into her sternum. She didn't react. He hit her sternum again. With a start, she coughed up water and turned to her side. Longinus carefully helped her into the foetal position as she vomited more water.

That was when he saw her reopened wound. He hadn't noticed it before, too focused on saving her, but now the smell of blood filled his nostrils. He stood up quickly and stepped away, turning his back to the assembled crowd so they wouldn't see him go pale. He coughed to disguise a bout of dry retching.

"Will she be alright?" asked the lad. It was one of the Varanguards. Longinus recognised him vaguely, although he couldn't remember his name, as with anyone not worthy of his full attention. And this lad, with his ineffectual fussing that could have cost Rory her life, was most certainly not worth anything more than contempt. Longinus focused on his anger, and it dispelled the nausea a little.

"She will be," he replied caustically. "And no thanks to you, imbecile."

"I pulled her out of the water," protested the lad.

"And what good is that if the water is still inside the lungs, you *dolt*?"

The lad coloured, but behind him, Longinus could see Rory sitting up. He only shot her the briefest of glances, not wanting to take his chances with the open wound in front of witnesses. Her skin was pale, her eyes rimmed with red.

"Rory, are you alright?"

He saw her nod out of the corner of his eye. "Fine," she replied weakly. "Someone give me something for my shoulder."

"Coming through!" came a familiar voice through the crowd. Spectators found themselves forcibly moved aside by Cruikshank. She knelt down next to Rory.

"You gave us a fright, lovey," she said.

Longinus saw that she was tending to Rory's shoulder — in fact, she was doing more than simply binding it: she wrapped it over and over again with fabric until the blood was all but hidden, although the smell lingered. He felt a surge of gratitude for them both, trying as they were to keep his secret.

A hush fell on the crowd.

"It seems my daughter and I owe you both thanks," said the Marchioness as she arrived.

Longinus turned to face her and caught sight of Lady Martha next to her. His breath left him like a wineskin emptying itself of wine. He had been too preoccupied that morning to really notice her, but now...

CHAPTER

45

Rory threw Longinus a glance, but he was merely staring at Lady Martha with such a glazed and idiotic air that, had she not known better, she would have thought he was simple. Lady Martha frowned and gestured again for them to take the two small bottles of liquid in her hand

"Your antidote," she repeated. "Please take it."

Rory took both bottles, wincing at the pain in her left arm as she moved it. She uncorked one bottle and guzzled the entire content so fast that she began to choke, but still she continued to drink. She finished, coughing and spluttering, and someone thumped her back.

"Thanking you, Lady Martha," she said between coughs. "Is that enough antidote?" She wiped her chin with the back of her hand where a little had trickled out and then carefully licked her hand.

The Marchioness laughed.

"It should be plenty, but just to be safe, my man will examine you both. He will also take a look at that wound on your shoulder, although Cruikshank seems to have done a stellar job with it. You have my thanks, Rory, and you, Viper. You will both come to see me tomorrow, but for now, I think everyone deserves a rest after the day's excitement. Until then, it goes without saying that you are both under house arrest."

"But we —"

"Yes, you have done me a great service today," interrupted the Marchioness, raising a hand. "But that doesn't change the fact that you are both criminals, a fact I won't forget simply because you saved my life."

"Not just your life, Damsport too," protested Rory.

"That's enough. No more discussions. Rafe, see that they return to Cruikshank's warehouse."

The Old Girl swept off, followed by Lady Martha, who gave Rory a small wink before she left. With the two women gone, Longinus sprang to life like a recently wound clockwork toy, and he downed his own ration of antidote.

"What was that?" asked Rory.

"What was what?" replied Longinus, stoppering the now-empty antidote bottle.

Rory was prevented from answering when Rafe stood next to her.

"Follow me, please." He gestured for them all to come with him, and a cluster of Varanguard flanked them, providing them an escort through the crowd.

When they reached a step, Rafe hovered by Rory, hands at the ready as though she might fall over at any moment.

"Careful, careful," he murmured.

"Stop that," Rory snapped. She wouldn't be babied by anybody, least of all Rafe. He started, surprise flashing across his face, quickly replaced with his usual sardonic expression.

"My apologies, Mistress Magnate."

"And stop calling me that."

"That's true, the name is no longer fitting. There is so much more to you than meets the eye. Your ability to drown, for instance, is second to none. Lucky for you I'm equally skilled in pulling people *out* of the water. When do I get my kiss by the way?"

"Excuse you?" Rory spluttered. "I ain't kissing nobody."

"Haven't you read stories? The love interest is always kissed after a daring rescue. Now, of course, in your case, it was I, the love interest, who rescued *you*. We're bending the rules a little bit, but let's face it: you're hardly going to save *me* any time soon, so we have to do the best we can with what we have to work with, don't we?"

"Keep on like that and my fist will kiss your face."

"Hmm, I think I'll have to wait for a better offer, then."

They had arrived at Cruikshank's workshop, and Rafe disappeared before Rory could shout after him that there was never going to be a better offer. She was annoyed at herself for being too slow with her comeback, blaming it on her spinning head from the walk back. As soon as she crossed the threshold into Cruikshank's workshop, all thoughts of Rafe were pushed out by the overwhelming desire to lie down.

CHAPTER

46

The following morning, Longinus was in a state of agitation worse than anything Rory had ever seen. They had just received word that they were to go see the Old Girl at the mansion later that day. Rory watched him pace the workshop as she gently prodded her now-expertly patched shoulder. The Old Girl's doctor had been nothing short of a miracle worker, and already the pain in her arm was fading to a dull ache.

"I *cannot* go to see the Marchioness dressed like this." Longinus gestured at his combat-weathered silks. "I must go to my tailor, and immediately. Do you hear me?" He shouted at the door, on the other side of which were a gaggle of guards. "Immediately!"

"That's the problem with house arrest, Longinus," replied Rory. "Makes it hard to go out, don't it."

"But Lady Martha will see me like this!" he wailed. "Oh, what will she think? It was fine for me to appear in this state straight after combat, but now? She will see just what an unworthy, what a lowly…" He sighed miserably. "She is an angel from heaven, I could compose odes to the nobility of her brow, the elegance of her neck, the straight perfection of her nose, the sparkle of her conversation, the breathlessness of her wit…" Longinus faltered and frowned. "No, the, er…"

"You've never heard her wit."

"I don't need to hear it to know it is simply…perfect," he finished lamely. "I need a pen and paper. Cruikshank!"

From the suspended runway above came the thud of footsteps, and Cruikshank's door flew open.

"Will you be quiet down there, I am trying to read!"

"Then give me a pen and some paper, and I will be as silent as a stone, for I shall be enraptured by the Muse — whom I can hear whispering to me now."

"The desk."

Longinus rummaged amongst the mess of sketches and notes until he pulled out a ream of paper and a pen. A little more searching revealed a grime-covered pot of ink.

"Aha!"

He sat down to write and stood up before having scratched a single word.

"I need to change my clothes, I cannot write like this. I cannot focus, this is just unbearable!" He opened the door for the umpteenth time to check on the guards outside and slammed it shut. He began to pace up and down the workshop once again.

"To think that this celestial being will see me, unworthy as I am, and not even in appropriate clothing! Oh!" He pressed a hand to his chest.

"Longinus," said Rory.

"What?"

"You know how assassins are supposed to be all dark and silent like?"

"The word you're looking for is laconic," said Cruikshank as she climbed down the ladder, obviously having given up on her book.

"Yeah, laconic and all that," said Rory.

"Your point?" snapped Longinus.

"Shut up."

He opened and closed his mouth a couple of times, his face a perfect mask of outrage.

"She's right, lovey," said Cruikshank, reaching the ground. "Trust me, I've read many a romance novel. Assassins should be dark and mysterious. Men of few words. Women love that."

That gave him pause.

"They do?"

"Absolutely. You can't be spouting all that, er, poetry at Lady Martha, you'll ruin the illusion. She needs to have time to 'melt' your sullen exterior first. And your tattered silks add to that illusion. You're a combat-seasoned assassin, a trained killer. You should look a little rough."

Longinus nodded, his eyes staring into the middle distance.

"Yes, I can see it. The Viper, silent and deadly, sacrificing elegance for the safety of his beloved. Yes!" he snapped his fingers. "Where is that paper, I've just had a superb line."

He sat down and began to write once more. "Wait." He turned and faced the two women. "If I don't talk, how am I supposed to communicate?"

"Through me," said Rory with a grin.

"Absolutely unacceptable. You are coarse, you swear, and worse, you are grammatically incorrect."

"Well, I'm supposed to be, ain't I? You're the laconic assassin, I'm the cheeky urchin. That's how it works."

Rory turned to Cruikshank. "Do you think we'll get a medal or something?" she asked. "You know, for saving the Old Girl and Damsport? It would go nicely with my collection." She ran her fingers through the trinkets around her neck, thinking of Lady Martha and her wink. Maybe that had been a way to let her know that the Old Girl's severity was all for show.

"I don't know," said Cruikshank. "You saved her and her daughter, and the Marchioness is nothing but fair, but then again you should be held accountable for your crimes."

"She ain't going to arrest us, surely? Besides, I ain't an assassin."

Cruikshank sighed. "I really don't know, lovey. The Marchioness is a difficult one to read."

"She's a difficult woman, full stop," replied Rory, the memory of the enforced poisoning still fresh in her mind.

"Best not to say that too loud," replied Cruikshank.

***

It was a quick, if tense, trip to the Old Girl's office. Longinus had assumed a dark, glowering expression. It had taken a little practice, but he now had it just right. Rory was to speak for them both, and she felt strangely excited. So long as it wasn't to answer a sentence to the galleys, of course.

The Marchioness and Lady Martha entered by a side door.

"Ladies. Viper." The Marchioness sat down at her desk, and Lady Martha stood behind her.

"Our thanks to you both," she said with a smile. "You saved my mother and me, and for that I am eternally grateful."

"Yes, you have my thanks too," said the Marchioness. "That was good work. We wouldn't have been able to stop Myran without your help."

"We didn't *help* you stop her," corrected Rory. "We stopped her ourselves."

"Some people find insolence endearing. I do not." The Marchioness' face was hard. Rory found herself suddenly very ill at ease. "That said, I also understand that youth has to happen. So, keep your tongue in your pocket and we'll get along fine."

Longinus very discreetly shifted his foot and stepped on her toes. Luckily, her iron inserts took all of his weight, and she resisted the urge to throw him a dirty look.

"Before we get to you," continued the Marchioness, "we have another matter to address."

Lady Martha pulled the silken cord next to her. The double doors opened and two guards entered, dragging between them a snivelling Norman.

"Now, Norman," began the Old Girl.

"I didn't know it was a crossbow! I swear!" He threw himself on his knees, sobbing. "Please, Ma'am, don't send me to the galleys, please. I swear I didn't mean you any harm, I swear it, please!"

"Quiet!"

Norman hiccupped, swallowing his sobs.

"You'd better start by telling me everything from the beginning," said the Old Girl. "And if you lie, I will know."

"Well, it was like this. The woman, the one with the scar, she came up to me one night at the Pickled Heron, and she asked if I wanted to make some extra money and —"

"You were *paid* to help assassinate me?"

"No, no, no," cried Norman, shaking his head. "It wasn't like that. She said it was a joke, she wanted to play a prank on one of the performers. Just a harmless bit of fun, she said. All I had to do was tie something she would give me to the top of the mast."

"And you believed her?"

"I was pretty drunk, and…"

"Marchioness, can I please intervene," said Cruikshank. "The boy is clearly an idiot. But despite his stupidity, I know he wouldn't have meant any harm. His mother is one of my closest friends, I have known him since he was a baby. He's a good lad, very proud of the Damsian independence, and his heart's in the right place." She swallowed. "Please be lenient."

The Marchioness lifted a hand. "I'm not in the habit of executing teenagers, nor is stupidity a capital crime."

Norman mumbled something about eternal gratitude, sniffling loudly.

"That said," continued the Marchioness, "he will need to answer for what he did, but I haven't decided on a suitable punishment yet. Have someone fetch his mother," she ordered one of the guards. "Have them wait for my decision."

The guard nodded and picked Norman up from the ground, taking him back out.

"The gods damn the Emperor," said the Marchioness, slamming a fist against her desk. "He is even exploiting weakness in Damsian teenagers!" She rubbed her forehead. "Well, this brings me quite neatly to what I have planned for you both." She turned back to Rory and Longinus. "I have never before resorted to underhand tactics like spying. I like to look people square in the face when I take them on, but I've come to realise that isn't the way to deal with Airnia." A brief smirk flitted across Lady Martha's face, and Rory wondered how much of a hand she had had in that realisation. "You will both be the first of my spies; you will be my eyes and ears on the ground. You will sniff out any future attempts by this Myran and by the Emperor. If I need something done discreetly, you will do it."

"Hang on," protested Rory, "we ain't spies, we're assassins. We should be getting some reward for saving you and Lady Martha, not getting punished."

"Your reward is not being sentenced to the galleys for the people you have killed."

"Well, hang on a moment then, 'cause I only killed one."

"That's one too many. This isn't up for debate, Rory. Cruikshank will be your handler as well as your supervisor, and you'll be based in her workshop."

Cruikshank stepped forward at that. "What? That's not —"

"Your punishment for knowingly harbouring criminals, Eleanore. Don't think I forget anything."

"But I have my own work as a machinist to get on with."

"Yes, and most of the time you won't be interrupted. Your workshop is large enough to accommodate two more people. You can always set them to work when I don't have need of them."

"Now wait," said Rory, before Longinus could speak up. She could see that his impassive expression was in danger of cracking. "We're assassins. We can spy, but we ain't doing no manual labour. Our hands gotta stay delicate on account of all the poisons we use, right."

"Does the Viper ever speak?" asked Lady Martha.

"Only in case of dire need," replied Rory. "Death should always be silent." Out of the corner of her eye, she saw Longinus' face twitch, and she felt pretty sure that was a good line. She wondered whether he would write it down later.

"One of my Varanguards will be in plain clothes going forward," continued the Old Girl, "and he will relay any of my instructions. He is outside and will escort you back to the workshop."

The Marchioness stood up to signify the end of the meeting.

"What if we refuse?" said Rory stubbornly.

"You know how persuasive I can be," replied the Marchioness. "But I'd hope it won't come to that."

"No, it won't," said Longinus. Everybody looked at him in surprise. Rory wasn't sure if it was her imagination, but his voice sounded lower than normal.

He sketched a small bow and turned on his heels, making for the door. He clicked his fingers at Rory, who glowered at his back but couldn't do much other than follow him.

When she stepped out of the Old Girl's office and saw Rafe waiting there in plain clothes, she groaned inwardly and hurried after Longinus. She was relieved when Rafe fell into step with Cruikshank, leaving her and Longinus alone.

"I never thanked you for saving me, by the way," she said to Longinus. She had meant to thank him earlier, but there had never been a right time. She kept her gaze carefully focused on the ground; it was an odd feeling to know she owed her life to someone other than herself.

"Say nothing of it."

"No, I want to. Thank you. Really. For both times."

"Yes, yes, no need to get emotional." Longinus cleared his throat. "I saved your life because I shall be in need of an assistant and despite being a disaster, you do come in handy from time to time."

Rory raised an eyebrow. "From time to time? Anyway, I ain't your assistant, I'm the one who blackmailed you so that makes me the one in charge. *You* can be *my* sidekick."

"Sidekick? You are *joking*. The Viper is nobody's sidekick. Anyway, if you were to stop being my assistant, then my promise not to kill you is no longer valid."

Rory stopped in her tracks. "What?"

"Well, I mean, if you're not my assistant, what's to stop me from killing you?"

"You mean to tell me you're blackmailing me into being your assistant?"

"I guess so." Longinus smiled, and Rory wasn't sure whether to laugh or shout at him.

The Adventure Continues...

An old friend drained of his blood.
A shortage of black silk.
Rory and Longinus face their greatest crisis yet.

Go to **celinejeanjean.com/blackorchid**
to grab *The Black Orchid* now

PS: leaving a review is like giving an author cake.
Did I mention that I love cake?

Dear Reader,

I hope you've enjoyed getting to know Rory and Longinus so far. If you want more, I've got lots of goodies for you.

In *The Assassins' Guild*, they're hired by the head of the Guild of Assassins to investigate an attempt on her life. If they fail to get to the bottom of this, the consequences will be…unpleasant.

Can they navigate complex guild politics, survive deadly assassins, *and* do it all without arguing?

Then in *The Pickpocket*, discover Rory's origin story.

Lastly, you can get three bonus scenes that accompany some of the later books in the series. Go to celinejeanjean.com/bonuses

Printed in Great Britain
by Amazon

77852390R10212